Heirs to the Kingdom

Book One

The Bowman of Loxley
(Revised Edition)

Robin John Morgan

www.heirstothekingdom.com

First Published in 2009
ISBN 978-1-84944-003-5
Published in 2014 by Violet Circle Publishing.
ISBN 978-1-910299-00-5
Digital ISBN 978-1-910299-10-4

Cover illustrations provided by
Cover concept and design Robin John Morgan.
'The head of the wolf' By J. M. Bailey.

All characters and scenarios in this publication are fictitious; any resemblance to real persons, living or dead is purely coincidental.

British Library Cataloguing in Publication Data.
A catalogue record for this book is available from the British Library.

Violet Circle Publishing, Manchester, UK.

www.violetcirclepublishing.co.uk

Robin John Morgan.
(Fiction/Fantasy/Slice of Life)

Heirs to the Kingdom.

Book One, The Bowman of Loxley.

Book Two, The Lost Sword of Carnac.

Book Three, The Darkness of Dunnottar.

Book Four, Queen of the Violet Isle.

Book Five, Crystals of the Mirrored Waters.

Book Six, Last Arrow of the Woodland Realm.

Book Seven, Bridge Of Sequana.

Book Eight, The Circle of Darkness.

The Curio Chronicles.

Part One, Abigail's Summer.

Part Two, Curio's Summer.

Part Three, Curio's Christmas.

Other Works.

Rise Of The Raven

The Countess Of Darkness

Han's Cottage.

In Loving Memory of,
My First Granddaughter.
Rowan Elizabeth.

Born Sleeping January 24th 2013.

He stood on the bank, as the barge drifted slowly into the mist across the Glass Lake. His heart was heavy, for he knew that this was the passing of an era, and he bowed his head in respect.

"Good Sir, tell me why you bow to the dawn mist?"

He turned, and faced a young girl dressed all in white, with a hood pulled over her face. "I mourn the passing of my lord, for there will never be another as kind, fair, and even handed as he was."

The young lady lifted her arm, and touched him gently on the elbow. "Know that there are those who can see what will become in the times ahead. This I tell you today as truth, another will come, for his line has not been broken. Throw down your sword good sir and pick up thy quill, and write down what has been said here today."

"How can this be my young lady? No man knows what will become of the world?"

"Believe what has been said today, and tell the world to watch for the Bowman, for he will herald the start of new days." As the lady in white turned, he saw a flash of blue from under the hood. He stood as if spellbound, and watched her depart through the trees.

Turning, he headed for his horse, and left that sacred place, to head for Almesbury, and his father's church, where he would begin to write the history of his lord, and the hope for the future.

(Translated text of Geoffrey of Almesbury AD 421)

Introduction

LOXLEY AD: 2038.

The Lox family was the oldest family in the area, they could trace their family back over hundreds of years, and in the town of Loxley, they were highly respected. Since the dreaded Red Death, the family had played a very important role helping the other families around the area. What had once been a vast farm with many cottages for all the workers, was now a small town surrounded by a huge wooden wall, where people fleeing the terror of the red death had come looking for safe haven outside the cities.

The outbreak had begun in London in 2012, and within three years had spread across the whole country wiping out most of the population. It had been chaos, and people fled in panic out of the cities, the whole country just fell apart as death crept down every street.

Modern day transportation spread it worldwide within weeks, and the age of modern man began to fail. Power stations ceased to run as oil ran out, and the whole country ground to a halt. Bodies littered every street rotting and stinking, and people fought and killed each other in a mass struggle for survival. Riots exploded across the country as towns and cities burned to the ground, looters ran wild, and the cities and towns became desperate and violent places to be.

Within three years, it was gone but the country had become a very different place. Slowly nature began to take back what had been hers. Uncut grass verges became wild areas filled with coloured flowers, trees spread their seed in the gaps in cracking stone, and soon jungles of concrete created by man, became shrouded, and clothed in green.

People of the countryside adapted quickly, the old ways were not dead, and they used the skills passed down to them by their parents to help them survive. It had been tough times, but slowly as small communities banded together a new way of life began to evolve. Now as New Year 2038 began, the country had settled into a life more of that from the dark ages spliced with the remnants of modern day living. Electricity was scarce and yet some had the old knowledge, and wind turbines and solar panels provided lights and ran water pumps. Oil was now rare, and vegetable oil became the fuel of many.

Britain was now a hostile place; small communities defended the little they had against bands of brutal Cutters. The gun was a rare tool used; it was crossbows, and long bows that were the preferred weapons of the day. They were light and easy to make from surrounding resources, which was the way everyone now had to survive.

Living off the land, and with the land, was the only hope. The cottage industries boomed again, as life began to take on a different form, and old cars and vehicles were now just seen as a source of precious metals, used for the making of tools and utensils for survival, especially weapons for protection.

Robert Lox and his brother John were the local suppliers. John was a blacksmith and his brother a carpenter, between them they had been able to create quite a store of high quality weapons and tools, which they would sell or swap for goods at the fortnightly markets in Hathersage.

Long journeys were made back to the cities, to collect metal or cloth to use in day to day life, and trade started to grow in salvaged modern clothes and new woven garments.

Currency was soon introduced as communities reached out to each other, which were based on quarter ounces of pieces of metal. Most towns minted their own coins from jewellery they had, and gold, silver, and brass bits were now the price of those who had nothing to swap or barter.

As the snow blew in with the year of 2038, a deep sense of awakening stirred within the land, for the moment had finally arrived as the prophecy made long ago began its passage to fulfilment. Finally it was time, time for one man to walk forward and lead the way in seeking out the true Heirs to the Kingdom.

CHAPTER ONE

THE FINAL DAYS OF WINTER

Loxley is a town set deep in the wild moor, on the border of Yorkshire and Derbyshire. It is a small place, mainly made up from the local farms, with a few extra cottages for farm staff. It is not somewhere that you would easily find, especially on New Year's Day after a week of heavy snow.

The wind was wild, howling and rattling the windows; the air was crisp, as Robbie opened his eyes and peered out over the blankets. His door banged again, and then with a click, the light flowed into the room, as the door swung open.

"Come on lad, Billy's up, and John's already out in the barn. We have a busy day planned." The tall muscular frame of Robert Lox filled the doorway, as Robbie peered across the room.

"What time is it Dad?" Robbie yawned, as he began to move under the thick warm blankets.

"Time we're up and at it lad, come on your mum has breakfast ready." Robert Lox turned, and headed out of the room, as Robbie sat up and swung his legs over the bed. His dad's boots thumped as they headed back down the stairs.

Robbie stood up and shivered. "God it's freezing," he muttered, as he quickly grabbed his pants and pulled them up, and reached for his thick jumper. Dropping his feet into his boots, he stood and looked at the empty bed on the other side of the room; he hadn't heard Billy get up.

Robbie looked into the mirror, and was faced with a stocky boy of almost seventeen; his long brown hair was sticking out at all sorts of angles, and had flopped over the right side of his tanned face. His piercing dark eyes twinkled, as he tugged the cord out of the back of his knotted hair, and grabbing the old wooden brush, he began to rake his long hair straight.

"Robbie your food is getting cold." His mother's soft voice resounded up the stairs.

"Yeah, coming!" He held his hair back, and pulled the cord dropping his ponytail down his back. He smiled back to himself in the mirror, and then headed off down the stairs.

The kitchen was warm as Robbie walked in, his mum smiled, as she placed his breakfast of scrambled eggs and tomatoes on the table. "Come on love eat it while it's hot."

"Cheers Mum." Robbie sat, and began shovelling his breakfast down. Billy was sat staring out of the window chewing his toast; he glanced across at Robbie.

"Flights or points?" It was going to be another day sat in the back of the old barn, putting the arrow tips and flights on the arrow shafts. This would be the sixth day doing it, and Robbie was not looking forward to yet another long and monotonous day.

"Points," he sighed, and Billy smiled, he knew out of all the things they could do, this would be the worst.

"I need a path clearing first to the greenhouse." Jess leaned over the sink, and peered through the window at the large snowflakes and across the garden, to where the outline of two very large greenhouses stood framed in white. "Must have had about a foot and half last night boys, make sure you check the stoves, and keep them stoked up."

Jess Lox, was the gardener in the family, although gardener was hardly the word to use. Her Mother was an ex-teacher of Botany and Horticulture, and Jess had grown up surrounded by plants from all over the world. With her sister-in-law Beth, they grew all the food that they ate, as well as a whole host of other types of plants including spices, coffee, and tea. Her orchard was the biggest for miles, and provided them with a good income from the market during the late summer months.

Robbie smiled back at his mum. "No problem," and slapping Billy on his shoulder, he jumped up, and headed to the door, and the coat rack.

The snow now was well over three feet deep, as it drifted across the fields and on to the house. A small channel had been dug from the door to the large barn, where the sound of hammer on steel rang out. A red glow emitted from the gap in the doors, John had the furnace on full heat, and was pounding the steel of new sword blades as they entered. He looked up, his face bright red from the heat of the fire, and his bare muscular arms glowed with sweat from the effort of his labour.

"Morning lads, happy New Year." He gave them a huge smile, as they picked up two shovels and looked down, as he pulled the long piece of steel out of the fire, and laid it on the anvil, and then pounded it with his huge hammer. Sparks flew off in many directions, and the ring of the steel was deafening.

John Lox was the youngest of the three brothers. He was tall and heavyset, with dark short scruffy hair. To meet him you would be wary, but to those who knew him, he was a mild mannered and jolly man, who was always the first to smile. He had only been angered a few times in the past, yet the tales of the damage he inflicted on those that had crossed him, were still tales told regularly on market days.

Billy and Robbie were glad to be out in the air, it was deathly cold, and the wind seemed to bite at their faces, but they felt a light heartedness at being able to mess about, and not be cooped up in the back room of the barn. The snowflakes were large and fluffy, as they floated down, and it was not long before the snowballs were flying across the path, as Robbie and Billy made the most of their time outdoors.

They made their way laughing and joking into the greenhouse. The whole of the roof was covered in snow, and the greenhouse seemed insulated, and the sound of the door closing was dull. Gasping for breath and laughing, the two boys made their way to the far end, where there was a large stove, and a tall round silver water tank. Billy shook his long blonde hair as he dropped his gloves onto the stove.

"Better check the supply tank, make sure that valve isn't sticking again." He stood on the stool, and lifted himself up to look in the top of the tank, that supplied warm water to the pipes running along the floor. "Thought so," he wiggled his hand, and the tank made a gurgle as water flowed back into the system.

Robbie dropped his gloves on the stove next to Billy's, which were now starting to steam. "Oh... that's good," he breathed, as he held his frozen hands just above it to warm them.

It was a vast greenhouse, of over a hundred feet long, and sixty feet wide. Robbie stared around at the hundreds of plants growing in rows up and down the house. This was his mum's turf, with help from his Aunt Beth and Cousin Alice; his mum grew most of the food they ate. Some were sold at market, and some were left to seed to provide for future years. Robbie loved the damp moist atmosphere of the greenhouses; they had a rich earthy smell that mingled with the scents of some of the flowers and spices his mother was growing. Robbie breathed a long satisfying breath.

He sat in the small chair in front of the stove and rested his boots on the edges, as his pants began to steam. Billy collapsed into the chair at his side, and passed him a steaming mug. "Now this is more like it, I am sick of seeing sodding arrow tips."

Robbie smiled. "Yeah, I don't think we have ever had as many in stock before, dad seems mad about making more and more, I think it's the Cutters who have him worried."

"It's got John bothered, I heard him talking to Len over Christmas, they have been moving north for some time now... I just can't see them finding here though, let's be honest, this place isn't even on the map it's so small." Billy took a long slurp of his drink.

"This place is pretty secure even if they did come, I can't see them getting in that easily, dad needs to relax a bit." Robbie looked at Billy; he seemed lost in thought, as he stared at the snow covered roof panels.

"I don't know Rob; in all my time here, I have never known your dad worry like he is now. Maybe he knows more than he is letting on, although I just can't see how they would get through. You and your dad are the two best longbow men in the whole area, and John is no push over with a sword. It would take hundreds to overrun this place, especially with all the guards. Even then, they would have the toughest fight they have ever had to win. Not to mention that they would have to get over the wall before anything else."

Robbie thought about his dad. "Maybe he just wants to make sure he is prepared, you know, keep plenty in, just in case."

"Maybe, I suppose it won't hurt." The greenhouse door slid noisily open, as the slender figure of Alice stepped in with two large watering cans in her hand. She smiled when she saw them sat in front of the stove.

"Morning guys." She trundled up towards them, the two cans slopping water on the floor as she walked. "Don't let Aunt Jess see you drinking that, she is getting low on beans, and the new crop is not ready yet, you know how she loves her coffee?" She set the cans down, and flicked her long brown bushy hair out of her eyes and over her shoulder.

Billy leaned forward and looked at the cans. "Erg, what's that, it stinks?" The cans had a muddy green liquid slopping around inside them, and it smelled like rotten cabbage.

"It's plant feed, we make it with comfrey, nettles, and a little manure, it's really good stuff, got everything we need to create strong plants." She smiled smugly. "It's a recipe of my own."

Billy looked disgusted. "Please tell me you don't put that on the food we eat?"

Robbie smiled, as he watched Billy retch, as he had moved just a little too close to the can, and got the full flavour of its foul reek.

Alice tutted at him. "You don't seem to mind too much when you are emptying the salad bowl on to your plate, it's this stuff that actually makes it possible for us to grow enough to feed you two. Anyhow one of you can give me a lift to get it in to the irrigation tank."

Billy seemed as green as the plants, so Robbie laughing at him, got up and lifted the cans, and made his way to the top of the greenhouse, where a large metal water vat stood. He lifted a can trying to hold his breath, as it was putrid. He tipped the can, and the contents slopped out in to the water tank. Alice smiling at his twisted expression, passed him the other can, and he poured it in. "Thanks Robbie... So, what are you two up to today?"

"Not bloody arrow making that's for sure." Billy took another swig of his coffee.

"I have plenty of seed to sow, and plants to water, you can both give me a lift if you want." Alice started back down towards the bottom end of the greenhouse. "I will be in the potting house if you feel like it, ok?"

Billy seemed keen, but Robbie didn't fancy doing it much, he felt restless and wasn't really sure what he wanted to do. He walked back towards the stove and sat down; Billy was watching Alice as she headed out of the door, and across the snowy yard to the potting house. Robbie smiled to himself. "Why don't you go and help her?"

Billy blinked, as if coming out of his thoughts. "What?"

Robbie nodded towards the greenhouse door and smiled. "Go and help her... You know you want to." Robbie laughed, as Billy looked surprised.

"What's that supposed to mean?"

"God Billy, it's so obvious that you really like her... Just go and spend some time with her, I will be fine in here."

Billy looked down at the floor, he was amazed at how Robbie had picked up on his feelings for Alice, he had been so sure he had kept it hidden, he looked up at his friend and smiled. "You don't mind then?"

Robbie lifted his feet back up on to the stove and laughed. "Alice really likes you too; I don't understand why you have to make such a big pretence... To be honest it's sickening the way you stare at her, and pine away in secret... Go on, get out of here and give me some peace."

Billy seemed unsure, the fact his best friend had rumbled him did quite surprise him, but he was also glad that Robbie knew. Alice was Robbie's cousin, and he was very close to her. Billy had somehow thought that he would not like it; after all he was just a guest in the Lox household.

He smiled back, and got out of his chair. "Cheers Rob... Shout me if your dad wants us." Billy wandered down the greenhouse, and out through the door, Robbie settled back in his chair, and enjoyed the few moments alone that he was about to get. He leaned back and closed his eyes; the peace and quiet created by the snow-covered greenhouse was bliss. His mind wandered around his many thoughts, finally coming back to rest on Billy.

His mother Jess had found Billy nine years ago battered, bruised, and freezing to death on the old moor road. He was barely alive when she had brought him home, and it had taken weeks for him to recover fully enough to tell them what had happened to him.

Billy had lived in the country somewhere outside of London, with his parents, Kate and Arnold Avalon. The Cutters, who killed his parents, and burned the place to the ground, had attacked their house in the daytime. Billy who had been playing in the nearby fields had been terrified, and hidden in some thick bushes, where he saw his parents dragged out and murdered.

He had stayed in the same spot for two days, until his Uncle Tobias had arrived. Tobias had taken him back to his place and set him to work on a loom, but he was a brutal drinking man, and when things went wrong, it had been Billy who had suffered horrific beatings.

After one specific very bad beating, Billy had waited until nightfall, and escaped through the pantry window, and run north to get as far away from his uncle as possible. Somehow, Billy had lost his way on the road during a bad blizzard, and found he was up on the moors lost, unable to find a way to a village. He had collapsed in the road, and was very lucky that Jess had been the one to pass him in her cart.

Now Billy was a member of the family, he was more like a brother to Robbie than just his friend. It now felt like they had grown up together since birth, Robbie could not remember a time in his life, when he had not had Billy at his side.

Billy's only possession had been a golden chain round his neck, with a silver lion, and a golden dragon on it. Robbie slid his hand inside his shirt and pulled on his own chain, and looked at the silver lion with two small diamonds for eyes. They glinted as he turned it around in his hand. He thought of the time on his 14th birthday, when Billy had undone his chain and slid it off, and given it to him as a gift.

Robbie had known how precious it was to Billy, and had refused it, but Billy had been so insistent, and deep down inside he knew how thrilled he was to have it, and how deep a symbol of friendship it had meant to him. To Robbie that moment had sealed their kinship, and he had thought of him ever since as more of a brother than a friend. Yes, Billy was now family in his eyes.

The large water tank gurgled, and Robbie came out of his thoughts. He stood up and looked at the tank, and the pile of wood at the side of it. He crossed over to the woodpile, and lifted several pieces into his arms. With a block in his hand, he rapped the catch on the front of the stove, and slowly tapped the door open, to reveal the small bright embers inside. He pushed several pieces into it through the door, and watched the red sparks fly, as the wood settled in the midst of the heat. He closed the door with his foot, and knocked the catch back with the small block. Picking up more wood, he headed off to the other stove, on the other side of the greenhouse.

With all the stoves full and burning, and the under soil pipes heated, the plants would be kept at a good temperature, to protect them through the cold snap. Robbie pulled off his coat, and loosened his sweater. The air was warm and moist, and he enjoyed walking around the growing crops and having the space to think.

He peered through the glass at the two stone houses stood side by side across the yard. The snow seemed to have lessened, as the flakes were a lot smaller now and falling less frequently, he loved his home, and yet he had a nagging doubt about it that had been in his mind more and more.

The farm was now the centre of what over the years had become a community. Just under a quarter of a mile away was a group of fourteen houses, which as he had been told, was once the residence of all of the workers from his grandfather's time as farm owner. Now they were home to a whole host of assorted families who had escaped the red death, and they all looked to his dad as landlord and local leader.

Over the years, the huge forest that had surrounded the farm had been thinned, and the tall wooden trunks had been sunken into the ground, to form a huge perimeter fence. Everyone now called the farm, 'The Stockade,' and it was a small community, bound and enclosed behind the high rough wooden walls. Loxley was now a protected town surrounded by dense forest, and those who did not know of its existence, would find it very difficult to locate.

On New Year's Day surrounded by three feet of snow in a blizzard, it felt like the most remote and isolated place on earth, especially to Robbie who was used to being able to wander and hunt outside the walls. Winter had felt like a very long time this year, and as Robbie stared through the glass out into the white of the winter scene, he felt more trapped than ever. Spring was only seven weeks away, and he could not wait for it to bring him sunshine, green grass, and a chance to slip out of the walls and roam in the forest.

Figures moved in the greenhouse opposite, and he noticed Billy all smiles, talking to Alice as he carried a large sack of compost on his shoulder. Robbie smiled to himself, to see Billy and Alice talking away as they worked, they seemed so much happier than he felt.

Alice was very special. Although they were cousins, it was mainly due to the fact that she lived in the house next door, yet spent most of her time either in his house, or working with him. Robbie had grown up side by side with her, and she was more like a younger sister to him. She was also one of his best friends, and he had on many occasions shared many of his secrets with her, which she had always kept to herself.

The irony of the day hit him, and he laughed to himself. Fancy telling Billy to stop pining and go and talk to her, when all his free time of late, had been spent alone and thinking about Rune. He had not seen her since Christmas, where he had to admit that he had watched her all day, and had only had the briefest of moments with her, at which point he had felt so awkward that he had hardly been able to express an audible word. "Fine one you are Rob to preach to Billy," he said out loud.

The pictures flooded into his mind of the pale slender figure with waist length red hair, streaked with golden flecks. What he would not give now to look into those sapphire blue eyes, which seemed to him, to hold such a life force. She was everything he imagined a woman could be and more, and yet the sight of her would send his heart racing, and he became so nervous he could hardly speak. His embarrassment at all of the other occasions, when he had made such a fool of himself in front of her, rose inside him.

He kicked the watering can and felt like an idiot, it rattled on the floor, and fell over clattering on the stone pathway. Robbie pushed his hands into his pockets, and walked past it as he headed back to his chair by the stove and flopped down. His gloves were now dry, and felt stiff as he threw them onto the floor at the side of the chair. He reached over for the coffee pot and poured another cup full.

Robbie sat in the old chair sipping his drink and lost in thought for some time, the house door banged shut, and a figure in a black cloak walked up towards the greenhouse. Jess Lox opened the large sliding door and stepped inside the greenhouse. She looked up the path at her son sat lost in thought in front of the stove. She smiled at him as he looked back at her. "Go easy on that coffee, it is getting a little low, and the new beans are not ready."

Robbie smiled back at his mum. "Don't worry your secret sack is still unopened," and he laughed. Robbie knew about the sack in the potting shed that she had hidden at the back of all the large plant pots. His mum looked surprised.

"How do you know about that?"

"Not a very good place to hide it was it? John wanted some big pots last year, and I had to move about a dozen to get to those really large ones at the back. I saw your stash tucked down behind all the bell pots."

His mum shook her head and laughed. "I will have to find a better place now."

"Don't worry Mum I won't tell." Robbie grinned as his mum walked up towards him, and sat in the chair opposite.

"So why are you here all alone and not helping the others? Don't fancy being a gooseberry?" Her hazel eyes glistened with glee.

"I just felt like being alone with my thoughts for a bit."

Her eyes seemed to fill with concern. "Winter gets to us all you know? Somehow, I think you suffer the most. Don't worry spring is almost around the corner, and life will feel full again." She leaned forward and patted his leg, as she rose up and moved to the table to gather her basket and knife.

Robbie sat back in his chair, as he watched his mother cut away the sprouts on the stored canes. She expertly pinched the tips of the spinach and laid them neatly in the basket, and pulling hard on a stem, she lifted a potato plant out of the loose earth, and shook it so that the hundreds of small new tubers fell onto the top of the soil. Collecting them carefully she wiped each one on a rag hanging from the cord of her apron, and placed them into the basket. Those that were left; she gently pulled into a pile, and covered them with the loose earth for next time.

"I've told your dad to give you all a day off from arrows, it used to drive me nuts as well. What with thousands of the things filling the cellar, I think one days break won't hurt." She smiled as she stood up, and picking up her basket she began to walk back to the door. "Keep the stoves hot won't you Robbie dear?"

"I will Mum.... And Mum?"

"Yes Robbie?"

"Thanks, I bloody hate arrow making."

Jess smiled as she pulled the door closed, turned, and headed back to the house. Robbie took a long swig of his coffee, settled back down into his chair and breathed a long sigh.

Over the following week, the dark brooding sky seemed to lighten, and as the winds picked up the snow ceased, and the sun broke through turning the whole area around the farm a dazzling bright white. Icicles hung from the gutters, and dripped sparkling like jewels, the whole area began to come alive, and work began clearing paths and roads.

It was a busy time, and Robbie's sense of foreboding seemed to lift as he joined Billy and his dad clearing the snow, and getting the road down to the cottages open. It was hard work, but with a few snowball fights with the local children, and a lot of laughter, the task seemed to flow by quickly, as did the time.

The small cottages built in two rows, formed a little Village Street of fourteen house's each with its own courtyard, and in some cases the homes of the residents doubled as shops, and one such resident was Len Rimmer.

Len Rimmer was an older man, whom seemed to be very wary about giving his true age. His role in the small community was that of chemist and medic, and he could often be seen walking down the street with his little bag of potions clutched tightly in his hand, and his long snow white hair blowing behind him, with his goatee beard twitching in the breeze.

Len was often a topic of talk in the small community; for his age he appeared to be a remarkably fit man. He looked at least sixty years old, and yet he had the strength and vitality of a man half his age. His eyes were the brightest of green, and when you looked him in the eye, you somehow felt that the life behind them was young and powerful.

Robbie liked Len a lot, there was something about him, an air of mystery, and yet somehow he always felt that when he spoke with him, Len understood more about him than he had revealed.

The house next door to Len's was Robbie's favourite; it was the home of Len's daughter Steph. Stephanie Rimmer Lane was the local weaver, and supplier of clothing and jewellery. Outside her home, Len had built a large wooden roof over the yard to give her the protected space to sell her clothing, and set out her jewellery.

The real reason that Robbie loved this place more than any was not because of the clothes or the jewellery, which were of the highest quality. No, he loved it because Steph had two daughters, and one in particular was the focus of all his spare moments alone thinking.

Jade and Rune were as alike as chalk and cheese. Jade had her grandfather's green eyes and blonde hair, but she was more of a tomboy who dressed in collarless shirts and dark canvass pants, which were usually patched. Jade made the jewellery, and was at her happiest working in the back yard with her small furnace and metalwork tools.

Robbie liked Jade; she had a great sense of humour and was always looking for fun, even if at times she could be loud and rough with some of the smaller boys in the village. They had always got on well, but her sister, well she was something to behold.

Robbie took a break and leant on his shovel. He had just cleared the yard for Ann and Alice Kirk, who were now busy putting up a table, so they could get out the daily stock of fresh baked bread. The smell wafted out into the street and his stomach rumbled.

Across the road Rune was hanging garments on the clothes rail. Her long red hair glinted in the sunlight, and shimmered as she moved. Robbie watched as she moved elegantly around the rail, making sure all the garments were neat and orderly, her bright blue eyes darting from side to side as she inspected each garment.

His eyes covered her whole slender body, as he took in the vision before him; her delicate wrists and hands covered with silver bangles, bracelets, and finely crafted silver rings. He absorbed the pictures in his memory of each fold of her long flowing top in the richest of dark purple velvet, as it flowed down and over her matching heavy flowing skirt, down to her delicate boots.

"Pretty, isn't she?"

"What?" Robbie turned to see Anne Kirk smiling up at him. "Sorry Miss Kirk, what did you say?" He felt a little awkward having been caught staring at Rune.

Anne's eyes twinkled. "I said she is a very pretty girl Robbie." He felt his face warm with embarrassment, and looked down for a moment. Anne laughed. "Don't be shy boy, she is a very lovely girl, and you could do a lot worse than Rune." She patted his shoulder and pushed a small bag of warm scones into his hand. "Thanks for clearing the yard, maybe you should wander over and offer her one of these whilst they are still warm."

Robbie smiled. "Thanks Miss Kirk." He lifted his shovel up on to his shoulder, and stepped out of the yard as Anne Kirk walked back into her shop, and in a light hearted mood; he took one of the scones out of the bag and bit into it. He stood for a few moments and considered the point, why not he thought to himself, and stepped into the road. Robbie walked across the street towards the small stonewall that surrounded the front yard. Len stepped out of the door as Robbie approached.

"Robbie lad?" He smiled as he stepped down into the yard; Rune peered from between the garments, and seemed to be a little pink around the cheeks as her bright blue eyes sparkled.

Robbie nodded at her and gave a weak smile. "Hi Rune." He turned to Mr Rimmer who was now almost at the gate. "Hi Mr Rimmer, how are you?"

"I'm fine my lad, yes fine." His bright green eyes sparkled as they looked Robbie up and down, and made a note of every aspect of him. "I see you have come to the aid of the good ladies Kirk, that's very good of you Robbie. I like a man who will always aid others."

Robbie now felt a little out of sorts, he had wanted a chance to talk to Rune, but he was faced with having to talk to Len, he considered his position whilst noticing the two blue eyes that flashed through the garments, as Rune continued her work. He looked back over at the small bakery, and then back up at Len who was watching his every move. He held up the bag of scones. "I was given these by Miss Kirk, and thought it would be nice to share, after all it was not really my idea, you know?" Robbie moved his cold feet from side to side. "My dad thinks we should all muck in and help out."

"He is very right my lad, very right indeed. In times like this it is more important than ever that we all should stand together and help each other." Len smiled a warm and friendly smile. "Never the less my young friend, you chose to share your earnings with this household, and I am very honoured by the gesture, so I feel it only right to offer one of my own."

Len rubbed his hands together, and then pulled open the tiny gate. "Would you join myself and my granddaughter for coffee, to wash down such fresh baked delights?"

Robbie looked up at Rune who was appearing around the end of the garment rack. He could feel his throat constricting as it always did in such close proximity to her. He coughed. "That would be very nice." He smiled and stepped through the gate.

With a swish of her garments, and a tiny rattle of bangles, Rune disappeared through the door in front, leaving Robbie alone in the yard with Len. Len patted him on the back softly. "Come along lad; let's get in where it's warm, I feel it quicker these days." He briskly rubbed his hands again and led the way into the house.

The old cottage was home to three women who were all gifted at the crafts that they did, and the house reflected it. The front room was just like an extension to the front yard, and was filled with fine clothes and jewellery, all displayed with care and labelled very neatly. There was a small table by the door, which Robbie assumed was a counter, and all around the fireplace there were endless items from sculpted metal, to picture frames, as well as more jewellery. The fire crackled in the hearth, which had large baskets either side filled with shawls, and intricately embroidered cushions. Robbie's eyes wandered around trying to take in every item in the room. "This place is fantastic," Robbie muttered.

"All my girls have far more than their fair share of talents. You would be surprised what they can do if they put their minds to it." Len spoke with pride, even though his tone was kind hearted, Robbie could see how important they were to him. "Now my boy let's move through to the back room, where we may sit and enjoy our delights and talk as friends." Len moved through the small wooden door at the other side of the room, and Robbie followed.

The back room again had a roaring fire, and a large rug decorated with a mighty coat of arms surrounded by a black and white circle. Three large comfy chairs were placed around the fire, and a long old three-seated settee was pushed up against the wall. All had the same cushions, and were covered with bright hand woven throws. Len gestured to a chair by the fire, and Robbie loosened his jacket and then sat down. Len sat opposite smiling. "That's better... Nice and cosy here, it's so much better than my shabby old place."

Robbie's eyes wandered the walls looking at the many paintings that were hung there. Most of them were of places he recognized, as they were all painted within the walls of the stockade, a few he did not recognize and yet he felt they were familiar, which was unusual to him. Len watched with a satisfied look on his face as he studied each painting from his seat.

"You like my daughters work Lad? She is a very fine painter. I just wish she had more time to do it, she has a very natural talent."

Robbie nodded to Len as he spoke, but his eye was drawn to one painting in particular. It was an old ruin surrounded by trees. Whether or not it was the way that the sunlight broke through the dark clouds he could not tell, but as he looked harder at the picture, he could just make out a small stone slab hidden under the low shrubs. It was as if one beam of sunlight seemed to find its way through the dense growth and illuminate that single stone.

"You like that one, do you?" Len's voice seemed soft in Robbie's ear.

"Very much so... Yes." It was almost a whisper as he nodded. "Where is it?"

"That's the old Priory at Kirklees." The voice was soft and caring. Robbie looked round as Rune placed a large tray containing plates and cups of hot steaming coffee on the table at the side of him. Her face was almost level with his, and he could see her white pale skin with faint freckles, and long red eyelashes decorated with the finest amount of lilac pale powder. She gave him a small shy smile and began to pour.

"The Priory was a convent many hundreds of years ago." Len leaned forward to pick up a cup and passed it to Robbie. He took the scones out of Robbie's hand, and passed them to Rune, who sliced them and added fresh butter and strawberry preserve. "They say in legend that is where the son of the Earl of Huntingdon was buried."

Robbie had no idea of who that was; he just loved the picture, and felt strangely drawn to it. He put his cup to his lips and drank the hot fresh coffee as he looked back up at it.

There was movement and a faint tinkle of bangles. Robbie looked down from the painting, and his eyes met Rune's, she was watching him very closely. Her bright sapphire blue eyes seemed to dance with life. Len was still talking and his voice seeped back into Robbie's ears as he awoke as if from a dream.

"Yes it is so sad, it was one of the best examples of architecture for its time, such a shame most of it has gone forever now, this country has lost so much since the red death, now it's just a wasteland of ruins." A bell rang in the other room, and Rune jumped up, and walked past him into the shop, Robbie's eyes followed her through the door.

"My granddaughter is very beautiful is she not?"

Robbie felt the flush of embarrassment rise to his face, as he turned to Len sat opposite in the chair; he smiled knowing the old man had noticed his attentions. "She is sir."

Len let out a mighty chuckle, and his eyes twinkled with delight, he leaned forward laughing and patted Robbie's knee. "Don't look so worried boy... You are a young man; I would be very concerned if you did not take notice." He sat back in his chair and his old green eyes danced with delight.

The moment was long, as Len seemed sat in thought as he stroked his small goatee beard. Robbie took another sip of his drink and looked at the floor. He finally spoke and his voice and manner seemed very reflective. "I am a lucky man young Robbie; I have a very beautiful daughter and two very beautiful granddaughter's, all of whom have exceptional talent." He seemed to pause and spoke more to himself than Robbie. Robbie sat watching the old man who seemed lost momentarily in thought. "Yes lad, even I never realized how gifted the three of them are, they have gone well beyond what was expected of them."

Len moved forward slowly in his chair, and lifted a scone off the plate. "So young Robbie, soon you will be old enough to choose your own path in life, I have seen you grow into quite a man, not unlike your father I might add. Tell me, will you stay here and make bows and hunt, or will you leave this prison of a stockade?"

The question seemed to come right out of nowhere, and Robbie felt the surge run through him as the surprise hit him, did Len know of the feelings of restlessness inside him? Was it so obvious to all around him? His words faltered a little.

"I err... I have not really thought about it, I guess for now my place is here, my dad needs me up at the farm, and at the markets I suppose."

"For now you say?" Len considered the phrase. "Well, it is still early, you have youth and there is still plenty of time. All men have their own destiny young Robbie, don't ever forget that. You have a path to follow like all men, and if it forks from what you know into the unknown, do not be afraid to let your instincts guide you. I can see you are already questioning your path, which is a good thing. Time will lead you to where you need to be."

He gave him a kindly smile and Robbie smiled uncertainly back. His words had resounded deeply within Robbie, and he was not sure if Len knew more than he was letting on. One thing Robbie did know was that this old man was no fool, and he had spotted something inside himself that no other had spotted.

"How well are you schooled?"

Robbie was surprised. "How do you mean? My mother has taught Billy and myself for most of our life, like all the other families around here."

"Aha, you're Mother." Len nodded. "Of course, her mother was a school teacher in the days of the old ways; I would say you are well grounded in English, Math's and Botany, but what about sciences?"

"I am not sure sir; I think I know enough if not more than most people around here, my mother was always very insistent we had a good education."

"I have no doubt that with Jess as a teacher you have a very advanced education young Robbie. I just think that somehow you are the sort of person who would benefit from a little; well let's just say more advanced education. I was once a professor at a university in the days of the old ways, I could offer you a chance to let that enquiring nature of yours, let's say, explore other avenues."

Robbie looked at the old man and considered his point, he had after all read every book at home, and he was the one who was always asking questions. "I would have to discuss this with my father first, he has a heavy work load and he will have to let me have time off."

Len shook his head. "Of course lad, you must have your fathers approval, I will speak to him if you want? Although the lessons will not be free of charge, you will have to do a little teaching of your own in return."

Robbie was very surprised. "What can I teach you?"

The old man smiled. "Not me my dear lad, my granddaughter's."

"What?"

Len leaned forward in his chair. "I believe if rumours are true, you are quite a dab hand with a long bow. In fact, if rumour is correct, you are probably sharper than your father, which I have to admit, would be quite something to see."

Robbie nodded. "I can handle a bow."

"You can do a little more than handle one from what I have heard. Therefore, I will fill in the gaps in your education, and you can give my granddaughters guidance in using the long bow. Is it a deal?"

Robbie smiled with a little relief. "Yes sir, it's a deal."

Ten minutes later, Robbie entered the shop with Len Rimmer, as Rune handed the neatly wrapped package to the young girl, who left the shop. Rune smiled at the two of them, and her eyes seemed to sparkle, had she heard their discussion in the back room?

"Well my dearest granddaughter, it appears that you have some company for your lessons with your old bookworm, and in return I have found you a very accomplished teacher of the long bow. I believe young Robbie's visit here today has been just the moment we were looking for." He patted Robbie hard on the back.

Robbie felt a little foolish in front of Rune now, and his stomach seemed to squirm slightly, especially considering the large smile on her happy face.

"That's wonderful grandfather, so Robbie, I hear you are very good with the bow, I will really look forward to my lessons."

Robbie felt suddenly very hot, but also very happy. Half an hour later, as he walked slowly back up the lane towards the farm, he found his thoughts drifting around at the prospect of being alone with Rune, and showing her the subtle aspects of bowmanship. It was something that seemed to fill him with great warmth, and he smiled as his pace quickened. Teaching Rune was definitely going to be the highlight of his week from now on, and he broke into a run, to go and find his father, and ask him about lessons with Len Rimmer.

CHAPTER TWO

ARCHERY AND LESSONS

The weeks slowly passed in a blur of arrow making, and repairs around the farm. The wind turbines were given a full service, and the solar plates on the roof were cleaned. Fencing was repaired, and tools sharpened ready for the coming year. Robbie spent a lot of time working with his dad, as Billy helped John with the metalwork on the carts to ready them for the market.

The sun broke out, and the snow disappeared, to be replaced by rain or frequent showers, and the signs of spring began to show everywhere. Aconite popped their heads above the soil, and the primroses began to bud up. During the sunny days, Jess opened the vents on the greenhouses to allow a little air inside, and new green shoots appeared on all her plants.

Jess was more delighted to see that the first crop of coffee she had forced into bloom over the winter was now producing large succulent beans. The salad was growing much faster, and it was noticeable as Robbie and Billy scooped large quantities on to their plates.

Robbie's mood lifted, sunshine and work kept him very busy and he had less time to think, and more time to plan his first hunting trip. It was the first week of February when Jess stopped Robbie and his dad, who were carrying five large pieces of timber down the driveway to replace the fence at the front of the house.

"Rob darling, could you have a talk to Alf Smith, and find out how his stocks are? We are starting to run low, and I think now would be the time to start preparing another trip out into the forest." Robbie's ears pricked up, and his heart jumped for joy, finally a chance to get over the wall and roam free. He watched his dad's expression carefully.

"Right love." He scratched his chin, as he balanced the stack of timber on his shoulder. "I wanted to pop into the village, so I will nip down tonight when we are finished and have a word OK?"

Jess smiled at her husband, and turning round to face Robbie, who was stood shouldering the weight of the timber, she winked and smiled at him. "Oh, and that reminds me." She turned back to her husband. "You haven't heard from Harry, have you? It's just that the freezer is on the blink again, and I think it should be looked at before we fill it up."

"I think John heard something last week, it might be better to have a word with him. You know our Harry though; it could be months before we see him again Jessie love."

Robert Lox seemed to smile at the thought of his brother. Robbie really liked his Uncle Harry; he was to say the least a bit of a wild card. Harry enjoyed his life, he would spend months on end digging out stone from under the local hills and polishing it up, before setting off to trade it with the jewellers all over the country.

Harry liked the joys in life, such as good food, good women, and good wine. His main passion in life was restoring old motorbikes, and he knew every place in the country where they could be found. He would clean them up, and convert the engines to run on a mixture of rapeseed oil and moonshine, which he acquired from Joe.

Joe Whitmore was a woodsman who lived deep inside the forest; he was also Harry's best friend, and Jess's older brother. Harry would spend his time searching out copper pipe and yeast, and other relative ingredients, so when he returned home, he could deliver the goods to Joe who would brew the lethal concoction he called whiskey. It was without doubt powerful stuff, and John often kept a bottle in the back of his furnace house, although he never drunk the stuff, he just used it to strip imperfections off the metal of his sword blades.

Jess wandered off up to the furnace, and Robert winked back at his son. "Well lad it looks like it's time to polish the old bow, and sort out your best arrows, you and Billy boy will have a day's work coming from Old Alf."

"I can't wait," beamed Robbie, as they trundled off down the pathway to the front of the house, towards a row of fence poles waiting for new crossbeams. It was later that afternoon that Robbie and his dad set off down the road towards the village, and past Oscar Hargreaves bookshop, to the very last house on the street, where a large stone extension had been built.

Alf Smith was a tall stocky man in his mid-fifties. He had a reddish complexion to his large round face, and he always wore a smile. He was in his shop, which was gleaming with the white tiles that were on every surface, stood next to a large stainless steel table, where he was cutting thick slices of meat, and tossing them into the weigh scales.

"Mr Lox?" His large voice boomed as Robbie walked in with his dad. Alf laid the large silver knife down, and grabbing a cloth, he quickly cleaned his hands, dropped the cloth on the table, and walked over to Robert and shook his hand vigorously.

"Young Master Lox? It is nice to see you both looking so well." His face beamed with its usual large smile. "What can I get for you gents?"

"I think it's more a case of what we can get for you Alf, we are planning a trip out this week, and wondered what you might be low on."

Robbie stood just inside the door watching his dad and Alf as they wandered into the large cold room, and observed the meat hanging in rows, and discussing the game that might be available. The old butcher with his large round belly and big red rubber apron, waddled about at the side of Robert Lox, who was just as tall but stockier. His very long dark ponytail hung down his back, and swished as he nodded in agreement with the old butcher, and his dark eyes flickered in his tanned face, as he negotiated a deal for anything that Robbie and Billy could bring back with them from their hunting trip.

Robbie wandered out into the street and leaned against the wall; the excitement had been building in him all day at the thought of going out into the woods. It was his favourite place, and he knew the woods and the surrounding area like the back of his hand. The delight of being able to wander all the familiar paths again, filled his mind with pictures, and he daydreamed of the moment when he would be there again.

"Hey Robbie, what you up to?"

Robbie opened his eyes and looked up. "Hi Jade."

Jade Lane was wandering across the street' her hands in her pockets, her heavy boots scrapping the floor, as she dragged her feet in a lazy way. She was wearing a heavy suede coat and a wide brimmed hat that was pushed down hard on top of the blonde curls, which flopped down to her shoulders. Jade always reminded him of a female version of Billy.

Jade turned her back, and leaned against the wall at the side of him, her green eyes twinkled with the mischief Robbie always expected from her. "So... I believe you are going to be my new archery instructor... that will be interesting."

"Yeah...your granddad thinks you and Rune should learn to shoot, I didn't mention you could be just as dangerous with a knife."

Jade slid her arms inside her coat, and pulled out two long silver daggers, from the holsters that she had attached to the back of her belt, they glinted in the light as she turned them slowly. "Don't think he approves of me having these." She spun them in her hands and then slid them back.

Robbie liked Jade, she was like a male friend, just as rough and equally as strong, but she had no pretence about her. Although most of the local women would show their disapproval of a young woman dressing and acting like a man, Jade did not care, and Robbie respected that.

She turned her tanned face to his. She was not unattractive, and had most of the looks of her sister; only she was slightly stockier, with a darker complexion. "So, when do we get to pull on your bow?" She winked and smiled.

Robbie laughed. "Behave Jade." He leaned back on the wall. "I will be practicing on Thursday for most of the afternoon, if you and Rune want to come up the house, I have got the small range set up behind the barn, you can have a bit of target practice.”

“Sounds fun, you and my sister alone behind the barn.” Her eyes twinkled more with devilish delight. “Maybe I would be in the way.” She winked and Robbie felt a twinge of embarrassment, as Jade burst into laughter.

He laughed back at her, but it was a thought that had preoccupied his week. Being alone with Rune was something that made him feel very nervous, but with Jade and her constant stream of innuendo as well? That did worry him a little more than he was willing to admit.

“Don’t worry pal I will behave, actually I have been thinking about it, and I could use a lesson or two, you never know when it might come in handy.”

Robbie nodded his head. “If you can be as accurate with a bow as you are with those knives, you will come in handy if this place is ever attacked.” Jade leaned closer and lowered her voice.

“Has anyone mentioned the Cutters to you recently?”

“No, why?”

“Could just be me Rob, but somehow it feels like there is something going on, that not all the old ones are talking about to the rest of us.”

“What makes you think that?”

“Granddad for one… He keeps going on about making sure we are always on our guard, and being able to protect ourselves. It’s like he is on a mission.”

“Is that why he wants you to take lessons?”

“I could be wrong Rob; I just don’t think I am… there is definitely something going on.”

“It is probably just nerves, I think a few have been spotted further north and it’s worried some of the community, I know dad has had it on his mind. John and your granddad discussed it at Christmas. If it was a real danger, we would all have been told, and more of us would be on lookout duty.”

“I suppose so, anyhow my old pal, I have a lot of work to do, don’t fancy it much today, but with the first big market coming up, I better make the effort. See you Thursday after dinner Robbie.”

“Yeah, see you Jade.”

Jade walked off slowly up the street dragging her boots, her head down, and Robbie stood watching her leave, wondering if she was right, and there was something going on. He did not even notice as his dad came out of the shop.

Seeing his dad in front, Robbie jumped forward, and hurried to catch him up. It looked like his dad was deep in thought; they walked slowly up the street as the sun began to fall on to the skeletal hawthorn edged lane. It was getting cold and Robbie shivered, the movement seemed to pull his dad out of his thoughts. “You could do with a good cloak; I will have a word with Len and get Rune to knock you one up.”

They walked along a few paces, and then his dad stopped and turned to him. He paused as if choosing his words carefully. "Look Robbie...I want you to keep a bow with you at all times from now on, and keep a good stock of arrows close to hand." He could see the concern in his dad's face, and it began to worry him.

"Is everything alright dad? It's just...Well things are being said... You know about the Cutters."

His dad sighed, and put one of his large hands on Robbie's shoulder and squeezed it gently. "Robbie you are so important, do you realise that?"

He smiled. "I love you too dad."

Robert Lox laughed a deep laugh, and nodded his head. "You're my son and yes, I love you, but that was not quite what I meant." Once again Robbie felt like his dad had something important to say and was picking his words with caution.

"Rob... There is more to what I do around here than you know. Very soon, you will be 17 and more will be made clear. There are raiding and scouting parties of the Cutters getting closer by the day, and soon we may find that we will have to fight to defend what we have built. Do you understand what I am saying?"

Robbie felt a jolt in his stomach, the reality of having to stand against a legendary force of evil began to wash over him. He nervously looked up into his dad's darkened eyes. "Yes Dad, I understand."

His dad smiled. "Robbie, I lead this community and one day so will you. It is not an easy task, but it is one that has been passed on to us, and we must do everything we can to protect the people here, they are very valuable to all."

"It's Ok dad I understand... I won't let you down."

His dad smiled and patted him softly on the side of the face. "I have never thought for a moment you would." He put his arm around Robbie's shoulder, and patted him on the back. "Come on let's get home to supper."

They walked along the lane, the lights of the house in sight as the darkness slowly folded over the fields around them, and finally reaching the group of houses with the tall barn, and large greenhouses in the background, as dark silent shapes they entered through the kitchen door.

The meal was an interesting affair as Robert and John finally began to open up about what they knew, and what they thought about the current activity of the Cutters. They had made two large raids just outside of Lincoln, and it looked like there was now a marauding band of about eight hundred. Scouts and small groups had been spotted further north, and there had been a few skirmishes around Old Gainsborough.

Robbie had never seen John so worried, Billy kept giving him anxious looks across the table, although his dad seemed less concerned, he made a good case about the fact that they were still very far away. It would take weeks before they could move such a large host this far. The stockade was well built, and all the surrounding communities were on the alert, so the first local sighting would reach them well in advance, which would give them time to prepare.

He listened carefully, and he understood that his dad was informing the family, but also giving him a unique insight to how he thought things out; Robbie had never heard his dad talk so openly or frankly about his role as community leader.

That night as he lay in his bed, Robbie had a lot to think about, would he one day be the leader of this community? It was something he had never ever thought about before. He had always seen his dad negotiate and organise the locals, never once in that time had he even envisaged a time when his dad would not be there.

What made him think the most was his dads' comment about how members of the community were valuable to all. Did he mean all of this community, or did he mean all of the country? He lay in the dark listening to Billy snore across the room, he thought about waking him up and asking him what he thought about it all, but then Alice came to mind.

Alice had a great way of working things out. She got to hear a lot around the house and the greenhouses, because she worked with his mum and his Aunt Beth. Yes, Alice would be the one to fill in the blanks, and so he decided he would talk to her tomorrow.

The following morning as they took a break, Robbie sat with Alice on an old stump at the far end of the yard. They were next to the compost heap and out of earshot. Robbie told her of his conversation with his dad the night before. "So, what do you think?"

Alice took a large bite out of her apple. She chewed as she thought about everything. She extended her finger still holding the apple, and poked the air in front of Robbie. "You know what? I have never really thought about it that way before, in theory you are the first son of the first son, which means you will inherit your father's mantle. It's sort of weird to think about it don't you think?"

"What do you mean weird? I bet I will do as good a job as my dad."

Alice smiled. "I wasn't saying you will be no good silly, what I meant was that the land and the farm will be divided amongst the three brothers. But in the community, you will be seen as the rightful heir, no matter what may happen, it will be you who is looked to for leadership." Alice took another large bite of her apple and continued to chew.

"I've got to admit it Alice, it sort of scares me, you know, it's a big task and I am not really sure I will ever be able to fill my dad's boots... I mean he is so good at it, look at how much respect he has got."

"And you haven't?" Alice tossed the apple core on to the compost heap. "You obviously haven't heard the way the kids around here talk about you."

"Yeah, but they are just kids, it's not like they have much sway around here, is it?"

"That's very true Rob, but you are missing one point, a very important one I might add."

Robbie looked up at her and shrugged. "And that is?"

Alice smiled smugly. "By the time you take over from your dad, they won't be... Kids that is."

Robbie knew talking to Alice would help; she had just put everything into perspective. Firstly, it would be quite some time, by which point he would have the backing of the community, and would be more able to cope. It gave him a sense of relief. It must have shown because Alice gave him a big smile and softly spoke. "You know Rob, no matter what happens in the future, I will always be here for you."

It seemed to matter to him a great deal to hear her say it; he had always thought she would be. Hearing the words touched him deeply, Alice was very special to him, and although he rarely told her, he just knew that she was aware of it.

"So, what do you think about this having to protect everyone because they are important to all?" Robbie watched as Alice pulled a pear out of her apron pocket, she passed it to him, and pulled another one out for herself.

"I have got to admit it Rob that does seem like an odd way to phrase things. I am not sure what your dad meant."

"I think, he either means important to us here in the stockade, or to everyone left in the country."

Alice looked puzzled as she bit into the soft fruit and sucked, as the juice ran down her chin. "Well, everyone in this community is important, because we all depend upon each other for our whole survival." She took another bite of her pear. "Wow these are juicy, go on have a bite these are the best we have grown."

Robbie bit into his pear, she was right, the juice flowed down his chin and he wiped it with the end of his sleeve. "But what about the rest of the country?" He swallowed deeply and looked at Alice in thought.

She chewed slowly as if it helped her think, and then swallowed. "Len Rimmer was very well known before the red death; maybe somehow he has something more to do with the outside world than we know."

"Like what? He was just a university professor."

"Also, a very well respected historian, I have read one or two of his papers about the Celts. He possibly knows more about our early times than anyone else from his generation."

"So, what you are saying is, he somehow knows something that could change our world forever?"

Alice finished her pear and wiped her mouth on her hankie. "It is possible. The problem is we do not actually know what is going on outside these walls, do we? Perhaps he is a very important man."

"What like a king?"

"Well, I am not sure he is a king, I think if he was, we would all have to bow to him or something. I just think he has got something to do with whatever is happening."

Robbie thought for a moment. Alice was much brighter than he was, and he knew that eventually she would puzzle things out. "I will tell you one thing Alice, I always feel like he seems to know more, and understands more than he actually says."

Alice looked up at him. "You know what you should do don't you?"

Robbie shrugged. "What...?"

"You should talk to Rune; she will know for sure."

Robbie's stomach twisted, talking to Rune was not something he could easily do, even when he practiced his words, as soon as she appeared everything seemed to come out in the wrong order. He could not tell Alice that though. "Why Rune and not Jade?"

Alice smiled at him. "Two reasons really, firstly she spends more time with Len than anyone else in the community, and secondly she really likes you."

Robbie started to blush, and he looked down at his feet. "Whatever makes you think she likes me?"

"Well, she always asks about a hundred questions about you for one thing." Alice gave him a huge smile. Her voice dropped to a calm softness. "You know Robbie; you should relax a bit around her, and talk to her like you do me."

Robbie felt very awkward. "I try to but she makes me nervous."

Alice patted his knee. "Rune is a really nice person when you get to know her, you should try to get to know her Robbie, I think you will find you have a great deal in common."

Robbie really wanted to get closer to her, and he knew Alice was right, but somehow his body just refused to listen to his brain whenever he was around her. He gave a long desperate sigh. Alice stood up. "Come on, we still have about two hundred tomato seedlings to pot up, if we don't get on with it, we will be up all night."

Robbie followed Alice back into the greenhouse, and spent the afternoon lost in thought, and trying to find ways he could talk to Rune without making himself look like a complete idiot. The tomatoes were all potted by teatime, and after tea he headed up to his room to be alone. The following day would be Thursday and suddenly he wished he had not eaten so much. His stomach danced as he lay in bed thinking of the archery lesson the following day. Sleep crept slowly up on him, and he drifted into dreams of being the world's best archer, and he stood on a large podium holding a golden arrow, as Rune looked up adoringly at him.

The range was a section of field directly behind the barn. It consisted of a long narrow area of short grass hedged on either side. At the far end, which was 200 meters away, was a heavy wooden wall, and in front of that, were three large round straw targets. A white sheet with the markings of three large circles was stretched tightly over each of them. Down one side of the range ran distance poles, which showed how far away from the target you were.

Robbie slipped his fingerless leather glove onto his left hand, and gripped his bow. Drawing an arrow over his shoulder from his quiver, he laid it across the grip. Fitting it to the wire with his two middle fingers, he pulled the string back.

It felt good to feel the wire tense against his fingers; he raised the bow and took aim, bringing the arrow level with his eye. The string vibrated as he gave it just a touch more tension. Looking down the arrow he saw his mark, and slowly released his breath, the arrow took flight as he released it, and it whistled at speed, a sound that brought joy to his heart. Thud!

The arrow hit the target piercing the bull. Not bad he thought considering he had not practiced for over a month. He loaded his second arrow, and it swished, and then thud! Two arrows stood out from the target side by side. He felt the burst of excitement as he loaded the third, God it felt great to be shooting again.

His third arrow swished down the range, and with a thunderous crack, it entered between the two other arrows and spread them apart. From behind him came small gasps followed by clapping, he lowered the bow and turned. Jade and Rune were stood smiling, and clapping their hands together. Rune looked positively impressed, her eyes sparkled flashing bright blue, and her cheekbones seemed highlighted by the happy smile she wore.

Jade walked slowly forward her eyes fixed on the target, her voice was quieter than normal, and she actually seemed impressed. She looked at him and back at the target as she spoke. "That Robbie... Was not too shabby."

Robbie glanced at Rune and back over at Jade. "Want to try one yourself?" He held out the bow to Jade. Knowing her well enough, he knew she would not resist, she did not disappoint and took the bow with a smile. She stood level with the marker and held the bow out at arm's length. Rune came up to the side of him as he drew an arrow from the quiver and handed it to Jade.

Suddenly he felt a little nervous, and he focused on Jade. "OK... Hold the arrow back at the end behind the flights and fit it to the string." Jade fitted the arrow and pulled back slightly as she raised the bow. "Right, now... Look down the arrow and past the tip to see the target... Now pull back, keeping the arrow on target... Breathe out a long slow breath, and as you do, lock your elbow and release the arrow."

Robbie stepped back a little as Jade took full aim pulling back on the string. She released, and the arrow thundered down the range and into the target. It struck deep into the outer ring. Jade lowered the bow and gave them both a massive smile. "I hit the target, that's something."

"That was good for a first time, honestly Jade, I missed the target completely on my first ever shot." He handed her an arrow and walked around behind her. She fitted it and brought the bow back up. Robbie cupped her extended elbow. "Lock it so it is really stiff, you are shaking just a little." He put his hand on her shoulder. "See here, lean into it a little." He pushed her forward. As he spoke, he looked up at Rune who was now watching everything he was showing her sister to do.

Robbie felt a little confidence grow inside him, and he looked Rune right in the eyes. "It's all about balance, if you can steady yourself, the bow won't pitch, and your shot should be true." She gave him a huge smile and he felt his cheeks warm slightly.

Jade released the arrow, it hit a little closer inside the rings, and she whooped and jumped up. "Look at that one!" Rune looked down at the arrow and back at her sister.

"Wow sis I am really impressed, I hope I can be as good." She looked straight at Robbie.

"Only one way to find out." Robbie took the bow from Jade's hand and held it up to her. She took it, and stood just in front with her back to him. He pulled an arrow out from the quiver and passed it to her. Rune fitted the arrow and raised the bow.

Robbie looked at her stance. "Ok lean into it." He placed his hand on her hip and pushed her forward a little. His heart raced, and he swallowed deeply as he moved closer to her. He could smell the soft scent of jasmine and honeysuckle. He raised his left arm and supported her under the elbow. His voice was soft, if not a little higher than normal.

"Ok Rune... Take a long deep breath and aim... Look down the arrow... Bring it in a little closer to your err..." He looked down at the laces that were loose on her top and revealing her soft white skin. "Err... Chest!" He swallowed deeply. Rune smiled. "Right, breathe out and release." He stepped back a little.

Rune sighted the arrow pulling back with a determined and focused look on her face. He heard her soft breath as she breathed out. There was a swish and a thud. Robbie glanced at the target. "Wow!" He looked back at Rune's very happy and satisfied face. The arrow had hit just inside the bull. Jade was bouncing about.

"I knew it... I did... Didn't I tell you?" She grabbed her sister and pulled her into a hug. "I knew you would be better than me." Robbie watched as the two sister's happiness showed. He had never actually seen them together; they were always so busy, that one of them was always off doing something, whilst Robbie had talked to the other. They were very close it was obvious.

Both the girls stood in front of him all smiles and very happy. Robbie laughed; he was still very nervous. "That was amazing." Rune looked down smiling and began to blush a little. He walked over to the hedge and picked up two more bows, and a bucket of arrows. "Ok, practice makes perfect, so I want you to shoot a few more to really get the feel of the bow." He dropped the bucket in between them and turned to Jade.

"Jade you use the right target, and Rune you use the left." Both the girls excitedly took an arrow each and fitted them to the bows. Robbie noticed Jade's stance was out and stood behind her. He put his hand on her hip and pushed her forwards a little. "Balance..." Jade pushed her buttocks back into his groin and wiggled it. "Hey behave." Rune giggled behind him as Jade laughed out loud. Jade winked up at him.

"If you're lucky Rune might let you do that," she whispered. Robbie felt his face burn as Jade giggled.

"Shut up and shoot."

Twenty minutes later the arrows were flying, and everyone was very relaxed. Most shots hit the 10-inch bull, which from 100 meters was very good. Robbie walked them down to the 150-meter mark.

"Right, you will be shooting further, so you will have to concentrate and aim harder. Pull the string back a lot more, and keep it taught." He took aim, and the arrow whipped with far more pace down the range and into the very centre of the bull. Billy came around the corner of the barn with his bow on his shoulder.

"How goes it ladies?"

Robbie looked at the two girls. "Show him." Robbie walked back towards Billy, and both of them stood watching. The girls loaded and took aim, Jade let fly first, and Rune's shortly followed. Both arrows hit bull, Robbie watched Billy with a satisfied smile on his face, as Billy's jaw dropped. Both girls turned to see his surprised expression. Billy was speechless. "I think we are getting the hang of it, what do you think Rune?" Jade looked at her sister who glanced back at the target and then back at Billy.

"There is room for improvement, but yes... I think we are getting there." The three of them laughed.

"What's up Billy? Didn't think girls could shoot?" Jade smiled at her sister.

Billy shook his head. "That was really impressive, I must admit I was not sure how well you would do, what about moving targets?"

"One lesson at a time I think Billy." Robbie walked up towards the marker. "Ok a little more practice at this distance, you don't want to overdo it, no matter how good this feels, tomorrow your arms will ache."

"Are moving targets harder?" Rune was more relaxed now as she asked Robbie the question, and he felt a lot more comfortable around her. He still felt the intensity of her eyes as she watched him.

Robbie looked at her and smiled. "It takes a lot more concentration, and you really have to practice to get your reaction time quicker."

Billy pulled an apple out of his pocket. "Want to go for it Robbie?"

Robbie drew an arrow from his quiver and fitted it to the string. He nodded at Billy. Billy launched the apple into the air with all his might; it shot like a bullet into the sky. Robbie's reaction was instant, he pulled back the string, sighted the bow, then released. The arrow sped through the air hitting the apple and slicing it completely into two, the girls gasped at the speed of his reaction and accuracy.

Robbie smiled at their obvious praise. "That takes a little more practice." He winked at Rune and smiled, he knew as she beamed back, her esteem for him had just suddenly risen. A warm happiness rose inside him like a phoenix.

Robbie sat back against the barn wall on the log pile, as he watched the three of them shoot. Jade was quite good and could match Billy shot for shot. Rune however seemed to have a very natural talent, and was putting more shots closer to the bull. Alice appeared round the corner with a tray of cakes and drinks. "Hi Rob, how is it all going?" She put the tray down on the logs in front and sat down near his feet.

"Actually, it seems to be going a lot better than I thought. I have enjoyed it more than I thought I would."

Alice laughed. "Jade has behaved then?" Robbie smiled and nodded. "That's good... Wow Rune that was an incredible shot." Rune had managed to recreate Robbie's shot from earlier, and she beamed a huge smile back at him, as he saw the two arrows split sideways by the new arrow set between them.

Alice walked up and congratulated her. Rune handed the bow to her, and then walked slowly back towards Robbie, and sat down beside him. She lifted a drink and began to sip it. Robbie turned slightly to her. "You have a very natural talent with a bow, I think I had better watch out, or the whole town will be praising you instead of me." He laughed.

Rune seemed a little embarrassed. "I am not sure I could cut an apple in midair."

Robbie nodded. "With practice I am sure you will."

Rune looked up at him; she was a little pink around the edges of her cheeks. She was so beautiful, and he smiled at her as her eyes danced. "Thanks for today Robbie, I have really enjoyed myself, it seems like a long time since I have left the loom and gone out."

Robbie took a big swig from his drink. "Maybe you should come up here more often. I could always use the company when practicing."

"I would really like that Rob."

"Yeah, so would I." Rune gave him a very large grin.

Robbie pointed. "Watch this, Alice is a really great shot, she will rip Billy's arrow clean out of the target." Robbie leaned forward bringing him right up against her side. "See how well balanced she is? Look at her legs and how she leans into the bow."

Rune nodded and turned to him; her breath blew across his cheek making the hairs on his neck stand up. Alice released the bowstring and thud! Her arrow whipped straight at Billy's, hit the target and his arrow shattered and flipped out of the target and on to the floor.

Rune gasped. Jade whooped, shouted, and danced around before running up to Robbie and Rune. "Did you see that...? Did you...? How cool was that? Wow you guys are so good at this... God, I hope you can teach me that Alice, it was incredible."

Billy had a very long face. Robbie laughed. "Oh never mind Billy, better luck next time." Everyone started to giggle, as Billy shook his head.

"What gets me is, I spend bloody hours out here practicing, and she comes along once a month and look at her. I can never ever beat her."

Everyone laughed and joked all afternoon. Robbie had not had as much fun in a long time. By the end of the afternoon, he found everyone seemed to be relaxed and was having fun. He now felt a growing confidence, and he found he could actually string together whole sentences that actually made sense when talking to Rune.

It was finally time to leave, and everyone gathered up the arrows. Rune and Jade brought their bows over to him. Robbie smiled at them. "Those are now yours; you must practice whenever you can."

Jade gave him a huge hug. "Thanks Robbie you are a real pal. I have had a great time today." She loosened her grip on him and winked at him.

Rune stretched up and kissed him on the cheek. "Thanks for the bow Rob; it is really sweet of you." Her eyes twinkled and he blushed a little.

"It's my pleasure; I have really enjoyed teaching you." They all began to walk around the barn, and head down the path. Robbie was last as he picked up the arrows and followed. Rune seemed to slow, and he caught her up and walked down to the gate with her.

"You know I am going into the old wood on Saturday to hunt, I would love it if you came along. It would be a really good chance for you to use your skill with a bow. Billy will be there so you could bring Jade along, we could pair up."

Rune turned at the gate. "I would really love to... It's just... Well, we would be outside the walls, I am not sure my mum would allow it." She looked disappointed.

"Try asking her and see what she says. Tell her you will be by my side at all times, and there really isn't anyone who knows those woods as good as Billy and Me. We have never ever seen anyone in years of going into them. It's worth asking, isn't it?"

Rune nodded. "I will ask, will you be in the village tomorrow?"

"It seems I have a good reason to be now." Rune gave him a broad smile.

"See you tomorrow then."

Robbie stood at the gate and watched her walk down the lane and out of sight. Alice came up by his side. "See I told you... Just relax... Come on tea is ready."

It was a bright happy morning when Robbie walked down the street with Billy. Both laughed and joked, and he felt on top of the world. Billy patted his back as he made his way to the bookshop. "I will see you later Rob... Good luck." He winked and Robbie smiled. He had smiled all morning, and it just seemed to broaden as he walked down the street towards Rune's house. He waved to Alice and Anne as he passed.

Rune stood by the gate, and her eyes sparkled with delight as her face broke into a huge smile. She looked radiant, in a long dress of burgundy velvet with a silver belt of hoops. She opened the gate as he approached, and stepped out. "Hi again."

He beamed. "Hey Rune."

Stephanie Rimmer coughed. "Hello Master Robert."

Robbie looked across the yard, and saw the green eyes of Rune's mother watching him. "Good morning Mrs Rimmer."

She flicked her long blonde hair over her shoulder and closed her book. Steph smiled a gentle and warming smile, and then leaned forwards in her chair. "Won't you come in and sit down Young Robert."

Robbie came through the gate as Rune sighed. "Oh, Mum do we have to be so formal, he is called Robbie."

Robbie sat in the chair opposite, as Rune sat on the wall at his side. He felt very nervous as he looked across at Stephanie Rimmer. She smiled at him warmly. "My daughters tell me you wish to take them hunting in the old wood outside the walls tomorrow?"

Robbie shuffled a little. "Yes Mrs Rimmer, they are both very talented with a bow, and I thought it would be good to let them see the skills we use to hunt with the bow."

Steph nodded as he spoke. "Although the woods can be a dangerous place Robbie?"

"I do not think so, Billy and I have been in there alone thousands of times, both of us are trained woodsmen, and without boasting, there is not too many who could spot me in the woods."

"I don't doubt it Robbie, but you will not be alone, will you? My daughters will be with you." Steph sat back in the chair. "Robbie, I know of your skills and your talent with a bow. You have an impressive reputation around here, and I believe you will one day be very well known for your talents. Please understand that my daughters are very special and precious, and I would not trust their safety to just anybody."

Robbie understood her perfectly, but he did not agree with her. "They won't just be with anybody; they will be with the two best that Loxley can offer Mrs Rimmer."

Steph laughed, and sat forward in the chair. "Well Robbie you certainly have some of your father in you that is for sure. You can relax, I have discussed this with my father, and we both agree that you above all others would be most qualified to take my daughters into the woods. If I have your word you will protect them at all costs, I will feel reassured that they will be safe."

Rune gasped as Robbie gave her a big smile. He looked at Steph and solemnly spoke. "You have my absolute promise, that I will give your daughters my total protection Mrs Rimmer."

Steph stood up with her book in her hand. "That is good enough for me Robbie." She walked towards the door, stopped, and looked back at him. "Robbie for god's sake, please call me Steph. Mrs Rimmer makes me sound older than my father."

He smiled at her, as Rune giggled. "Yes Steph."

CHAPTER THREE

HUNTING AND HUNTED

It was just before dawn and Robert Lox stood at the gate, as Robbie and Billy headed towards him. Robbie was shouldering two quivers, with fifty arrows in each, as well as his best rowan-wood bow. Billy at his side was wearing a wide brimmed hat, and his long curly blonde hair blew back in the breeze. They approached Robbie's dad smiling.

"OK you two, I will be at Joe's place just after dusk to pick up whatever you get, I know you know the whole area better than anyone Robbie, but I want you to promise me you will be extra careful today. I don't want your company put at risk; Steph has put a lot of trust in you to let her girls go out with you into the forest, so think on at all times."

"We will be extra careful Dad I promise." Robbie could see the concern in his dad's eyes, but he also knew that his dad had a great deal of faith in him, and he appreciated it.

Robert Lox was holding a piece of soft leather in his hands, and he began to unwrap it, revealing two silver daggers in new leather holsters. "I got you both a present here from John, thought they could be useful in a bind. From this moment on you both wear these at all times; it will give me some piece of mind."

He handed both of them the daggers. "Wow Robert this is fantastic, tell John thanks for me, won't you?" Billy eyed the glittering blade.

"Yeah, thank Uncle John for me as well will you Dad? We will meet you later." Robbie slipped his belt through the holster, and slid it round to his side. "Well, we will be off then."

"Ok boys, have a good hunt and I will see you at Joe's." Robbie and Billy set off down the lane towards the village, where they would be meeting up with Rune and her sister, they moved quietly talking to each other, and now dressed in colours to blend into their surroundings, and it was not easy to see them pass.

Both wore loose fitting dark green shirts and canvass pants, Robbie had on a suede long waistcoat that had extra pockets for his hunting knife, and his small pocket telescope. Billy had a sleeveless brown cord jacket on, and both were wearing their softest boots. Comfort was the most important thing when lying in wait for a strike.

They reached the small quiet village that was almost in darkness. Alf and the Kirks were the only houses that had lights on. Two dark figures stood by the wall outside Steph's house, and Robbie knew they were there waiting. "Hi guys," whispered Jade as they walked up.

"Hey Ladies." Billy stopped, and dropped one of the quivers off his shoulder and handed it to Jade.

Robbie could see the bright eyes of Rune as he approached her. The dim moonlight reflected off her pale face. "Hi... Got your bow?"

"Hi Robbie... Got it here and I got you this, sort of a thank you for the bows." Rune handed him a large folded piece of cloth. "Mum said your dad had ordered a cloak, and I thought it would be nice to have it today if it rained, we have them, look." It was still quite dark and hard for Robbie to see. Billy obviously had one off Jade, because Robbie felt the breeze as he flung it over his shoulders.

"I know it's still dark but you will see it better when it gets light. Yours is sage green, I hope that is alright, it is a proper woodsman's cloak."

"Wow Rune I am really lost for words; it is really nice, thanks I love it." Robbie swung the cloak round his shoulders, and felt the large hood drop down on to his back. He gripped his ponytail and gave it a flick, so that it dropped down outside the cloak; Rune took the tie strings, and tied it round his neck smiling. It was quite a large cloak, and yet it felt very light, and it seemed to flow around him, it was very comfortable, and as he moved it felt so light; it was as if it was not there.

Robbie peered around at the others. "Has everyone got everything? Right let's go." The hunting party set off quietly down the street, and onto the lane that led out of the village towards the stockade walls. Robbie felt alert, and his senses were at full power, as he knew once in the forest every sound would give him the clues as to which direction to take. Rune was by his side and he turned his head to her. "Excited?" He whispered.

"Very," came the soft giggle, and he felt her small, warm hand slip into his.

They followed the road until the large wall of buried stumps was in sight; the daylight was starting to increase, and just over half a mile from the large main gates, Robbie stopped. "Right, this is where we leave the road; this is a way out of here only known to Billy and my dad, you two must promise never to tell another living soul about this."

Rune smiled and nodded, as Jade smirked. "Chill out Robbie, you can trust us. Hell do you honestly think we would let anyone else know that there is a secret exit out of this prison?"

Billy smiled. "I think it's safe to say the biggest rebel in the whole community is not going to give away a secret of this magnitude Rob."

"Too right I'm not." Jade looked round. "So where is it? I can't wait to get outside these walls."

Robbie turned, and started to walk across the field. "It's this way, come on." Still holding Rune's hand, he headed for the large wall of heavy timber.

"How will today work Rob?" Rune's eyes shone brighter as the light began to increase.

"Just through the wall is dense forest, but there is a clearing a short way in. We should bag quite a lot of rabbits there. After that, we will head into the deep wood and higher up to where the deer are. On route, we usually track a few boars; Joe tends to leave us a few trolleys dotted about the place, so we load up and head for his house. Dad will pick us up there later, and we will bring back the load for Alf."

"Quite a busy day then?"

"It can be, but with extra bows at work you never know, we should have a little more time than we need, if we can get to Joe's early enough, we could spend a little more time with him than normal. You will like Joe, he is a good guy and a real woodsman."

After about fifteen minutes of walking, they arrived at the large rough wooden wall that defined the edge of safe land. Rune and Jade stared up at the tall thick heavy tree trunks that rose up to seventy feet in the air. The tree trunks had been sunken deep, and were set together touching so that nothing but air could get between them.

"Whoa! That must have been one hell of a fencing job?" Jade looked from left to right. As far as the eye could see the huge wall ran on either side, Jade looked at Billy and Robbie. "How long did it take to build this? I have never imagined it was this big."

Billy looked up towards the top of the wall. "Rob's granddad started it, and then his dad took over. It took 14 years from start to finish, all the men worked in shifts, and each wall is five miles long forming a perfect square. There are 150 farmers working this land, and twenty miles of woodland all the way round it. Joe and a crew of thirty men planted thousands of trees to bulk the woodland area back up."

Robbie looked at a very impressed Rune. "My Uncle Joe still grows and plants hundreds of trees every year to increase the size of the woodland."

"It's hard to get it all in your head; I mean it's just so vast, I never imagined it was this big. The gateway looks much smaller when we pass it to the market." Rune's eyes darted all along the top of the huge wall.

"The front wall is only forty feet high because it is guarded day and night, round here is a little deserted, so it has to be a lot bigger just to make it harder to get over, unless of course, you know about this." Robbie pulled on a large spring retained lever, and a small door four feet high and three feet wide swung open in the wall.

Through the door, the trees could be seen, and Jade was through in a flash followed by Robbie, and then Rune. Billy came last pulling the door shut, until a loud spring clicked to let him know the door was now locked again.

Robbie slid the two arrow quivers off his shoulder, and undoing the bottom straps; he tied one around his waist, and then gently passing the ties around Runes slender waist as she lifted her arms, he secured it so that the quiver hung from her hip. He stood up slowly, and found himself face to face with two big blue beautiful eyes. "Not too tight is it?" She smiled at him, and he could see all the faint freckles on her soft white face.

"Perfect," she whispered, and he felt her breath blow across his skin. He swallowed deeply.

"God you two... One sniff of freedom and you're almost at it, give it a rest."

Robbie smiled at Rune and slowly stepped back. Billy was laughing quietly, and Jade was stood with her hands on her hips, a look of disgust on her face.

"Ok Jade... Get your bow ready and let's hunt." Robbie pulled an arrow out of the quiver and rested it on the grip of his bow. He showed Rune how to hold it there ready, and she followed suit.

The trees all around were still bare, and the floor was covered with brown dead leaves. Dense patches of tall brown bracken grew all around, and the wild Primula littered the sides of the path, their yellow flowers were starting to open everywhere, and spikes of green were pushing through the masses of leaves, which would flower over the weeks as the wild narcissi bloomed.

Robbie led the way quietly, outside the walls, and in the woods, he began to feel alive. The damp earth smelled musty and he loved it, and breathed deeply as he followed the leaf buried path towards the clearing, where he knew rabbits in abundance would be coming above soil to eat their first meal of the day.

His pace slowed, and Rune came up at his side, the sun was starting to climb in the sky and he could see where the trees broke up ahead. Billy came up silently to his other side. "Same routine as normal Rob?"

Robbie nodded. "You take Jade and give it about ten minutes before you come in Ok?"

"Got you Rob." Billy patted his shoulder, and very silently he guided Jade off along another path.

Robbie pointed to a gap in the trees on the edge of the clearing. "Billy and Jade will fire from there." Swinging his arm slowly left he pointed to two large trees. "We will fire from between those two, that way we will only hit the rabbits and not each other." Understanding, Rune gave a nod.

"I wasn't too sure at first, but I see what you mean now." Robbie held his hand backwards towards Rune. She grabbed it, and he slowly wove her through the dense twigs and bramble to the shooting spot. He crouched low, and moved forward very slowly towards a patch of dense bracken, Rune came slowly up to his side.

"See?" He whispered very quietly. The clearing was quite wide, and there on the grass feeding in the sun, were at least three hundred rabbits. "They are breeding very fast up here alone, in a way we help keep the numbers balanced, as we only ever take what we need to ensure the community survive."

Robbie fitted the arrow to his bow, and Rune followed. "We will shoot in pairs taking our time. After we have shot, wait for Billy and Jade to shoot, and then we shoot again. If we fire off too quickly it will panic them and they will head underground, so don't rush, Ok?"

"Got you."

Robbie took aim, and Rune raised her bow. His arrow shot silently with just the faintest rush of wind, one of the rabbits hit the floor quietly, and did not move again. Rune followed, another rabbit fell and did not move, the arrow sticking out of its head.

"You alright?" Robbie whispered and Rune nodded looking sickly. He remembered his first time with his dad; it had made him feel sick to kill an animal. "This is survival for our people." He spoke quietly to the sick looking Rune, as two arrows shot out from the trees just to the right, and two more rabbits fell. Robbie took aim, and it started again as more rabbits silently fell.

Rune leaned over towards him. "Why don't the arrows make that whooshing sound like they did the other day?"

He slipped out another arrow, and showed her the feathers on the flight. "I clip the ones I use to hunt with a little shorter, it cuts down the wind resistance so they are a lot quieter." Rune smiled, and nodded, as she understood.

It was about forty minutes later, and they were all in the clearing, as Billy tied the rabbits into bunches that could be slung over the shoulder and easily carried. They had seventy-six rabbits, a lot more than normal. Robbie and Rune collected all the arrows and cleaned the tips on the grass, Robbie handed Billy some of the spent arrows back.

"Good haul, we need to make it up to higher ground now, and track the deer across to Joe's place."

Billy smiled. "Useful pair these two... Just look at em." He chuckled.

Jade was stood in front of Rune wearing a very happy face, and moving her arms to mimic the shots she had taken, and talking very excitedly. "Oh wow... I mean... I just crept up so quietly, and then I saw it and I lifted the bow, waited... Then swish! I couldn't believe I actually hit it, although I didn't think there would be that much blood and stuff."

Rune stared blankly, as Jade went on about her next kill, Robbie got the feeling that she was not enjoying hearing her story again. He walked up and looked at Rune sat on the grass, and then to Jade. "We have to get moving, there is still a lot of distance to cover." Rune slowly stood up, and Jade skipped over to Billy, and continued her excited conversation. Robbie looked at Rune's pale face. "It's not an easy thing to do, is it?"

She blinked. He could see some of the sadness she felt. "It is a shame they have to die so that we can live... I don't know... They were so full of life, and now look at them." Robbie lifted the bundle of rabbits on to his shoulder.

"I hated my first time hunting, I was actually sick."

"You were?" Rune seemed very surprised as she turned to look at him.

Robbie nodded. "My dad thought it was really funny after all the boasting and bragging I had done to get him to take me." Robbie seemed lost in a thought for a moment, and he smiled, he looked up to see Rune watching him and listening to his every word. His eyes met hers. "He patted me on the back, and said it's a good thing you feel like that my lad... It's a hard thing taking a life, and not something that should be done lightly."

"And what did you say to him?"

Robbie gave her a grin. "Nothing... I was sick again." Rune gasped a small laugh, and Robbie chuckled. He held out his hand, and smiling she took it, and they began to follow Billy and Jade up the path into the deep wood. "I have never forgotten how I felt that day Rune, and you shouldn't either... I only ever take what we will need at the Stockade; any meat that Alf sells on the market does not come from my bow. My job is the survival of the community, and Alf understands that." Rune squeezed his hand, and he turned to her, Rune understood him, and she knew that even though he was leading the party, he too felt the same way.

The sun was climbing higher in the sky, and hand in hand, they walked through the forest of old trees. The grass was lush and dark green, carpeted around the now thickening pale fronds of the newly emerging bracken, old acorns and beechnuts littered the floor, and crunched as they walked, and not too far away, came the sound of water trickling on stones.

They stopped at the side of the stream, and whilst Jade and Rune crouched to fill their canteens, Robbie scouted the bank with Billy. "Two here Rob." He winked. "And not that long back looking at it." Robbie came over and looked at the fresh tracks in the mud at the side of the stream. The girls came up and looked down.

"Deer... They passed this way earlier." Billy showed them more tracks, which headed across the stream and up the bank on to the stonier ground. They crossed the stream, and watched them until they hit the rocky scree where they disappeared. Jade looked back to Robbie who was slowly standing up, still reading the markings on the floor.

"They just vanish at this point; how can we follow them?"

Billy pointed back to Robbie. "That is his job... Best tracker in the district, no one is better, not even Joe."

The girls watched, as Robbie with his head down, walked along the bank of the stream and back again. He then stepped over the stream, and came towards them.

He passed Jade and Rune, and stepped up to Billy, and softly whispered to him. "Keep your bow ready, we are not alone." Billy looked stunned as Robbie passed him, and headed slowly along the path in front.

"Is everything alright Billy?" Rune looked up at him with a puzzled look on her face.

"What...? Err yeah... Fine, come on then let's get going, Rune you follow Rob, and Jade and I will take the rear." He smiled an unconvincing smile, and slid an arrow out of his quiver and laid it across the bow. Jade walked up to him.

"Are we that close?" She looked at the arrow lay on his bow.

"Err... Yeah, you have to be fast when you are tracking deer, slightest movement and they are off."

Jade pulled an arrow out, and fitted it to the bow, then followed her sister up the path. Billy stood with his back to them for a moment and surveyed the woods slowly; happy it was clear, he turned and followed up the path, his eyes darting left to right.

The site of fresh boot marks worried Robbie. There had been three different types of partial sole prints a little further along the stream on the bank, Robbie knew Joe's tracks, and he also knew Joe well enough to know that he would not bring anyone easily into the wood.

Joe was a true woodsman, which meant he was a very private and solitary man. Robbie and Billy were only two of a short list of guests, Joe allowed free reign. Robbie's senses were now in overdrive as he scanned the floor, and all the trees and branches on either side of the path. He wanted to spot any clue that would give him some idea of who else was in the wood with them.

Silently he moved forward as the ground in front began to rise steadily upwards, he was following the deer tracks to the top of a large limestone escarpment, which he had originally thought would make a great place to stop for a rest and something to eat. Now his mind turned to using it as a good place to look out over the woodland, to see if he could spot any signs of the others in the forest.

His ears were straining, as he tried to listen for anything that was odd, above the birds singing in the trees. His eyes spotted fresh deer tracks, and he stopped and crouched low, Rune came up beside him and lowered herself to look at the prints. Robbie turned, as her face came down at the side of his. He pointed at the hoof print. "See how dark the soil is around the edge? That dampness tells me it's less than an hour old. We are getting very close now they must be around here somewhere."

Rune looked down at the soil and smiled. "That's pretty amazing Rob, I had no idea... But I can see now how you work it out, that will turn grey like the rest of the soil over the day wont it?"

Robbie nodded. "You will hardly even notice it in an hour; we will have to take it really slowly and quietly now."

Billy and Jade crawled up to them. Robbie pointed at the track, and Billy nodded. "We are close then Rob?" Billy looked him in the eyes. "Any other signs?"

Robbie knew what he was thinking, "nothing yet." He looked at the two girls. "Ok this is how we will play it. We stay in pairs and move up as slowly and quietly as possible, do not break cover, and expect a long shot. These deer will not let us get too close, so stay below cover and take aim."

"Pointless going for more than two eh, Rob?" Billy had a point; the odds were high that the girls would not manage to carry one, whereas Billy and he could take one each.

Robbie thought for a moment. "It may take two shots for each deer, so pick your mark, and both shoot for the same one. Go for the top of the neck just below the base of the skull; it will be fast for the beast." Robbie looked up the path. "Ok Billy, you and Jade go for anything to the right of this path, and Rune and me will aim left of the path, at least that way we will be sure to go for different ones. Billy, keep close to Jade so you can talk your instructions to her, I will give you the usual hand signals."

"Ok Robbie, see you at the top... Come on Jade, you follow me."

Jade looked very excited; her eyes sparkled as she gave a little wave to them. "See ya!"

Robbie looked back at Rune; she was sat on a small rock, and gave him a sweet smile as he came up to her. "You alright?"

"Yeah, I'm fine."

"I won't mind if you don't want to shoot... It's up to you, but if it upsets you, and you don't want to I will understand." Rune gave a sigh.

"No, it's alright, I will shoot... I can see how controlled you are over what is taken, you are right, this is about survival of the community, and you will only be taking the two, won't you?"

"Two deer will feed a lot of people Rune, I think it's enough, and it's all I will take whenever I need to... I think I will head for that gap between the two trees, stay close and keep low."

Robbie pulled the hood of his new sage green cloak up over his head. It seemed stiffer at the front of the hood, which allowed him to use it to shade his eyes.

Slowly he moved forward keeping a watch across to the right. Billy and Jade were about twenty feet in front of them just off the side of the path. Robbie raised himself up slowly to peer forward.

He saw a large antler move at the edge of the clearing on the escarpment, and lowered himself slowly down, and signaled Billy. Rune was watching him crouched frozen in the grass; Robbie smiled and pointed up front. She slowly moved up to his side. Robbie pulled two fern leaves off the plant, and taking Rune's bow, he took a small piece of twine out of his pocket and tied it to the top of the bow as he quietly spoke.

"That will give the bow cover when you shoot; the deer won't notice it in amongst the trees."

Rune nodded. He did the same with his bow, and then on hands and knees, they began to crawl forwards very slowly. Just up ahead was a small holly bush, surrounded by large ferns. Robbie and Rune peered through the undergrowth; Rune drew a breath at the sight of the mighty stag that stood proudly watching the rest of the herd. She raised her bow and took aim.

Robbie's hand touched the tip of her arrow and pushed it down. Rune turned to look at him. "Him we leave," he said softly. "That one is special, he belongs to Hearne."

Rune looked surprised. "You believe in Hearne, the Green Man?"

Robbie winked. "There is a lot more in this world than people realise Rune. I have sat with that stag many times over the years; he knows he will have safe passage from me. I am a woodsman; I will not kill that which deserves to live." Rune smiled at him.

"My granddad was definitely right about you."

"What's that supposed to mean?" He frowned at her.

"Don't worry its nothing sinister, he told me that he thought you had many layers, but most importantly that you are at one with the land. To him that is very important."

The stag moved up ahead, and Robbie looked up, Billy and Jade were crouched low in some small bushes over on the other side of the path. Robbie signaled to get ready. Rune and Robbie rose together, their bows fitted with arrows and their eyes already at the aim. Frozen they stood as the herd moved grazing forty feet in front of them. A large doe was closest to them, and Robbie breathed his words out slowly to Rune.

"The doe... On my count... One...Two...Three." The arrows shot straight and true, silently crossing the front of the clearing. The doe had no time to react, by the time the rest of the herd realised what was happening, the doe lay still on the ground. Robbie stepped forward fitting another arrow, but it was not needed, both arrows had flown true and hit the doe at the base of the skull. It was a fast, instant, painless death.

Robbie pulled the arrows out and wiped them on the grass, and dropped them into his quiver. Across the clearing, Billy was doing the same; he lifted his deer onto his shoulders and began to walk over to them. Robbie scanned around the clearing to ensure they were secure. He picked up the doe, and carried it back to the place where he and Rune had hidden. He dropped it to the ground next to the rabbits.

He walked back to the edge of the clearing as Billy and Jade arrived, Billy walked through and dropped his deer at the side of Robbie's, and came back. The four of them stood together just inside the tree line. Robbie pulled out his small telescope, and pulled it so it extended out. "I want you all to stay here a second while I check the tree line, this seems like a good enough place to have a break, it's not quite mid-day yet, but something to eat would be nice."

Robbie walked towards the edge of the overhang; he kept low and close to the tree line. At the edge he crouched down, and looked through the scope scanning the whole forest. A column of smoke rose into the air, near Joe's hut, Robbie knew he had the still burning; slowly he scanned the forest backwards towards the base of the escarpment. Billy crawled up beside him. "Any sign?"

Robbie passed him the scope. "Nothing, but let's be honest, if they are under the tree line, even without leaves they will still be difficult to spot."

"What you going to do Rob...? Do you think we should tell the girls?"

Robbie sat back against the stump of the small oak and thought for a moment. "I think we should yes. We all need to be very alert, it might be nothing but I don't want to risk it. This is our turf we have the advantage here."

"Ok Rob you're the boss around here, let's tell em and eat, I am starving."

"No fire Billy."

"Yeah Ok, I will tell them, you keep your eyes open." He handed the scope back to Robbie.

Robbie sat looking out across the woodland, his eyes panned right to left trying to glimpse anything that could give him an idea of who was in the woods. He had seen three different sets of boot marks, so he knew at least there was an equal match for the group.

Rune came over towards him; she kept very low and sat beside him near the high edge. "I brought you a sandwich." She passed him a small package wrapped in brown paper. "Is what Billy said right... do you think there are Cutters here?"

Robbie opened the paper, and took out the thick wedge of bread and cheese. He bit down hard and began to chew, and chose his words carefully. "The problem is, I just saw three sets of boot marks, but I have no way of knowing who owns them. What I do know is, they were made today."

Rune slid her arm inside his, it surprised him a little, and he took her hand in his. "I think we will be alright... Let's face it we have our bows and with your tracking knowledge, and your ability to navigate these woods, it must be possible to avoid contact with anyone?"

"That's what I have been thinking. All we have to do is get over to Joe's place safely, and we should be fine. I have tried to see if anyone is down there, but there is no sign of life at all. I suggest we just enjoy the day, and if something crops up, then we will deal with it."

"I have really enjoyed being with you today Robbie. You really do look the part in your cloak and hood." He turned to tell her how much he liked it, Rune moved in close and before he knew what was happening, her lips met his. His heart missed several beats as she kissed him.

Her soft pale face moved back a few inches, and he gazed in wonder at her bright blue eyes and long red eyelashes. "You should wear your hair down more, like a woodsman does." She smiled, her eyes radiated happiness and peace, and he felt very calm and relaxed. She really was very beautiful, and he felt so lucky that she was here with him. For so long he had watched her from a distance and wanted her close, and now that she was, he felt that there was nothing he could not achieve.

Rune took his hand and gently pulled him back. "Come on we should move." Robbie slid back, and skirting the tree line, they headed back together to the others. Jade was wearing a big smile as they approached together; Billy was examining the deer and stood up as Robbie approached. Jade began talking hurriedly to Rune in the background, and Robbie heard the giggle as he came up to Billy.

"So Rob, What have you got in mind?"

He scratched his chin and looked down at the two deer, and the bunches of rabbits. "Carry on as planned I think, but be extra vigilant, and at the first sign of trouble we stash these, and get the hell out safely to alert the community."

"Sounds like a plan to me pal, come on then let's make a move, you track and I will cover the rear." Billy lifted the doe on to his shoulders; it was the biggest and the heaviest. He knew Robbie would need to scan the floor and all the plant life, if he was going to keep them clear of trouble. He would manage better with the smaller deer on his shoulders. "Ladies can you handle a few rabbits?" He crouched down and managed to thrust one of the large bunches of rabbits to saddle the deer, and then stood up.

Rune and Jade grabbed a bunch each, and threw them over their shoulders, as Robbie lifted the second deer over his broad back. "Ok, is everyone alright?" They all nodded. "Right let's move, and don't forget keep alert if you see or hear anything sing out."

Robbie led the way across the top of the escarpment, and through the trees to the other side, where the path descended back towards the lower forest floor. His senses were as keen as they had ever been, as he checked the plants and trees for any signs of damage, and the floor for prints. Looking all around as he walked, he checked the path up front and the surrounding woodland.

Everyone seemed on high alert, Rune and Jade walked besides each other and strained to see if they could hear something, both of them glanced from side to side as Robbie led them off the path, and through dense trees and bushes. Billy covered the rear checking behind him as he went. It was slow going, but he knew the trail Robbie had taken, and he understood the short cut. Robbie wanted the girls safe as quickly as possible.

It had been over an hour when Robbie slowed and turned to the others. "There is one of Joe's tree carts, we will take a break there and load it up." He pointed through the trees, and Rune could just make out two long pole handles sticking up in the air.

The cart looked like horses had once pulled it. It had two large wooden wheels edged with steel and a flat base. Joe used it when he cut rowan poles; he would stack the cart, and pull it back to the cabin. Robbie pulled down on one of the poles to bring it level, and then rolled the deer off his shoulder and on to the flat base. He held it steady as Billy dropped the large doe on to it. The cart had a small leg at the front so that the long poles did not fall to the ground under the weight, and once it was set level, he lifted the rabbits off Rune and Jade who both sighed in relief.

The girls were very red faced, it had been a long walk, and the rabbits had been surprisingly heavy. Robbie walked over to a tree stump, and lifted a pile of moss out of it. He pulled two large bottles of lemon juice out and passed one to Jade. "Secret stash of Joe's." He winked at Rune and she smiled. Both of them drank heavily. He sat down on an old log, and dropped his hood. Pulling the cord out of his hair, he shook it so that his long dark brown hair dropped over his shoulders. Rune's face was all the approval he needed, and he smiled as he looked at the floor.

Jade was sat on the grass rubbing the back of her calves. "God my legs are killing me, I haven't walked this much in years." She looked up at the others. "I am not complaining, it's just that there isn't really any place to walk to in the Stockade is there?" Billy nodded.

"Never actually thought of it like that before, I suppose Rob and me spend so much time running up and down the greenhouses, and to and from the barn that we must travel miles in a day."

"I just go to the yard and back, or across the street, you must do quite a bit Rune, on those loom peddles?"

Robbie looked up the track. "It's not that far now, Joe's place is just up through the trees behind that small hill. We can push the cart along the track; it won't take us too long." He stood up and walked slowly up the track to where he had a clear view. He felt nervous, seeing the boot marks had bothered him, but not nearly as much as not hearing or seeing any signs of who made them.

He felt the arm of Rune as she came up beside him, and slipped it around his back. He raised his arm upwards and put it around her shoulders pulling her close. "You seem uneasy Robbie what is it?"

He looked down at the shiny red hair and her pale face. "Something is not right Rune. I just cannot put my finger on it. It seems to me that those prints were left this morning, and yet there has been no sign of anyone all day. There are very few who can navigate these woods, I did expect to run into whoever made those prints."

Rune pulled her arm tighter. "You don't think they are after your uncle, do you?"

"That is exactly what I think, and it bothers me in ways I cannot even comprehend. The only good thing about it is Joe's place is very hard to get to if you don't know the way. He is the only person I know who still owns guns; I guess if they try to take him, we will hear the noise miles away."

"Maybe we should get moving rather than hang around here; the closer we are, the quicker we could help him." They walked back to the cart and Robbie heaved it up. He turned around and started to pull the cart, Billy pushed from behind, and it rolled along creaking quietly. Robbie put his head down and scanned the floor for signs; there was nothing, only the odd animal track.

They pulled for an hour, and the sweat dripped off Robbie's brow, as he moved slowly up the track. His eyes peered through the dense trees from side to side, and back down at the floor. He looked up at the green mound rising before him, and he knew it would not be too much longer before they came across the winding path that led to Joe's cabin. Robbie looked down at the ground and his heart skipped a beat, he came to an abrupt halt staring at the floor.

"What is it Rob?" Billy had bumped into the cart as it stopped. Robbie lowered the cart on to its foot and Billy and the others came forward to see what Robbie was now inspecting on the ground.

Billy looked at the boot prints. "Shit." Robbie looked up at him.

"You are telling me Billy. There is about ten of them, and it looks like they are definitely looking for Joe."

"What do you need us to do?" Rune and Jade stood side-by-side, bows in hand.

"I am not sure yet, maybe we should ditch the cart for a while and get closer just to see." Robbie looked up to Billy for reassurance.

Billy winked at him. "Sounds like a plan to me."

Robbie turned to the girls. "This could get hairy; I don't want you two getting hurt."

Rune and Jade's eyes glared with defiance, Rune looked at Jade and then to Robbie. "If we stay with you two just as we did for the hunt, we won't, will we?"

"I am not sure Rune; I did promise your mum I would not place you in harm's way."

"I don't see how you have a choice. None of us know who these prints belong to, so you cannot leave us here just in case they come back. Not that we would for one moment stay put, we would follow you anyhow."

Robbie smiled; he knew when he was being out smarted. "Alright we will stay in pairs as we did this morning, but promise me you will not take any risks, and you will do as Billy and I instruct you. Let's say this is just another hunting lesson alright?"

"Agreed!" Jade and Rune nodded and spoke together.

"Right Billy boy same as before, you get the right with Jade, we will handle the left. Stay low and move slowly. And keep as quiet as possible; these could be a little jumpier than a deer."

"And they could bite back." Jade's voice carried a note of caution.

With Rune at his side, Robbie moved off the path, the track was the long route round, and he wanted to get there as quickly as possible. Silently they moved through the trees and the shrubs, skirting large patches of bracken and brambles, until they started to climb the small mound that would give them an overview of Joe's place.

It was about twenty minutes later, when they reached the top of the mound in amongst the heavily overgrown trees. Robbie's hand signaled to stop. They all instantly sank to the floor; Robbie crawled forward and peered over a fallen log into the large basin below.

The old cabin was sat in the middle of a large clearing; smoke issuing from the thin metal chimney. All seemed to be all right, Robbie pulled his hood back over his head as he raised himself up. His bow was loaded ready as Billy appeared a few feet away at the base of a tree. He had stuck ferns in the rim of his hat to blend in.

Robbie was about to mouth all is all right when he saw it. Half way down the bank on the other side of the basin was a glint, as the sunlight struck something. He dropped like stone behind the log, and Billy who was watching pulled back behind the tree.

Rune looked at him a little startled. "What is it?" She whispered peering over the top of the log. Robbie ripped out lumps of grass and two large fern leaves and bound them to the end of his bow.

"Joe has company, and I am sure he is not aware of it. I have got to warn him."

"How are you going to do that?" Rune's face paled a little. "You are not going down there are you?" She gripped Robbie's arm.

"Rune there are times when I can be really stupid, relax this is not one of them." He leaned forward and kissed her. She was stunned at the speed in which Robbie, popped up from behind the log, took aim and fired; he fell back down beside her and smiled.

The arrow hit Joe's door at a horrific speed. Such was the power of the shot that the wood split, and the tip came through on the other side. Robbie knew that Joe would recognise his arrow, and would then realise that there was trouble, the cabin door creaked open a jar. The distinctive clipped flight of the arrow was enough to let Joe know Robbie was about. Joe knew wherever Robbie was, so would be Billy.

Robbie peered over the log. His new sage green hood gave him perfect cover, as he scanned along the bank where he had seen the glint earlier. The bracken moved; he knew someone was trying to crawl through it. He signaled over to Billy.

Robbie pointed to his wrist, and then lifted ten fingers; Billy nodded and whispered something to Jade. Billy raised his bow ready; he had known Robbie long enough to know what he planned.

"Ok Rune, are you up for this? I need you fast and accurate. In a few moments on my signal, Billy is going to stand up and shoot directly at our ten O clock position. When he does it, he will give himself away; they know someone else is here now because of my shot at Joe's door." Rune nodded understanding what he was explaining.

"When Billy stands up, he will become a target, I need you to cover all of the right side, so I can cover the left. I will bet my bow some smart arse down there will break cover to shoot Billy. If it is on your side, you must get them first, Billy's life will depend on it." Rune suddenly looked very nervous. "If you are not up to it, that's alright, just tell me now." He gave her a soft smile. Rune swallowed deeply.

"I can do it Robbie."

"Good girl... As soon as you have fired, get yourself back down fast... Ok here we go." Robbie gave the signal to Billy, and pulled his wire taught on his bow. Rune fitted her arrow and pulled back. Robbie nodded, and Billy stepped out from behind the tree. He took aim and fired.

Robbie was up in a flash, as the undergrowth parted and a small fat man with a brown felt hat appeared with a crossbow. He unleashed the arrow with great force; Rune's bow sung out, Robbie had another arrow fitted and ready before the fat man hit the floor. There was a scream from the right and another man fell dying, an arrow right through his throat.

Rune had her eyes closed as she lay on her back behind the stump. Robbie leaned over her and blew her eyes softly. She opened them and looked up at him. "That was a great first shot," he whispered. "I am sorry Rune; I know this is not easy for you."

"I killed him, didn't I?" Her voice was quiet and a little shaky.

"You saved Billy and my uncle, which has to be worth something. The man you shot has probably killed many innocent people; he would kill you in a flash without thinking about it." Rune nodded up at him, she understood what he was saying. There was an almighty bang that echoed around the woods, Robbie and Rune jumped. One of the Cutters fell out from behind Joe's fence.

"Looks like Joe got my message." Robbie peeped back over the log. Three Cutters were down, Robbie guessed there had to be at least another seven dotted around, and he looked for the signs of activity. To his left an arrow shot off, the foliage at the ten O'clock position parted and a body rolled out. Billy lowered himself back into the under growth.

Twigs snapped in front of him, and his eyes darted across the area of the sound, but nothing moved. Rune crawled to the end of the log and peered round. She was flat on the floor hidden by her deep green cloak and hood. Rune patted the log, Robbie looked, and she raised two fingers. She closed her hand and then flashed five fingers, and then another three.

Robbie looked to the eight O'clock position, and sure enough, he could see two men sat together in the top of an old oak tree. He pulled two arrows out, and pulling out his knife, he cut one of the four flights off both arrows. He loaded the two arrows together on the bowstring. Rune was staring up at him as he slowly rose up, took aim and fired.

The two arrows shot through the air, and then as they neared their target, they split apart and a gap widened, as one arrow each hit both men in the chest, they looked shocked as they fell out of the tree.

Robbie looked up at the sky, the afternoon was starting to draw in and soon it would begin to grow dark. He didn't like the idea of being out in the open after dark, especially with at least another five Cutters hanging about. There had to be a way of getting them out in the open.

"What you thinking?" Rune was sat up watching him.

"It's going to be dark soon, and I don't fancy sitting here all night waiting to get my throat cut, apart from all that, it won't be that long before my dad gets here, and he has no idea what is going on."

"How do you flush out animals when you are hunting?"

"Hail."

"What?"

"Rune you are a genius." He grabbed her and kissed her, she looked dumbfounded, but Robbie was already signaling to Billy and Jade. They crawled over into the small space at the side of Rune and Robbie.

"What's going on guys?" Jade seemed to be really enjoying herself, she had a very dirty face and was smiling broadly.

Robbie leaned against the log. "Time is getting on and we need to find the rest, Billy what if we create a little hail for our guests?"

"Brilliant." Billy nodded his head vigorously.

"Ok ladies time to learn to shoot two arrows at a time." Robbie pulled out two new arrows, and showed them how to clip off some of the flights. He put the flightless sides of the arrows together, and fitted them to his bowstring. He raised his bow, and shot them into the air. They glided over the cabin and then split in mid-air, and fell to earth.

Rune, Jade, and Billy loaded their bows. "Alright, if your arrows flush anyone out, I will take care of them. Let's start at nine O clock and work round." A few moments later, Robbie was waiting, his bow ready. Six arrows shot into the air, and rained down on the bracken just up from the cabin. Nothing moved.

"Alright let's try eleven." Six arrows rained down on the scrub and bushes. There was a squeal, a man ran out from the left of a tree, Robbie fired, and he hit the floor dead. "Twelve."

Again, the air rained arrows. The trees parted, a man ran out with terrific speed, heading for the shelter of the cabin wall, before Robbie could let the arrow go, there was an almighty bang. The man lifted into the air, and shot backwards on to the floor. Robbie noticed the smoke around the cabin door. Joe had his shotgun pointing through the gap.

"One O clock." Nothing happened.

"Two O clock." Nothing again.

"Three O clock." Two men ran out in opposite directions, Robbie took out the one running away from the cabin, the loud blast signaled the others demise. They had covered a full arc in front of them, and as far as they now knew, the area around the cabin was clear; Robbie gazed down at the bodies, and the surrounding trees and scrub looking for the slightest movement.

"So, is that it Robbie my boy, or do you think there are more?" He turned to look at Jade, who he felt was having the time of her life.

"I am not sure... Those tracks I saw could have been just one group of a few... What do the rest of you think?"

"That does seem to be the lot Robbie; we have pretty much covered the whole area in arrows." Billy was still looking out over the scene as he spoke, Robbie could tell he was nervous.

Rune looked across at the cabin and then back at Billy. "I don't fancy our chances up here in the dark... But I am not over excited about walking down there either; it will only take one arrow to lose one of us."

"I am not sure we have much of a choice, let's face it, up here we are sitting ducks come night fall. Robbie, I think we have to move and move now, just in case there are more on the way." Jade looked at the other two. "Come on guys, I am right we have to get down to the cabin."

Robbie nodded. "You are right Jade... We have to be with Joe when my dad arrives... I think the only way to go is two at a time." Robbie peered over the log. "See that big tree with the stump at the side?" Billy nodded as he picked out the point Robbie was looking at. "Rune and I will head there first, while you two cover; we can cover from both sides as you two come down behind us."

They began to get organised, as Billy and Jade loaded their bows and took up a central position side by side. Robbie looked down for the best route and then turned to Rune. She looked nervous, and he took her hand in his. He looked at the pale white skin and the delicate fine fingers that glistened with the rows of silver and jewelled rings. "Don't be scared... I want you to keep right behind me at all times... Just follow my lead, and I promise you will be safe." He smiled, and she smiled back. "On the count of three... One...Two... Three."

Still holding her hand behind him, he set off guiding her through the trees down the slope. His eyes moved from side to side picking a safe course that kept them behind the trees. The stump came into view at the side of the large tree, and turning his back to it, he slammed up against it, catching Rune in his arms and holding her tight. His heart was hammering on his chest, and he felt the soft warm body of Rune pulled tight up against him. She was trembling slightly, her breath coming in small gasps. He put his head on her shoulder. "So far so good, are you alright?"

Rune moved, and he loosened his arms as she looked up. Her hood had slipped down and her fiery red hair shone in the last of the afternoon's weak sunlight. "I'm fine... Shaky... But fine."

"That's my girl... Ok let's get ready for the other two, you keep cover from here, I will watch from the tree." Rune loaded her bow and lifted it ready. Robbie signaled Billy, and turned to face the open ground across to the cabin, he raised his bow.

Billy and Jade came half running, and half tumbling down the hill at great speed. Rather than run in zigzags as Robbie had done, they just ploughed through the under growth in a direct line. Both of them fell in a heap at Rune's feet.

Jade sat up smiling, moving Billy's out stretched leg from her face. "That was sort of fun." She grabbed Billy's arm and heaved him into the sitting position. "You ok there Billy boy?"

Billy sat up spitting dirt and grass out of his mouth. "I'll settle for not being dead."

Robbie had not seen so much as a leaf move, it made him more nervous. The cabin was fifty feet away across low grass; he could see the black end of a shotgun pointing out through the gap in the door. Without looking back, he spoke. "I think this time we all go together. We will walk with bows loaded, compass points, and keep your eyes peeled. Billy you're south, I will go north. Ladies keep close side by side between Billy and me... Right nice and slowly let's move."

With bows raised, the group walked out. Robbie could feel the pounding of his heart in his ears, as he waved his bow slowly from side to side across his field of vision. The others followed packed in a tight bunch close together, their attention solely fixed on the woodland all around them.

Twenty feet from the cabin, Robbie shouted. "Woodsmen on foot," and the door moved slightly. They reached the steps of the cabin, and moved swiftly up, Robbie stepped to the side of the doorframe, as the door opened and the others entered. After one final look, he walked slowly backwards, his bow still high, into the cabin. The door slammed shut with a bang.

Before he could move, two large hairy arms pulled him into a hug and he felt the heavy patting of his Uncle Joe's embrace. "God lad that was something... Hell I am glad you were here Robbie."

He lowered his bow and gave his uncle a huge hug. "Not half as glad as I am to know you are still here." Robbie turned as his uncle released him from the hug, and looked at the other three stood by the old wooden table. "Is everyone alright?" They nodded, and Billy walked forwards to embrace Joe.

Robbie crossed over to where the girls stood silently smiling; he put out his arms and pulled Rune into a big hug. Raising one arm, he slipped it around Jade and pulled her into a hug with her sister. "You two have been pretty fantastic today, I am sorry it didn't turn out to be the fun day you expected, but thanks for everything."

Jade pulled back and looked at Robbie, and then Billy who was still hugging Joe. "Are you nuts? This has been the best day I have ever had. You guys are wild; I can't wait for the next time." She beamed a huge smile at them.

Rune and Robbie started laughing, as Billy and Joe stood looking at her a little in disbelief.

CHAPTER FOUR

FAMILIES AND SECRETS

Robbie sat in the corner at Rune's house. His father informed Steph and Len Rimmer of the day's events, and how on his arrival at Joe's cabin, he had found one very relieved brother-in-law, and four very tired, yet victorious teenagers.

He described the scene of the dead Cutters, and how after ensuring the cabin was safe, how Robbie, Joe, and he, had gone back out into the woodland to check their trail, and make sure there had been no others. Robbie and his father had tracked all the prints to a clearing, where it appeared that all the small groups had met up.

Robert had been convinced that their progress had been too smooth going, and he had looked at both of them, and suggested that the group must have been using a map. It was disturbing because Robbie and Joe were the only two who knew the woodland that well. Joe was flabbergasted at the notion of anyone doing something so terrible. It had frightened Robbie to think that there was a spy amongst them.

They had returned several hours later with the cart containing the deer and the rabbits, and loaded up, then returned to the Stockade. Joe had refused to leave his cabin; even though Robert had done everything he could to convince him it was no longer safe. It was a smiling Jade and Rune, who had pointed out to their mother, how careful Rob and Billy had been, and how they had been protected and felt safe at all times.

Rune was sat next to her grandfather, and both of them had not taken their eyes off Robbie for the whole time they had been talking. Robbie was tired, and sat quietly with his bow across his knee, staring at the floor. Steph Rimmer sat calmly listening to Robert Lox, and Billy sat on the chair, set to one side of Robbie.

"We loaded up the cart and headed straight back, Billy here drove the cart, and I sat the girls in the back out of sight, whilst Robbie and I sat on the top and kept a good watch with our bows on hand. We saw nothing at all on the way back, and that's about the size of it Steph."

Steph Rimmer had listened for an hour, and she thought about all that she had been told. Robbie now expected the explosion, and he tensed as he waited for her to accuse him of endangering the lives of her daughters. Her voice was calm and quiet as she spoke softly. "Thank you Robbie, for keeping your word to me, you have been true, and I owe you my gratitude."

"What?" Robbie slowly looked up into the kind face of Steph Rimmer. "I thought you would be angry with me. You knew of the risk and warned me, but I did not listen."

Steph leaned forward and touched his leg. "I must admit I considered the possibility Robbie, but even I had not expected them this soon. You faced them today and protected my family as a true woodsman would, I am not angry, I am proud of you all." She smiled at him. "You have all been very brave."

"Here... Here...?" Len raised his cup in salute to them all; Robbie looked back at the floor. It had all happened so fast, and now he sat in the corner, as the events of the day began to impact on him. For years he had listened to the stories of the Cutters, and their deadly attacks, and now suddenly they were not just some tale, they were here amongst them. Somehow, he knew life was never going to be the same again.

Jade was talking again, and telling everyone about her first hunt, her excited voice seemed to blend into the background, as Robbie was lost in his thoughts and his memories of the day. He had hunted for years and killed animals many times, today he had been forced to face and kill men. Four men lay dead, and now buried in the old woodland because of his arrows.

His stomach churned as he saw the faces of the dead men in his mind, their eyes open yet dull and lifeless. It had happened so fast, and he had not given it any thought at all, it had been an instant decision, and somehow it had come too easy to him. Easy... How could he think that...? Yet it had been. In the heat of the moment just like with a deer, he had lifted the bow and taken his shot.

Four men now lay dead because he had shot them. He found it difficult to understand how exactly he felt about that. His emotions seemed to be bumping around inside him. Rune was safe, he had killed to protect her; Joe had been saved from being overrun. Four men lay dead with his arrows inside them, confusion swept over him.

Two small soft warm hands closed gently around his. One took the bow, and lifted it off his knee, and stood it at the side of his chair. Robbie looked up at the pale white face surrounded with red hair, and two sapphire blue eyes that burned with life. It smiled and spoke very quietly. "Hey... You alright...? I am making everyone drinks; will you come and help me?"

The hands pulled, and coming back to his senses, he rose out of the chair and followed Rune through the door into a small kitchen. She pushed the door shut gently, and turned back to him. Rune slid her hands around his waist and pulled him close. Her soft warm lips met his and Robbie began to slide back to life, as he lifted his arms around her.

Rune put her head on his shoulder and squeezed him. Happy just to be alone and holding her, he leaned his head down on to her and breathed a long sigh of relief. Rune pulled him closer. "Are you going to be alright now Rob?"

"I killed four men today Rune, and I do not know how I should feel about it."

"You also saved four lives." Her soft voice came from his chest below his chin.

"I did not think or feel, I just reacted, and they were dead. Everyone is thanking me, and yet I do not find it something to be proud of."

Rune leaned back and looked up at him, her bright blue eyes glistened. "You have to understand Robbie; you had no choice; you did what you had to in order to save your uncle and protect us. Didn't you say in the woods you only killed what was necessary to ensure the survival of the community?"

"I was talking about deer, not men."

"I don't see the difference." She raised a hand and swept his long hair back to look at his face. "Robbie, you took two deer to feed all of us, and you killed four men to protect us all. You said today, it was your duty to ensure everyone's survival."

Rune's faith in him surprised him, her words resounded around his head, he smiled, and she smiled back at him. "When did you become teacher, and me the student?"

"When you doubted yourself, after showing me the man and leader you will one day be... I tell you what; let's just say that it is a good thing that you feel this way."

"How can this be a good thing Rune?"

"Think of it this way Rob, feeling as you do is not going to make you a cold and oppressive person, is it? I would say, that if anything it would make you more just and fair. Come on, let's not think about it anymore, help me fill the kettle." Rune slid out from his arms, and crossed the kitchen to a large black metal kettle; she picked it up and passed it to him. "There is a pump just outside the door."

Robbie stepped out into the cold night air and looked around; there was a large pump just at the side of the door. He grabbed the handle and pumped it up and down, as water flowed into the kettle. For a few moments, he stood and breathed the night air. He felt his head begin to clear, and his insides seemed to have settled a little.

Maybe Rune was right, he thought about her words and the reasoning behind them. Rune had made some very good points, and she made a great deal of sense. Beautiful with brains he thought to himself. It did matter to him that he had taken human life; it was not something he had ever thought he would do. The Cutters were taking more lives every day, and Rune was right, if they had come across them in the wood, he was under no doubts that maybe some of his friends would be dead.

Robbie looked down at the over brimming kettle in his hands, and turned back to the door. He was tired and it had been a long day, it was better he thought to think about it after a good night's rest. He took one more long deep breath and returned to the kitchen, He stood for a moment and watched Rune who was humming an old Celtic tune as she moved around. She noticed him standing by the door and smiled. "How long have you been there?"

"Nice tune."

"It is, isn't it? I have no idea what it is, I guess I picked it up from mum, she hums it while she embroiders."

"I like it; somehow it is sort of calming." Robbie carried the kettle over, and put it on the stove to boil. "What do we do now?"

She came over and slid her arms around him. "Funny you should say that, we have to wait for the kettle to boil. It could be some time."

It was some time later when a smiling and joking Rune and Robbie appeared from the kitchen with a large tray, containing cups of Jasmine tea and cakes. Everyone was sat around discussing the events of the day, and their minds were suddenly distracted by the arrival of refreshments.

Robbie sat back in the chair, and Rune came over and sat on the chair arm next to him. Len was watching him carefully; Robbie looked up at him and thought for a moment before asking him a question. "Mr Rimmer..." Robbie picked his words carefully. "You come from the south, don't you?"

Len gave a knowing smile. "I do Robbie you are quite correct."

"You must have seen quite a lot of the Cutters; after all, you came here for protection did you not?"

"Once again Robbie, you are quite correct, your Uncle Harry and your father have both done me a great service. One I fear I will never be able to repay."

"I was led to believe; you were in some sort of trouble with the Cutters. Am I right?" Robbie could see the face of Steph change as he asked her father each question, and she looked nervous.

Len seemed calm and unfazed by the questions. "You are right, in many ways young Robbie, I did come north to avoid the Cutters, but I also came north to oversee a task that was set for me."

"Dad that is quite enough, now is not the time, you know better than this." Steph suddenly seemed quite annoyed with Len. She looked over to Robert. "This is not the time or the place Robert and you know it too." Robert nodded. There was a sudden understanding between his dad and Rune's mum, and Robbie looked at both of them before turning back to Len who had started to speak again.

"Robbie, you have to understand, there are many things in this world that you have no knowledge of. I cannot give you answers to everything just yet. There is a time and a place, and soon you will see that. My daughter is in many ways right, however, I think after today you do have a right to know some of the answers to your questions. I will answer what I can if you ask me."

Robbie felt Rune straighten a little as her grandfather spoke. She seemed as keen as him to get some more details about what was going on. He sat for a moment his eyes fixed on Len. "Can you tell me who the Cutters are, and why they wish to destroy us?"

Len Rimmer sat back in his chair and folded his legs. He lifted his cup as he thought about the question and sipped his tea. He leaned forward and put his cup on the table, and gestured as if to speak. He gave a long sigh, and sat back. Every eye in the room was now on him, the silence was such, that you could have heard a pin drop.

"Let me see now...The Cutters... Robbie, the Cutters are in a way a sort of private army. They are called the Cutters, because they originally started out as a group of ruffians who would cut the crops of the local farmers in Devon, and take them as payment for their employer, who had pronounced himself the Overlord of Devon and Cornwall."

Robbie thought about what Len had said. "So, if I understand you Mr Rimmer, this lord taxed people in goods, a little like Richard the Lionheart did back in the dark ages."

"You know a little history Robbie that is pleasing to me. Curious you would mention King Richard, I find the comparison quite similar, yes the Cutters were initially a tax collecting body of ruffians."

Robbie seemed pleased that Len was at least considering his questions. "So, who was this overlord?"

Len smiled a big smile. "Err, now my lad you have hit the nail right on the head. The so-called, self-proclaimed overlord was once known as Mason Knox. He now calls himself the Duke of Cornwall."

"So who is this Duke of Cornwall, and just what is it he wants?" Robbie was a little surprised to hear Rune asking the question. He looked at everyone sat in the room and they all seemed to be as interested as he was, with the exception of Steph, who was still looking a little nervous.

"Mason Knox was a professor of history at Cambridge University. His speciality was the old text relating to the kings and queens of this country, especially the ancient lines of the Celts and Anglo Saxons. I knew Mason very well as he was a colleague of mine, who often asked my advice on certain aspects of Celtic culture. My subject was science, but my pastime for a great deal of my life in private, was the study of Celtic literature." There was an audible gasp around the room as he spoke; the fact that he knew the leader of the Cutters personally was quite a revelation.

"The thing was, Mason found some writings that led him to think he was the rightful heir of the original Duke of Cornwall. Cornwall was the man whose wife was coveted by King Uther Pendragon, and had a son who he named Arthur. Mason proclaimed that he was the rightful heir to the throne of England, it created quite a stir at the time, which was sometime around 1998."

Jade sat up and looked at her grandfather. "So what did that have to do with you?"

"Well, my dear child, I was the one who the university approached to check the documentation that Mason had used, it created a lot of upheaval, and the University did receive a lot of let's say, bad press. I spent several months looking at the documents he had used and translating them, I very quickly discovered that he had in fact translated them wrongly, and his mistakes led me to believe that he had no claim on the title."

"Wow, so what did you do grandfather?" Jade's eyes sparkled under her long straggly fringe.

Len looked at Jade and then gave a knowing look at Steph. "I gave the facts to the university, who publicly denounced Mason, and I took my translations and hid them to protect the truth. Mason was dismissed from the university, and he never forgave me for what I did."

Robbie looked at Len. "You are not going to tell us what it was exactly, that you are keeping secret and hidden are you?"

Len looked at Robert and then back to Robbie. "Alas Robbie, now is not the time for that information to be known. One day all of you will know, just not yet."

Rune stirred next to Robbie. "What happened next Grandfather?"

"Then came the outbreak of the red death, the whole country fell into chaos as it swept with ferocity from town to town. Millions died, as you all know, it was a time of great pain and loss. Cambridge was becoming a very dangerous place, and my wife Opal and I headed for the only place we knew we would be safe. The seat of my ancestral home was in South Wales; there for a time we found a haven to ride out the plague that had destroyed the country."

"I have a grandmother?" Jade was staring at her mother.

"Yes my daughters, you both have a grandmother who is still in Wales. She became ill and was unable to travel with us here. She now has duties of her own to oversee as her father died shortly after we left."

Rune seemed really surprised, and her voice was very quiet. "Why have you never told us this before?"

Len sat forward before Steph could speak. "It was my decision to keep these facts from you. I cannot tell you as to why, just believe me when I tell you that it has been necessary to keep certain things secret to protect you."

Jade looked at Rune and then back at her grandfather. "Protect us from what... The Cutters?"

"Mason Knox and his Cutters would kill you if they discovered your link to me. I have always tried to hide you from him, and it is here that Harry and Robert enter the story." Len sat back in his chair and pondered his thoughts for a moment. "The first that I knew of Mason's survival was when Harry rode into our town. I had known Harry in his younger days." Len looked up at Steph and smiled. She gave him a brief smile. "Peter Lane was Harry's best friend and a motor cycle fanatic." Rune gasped.

"My dad was Harry's best friend?"

"Harry was a little more than that my dear, Harry is also your godfather, and was the best man at your parents wedding."

Robbie looked up at the smiling Rune. "I have a godfather; I had no idea." She beamed with delight and Len continued.

"It was Harry who had been travelling around, and found that all roads into Cornwall had been blocked by Order of the Duke of Cornwall. I knew then he was alive, and had used the red death to his advantage. Mason had set himself up as a lord, and cut all of Cornwall off from the outside world. As far as we know, this saved a great many of the people, and they all now looked to him as lord and protector. Within three years, he had moved slowly north and had cut off Devon expanding his kingdom."

Steph looked at Rune and then at Jade. "Harry and your father were very brave at that time. I left Wales and came to live in Stratford with your grandfather, who knew that being in Wales was much too close to Mason. He had begun to send out raiding parties, and it was not long before he attacked many towns in Wales. Peter brought your grandfather and I to his father's house there, both his parents had been lost in the red death outbreak. We fell in love and were married, and you two were born within five years. Harry and your father traded with some of the Cutters, and spied on Mason to provide us with an idea of what he was up to, he had by that time become a very powerful man."

Len put his hand on Jade's shoulder. Rune seemed to know what was coming and her hand fell down to Robbie's, he took it and gave it a gentle squeeze. Len looked suddenly very sorrowful. "Mason discovered I was alive and in hiding. He had planned to use his old documents incorrect as they were, to prove he was the rightful king of England, and assume supreme power as the true heir to the kingdom. He knew if he tried to take over, then eventually I would resurface and prove once again he was not. He also knew that I was now aware of the true lines of kings, and so he began a wide search to find me and destroy me."

Len looked up at his daughter, and a tear welled in his eyes. "How he found out about Peter I will never know, I am so sorry my darling, how could you ever forgive me?"

Steph raised herself out of the chair, and threw her arms around her father. As she wept, she sobbed her words of comfort to him. "It was not your fault, he knew the risks, we have discussed this dad, and you must not punish yourself this way." Rune had tears in her eyes as she watched, Jade stared around the room at everyone, until finally her eyes fell on Robert Lox who looked on Len and Steph with a sad look on his face.

"Mason killed my dad?" Jade's words seemed to trail off as Robert looked down at her. Robbie felt Rune slide on the chair, and he moved across allowing her to move next to him. Her arms folded around his neck and he pulled her close. His eyes stayed fixed on his father, Robert looked up at him and Rune, and then back to Jade.

"Your father is alive... Well, the last time we heard he was." Rune and Jade gasped at the news. Robert nodded. "He was taken by Knox, and is held prisoner somewhere in the Devonshire region, we have been trying for a very long time to find out where so that we could rescue him." Robert Lox gave a long sigh. "Your father knows of the old lines that still exist, and we think that Knox has tried to get him to give up what he knows. The fact that we have not been attacked has always informed us that he has not given Knox anything. It is why you and your mother were brought here with your grandfather."

Rune seemed to squeeze Robbie even tighter, and he felt her tremble slightly in his arms. Jade looked stunned and at a loss for words. The room was silent for several very long minutes. Steph got up from hugging her father and sat back in her seat. She dried her eyes on her shawl as she sniffed. Jade seemed to be building up to something, and Robbie watched as she turned to her mother. Her face seemed to grow taught and her eyes began to blaze. Jade's tone was filled with accusation. "You lied to me! I thought my father was dead, and he is still alive being tortured by that evil man. How could you lie to me about something so deeply important to me?" The tone of her voice grew louder and louder as she spoke.

Steph's voice was quiet. "Jade you do not understand, you only know half of it. We had to protect you and Rune from him. He wants you all dead." Jade burst up from the floor, her face red with anger.

"YOU SHOULD HAVE TOLD ME; HE IS MY FATHER!" With tears streaming from her face, she burst through the door. Before Len could get up to stop her, the door slammed with an almighty bang. Every one recoiled from the sound.

Steph looked at Rune who was now sitting upright, tears in her eyes. "I had to; I had no choice... I could not risk losing you two as well." As she stood up to move towards her, Rune jumped off the chair, and flew into her mother's arms. Steph sobbed as she clutched her daughter, Robbie felt a lump rise in his throat as he watched mother and daughter sobbing in each other's arms.

He got up slowly and crossed the room towards the kitchen door. Len who was on his feet looked across at him, and Robbie knew he had the same thing in mind as him; he raised a hand to Len. "Leave her, let me talk to her." Len nodded, and Robbie slipped through the door and across the kitchen.

Outside in the yard he could hear the sniffles of Jade just inside her workshop door; he walked across the wide flat stones, and passed a small anvil to the doorway. As Robbie looked around the doorframe, he saw Jade sat with her head in her arms on an old stool. She sniffled. "Want a bit of company?"

Jade turned around, her eyes were red and she lifted her sleeve to dry them. "Bet I look a right sight?" She gave him a slight smile.

"Really awful actually, but since when did you care?"

Jade gasped a small laugh. "I don't normally... I don't know what got in to me, I have so little memories of my dad, I thought he was dead, and now to hear them tell me he is alive, I just lost it Robbie, I am really sorry."

He slid another stool with his foot across in front of her, and sat down facing her. "You have nothing to be sorry about, we are friends, aren't we?" Robbie smiled at her. "I mean if you can't lose it once in a while, what is the point eh...? I cannot imagine how much hurt you must feel about now."

Jade looked up at him, she was normally so tough, and yet here he was looking at a very vulnerable side of her, and it did surprise him. Two new tears rolled down her cheeks. "There have been times when I have missed him so much." The tears dropped off her jaw and onto the stone floor. "I only have a few memories, but all of them are so precious. He used to throw me in the air and tell me how much he loved me." Her shoulders began to shake as she started to sob and she put her head down.

"Hey come on Jade." He leaned forward and put his arms around her. Jade lurched, throwing her arms around him and burying her head into his shoulder, her sobs rose higher. Robbie held her tight and rocked her, as she wept uncontrollably.

When Rune appeared at the door about ten minutes later, Jade had cried out most of her tears and was sat back on the stool, she was talking to Robbie.

"Sometimes Robbie, I just get so lonely here. The women are not exactly fans of mine, and you are so busy, and Alice has not been in town for ages, I just feel so isolated and alone at times."

"Rune loves you Jade you should talk to her; I think you might have forgotten that she too has just found out her dad is alive." Jade looked up and Rune stepped into the workshop.

"I have always been here for you, and you know I always will be." Her bright blue eye's glistened, Jade stood up as her sister embraced her.

"I know sis."

Robbie walked slowly out of the door and left the sisters together. As he walked back into the kitchen, Steph and Len both looked at him. Steph was pale and looked really worried. "It's alright, she is fine, it was quite a shock for her. Rune is with her at the moment, I felt they should sort it out together."

"Quite right Robbie." Len patted his arm.

"I think it would be better now if we all got home, it has been a long day, and I know I am exhausted, I think a good night's sleep will do all of us good."

Steph turned to Robbie and smiled. "Thank you Robbie." Her voice was faint and weak. He smiled back.

"Jade is the tough one don't forget, she will be fine don't worry."

Five minutes later Robbie, Billy and his dad walked up the dark country lane, they had left the cart at the side of Alf's shop for him to unload, as he prepared the meat for his cold room.

Robbie had a lot to think about, and his mind swam with all that he had learned today, he realised that suddenly he knew so very little about the world outside the Stockade. The whole world seemed to have shrunken, and the uneasy feelings he had felt all winter, began to creep back up inside him. His words seemed to just come out as he thought them. At first, he was not even aware he had said them. "Knox knows about Len and his family being here."

"He has an idea but he does not have the proof yet." Robbie felt his dad's heavy arm on his shoulder.

Robbie thought for a moment. "He sent his men into the woods today to find Joe. There is a traitor in this Stockade dad."

Robert Lox stopped and looked in the dark towards his son and Billy. "I cannot believe that Robbie. I think someone in these parts is passing information back to Knox, to be honest John and I have thought it for some time. Neither of us thinks it is anyone living in the Stockade."

Billy had been silent all night, and finally he spoke, Robbie had almost forgotten he had been there. "How can you be so sure? Information on this place can only come from within the walls." Robbie nodded in the dark, Billy was right.

Robert's large boots shuffled. "Don't you think we have spent a great deal of time and effort watching everyone in here? No, I am absolutely certain that it is someone who comes into the stockade and looks for gossip; they then report it back to Knox. All the families here are protected for the very reason that he is out there, not one of them would help him, and they have all suffered because of him."

"But how do we explain the woods dad? You saw the tracks, they knew right where to go, I followed them backwards, and they had a clear route. Anyone else in those woods would have wandered around for hours trying to find their way. Hell, it has taken Billy and me years to learn to navigate those trees."

Robert Lox knew his son was right. It had bothered him all night. "I must admit boys it is the only thing in all of this that has worried me. Joe has never seen anyone in those woods before today. Someone has definitely mapped them out; the trouble is somehow they have been undetected all the time they were doing it." Robert gave a long sigh and Robbie could just about make out the movement as he shook his head. "I cannot believe they could get passed Joe or you two without being spotted."

Robbie and Billy had spent the last seven years of their life going into the forest. Robbie knew every leaf and stick in the place, he spotted the tracks instantly, and he knew that over the years he had only ever seen Joe's tracks. On many occasions, he had followed them and tried to sneak up on Joe, only to find Joe waiting to jump out on him with a smile.

Today Joe had been surrounded and was unaware of it, was he getting old and slow, or were these Cutters more organised than everyone thought? They must have had some woodcraft training. "Dad these Cutters really knew what they were doing today. They were no match for our skills, but they knew their way around the trees without being seen."

"I know lad, it is the one thing that has got me more concerned than anything else. We have always seen the Cutters as a wild bunch of ruffians. These today were controlled and ordered; I have a funny suspicion Knox has been training an army."

"Maybe now would be a good time to start teaching our skills to some of the others." Billy had a good point. "You know war is coming and we should prepare."

"I think it is time for a town meeting, I want to speak to Jess, John and Beth tomorrow, and then call on all the surrounding area to attend. If I am right, we could be holding up here for some time, after today I think it is time we introduced you to another level of life here."

"What do you mean Dad, another level?"

Robert began to walk slowly forward up the lane. Billy and Robbie were suddenly very keen to hear more, and moved quickly up to the side of Robert Lox. He put his arm out and brought it round Robbie's shoulders. "As you have both witnessed tonight, there are a lot of things that go on around here that only a few have knowledge of. Well, I think it is time that you two and Alice, were made more aware. I had intended to leave it until you were 18 Robbie, but today you have shown me beyond doubt, that you are ready to be more involved with the true way of Loxley life."

"The true way, what does that mean?"

"That's enough for now I think, you will see."

T alk around the table the following morning was more open than it had ever been. Robbie noticed the moment he walked into the room, that his mum and aunt both now had silver daggers on their belts. Jess Lox looked up as she slid Robbie a large plate of beans and fried eggs in front of him. "Robbie, you have your hair down." Her hazel eyes sparkled as she smiled at him.

"Wonder why that is?" Alice giggled.

Jess gave him a knowing look. "I used to make your dad wear his hair down when I first met him." Her eyes seemed to glint with delight. "He was very handsome, and I would think that Rune feels the same way as I did, she is a smart girl that one."

Robbie felt his cheeks burn, and he looked back down at his food and focused intently on eating for a few minutes. Alice leaned over to him; he looked up and could see the excitement on her face. Alice whispered quietly. "Billy told me all about yesterday, was it really frightening fighting the Cutters? Billy thinks you are really brave, he said you were a born leader like your dad."

Robbie thought of the day before, and the sickness he felt the previous night seemed to raise itself inside him. "I didn't have time to think much, it just rather happened. Afterwards when we were sat in Joe's place, I felt sick and I realised how frightened I actually was. Any of the others could have died, and death comes very quickly with an arrow."

Alice suddenly looked very sober, she knew him well enough to know, that if he was scared and actually admitting it, then it must have been bad. "Billy said you took four out, and you were so accurate and fast they did not even realise they were hit. He said it was almost surgical."

Robbie pushed his plate away, his appetite had gone and as he looked up, he realised that there was only Alice sat at the table. He felt two hands on his shoulder and looked up at his mum. She gently squeezed, and then pulled the chair out at the side of him, and sat down beside him.

Jess softly stroked the hair from his face like Rune had. Her voice was soft and gentle. "You have grown up so much recently Robbie, I had not noticed how fast. I am so very proud of you, not because I know you can now kill a man, but because I now know you will only take a life if there is no other option." She smiled at him and took his hand in hers. "You are so very like your father; I see it more and more every day. He too is a man of high honour, and I have seen him spare the life of many in my life with him."

Robbie was surprised; he had always thought that if it came to a fight his dad would be a warrior of terrifying ability. "My dad doesn't like killing either?"

"Your Father has saved more lives than he has ever taken, I have seen him pin a man's hand to a tree with an arrow, just to stop him using a sword. Anyone else would have killed them, that man helped us find out that Peter Lane was still alive. Your father spared him, and it might with luck save the life of another." She stroked his hand softly. "I can think of worst things in this world Robbie than growing to be like your father. I also would like to think you have his excellent taste in good women." She smiled, and Alice started to laugh.

Robbie smiled, and a small laugh came up inside him. "Thanks Mum."

Jess Lox put her arms around her son and he hugged her back. "Rune is a very lovely girl Robbie; I have always liked her."

"Jade is really very nice when you get to know her as well Mum."

Jess flashed her eyes at Alice and spoke. "She is more Billy's type; he prefers his rough." She winked at Robbie, as Alice looked scandalised. Robbie and Jess burst out laughing. Jess bent down and gave Alice a small kiss on the head. "Don't you two think meeting late at night in the barn is quite obvious?"

Alice turned purple. "How do you know that?"

"Alice my darling, how do you think me and Rob got together? Come to think of it, your parents were worse than us two." Jess chuckled as she picked up the plates off the table and headed to the sink. "If that barn could talk, all of us would be in big trouble." She dropped the plates into the hot water and turned back to the table. "Right you two, up and off, I have work to do."

As Robbie and Alice came out of the kitchen door and into the yard, John Lox walked out of the barn. "Either of you two seen Billy?" He shouted from up the path, both of them shrugged and shook their heads. "Never here when I bloody need him these days, lazy bugger that one." John swung round and went back into the barn.

The two of them walked slowly round to the front of the house, where Robert was painting the fence that he and Robbie had repaired the other day. "I want you two to go down to Lens today, he wants to start your lessons, and I think you too Alice, should be a part of them."

Alice looked surprised. "What about Billy?"

"We have other plans for Billy boy, his talents lie elsewhere."

Billy was very able with a sword. There had been many times during the making of swords that John had used Billy for help. Billy was muscular and could handle the heavy work easily; John had noticed that after polishing the swords up, Billy had a very natural way of spinning and swiping a sword to get the measure of it. John was an excellent swordsman and on occasion had duelled with Billy. Billy had a lot of natural talent, and so John had started to give him private lessons.

Alice and Robbie walked down the centre of the street. Rune was standing outside her grandfather's house, she smiled as the two of them walked up and then she stepped forward slipping her hands inside Robbie's cloak. "Hi."

Robbie smiled as her warm body pulled in close to his. "Hey... How are you?"

She kissed him on the cheek. "I am fine... Are you alright after yesterday?"

Robbie knew that she was referring to his feelings about killing four Cutters. "Yes, I really am alright now... So, what are we in store for today?"

"Not really sure, you know my grandfather, we could be studying anything. Hi Alice are you joining in as well?"

"Hey Rune. It looks like it, although I am a little surprised."

"The more the merrier, eh Robbie?"

Robbie was looking at the shabby old door behind which he could hear shuffling. "What... Oh Yeah." The bolts on the back of the door slid back, and

Len's smiling face appeared.

"Ah ha, come in everyone we have much to discuss." Robbie stood back allowing Alice and then Rune to enter; he followed at the back feeling a little apprehensive. This was the first time he had ever been in Len Rimmer's house.

Somehow, the house did not disappoint. The walls of the front room were filled with medical charts showing every aspect of the human body. Every inch of wall space was filled with shelves on which one side was entirely filled with books, and the other glass jars of herbs and potions.

In the centre of the room was a large desk with two chairs. The desk was surprisingly neat with pencil holders and inkwells; there was a chair on either side of the desk. This was where Len would hold his surgery on a Saturday morning for anyone in the area to come and seek his help.

Robbie noticed Alice looking around with the same curiosity as he did. Len appeared at the small door on the other side of the room. "We will be comfier in here I think." Robbie and Alice followed Rune into the other room, which was very similar to Steph's house.

There were two large comfortable heavily padded seats large enough for two to sit on, and two very elegant cottage chairs. All were covered with throws and elaborately embroidered cushions. Alice sat quietly down in one of the cottage chairs, as Rune grabbed Robbie's hand and pulled him on to the large padded seat. They all looked at each other and smiled, as Len moved the other cottage chair into place where all of them now faced him. He sat down and gave a large smile.

"Well, I must say this is very exciting for me, I have waited a long time for this." Len leaned back in his chair. "Let's see now where do we begin? Today we are sat together in what was once known as the hamlet of Loxley. From here, and over two hundred miles was a vast forest with small towns and villages hidden within it. This is and always has been the birthplace of our most famous son Robin of Loxley; he was son and heir to Robert Fitzooth the true and rightful Earl of Huntingdon.

"Robin Hood... No offence Mr Rimmer but we all know the legend." Alice seemed a little disappointed.

Len smiled. "So you should, you are a Lox which makes you a distant relative."

Robbie leaned forward on the seat. "Are you saying that the legend is all true, and he really did exist, because no one will ever believe that?"

"Mason Knox does... In matter of fact, it was he who worked with me in finding all of the relevant documentation to prove it. How do you think he discovered about his own family line? The papers were all hidden together here in this area."

Alice still looked very skeptical. "You have these documents, and you can prove it?" Len smiled, and rested his hands on his lap. "I know where they are, and in good time you will see them... Let us just say for one moment I am telling the truth, shall we? It will save us a great deal of time." Robbie looked at Rune who had been sat very still and not said a word.

"You know this already, don't you?"

Rune looked a little embarrassed. "I know some of it, but not all Robbie."

Len coughed to clear his throat. "Robin of Loxley was born in 1285, and lived here in Loxley in what today is your home, Robbie. Like you, his first name was Robert, and it was time and his deeds that had him named, 'Robyn in the hood', for that is what the locals at that time called him." They all settled into their seats, as it appeared this was going to be a long day.

"He was raised here with his mother, and taught the only real trade that existed in these parts; he was a woodsman and a very gifted one at that. After his death a prophecy about his line was discovered, that was written in 421 AD, a good seven hundred years earlier, that made clear that the future line of Loxley would herald the coming of a true heir to this kingdom, and such was the overpowering evidence, that his son decided to prepare for such a future time." Len stretched his legs forward in the chair as he looked at the confused faces of his guests. "Are we all up to speed now?" They nodded, although Robbie was finding most of this fanciful and hard to digest; Alice however seemed to be swallowing every word with her eyes fixed on Len, and nodding to him as he spoke.

"The Fellowship of Bowman was first set up by Marion of Blidworth and her son ten years after Robin's death in 1341. It has since followed an unbroken line to this present day where Robert heir to Loxley sits here listening to an old man."

Alice looked across the room at him, and Rune was watching him sat at her side. He turned to her as she put her hand on his and she smiled at him. "Robbie it is true I have seen the documents."

"It just all seems so... I do not really know what to think... I grew up playing Robin Hood with Alice and Billy. That's how I learned to use a bow."

"You have never had lessons in how to use a bow have you Robbie?" Len's eyes seemed to twinkle as he asked.

Robbie looked back at Len. "No, I just picked it up as I went along."

"Yet you are the most gifted bowman this area has seen in over a hundred years... You even surpass your father's talents." Alice had spoken so quietly at first Robbie had thought she was thinking aloud.

Rune squeezed his hand. "Think about yesterday Robbie, the speed with which you took aim and fired was incredible. It made my head spin; I was very impressed."

"You were?" Robbie's broad grin broke across his face. He liked the idea of being able to impress her.

Rune turned a little pink. "Oh yes Robbie, very." Her bright blue eyes fluttered as she looked down.

"Yes, well err... Let us continue. The Fellowship of Bowmen has over the years become the guardians of all the true lines of Saxon and Celtic origins. There are many families across this land that contain the true heirs to this kingdom, it is, or one day will be your job Robbie to take the mantle from your father and continue until the rightful heir to the throne is found and seated."

Robbie turned back to look at Len. "This Fellowship thingy, do I have to join them, who are they?"

Len moved forward in his chair. "All in good time young Robbie; you shall meet all of them tonight when the three of you are initiated into it." He got up out of his chair and moved towards the kitchen door. "Tea everyone?"

The room filled with gasps, and Robbie got up from his seat. "Hang on, what do you mean initiated... All of us?" Len's Voice came from the kitchen.

"Oh, did I not mention it? How forgetful of me."

Alice looked dumbfounded and she turned to Rune who actually looked more shocked. "Did you know about this?"

Rune looked bewildered as she looked up at him and shook her head. "No... Honestly, I had no idea. I thought it was an all-male thing."

Len popped his head back round the doorframe and smiled. "Marion was a very accomplished bowman, well woman. Who has sugar?" Len grinned at the three of them.

CHAPTER FIVE

THE WOODSMAN & THE BOWMAN

The smoke wafted through the clearing, on the same breeze that rustled the brown dry leaves still clinging to the beech trees. Red sparks and embers hissed and crackled as they shot from the charred wood that was only hours earlier a cabin. Now it was reduced to a mound of blackened and glowing cinders, which would glow bright red and orange as the breeze wafted across the clearing.

The smoke parted and the figure of a teenage boy with sooty clothing, staggered through the parting swirls of smoke towards the long hole dug in the ground, beside which was two raised mounds of freshly dug earth. In his arms lay the limp body of a small female child. Her bruised and blacked arm swung from side to side as he staggered, her long golden blonde hair flapped in the soft breeze.

He fell to his knees, and leaning over her, he pulled her close and started to sob. He rocked her gently backward and forward as he wept, his tears falling across her face and leaving soft white patches on her blackened and dirty delicate skin. His shoulders shook and the muffled wails seeped out from under her, as the loss of his parents and his little sister tore at his soul.

For some time he did not move, the whimpers became less and finally he sat up, his eyes red from the smoke and the tears. His face was black, and as his grey eyes filled with hate lifted to the sky. He screamed. "Hearnnnnnnnnnnnnnne!"

With the grace of an angel, he lowered the tiny body into the hole. He pushed his hand into his shirt, and pulled out a clean green cloth. Tenderly he wiped her face, and then placing two small copper coins on her eyes, he laid the cloth over her face.

The soft damp soil easily fell into the hole, and slowly she disappeared back into the earth from which she came. Soon the mound was complete, and lifting his spade, he thrust it down on to the makeshift cross, and hammered it hard into the ground. He laid the small longbow and two small arrows on to the top of the grave. The pain rose inside him and the tears welled in his eyes, he fell back to his knees hugging the cross and weeping bitterly. The soft breeze blew into his ears as if whispering to him. "Hearne."

A deep rich voice entered his head. "Woodsman." He thought he was going insane. "Woodsman, hear me." Through blurred eyes he looked up and across the clearing and over the smoking cinders, where a tall handsome stag stood at the edge of the trees staring at him.

"Woodsman my daughter awaits you by the lake, go to her." Slowly he rose to his feet, it was as if dreaming as he stared at the stag. The tall handsome animal bowed its head, turned, and walked from the clearing. He stood frozen watching as the breeze swirled around him and the stag was gone.

The boy, picked up his bow and quiver and took one last look at the three graves, he bowed his head. "May Hearne protect you." His voice was hoarse and struggled from his dry mouth. He turned and walked from the clearing.

He stood alone on the bank of the lake and gazed across the calm water. He was sticky and dirty, and slowly he walked into the cold clear water to clean the stench of death and fire from his clothes.

He stood, the ice-cold water surrounding his waist, and scooping two large handfuls, he threw it across his face. The freezing water cleared his mind, and he shuddered with the shock of it, and then almost with urgency, he began franticly splashing the water all over him in a bid to get clean.

His top sleeve was torn, and below it was red and purple, as the deep gash stung from the water. He gritted his teeth as he applied more to clean the open wound. Finally, he was calm and walked from the lake dripping, but washed and clean as if re born. He picked up his bow and quiver. "Woodsman hear me?" The voice was soft, gentle, and had a calmness that seemed to ease him; and he turned in the direction from whence it came.

Against the trees edge, there stood a young woman dressed in a long white robe, her face hidden behind a white hood. She began to move slowly towards him. "Fear me not woodsman, for I have been sent to you by my father."

He watched frozen as if entranced, as she approached, the water still dripping from his hair and chin. She stood before him, and raising her arm, a pale white hand with a silver ring of an oak leaf woven around her finger, slid from under the crumpled sleeve. He watched as she touched his open wound, and all pain left his arm and his heart lightened.

"You have been wronged woodsman, and my father has called you to his service, as there is now a task of great importance to be done." He felt no fear, yet marvelled as he looked at his arm to see only a pale white scar in the shape of a longbow. "You must leave here and all traces of whom you are. What is your name Woodsman?"

"I am Dirk My Lady."

"From here on you will be Rowan the woodsman, and shall no longer except your name of old, for secrecy will be your true identity. In the hollow of the mighty oak across the path, you will find something of great value. You must make great haste, for tonight the Bowman will be revealed to all." Rowan nodded as she spoke.

"This task is of great importance to all of us Rowan of the wood. Look for the name of Lox and trust no one, deliver this possession of great power to the bowman himself and no other. Tell him his fight now is the truth, and this heirloom of our house shall not fail the man who seeks it."

Rowan looked upon the figure in white. "Please My Lady, if this task is so important how will I know I truly am speaking to this bowman?"

"You will know him when you see him, but if you are concerned, then a silver lion will confirm him. You will find food and better weapons in the stump, use them wisely woodsman, and fear not for your family will be honoured and watched over always. Your path now lies in the north, go with speed."

The woman turned, and walked slowly back to the trees, a tiny glint of red and gold flickered from a single hair that blew from under the hood. Rowan gasped in awe. "Farewell woodsman, happiness will be yours again; if you lose your way, shoot the white arrow and it will guide you." Her voice faded as she walked.

He stood and watched as the woman in white disappeared through the trees, and suddenly he realised he was alone on the bank of the shore, with only the lapping of the water at his heels, and the birdsong from the trees. Rowan looked across the path, to the trees, which were starting to bud. In amongst them all stood a mighty stump from a fallen oak tree.

All his life he had lived in these woods, and yet he had no memory of the stump. He knew every inch of this woodland; how could he miss something so large? Rowan began to walk towards it cautiously. Was this the magic he had heard of so many times as a child? There had been strange tales told him of the green man who could turn himself into a stag.

Rowan very carefully peered into the stump, there deep inside he saw a bundle of dark green silk, and he lifted it gently out of the hollow and looked at the long package. He could feel arrows inside, and he pulled on the green cord, and the silk fell away revealing a beautiful rowan wood bow. Ten arrows were tied with silk string, nine of them black with white feather flights, and one of them was pure white. He looked back into the stump and another bundle was there.

Rowan lifted it out. It was thick and woolly; he slowly unrolled the light brown material and inside was a sage green package bound tightly in cloth. He knew this was the precious object he must deliver. It had a line of woven green silk tied at each end, so Rowan slipped it over his shoulder, and slung it across his back. There in the centre of the thick cloth was a golden brooch. It was the finest thing he had ever seen, two golden oak leaves with two golden acorns. He held it up and gazed in wonder at the craftsmanship of it.

The breeze lifted, and the fabric on the floor stirred and unrolled, Rowan looked down at the hooded cloak. Taking the lightweight cloak up, he cast it around his shoulders and clipped it together with the golden brooch.

A bumblebee buzzed up out of the stump, and once again, Rowan peered over the edge inside, where a small leather bag sat at the base of the stump. He could smell the sweet scent of fresh fruit and cheese, and freshly baked bread. Pulling the bag out of the stump, he knew it was time to leave. He looked from left to right, had she said north he thought to himself.

Rowan looked up to the sky and the placement of the sun, he pointed to the end of the track on the far side of the lake. "North," he whispered to himself. He slung the leather bag on to his shoulder, and set off along the edge of the lake towards the far side, and his new task. 'Lox' he thought to himself that was a name he had heard before.

He made the track with speed, and began the climb up the steep slope that would take him out of the woodland and Lake Basin, and onward north in search of a new life and a new destiny. At the top of the ridge an hour later, Rowan halted and turned back to face the forest; below him in the distance through the roof of the trees, he could see a thin wisp of smoke rising.

There was his old life, and a home he had known for 18 years, a father who trained him from a small boy in his craft, a mother, who had loved him and cared for him, and his small sister who he had loved more than anything else on earth. The picture of the three graves in a row was bright in his mind as he wiped away the tears that had come suddenly to his eyes.

He knelt down before them and said quietly to himself. "I will give up my life and my name, but I will not forget those who I loved. I will never forget you, and one day I will avenge you. This I swear as a true woodsman and in the name of Hearne."

Rowan stood up and the breeze whipped around his cloak. There to his left on the other side of the ridge was the large stag, Rowan bowed to him. "I will honour your task My Lord, but one day I will return to see my family avenged. I have sworn it."

He turned, raised his hood over his head and face, and walked into the trees and did not look back again. Now he was Rowan the woodsman with no past, present or future. He was on a mission to fulfil his master's request. The bowman was his destination, and also his destiny.

Stephanie Rimmer was sat in her chair sewing an emblem on to Robbie's cloak. It was the Bowman's coat of arms depicting a wolf's head, with black and white crossed arrows below. She paused and looked up at Len Rimmer. "Father it is done, the woodsman is coming."

Len smiled. "Good, let us prepare, our new bowmen will be growing impatient."

Robbie sat next to Rune on the seat, with Alice sat opposite, Rune was lost in thought and stared at the rug. Alice would sigh and then smile at him. "Well you two, what do you think it's going to be like? I must admit I am feeling very nervous."

Robbie looked at Rune. "I don't suppose you know anything that might help us?"

Rune looked sadly back at him. "I know they go to these meetings, but they are so secret no one really knows what happens. I just want to get on with it, what do you think is taking so long?"

The initial shock of finding out they were going to be initiated into the Fellowship of the Bowmen had now started to wear off. All of them knew that it would change the life that they now lived; from that night onwards, they would be considered a higher status amongst the residents of the community. It was Beth Loxley that entered the room and greeted them. "Good evening Master and Mistress's of the woods."

"Mum what is going to happen tonight? We have been waiting for ages, and do you know what they will require us to do? Is there a test because I really don't like the idea of that?" Robbie thought Alice was about to talk herself hoarse, or at least talk her mother to death.

"Alice, settle down... Right you three; there is nothing to worry about. I will be with you at all times. It is a simple ceremony which will be explained in full to you all."

Beth gave a warm and reassuring smile to all of them. Her bright blue eyes showed her excitement, and she pulled her robes around her plump stomach, stood back, and looked at them. Robbie loved his Aunt Beth she was very kind and always seemed to be able to find something funny in every situation. Knowing she would guide them through the ceremony seemed to calm his nerves a little.

"Alright my darlings, we need to get you ready, Robbie put a brush through your hair, and straighten your shirt. That belt needs adjusting, and all of you from now on you must wear your daggers on the right. Rune my sweet, would you like me to braid your hair? It is traditional at all ceremonies for the ladies to wear their hair down and braided at the sides. I have these hair slides for both of you girls." Beth pulled out of her pocket two golden slides both made of two oak leaves and two acorns. Rune smiled as she looked at hers.

"These are the mark of Hearne." She looked back up at Beth who smiled.

"They are the mark of a woodsman and the bowmen; we are all guided by the lord of the woodland."

Robbie smartened himself up, whilst Rune braided her fine red and golden streaked hair. Beth helped Alice tame her bushy hair, and finally got it flat and braided with the help of one of Rune's herbal oils. The three of them stood together as Beth beamed at them and clasped her hands tight together as she chuckled. "This is very exciting, isn't it?" Her eyes danced.

Once they were ready, the three of them led by Beth made their way down the small village street, and up the track that led to the Village Hall. The hall was a very large building made of logs. This was the place where all the meetings and weddings of the community were celebrated, and unknown to the three new initiates; it was where the Fellowship of the Bowmen met regularly.

Instead of entering by the front doors, Beth took them around the back to a small door. She knocked four times, and the bolts drew back and the little door swung open. Steph smiled at them as they stepped in, Robbie was startled as he saw her.

Steph Rimmer was dressed in a long white robe tied at the waist with a silver belt of woven oak leaves. Her hair was braided and decorated with small yellow primrose flowers that seemed to highlight her long blonde hair. Her green eyes sparkled.

From her shoulders, held in place with an oaken clasp, hung a fine silk powder blue cloak. The hood hung neatly behind her. "Mum you look so beautiful." Rune stared at her mother, and Alice stood speechless for the first time in a long while.

"Thank you my darling," she whispered. "You must wait here for a while longer. Beth will guide you. Oh I am so proud of all of you." Steph hugged them one by one and then raising her hood, she winked at Robbie. "I will see you all in there."

Steph passed silently through the door into the meeting hall, and closed it behind her, Beth smiled. "Have a good look round it will be a few minutes yet."

Robbie took a careful look around the room. Like the rest of the building, it was all highly polished wood... Large ornate arched windows allowed the light to flood in, yet this evening, heavy dark green curtains were drawn to keep out unwanted eyes. The walls had various tapestries hung on them, which were easily identified as the life and times of 'Robyn in the Hood.' There was a large carved wooden crest of a wolf's head with arrows, and the oaken cluster of Hearne above a large mahogany desk, set at one end of the room.

Robbie noticed Rune looking into a long glass display cabinet against the wall next to the door that led into the meeting hall. He walked over to her and she looked up utterly bewildered. "Robbie look, these are his."

He looked down into the cabinet, and there laid out for all to see was a collection of artifacts. It took a few moments to fully grasp the facts. The long old wooden bow, the crude arrows and old leather and canvass quiver, a very old and tatty green cloak with a long hood, and a silver belt with an old dagger.

"No way... This is not real." Robbie looked back at Beth who nodded and smiled, Rune put her hand on his.

"Robbie these are the actual possessions of your family... It is hard to believe that these belonged to the very first Robert of Loxley, Robin Hood himself." Rune gave him a huge smile.

He had found it hard to believe sat in Len Rimmer's house, and yet here he was in front of proof. The most convincing item was a book laid open that showed the registry of the wedding of Robert of Loxley to Marion of Blidworth, at the church of St Mary at Edwinstowe. Alice who had come up at the side of him gasped in awe. Her pale blue eyes twinkled with delight. "He is actually a member of our family Robbie, how cool is that?"

This all seemed a little too much for Robbie; legends were coming alive in front of him. Stories he had been told as a child and had always believed were fantasy now seemed to be the actual truth. It took a lot of understanding. Rune slipped her arm around him. "It is quite a lot to take in isn't it?"

"You are not kidding... Do you realise that if this is right, then technically I am the next Earl of Huntingdon?"

"Wild, isn't it?" Alice was positively beaming with excitement.

Rune leaned into him and quietly whispered. "Want to know something really spooky?" Robbie looked at her cautiously, not entirely sure if he wanted to hear what she was thinking. "Go on," he hesitantly replied.

Rune grinned. "Well, when your dad asked me to make your cloak, he wanted a Lincoln green one like his." Rune paused and looked a little embarrassed. "Well, the thing is I could not find the material anywhere. Honestly I emptied the house looking for it; I have a really large bale because it is the chosen colour of the head bowmen."

Robbie was not sure where this was going. "What exactly are you getting at Rune?"

"Look at the colour of his." Robbie peered over at the sage green cloak beneath the glass. "Sage green was the only green cloth I could find, so I made your cloak out of a colour no one uses... Or as it appears has used in over 500 years. How weird is that?"

Robbie looked back at the cloak and then up at Rune. "Please tell me you are having me on?"

"Honestly Robbie I swear... Ask my mum it was the day after I made it that I found all the other green cloth under the table where I had searched about fifty times."

Robbie was now getting a very strange feeling. "You think this is all something to do with destiny, don't you?"

Rune blushed. "I think you are the Loxley that will return this country to the way it should be.... In addition, I think it has a direct connection with the first son of Loxley. I also think tonight is the start of something big for you Robbie."

He flopped down in the chair besides the case. "This is just too big for me, I am not ready, my dad is so much better at all of this, honestly Rune I really don't think my shoulders are broad enough to carry all this."

"Too late now Robbie it's almost time." Beth came up carrying his cloak. She opened it up for him to step into it and he noticed the new crest that Steph had sewn on to it. His heart began to beat faster. "Come on Robbie put this on, and girls you too. Right Robbie, everyone in there will be hooded, but you must all keep yours down until you have been sworn in, at that point you lift your hoods."

Beth gave him a big smile. "Do not worry about it... You will be smashing." She leaned forward and kissed his cheek. "I always knew you were special... I am never wrong." She winked at Rune.

A loud gong boomed from within the meeting room. The Fellowship of the Bowman had been called to order. The large room of the Village Hall slowly filled as the bowmen entered. The main room of the hall was very large, it had been designed for any event the community would require, but more importantly had been built for the large annual gathering of woodsmen that happened every Easter.

The whole building was made of wood, and had been constructed somewhere around 1377. It was to say the least, a very ancient looking building, from its vast exposed roof beams, to its highly polished wooden floor. At the top of the main hall was a platform on which three large chairs sat. The central chair was made of oak and was carved with great skill. It was covered with Celtic and Saxon runes, and decorated with carved oak leaves and acorns; the back of the chair depicted a mighty oak tree standing alone. The four legs were carved lions sat staring forward. The two chairs either side were smaller in stature although they were as intricately carved, and they seemed to add greater importance to the one in the centre. Below the platform was a long wooden table that was covered with a thick deep green velvet cloth, that had golden tassels hanging all the way round.

The table looked almost empty apart from a carved bone horn of great age, and a long silver sword. At the far right hand side of the table, sat a large golden gong. Seven chairs were pushed neatly under the table as the bowmen of Loxley entered to prepare for the ceremony.

Beth fussed, as she made sure that everyone looked his or her best. "Right my darlings when the next gong sounds you will walk into the room. There will be three chairs set in the centre of the room, walk up and stand in front of them. Rune you lead followed by Robbie dear, and then Alice my love, you will be last. I will stand behind the chairs to guide you through the ceremony." Beth pulled a rolled parchment out from inside her cloak. "Robbie you will need to see this before you go in." She handed it to him and he nervously unrolled the parchment and looked at it.

THE FELLOWSHIP OF THE BOWMEN

WOLVES HEAD
(GRAND MASTER)

ROBERT JAKE LOXLEY

HIGH MISTRESS	*GUARDIAN OF LINE*	*HIGH MASTER*
JESSICA LOXLEY	*STEPHANIE MOON LANE*	*LEENARD RIMMER*
MASTER OF ARMS	*MASTER WOODSMAN*	*MASTER GATES*
JOHN H LOXLEY	*JOESEPH WHITMORE*	*DAVID WILLIAMS*
ARMS MEN	*WOODSMEN*	*GATE KEEPERS*
ASSEMBLED	*ASSEMBLED*	*ASSEMBLED*

THE BOWMAN OF LOXLEY

ROBERT JOHN LOXLEY

ABLE BOWMAN	*ABLE BOWMAN*
RUNESTONE LANE	*ALICE VICTORIA LOXLEY*

THE BOWMEN OF LOXLEY

ASSEMBLED

Robbie looked into his Aunt Beth's eyes. "What does this mean? Why am I a Bowman and what are Able Bowmen?" Beth smiled and patted his shoulder.

"Robbie my dear boy, soon you will know all there is to know. Be patient for a few minutes more."

Robbie looked at Rune, and then back at Alice, both of them smiled. He turned back to Rune. "I didn't know your full name was Runestone."

Rune shrugged. "Parents what can I say? Mum says we're so precious; she had to name us after gemstones. Apparently, I have a cousin somewhere called Jett, and another called Sapphire, although that's my middle name as well, Runestone Sapphire." Rune nodded. "Blue eyes, you see?"

Robbie smiled. "It really fits you; I noticed your sapphire blue eyes the first time

I ever saw you, and they are really beautiful." Rune blushed as she smiled a broad smile.

"I bet you cannot guess Jade's middle name?"

Robbie thought for a moment. "Well, green eyes has to be the Jade, and she has blonde hair, but no I cannot think of a blonde coloured stone, apart from a pebble, please tell me it's not that?" Alice and Beth both began to giggle and Rune burst out laughing and shook her head.

"No silly, it's Opal after her grandmother." Rune put her hand to her mouth to suppress the laughter. "Pebbles!" She started to laugh again. Her bright blue eyes danced with happiness as Robbie smiled back at her. She was very beautiful and somehow it seemed to stick in his mind.

He felt light hearted as the moment welled inside him, and he put out his hand and touched hers. Her soft fingers closed around his and he felt his nervousness settle. The loud gong, rung out, Beth walked to the door. "Alright now my dears, walk nice and slow, and stand straight. Good luck and most importantly, enjoy the moment." Beth pulled the door open and Robbie watched the shimmering hair of Rune in front of him, as they moved forward, and walked slowly into the room.

Robbie looked round at the assembled crowd. To his right, stood against the wall, was a long line of men in cloaks of black with their hoods up so that their faces were hidden. On the left of each cloak was a coat of arms of two oak leaves with crossed swords of gold underneath. Down the left hand wall of the room, was a similar line of hooded men, their coat of arms was an oak tree with a crossed sword over an arrow. Behind the three chairs, stood row upon row of hooded men wearing Lincoln green cloaks, their coat of arms was the same as Robbie's. There was a wolf head under which were two crossed black arrows. He looked down at his own coat of arms. One of his arrows was white; it was the same as Rune's and Alice's.

They came to the three seats, stopped and stood in front of them, Beth moved behind them. Robbie now felt very nervous, as he saw the large chairs and the long green table. A door to his right opened and a long line of hooded men in long black cloaks walked out, they had a coat of arms, which was a bright golden gate.

They walked across the front of the table; each had a dark black long bow in his hand. Robbie knew them well he had polished them all after his dad had made them. He knew that these men were known as the Keepers of the gate. These were the men and women who guarded the stockade night and day.

The men halted and then broke into two groups. They walked down the room to the back and formed a line across the bottom of the hall. A gong rung out and Robbie looked up to see a hooded man in a black cloak with a golden gate crest that had two acorns below it. He placed his hand on the gong to silence it.

Six people walked out of the door and along behind the green table. Each took their place behind one of the seats, and the man in the black hood moved around to fill the seventh seat.

Robbie looked from left to right. The first wore the same brown hooded cloak, and had the oak and crossed swords crest, although his was bright gold. The second had a Lincoln green hooded cloak and the same crest of an oak tree with crossed arrows in gold. Robbie tried to remember the parchment. Master of Arms, and the Master Woodsman.

The third person he knew, even though she was wearing a hood of the purest white. All he could see was her smile below the hood; it was his mother the High Mistress of Loxley. Next to her in a hooded robe of Lincoln green and wearing a wolf's head as a headpiece, he knew was his father, the Grand Master, or Wolves Head as it had said on the parchment. His father's eyes glistened through the mask.

Stephanie Rimmer Lane, he had already seen in her white robes and powder blue cloak. Beside her was a man in long deep red robes with a red hooded cloak. His hood and cloak were edged with bright gold clusters of oak leaves and acorns; this had to be the High Master? Beside him, was the man in black who he had already worked out was the Master of Gates.

He glanced from side to side. Alice appeared to be quite nervous, and she was slightly trembling, Rune nervously bit her lip. He was not really aware of why he did it, it was more out of instinct, but he moved both of his arms sideways and took hold of the hands of the two girls.

From below the white hood, he saw the smile broaden, Rune squeezed his fingers and he glanced at her smiling face. Robbie turned to look at Alice, she was very pale, but she gave him a small smile. He winked at her and her smile widened.

The group at the table sat down. "You can sit now," whispered Beth from behind them. Still holding hands, the three of them sat down.

The Wolfhead stood back up and raised his arms. "Fellows of the bow, greetings."

Greetings resounded from under the hoods all around the hall. The Wolf head leaned forward and peered at the three new arrivals.

"My distinguished guests, I greet you on behalf of this fellowship. We are honoured to have you here tonight."

"Well greet the Grand Master then," whispered a voice from behind them.

"Greetings Grand Master." They all spoke with much higher tones than normal.

The Grand Master smiled. "Good fellowship and distinguished guests. Tonight has been long in the coming, and yet it has been spoken of before, would our guardian of the line please remind us of our duty tonight?" He sat down as the guardian stood up.

"My distinguished guests welcome to the Fellowship of Bowmen, I bring you great tidings, for tonight we will fulfil the prophecy of old as told by Geoffrey of Almesbury in 421. It was told to him that a bowman would return to begin the start of a new era, and the return of a line of lords to rule the land. Tonight we will greet the first heir to our kingdom, for tonight the hooded man will return." There were murmurs all around the room as Stephanie Lane sat back down.

Robbie and Rune gasped. Alice squeezed his hand very tightly, so tight it hurt, he turned to her white startled face, she could hardly talk. "It's you," she barely whispered.

"What is?" Robbie frowned at her.

"Shush." Quietly came from Beth behind them.

The murmurs died down and the red hooded man stood up. Len Rimmer's voice rung out from below the hood. "Runestone Lane... Alison Victoria Loxley step forward."

"Go on my dears walk up to the table." Beth followed, as nervously the two girls stood up and hesitated. They glanced at each other and then slowly moved forward. The Master of Gates came forward with two purple cushions and placed them on the floor. He bowed to them.

"Please kneel." The girls lowered themselves on to the cushions. The High Master walked around the table as the Wolfhead stood up. Len Rimmer in his red robes lifted the large silver sword off the table.

"I hold the sword of 'Robyn in the Hood.' Here tonight I bear witness that in his name, his servants will fulfil their destiny, and return the heirs of this land back to their rightful places." He held the sword upright, pushing its tip to the ground. "Raise your right hands."

The two girls raised their hands, and he placed them one on each side of the sword hilt. The Wolfhead spoke. "Do you swear to defend and protect the heir of 'Robyn in the Hood' to your best ability?"

Len whispered, and the girls said out loud. "We do Grand Master."

"Do you swear to stand by his side as he fulfils his destiny?"

"We do Grand Master."

"Will you guide him with wisdom, and advise him so that he may lead his people?"

"We will Grand Master."

"Stand." The two girls stood up as the High Mistress of Loxley came around the table to them. From under her cloak, she took out two tiaras made of woven gold, each decorated with oak leaves. One at a time, she placed them on the heads of the two girls, and then pulled their hoods up over their faces.

"Welcome Daughters of Loxley." She took them by the hand, and led them behind the table to the two seats at the sides of the central large carved seat. The two girls sat down. "Behold good fellowship, the daughters of Loxley and Able

Bowmen."

Everyone in the room bowed. An icy shiver suddenly trickled down the back of Robbie. Alice's words from earlier became apparent, as his mind struggled as if some crazy notion had been suggested to him. "It's you," echoed through his mind.

"Robert John Loxley step forward."

His whole body suddenly felt numb. He shakily stood up, not quite sure why. This had to be a mistake, his father was the current heir not him. He was too young to lead this community, he had years of learning before it was his turn, Alice had said so.

"Robbie, for god's sake go to your father." Beth's whisper was rising in his ears, he felt her hand push him in the back, and he took a step closer to the table.

Slowly he took another step, the ten feet before him felt like miles, and took an age to cover before finally there were a few feet between him and his father wearing a Wolfhead mask. Len Rimmer and his mother came up to his side, his mother whispered very quietly.

"It's alright sweetheart, do not be afraid, we are all here with you. Robbie, kneel down." His legs folded, and he slowly descended to the cushion.

"Fellowship of the Bowman, will you take Robert John Loxley to your hearts?" Robbie peered up at his father as he spoke, his arms raised in the air.

"WE WILL!"

The response was so loud it was deafening. Robbie noticed the small smile on his father's face. "Robert John Loxley, will you lead us all in the quest to return the true heirs of this kingdom back to power?"

"I…Will Grand Master." Robbie had no idea why he was saying it.

"Will you be loyal and just, and fair in your duty to the people of this country, and to the honour of Loxley?"

"I will Grand Master." His voice was strained as his mouth constricted with the dryness it now felt.

Len Rimmer lifted the sword and placed it on the top of his head. "Robert John Loxley, 51st Earl of Huntingdon, you stand before us charged with the duty of returning a true heir to the throne. You have sworn before us here tonight, and it has been witnessed." Robbie's heart pounded; he had no idea why he was going along with this. He had no idea how he would even begin to find a leader of the country, let alone lead the community.

The High Mistress came around in front of him. "Stand up Robbie," she whispered. He struggled to get his wobbly legs off the cushion, and he rose unsteadily. His mother's smile and bright eyes met his face, as his legs straightened. "Nearly over now sweetheart."

The Grand Master handed her the horn of 'Robyn in the Hood,' and she took her sons hand, and led him around to the large wooden seat. "Robbie stand here, don't sit until I nod, alright sweetheart?" Robbie nodded, as his throat was so dry now he could hardly speak. She placed the horn in his hand.

The Master of Arms walked down the table, and rolled the green velvet cloth up. Two Armsmen, and two Woodsmen came forward and pulled the table apart, moving it away as the seven leaders of the fellowship formed a line in front of him. His father stepped forward, and in a loud and clear voice, he spoke. "Robert John Loxley, if you will honour your vow, then pull forward your hood and become the hooded man. Be known from this day as Robbie, Hooded Man and the true Bowman of Loxley."

His Mother smiled, Robbie felt the hands of Alice and Rune as they lifted his hood over the top of his head and covered part of his face. Rune whispered. "Your mum says you should now blow that horn."

Panic rose inside him. He had never blown a horn before, and his mouth was so dry he was not even sure he could. He licked his lips and lifted the cold mouthpiece to his dry lips. Breathing deeply, he took a huge breath, and then blew with all his might. The horn struck a perfect deep resounding pitch that was deafening; everyone in the room went down on one knee and bowed to him. Standing up they removed their hoods to reveal their faces, and Robbie was the only hooded figure in the room.

Robbie noticed his mother nod and he gratefully sat down in the large carved chair, his legs now felt so weak, he thought that they would not have held him up a moment longer. Rune turned to him and took his right hand. At the same time, Alice took his left. Rune slid a ring of golden oak leaves on to his right index finger, as Alice slid a bracelet of silver interwoven oak leaves and acorns onto his wrist. Both squeezed his hands.

"Hell, I am glad you two are here with me, I am scared stupid." Alice giggled, and Rune's bright blue eyes flashed at him.

"I love you Robbie in the hood." She held his hand tightly; as his father came up to him his eyes sparkled with pride.

"You did well, I am very proud of you." He bowed.

Robbie's mother, tears in her eyes came up and kissed him warmly on the cheek. "You're my son before my lord; don't think you can get off picking apples in the summer." Robbie smiled.

"I love you Mum." The tears rolled from her eyes.

"I am proud of you, My Lord." She bowed.

John, Len, and the others followed, all bowed and all called him Lord, it was the strangest feeling he had ever known. Suddenly there was Billy, and he was dressed in the robes of an Armsman. He took Robbie's hand and held it. He bowed. "My Lord," and he turned.

Robbie grabbed his hand and pulled him back. "Billy, I am Robbie, your brother." He pulled the chain from round his neck to reveal the silver lion.

"Nothing has changed, we still hunt as two."

Billy smiled. "I know Rob, here and in public though you are Lord Loxley." He pulled at his cloak. "I am an Armsman in your service." He winked at Alice. "See you later." Billy walked away, and Robbie felt a knot form in his stomach.

Woodsmen from all over the area followed more men and presented themselves over what felt like an age, as a long line of bowmen who it appeared were now his to command. Joe introduced them one by one until finally the last one stepped up.

"Wow Robbie you are such a lucky git, and I thought I was being cool by training as a woodsman." She threw her arms around his neck and gave him a huge kiss on the cheek. "Sloppier than my sis I bet?" She winked at him. Joe coughed; Jade smiled. "Sorry My Lord." She swept him a long bow, and beamed a huge smile at him, Joe scowled at her.

"It's alright Joe; this one is not like the rest of us. Believe me she grows on you." Robbie smiled at Jade. "Go on Pebbles go have fun." Rune and Alice both burst out laughing as Jade descended the steps.

Tables appeared, and were laid with great speed, and soon everyone was happily tucking into the feast. Robbie sat at the top of the table surrounded by the masters of the fellowship and his two faithful escorts. Rune slid close to him. "Some night eh Robbie?"

"Weird as hell... How can they expect all this of me Rune? I am not ready for this."

"To be honest Rob, I think you are... You just don't know it yet." She pushed her arm through his and pulled him closer.

"At least I have you and Alice, which is some comfort."

"You also have your mum and dad, not to mention my mum, and my granddad, honestly Rob I think everything will work out fine."

"Oh, I don't know Rune."

"Honestly trust me I am right... I know stuff." Somehow, he believed her, which maybe had a lot to do with the fact she believed in him. Rune had her quiet moments and even her shy times, but over the weeks, he had seen her in other lights. Her courage and determination had become clearer. He certainly saw a lot of inner strength and bravery in the woods, she had greatly impressed him that day.

Robbie looked over to Alice; she had always been there for him. There had been so many times when he had looked to her for advice, and she had never let him down yet. A ray of hope seemed somehow to grow brighter inside him, and he felt a little calmer by the thought. He smiled to himself, maybe this might work, and he could only try.

The evening seemed to last a long time, and just before midnight he found himself outside with Alice and Billy. Rune had her arm around him, and Jade bounced around in front as they walked slowly back to the village. The title of Lord was gone and he was glad, here amongst his friends he was just Robbie again. "So, Robbie." Jade bobbed about in front. "How exactly do we find these heirs?"

"Well, my dear Pebbles," Jade had been filled in on the joke, but quite liked the nick name. "I was wondering about that very point."

Billy looked over at Jade. "How do you mean we?"

Jade grinned at him. "Us... Well, we cannot let Robbie here do it on his own can we? Anyhow, I just thought that we would naturally be the ones to help him."

Rune squeezed him. "What did I tell you, where you go, we go."

Robbie felt a strong bond with this group, to him they were his own family and he loved them all dearly. "I think I need to spend some time with Len, and then talk with my dad. I would imagine that they would have the leads that we must follow."

Jade stopped bobbing about. "Glad you said we." Robbie laughed and looked down the tiny village street. "You two go on, I will be back in a bit." Billy smiled at him; he knew he wanted some time alone with Rune, just as he wanted to be alone with Alice. Billy said goodnight and turned with Alice pulled close, and headed off up to the farm.

Robbie and Rune headed down the dark street towards her house. At the gate, she leaned against the wall and he slid his arms under her cloak, and pulled her close. Jade wandered into the house and he was alone with Rune at last.

"Been a busy week, I thought we would never be alone." She moved forward and she kissed him. It felt like heaven, and was surprisingly long. He pulled back and looked into those beautiful eyes; her hair sparkled in the light behind her.

"I am so crazy about you Rune; you know that don't you? All of this other stuff is meaningless without you." She pulled him close, and he could feel the heat radiate out of her and into him.

"It is very important Robbie, more important than I am, but I swore an oath, and even without that I will still be with you no matter what." She laughed. "Somehow your pal Pebbles will be at your side. She is very fond of you Robbie... She told me she sees you as her best friend, you have never once sat in judgement of her. That has meant a lot to her, and to me." She squeezed him tighter. "If you approach everything in the way you have my sister, you will always make the right choices."

"And if I don't?"

"How many times do I have to tell you? Trust me I know stuff." Rune kissed him again. "I will see you tomorrow, go on you look tired, go and get some rest."

"Ok... I am going, goodnight." He gave her another kiss, and slid back so she could go through the small gate. "Rune?"

"What Robbie?"

"I do love you... You know that don't you?"

"Of course... I told you, I know stuff." She smiled and walked through the door, and turned, then blew him a kiss. "Goodnight."

"Night Rune."

Robbie walked slowly back up to the farm, it had been a long day and he needed to think. Everything had gone so fast; he really had not had the chance to let it all sink in. He slid his bow onto his shoulder, and put his hands in his pockets as he walked through the darkness home.

CHAPTER SIX

RETURN OF THE HOODED MAN

It had been a very long day and Robbie had crashed into bed absolutely exhausted, and his mind was ablaze with the day's events. His sleep had been filled with uneasy dreams of a lady dressed in all white, who had called him from the trees, saying, "Lord Loxley he is coming, look for the mysterious swordsman, he will bear a white arrow." She faded into smoke and a large stag appeared.

"Hear me Lord Loxley you must act now. Bring together your people; trust only the two who choose you." Then there was screaming, and burning, and women and children crying, a flash of light, and a roll of thunder and he was stood on the top of a tall balcony, his bow in hand, the string sung as he released the arrow, but it missed whatever he was shooting at, and hit Billy.

Robbie sat bolt upright in bed, sweat was rolling down his face, the picture of Billy's dead face was still in his mind. He sat trembling in the dark, as he slowly came back to his senses. Robbie breathed deeply. "Just a dream," he told himself with a tone of relief. It had felt so real and had given him quite a scare.

Slowly he lay back in his bed, and the room lit up as a bright blue flash exploded outside the window. Heavy drops of water began slowly to tap on the glass; he lay there and listened as they began to steadily increase in speed. The air broke with an ear-splitting rumble, and the rain beat harder on the window.

Robbie lay awake; he knew there would be no going back to sleep now, he felt alert and wide awake and lay in his bed, as the storm outside continued to rage. The room lit up as another flash streaked in, Billy's bed was empty. Robbie smiled, somehow, he thought that the barn would be the place to find him, and he knew he would not be alone. Somewhere during the storm, he had fallen back into sleep, and as the sun rose, there was the familiar banging on the door that told him the rest of the family was already out of bed.

It was sometime later; when Robbie sat down to eat. Billy had already gone off with John, and his father had now left for the village. Jess placed a hot mug down in front of him, and filled the half empty cup in Alice's hand. "Considering how late you slept this morning Robbie; you look like it wasn't enough."

He looked up at his mum, who was standing by the sink holding her large coffee cup in both hands. "I had some very strange dreams last night," he yawned. "I didn't get much sleep with them." He lifted his cup and took a deep swig.

Jess looked at him sympathetically. "I am sorry Robbie, I know how your dad felt when he took on his role round here, he was about thirty and not really ready for it. You must not think this is just your burden; everyone will be behind you every step of the way. I told Len it was too soon; I just wish he had listened."

"I am fine mum honestly, it was just a lot to take in yesterday, I have had time to think about it all now and I really think that this will be good for me. It will keep me busy which you know is what I need." Robbie watched his unconvinced mother, she knew him too well and somehow, he knew she could see some of the concerns he felt about suddenly and unexpectedly being a Lord.

Twenty minutes later, he walked down the country lane with Alice at his side, heading for the main road of the village. He had talked to Alice about the shock, and the dreams, and how he was actually quite worried about the huge burden of responsibility that had been shoved upon him.

"I know how daunting a task this is Rob, but as your mum said you really are well supported. Rune and I will never desert you, and I know how important you are to Billy. He would die to save you." Alice chuckled. "Even Pebbles will do everything she can to help. She is very fond of you Robbie."

"I guess so, to be honest I am not even sure what it is I have to do." It started to rain, and both of them pulled up their hoods and pulled their cloaks around them. They quickened their pace into the village, and headed up the street to the shelter of Rune's front yard.

Rune sat out in the yard with her mother, both of them stood up as Alice and he walked up. Rune beamed a huge smile. "Hi Robbie." She was dressed in the lightest of lilacs and she looked radiant, he grinned back.

"Hey."

Steph nodded her head at him. "Good morning My Lord." He was so unprepared for her comment, that his happy hello stumbled.

"What...? Oh.... Mrs Rimmer, do we have to be so formal at home as well? It makes me nervous."

Steph smiled. "I am sorry, but you have to understand the importance that has been placed upon you. It is now very important that you get used to being called Lord Loxley, I am sorry to say it Robbie, but it is how they will address you from now on."

Robbie sighed. "Alright I tell you what. In my house or in your house you call me Rob, and I will call you Steph. Everywhere else, you call me Lord Loxley. Is that a deal, because I really need some of you to be normal with me?"

Steph Rimmer burst into laughter. "Come here young Robbie," and she put out her arms and pulled him into a hug. "Is that normal enough for you My Lord?" Robbie smiled at Rune whose eyes twinkled as she laughed.

"That's perfect, thank you."

"Right then, are you ready for your first official duty as the Lord of this area?"

"What so soon?"

"I am afraid so Robbie, today you will meet with the high masters to discuss the future of Loxley and its surrounding inhabitants. We need to bring you up to speed so that you are aware of all that is happening. I know your father has given you some information, now you need the rest." Steph grabbed her cloak from the back of the chair. "We meet at the village hall in twenty minutes so don't be late."

Rune looked disappointed. "I was hoping I would see you today to talk." Robbie looked down at the floor.

"Yeah, me too."

"What on earth are you two talking about, have you forgotten your oath Rune? From now on, when its official business, where he goes you go. Same for you as well Miss Loxley." The two girls beamed with delight and Rune grabbed her cloak and linked Robbie's arm.

"We are ready Mum."

Steph smiled and shook her head. "Come on then let's get a move on."

In the Village Hall, in the small back room, two tables had been placed next to the large wooden desk. Robert and Jess Lox sat with Len and Steph Rimmer, Joe and Robbie's Uncle David sat at the far end. Robbie, Rune, and Alice, all sat down and looked at everyone, there was a bang of a door and John hurried in.

"Sorry folks, had a little trouble with the furnace, got a little side tracked." He dropped down into a chair opposite Robbie and winked.

Robert Lox sat back. "Good morning My Lord and kinsmen." Robbie turned to look at him.

"Can I say something?" Robert Lox smiled.

"You are the Bowman of Loxley, this is now your domain, and we are here to hear anything you want to tell us."

"Good... Firstly, I have known all of you for most of my life. I am not all together happy about the way you just thrust all of this on my lap; a little advanced notice, and maybe some training would have been appreciated. You are my family and my friends, so when we meet here in private drop all this lordship bunk and call me Robbie." He sat back in his chair and folded his arms, a determined look on his face.

Robert Lox gave a deep booming laugh. "I fear my friends we have offended our Lord and Master in less than one day of his reign." Robbie scowled at his father. Robert Lox lifted his hands up still smiling. "I am sorry Robbie. All of us here understand the surprise you must have felt last night, but you have to understand that things are moving very fast. I think with a little hindsight we should have prepared you a little better, please, we are truly sorry.”

Robbie deflated and his face softened. “How do you know that I can even do what is asked? Dad you have spent all your life preparing for this, shouldn’t you be the lord of this realm?”

His father smiled. “I am honoured that my son holds me so high in his esteem. Robbie, you have to understand that all of us have a role to play; yet none of us choose those roles. We are governed by a higher power than mortal men, all of those here have been chosen for this very moment. All of us have the one purpose of helping you achieve a destiny that was set for you hundreds of years ago.”

Robbie felt his stomach lurch as he thought of this being his destiny.

“But how do you all know that I am the one?”

Jess looked across at her son. “The one to lead will be marked with a silver lion. The night I found Billy on the moors and brought him home, I bathed his wounds and changed his clothes. It was then I knew that one day he would pass that pendant to you. Billy was sent to us to tell us that you would one day lead these people. It is the destiny that has been set for you Robbie, and none of us may prevent it.” Robbie looked down the front of his shirt at the silver chain, and then back to his mum. She smiled and nodded.

“We must get on there is a lot we must discuss.” Len Rimmer looked around the table. “We have had more news of Knox. He is now moving further north and fanning his men out, I think it is clear that he is looking for Loxley. Our greatest fortune is that in later parts of the days of old, this place was so small they did not bother to put it on the map. That will hold him up a little, but not indefinitely. His men are now encamped at Matlock and old Chesterfield. His scouts are on every road, and small bands are attacking lone farms all over this area. He is getting closer every second. Now is the time to act.”

John moved forward in his chair. “As I reported last night, Malcolm Hopewell of Hathersage has asked for us to allow him to bring the regular markets within the walls of the stockade.”

“Why not bring everyone into the stockade and give them protection?” Rune turned a little pink as everyone turned to look at her. Steph smiled at her. Jess looked at Robbie.

“What do you think Robbie? Should we protect anyone who wishes to come?”

Robbie looked across at his father. “You and granddad brought most of the people in this community here during the red death to save them, should we do that again?”

Robert Lox sat back in his chair and thought for a moment. “My son has great heart and I see some wisdom. I cannot deny that it would benefit us to have more inside this stockade. We certainly have the space, and you all know I have thought for many years, the market should be here in Loxley. The only drawback that

I can see is time. John, you understand these Cutters better than any, how long could we hold off their army?"

John scratched at the stubble on his chin. "From a military point of view and I am sure David here would agree, from what we have seen of their forces we could hold them off indefinitely. As for those who are in here, it would be feeding them and giving them shelter that could be a problem, well that would be more Jess and Beth's department they grow the food that feeds most of this area."

"We should have enough food stored or growing on the farms within the stockade to keep us going for most of the year. We could also ask anyone coming to bring as much as possible." Jess looked at Alice. "You know your mothers work, do you agree?"

Alice nodded. "My mum has always said if it wasn't for the Lox family farm, we would all be dead now. I think Aunt Jess is right. The question I want to know is, if we hold off his army will we have time to defeat him?"

"The only way to defeat him is to find the heirs, I am right am I not Mr Rimmer?" Robbie was looking at the face of Len as he spoke, and he knew that Len understood what he was suggesting. Len nodded to him.

"You are right young Robbie; I understand you perfectly."

"Then it is settled, and that is what we will do." Everyone looked at Robbie and then Len with puzzled expressions. Rune had grasped the facts and understood; she looked at him and nodded. Dave Williams who had not yet spoken looked around the table.

"Maybe I missed something. Just what exactly are we going to do?"

"I will leave with a small party and seek out the heirs, and collect the proof that we need to destroy any attempt that Mason Knox makes to crown himself."

Robbie sat back whilst the others thought about what he had just said.

Robert sat up in his chair. "You know what you are opening yourself up to here Robbie, don't you?" His face had concern all over it. "This will be no picnic for any of you."

"If Knox finds out, he will leave you all and come after me. Yes, I know what will happen, is this not my destiny? Would the powers that be, not have chosen me if I could not do it? I am a woodsman and the Bowman of Loxley; he will not find it easy to catch me."

"Who will you take?" Jess looked very worried.

"I will take those who know me enough to follow my lead, and three of our best bowmen."

Jess looked down at the table. "Billy and Alice?" Robert put his hand on his wife's arm.

"You know he is right Jess love, they have hunted with him, and in a difficult situation they trust his lead, he will need to know those around him are dependable."

Jess looked up with tears in her eyes. "You are all I have please be careful and take care of my family."

Robbie got up out of his chair and walked over to his mother. He crouched down and put his arms around her. "I love you Mother, and would never see you in pain. I promise I will return with everyone. Please trust me."

A soft voice spoke. "He will not be alone Jess. If he is taking my daughters as I know he will, I will also be going with them." Steph looked as Robbie lifted his head. "Rune has not yet received the gifts of my line, you will need me Robbie." He nodded.

Robert Lox stood up. "Then it is done, I expect everyone to assist my son in every way possible. Robbie let each man know what you need and seek their advice for they are very well versed in each of their fields. When will you leave?"

"I will have to discuss matters with Steph and with Len; I will let you all know shortly. In the meantime, we should start getting as many people around the area under our protection." John stood up and bowed to Robbie.

"With My Lords leave I will begin straight away."

"Uncle John, in here I am Robbie."

John walked over to him and clasped him by the shoulders. "Robbie is a young boy who nips off to the greenhouse to avoid work." He smiled. "The man I see before me is my brother's son, and I call him Lord with great pride." He pulled Robbie close and patted him on the back. John nodded to the others and then left the room.

T he word soon got out that Robbie in the hood had returned, and was calling on everyone to join him and come to the stockade to help defend it and seek protection. All were told to bring supplies, and soon a trickle of carts began to appear. Timber was felled and all along the inside walls of the stockade small huts began to appear. As people arrived, they were put to work helping to build, or farm so that everyone had a sense of purpose.

Robbie spent his time going from one member of the fellowship to another. Rune and Alice were always by his side, and they heard what he heard, and once alone, they would discuss the day's events, and formulate a plan. Each night Robbie would talk to Billy, and Rune would update Jade and her mother. Steph was going to be one of the last people he spoke to, as her input in the final decisions would be crucial.

Robbie was beginning to see that she had many of her father's abilities. She too seemed to understand him without having to say too much, a quality that had on occasion been noticed in Rune. Jade remained clueless but brought other qualities. She had been spending a lot of time with Joe, and her woodcraft skills were noticeably greatly improved. Joe seemed to be drinking more moonshine than ever. "She would drive a saint to drink that one; God knows what Hearne has planned for her. Whatever it is you can bet your last bit it will be bloody noisy."

There were only a few days to go before Robbie was intending to leave. He had decided not to mention anything until the very last minute; he thought that it would be better that way, as it would give less notice to anyone. He felt he should trust no one, and keep his plans as secret as possible, the last thing he wanted was Knox to know in advance he was leaving.

It was early evening and he was sat in the chair in the back room of Rune's house. They had been so busy recently that they had not spent much time alone together, Rune brought in drinks and having set them on the table, she sat on his knee and curled around him with her arms around his neck, and her head on his shoulder. "You plan to go very soon, don't you?"

"Within the next few days, yes. I have kept quiet as I think we should leave unnoticed."

"You still think there is a spy in the stockade?"

"I don't care what anyone thinks; those Cutters, who attacked Joe, went straight to him. They knew just where to find him, so if there is a map of the woods you can be sure there is a map of in here. If we just disappear it will cause confusion to the enemy, and will buy us some safe passage."

Rune pulled herself closer and snuggled into him. "That does make a lot of sense. Will you go to the priory?"

Robbie looked down at her. He had not once mentioned the priory in Kirklees, even though he had been thinking about it a lot. "What makes you say that? How did you know I have been thinking about it?"

Rune glanced up and smiled. "I keep telling you, but you don't listen."

"Yeah... Yeah I know... You know stuff." Rune giggled, and he felt her soft light body shake. He put his arms around her and pulled her tight. "I have missed being alone with you."

"I know."

"It's peaceful here, sharing with Billy can be hard."

"I know."

"Pack it in Rune, it's spooky."

"Yeah, I know." She burst out laughing.

"Ok if you know so much, what am I thinking about?"

Rune sat up and looked at him. She blushed. "We can't, Jade will be here soon."

Robbie sat still and stared. "There is no way you could have known I was thinking that."

Rune smiled. "I just guessed. I figured you want to shock me, or embarrass me. You being a young male, and me being your girl, I wondered when your mind would finally move to that. Simple really and very predictable, most women would have seen that coming."

"So, you can't read my mind then?"

"That's not how it works Rob."

Robbie breathed a sigh of relief. "Thank Hearne for that, you had me going for a moment."

Rune smiled, and curled back round him. "I have thought about it too." She stretched up and kissed him, the front door banged. "See told you." Jade burst into the room with four rabbits in her hand.

"Hey guys," she lifted the rabbits. "Not bad Eh...? I tell you Joe is one of the coolest blokes round here. He is not like the other old ones. He moans like hell, but get him alone in the woods and man he knows wood craft, I swear he does not leave foot prints." She flopped into the chair opposite dropping the rabbits at the side of the chair. "So what have you guys been doing, or shouldn't I ask?"

"We are waiting for your mother; there are a few more things to sort out before we decided on what day we leave here."

"Cool, well if you don't mind, I am going to go and prepare these, I will make some stew after if you are hungry, see you later guys." Jade got up and collected her rabbits, and headed off through the kitchen.

It was not that long before Steph arrived back, the sounds of cooking came from the other room, as Robbie settled ready to talk to her.

"Before we begin Robbie, I think there are things that Rune and you should know."

It seemed fair to let her speak and Robbie nodded. "As you know Robbie my father has spent a great deal of his life in study of things relating to Saxon and Celtic lines of descent. I have spent much time with him in the past helping him out. What I mean to say is that dad has passed on a great deal of his knowledge to me. You are not aware of it, but my father's line is long, and so is mine. We are two of the oldest families in this country, and you will learn things about us, but you must at all costs protect what you hear and speak of it to no one."

Steph was suddenly very serious and Robbie stiffened in his seat. He could feel Rune tense as she sat beside him; somehow, he thought that she too was about to learn something she did not know. "Steph you have my word, your family will be protected at all costs by me."

She relaxed a little but looked nervously at her daughter. "I prevented my father from speaking the other night because there are things that I do not want your father to know just yet. You are the true heir, and you alone I trust, I hope you realise how important the things are that you will learn in the coming weeks."

"I will treat nothing lightly that is spoken to me; I can assure you of that."

"Robbie I can see that you love my daughter, and that brings me great joy. It is for that reason that you will learn of the truth of my family. Now is not the time for all things but you should know that one day Rune will have a power that will surpass my own. She already has the gift of limited sight; it will increase in time." Rune gasped.

"I knew it; I have had dreams that have come to pass." She stared at her mother.

"Soon my child you will see more clearly than you realise. Your sister will not have this gift, and I want you to promise that for now you will not tell her. She is not ready for the destiny that has been deemed hers."

Rune's words were soft and quiet. "I promise Mother."

"Robbie we must leave within the week, do you know where to go?"

Robbie looked up at the wall, and the picture of the old priory. "I knew the day I saw that picture that I would go there, I dreamed of it as a child many times, when I saw it the restless feelings I have always felt stopped. I suppose it was suddenly like I knew I would leave here and travel there."

Steph nodded as she looked up herself at the picture. "Many answers lie there, and questions. I know you think you are ready, but there will be one more piece in the puzzle before we leave, I expect more information to arrive in the next few days, can we wait that long?"

"I have been thinking of departing in about three or four days so that should not be a problem."

Steph looked at him very carefully, and Robbie felt like she was looking inside him as if he felt her father did sometimes. "Robbie who have you told about us leaving in four days?"

"Just Rune, and now you, why do you not think it safe?"

"I know it is not, so do not tell anyone else... Robbie I mean anyone. Do you understand me?"

He shook his head. "Yes, I understand you."

"Good. It will be better to just suddenly disappear; it will make people think we are just busy in our homes or working. I have started to tell people that I have fallen behind, and will have to spend a week on the loom just to catch up for the market, you would be wise to do something similar."

"I will."

"Ok let's eat, please trust me, when we are out of here it will be safer to talk."

"To be honest I am glad you will be coming along with us, somehow, I think that you will fit in to the group very well, what are your woodcraft skills like?"

Steph smiled a knowing smile. "Let's just say they are superior to Jades."

The evening passed slowly, the food was great, and Rune and Jade larked around making him laugh, and by the time it was time to leave Robbie felt happy and relaxed. He kissed Rune goodnight after holding her in his arms for what seemed like an age, and taking his bow, he began his way through the dark home. Winter was gone and apart from the rain, that had seemed more this year, spring was starting and the trees were beginning to open their leaves as the daffodils flowered and the days began to warm.

It was dark and quite cool, especially after sitting in front of the roaring fire at Rune's house; Robbie shuddered as he walked down the street, and pulled his cloak around him. He lifted his hood to take the cool breeze off his neck.

At the end of the street, he turned into the lane that led to his home, it was pitch black and yet he knew every inch of the way back, avoiding any potholes or puddles. His thoughts began to swim around, especially his thoughts of Rune. She was going to have powers but what would they be?

She was starting to work out her dreams, and Robbie sensed that Len and Steph were far more powerful than they let on. There was something there he had not yet spotted, something just below the surface that he could not quite put his finger on. Whatever it was it would pass to Rune, and what was planned for Jade?

The feeling seemed to suddenly creep up on him as the hairs on his neck lifted. Robbie had the odd feeling he was not alone. He slid his bow off his shoulder and pulling an arrow out of his quiver, he quietly fitted it to the string. His hearing sharpened as his pace slowed, and he peered through the dark. Slowly he moved into the edge of the hedges, trying to absorb himself into the trees in hope of making himself invisible in the darkness. His ears strained as he lifted his bow, and slowly drew back the string. A very quiet voice spoke.

"We are not alone, and for god's sake do not shoot that at me."

Robbie leaned forward his eyes straining in the darkness. He had not been out long enough to get his full night vision. "Alice?" He almost breathed the words.

There was a glint of moonlight on a blade, and a quiet voice came back. "I am here." He moved close to her putting his back to the hedge.

"Where are they?"

"Just down on the left near the farm gates, I think there are three." Robbie looked up the track trying to see anything that moved. On the left of the track, there was slight movement. A figure was there and he could just make it out, he lifted his bow and took aim. The arrow sung out as it left the bow, almost instantly there was a scream, and two figures headed into the lane running towards them. Another arrow was on the string as he stepped out in front of the advancing figures. "Stop or I will shoot."

There was a shriek, and a skidding of feet on the rough track and a high-pitched voice squealed out. "Please don't shoot us Mister."

Robbie held his bow high, and aimed at the figures now on their knees on the floor up in front. Rune came up at his side. "Hi gorgeous."

Robbie looked at her blue eyes flashing in the dark. "What are you doing here?"

"Had a vision, thought I would check it out... Told you."

Robbie smiled. "I know."

Alice shouted back. "It's alright, it's just kids."

Robbie and Rune moved forward and looked up the track. Alice stood holding two small boys by their shirt collars. Robbie looked down at them. "What are you doing creeping about in the dark at this time of night?"

Rune lit a match, and lit a small lantern that had been hanging from her belt. Two very white and frightened faces looked up at them. "Please Mister we meant no harm; it was his fault." A dirty looking blonde haired boy pointed to his dark haired friend who began to cry.

"It's not my fault, Jimmy said that Robin Hood was up here, and we only came to see if he was, and then someone shot him. I do not want to die. Please mister, don't kill us."

Rune turned to Robbie. "God Robbie, you haven't killed one have you?" Her face was becoming as white as the two small boys.

Robbie smiled. "I thought you knew stuff?"

"I do."

"Then how come you don't know I just pinned his cloak to the fence?"

Robbie walked up the track and Rune followed. Alice came up behind still holding the two small boys by the collar. Robbie looked at the small boy hanging out of his cloak. "Aw look, the poor little sod has fainted." Robbie pulled the arrow out of the fence post, and holding the small boy, he patted his face gently. The boy jerked awake; his wide eyes stared up for a minute as the panic within him surged.

"Easy there little fellow, no one will harm you." Rune crouched down to look more closely at him and she smiled. He sat up and looked around and seeing the two boys, he lifted his arm up and pointed.

"They made me do it, honest Mister." Rune laughed, as Alice gasped and tutted, she sounded a little like Beth. Rune lifted the small boy up and stood him next to the other two, who were still firmly gripped by Alice.

"So young gents, you came to see if Robin in the Hood lived here, did you?" All three looked at Rune, and then put their heads down in shame. She looked up at Robbie and smiled. "Sort of cute, aren't they?" She turned back to the three boys. "Why do you look at the floor? You won't find him there."

Robbie slid his hood back over his head and stood with his bow in his hand. The three boys looked up and gasped in awe. "Robin Hood," they all whispered together. Even Alice had to smile, and she let go of their collars.

Robbie looked down at the three tiny smiling faces. "What would three noble woodsmen want so badly that they would endanger their lives, to seek out the hooded man on such a night as this?" His voice seemed deeper than normal and Rune looked at Alice who was trying to hold back her giggles.

Little Jimmy stepped forward. "Please sir, are you real?"

"Was my arrow young master woodsman?"

Jimmy nodded vigorously. "Yes sir, I thought I was dead."

Rune could see Robbie's shoulders shake as he held back his laughter. "My

Lord is too good a shot to kill a young master such as you. He only meant to hold you until he could decide if you were a Cutter or not. The Lord Loxley will only kill if he is forced too; he is a kind and gracious Lord." Little Jimmy nodded and Rune smiled at him. "Lord Loxley commands all this land, and the people within it. If he was to command you, would you obey him?"

Jimmy beamed a huge smile and then went down on one knee. "Command me My Lord." Robbie knelt down in front of the small boy and lifted his face to look at him. "What is your name boy?"

"Jimmy Perkins, My Lord."

"What will you be when you get older Jimmy?"

"I want to be a bowman like you, My Lord."

Robbie slid back his hood and smiled. "Will you be loyal to Loxley and all who live here Jimmy?"

"There will be no one more loyal My Lord, I swear it." A tear welled in Rune's eye as she watched the tenderness of Robbie, who was very touched by this young boy before him.

"To become a bowman of Loxley, I demand only the best with a bow." Robbie handed his rowan bow over to Jimmy. The young boy's eyes widened. "Take this and practice day and night, for one day Jimmy Perkins, I would hold you to your word, and ask you into my service."

His two small friends gasped as Jimmy took the bow as if he had been handed something of immense value. "Thank you My Lord, I will not fail you."

Robbie smiled. "I know you won't." He stood up and pulled his hood back over his head. "Will you be safe going back in the dark my bowman?"

"I will fear nothing again My Lord."

"Then off you go Jimmy and I will see you again in a few years."

Jimmy Perkins bowed low to his lord, and he turned and ran down the lane into the darkness, his friends bowed, and then turned and ran after him. Rune came up close as she wiped the tears from her eyes.

"That was a very sweet thing you just did."

Robbie smiled at her as he pulled her close. He looked at Alice who was wiping her face. "Are you two always going to pop out of nowhere when I need you?"

Alice burst into laughter, and hugged him. "Really Robbie that was a very nice thing to do."

"I suppose I will have to get use to the idea wherever I go from now on, although I must admit Jimmy was a brave little bugger, I am not sure I would have been that brave at his age."

Little Jimmy Perkins never forgot the night he met Robin Hood. He was true to his word and practiced every day before and after school. If anyone ever told him to rest, he would always say, "I have to be the best when Lord Loxley comes for me," and he would continue to shoot.

The following day the anticipation was beginning to grow in Robbie, he was sat next to his father above the tall wooden gates, looking into the stockade at the small wooden town that was now growing day by day. "Do you think there will be enough to hold out Dad?"

Robert Lox patted him softly on the back. "You worry too much, your granddad was the same, as soon as he heard about the Cutters, he was out here marking out the soil for where the wall would go."

Robbie thought for a moment before speaking. "Dad it has bothered me ever since I met the Cutters in the woods, they are organised and well trained. I just cannot get over how they just crept up on Joe. Mason has got a lot more up his sleeve I am sure of it."

"Robbie lad you listen to me now, and understand what I tell you. We are woodsmen born and bred; our life is the way of nature. We live on the land, and with the land and that is a special sort of life. It is a hard life but we do not always notice that because we are accustomed to it. These southern boys they do not live like us, they never have, and it has always been different between them and us. Folk of the north are tough; they have to be because life up here has always been hard."

He looked out across the Stockade. "See for yourself, look at em... They are all working hard to put another part of Loxley together. Twice now, we have rebuilt to keep out death, and it is only folk from up here that can do that. I will bet you Mason is prancing about in a flash dwelling, and eating rich food and having a right old time of it. He is not the type that will have splinters in his hands and an ache in his back. You mark my words no matter how many men he has, they will stand the measure of the men of Loxley."

"I really hope you are right dad."

"I am... Rune told me, nice girl that one, you have done well there. First time I saw her I said to myself, now there is a girl who knows stuff." Robert started to laugh. Robbie looked at his father's jolly face. "Not you as well?"

Robert laughed harder and slapped his son on the back. "Just kidding, I was talking to her yesterday and she told me. Good to see a smile on your face boy. Seriously though Robbie lad I do like her a great deal, she has a lot of young Jess in her, and that is the biggest compliment I can pay the girl believe me." Robbie smiled he knew how much his parents loved each other, and it felt nice to know that maybe he might one day have what they had with Rune.

"I mean it Robbie. Don't you go worrying about this place; you concentrate on what you have to do, leave the Cutters to John and me. I promise you this, they will need more than muscle and sweat to bring this place down."

There was a deep rumbling down the old road that led to the reservoir, Robert

Lox straightened up and listened. "Now that is a sound I have wanted to hear," and he jumped to his feet and looked over the wall, Robbie scrambled up and stood by his father.

He looked over the wall and could see a large dust cloud in the distance. "What is it Dad?"

Robert beamed a huge smile at Robbie. "That if I am not mistaken is a motorbike, which can only mean one thing."

Robbie glanced over the wall and then back at his dad as his face broke into a smile. "Harry."

"Took his bloody time, I tell you, I was getting a little worried, come on lad let's give your crazy old uncle a welcome." Robert disappeared down the ladder to the bottom of the gates, and Robbie followed. A few minutes later in a cloud of dust, Harry rode into the stockade, and was greeted with a huge hug from his eldest brother. Harry was released by Robert and turned to Robbie

"Man, you have like shot up a foot since I left." He threw his arms around Robbie and lifted him off the floor. He dropped him back on the ground and stood back to look at him. "Well, my cosmic young Hood, you will be surprised to know man that you have become like a very famous man, it's totally cosmic." He slapped his arm around Robbie's shoulders. "It's kinda weird cause you are my nephew, but I tell you Robbie dude, folk are like talking about you all the way past Birmingham." He lowered his voice. "I heard you finally got it on with the Rune chick. Good on you Robbie dude, always fancied her mum, she liked my mate better, what can I say eh...win some lose the best."

Robbie smiled. "I am really pleased to see you Harry, I thought for a moment you would not get back in time."

Harry laughed. "Not me dude, I always pop up if there is trouble."

CHAPTER SEVEN

PLANNING AND PREPARATIONS

Robbie climbed up on to the back of Harry's bike and clung tight to him. Harry kicked down the pedal and the bike roared loudly. He could feel the throbbing in the seat as Harry gunned the engine. "Hold on tight dude this is going to be a ride like you have never known, it's like vibe building, man." With a loud burst, the bike leapt forward and Robbie spat out the dust that filled his mouth. Harry laughed wildly.

"Man, I love this beast," and the bike whizzed up the dirt track towards the village at a horrific speed. Robbie hung on for dear life although he loved the power and the speed and laughed loudly as they tore down the track and into the village. The bike skidded to a halt outside Rune's house and Harry threw his leg over the tank and hopped off. Robbie was all smiles as he slid off the back of the bike. The screams and howls of happiness that came from inside the house announced Jade was on her way.

With a huge smile on her face and tears in her eyes, Jade flew through the door and vaulted the wall. "Harry, Harry, you made it."

She tore across the street and leapt into Harry's arms. Harry held her tight and spun her round in the air hugging her. "Hey baby girl, whoa I've missed you." He put her down on the floor and held her back to look at her. "It is really cool being home baby girl, man you look good." He pulled her back into his arms and hugged her again.

"Oh Harry, I have missed you so much, I thought you were never coming back."

"What and miss a welcome like this? You know better baby girl."

Harry turned to see Steph stood at the gate, and he grinned at her, and held out his arms and walked towards her. Steph smiling with tears in her eyes put her arms around him and squeezed him very tight. Harry held her close and kissed her cheek as she sobbed. "Hey come on girl no need for tears. Oh Stephy, I have missed you, how are you holding up girl?"

Robbie saw a different side of Steph as he walked slowly towards them. Jade was busy looking at yet another new bike for Harry. Steph sobbed into Harry's shoulders. "I miss him so much Harry, have you heard anything?"

Harry leaned back and stroked the hair from her damp eyes. "Listen to me girl, there is talk. He is still with us so do not give up on him. I promised I would get him home and I will. I think Knox is about to make and big mistake and when he does, believe me chicken I will snatch him back for you quicker than lightning... I promise." She sobbed a smile and he released her. "So where is this hot chick who Robbie here has snatched up, before I can get to her?"

"Hi Harry." Rune stood at the door her long pale yellow skirt flowing in the breeze, her silver jewellery shimmered in the pale sun. Harry looked up at her and smiled.

"Whoa baby girl, and haven't you become the fairy princess?" Harry held out his arms. "Don't the old man get a hug?" Rune smiled, and came down the path and gave him a hug. Harry looked back at Steph. "Two of the most beautiful women on earth, both snatched from under my nose by better men. Man, life can suck." He grinned at Robbie, and winked at Jade. "Hey baby girl, you going to make your old Uncle Harry a brew?"

Jade ran over and put her arm around him. "This way Dude." Harry took his black velvet hat off and dropped it on her head.

"Cool... Lead the way baby girl."

Rune slid her arm around Robbie's waist. "You realise Jade is going to be hell to live with while he is here?"

"Bummer baby girl." Robbie ducked as Rune swung her arm up, Steph burst out laughing with Robbie, as the three of them followed into the house.

Harry was wild there was no doubt. He lived on his bike but loved his family, and his arrivals home were always a cause for celebration. All the women in the town loved Harry. He was tanned with waist length straight silky brown hair. His clothes were always black, from his silk shirt with silver collar tabs to his straight leg denim pants and black suede cowboy boots, with silver spurs.

Somehow the fathers in the area never seemed as enthusiastic when he turned up, and Robbie thought how at this very moment men all over the district would be dragging their daughters indoors for their own protection. Harry did have quite a reputation.

The truth was that he just had never really grown up. He lived a life that let him be the person he wanted and Harry felt no guilt or shame at doing so. Harry's travels got him all over the country and so over the years he had been a vital link for news. Robbie knew his time with Harry would come and he would learn more about Knox and his plans.

Harry was Jade's hero. She adored him, as he did her, Jade like him felt something of an outcast and she identified very strongly with him. Wherever he went over the coming weeks she would be beside him, which did not enhance her reputation with the women, but like Harry, she did not care.

Harry arrived later on at the farm and chased Jess out of the greenhouse shouting. "Hey Jessie baby," and he finally caught her, spun her in the air, and gave her a huge hug and a very sloppy wet kiss whilst she protested.

"Harry, I mean it... cut it out and put me down.... Oh Harry, please behave yourself, what will Rob think and the boys?"

Harry bellowed with laughter. "I don't care you are the woman of my dreams Jessie Lox." Finally, he put her down and smiled at her. "I miss you the most when I am away sis."

Jess smiled. "You miss my cooking and my coffee... Don't try and flatter me Harry Lox, I have still not forgiven you for the last sack of beans you whipped." Harry blew her a kiss. He still had a boyish smile and Jess soon crumbled. "You want to take more care, look at you... you have lost weight." Harry shrugged.

"I am a growing boy and no one feeds me like you Jess."

Jess laughed and shook her head. "Never turn it off do you Harry?" He smiled.

Meal times with Harry were fun. He would tell every one of his adventures and how the rest of the country was recovering. New communities were starting to form and trade was improving. There was rumour that some sort of postal service might even be brought back to speed up contact all over the place. Billy was delighted when he walked in to hear the familiar, "Billy Boy."

Harry raised his flat palm and Billy slapped it as he sat down. Beth screamed and ran back out as Harry raced after her shouting, "give me some love Beth baby." Both had come back laughing, although Beth was beetroot, and Harry winked at John and smiled. "Lucky old dog Johnny boy."

Alice had given him a huge hug saying. "God Harry you are sexy," and kissed him hard on the lips, which had momentarily thrown him and he laughed as everyone realised he had been caught out. Alice winked at him. "Got you at your own game Harry, you are getting slow." Harry bowed to superior talent.

The meal was loud and happy. Robbie noticed as Jess stood at the sink watching everyone enjoying themselves. Robbie knew that she more than most was dreading the moment when he would leave taking some of her most precious family members with him.

The meal moved on and slowly one by one the family excused themselves to go off to attend to their duties. Robbie sat alone with just Harry and his father. Robert Lox sensed the time was now right, and he moved into the discussion that would most affect everyone. "What is he up to now Harry, have you heard anything?"

Harry looked at his brother and then at Robbie. "It's not good guys." There was a serious tone to his voice, which Robbie had never heard before and it worried him. "Mason Knox has been a very busy little bee. He has spent a lot of time holed up in the south and now he is stretching his arms out." Harry leaned forward on to the table, "I will tell you this Bro, they are one hell of a lot longer than any of us thought."

Robert's eyes narrowed as he looked at his brother. "How long?"

Harry took a long drink of his wine; he looked at Robbie and then his brother and let out a long sigh. "Here."

A cold shiver ran down Robbie's spine. "What do you mean Harry?"

"What I mean Rob is very simply that Knox now knows you have the one thing he wants more than anything, and he is coming to get it."

Robert had no doubt in his voice. "He knows we have Len." Harry slowly nodded as if in thought.

"He wants this place for his own Rob. He plans to make this his next fortress to enforce his will in the north. I tell you man, he will not stop at anything to gain control of Loxley."

"He will get a fight worth fighting; I won't leave my father's land easily."

Harry nodded. "I think it might be his first big mistake. This guy is really off it with power Rob; I mean the dude thinks he is like really invincible." Harry looked at Robbie. "You got plans to go after him man?"

Robbie nodded. "I am the one to stop him Harry." Harry smiled.

"Cool... I'm in."

Robbie looked a little shocked. "What do you mean? You want to come with us?"

Harry winked and smiled at Robbie. "That is a gig I aint goin to miss... Man it's goin to be cosmic." Harry pulled down on his neatly shaped goatee, and he leaned across at Robbie. "Look dude, this guy thinks this place is a walk in the park. The way I see it is he will lob everything he has at this place. But my old pops built this place to keep out more cosmic things than him. The way I see it, if we just kinda pop out unnoticed like, we can shimmy on down to his pad and kick his ass."

"I am not so sure it will be as easy as that Harry." Robbie admired his uncle's courage but his idea appeared as nutty as he was.

Harry waved his hands about. "Look... Wow Robbie Man ... You got to see the whole picture. This dude has the Cutters all over the shop kicking ass, but they aint the problem. I am telling you man, I have seen what he has behind the scenes." He lifted his glass and emptied it.

"This man has some serious beef on his side; we are talking rough and nasty but trained like a real army. Man, they are some seriously heavy dudes, I have seen towns all over the country living their nightmare man. There are folks down there who join him to protect themselves and their family." Harry poured another glass of wine.

"He has spies everywhere then?" Robert Lox seemed very concerned.

"Look Bro that is what I am saying, that is the dude's weakness. They hate him man, but they kiss up to him because it like keeps them alive. Pop him and I tell you the whole house of cards will drop like a really cosmic stone."

Robbie was already hatching some sort of new plan in his mind. "What does he intend to do after seizing Loxley?"

Harry smiled. "I got to admit this is where you got to really admire the dude. Man, he is barking... The dude is goin to Canterbury to make himself the king. How totally weird is that?" Harry laughed and shook his head. "Really off his tree man, I am telling you."

Robert looked at Robbie and patted the table as he thought. "So, what you are saying is that he is going to use the attack on Loxley to silence Len, and create a diversion to crown himself King?"

"Totally guys."

"What do you think Dad?"

"I think Robbie that your uncle here has the maddest plan I have ever heard... But mad as it is, it could work if planned properly."

Harry smiled. "Cool."

Robert Lox stood up and looked at his son. "This will need to be looked at Robbie I am going to go and see Len, and see if we can get everyone together in the morning. I will see you both later." He walked across the kitchen and out of the door leaving Robbie alone with Harry who was swallowing yet another glass of wine.

"Robbie man, are you off to your chick's house tonight?"

"She's not a chick Harry, Rune is my girlfriend."

Harry frowned. "That's what I said man."

Robbie laughed. "You know Harry you are as loony as a fruit cake, it's a good job I love you."

"Cheers man... You know I really love you too dude, don't you?"

"Come on, and leave the wine here you are getting stranger by the minute drinking that stuff."

Robbie and Harry walked down the roadway and on to the track that led to town. Robbie walked; Harry somewhat staggered a little. "Glad we are alone man. I like am really needing to talk to you... You know they took Steph's man and locked him away? Well Pete was my total bud you know? Man I love that dude... Thing is Rob they are going to move him from the prison he is in and take him through this really huge wood to a castle in nowhereville. I was sort of thinking of getting the guy free you know?"

"Are you talking about Rune's Dad?"

"Yeah man... You up for it? We can totally do it on the way to popping the king dude."

"Tell me more Harry." Robbie and Harry slowed their pace, one because it was easier to talk, and the other because Harry was now so drunk, he was finding it hard to walk. After a lot of translation from biker dude talk into English, Robbie began to make sense of what Harry had told him.

Peter Lane was alive and still imprisoned at Tintagel Castle in Cornwall. It appeared that Knox had completely rebuilt the old castle, which was the ancestral seat of the Duke of Cornwall. His plan was to move Peter by boat further up the coast to a place called Richmont Castle. This was as far as Robbie could work out, was near a place called Axbridge.

They would land on foot at Burnham and travel across land through the Cheddar Gorge to the castle. Robbie had no idea where these places were, he just understood that the later part of the journey would be through woodland. He knew enough to see why Harry had mentioned it. Robbie was locally renowned for his woodland skills, and Harry knew that he would be able to track and attack the party that escorted Peter Lane to another prison. This had been the only chance created to get Peter since his capture, almost ten years ago.

By the time they arrived at Rune's house Harry was very drunk. He flopped into a chair and was asleep in minutes, Robbie had not realised the wine was made by Joe, which possibly meant it was moonshine based. Harry had drunk over a litre, and Rune worked out that it would possibly sedate him until the following mid-morning.

Robbie sat with Steph and Rune and told them what Harry had said, he sat back and waited for a reaction from Steph. She was very quiet and stared at the rug, Rune watched her mother with hope in her eyes. Steph finally looked up. "I miss him so much and I know my children need their father, but I cannot put my needs above those of this community Robbie, you know that?"

Robbie nodded. "That is not what I am saying... I think it is possible on route to pass this area and make at least one attempt to free your husband. If Harry is right, it should be an easy task."

Steph had a deep sadness on her face; he knew she did not dare hope just in case. A single tear ran from the corner of her eye. "I would die to save him Robbie." He stretched out his arm and put his hand on hers.

"Let me try, and I promise I will do all in my power to get him." Steph nodded unable to speak. Robbie squeezed her hand. "Both of you must promise me, you will not mention a word of this to anyone, especially Jade. If Knox finds out what we plan, you will lose him forever... I do not trust many at the moment."

Steph nodded. "I promise you Robbie. Thank you." He turned to Rune; she smiled with eyes that glistened.

"You have my word."

Robbie sat back up in his chair. "Where can I get a map of this Cheddar Gorge area and Burnham?"

Steph looked up. "Burnham?"

"You know it?"

"It is not far from where my family started. I have some knowledge of the area, and I know just who to ask for help down there. There are woodsmen I know who visit that area regularly." As she spoke her voice returned to normal and hope slipped in between her lines of speech. Robbie now felt more encouraged.

"Ok we leave here the day after tomorrow, and we travel to Kirklees to the old priory. Once we have the facts we need, we can head south and contact your friends, with luck they will help and we should free your husband. Then we head for Canterbury and try to stop Knox. We can work out all the details with Harry and yourself on the journey."

"Harry is coming with us?" Steph seemed surprised.

"He asked especially to come tonight; I said he could because Harry has a lot of contacts that might prove useful."

"He will be good in a fight; you have never seen him with his swords, have you?" Steph looked impressed.

"No is he good?" It was a part of Harry that Robbie had never thought about.

"If he pulls those two blades, sit back and enjoy the show, I am telling you Robbie he is a master of the Samurai sword."

"What's a Samurai sword Mum?"

Steph gave a knowing grin. "Wait and see you will learn a lot." Harry grunted in his sleep, he hardly appeared to be a master swordsman to Robbie at the moment.

Steph sat sipping her coffee in the chair; she was lost in thought and stared into space. Robbie sat looking up at the picture on the wall. The old priory stood in a glade surrounded by trees, its brickwork looked crumbled and shabby, and the stone surrounded by railings, under the shrubs seemed to stand out more and more. His answers lay there below the surface of the ground. What had Len found that Knox wanted so desperately?

Rune was curled besides him and disturbed in her sleep. She whimpered a little and Steph looked down at her, her eyes moved to Robbie. "It's starting." She spoke quietly as she watched her daughter twitch and murmur in her sleep.

Robbie felt a little alarmed as he watched Rune, who moved and moaned quietly. "What is starting?"

"Her powers." Steph smiled. "Mine came late, it would freak Pete out, he would get all concerned and worried when he could not wake me up. She has started very early; I think she will be as powerful as her grandmother."

Robbie looked back up at Steph. "Should I do anything?"

"Leave her and she will be fine, it looks worse than it is. She will have strange dreams and then flash backs, and after that, she will settle as the true sight comes. It takes a few weeks but you will not notice much, until one day she will tell you something and it will happen exactly as she says. Then you will know her powers have matured."

Robbie sat and softly stroked her hair, and she seemed to settle more. He gazed at this beautiful young woman lay across his lap. Her soft white skin with faint freckles seemed to glow in the light, her red eyelashes seemed to curl away from her eye. He had never been able to look at her in such detail before. "She is very beautiful, isn't she?" Steph was smiling at him with a look that showed him she understood how important she was to him.

"You said you would die to save Peter, I would for Rune." His eyes did not leave her as he spoke and when he looked up Steph nodded.

"She would for you. I am not sure if you really know how long she has waited for you to ask her out. I have seen her sat in front of her loom staring out of the window all day watching you work in the street. Rune is very deep, not at all like Jade."

"Jade is deep." He looked back at Steph. "She pretends like she is not, but I have seen it. I think Jade and I are a bit like you and Harry."

Steph looked over at Harry who was fast asleep and she smiled. "For all his wild ways I do love him. He is without doubt the greatest friend I have ever had Robbie, he loves Pete like a brother and although he does not show it, he feels the loss more than any of us. That is why he leaves here so much." Robbie did not quite understand, Steph could see his confusion.

"Jade is very like her father and Harry can see the Peter in her. Rune is just like I was at her age. Pete and Harry were both in love with me, it was hard to choose, but Pete asked. Harry and I changed from that day onwards, I think if anything the love grew deeper between us because we had one thing in common, we both loved Pete. When Harry comes home, he has Jade, Rune, and me, to remind him that he was with Pete when he was captured. He blames himself for it, even though they were completely outnumbered, and so he spends all his time here drinking that poison of Joe's to ease the pain he feels."

Steph sighed as she watched him sleep. "He is such a great man with the biggest heart I have ever known. It saddens me to see him like that." She turned to Robbie. "Actually, Robbie you could do me a great favour."

"Name it."

"Robbie you will lead this party out of here, and you will be the one in charge, won't you?"

"Yes, I suppose so."

"Good... You tell Harry before we leave you will not tolerate a drunken fighter. Make sure he leaves all that booze from Joe behind, believe me if you straighten him out a bit you will have a truly able woodsman with us."

"I can do that no problem." Steph smiled at him and she got up and pulled a blanket off the back of her chair. She gently pulled it over the sleeping Harry, and kissed her fingers and touched the top of his forehead.

"It's late Robbie I am going to get some sleep. If you want to stay there you can, there is a blanket on the back of the chair. Goodnight." Steph crossed the room to the door where she hesitated, and turned back. "Thank you, Robbie, for tonight. If you can find a way to help Pete on route, my children will never be able to thank you. You have Harry's heart." She left the room and he heard the front door bolt shut.

Robbie looked down at Rune as he pulled the blanket off the back of the chair and laid it across her. She had settled a bit and was now sleeping more peacefully. He slid down carefully beside her and pulled her close. He closed his eyes, and suddenly seemed to feel an enormous tiredness flow over him. The fire flickered and crackled, Rune moved rhythmically as she breathed, and he felt her soft breath on his cheek. His eyes struggled to stay open as the calmness and relaxation washed over him, his eyes closed.

He slept deeper than he ever had before; maybe it was Rune beside him or the safe atmosphere of the house, whatever it was it was like letting go of everything and just drifting away like a cloud.

Robbie opened his eyes. It was very dark; he was startled for a moment unsure of where he was. Two eyes seemed to glow in the dark in front of him. He felt pressure on his chest, his shirt was open and he felt the warm soft skin of her hands stroke him. The eyes came closer and he felt her lips touch his. The kiss was soft, tender, and sweet, and he felt his body relax. "Hi gorgeous," she whispered, as she lifted her face from his.

"Hey beautiful." He slowly sat up to face her as she sat straddled over his waist. All he could see was the bright sparkle of her eyes, she moved as she slid her top over her head and dropped it on the floor. Robbie pulled her close and stopped. "Where is Harry?"

Rune pulled his shirt down his back. "Don't worry he won't wake up for hours that was Joe's recipe. She pulled him close and kissed him softly, and then pushing him back slowly to the cushions, she pulled the blanket over them.

The strong smell of coffee mingled with cherry shampoo wafted into Robbie's brain. He opened his eyes; Rune was curled up with her back to him still asleep. Jade smiled her green eyes dancing. "Here." She showed him the coffee and put the two cups on the small table. "I err...Would put these back on if I was you, mum will be up in a bit." Jade dropped his pants on to Rune who jumped up startled. Jade smiled at Rune. "Lucky bugger."

It took a few seconds for Rune to come around, and as she looked back at Robbie, and then under the blanket, the memory of last night came back. Rune smiled and turned to him. "Wow." She kissed him quickly, and then grabbing her skirt she pulled it under the blanket. Slipping her top on, she slid from under the cover and passed him his pants, she gave him a big smile.

Robbie pulled them on and grabbed his shirt as he threw the blanket off and put it on. Rune gathered her remaining clothes and a coffee, and beaming she headed for the kitchen. Robbie sat on the edge of the chair and stretched. He felt rested and strangely alive; he picked up the coffee and started to sip. Harry was still dead to the world.

The sound of Jade's titter came from the kitchen and he smiled. Movement upstairs told him Steph was up and he grabbed his boots and pulled them on. Robbie stood up and stretched, he picked up his cup and headed into the kitchen, Rune was combing her hair at the window, she gave him a huge smile and the happiness he felt broke across his face. Jade coughed.

"Yes... Yes, we know, God, you should see yourselves, get a grip." Jade picked up her cup and walked out of the room, Robbie walked over to her and she raised her arms pulling him close.

"Good morning My Lord." She kissed him.

"My Lady." He felt like the luckiest man in the world as she squeezed him tightly.

"Good morning." Robbie released Rune as Steph walked in. "Robbie, do you want to give Harry a kick? Be warned do not get too close." He felt concerned at the tone. Was Harry dangerous when woken quickly? Steph laughed as she picked up a pan. "He will be a little tender today, and he could be a little grumpy, do not startle him." Rune gave him a knowing smile as he slowly peered around the door at Harry still flat out in the chair.

Robbie approached Harry as if facing a dangerous hog. Rune tittered from the doorway as he stretched out his leg and knocked Harry's foot. "Harry...Harry." Nothing happened.

Jade came in and looked at Robbie's feeble attempts to rouse Harry from sleep. She bent down close to his ear and screamed with all her might.

"HAAAA....RRRRY!" Harry shot out of the chair swinging his arms madly.

Robbie ducked just in time as Harry's arm hurtled towards him. Rune collapsed in the doorway in hysterical laughter at the look of shock on both Robbie and Harry's faces. Harry blinked and smiled.

"You want something Jade? Morning Rob." The sudden impact of last night clouded over Harry as his smile faded and he groaned. He put his hands to his head. "Oh man I have a bummer head." He very slowly sat back down and Robbie gave him his coffee. "Cheers dude." Harry sat very still holding the cup close to his lips. It was as if just simple movement was too loud for him. Steph came in and handed him a glass of fizzy green water. "Cheers Babe." Harry drank it down and closed his eyes.

Breakfast was hearty. Robbie felt strangely very hungry and tucked in to bacon, eggs with beans and masses of toast. Steph informed him that his dad would be meeting with Len later; she had just come back from taking him his breakfast. Len had asked if he would go down to the range later and keep an eye on the bowmen as they practiced. It seemed he would have been helping out, but now had to attend the meeting. Robbie liked the idea of seeing who could shoot and asked Rune if she fancied it, Rune nodded, as she finished washing her plate and put it on the drainer to dry.

It was two hours later when Robbie with Rune on his arm and a rather subdued Harry walked down the street towards the target ground behind the village hall. Alice came running up as they entered the site.

The target range had twenty long rows all marked off with wooden posts, at the end of each range was a large round straw target. Bowmen lined up in front of their own target, and on command, they took aim and fired. John Lox walked along the range behind bowmen and looking down at the target; he would tap them on the shoulder, and tell them, in, or out. Those who were out would lower their heads and walk back to the seats at the back of the range. John came back down the line towards them he lifted a thumb towards the crowd of two hundred young hopefuls who watched eagerly. "New recruits."

Robbie glanced at them and smiled. "That's good John, we need them."

John shook his head. "They cannot shoot for sh..." He noticed Rune watching him. "Err toffee." She smiled.

"Maybe they just need a little instruction." Rune looked at one of the hopefuls who had barely hit the target and was walking back to the bench dispirited. "You... What is your name?"

He turned round looking at Rune and stopped. "I am Eric Tanner of Bamford Mistress." Rune beckoned to the target.

"Shoot again." He turned with a smile and almost ran back to take up his position. All of the others watched as Rune and Robbie began to walk back up the range towards Eric. "These boys have heart Rob they need to be encouraged, with a little training and their own pride they will defend this place to the death." Robbie stood a little way behind Eric as Rune went to his side and gave him a few pointers. She stood in line with the next range as she spoke, and drew out one of her own arrows. She took aim and prompted Eric to follow.

Robbie smiled as Alice and Harry came up beside him. Rune bent her knees as she spoke to Eric and he followed. She sighted the bow, and unleashed the arrow. It hit the dead centre of the bull. Eric's arrow followed and hit just outside the bull; his first arrow still hung limp at the far edge of the target. Rune patted his shoulder and turned to walk back to Robbie, a broad smile of satisfaction on her face.

Robbie beamed as he stood with his legs slightly apart and his arms folded, his hair blowing back in the breeze. Rune came up slowly towards him, Eric who was thrilled ran up behind her. "Excuse me Mistress... Thank you... I hope you do not mind me asking? But who are you so I can tell my friends about your remarkable shot?"

Robbie looked at the young lad. "This is the Lady Runestone and Able Bowman of Loxley." Eric's eyes widened as she smiled at him and slipped her arm through Robbie's. He looked at her arm entwined in Robbie's and suddenly he realised who he was talking to.

He dropped to one knee. "My Lord Loxley, forgive me I did not recognise you."

Robbie stepped forwards. "Come lad." Robbie walked back towards the line. "How old are you Eric?"

"I will be 16 next month My Lord."

"So, you want to be a Bowman of Loxley?"

"I do My Lord very much so."

"Very well let us see if we cannot pull some of that desire into your bowstring." Eric stood at the top of the range with his bow ready. He lifted the bow. "Who do you fear more young Eric, the Cutters or me?" Eric's arm was shaking nervously.

"You, My Lord."

Robbie started to laugh; he lowered his voice a little. "You should have no fear of me, I want you only to do what you desire. So, if you wish to be a Bowman better that last shot and I will award you your crossed arrows." He stood close and stared at him increasing the pressure that Eric now felt. Eric raised his bow; he focused all of his concentration on the target.

The arrow released and swept down the range plunging into the target two inches closer than the last, Eric gasped with relief. Robbie patted him on the shoulder. "You did well under pressure Eric; you have earned your crossed arrows, welcome to my Bowmen." Robbie held out his hand, Eric hesitated then took it and smiled as he shook hands.

"Thank you, My Lord; my mother will be so proud."

Robbie smiled. "Go and tell all the others they will shoot again, this time for the Able Bowmen of Loxley. Instruct them as my good lady did you."

Eric ran down the field to the others as John came up towards him. "May I steal your class from you John? I am sure Dad could use your advice."

John smiled. "To be honest I was rather hoping you would." He handed Robbie a list of all the applicants, "just put a cross next to their names if you think they will do and I will see they get sorted into their new groups."

The group gathered around Lord Loxley. Rune, Alice and Harry stood on the range and took aim. Robbie talked the recruits through the process as each of them fired. They all hit the bull smack in the centre. Robbie continued to talk over the gasps as he slid one of his own arrows out of the quiver. He stood at the top of the range and looked at the arrow Alice had place perfectly in the centre of the target, he continued to talk. "You lock your elbow and hold the arrow just for a moment longer whilst you ensure it is correctly sighted." He raised the bow and

took aim. "Look down the arrow and focus. Put all distraction out of your mind."
He released the arrow. "Once it's gone do not watch it, load another arrow."
There was an almighty gasp as his arrow hit the centre of Alice's and split it right
down to the tip. He released his second arrow. Once again, he hit the arrow in the
target, and it splintered as it tore apart allowing the arrow into the same spot as the
previous one. "Remember where your mark is and don't lose your focus, that way
you will hit again and again." Robbie smiled at the silent and dumbfounded group
in front of him.

Alice and Rune chuckled. Alice looked at Rune. "He has always been a show off
you know?" They both started laughing.

"Right, everyone take your target and show us better than last time." Robbie
smiled at the other three. "Come on you are here to help as well, help this lot
improve we are going to need every able shot we can get."

Robbie spent most of the morning with the others walking up and down the line
instructing as he went. He spotted some very talented shooters and devoted a lot of
his time to improving them, whilst the others helped instruct those with less ability.

By the end of the morning, he instructed them all to take a break and have
something to eat and drink. "I want all of those chosen back here in one hour to
continue." Robbie sat on one of the benches and watched as they left with their
heads held high and bright smiles on their faces. The others came up and sat
down.

"How's the head Harry?" Rune smiled at his blood shot eyes and pale face.

Harry screwed his eyes a little. "It is clearing slowly, man that was a strong one.
Really sort of cosmic." Robbie smiled; Harry was almost talking normal again,
which meant the moonshine was wearing off. Steph came down with Jade and
a large basket. She had prepared a lunch and had decided that Jade and herself
should get in some practice to sharpen them up for the trip. After a good hearty
feed, most of them headed back to practice. Robbie sat with Rune on the seats
observing them closely.

"Your mum is good with a bow." His eyes fixed on Harry and then Jade. "Your
sister is much better as well, mind you she has spent a lot of time with Joe, and he
would have shown her a few tricks."

"They will be fine Rob don't worry so much." She squeezed his leg and then lent
on it.

"My mum is already upset about all of them coming with me, can you imagine
what your mum will be like if anything happens to you or Jade? To be honest if
there was anyone better, I would use them, but this group is the very best Loxley
has. It will take only the best to beat Mason I have no choice."

"You are a man with good instincts trust them as you do in the woods, and we
will all be safe. You have a lot of loyalty here, and you know we will all stand by
you no matter what." The hour passed by and the new recruits came back to

continue their lessons. The word was out that Lord Loxley was at the target range, and it was not long before most of the children in the stockade appeared at the fence line to watch. Many of the recruit's parents had also shown up to see their children being instructed by Lord Loxley.

Rune was also getting a lot of attention from the crowd, every time she hit the bull, which was always, the assembled crowd cheered and Rune blushed. The atmosphere lightened as the day wore on and the new recruits improved, with the crowd behind them they seemed to smile more and start to laugh at each other. With Harry right in the middle of the line, there were plenty of jokes to be had.

A competition began as he ragged Rune, who responded by out shooting him, Alice did likewise, very soon the recruits were watching as Jade joined in and finally Robbie. Shot after shot saw Alice Robbie and Rune tie until eventually it came down to a match off between just Robbie and Alice.

Alice waited until the target had been placed at its furthest point, of 300 meters. The target looked so tiny it would be a wonder if anyone could hit it. She lined up her bow and took aim; the arrow was true, and swept down the range planting itself firmly in the bull. The crowd cheered and sang as Alice walked back to the safe area with a big smile on her face.

The cheers grew louder as Robbie walked up to the firing pitch. He loaded his arrow and raised his bow, Harry and Steph started to cough loudly. "Missit"

Robbie lowered his bow and smiled as fits of giggles broke out in the group. He raised his bow and took aim. He smelt the scent of fresh cherries close by. "I want you naked again after this." It was Rune's soft voice.

"What?" Swish......... Thud! The crowd roared. Robbie's arrow was outside the bull, Rune stood laughing and blushing slightly as Robbie turned with a huge smile on his face. Everyone was hugging Alice who was beaming, Robbie looked back at Rune.

"That was dirty." He wagged his finger at Rune, who came up and hugged him. Robbie restored his credibility when Harry suggested moving targets. Robbie hit every apple that was thrown, and cleanly sliced it, at which everyone cheered. By now, it felt like the whole town was watching the noise was so loud.

It had turned out to be a very fun day, for many this had been their first sight of Lord Loxley and the impression he had given was one of a lord who commanded great loyalty and respect, but also one who was fair and a man of his people.

Everyone went home that night with fond memories of the day and even fonder memories of Lord Loxley the Hooded Man returned. That night Rune joined Robbie at his house for tea. The table was once again happy and fun and she joined in with the day's jokes, it was Harry who suddenly looked up at her and asked.

"Hey Rune... What was it you whispered that made him miss the target?"

Rune swallowed hard. "I err... What?" She began to go slowly pink.

Harry smiled. "Not just dirty, but really naughty eh Rune?" He winked at her and she turned scarlet.

"Harry, leave the poor girl be." Jess pulled an arm around her. "Ignore him Rune, honestly Harry you should not embarrass the poor girl like that." Harry nodded at Rune

"Sorry my sweet girl, or should I say lady?" He winked at Robbie.

By late evening, Robbie was sat with Rune and Alice. Harry sat back in his chair and Robert and John who had arrived late were eating. Jess was drying a large pan on the side of the sink. Billy walked in having been checking the stoves in the greenhouse. "We leave tomorrow. I will exit by the usual means and head to Kirklees; make sure you all have your things ready. I want you all to make your own way to the exit gate. Billy you and Alice go together, Rune will be with me. Harry, you come along with Steph and Jade. No bike." All of them nodded.

"Alright everyone prepare yourselves, John who are the two best Bowmen we have?"

John considered the question. "Well Martin Reef of Hope is probably one of our best."

"Don't forget John Styles the foreman of bottom farm, he is as good as they get for these parts." John nodded his head as Robert spoke.

"Alright then I want them to join us as well as young Eric Tanner from Bamford, he has earned himself some more lessons with the more experienced. Call them in and have them ready at the gate tomorrow. I will go and let Steph and Jade know now and see you all here later."

Later that night Robbie and Billy sat on their beds in their room, it had been such a busy time that Robbie had felt he and Billy had not had much time to be together. They had caught each other up on how things were progressing and now faced the daunting task of finding the evidence to stop Mason Knox.

"What do you think Rob; do you think we can stop him?"

Robbie shook his head. "Do you want an honest answer or would you prefer that I lie?" Billy smiled at him.

"It's that bad eh?"

"It is a challenge that is for sure, we could pull it off, but there again we could as easily fail. I am not underestimating Knox at all. I have not forgotten that day in the woods and how well his men seemed to get about without being spotted."

Robbie leaned back against the wall and looked at Billy. "Please Billy, watch your back, these guys are good just keep your guard up at all times."

"Come on Rob don't worry so much; you know how we work when hunting. Well, it will just be the same only Cutters instead of hogs."

Robbie was still concerned. "Just keep Alice close and keep Jade and Steph between us at all times, let Harry and the others watch the flanks." Billy nodded and smiled at him.

"That my friend sounds like a plan to me." Robbie smiled; it felt a little more like old times.

"I am glad my cousin chose you, and I am glad you will be at my side through this Billy, it does make me feel more secure about things."

"So Robbie my boy, what's it like to be Lord Loxley?"

"Honestly or do you want me to lie?" Billy started to chuckle and Robbie smiled.

"Oh please Billy don't ever treat me like you did in the hall again, I hated it. It is so weird with everyone bowing all the time, it takes me three times longer to do anything. I tell you it's driving me nuts, thank Hearne for you, Rune and Alice, I think without you all I would go mad."

"Yeah, it wasn't good, was it? I am sorry mate; they told me when I arrived that you had no idea of what was coming. Actually, I thought you was pretty cool about it, not so sure I would have been, John did tell me you had a bit of a go at them after. Still, it's done now... I know this sounds mad Rob, but aren't you a little excited to know we will be getting well away from here for a bit?"

"I suppose so, I have not had time really to think about it, it's all gone so quick. It will be nice to walk in pastures new and see a bit more of the world than Stockade walls. I find it hard to believe really that only a few months ago, I was sat in the greenhouse hoping to get free of this place one day. And here we are about to."

Billy looked at the old clock in the corner. "You don't mind if I ... you know slip off for a bit?"

Robbie smiled. "A bit of what... Alice?"

Billy grinned and his eyes danced. "We are not going to have much time after tonight, are we? There will be loads of others about."

"Yeah, go on, I have a lot to think about."

"Cheers Robbie." Billy jumped up and silently slipped out of the door. Robbie sat back on his bed and thought about Rune.

"I wish I had one more night alone with her."

CHAPTER EIGHT

A RELIC FROM THE PAST

The day had finally arrived, and as Robbie sat up in his bed and stretched, he felt a surge inside him that made his stomach twist slightly. There was a pile of clean clothes in green at the foot of the bed, and he knew that at some point his mother had slipped in and left them for him.

He had a new lace up shirt and thicker green pants, although these were slimmer than he was used to wearing. There was a long sage green sleeveless canvas waistcoat, which by the look of it was definitely Rune's work. She had tailored it perfectly, and as he fastened his belt with his dagger on it, he felt like a true woodsman. He collected his hunting knife and telescope, and put them into his pockets and then headed out of the door and down the stairs. Billy was almost identically dressed, although he was in Lincoln green and light brown.

Jess smiled at him as he walked in through the door. "Oh Robbie love, just look at you. My son is a true woodsman there is no doubt now." She put her hankie to her mouth and the tears began to flow. "Oh I am sorry Robbie; I promised myself I would not do this."

He walked over and put his arms around her. "Come on Mum don't cry now."

Jess sobbed and tried to swallow the tears. "You are my boy no matter what others might think, please take care of yourself and watch Billy and Alice for me." Billy came across the kitchen and put his arms around her too.

"Come on Mum it's alright we will be side by side watching each other, and don't forget we will have Harry with us." Jess sobbed even louder.

Robbie looked at Billy and grinned. "I am not sure that has reassured her that much. In fact, it has not reassured me a hell of a lot."

Jess tittered and tried to smile. "Oh boys please be careful and promise me just one thing?"

"What?" Both answered her at the same time? Jess looked up at them both with a very serious look on her face.

"If Harry looks at you and says, trust me man. For god's sake don't."

Robbie and Billy both looked at each other and then burst out laughing. Even Jess started to laugh. "It's not funny boys." She started to giggle. "Every time he says that he gets deeper into trouble." Jess began laughing with them as she wiped her eyes. "He is a bloody liability so be very careful." Her giggles continued and she pulled them close and squeezed them enough to last until they returned.

Harry walked in dressed in all black, with a very shiny silver knife on his belt, and two long handled swords crossed and sheathed across his back. He pushed his black hat up with one finger.

"Hey Jess, I don't want you to worry now. I love these guys and I won't let any harm come to them. Trust me Man." Robbie, Billy and Jess looked at each other and burst out laughing again. Harry looked confused as Jess howled with hysterics.

"Wow Jessie you are taking this way better than I thought you would." Shaking his head and still laughing Billy patted him on the back and walked out of the kitchen. Robbie gave his mum another hug as she calmed down and she kissed him on the cheek. "See you soon mum."

"Take care my love." Robbie walked past Harry smiling and out into the yard where Alice and Billy stood next to Robert Lox. He pulled Robbie into an embrace and patted him on the back.

"Keep your eyes peeled and post three to watch at a time at night, if in doubt shoot first and question later, here, you will find the tension on this one is more suited to you." Robert Lox turned and lifted a new bow that had been leaning against the wall. "It's rowan, a good one, probably the best I have ever made."

He handed Robbie two quivers each with fifty arrows in each. "I have already clipped the flights to keep them quiet, I dropped spare arrows off early this morning for the girls and Steph." He handed Robbie a roll of fabric. "This is an arrow repair kit; it will allow you to reuse arrows and repair any that get damaged. There is also a moneybag in there with one hundred gold pieces. They were all minted in different towns; you will not find a single Loxley coin in there."

Robbie looked at the roll. "Why no Loxley coins?"

"It's the easiest way to tell where a man comes from. We all mint our own coins; so the more you have from one town, the more likely it is you come from that town. No Loxley coins will make someone think you have never been here; it could save your life Robbie."

"Thanks Dad." Robbie smiled but felt the tears starting to rise; he threw his arms around him and hugged him hard. "I love you dad, just keep safe if he attacks before I get back, and look after mum and Beth."

"I love you too son, remember travel fast and keep to the trees, you above all others know how to use the cover of the land to remain invisible. Be true to the Hooded Man and be a ghost." He patted him hard and then squeezed him like he never had before. "Go with speed my Lord of Loxley, make me proud."

Robbie picked up his bag and put the kit inside. He slung his cloak over his shoulders and fastened it. Jess came silently out and gave him another hug, and with tears in her eyes, she pulled his hood up over his head.

"You are a boy no more Robbie, you are indeed the Hooded Man." She touched his cheek with her hand and smiled. "I love you."

Robbie turned and walked down the path to the track that led to town and eventually to Rune's house, Billy and Alice hugged and said goodbye to Robert and Jess and they too headed down the path towards the village. Harry hugged Jess and Robert.

"I will not fail them. I promise I will die before I allow any of my family to be hurt, you have my word brother." Robert and Jess looked a little shocked. Neither of them had seen Harry remotely as serious. Harry smiled at them. "Later Dudes," and he winked as he walked away.

Robert and Jess stood at the gates and watched as their boy walked down the track and out of sight. When he had gone, they turned, and arm in arm they walked back to the house.

Robbie took the direct route to Rune's house, and as planned, Billy and Alice turned off the track half way down and headed across country towards the gates. They walked hand in hand their bags carefully concealed under their cloaks. Harry walked down to the Village Hall and followed the footpath past the shooting range to the market ground. Jade and Steph were walking round looking at the stalls.

Most people asked why their stall was not there as usual, and they both replied that there was not much need as their shop was in the village, where they could offer more. Len was in the shop as normal and they were taking a break from weaving and jewellery making.

Jade was now a woodsman and so the fact she was in full male woodsman attire with the crest on her cloak did not surprise anyone. She usually wore male clothes so she actually appeared normal, and more and more of the men now wore their military attire. Harry walked up and greeted them loudly. He lifted his bag up to show them. "Been doing a spot of shopping never know when you have to split so I kinda grabbed some bits you know." He did somewhat over play the part but no one really noticed as most people thought he was loud and mad anyhow.

Rune sat on the wall with her grandfather. She was in a sage green tunic and had brown tight fitting pants with her cloak pulled over her bag. The able bowmen crest provided her with ideal cover; she was also the girlfriend of the hooded man and so naturally expected to look the part. Len smiled as Robbie walked up. "You are all prepared My Lord?"

Robbie nodded. "I have given my daughter very specific instruction, which she will divulge to you on route. Just listen to her carefully and you will be fine."

"Thanks, Mr Rimmer. I appreciate all you have done to help." Rune slid her arm around him. Len smiled at them both.

"You look like a very lovely couple; take care of this one Robbie she is very special to me." His eyes glistened, he had not been parted from his family since he had arrived at Loxley, and now he was going to be parted from all of them. He pulled Rune into a hug. "Be careful my precious child I cannot bear the thought of being parted."

Rune's eyes splashed tears down her face. "I love you Grandfather, don't worry I will be back, it has been seen."

Len smiled. "Your power is coming?"

"It's already here and has been for some time." Rune smiled, as her grandfather seemed to relax. "We have to go, see you soon." Rune pulled away and began to walk down the street; Len patted Robbie on the shoulder.

"Watch over her My Lord."

"I have for some time." Robbie smiled and set off after Rune.

They walked out of the village hand in hand, people nodded as they passed them and once down the lane and out of sight, they crossed the fence and headed across the fields. Robbie glanced at Rune and she knew what he was thinking, she stopped and looked at him.

"Don't look at me like that Rob. I had to lie; how could I leave him to worry himself to death? If he thinks I am coming back, he will relax more. He has never been without us Rob, and it will be hard enough for him as it is. I hate it but I had no choice."

Robbie thought about it for a moment. "Ok, I see your point; it confused me a little because I know your powers are coming sooner than expected. I just thought you had them now."

"How do you know about my powers coming?"

"You know the other night when you woke me up." He smiled, it was a nice memory, Rune smiled back, she thought so too. "Well earlier on you were moaning in your sleep and twitching, your mum told me it was the start of your power coming."

"I see, I hadn't realised, it was a strange night all around."

Robbie grinned. "I thought it was a great night." She started to laugh.

"Why doesn't that surprise me?"

Aunt Beth sat with John on the cart next to the small door in the high wall, three bowmen stood around looking up at the high wall. Robbie and Rune came down the side of a wheat field and climbed over the gate. Beth waved as they came up and John jumped down off the cart, the three bowmen bowed as Robbie came up to John. "Any sign of the others?"

John nodded and embraced Robbie. "Not as yet but it is still a little early." They walked round to the rear of the cart and John slid off two packs. "There is plenty of food here, bread and cheese and the like. Jess has packed you some dried vegetables and herbs, I know you will not go short for meat but you can chuck a few handfuls in a pan and it will give you all a good stew. I made you a special set of pots and pans that all fit together so they do not take up space. They are very light to carry."

Beth climbed down off the cart and came around to him, she wore a huge smile and she pulled him into a big hug. "Now you take good care of yourself and be careful, you will look after Alice for us won't you? I know Billy will be with her but keep one eye on her as well for me Robbie."

"Don't worry Aunt Beth I will take care of everyone, and please both of you look out for mum and dad for me. If the Cutters come before I get back keep your heads down and watch each other." Beth pulled him back into another hug and tears began to well in her eyes.

"Oh, look at me crying like a baby, honestly these days I don't know where it comes from. First thought of Alice or you going off and I was bawling." She patted her eyes with a small lace hankie. "No doubt Jess is the same; I think it's something to do with our age."

Rune came up and hugged Beth. "Oh my, here I go again. Oh, Rune my sweet girl you are all so brave please be careful and watch Robbie for us."

"I will you can be sure. Mrs Lox if I could ask a favour of you, I would be very grateful."

"Rune sweetheart anything, anything at all I can do I will." Beth began to wipe her eyes as Rune spoke a little quieter.

"Would you keep an eye on my grandfather? He has not been without any of us since we all came here and I think he will miss us all a great deal. I will worry knowing he is alone and he will not feed himself properly."

Beth beamed at Rune. "My darling that would be my privilege, of course we will watch out for him and as for feeding him up..." Beth smiled and patted her round tummy. She winked. "That's one of my best areas of expertise." Rune smiled.

"Thanks, it will ease my mind to know he is alright." Rune hugged her again.

Robbie and John walked over to the bowmen, and John introduced them. Each bowed as John spoke their names. Martin Reef was tall and slender with very tight curly brown hair, his dark eyes burned bright as he bowed.

John Styles was a very stocky bald, bearded man with bright blue eyes. Apart from his bow, he had a sword on his belt and he gave the impression he knew how to use it. Eric Tanner radiated pride; he was short but had the makings of a good woodsman. Robbie knew that Eric had the drive to prove himself and for that reason alone, he had brought him along.

Robbie looked at the three and smiled. "Gentlemen you have been chosen for this mission because of your own abilities of which I am assured will aid our cause greatly. Here in this stockade, I am Lord Loxley, when we enter the wood, I am Robbie in the Hood. Our mission is very secret and of vital importance to the survival of this realm, we must be fast and invisible and ready to be challenged at all stages do you understand?"

All three spoke as one. "Yes My Lord."

"The rest of the group will be here shortly let's prepare." The three bowmen busied themselves as John handed out bows and shared the food and supplies amongst each man; Robbie stood up on the cart and took out his telescope. Billy and Alice were in sight making their way towards him and in the distance, he could see the tall figure in black of Harry with his two companions.

The group finally all met up around the cart, Beth wept buckets as she clung to Alice who found her tunic was becoming damper by the second, as her tears mingled with her mothers. Harry beamed as he embraced his brother and the look they shared as they parted was one of understanding. In secret, John and Robert had spoken with Harry and asked him to guard their children at all costs.

Harry had not needed asking; he was a fierce fighter and knew his blades would be true in defence of his kin. Robbie stood by the open door, as the bowmen slipped through to ensure the area was secure. They took up their positions watching the wood with bows ready, as the others came through into the wood.

Alice walked to the gate and Robbie smiled at her. "Ready for this?" She nodded bravely and slipped passed him. Rune was last and she winked as she passed, Robbie turned to John and Beth. Beth sniffled into her hankie; Robbie put out his hand.

"See you all soon." John snatched him into a huge bear like hug and patted him on the back.

"You are young but hell boy you have true Loxley blood. Take care of my Alice Robbie and good luck."

"I will care for all of them and return your daughter safe, you have my word." With one last smile at his aunt and uncle, he slipped through the door and entered the woodland. The door in the wall closed with a loud click and he knew they were all going to be safe inside the stockade.

His mind turned to the task at hand, as he looked around at the others waiting his command. Robbie was on his turf, in his world, he was a woodsman and now back amongst the trees he felt his authority grow. "This way... Billy you take the rear with Martin, I will lead point, Harry you cover the right side and John you cover left. Eric, you stay close to protect the centre. We move swift but quietly, Rune, Steph, Alice stay close. Pebbles I want you up front with me; let us see how much Old Joe has taught you." Robbie gave the signal and they moved off heading for the escarpment that would take them over the back of the moors towards Kirklees.

The woods were now coming into their own, the season had moved and the trees had started to leaf. The grasses and ferns were lush and fresh, and the light was dappled as it now wove its way through the green leafy canopy to the floor. Birds sung, and the air was filled with the bees that were actively searching the flowers of the trees for pollen.

Robbie allowed Jade a few feet in front of him so that she could read the signs of the wood, Rune was close by his side and watched and listened as Robbie instructed Jade. It was clear to Rune that he too was instructing her at the same time and she made note as he spoke.

It was two hours before they reached the escarpment, and slowly they approached the edge of the tree line. Robbie gave the signal and everyone went down on one knee, and got ready their bows. Robbie and Jade edged forward; slowly they crept forward without making a sound. Two rabbits sat in the sun on a small patch of grass unaware of the figures rising at their side in the undergrowth. The arrows flew silently side by side and both rabbits lay down without realising they were dead.

The two hooded figures rose quietly from the trees, stepped out, and walked over to the rabbits. The shorter of the two pulled the arrows out of the rabbits and wiped them on the grass, the taller dropped his hood. "You have improved a great deal since we last hunted." He waved back to the trees and another hooded figure appeared. Jade dropped her hood and handed Robbie his arrow back to him.

"You have to give it to Old Joe, he knows his stuff and to be honest Robbie, I have always fancied wood craft, I like the adventure of it all." Robbie smiled.

"You will certainly get plenty of that over the coming weeks. We will take a break here, but let's stay close to the trees. I suspect there will be eyes wherever we go now."

The group settled down in the trees whilst Robbie with Rune moved across the top of the escarpment. This place provided a good look out across the woodland and Robbie knew if there had been any scouts this would be a place they would have visited. He scanned the ground for tracks and markings, and he was not disappointed.

Four feet in from the edge was a clear footprint, Robbie crouched with Rune and examined it. He showed her the dryness on the edges of the print and lifted a small piece of clay from the centre. It crumbled in his fingers. "This is at least two days old; see how dry it is at the centre?"

Rune inspected it and then looked in the direction that the print was heading. "Isn't that the direction we took when we headed to Joe's place?"

Robbie nodded. "Don't worry about Joe he is safe enough, my dad set a few of the best woodsmen we have to keep tabs on him after our last little run in with the Cutters. No one will make it close enough to harm him. That is why Jade was sent to be trained by Joe. Steph knew she was safer than us."

Rune smiled. "You are far more involved with the Loxley Estate than you let on.”

“Family business, what can I say. Tea time in my place is more like a meeting of the board.” Robbie stood up and looked out over the woods. “No smoke.” Rune looked across the wide plain that stretched up passed the reservoir and onto the distant moorland and Yorkshire.

“No smoke is a good thing?” She was not completely sure why.

“It is if there are Cutters about. They burn everything they come across; Harry told me there have been times when he was high in the hills that he knew exactly where they were. He just looked for smoke.”

Billy and Martin wandered over to Robbie as the others sat in the trees resting. Robbie pointed out the print. “At least two days old, but that does not mean we are alone. How much of this area do you know Martin?”

“I am not familiar with this side of the woods but I know the northern border well Robbie.”

“Good, I know all the area into the northern borders and so does Billy, I want you two to scout the area ahead and just see if we spot our woodland guests. I want no heroics all right? Just find out who they are and where they are, then get back to us. We will have a further ten minutes here and then follow on behind.”

Martin nodded and Billy slapped Robbie’s shoulder. “Leave it to us mate.” The two of them headed through the trees, and off north. Robbie returned to the group and sat down. Steph passed him an apple.

Eric and Harry sat at the edge of the group watching the woods they had travelled through, and the others talked quietly. Jade had tied the rabbits together and they now hung from her belt, as she talked to John quietly. Steph watched Robbie closely and smiled when he noticed her watching.

“What?”

She broke a piece off the slab cake she was eating; her eyes seemed to sparkle.

“I never understood why they picked such a young boy to do such a big task. I have to admit Robbie I wanted your father to be the lord, but seeing you in a woodland setting has made me realise.”

Alice looked at her. “Realise what?”

Steph swallowed. “How much authority he has out here.” She looked back at Robbie. “From the moment you left the stockade you have become something more, and now I see that they made the right choice. The way you move through the wood, you are not like others and they see that. You have a natural talent for this realm Robbie.”

Rune slipped her arm through his. “Of course he does, if we were seven hundred years earlier he would be the first hooded man.”

Steph smiled. “I believe you are right Daughter.”

“Alright we better make tracks; those two should be far enough ahead now. Harry, can you take the rear. Eric, I want you to cover the right flank, everyone else as normal."

They gathered their things and prepared to move out, Robbie grabbed Jade. "You swing out right and keep an eye on Eric for me, he is new at this and needs some instruction; teach him a few tricks for me."

Jade beamed, the fact that Robbie had so much faith in her filled her with pride and she almost grew in stature as she headed off right to accompany Eric. Steph smiled at him and he winked.

They moved across the top of the escarpment and down a different path from the one that led to Joes. The woodland here was growing a lot thicker and they slowed down a little to avoid making too much noise. There was less bracken and more grass that made walking easier, but Robbie was very aware that there was also less cover.

All of them were now becoming use to the hand signals he gave. Harry and John, who were able woodsmen, knew the signs; but the others had to learn on the journey up to the escarpment, Robbie had whispered his commands at the same time as signaling. Now he just signaled and they followed his lead.

After another two hours, their progress was good, although Billy and Martin were still ahead of them. Martin had left clues along the path for Robbie to spot, and now Rune was able to notice them as they moved. Jade discovered tracks and signaled to Robbie, his arm shot up and everyone sank low with their bows at the ready.

Robbie slipped over to Jade and looked at the earth. "Single guy, walking very slow as if he too is tracking something, and not that far ahead I would say." Robbie smiled at Jade as he looked down at the print.

"Well Pebbles, I think you have earned your place as a woodsman for sure today. I believe you are quite right." Jade was thrilled and beamed her smile at Eric and began to show him the signs as Robbie made his way over to the others and called them in closer.

"We have a guest, not that far in front but possibly between us and the other two. We must move quickly and stay closer until we find out who they are." Everyone nodded as they prepared to move in a single line spaced out five feet apart.

Robbie took the lead with Harry just short, the others followed and John and Eric took up the rear. Jade stayed wide following parallel on the right. Their speed quickened as Robbie scanned the earth for more signs. This guy was good but left a few small signs that Robbie could read easily.

The canopy thinned a little and more light streamed into the dim woodland, and large clumps of bracken began to appear as they pulled themselves up to the light. The track began to bend and weave as it started to climb up a steep bank, Robbie slowed and the others followed his lead. He signaled back and instantly they all began to fan out into the now thick scrub and undergrowth. They slowed to a quiet walking pace as Robbie neared the summit, and then up went his arm and they stopped.

Robbie pointed two fingers to his eyes and patted his chest. He was going to have a look over the top, he pointed to Jade and then to the cover near the top on his right, she gave him a thumbs up and silently moved forward. He pointed John left and he moved into position; Harry followed Robbie a few feet behind.

Crawling over the top, Robbie peered down the steep bank, it fell away to a small ledge and the path ran off to the right, and fell steeply to it. Below the ledge was a small clearing, and on the far side of the clearing, Robbie saw two figures crouched down by what looked like the remains of an old campfire. They were examining the contents and looking into the wood in front of them.

Robbie was about to signal them when on the ledge below he noticed a slight movement. Just in the tree line was a figure crouched down watching Martin and Billy, he wore the hood and cloak of a woodsman. Robbie signaled to Jade, she scanned the undergrowth and then spotted him.

John, who was watching Robbie, looked down and then gave the thumbs up. They took aim, as Robbie stood up, pulling his hood up to shield his eyes from the sun, he took aim. The arrow was swift and silent; it stuck in the earth at the side of the figure, who jumped with shock.

Robbie already had his second arrow in the string, and was aiming at the figure who looked up at him startled. "Who walks in my realm without my approval? Identify yourself or suffer woodsman." Jade, Harry, and John stepped through the trees and revealed themselves, their bows trained on the figure.

The woodsman lay down his bow, and slowly stood up lifting his hands. "I am alone and unaware I must seek approval to enter this realm. I am a simple woodsman with no malice in my heart."

"Yet you seek to track my kinsmen." As Robbie spoke, he noticed Billy and Martin slip into the trees, and train their bows up at the woodsman. Rune, Steph and Alice appeared through gaps in the trees, their bows ready. Eric came up at the side of Jade.

The woodsman looked fearful at the numbers appearing through the trees. He glanced back at the clearing below and knew he had no escape. "I was not aware that I tracked your kinsman sir, I was just exercising caution, I have nothing to hide."

"A man with nothing to hide can walk freely in these woodlands; it is those who sneak that are up to no good. Declare your name and your business in these parts."

"My name is Rowan of the woods, for I am bereft of a homeland. I travel here by order of Hearne the Lord of all forests."

Steph gasped. "Robbie, I know of this man."

Robbie looked across at her. "You do?"

"He has been sent to aid you, and if I am right, he will carry something precious for you, please spare him and welcome him to us."

Robbie looked across to John and Harry. "You two go down and escort him to the others below, I will follow shortly." Robbie looked down at Rowan. "Stand fast Rowan the woodsman I will have need to speak with you, my kinsman will escort you to safety; you will not be harmed if you comply."

Rowan stood still as John and Harry came down towards him, Harry picked up Rowan's bow as John took his dagger. With his hands on his head, he followed the path to the bottom, Robbie turned to Steph. "Tell me what you know of this man."

"Send the others down so we may talk privately, Rune you stay." Robbie signaled and the others moved down.

Steph looked at Robbie and her daughter. "As I told you Robbie you will learn things that no other should know. This man carries a great gift to you from Hearne himself; it is something of great power that will aid you in your most needed hour. This man seeks the wearer of the silver lion and will only surrender it to you. You must never allow any to use it, for this is your gift from the Lord of the woodland."

"How could you know this, when this is the first time you have left the stockade?"

"I have told you Robbie, Rune and I have gifts of our own, and for now that is all you need to know. More will be revealed in time. Now come let's get down there before one of the others wishes to remove his package from his back."

They hurried down the hillside and across the clearing to the edge of the trees. The group sat alert and on guard, Rowan sat in the middle with a rather menacing looking Harry. His hands were on his head as he sat cross-legged on the grass.

Robbie looked around at the others. "There has been a camp here spread out and find out how many and when." They all melted into the trees and Robbie looked down at Rowan. "You may rest your arms Woodsman." Rowan slowly lowered his arms; Rune passed him a bottle of water, which he gratefully took. "Do you know who I am?"

Rowan looked up as he drunk. "There has been rumour of a hooded man who has returned to these parts, I take it you are him?"

Steph spoke. "You were sent here by a lady in white. A daughter of Hearne, who to you is the stag, it is his wish that you find Robert Lord of Loxley and aid him is it not?"

Rowan's eyes widened as she spoke. "How can you know this?"

"I am Stephanie of Caerleon. I know you know of my line woodsman. You sit before the Bowman of Loxley, Lord of these lands and hooded man returned. This is the Lady Runestone, daughter of Avon, you should show your respects to the company you behold."

Rowan who was looking more and more shocked snapped to his knees. "My

Lord and Ladies please forgive me my ignorance; I have been alone too long in the woods and my manners have suffered."

Robbie looked at the woodsman bent double before him and pitied him. "Stand up Rowan for your quest is at an end, and you can relax knowing you have found whom you seek."

"I have no wish to offend you My Lord, but I was instructed to trust no one. Can you prove who you are?"

"Have no fear Rowan, I have what you seek." Robbie put his hand down the front of his shirt and pulled out the silver lion with the diamond eyes. They sparkled in the sun.

Rowan dropped to his knee. "Forgive me My Lord I was instructed to check."

Robbie smiled, and Rune put her hand on Rowan's shoulder. "Rise up woodsman your loyalty to your task is commendable, should we ask for that loyalty to ourselves?"

"I will give it freely My Lady, for I now know the truth and the enemy you fight, for he is my enemy also."

"Then join us Rowan of the Wood, and be at peace knowing you have friends here." Robbie offered his hand and Rowan took it. He pulled him upright and handed him back his bow.

"I have something of great value to aid you, My Lord."

Robbie held up his hand. "Here is not the time or place, carry your gift a little while longer, we will rest not far from here in caves that I know of. Tonight, we will eat and then we will talk privately."

"Yes, My Lord." Rowan gave a small bow.

"Rowan, do me one thing?"

"What is your request My Lord?"

"Here in the woods, I am Robbie the hooded man, address me as such, when I return to my home, I will be lord again."

"Yes my... Robbie." Rowan smiled and Steph and Rune grinned.

"Let us move for the light is starting to fade and I also fear rain is on the way."

The group began to move off and as they did so, the others one by one appeared out of the trees to join them. As Jade came out of the bushes and came up to his side, Robbie whispered, "I fear two rabbits will not feed all of us, track right and see if you cannot provide us with more meat, take Eric."

Harry and Billy came up either side of him, Billy looked back. "I take it our guest is going to join us...? We still have more company, but I think they are a couple of days ahead judging by the camp fire."

"There will be raiding parties all over this area now. They will want knowledge of Loxley and its defences; I think we will find more than one or two running around before we are through. Harry, we need to borrow your cave for the night, rain is on the way and it has been a long day for those who are not use to woodland life. A safe haven tonight will be very welcome I think."

Harry nodded. "My pad is dry and has a few comforts, consider it your own man."

Harry headed forward to lead the way and Robbie dropped back to Rune and Steph. "Not far now and we will camp for the night."

Steph smiled. "I am a bit out of practice, my legs are killing me, and Alice is looking a little tired."

It was twenty minutes later, when they came up to a large boulder sat against the face of a high rocky outcrop of limestone. They all stopped and looked up, Alice sat down on the grass and rubbed her legs.

"Please Harry; tell me I don't have to climb up there?"

Harry smiled. "Chill sis, we don't go over, we like go under." Harry walked to the back of the boulder where there was a huge pile of logs stacked. He pulled on a large piece of Ivy growing down the wall and the logs lifted up in the air to reveal a small doorway into the mouth of a cave. "How cool is that man, did it all myself, sometimes I can be really amazing."

Robbie was impressed, and followed him in through the door and into the cave. "Actually, Harry this is a pretty cool place you got here."

Harry flopped down on an old chair. "Buzzin."

Oil lamps were lit to reveal a large cave filled with wooden boxes, this was where he stored all his goods for trade, including Joe's moonshine and surprisingly to Robbie, some very large quantities of his father's weapons. There was a couple of tables and plenty of chairs as well as four beds; these were obviously meant at some point for sale.

The group spread out around the cave and either sat on chairs or collapsed on beds, Rune piled the stove with wood and lit it. Harry picked up a bucket and wandered off to a small stream he knew to get some water, Jade and Eric returned sometime later guided in by Martin, they had about a dozen rabbits which they passed to Billy who popped out his knife and took them outside to clean them. Eric appeared to be quite a cook, and soon helped Rune to get a good stew boiling on the stove.

Harry lifted five bottles of a dark wine out of a crate and Steph threw him a very disapproving look. Harry shook his head. "Awe, come on Stephy baby I promised, didn't I? This batch went wrong, it's sort of like strawberry juice, it would not ferment. Don't throw me those evils."

Steph reached up for the bottle he had just uncorked and smelled it. She lifted it to her lips and took a small taste. "All right Harry I am sorry to doubt you." She handed him the bottle back.

"Wow... Yeah... Cosmic man." Harry opened a box of old glass jars and began to pour the juice.

The meal was welcome after a long day. There was plenty for everyone and soon most of them were filled with rabbit stew. John however had a very good appetite, and Rune giggled as they all looked in amazement as she loaded his plate again. "Thanks miss, this is really wonderful."

Harry sipped his juice. "Man, I tell you, eat like that every day and we are going to run out of rabbits round here." John smiled.

"You are a weird guy Harry, but don't worry, I hunt more than I need."

Everybody seemed to smile. Jade took a plate to Rowan who was sat on guard duty with Martin. She gave him the plate and nodded to Martin. "You go and get something to eat Martin before John eats it all, and I will sit watch with Rowan for a while."

Rowan broke the bread and dipped it into the hot stew. "Thank you Miss."

"My name is Jade; some call me Pebbles." She sat at the side of him with her bow across her knee.

"You have goods skills in the wood, I watched you. Are all the hooded men and woman as good?"

"We all have skills that make us dependent on each other. You were not easy to track, I found you hard to follow, and it was Robbie who read your signs fully."

"It was you who discovered me?"

"I discovered your trail first; Robbie would have found you though."

"He is a very good woodsman. No man has ever been able to sneak up on me like that; I did not even hear his arrow. I would love to know his secrets."

"In time you will learn from him as I have, he is truly at one with the wood, this really is his kingdom." Rowan watched her closely with his deep slate grey eyes.

"You admire him greatly; I can see that."

"I will tell you something Rowan. He is my best friend and my hero; I love him dearly and would die to save him or my sister. They are special and you will see if you stay with us that there are no others who are fairer or more honourable."

"I will accept the word of the fair Lady Pebbles, and learn from her example." Rowan smiled, his face had a mysterious sadness about it, and Jade was happy to see it lift if only for a moment. He seemed so lonely and alone, it was something she knew herself.

Everyone sat around as Martin worked out the guard rota. Alice was exhausted and already asleep. Robbie sat with Rune who was leaning on him dozing; Steph sat close by her mind in thought as she stared at the high white lime walls. Billy sat with Eric and Harry, as Harry polished his swords. Billy was a keen swordsman and marvelled at the strange long thin blades. John had found several bags of coffee, he now wandered round with a coffee pot pouring out cups and handing them around.

The group had gelled well on the first day, and Robbie was pleased, he felt there was a balance that gave them an edge and kept them tight. Their personalities were all very different and yet they seemed to have found common ground with each other. Rune disturbed in her sleep. He twisted around and let her slowly lower herself to his lap. Sliding his hands under her, he lifted her up, and carried her to one of the beds. Slowly and gently, he lowered her on to the bed, and stroked her long red hair back from her face, she murmured and then settled. He came back to his chair and sat down.

"You should get some sleep you know." Robbie looked across at Steph

"I want to speak with Rowan first, afterwards I will get a few hours in." Steph nodded and closed her eyes. Harry dimmed the lights as they all settled down for the night, Robbie's eyes flickered and he was gone into the realm of sleep.

"Robbie... Robbie... Come on you must wake up."

"What's up?" Robbie sat forward and rubbed his eyes, he looked up at Steph. The light was dim and he had to focus for a moment before the blurred vision cleared.

"Rowan is here and we must now speak." Steph pushed a hot cup into his hand, "here drink this."

It took a few minutes to come round fully, he had slept deeper than he had meant to. He stared into the gloom as Rowan pulled the long bag from around his shoulders, and lifted it over his head. "My Lord this has been entrusted to me by the daughter of Hearne. I was given the task of ensuring it arrived to you and only you." Rowan placed the long green bundle on to his lap. "The Lady of the forest told me that I must inform you that the eyes of Knox are amongst your men, and that your fight will be the truth. I cannot say My Lord what that must mean, please accept my bow in your service, for if your fight is the truth, then we have the same cause."

Robbie looked up. "Thank you Rowan, I would indeed welcome a servant of our Lord Hearne by my side."

Robbie undid the ties and unfolded the cloth. Steph gasped, "I was right. The Sword of Truth." Steph blew a long breath out; her words carried the seriousness of the moment. "Robbie this a mighty gift you have been given; this is the sword of Gawain as given him by the Green Lord himself in his quest for truth. I have studied these things with my father and sister, but even I always thought this sword was a myth."

Her eyes ran up and down the blade as Robbie pulled it from the sheath. He held it in the air, and it glistened and sparkled in the dim light. Rowan's face was lit with the many colours that reflected off the blade. "Why Me?" Robbie looked at Steph. "I am a bowman not a swordsman. Billy would handle this blade better than me."

"Billy could not use this weapon Robbie. Only its allotted owner could wield it, and that has now passed to you.”

"It still does not change the fact that I am trained for the bow." Rowan came closer.

"That does not matter My Lord, I heard tales of this weapon as a boy. As long as the one whom weals it fights to uncover the truth none can defeat him, this is a sword of power and I know only of one other more powerful, and that has returned to the Lady of the lake."

Robbie turned the blade of gold around in his hand. The blade was inscribed with all of the leaves of the woodland trees; strange runes ran down the centre of the blade. The handle felt cool in his hand, and it seemed perfectly tooled to his grip. On the hilt of the handle was a small silver lion with two diamonds for eyes. Robbie pulled his necklace out of his shirt, and he gazed at the lion on the chain. "They are the same," he whispered almost as though his thoughts had escaped.

"It is yours Robbie it was foreseen many years ago. Read the blade."

Robbie looked up into the sparkling blue eyes of Rune. "I cannot Rune." He looked at Steph. She nodded her head.

"I know runes, but these are strange to me."

Rune sat down beside him and pointed to the blade. "Seekers of the truth shall be spared." She twisted his hand so he turned the blade over. "Those who deceive will perish." Steph smiled at her daughter.

"How can you read runes you have never seen before?"

Rune shrugged her shoulders. "I just seem to know."

Steph nodded. "It appears I named you correctly Runestone Sapphire."

Her eyes sparkled as she smiled at her mother. "I know stuff, he just doesn't listen." Robbie started to laugh, and he slid the sword back into its sheath, and then stood up and fastened it to his belt. Rune lifted his old sword and slipped it through the loops of her belt. Robbie stretched.

"I need some air; I think I will replace whoever is on guard, you fancy coming?" He reached down and grabbed Rune's hand. She stood up and pushed her arm round his waist. "You two get some sleep; it will be another long day tomorrow."

Robbie and Rune walked outside and replaced Billy and John who both looked very tired. The air was damp and the night cool, Robbie breathed deeply. "I love the woods at night it's so peaceful, just listen to that?"

"I can't hear anything."

"Exactly... I finally have you alone." He pushed her gently up against the tree and slid his arms around her waist.

"Why My Lord you have taken advantage of me sir." She smiled her face close to his. Her pale skin shone in the moonlight, and her eyes sparkled.

"I love you Rune." His lips met hers as her arms folded around him.

"I know My Lord."

CHAPTER NINE

THE WARNING OF THE WHITE LADY

The sea air blew over the castle wall, and the seagulls screamed as they were buffeted in the breeze that howled up the coast. She stood on top of the rampart and gazed out to sea, a strange feeling had come over her, and she was not sure, yet it felt like finally it was starting to happen. She was after all two years younger than her so it would be hard for her now.

The rain began to drop its heavy droplets on her very pale face, made paler by the contrast of her jet black hair that was being whipped round it by the wind. Her eyes remained closed as she struggled to focus and keep the thread between them. "Focus cousin," she said to herself, as she concentrated with all her might.

Her slender frame was battered by the wind and rain, and her robes of black edged with lilac stuck to her, and her sword dripped from its pointed sheath as the water ran down it. She was losing her; the noise of the wind and the gulls was too much; she could not focus enough to make the thread of connection. She opened her eyes as the wind blew across her. The pupils were dark and black, and yet somehow the whites of her eyes flashed blue with a faint lilac undertone.

Leaning into the wind and grabbing hold of the wall, she buried her long white fingers into the stonework. A surge came through her as she closed her eyes again and breathed deeper. One more time she thought to herself, and she focused her power, and then with a mighty push of her mind she sent everything she had in to one almighty burst of thought. *"HEAR ME!"*

Rune shot up off the bed with a scream. Robbie turned at the same time as Steph and rushed over to her. Rune sat shaking and breathing deeply. "Rune are you alright, what happened?" She seemed disorientated and she looked at her mother in fear.

"Those Eyes," she whispered.

Robbie looked at Steph. "Do you know what this means, was it just a dream?"

"Leave us Robbie. She will be fine let me talk to her." Rune was coming more to herself again and she looked to her mother for answers. Her face was very white and she trembled.

"Was it a dream Mum?" Robbie stood up and stepped back as Steph slid up to the side of her, she put her arms around her and pulled her close.

"What did you see Rune?" She looked up at Robbie and he knew not to meddle. He walked back to the table and the map that Harry and the others were looking at. He glanced back over at Rune who was pale and still seemed to tremble.

"I saw two eyes and then heard a loud voice scream in my ears."

"Alright, tell me about the eyes first." Rune looked at her mother a little afraid of what she had seen.

"They were black, as black as night, and they stared at me and through me. But what scared me was the whites of her eyes, they were almost lilac."

"You said her eyes, did she tell you who she was, or did you just know?"

Rune shook her head and thought for a moment. "I just seemed to know it was a woman."

"What about the voice, what did it say?" Steph pulled her close. "It is alright you have nothing to fear here, just tell me Rune."

Rune trembled and swallowed hard. "It just screamed at me, hear me."

Steph smiled and hugged her daughter. "Then you truly have nothing to fear, although I will have a word or two for your cousin when I see her."

Rune turned and looked at her mother. "What has she got to do with it?"

"You still have some way to go my darling and I fear that Jett is growing impatient. Those are her eyes, there is no doubt and she is looking forward to the bond that joins all of you being completed. I think she felt you and pushed a little too hard in her excitement to talk to you."

"Jett...? Our bond...? I do not understand."

"Rune my darling your powers are building and soon you will know the joy of being linked to your kin. You are the centre of a wide ring that joins everyone together. When your power is complete, you will be able to communicate using thought to all of your family. Even Jade will, although I am not looking forward to that at all. Goodness knows what trouble you two will get into."

"I thought I was seeing something evil."

Steph laughed. "Don't let Jett know that. She will not harm you Rune; you will have greater power. Jett loved you very much as a baby, I would imagine she has missed you; I know she feels lonely at times and she will want to speak to you as soon as she can."

"I do not remember her at all. What is she like?"

"You were only three years old when she left Avon. She wanted to come to Loxley, but her task was elsewhere and she returned to her sister in Wales. Jett has a lot of power, as I remember she had the power to hurt people simply by looking at them, although from what I have heard she seldom uses it, as she prefers the sword. She is a very accomplished swords woman. I think the best thing to do if she tries again is to just relax and think of her. If the connection is there, you will talk. Come and eat we will be leaving as soon as Harry finds the right map."

Steph kissed her on the head and got up. Rune took a few breaths and composed herself, and then stood up and came over to Robbie who had been nervously watching her. "You alright?"

She smiled and put her arms around him. "Just part of the process, I will be fine now." Robbie did not feel comforted at all. The thought of a power that terrified her disturbed him a great deal. He watched her closely all morning after that.

Harry was irritated. "Look man, I am telling you this is the cave, stop getting so heavy on me."

Alice stared down. "Harry there are sixteen caves on here. You are certain that this one here is the cave we are currently stood in?"

"Hey man I am not a fool you know? I know my own caves and I don't appreciate this heavy attitude, and you giving me all this hassle."

"Oh really Harry? Well tell me this then, we are in what you call your store pad yes?"

Harry looked insulted. "Totally."

"Would you mark it on the map as SP?"

"Yeah."

"So why is the one you are pointing to marked BP?" Alice shook her head.

Harry leaned forward and starred at the map. "Wow man it's moved, that's cosmically spooky."

"OH FOR GODS SAKE HARRY, WILL YOU LOOK AT THE MAP, AND SHOW US WHERE THE HELL WE ARE!"

"Peace chicken, chill out a little it's on here, I just got to get my map head around it and then it will be happy vibes and off we go." Alice slammed her cup down on the table and stormed out of the cave muttering.

"The man is a total loon, I cannot believe we are trusting him to guide us, he is not even on this planet let alone in this area."

Robbie had his head down as his shoulders shook, Rune pushed her face into his chest to stifle her giggles and everyone had their heads down, and had become occupied with their belts. Harry, who was completely unaware of all of it starred at the map. He turned it over smiled and announced. "See man, if you don't hassle me, I am sorted." He pointed to a cave marked SP.

Robbie coughed and smiling looked down at the map. Rune now had her head buried in his back and as he tried to read the map, he could feel the vibrations from her silent giggles passing through him. Robbie fought the urge to laugh with all his might. John spluttered and ran quickly outside closely followed by Billy, Robbie could hear them explode as they left the cave, and Steph tittered in the corner.

Robbie composed himself and swung a hand behind him to prod Rune out of laughing, muted squeaks emitted from her. Robbie swallowed deeply keeping his eyes on the map. "Ok according to this we are just outside Old Barnsley, so we need to move as fast as possible, some of these old towns have all sorts of bandits in them. Can I keep this map for now Harry?"

"Hey man, what's mine is yours you know?"

Robbie folded the map and looked up at Eric who was the only other one left in the cave. "Tell everyone to gather their things we leave in ten minutes." Rune dried her eyes and went out to pacify Alice.

Ten minutes later, they all gathered on the grass in front of the cave. Billy was marvelling at the sword in Robbie's hand, it gleamed bright in the sunlight and rays of coloured light cast small rainbows on the trees.

"Wow Robbie that is a serious piece of craftsmanship." Billy's eyes searched every inch of it. Robbie lowered the blade and passed it to Billy. He swung and lunged with it sweeping it round, Robbie was impressed at how his sword skills had improved. Billy handed it back to Robbie.

"It's a little heavy, but it has good balance, this will serve you well in a fight."

Robbie swept the air with it. To him it felt perfect. Jade inspected it. "It is very pretty, but I like something lighter that avoids smelling a Cutters bad breath." She opened her cloak and her belt now had eight shiny knives on it. Robbie smiled as he saw the neat row attached to her belt. Jade looked up at him and shrugged. "I figured you might need back up. Joe made me the belt; I taught him how to throw a few and made him a set as well."

"I am impressed Pebbles, and will be relieved to know you are not far away." She gave him a big smile. Robbie swung the sword up and dropped it back into its sheath.

Robbie looked around to make sure everyone was there, he signaled to Rowan who was leaning on a tree. Harry lowered the log pile back to conceal the cave entrance. "Rowan and Jade you take point, we head north. Stay alert and keep the chat low. Billy, you run left with John, Martin, Eric, right, Alice you go up front and Harry clear the rear. Ok let's move."

The group set off at a good pace, the rain was easing a little, but Robbie did not seem to mind. The whole area had a damp earthy smell that was wholesome and clean and he found it invigorating as he moved amongst the trees.

They followed the path to the side of a stream, and Rowan led them on down the side of it. He kept off the trail and stuck to the trees, and Robbie could see how accomplished a team Jade and Rowan made. They skirted a small lake and then headed into new territory, which he had never seen before; buildings that had been pulled into decay by plant life loomed up around them. This was the remains of a very large town although it was hard to tell. He knew that somewhere under his feet were concrete roads, which the trees and plants had finally torn through, as they took back their world from humankind.

The morning seemed to pass in a rush, and soon he could see the sweat on the faces of his companions, he signaled them to slow the pace and signaled Jade to find a safe place to stop. The rain had eased off, and the day was growing warm, Jade pointed through some broken down houses to an old building with large courtyard gates, and she moved close towards it.

Robbie signaled, and they all went down, he moved forward with Rowan, his bow at the ready. Jade stood with her back to the wall at the side of the gate. Rowan and Robbie took cover by a crumbled wall just in front. She stretched out her arm and gently pushed the gate, and it creaked open an inch. She took a quick peep round and pulled back.

Jade lifted five fingers; someone was there. Robbie signaled and everyone took cover, their bows pointed at the building. There was a scuffling sound over the wall, and a rough voice grumbled. "That bloody gate, it never bloody shuts properly." Harry appeared at the other side of the gate, and Martin crept up as Robbie signaled to John and Eric. Rowan stretched his bow, as the footsteps got closer to the gate.

A rough unshaven man in deep brown blood stained robes, stepped through and looked straight at Jade, she blew him a kiss. "Hi sexy."

There was a muffled grunt as Harry seized him and pulled him out of sight of the others in the yard. There was a flash of silver, and silently the man crumpled to the floor. Robbie was surprised at the speed of Harry, and the accuracy of his knife. He remembered Steph telling him about Harry and his swords, John and Eric came behind Jade, and Martin took his place just in front of Harry. Rune, Steph and Alice appeared either side of Robbie and Rowan. The scene was set as everyone lifted their hoods. Rowan nudged Robbie. "The windows." He gestured up. Rune and Steph heard him and raised their bows, Robbie signaled Alice and she took her stance. Jade winked, and Robbie winked back it was her call.

She pulled out her knives and then with all her might she slammed her foot into the gates. They exploded open, as the bowmen entered two Cutters fell dead instantly with silver knives in their throats, the rest fell with arrows. Faces appeared at the windows upstairs and screamed as Robbie and Rowan's arrows hit home, they reloaded with speed, by which time Rune and Steph had taken their marks out and Alice let fly her arrow.

Harry entered the building, his swords flashing in the sunlight, and there were screams as Cutters fled at the sight of him. As they jumped out of windows and scurried through doors, the arrows found them. In less than ten minutes, it was over, and thirty-eight Cutters lay dead. Jade signaled the all clear. Robbie solely stood up. "Alice, Rune, side of the gates, Rowan will you watch the street and signal if any more appear?" Rowan nodded.

"Ok Steph with me let's move with purpose." They all jumped over the wall and headed across the grass-covered street. Rune and Alice sped to each side of the gates and pointed their bows to left and right. Robbie and Steph entered the yard.

Harry was bent over one of the dead Cutters as he tore a large section of his shirt off. He stood up, and wiped the glowing red blades of his swords on it, and then threw it back on the body. "Now that man is how I prefer my Cutters, sliced and diced." He spat at the body.

The centre of the yard had a large cart with a cover over it. Two dead Cutters hung from the front with silver daggers sticking out of their throats. Jade walked up and pulled her daggers back, and let the bodies' fall to the floor. She climbed up on the cart and pulled off the cover. Robbie could see the food and weapons piled high. Jade beamed a huge smile. "To the victor the spoils."

Robbie looked up at her his voice contained anger. "That is not ours." Jade looked confused at him. "That was stolen from good people, it goes back." He looked around at everyone who was watching him closely. "If we take that for ourselves, we are no better than this scum." He kicked out at body on the floor. "If you want a share of this then take it and leave me, for I will not have any part of anyone who robs those who have little." Robbie turned to the gate and saw Rune smiling at him.

"Get the cart out of there and burn this place, it is the only way to clean up scum like this." He walked out of the gate and into the street, and felt a hand on his shoulder. He turned to face Jade.

"I am really sorry Robbie, please forgive me?" She threw her arms around him, and buried her head in his chest. Robbie stroked her hair.

"Come on Pebbles don't get upset, I know you have a big heart and would not hurt those who cannot defend themselves. You have done nothing to offend, just understand me when I say these brutes have destroyed countless lives. I want to repair some of the damage done." He squeezed her tight for a few moments; little murmurs came from his chest.

"I am sorry Robbie, I will not let you down again."

Robbie smiled. "You never have and I don't believe you ever will."

Jade stepped back drying her eyes, Robbie turned to Rowan. His face was solemn and his eyes glistened slightly, he moved forward and took Robbie's hand and squeezed it tight. "I shake the hand of a truly noble man; you honour all of us Robbie in the hood."

Robbie was just for a moment lost for words, as he watched Rowan tenderly put his arm around Jade and take her back into the yard to help clean up the mess. Rune and Alice came up to his side. "What just happened then, do you two know?" Rune looked across at Rowan, and then back to Robbie.

"There is a great sadness in his past, I have felt it since I first saw him, and I think the Cutters have wronged him deeply. I think you have just shown him the way to make up for it." Rune slid her arms around him and kissed him on the cheek.

Movement caught her eye, and in a flash, she pulled Robbie round and stood in front of him, Alice stepped up to her side. Two small eyes peeped over the wall. Rune stepped forward; she smiled down at the face of a small girl dressed in rags. "Hello sweet pea, do not be afraid no one will harm you." She crouched down in front of the wall so that she too peeped over like the little girl. "Hi."

"Hi," a whispered voice came back. "Is that Robin Hood? They said it is."

Rune smiled. "It is, would you like to say hello to him?" The little face on the other side of the wall nodded. Rune turned and winked at Alice. "Excuse me Robin Hood, but could you come down here for a minute?" Robbie walked over and lowered himself at the side of Rune. "Robin Hood, I would like to introduce you to..." Rune put her hand to her mouth. "I am so sorry My Lady I did not ask your name."

"Agatha," she whispered back from over the wall.

"Robin Hood, I present to you the Lady Agatha."

Robbie lifted his hand on to the top of the wall. "I am delighted to meet you Lady Agatha." Rune smiled as Agatha took hold of his hand and shook it.

"Nice to meet you Robin." With a giggle she turned and ran off shouting. "It is him; it is Robin Hood." Robbie stood, as slowly from all over faces appeared from behind decayed brickwork and behind bushes. A small man who was holding Agatha's hand came forward. He walked with a limp and Robbie could see others behind him, who were badly cut and bandaged as they struggled forward. They looked tired and worn and under fed, it stirred something deep inside him.

Somehow, he realised how lucky he was to live in Loxley where everyone was sheltered and looked after. As the small man approached, Robbie climbed over the wall to meet him.

"Oh bless you sir, and your men, we had heard the tales but was not sure they were true. I am the town leader Thomas of Cumberworth."

He looked at the small man whose eye was blackened and sunken. His face worn with hunger, his clothes were old and patched. His boots had part of the sole peeling off. Robbie shook his hand as he heard the rumble of the cart behind him. The gates creaked as they closed, Robbie turned to see Martin and Jade fire two burning arrows over the wall. Flames jumped up everywhere. Harry had found two barrels of moonshine and had soaked the place.

"You should have no fear of those Cutters sir; they have been taken care of. I have a cart of goods here, which I feel should be returned to the people. If you would guide us, we would be pleased to transport it to wherever you would require it."

Thomas looked up at Robbie and his face was enough to show the gratitude. All the hooded men lined up at the wall waiting, and the town's folk came close and began to shake their hands. They bowed to them and thanked them, and the entire group bowed their heads, for such was the power of the moment, that even the tough John Styles felt a lump rise in his throat. The gratitude of a people who had suffered such misfortune humbled them greatly.

Little Agatha took hold of Harry's hand. "What is your name?"

"Hey little baby girl they call me Mad Harry." He bent down and picked her up and walked down the line with her. "This is Rowan of the woods. He is one of the best woodsman round here, apart of course for Robin. Here we have Quiet Martin; you will not hear him shoot. Little baby girl this is Big John, he is a very tough dude, and this is Little Eric he is a very good cook, makes great stew. This is Billy the sword; Robin's best pal, and Lady Alice of Loxley. She is brainy and very brave. One of my favourites is this lady," he whispered. "Stephanie the wonderful, and her very special daughter and excellent tracker, and my best pal Pebbles."

Agatha said hello to each of them and they shook her hand. Harry turned to face Rune who had tears in her eyes. "This very beautiful lady is the very cosmic Lady Runestone, who is the kindest person I have ever known, and the cool cosmic guy next to her is Robin Hood, I believe you have met."

Agatha nodded her head and whispered into Harry's ear. "I have, he is very big."

"I know, he's my boss." Harry whispered back as he put her to the floor. Agatha stretched up and kissed him.

"Thanks, Mad Harry."

Harry stood up with tears in his eyes. "Man, this is a good job, I really love all you guys." He turned and walked up the street a little way, and pulled out a huge spotted hankie and blew his nose rather loudly.

Robbie turned to the people of the town. "I am afraid we have to move on, we have very important business, clear the cart quickly and use the weapons to defend yourselves. There appears to be food and clothes and supplies for many months on it, I trust it will help you through." He looked at the sad and dirty faces. "I wish we could do more; I am sorry."

Thomas took his hand and shook it. "How can we ever thank you Robin Hood?"

"You have no need to Thomas; I feel your daughter here has done it for you." Sniffles came from behind him as Rune, and Alice and Steph and even Jade wiped their eyes. So did John and Eric, but no one saw them do it.

Robbie turned back to Thomas. "If more Cutters come do not suffer for what we have done here today." He pulled out an arrow from his quiver with neatly trimmed flights. "Give them this, and tell them this is the arrow of Robin Hood, and I have others with their names on them. Tell them I will find them in any wood across this land."

Thomas grabbed his hand and shook it again. "Go with speed Robin Hood most noble of our kind."

Robbie gave the signal and the group began to move forward up the overgrown street, as everyone cheered and waved. Carefully they worked through what was left of the town and headed out in to the countryside and back into woodland. Robbie noticed how quiet the group was. All of them had been moved by what they had encountered, and all of them now had a great deal to think about. Robbie himself was quiet, it had made him realise that today the games he had played with Alice and Billy as a child had become a reality.

He had never given the role of hooded man much thought, if he was honest with himself, he was just trying to save Loxley and survive. Suddenly when he least expected it, he had taken on the role of his distant ancestor, and given back what was taken to the down trodden and persecuted. "I just hope Mason's middle name isn't John." Steph and Rune chuckled at his side; he turned to look at them, and smiled. "We will be robbing the rich next." Rune beamed at him and Steph started laughing, the atmosphere broke as they entered the trees and soon quiet happy banter began again.

Harry was in for some stick. "What do you mean Quiet Martin, I have just been thinking a lot recently that's all, and I chat for hours when I want."

"Billy the sword, you made me sound like a freak." Alice burst out laughing. "Well, it's alright for you, he gave you a decent name Lady Loxley, at least he didn't call you Alice the Arrow, or Rune the knife. Honestly, Harry that kid is going to tell everyone. I will have people all over this bloody country saying hey, here is the weapon boy."

Alice exploded into fits of laughter, as did Eric; Billy spun round on him. "I don't know why you are laughing? Little Eric, that's really going to impress the women." Eric suddenly frowned, and Rowan laughed aloud. Robbie walked on in the lead with Rune who was chuckling, a smile on his face and a sense of pride at the quality of his men. Harry was silent and kept his head down.

They had been walking for some time when suddenly in the trees was a road sign. Robbie had not realised that they were on a road at all. The sign read 'Flockton.' He stopped and pulled out Harry's old road map, he looked down and found it. He looked at the sky through the treetops and worked out the position of the sun, there was about two hours of light left. Looking at the map, he worked out how far away they were from the priory.

He sat on the grass and everyone broke apart, and sat facing different directions as they rested and watched the trees. "I think we should, with a push, make the Priory by dusk. If this land was flat, we could take our time, but with the thickness of this forest we might have a little trouble."

Alice looked at the map. "It's a pity these roads are not clearly defined, I had no idea we were on one, nature has certainly been busy up here."

Robbie opened his water bottle and took a large gulp, he passed it to Rune who swallowed a large mouthful, and then poured some on to her hankie and wiped her face. Taking a lace out of her pocket, she tied her hair back and then wiped her neck.

"Isn't that my lace?" Rune gave him a smile.

"You dropped it on that first hunting trip and I picked it up." He smiled at her and lay back. That first hunting trip now seemed like so long ago, he remembered her excited face at the rabbit shoot. He was so crazy about her and so nervous, and yet now here he was as relaxed around her as he was Billy. He opened one eye and she was smiling at him.

Life had been so simple then, all he did was watch her and hunt, and somehow in between then and now he had become a lord and hooded hero to children, and protector of Loxley and was now on route to saving England from a mad man. Where it had all gone so crazy, he was not too sure.

Rowan stood up. "We should make a move there is some rain coming. It will make it harder." Robbie sat up and pulled his things together; he lifted his bow and signaled them all to move out. Rowan led the way as they fanned out behind him. He was right, and soon the rain started to fall, and it came down in torrents; Robbie pulled the group in closer as they trudged through what was now thick mud, Martin shouted in from the right side.

"Hey Rowan, when you said some rain, I thought you meant a shower, not a bloody monsoon." Everyone laughed as they leaned forward to balance and pull their feet squelching out of the mud.

It was well after dark when they finally arrived at the priory. The crumbled outline could be seen up the short incline, silhouetted against the dark sky. The white silver birch trunks glowed as they passed them. Robbie stopped and took out his knife. He started to strip pieces of bark off. Rune came up to his side holding her hood out so she could see through the heavy rain.

"What's that for?" She had to almost shout the rain was that loud.

"Birch bark, it burns when it's wet, I think this is the only way we will light a fire tonight. We will need to dry out or we will freeze to death." Rune pulled out her knife and helped him cut away more. They all hung back in the trees as Rowan, Billy and Jade checked out the Priory. Billy gave the signal and they all moved with speed to get to cover.

Most of the priory was now in ruins, there were only small parts that still had a roof. It was as dry as they were going to get, and all of them huddled dripping as Robbie got a fire going. In places where the roof had collapsed, there was some dry wood so he built a fire and encircled it with wet wood to dry out for later. With no meat and no chance of hunting in such bad weather, Rune used the dried veg and herbs Jess had given them to make a rich broth. It was steaming hot and soon warmed them. They all sat huddled and steaming by the fire.

Robbie kept just one on watch by a window that overlooked the only sensible route in; the steep banks across the lawn that fell to thick woodland was something even the Cutters would avoid in such bad weather he thought. The evening pressed on and as each of them got as dry as they could, they moved to the sidewalls and unrolled their blankets.

Billy was curled up in the corner with Alice, with each other and two blankets they were much warmer. Steph pulled Jade up against her and soon both were flat out. Eric lay back to back with John near the fire. Rowan sat and stared at the flames, and Harry and Martin watched through the window. The fire crackled as he lay down and Rune snuggled up. "Wake me in two hours Martin and we will take over." Martin nodded. Robbie lay down and pulled Rune as close as he could. She was soft and warm and smelled of fresh violets and cherry shampoo. He kissed the side of her neck, she wriggled, and he settled down behind her. Sleep came quickly.

Rune's soft lips on his cheek stirred him from his dreams, and he opened his eyes. "Come on sleepy," she whispered. Robbie sat up and stretched. Across the crumbled room, Martin and Harry were slipping under their blankets. She pulled him on to his feet and handed him a hot cup of coffee. He felt disorientated and groggy; he shook his head and yawned. Rune pulled at his hand and he looked up at her.

"Robbie we are wanted, come on." He frowned, his mind was still cloudy, Rune pulled at his arm and he followed sipping his coffee, and trying to wake up.

Rune led him down the old corridor and into what was once the chapel. He looked around at the old decayed beams and the holes in the roof. Some of the pews still existed, as did the old altar, which was now just a slab of stone. Most of the stained glass was smashed and missing and ivy had grown in and up the wall. Steph was sat quietly in front of the altar on the front pew. Robbie's mind was clearing now as the coffee kicked in.

"What's Steph doing here?"

"Shush you will see."

They reached the top of the chapel and sat down beside Steph. Robbie lifted his cup to drink as a woman in white walked in through the wall. He lowered his cup. She was covered in a long robe and had a hood up over her face. He felt the hairs raise on the back of his neck as his fingers tensed on the cup. "Greetings my children." Robbie stiffened. Ghosts in churches after midnight did not appeal to him.

Steph stood up and opened her arms. "Mother," she hurried and threw her arms around the woman in white. Blue flashed from under the hood as the woman greeted her daughter.

"I have missed you my child and so have your sisters." The woman lifted a white hand to her daughter's face. Robbie's brain was struggling, Steph's mum, Len's wife, was a woman in white who walked through chapel walls; Robbie knew this had to be a dream.

The woman spoke quietly to Steph for several minutes; he could not hear what they spoke of and did not much mind. He took a large gulp of coffee as the woman in white lifted her hand. "Come my Granddaughter so I may speak with you."

Rune stood up, walked over to the woman, and embraced her. "Hello Grandmother," the woman in white stood back and looked at her.

"Your powers are almost here my child that is good; you will soon have need of them. Your cousin Jett awaits the moment eagerly, although she is sorry she startled you, do not be angry with her she has missed her favourite cousin." Robbie shook his head; he would wake up shortly he thought.

"You have done well Runestone, the Green Lord is proud of you and your companion, whom I must speak to, bring him to me so he can see I am no ghost or dream."

Rune came over to Robbie and held out her hand. "My grandmother wishes to talk with you Robbie."

Robbie stood up nervously. "What do I call her? I can hardly call her Rune's Grandmother, can I?"

"She is the Lady of the Woods." Rune squeezed his hand as he approached. Robbie bowed to her, and swallowed deeply, his voice trembled slightly.

"Greetings My Lady of the Woods."

"Bowman you have done well and my lord is pleased with you. Your consideration of his woodsman, has gained you great favour."

"Thank you My Lady."

"We do not have much time Robert of Loxley; there are things you must know so I must be swift. You have known for some time that your secrets are being past to the enemy. There is a traitor with a veil of darkness cast upon them, which prevents us from seeing who they may be. You must trust only your kin and my daughters. The Woodsman is true to you and the lord of the forest." Robbie nodded. "I have chosen this day to reveal the line of my kin to you Bowman because you now seek the truth, and my line is a part of your fate, guard well this secret, for the daughters of Hearne should not be angered."

Robbie bowed to the white lady. "My Lady I am honoured by your trust and will protect your line in all that I do."

"The secrets of the future lie here in the soil; I know you know where. My daughter will help you to understand them; you must get them to Canterbury and prevent the snake from becoming the king, as his rule will kill the lines of men forever. You will have help in places you do not expect them, keep my family close and safe Bowman, I have placed great trust in you. Travel west from here and head south after two days."

Robbie bowed. "I will not fail you My Lady."

"I will soon have to leave this place as my power is fading, leave me alone with my granddaughter for a moment." Robbie stepped back and walked back to the pew where he sat quietly and watched the lady in white. There was something familiar that he could not quite put his hand on. It confused him, and he thought as he watched the lady place her hands on Rune's head. Rune gave her a hug and then the lady in white hugged her daughter. "Farewell Bowman, we shall meet again do not worry." The lady in white walked back up the chapel and disappeared as she met the wall, Rune stood for a moment and then turned and walked with her mother back to the pews. Rune smiled. "I hope you liked my grandmother; I am glad you have met more of my family." Robbie, felt a little shaken, he looked at Steph.

"Harry is just bonkers, but you lot, hell Steph, she walked through a wall."

Steph began to laugh. "Oh Robbie, did it bother you?"

"Bother me!! I cannot even explain how I felt. I bet her house is safe, no need for doors with that one."

Steph and Rune began to laugh at Robbie's expression of shock; Rune grabbed his arm and pulled him close. "She is quite sweet when you get to know her, I promise."

"I can't wait for her and Harry to meet, now that will be really cosmic."

Steph laughed at Robbie and patted him on the back. "You are quite safe I can assure you; Rune and I will remain quite solid and continue using doors." Both of them laughed as they walked back to the others. Robbie remained quiet; it was too much excitement for one night.

Robbie sat up to watch as Rune slipped back under the blankets. Steph sat with him and handed him another coffee. Somehow, now he was wide-awake, as Steph spoke quietly to him. "You see now why Rune was so attractive to you. She is a daughter of the thing you love the most, nature and the forest. You will find in her everything you have found alone in the woods. I know how deeply you love her Robbie; I have seen it grow in you for many years." She smiled. "I would also say that your love of the woods and the natural way is the reason why she chose to fall in love with you. She has hidden deep feelings inside herself for a very long time; she will never leave you, and never stop loving you."

"I hope we shall never be parted, for although we have only had a short time together, I already feel as one with her and could not bear separation." He looked at Steph and she nodded softly at him.

"I believe you and that brings me joy to hear. You know her powers will not be noticeable, they will only appear when called upon, but she will have a force inside her that none will be able to stand against. Mason Knox knows this and that is why he will try to kill her."

"What?" Robbie sloshed coffee all over the floor? Steph put her finger to her lips. He settled down. "What do you mean Knox knows, how can he?"

"Tomorrow when we lift the box that contains the proof we need, you must let no other see what is inside it. Bring it straight to me, I want Rowan to guard it always. If my mother is right and someone in here is against us then we must prevent them from getting to it and destroying the evidence."

"I must admit I find it hard to believe Steph, that one of our group is a traitor." Robbie looked across the room at his men sleeping soundly. Each one had great merit and he honestly could not except any of them would do him hurt.

"Knox is very powerful Robbie: he has powers not un-similar to those of my family, his line is known to us, and we have clashed in the past. He will find ways to get to you that we will not see coming. Our road from tomorrow will be dangerous; the word is out that you are no longer in Loxley." Robbie watched her deep green eyes as she spoke. "The prophecy made told of the Bowman who will lead the change of his fortunes. You are now as big a threat to him as Rune is. My greatest hope lies in the fact that we are only eleven in number."

"Why is that to our advantage, wont Knox just send hundreds to attack us?"

"Robbie what would you think if you were him and had his power, and suddenly discovered this prophecy?"

"I am not sure; I would suppose that I would expect me to raise an army and attack him."

"Exactly, and yet you haven't. Instead, you have chosen stealth, the one thing that has always given the woodsman an edge and continued his survival. Do you not find it strange that up until the red death everything in this world was different and run by machines?"

"I am not sure what you mean."

"I was eleven when the red death came; I still remember the old days of modern man. Many of the traditional ways were dying, people back then did not care about the earth; they abused it and wasted everything. They had become lazy and did not want the bother of learning a craft." He listened carefully as she spoke.

"Nature will only endure so much. Millions died because they had lost the ability to live with the land, I have thought about it all my life. The red death was just a symptom of a much greater illness, apathy. Nature allowed those who respected her to live, and the woodsman began to flourish again as they had in the days of old. Traditional ways lived on, and woodsman adapted their craft to the new conditions as nature cleaned the land and returned it to how it should be." Steph placed her hand on his arm. "Robbie, we all live in a new world with a new way of life. In many ways, you are the standard-bearer of this new existence, Knox will try to return to the old ways of machines and greed; he has not learned anything at all. Why do you think that a lord was chosen who was born after the red death?"

Robbie thought about what she had told him. "I can only suppose that I can only live by the way that I know."

"Your father remembers more of those times than I do. He has chosen to live the life we have today, but fate will not trust one who was born before. That is why today you are the heir and not your father. You will forge a new path that is at one with all around you. It will be a better life for nature and for the people." Steph gave a big sigh. "I am very tired now Robbie and I must sleep; I will lift the sleeping charm on our friends here and sleep myself."

Robbie watched as Steph waved a hand and everyone murmured in their sleep, he could not believe it. She slid under her blanket and winked at him. Steph closed her eyes as Robbie smiled to himself. Eric sat up. "Is it my turn to watch yet Robbie?"

Robbie nodded and Eric rubbed his eyes. He poked John who disturbed and sat up, Robbie slid under the blanket next to Rune and pulled her close. She wiggled into him and he settled down and closed his eyes. Tomorrow was going to be yet another long day. His mind was filled with the pictures of the day, and thoughts of Rune and her powers, they all jumbled along through his head as sleep took him, and he drifted into dreams of white ladies and robbing Prince John.

Rune moved and turned over, her nose brushed his cheek and he opened his eyes. Her two blue eyes sparkled before his; he smiled as he gazed in to those deep blue pools surrounded by lilac... by lilac! He blinked and moved his head back to focus more clearly.

Rune's expression changed from the loving smile to one of concern. "What is it?"

"Rune your eyes... They have changed."

Rune sat bolt upright. "What do you mean they have changed?" Panic crossed her face. Robbie smiled.

"Calm down, they are absolutely fantastic and more beautiful than they have ever been... It's just that the whites of your eyes now have a lilac tinge to them."

Rune blinked and snapped at him. "You scared the hell out of me Robbie, never look at me like that again." Rune relaxed a little, and Robbie felt guilty, he got up and walked over to Alice who was pouring out coffee. He glanced back; she was sat with her head in her hands. He walked out of the room into the long corridor and leaned against one of the empty window frames.

The heavy rain had eased, and a patch of blue was breaking in the dark sky. He leaned on the window and breathed the fresh air as he sipped his coffee. Rune was upset, but he had not meant to cause it, her eyes were as beautiful. The trees swayed in the breeze as he turned his mind to what he knew about this place.

Robin Hood had been seriously wounded and his men had carried him here. His condition had steadily got worse and finally in a state of confusion, he had shot an arrow into the air and it had landed in the river over the trees. As his strength failed, he shot a second arrow and it fell in the trees at the top of the steep bank.

It was here that he had been buried after his death, Marion who was with child had remained in the priory in the care of the nuns, and later left to return to Loxley the home place of her husband. This was the birthplace of his whole line; it was here the legend ended and the facts of his family began.

Robbie looked around and pondered as to which window he stood at to shoot that final arrow. Maybe it was this one; his eyes scanned the trees and shrubs as he tried to remember the picture. Everything seemed so different now, so much larger and thicker, it was going to be a long job finding that stone.

He gave a long sigh and lifted the cup back to his lips. Steph came through the door and walked up the corridor towards him. "I wondered where you had got to, I have talked to Rune and she is fine, she is a little upset that she scared you."

"I was not scared, just a little surprised, most people's eyes do not change overnight. I had just woken up and was still a bit groggy, it took me by surprise that is all."

"She is going through important changes, and it can be quite scary at times for her, don't take it to heart Robbie. The fact that she has lilac whites to her eyes means the process is almost complete."

"I am not upset, I worry about her too, and I hate to see her distressed that's all."

"It all seems to happen at once, doesn't it?"

"You are telling me." Robbie breathed a big sigh and watched the trees sway in the breeze.

CHAPTER TEN

A ROUND DOZEN

It was a little after breakfast when Robbie had gathered Harry, and found Alice and Rune. "I have a job for you three meet me outside the chapel in five minutes." Robbie walked into the room towards Rowan. "There is a large Scot's pine out in the garden, could you meet me there in about ten minutes."

Rowan nodded. "Is everything alright Robbie?"

"Yeah, it is fine. I just need a private word." Rowan nodded and headed out of the door; Robbie turned to the other five as Steph had already left. They all looked at him, Jade spun one of her knives in her hand. "What is on your mind Robbie?"

"I received some news this morning which means we have to move out of here pretty quickly. There are Cutters everywhere and we need to find safe passage either east or west. I want you to divide into groups and scout out the surrounding area. Find us a safe clear route. I want you back within one hour, and I want to be on the road within 30 minutes of your return. There are things to be done here, and we will be ready by the time you return, and guys, please be very careful, heroes usually end up dead so make sure you all get back safely."

It took a few moments for them to gather their things and then they were off, Robbie moved quickly. He reached the end of the long corridor and called Rune to bring the others. He headed out side to where Rowan stood.

"Rowan under those trees at the top of the banking, is the answers to whom Knox really is. I believe if that information gets out, it will destroy him. Steph is the only one for now who can understand whatever it is, your new task from now on is to guard her, and whatever it is we find, and I mean guard her with your life. Trust no one who is not either hers or my blood, do you understand what I am asking?"

"You received your sword did you not?"

"She is more important to me than this sword Rowan." He nodded his head.

"I understand you clearly Lord Loxley, I will not fail you." Robbie smiled at him

"No I don't think you will Rowan." He patted his arm.

Minutes later Robbie and Harry had removed an old iron railing and were under the trees, as Rune and Alice stood watch. He found the stone quickly, and Harry and he heaved it up and laid it to one side. He had no spades, and so with their daggers they broke the earth and scooped it out with their hands. Harry pushed his dagger into the soil and there was a dull thud, he looked at Robbie. "Hey man I don't mind a little killin, but if this is not a box with like information in it, I will have to split man."

Robbie grinned. "You're not afraid of the dead surely?"

Harry waved his arms wildly, as his eyes looked about. "Whoa man don't talk about them like that, it's bad karma."

Robbie started to laugh. "Do you know whose grave this is? He has been dead for over five hundred years, Harry; he won't hurt you he is family."

Harry covered his ears with his hands, and closed his eyes as he started to chant repeatedly to himself, as he rocked back and forwards. Robbie still laughing scraped away the soil to reveal a small metal box. He pulled hard, and the soil came away as the box slipped out. "It's alright Harry you can look now."

Harry was still rocking with his eyes closed and chanting. Robbie shook his head. "Harry it's alright." Harry continued to chant; Robbie reached over and grabbed Harry's leg. Harry screamed out, and jumped banging his head on the branches. He fell backwards into the freshly dug hole and screamed even louder. His legs and arms flailed about as he tried to upright himself. Finally, with much screaming and yelling, Harry came flying out from under the trees like a scalded rat out of a hole.

Alice and Rune jumped back, as he flew on all fours past them and landed in a heap on the other side of the grass. Robbie his eyes red from his tears of laughter crawled still giggling, out from under the trees dragging the box. Alice looked at Robbie, and then at Harry. "What on earth happened?"

Robbie started to chuckle. "Harry thought the real Hooded Man had come back to thank him." Robbie grinned up at Rune. "He is afraid of the dead."

Harry sat up on the grass; he was very pale and trembled as he wagged a finger at Robbie. "That was not funny man." He shook his head slowly. "You are really twisted man; I mean really twisted."

Alice and Rune started to giggle, as Robbie got up and lifted the box. "Hey Harry can you fill in the hole, or should I come back?" Harry stared at the trees under which the hole lay.

"You are a sick man Robin Hood, like really twisted and sick."

Robbie and Rune were still giggling when they arrived at the chapel, Rowan opened the door and they entered, Steph was looking excited and worried. She took the box and pulled a small key out of her pocket. The lock clicked and she opened the box and looked inside. Steph smiled and looked up at Robbie. "My dad's all-time favourite inventions of the old modern world." She lifted the items out of the box. "Snap seal bags, and self-seal boxes."

Robbie and Rune did not quite understand, Steph smiled. "Here see snap seal bags are water tight and air tight but you can read through them." She popped the lid off the self-seal box. "Air tight you see, dry and clean." She handed them the plastic box to examine.

There was a lot more than Robbie had first expected. All were perfectly preserved, and air tight in the polythene bags. Steph seemed to understand the documents and worked her way down through the pile. She stopped and slipped two bags containing what looked like patterns painted on paper.

"This is it." She looked at the patterns and showed them to Rune, who then passed them to Robbie. He looked at the patterns, which were clearly different. One was labelled Anglo Celtic chromosomes; the other was labelled Mason Knox (Germanic Saxon chromosomes). Robbie passed them to Alice, and looked at Steph.

"I do not understand what these prove."

Steph took a deep breath. "Robbie this may go right over your head but here goes." She pulled an old copy of a newspaper article out of the pile. "Mason claimed that he was a direct descendant of Cornwall the Saxon warlord, who was Uther Pendragon's mortal enemy. The story goes that Uther wanted Cornwall's wife Igraine, and Merlin fixed it so that during the battle, Uther was transformed into Cornwall and snuck into the castle and had his way with her." She looked up from the papers to them.

"The result of the night was that Cornwall was killed, and Igraine became pregnant by Uther, the resulting child being Arthur the first true king of the Britain's. Mason believed he was the true line of Cornwall, and so therefore, the descendant of Arthur, and my dad proved that in some ways, he was, but the mistake that Mason made was that Cornwall already had a daughter. A daughter to a Celtic wife of a Saxon king." Steph watched them all to make sure they all were following her.

"Arthur was born of a Celtic king and a Celtic mother. In this lies the problem, because for Mason to prove his claim that his line is pure it must have been pure Celtic. These patterns are DNA; they show the lines of decent in a family tree. In order for Mason to prove he is a pure descendant of Arthur; he would have only Celtic traces in his DNA. Mason has no traces of Celtic at all, his roots are deeply buried in Saxon, which can only mean that he is part of the line of the daughter, or he is not even related at all. I really hope you understand this Robbie, because even I get lost in it; this is my dad's field of expertise."

Robbie nodded and looked back at the DNA and chromosome printouts. "I think I have the general idea, what is more, we have all your fathers' notes so if we need to, they can be read to prove the point."

Steph nodded. "Right Robbie we somehow have to keep these safe." Steph unrolled a small leather pouch and opened it.

"What is that for?" Robbie looked at the pouch with the long leather strap.

"I brought this to carry the notes in why?" Steph looked down at it.

"I just think it is a bit obvious, is there nowhere else you can hide it?"

Steph seemed to go a little pink. "Only my panties."

Robbie coughed. "Err... That's not quite what I meant, Rune is good with a needle can she not sow it in to your tunic or something?"

Steph looked at Rune. "I suppose it will fit in the lining, but what about this? I brought it along specially." She held up the pouch.

"Actually, that has given me an idea." Robbie took out Harry's map. "We won't be needing this anymore." He folded it, and then wrapped it in a piece of brown paper from the bottom of the tin box. "Put that in the pouch and guard it with your life. Never leave it anywhere."

Steph smiled. "Clever Robbie, very clever."

Robbie looked up the chapel. "Aren't altar stones hollow to hold the remains of a saint or something?" He walked up the chapel to the altar. "Give me a lift with this Rowan." The two of them lifted the top altar stone to one side and Robbie smiled. He took the metal tin and dropped it into the empty space inside the altar stone; together they pushed the large stone back. "Right, we know where the rest of the information is hidden, if anyone asks, we put it back in the grave alright?"

Everyone nodded. "Robbie what are we going to do about the rest of the information about other true lines?" Rune stitched her mother's tunic as she spoke to him.

"I have been thinking about that a lot. I think we should leave it here in secret, and then if we can defeat Mason, we will have the time to seek out others. With Mason still in the picture, it makes no sense to reveal and endanger others."

Rune nodded and smiled at him. "Good idea." She bit the cotton off her mother's tunic and let it fall to the seat. "All done, nice and safe now." Rune packed her little sewing kit back into her pocket.

The door opened, and Rowan went for his bow. Harry staggered in covered in mud. "Man, that was heavy, I put it all back as he would like it. It's a bad thing man to mess with em." Harry's eyes darted around the chapel as if looking for a spirit to come out and thank him. Alice and Rune both chuckled.

For the first time in what felt like a very long time, Robbie and Rune had a little free time. Steph had kept her father's pocket journal, and she sat outside in the priory grounds, Rowan sat close by keeping watch. Robbie and Rune walked around the overgrown gardens holding hands and talking quietly, once out of sight of the others they slid into an alcove and he pulled her close. His kisses were long as he relished each precious second alone with her, the time to move would soon be on him, and precious moments would be seldom.

Alice sat on a small chair by the trees with a needle and thread mending her cloak, which had been torn on a branch, as they had pushed through the woods in the rain, Alice looked at the crest of the able bowmen. She was so proud of it and had been thrilled to see how some of the other men had seen it on the range and shown her huge respect.

"You know Steph, maybe we should cover these." Steph looked up from her book. "They are a bit of a giveaway don't you think? I love it I have to admit, but if we want to blend in anywhere, a Loxley coat of arms would not be prudent."

Steph smiled. "I would not want to be you when you suggest that to Rune, she spent a whole day looking at it in the mirror when she got it."

Alice smiled sheepishly. "Yeah, me too," she giggled. "I won't take it off I just thought we could cover them."

"It might be worth mentioning to Robbie when he gets back, actually where is he?"

Harry leaned back in his chair and peered down the garden. He coughed, and quickly leaned forward in his chair. "The dude is safe I have my eye on him. He is not exactly in view at the moment, but whoa you don't want to disturbed him Stephy take my word for it, and believe me man, he is in very capable hands."

Steph gave Alice a huge smile as she noticed the slight reddening of Harry's cheeks, and she looked back at her book.

Robbie and Rune appeared all smiles sometime later, they walked down the garden laughing and joking their arms around each other, Steph watched them a contented look on her face, and she gave her daughter a smile as she passed with Robbie on her arm.

"Any sign of a return Rowan?" Robbie looked out into the forest. Rune looked down at Alice sat sowing.

"Why are you covering your crest?" Rune seemed horrified.

"I think if we intend to head south announcing Lord Loxley is in the area could be dangerous for him. I think it would be wiser for all of us to cover them."

Rune lifted her arm to her chest and touched the embroidered crest. Robbie smiled at her as she looked crest fallen. "If you want to leave it Rune, I will not mind, I am proud of mine as well."

Rune looked back at him. "No Alice is right; I will not be the one to give you away Robbie. I will still wear it under my patch."

Ten minutes later Jade and John came running through the trees and flopped down on the grass. Jade gulped air and tried to steady her breathing, John sat gasping and sweating as he wiped his face on his cloak. "We won't be going east Robbie." Rowan handed them both water bottles and they hurriedly gulped the water down.

Jade sat for a moment and gathered herself together. "We ran into one or two along the way Robbie, Knox has got a bloody big army based at Pontefract, it is about a fair few miles northeast of here. From what we can gather, he intends to strike twice at the same time. This lot up here are going to York; there is some lord up there who has been very organised. The old walled town has been rebuilt and the gates have been restored, and there appears to be a small local government ruling."

"That's great work, how did you get that information?" Jade slapped John on the back. "As you can see my big friend here has not had a shave for a day or two. We hit three Cutters on the way up and nicked their jackets and hats. John here came upon a group who were lost, he told them he was an officer of the Cutter forces and screamed at them for losing their way, he asked them what their orders were and they spilled the lot. He sent them off in the wrong direction, and we high tailed it back here." Jade beamed at John and then back at Robbie.

"That was a great bit of work you two, well done. Have a break and then give your cloaks to Alice and Rune, I want all Loxley crests covering. It looks like all of us will be appearing as something we are not soon."

Martin and Eric walked back into camp about ten minutes later. They had been scouting to the west and to date the area seemed clear of any large number of Cutters. There were scouting parties and raiding groups all over. Martin told Robbie of a skirmish they had on the way back with about fifteen.

"It got a bit hairy for a moment back there, Billy got separated from us, but as far as I can tell he got away. We both laid low for a while and then went back to check. I lost Billy's trail but it did look like he was on his way back here."

Robbie was anxious; he should have been back by now. Alice had put her needle down, and she was looking terrified. Rune clutched her hand and looked at Robbie. "We will give him a little longer, if there is no sign Rowan and I will go and look for him. I am not leaving without him; we have been through too much together to be separated now." Alice came up to his side, and Robbie put his arm round her shoulder. "Keep your faith cousin I will not leave him, you know Billy, he will come walking in smiling and love the attention." She smiled back at him and nodded.

"Yeah, he loves to show off."

Martin paced around the edge of the tree line anxiously. "Let me go back Robbie and find him, he could be in trouble."

Robbie patted his shoulder. "Just give it a little while longer. Billy is no slouch in the woods; we have hunted together for many years. He knows I will wait for a set length of time, and then come looking, we have done this many times before when hunting. Believe me Martin, if he is not back in another ten minutes he is in trouble and he knows I am coming. He will hole up and leave me the signs."

Robbie and Harry paced up and down the garden, the clouds were rolling in and it looked like rain again, finally Robbie stooped and picked up his bow and quiver. "Rowan, Martin, take extra arrows, Harry you guard this place with your life. Everyone get your things together and be ready to move at a moment's notice. Jade, Eric, I want you in the forest fifty yards down, if you see anything get back here and get everyone out of here pronto. You weave round and lay low, and when trouble has passed pick up my trail. Jade I will be using Joe's signals alright."

Jade nodded. "Right you are Robbie."

Robbie turned to head for the forest as Alice ran passed him. She threw herself into Billy's arms sobbing wildly. Billy winced as he lifted a badly cut arm and lifted his bow to greet Robbie. Robbie breathed a long sigh of relief as Billy hugged Alice, and spoke softly to her. "Hey come on now I am fine, I just picked on the wrong guy, and it took a little longer than expected to convince him I was the good guy." He smiled at Robbie as Alice cried.

Robbie walked up and looked at his arm. "That will need a stitch and a good cleaning, it was a dirty blade." Robbie leaned over Alice, and putting his arm around Billy's head, he pushed his forehead against Billy's. "You scared me Brother."

Billy smiled. "Scared myself to be honest." Robbie squeezed his shoulder. "Alice sort that arm out for him, ok everyone we move in ten grab your gear."

Alice was shaking too much, so Rune sat at the side of her, and while Billy and Alice calmed down, she sewed four stitches into his arm having cleaned the cut thoroughly. "No sword play for a while or you will burst the stitches, and it will be as stiff as hell in the morning, but you will live." She leaned on Alice to get up, she smiled at Billy and he nodded his thanks. Rune stood up and looked back at Alice; there was an odd look on her face.

Ten minutes later, they were in the trees tracking west. Everyone was on high alert and Robbie took point with Jade and Rowan at his side. Martin and John were wide on the left, and Harry and Eric cleared the rear. Billy was in pain and travelled with Alice in the centre. Rune and Steph kept close to Robbie who was just ten feet in front.

Steph closed her thoughts out and then concentrated.

"Hear me Rune."

Rune jumped and looked at her mother who smiled.

"Rune don't talk, think."

Rune tried hard to concentrate; she pictured her mother's face in her mind.

"Is this working Mother?"

Steph smiled.

"You are ready my child. Now tell me what is wrong. I know you felt something back at the priory."

Rune kept looking forward at Robbie.

"God he is gorgeous, oops sorry Mum, still trying to get the hang of this."

Steph laughed aloud, and then looked at the floor.

"Are you still there Mother?"

Steph smiled and focused.

"I am here. Tell me what you felt at the priory, and do not think of Robbie," Rune chuckled.

"I had a really strange feeling, I cannot explain it, I had finished helping Billy and I touched Alice. I went all cold inside, Alice cannot be the traitor, and I cannot believe that, so what was it?"

"I am not sure Rune, but believe me Alice would die for Robbie; you may just have touched on her pain. She was very upset about Billy; you will feel the pain in others at times. Have you tried talking to Robbie?"

"Hey sexy can you hear me?"

"Rune I meant the normal way."

"Oh sorry Mum."

Steph began to laugh again, and Alice came up at her side and looked at her.

"What's got you?" Steph smiled and tittered.

"Oh it was just this morning. You know Harry and his ghost fear. Robbie was really tickled by it and told me later, it just came to mind."

Alice chuckled. "It was so funny. You know he is such a big tough guy, but if you had seen him sat on the grass panting and as white as a..." Alice chuckled again. "You know, ghost?" She started to laugh more. "It really was very funny."

Rune looked over at her mum and smiled, her lilac blue eyes danced. The rain began to fall and they all pulled up their hoods and closed in to tighten the group. Rune was thrilled that she finally had the chance to use her power and talk to her mum without moving her lips. If only she could talk to Robbie, she thought of all the possibilities. It would be great for hunting and in a fight. She smiled to herself and thought hard about him.

"Robbie... Robbie... Hey sexy butt."

"Rune don't shout you almost deafened me."

Rune gasped aloud, and then smiled.

"Robbie is that really you?"

"You were hot this morning."

Rune gasped with glee.

"Robbie this is great, it was wonderful, wasn't it?"

"I can't wait to get you all to myself again, this time I am going to..."

"Cut it out Jett she is still only learning."

Rune jumped and looked at her mother.

"Sorry cousin just having a little fun, hi Aunt Steph how are things up there, mum sends her love."

"We are all fine; it's nice to hear from you again. Now Rune is growing in strength I will look forward to hearing from all of you."

"Hey Rune, I am so excited to be able to speak to you at last. Is Robbie as hot as I think, you will have to find me some hunk from the north and we can gossip all day about them?"

"Hi Jett, you stay out of my mind when I am with Robbie, and I will bring you a hot one."

"I am sorry Rune. Honestly, I did not mean to pry, but you did kinda lose it there for a moment, and well you did broadcast it to me. It almost made me blush."

"What do you mean I broadcast it?"

"What Jett means is that you got a little carried away and a few of your thoughts got sent round the family? Don't worry we have all done it."

"Oh god you all felt it?"

"I tell you cousin that Robin Hood must be an animal."

"I won't tell you again Jett, don't tease Rune like that."

"Sorry Aunt Steph."

Rune sniffled as she wept under her hood; Steph put an arm around her. "Come on Rune don't cry," she whispered. "It happens sometimes if we lose control for a second. That is all it was, just a second, we all got hit with a very loud, oh god Robbie, and that was it. There was nothing deeply personal, if anything it just made us all jump. Your power was very strong, come on now do not cry it's going to take a little time to adjust that's all. I tell you what; tonight, I will give you some lessons to help you control it. I will teach you to block it, alright?"

Rune wiped her eyes. "Thanks Mum."

Steph gave her a squeeze. "He is very sexy you know? If I had been a little younger, I don't know Rune, you could have had a run for your money." Rune laughed and lifted her arm round her mother.

"I am really glad you are here Mum." Steph kissed the top of Rune's hood. "Me too."

It had felt like a very long day when shortly before dusk they skirted the edges of Huddersfield. Harry knew this area well, and he took them by routes that cut out many of the built up areas. They crossed the moor and dropped into a deep valley. Harry had assured Robbie that even in the modern age, there was only about two or three families that had lived this high up.

Harry had a friend who lived in the valley. She had a small place with a large barn and he was sure she would give them shelter for the night. Robbie stood on the top of the hill looking down at the forest below, with wind and rain driving in to him. The others crouched down more to get out of the wind that was belting the rain with force into their faces. "We could do with some warmth and some shelter tonight Harry; this place feels like hell."

"Sorted man, I will move ahead and go down to see her, it's been a while she is a cool chick man, I know she will help."

"Alright Harry I will get everyone under the trees near that old bridge over there. Take John with you, and we will wait for your signal."

Harry and John set off down the hill and Robbie pulled everyone together. "Look I know you are all tired, but we must not slip. We have to make it to the trees down by the bridge, I know this is the middle of nowhere but let's not make any mistakes just in case. Jade swing round and give cover from those shrubs. Martin, Eric, you cover the far side there. The rest of you take it easy and quietly, and let's get through the gap. I will be happier with trees above my head again."

Jade silently sped off, and Martin and Eric quietly made their way down the bank. Once they were in position Robbie led off, and one by one, they descended the bank with Rowan taking up the rear. Robbie wove through the shrubs and thick heather down towards the trees. He came to a stop just short of the forest edge and waited; Rune crept up and put her hand on his shoulder. "Wait. We are not alone."

There was something about the way she looked that told him instantly there was trouble, his arm went up and signals moved back up the line. Everyone melted into the undergrowth. He looked towards Jade and pointed to his eyes. She shook her head there was no sign of anyone. He turned to Martin. He signaled no sign. Robbie turned to Rune. "Where are they Rune?" She closed her eyes and let her mind wander.

Harry walked around the corner of the house and straight into a crossbow, and he raised his hands. Rune thought harder, she turned her head from left to right. There were men in red cloaks lining the road lay behind logs waiting to attack. She opened her eyes and they blazed blue and lilac. "There are about fifteen men along the side of the roadway lying in wait they have Harry; I am not sure about John. They have red cloaks on, that is all I can see."

"It's enough, good girl." He kissed her and she smiled, not because he kissed her, but because he had taken her word without question, he just instantly believed her. Robbie signaled and they all closed in to him. "There are about fifteen of them along the road, they are in red, we are in green and the light is fading. Let us keep it tight and quiet, Jade Rowan and Rune up front with me, Martin you keep everyone back bows at the ready on my signal come out of the floor and let's show them who is boss."

Everyone nodded, Robbie slipped out of the undergrowth and into the forest. Rune was close and Jade to his left with Rowan far right. They wove through the trees keeping low and silent.

The road came into view through the trees and Robbie signaled to slow down. They dropped their pace and slowly Robbie saw the cottage just off the side of the road. Harry stood against the wall, where a man in a red cloak was holding a crossbow to his chest. Robbie looked round, as Jade pointed to a row of men lay on their stomachs along the edge of the tree line watching the road. A young woman with short spiky hair was arguing with a man in front of the cottage. Just five feet in front of him, a man stood up, and Robbie pulled back behind the tree.

"What the hell is she saying sergeant?"

Robbie looked back and Martin signaled, everyone was in position and ready, Robbie turned back and caught Rune watching him. She smiled and he winked. Robbie signaled Jade, no throwing knives she looked disappointed. The Sergeant shouted into the trees. "She says he is an old friend sir not a Cutter."

Robbie signaled Martin and then turned to Rowan, he pointed to the man sat on the ground next to the one standing up in front of him. The man stood up shouted back. "Well how do we know she is telling the truth?"

A silver dagger, came around the side of his face and touched his throat, he swallowed hard. "Because I say she is." The man who was sat down suddenly shot backwards, and found Rowan's knife at his throat. He lay very still. The rest of the group stepped passed Robbie and stood in a line behind the men lay down. The sergeant turned pale.

"What should I do sir?"

Robbie looked up at him. "Release my uncle for starters." The men on the ground turned round, but it was too late. They let go of their weapons and raised their hands, Jade smiled at the man below her. "Cute Butt."

Steph looked across at her. "No this one's much cuter." She winked at him; he gave her a worried smile. "Up then." She gestured. They all stood up hands in the air and walked out on to the road, the Sergeant dropped his sword, Billy picked it up.

"That's a nice blade don't be so rough with it." He spun it in his hand and then very gently laid it carefully on the floor. "See."

Robbie walked the officer out of the trees and on to the road. "Sit." The men instantly fell to the floor and the hooded figures surrounded them. There was a bench against the wall, Robbie spun the officer around and dropped him on to it. A man in red came flying through the door and landed sprawled on the floor.

"Wondered where you got to John."

John smiled. "Found this one sneaking out back, they never learn, do they?"

The officer looked up at Robbie. "Look no offence, but who the hell are you?"

"I am the hooded man, who the hell are you lot?" Robbie slid his knife back into his belt.

There were a few gasps, the officer looked very suspicious. "I thought your lot were over in Loxley?"

Robbie looked down at him and slid back his hood a little. "You know how it is, the forest has expanded and there are a lot of us." He turned and looked around the place. "We thought we would do a little sightseeing, starting with my uncle's mate here, which by the way it's nice to meet you. Robert of Loxley, didn't catch your name, Harry here sometimes gets forgetful."

The young woman smiled and did a strange sort of curtsy. "Kate."

"Well Kate, it is nice to meet you, have you met Lady Runestone Loxley?" Rune dropped her hood and smiled.

"Have you quite finished? We have the small matter of this incident to sort out."

Robbie turned slowly round to the officer who looked up with an annoyed look on his long pale face. "One should always observe the niceties when in someone else's home. Right, who are you, and what exactly are you doing round here?"

"I am Captain Patrick Smith, and these good men are the Saddleworth Constables. If you are who you say you are, then oddly enough we are on the same side."

"Well, we are, but we are not if you get my drift. Last time I looked in the mirror I was Robert of Loxley, as for sides I do not favour sneaks who set traps." The captain was outraged.

"You call us sneaks; what do you think you have just done?"

"Evened the odds." Jade smiled. "We just walked right up to you, if you had been making less noise you would have heard us."

"Exactly." Robbie bowed to Jade.

"That's beside the point what are we going to do about this?" Captain Smith was starting to redden.

"Well, we need a meal and a good night's sleep; I suppose you should reset your trap and keep the noise down. You are I presume expecting a raiding party?"

Captain Smith looked dumbfounded. "You are not going to help?"

Harry picked up his swords. "Not our jurisdiction man." He slid the blades back into their sheaths. "Put the kettle on Kate baby." He walked into the cottage.

Robbie shrugged. "It's brew time, down tools boys and girls." He put his arm around Rune and followed Harry into the cottage laughing.

The Cottage was quite small so with eleven guests in the house it was a little cramped; Kate was very cheery and passed out cups to everyone. Harry sat in the kitchen with Rune and Alice. Robbie looked at his men. "It has been a long day but we could have guests so stay sharp. I want lookouts both sides. Have a warm drink first and try to dry off by the fire, let our locals here sort them out. Rowan if it comes to the pinch, we could use any help we have, so give them a few pointers will you? Billy, see if you can get that Smith to be a little more organised. The rest of you crash out for a while." They all nodded.

Robbie came into the kitchen and took his dripping cloak off he threw it onto a hook on the door where four other cloaks dripped. "Thank you for this Kate, we won't inconvenience you for long."

"No problem, family is always welcome." Alice almost choked on her tea.

She looked up at Kate who was smiling and then at Harry as she coughed. He gave her a slap on the back and she choked a large cough. "Thanks Harry."

Rune looked at Robbie, and then at Harry who now had his head down. "Harry is there something we should know?"

Harry fidgeted for a moment as Robbie looked up at Kate, who he thought bore a distinct resemblance to Alice. She was obviously Lox. "Kate is my baby girl." He smiled up at her. Alice looked very shocked.

Rune smiled at her. "How old are you Kate?"

"I am sixteen My Lady."

"I am Rune, this is Robbie, and that is your cousin Alice, there are no titles in family."

"Sixteen! Harry just when exactly were you going to tell us about this?" Alice glared at him.

"Now don't go hitting me with them evils again Alice, I only knew about three years ago. I have always called here for a break on the road. It was only when her mum got sick she told me."

"Three years, a break? Harry that is not a break, that is a person, what were you thinking? You should have brought her to us as soon as you found out. What is the point in family otherwise?" Alice scowled at him.

"Err Alice is it? He has been taking care of me here; he just nips off for a bit and comes back."

"I think what Alice is trying to say is that family belong together Kate. It is very important to the Loxley family that they look out for each other." Rune pulled out a chair and signaled to her to sit. Rune smiled a sweet smile. "Kate, do you have any of your mother's family round here?"

Kate shook her head. "No Miss."

"I'm Rune, alright then." Rune looked at Robbie. "We have no idea of the road to Loxley it is probably crawling with Cutters now. Considering where we are heading... Hold on Robbie, mums listening in and wants to ask me something." Rune seemed to stare at the table for a moment. "Mum wants to know if she has any skills that Harry has taught her."

"She is cool with a bow, but really cosmic with the old samurai, taught her all I know." Harry beamed with pride at his daughter.

Robbie sat back in his chair and looked at Rune. "She is family and she is able, she is coming. I like the idea of a round dozen."

Rune nodded and Alice agreed. Robbie stood up and looked at Harry. "Shame on you Harry we should have been told. Kate welcome to the family I am sorry its short notice, but I cannot have a sixteen year old left alone while her stupid father fights up and down the land. When we leave, you are to come along as one of us. Alice, Rune help her find the right clothes and show her what to pack. There will be time for her to get to know everyone on the road."

Robbie stepped out into the night air; Steph sat cleaning her bow in the small porch. "Just how exactly do you listen in?" Steph smiled as she dried the wooden handle.

"Rune can talk to me and her cousins just by thinking. She can also let us see and hear what she sees and hears, what I didn't realise, and she does not know, is she has a gift we don't have. Rune can project herself and gain another person's perspective, which is what she did tonight. I could see the pictures clear in my mind so I knew what you knew the moment she saw it."

"Do you see everything she sees?" Steph laughed.

"Oh Robbie, I think I have had this discussion once today already. Rune only shows what she wants. She has her privacy just like the rest of us."

Robbie smiled. "Oh good."

"So, we have yet another Lox? Don't you go getting worried about her I will keep her close, I seem to be becoming mum to everyone else, one more won't hurt."

The night passed quietly and with an armed guard outside, Robbie eased up and let everyone relax a bit, he was feeling very tired and went upstairs and lay down. Tomorrow they would head south and for the rescue point, and hopefully get Peter Lane freed for Steph and Rune and Jade.

He lay in the dark thinking there was now twelve of them, and he wondered about his conversation with Steph the previous night. Knox had a large army, which he knew could not be far away from Loxley now. But Knox had halved his army to send another group up to York. That was two places that Knox was hell bent on destroying. What is in York he asked himself, why is it so important when it is so far away from the capital?

Lack of news was Robbie's biggest problem he had to find a way of getting more information, news was about but who was bringing it. Being out of sight in the trees would help his tactics of stealth, but he was cutting himself off from the world outside and he now needed to find a way to connect again without blowing his cover. The door opened and a slender figure slipped in. Her hair shimmered in the moonlight and her eyes shone at him as she crawled beside him and curled up. "Hi." The bed moved. "Oh, I didn't wake you, did I?"

"No, I was just thinking, I was not asleep." He pulled her close. "How are your powers coming along?"

"I am getting better; mum has been helping me get used to them. My head is really hurting now though."

"You need to rest. Maybe you have overdone it for one day." Robbie suddenly realized that one of his problems could be answered. Rune can talk to all her family, and they would have some news. He closed his eyes feeling her warm body beside him; tomorrow he would solve his other problem.

Robbie was up before the rest of them. He wandered outside with a drink and into the forest; it did not take long for him to find Captain Smith. Jade sat above him in the tree watching. "Captain, quiet night? That's good my lads needed a rest. I was wondering if you would care to join me in the house for coffee, and if you bring one of your lads, I am sure we can rustle up some tea or something for your men. "That is very decent of you Lord Loxley."

"Call me Robbie I am only really a lord at home, out here I use the hooded man thing, by the way you have met Pebbles, haven't you?" He handed her the hot cup of coffee, and she winked at the captain.

"Your people are quite remarkable. I had no idea."

Jade raised the cup and took a sip. "Just helping keep an eye out Captain."

Captain Smith followed Robbie into the house, where he was given a cup and invited to sit down. A young boy in a red cloak came in and busied himself making drinks. "Captain I wanted a quiet word and a little advice if that is acceptable?"

"What can I do that would help you?"

"What I need is a way of finding out what is going on around the country. News must travel but being deep in the forests and woods it is not always easy."

"Communication problems eh? I must admit, for us it is not that big a problem, the postal run is through our town so we get to hear everything."

"So there is post going up and down the country? I had heard that some towns wanted to get it going. I did not know it was there yet."

"Well, you see it is only the west side of the country that has it at the moment. Too many Cutters fouling things up in the east."

"So what do these postal run people look like, I would hate to shoot one by accident."

"They are all volunteers at the moment and they all look different, we spot them because they ride like the wind, not very easy to stop you know."

Robbie thought hard but a plan was forming. "Who is in York and why are the Cutters sending an army up there?"

"You seem well enough informed to me if I may say so. York, that is what's his face, Sir Giles Phillips. He is very well organised from what we hear, got the whole place fortified, and has all sorts of traders coming and going. He wants to reform the government, but that Knox fellow is making it hard, he keeps killing his ambassadors. I am surprised you have not heard from him, Loxley from what I have heard is just as well organised."

"We hadn't when I left."

"If you don't mind me asking, why are you so far away from your home when it is at risk?"

"I have many roles Captain, and all of them for now are secret."

The captain smiled. "I understand, you know they say you are the one bowman that will bring this country back from the brink. You will be the one to stop Knox and bring back better times."

"They do? And what do you say Captain?"

"I say Robin Hood is a fair and decent man who leads with an even hand. I would even go so far as to say they could be right."

"We will have to see, won't we Captain?" Robbie smiled as the young boy rattled past with a tray loaded with hot cups. The captain stood up and offered his hand. Robbie took it and they shook.

"It has been a pleasure to talk, take good care Robin in the Hood and good luck."

The captain took his leave and went back to his men. It was over an hour later when everyone had been fed and had gathered their dry things ready to leave.

Harry locked the door of the cottage, and took his place in the line, as Robbie faced everyone. "Well, my merry band now we are rested it is ever on. This is my Cousin Kate; she has not earned her nick name yet but I am sure she soon will."

"Actually dudes, I call her Blades." Harry smiled. "She is a radical swords woman."

"Well that settles it, everyone meet Blades."

Kate Lox was dressed in full brown woodsman clothing of tunic waistcoat, cloak, and two long thin sword handles protruded above her shoulders. Her short spiky blond hair gave her a boyish look, she smiled at everyone and her pale blue eyes twinkled. "Hey guys."

They all nodded and greeted her; Robbie looked to the trees ahead. "Right let's make a move today we go south, Pebbles you can take point, the rest of you, usual places. Rune, Alice stay close. Blades you follow with Steph. Right let's move out."

The group moved into the trees and mingled in to the background, and soon it was as if they were ghosts silently moving along unnoticed by any. Captain Smith stood with his Sergeant and watched as they disappeared. "He is very young, but did you feel his presence? I am telling you now Sergeant, in a few years he will be a very powerful man, and I actually think that will be a good thing. You just witnessed history Sergeant... Right let's get the men back it's almost breakfast time."

CHAPTER ELEVEN

SHOPPING WITH SMOOTH BILLY

They had been walking for over two hours and Robbie slowed his pace. Billy looked across at him. "What is up?" Robbie signaled the stop. Every one scattered and took cover, he stood and watched as the group just suddenly blended into the trees, and smiled to himself, as he saw how much they had all improved in such a short space of time.

Billy swiftly came over. "What is the matter Robbie, there is nothing around, why have we stopped?"

Robbie sat on the grass as Rune moved up closer. "Billy we are going in blind, I have no idea what Knox is up to or even where he is. I have to find some way of getting hold of up to date news."

"You know what we need pal don't you?" Billy glanced around. "We need a market where everyone is meeting and talking. It is where we always got to know what was going on."

Robbie smiled at Billy. "I cannot believe I did not think of that, of course anywhere people meet there is gossip."

"What about your new family member? This is her turf why not ask her." Billy nodded back at Blades who was crouched in the grass next to Steph. He seemed to look at her with distaste.

Rune looked up at Billy. "Don't you like her Billy? She seems quite sweet."

"A couple of flash swords don't make a warrior."

"Billy, I cannot believe it." Rune looked almost shocked and surprised. She gave a knowing smirk. "You are jealous of a young girl because she has two swords, which I might add are as precious to her as that pendant you wear, because they were a gift off her father." Rune frowned at him. "I expected better of you Billy."

"I am not jealous Rune." Billy snapped, and he seemed to be getting angry. "I don't see why we had to bring her. She is too young and will slow us down."

Robbie reached out and grabbed Billy's arm. "You trust me, don't you?" He spoke quietly and calmly.

Billy looked at Robbie. "What is that supposed to mean?"

"It means Billy, that it was my decision to bring her along. If you do not agree with me then let us talk about it. I hope you will not take this out on her Billy she is family and needs our protection."

Billy shrugged Robbie's hand off his arm. "Sorry just speaking my mind, I did not think it would upset you Lady Loxley." Billy got up and walked off. Robbie watched him as he wandered back into the trees.

Rune glanced back at Kate who looked nervous. "You need to talk to Billy and sort this out soon Robbie, I don't know what his problem is, but the quicker it is sorted the better. We have enough trouble."

"Yeah, I will." Robbie was still watching Billy, and was deeply puzzled by his behaviour. "Talk to Blades for me will you, and find out if there are any local villages or markets where we can find out what's going on, and tell Alice I want to talk to her will you."

Rune nodded and moved back towards the others. Robbie looked over at Billy who was sat with his back to a tree. Alice came over to him, and Robbie turned to the others. "We will take a break fan out and relax, but keep your eyes peeled."

Robbie turned to Alice. "Walk down here with me and tell me what is eating Billy up?" They walked into the trees out of sight of the others, there was a small stream and Robbie crouched down and washed his face.

"He was in a bad mood yesterday; I know he is in pain with his arm and maybe it is just that. I think he is restless; he has been in a funny mood recently."

Robbie sat on the bank and looked at his cousin, he had a lot of respect for Alice and he valued her opinion higher than most others. "Do you think he is jealous of me?"

Alice looked at the floor and Robbie knew he was right. Alice looked back at him and she fidgeted. "He loves you Robbie, and maybe he feels a little pushed out."

"Thanks Alice, I know how much you love him and would do anything to protect him. Your honesty to me does you justice; I know I put you in a tight spot, I am sorry."

Robbie stood up and turned back to camp, he walked quickly back through the trees, Alice jumped up and ran after him. "What are you going to do Robbie? Please don't fall out or fight."

Robbie stopped and looked back; Alice stood by a tall tree and nervously bit her lip as she wrung her hands. Robbie smiled at her. "I will do what I should have done a while ago." He smiled warmly at her. "Trust me."

He walked back into the camp past Rune, and Kate, and straight over to Billy. Robbie looked down at Billy who frowned up at him. "Walk into the woods with me Billy." Robbie walked off parting the trees as he went. Billy's reluctant steps followed him. When they were far enough away Robbie turned to face him. "I want you to know and understand now. I wanted none of this Billy, if I had my way, I would be sat at Joe's hut cleaning my knife after a good day's hunt with you."

Robbie kicked a large rock under a big shrub in frustration. "I am stuck with this Billy, it cannot be undone, now you either are, or you are not my brother and I need to know now. Can I depend on the one man I trust above all others?"

Robbie's eyes blazed as he spoke.

Billy looked at the floor. "I cannot believe you would have to ask me that."

"Neither can I but there you have it."

"I am sorry Rob, I didn't mean what I said, and I would never upset Rune, I was out of line."

Robbie's voice softened as he walked up and put his hand on Billy's shoulder. "You must always be honest with me; you above all, know that you can speak openly with me. Maybe I have not shown you the respect I hold for you and for that; I am also very sorry Billy. You are and always will be the only man I will want at my side. You are my brother and also a Loxley."

Billy looked up at Robbie's face and he smiled. Robbie patted his shoulder. "You know Billy suddenly I am Lord Loxley, and Alice is Lady Loxley, have you not realised that you are now Lord William Loxley? Just as our new family member is now Lady Katherine. You cannot avoid it forever, the mud sticks." He smiled at Billy and then left him to think as he made his way back to the camp.

Rune stood close to the tree as Robbie walked up, she looked nervously at him. "Is everything alright?" Robbie nodded.

"We needed to clear up a few points he will be fine now." Rune looked back at the trees from where Robbie had just walked and stared for a moment, and then turned and followed Robbie to the others.

Everyone was sitting on the floor spaced out in a wide circle; Harry had one of his boots off as he inspected a blister. It was still very early and the sun was starting to brighten into what looked like a warm day.

Robbie stood in the centre of the circle as Rune came up to his side. "I want all of you to gather round a moment." The group all stood up and closed in on Robbie, as Billy walked back through the trees. "I have been talking to my brother and we both feel that here in the woods that we are becoming isolated. We need news of the rest of the country, and my brother thinks it would be wise to find a market town, there we can mingle and find out what is going on." Everyone seemed to agree and nodded.

"Right, what we will do is divide into groups at the first town we find, it will not be wise to enter on mass. Billy will lead you all in and then we want you to circulate and get as much information as possible without being too obvious. When we all meet back up again, we will discuss our findings. Agreed?" Everyone smiled and nodded their heads. "Just in case they have it, only one glass of beer each, right let's get active."

Robbie stood up and Rune turned and looked up. "Is this really wise? They will be looking for you now the word is out." Robbie smiled at her.

"I will be safe I won't be going; Billy can handle this one and give me a day off." Rune smiled a huge happy smile. "Ooooh time alone."

Rune filled in Billy on the local market town, and Robbie assigned Kate to Billy as she had the local knowledge, he also thought by throwing them together it would help them to get to know each other; Harry was also going to be close to his daughter. They headed off through the woodland and after forty minutes of walking, they reached the town.

Robbie sat on an old stump at the edge of the small copse. He was sat high above the town at the top of a hill, and he looked down his telescope and out on the town. It was small with a few roads in and out but seemed quiet enough. As he looked through his telescope, he could see the market traders setting up for the day, as they unloaded their carts and placed their goods neatly on display. He passed Billy the scope.

"Right Billy, I will have a good view of you all, so if anything goes wrong, I will be able to get to you fast. Give everyone plenty of time to enjoy themselves, and find out what they can. Meet back here at dusk, this is your show enjoy it, but Billy be careful the word is out."

Billy handed back the scope and patted Robbie on the back. "Enjoy your day off, and I am very sure that you won't get bored, I would imagine Rune will see to that." Billy smiled, and set off to meet the others. "Just stop worrying we will be fine."

Robbie watched as Billy and Alice walked arm in arm down the slope to the town. Harry and Kate came out of the trees fifty yards further up with Eric and walked across the field. Five minutes later John and Martin walked in followed by Rowan and Steph. Jade he noticed was already there; she had skirted the town and was sat eating bread in the square.

Rune sat down beside him and hugged his leg. "It's going to be a long day." Robbie softly stroked her hair. "They all need a break it's been a long walk so far; I want a break too. I have not had time to really think about what is coming." He lay back in the grass and looked up at her smiling face and dancing blue eyes. "I will think later come here."

Rune cuddled up to him. "Happy?" She asked.

"Never happier." She kissed him softly.

The town was small with a dozen shops and a large market square with rows of wooden stalls. It had a small Town Hall and even an Inn. Here nature was not winning the fight and the plant life was still kept at bay and under control. The people who had survived the red death had also managed to keep their hometown intact. Roads were still concrete and tar with no cracks filled with trees. The paving was swept and orderly, and the houses free of ivy and clear of decay.

The market was busy and soon people were flowing in from every direction, the group mingled in and started to relax a little. It felt like a long time since they had left Loxley and soon, they were chatting and enjoying themselves as they toured the stalls, and haggled the prices down on things they needed. Alice had a large bag over her shoulder that now contained bread, some fresh veg and some cheese.

Steph looked at the jewellery and bought a small silver bangle for Rune, and a money pouch for Robbie. Jade felt uneasy and moved close to Rowan who was sat watching Steph just in front of him. "They have wanted posters up for Robbie." She handed one over to Rowan who glanced down at it.

"That is why he did not come; he knows how they think, although this disturbs me." Rowan pointed to a small line printed across the bottom.

All towns will be appointed new town marshals to bring order and justice to the country by order of Cornwall the newly appointed Governor of England.

Rowan looked around the market place. "Let everyone know Jade, they are now on the lookout for us."

Rowan walked up to Steph's side. "Keep your eyes open they have marshals looking for Robbie." Steph nodded and moved on to the next stall, glancing round to see if there was any sign. Martin sat with John at a small table outside the inn. John talked to an old trader who had left his wife on the stall and was having a quiet drink. Martin leaned forward watching the Town Hall.

There were men in blue tunics coming and going. The sight of similarly dressed people smacked of organisation, and although he could not see the badge on their tunic, he knew this could be dangerous. A large man in a long black coat came down the steps; he stopped as he spoke to an even larger brute sized man in blue. The man pointed across the market and Martin followed the line of sight to where Harry sat with Kate. Jade was making her way towards them when she spotted Martin watching.

Jade nodded, and then pointed two fingers to her eyes. Martin knew to watch, he leaned back and patted John on the shoulder, then picked up his bow. Harry sat with Kate on a bench at the side of the Market Square. He was thrilled having found a small set of spanners, and smiled at Kate. "I can fix that old Harley in your barn now." Jade dropped down at the side of them.

"Seen this?" Harry leaned forward and looked at the paper. The sun was blotted out as a tall man stood in front of them; he eyed Harry and Kate's samurai swords on their backs.

"Bounty hunters?"

Harry looked up. "Like you care man." The tall man had greasy matted hair, and his round fat face with an under trimmed moustache, broke into a ghastly black toothed smile.

"Actually, I do, this is my town now." He opened his jacket to reveal a blue tunic with a bright silver 'M' embroidered on it.

Jade looked at Harry and back up at the Marshal, she sized up his large frame, and looked at the silver sword hanging from his belt. Just inside his jacket, she could see the dagger in its sheath. "We want the reward money. There is nothing wrong with that." She smiled. "You have to earn a living using whatever skills you have." She lifted her bow slowly to her lap.

The Marshal smiled. "He is in these parts, bring him to me first and I will double it." Jade nodded.

"What about his men?"

"Fifty a piece, two hundred for the Runestone bitch, and five for him, and that's gold bits not silver."

Jade smiled and nodded. "We will be in touch."

The Marshal smiled, and heaved out his self-important chest. "I am in the Town Hall over there with my men whenever you need me." He walked off across the market. Jade signaled to Rowan who was watching carefully, she put two fingers to her eyes and then pointed to the tall man walking away in a long leather coat with the large silver sword hanging from his belt. Rowan nodded and grabbed Steph.

Billy was looking at new shirts, his was ripped, and even though Alice had sewn it back up it was still blood stained and he needed to replace it. Alice was pulling at a pile of coloured shirts, and slipped out a deep green heavy cotton shirt that had tie strings like Robbie's. "This one is really nice Billy." He picked it up and looked at it. He showed it the old woman behind the Stall.

"How much?"

She looked from side to side at it. "Five silver."

Billy smiled. "Three."

The old woman, looked poker faced and then grinned, she had no teeth. "You have a nice smile, four and it's yours."

Billy nodded and handed the money over. He gave her another smile, as Alice took his hand and they walked over to a seat on the edge of the square. Billy pulled his shirt slowly over his head, his arm really hurt and it was throbbing, and he struggled. Alice helped him slide his new shirt over his head. He tucked it into his pants and looked up as a sword touched his chin; he froze and slowly looked up. Alice screamed with surprise as she was pulled backwards, and hung wriggling in the arms of the large brute of a man in a blue tunic. His face was badly scared, with a long red line from his temple to his chin.

The Marshal slid his sword into the collar of Billy's new shirt, and pulled back the cloth to reveal his blood-stained bandage. Alice fought and struggled. "Been fighting have we?" Billy rose slowly to his feet.

Over the Marshal's shoulder, Martin watched, he nodded slowly to Billy. John was a few feet to his side.

"Had an accident when my axe head came off, that isn't a crime is it?" Five Marshals with drawn swords appeared in front of the crowd that had stopped and looked on. They tried to push them back away from Billy and the Marshal, as if expecting a fight. The Marshal watched Billy very closely; Billy's hand was on the hilt of his sword and his fingers twitched.

Stamping feet announced the arrival of a small squad of the Marshals men; all of them wore blue tunics and carried crossbows. The Marshal stepped back. "Fancy yourself with a sword do you Loxley?" He gave him a foul grin. "Yes, we know who you are Billy, and how you got hurt, the duke has faster ways of getting his news around than the post." The Marshal pulled a wanted poster with a very good likeness of Billy on it from inside his coat. "He wants you alive, aren't you the lucky one? I prefer barely myself; it makes for good sport."

Billy went for his sword, and over his head somersaulted a small figure, which landed in front of him like a cat. There was a flash of gold, and Blades spun her samurai swords in front of the Marshal. "Do pardon my intrusion but that's my cousin there, and I am sorry but he is late for dinner, we have to get home."

An arrow swished through the air and pierced the neck of the brute restraining Alice, the crowd gasped, and as he let go of Alice she shot in front of Billy. The brute fell gurgling to the ground, a large pool of blood seeped forward across the floor. The crowd murmured loudly; the Marshals head snapped to the direction the arrow had come from. Robbie and Rune stood on top of a cart, bows in hand, and hoods up pointing at the Marshal.

Hooded men appeared from nowhere alongside the Marshals men, their bows aimed at them. The men looked startled at the speed of their arrival, and they lowered their weapons, and let them fall to the floor. Robbie pulled back on his string of a newly fitted arrow. "You heard our cousin there, my brother is late for dinner, I would strongly suggest you lower your sword, you do not have to die today."

Harry climbed up on the cart. "Billy, dinner's getting cold." Billy slid his hand forward into Alice's hand, and slowly pulled her to the side, his eyes never left the Marshals.

"Go Alice, Blades move back." The Marshal's face looked fierce, and Billy kept his eyes locked on to his. Alice moved slowly backwards and Kate slowly walked swords up, until she was five paces away, both of them turned and ran to the cart. Billy held his ground until they were clear. He took one step slowly to the side. The Marshal screamed raising his sword, and lunged at him. Two long thin arrows pierced his chest as Billy sidestepped out of the way and turned to the cart. Robbie and Rune reloaded in a flash as Alice and Kate jumped up onto the back. Billy vaulted up behind Harry and slid over onto the seat at his side.

Robbie and Rune swung their bows over the crowd, as the others climbed on and aimed at the Marshals. "Tell Cornwall he has no business appointing himself as lord of this land, and if he wants peace, he had better find more qualified Marshals." The crowd cheered as Harry lashed the horses and the cart lurched forward.

Robbie and Rune dropped to their knees in the back of the cart and aimed at the Marshals men. None were stupid enough to pick up a crossbow. The cart raced out of town and Robbie winked at Rune. "Some day off eh?" He turned and climbed over the others to the front seat and slid down next to Billy. "You alright?" Billy slapped him on the leg and laughed.

"Now that's my idea of a shopping trip." He looked at Robbie. "Cheers Bro."

The cart hurtled at speed down the bumpy lane out of the town and everyone bounced around in it, until Jade shouted out in a very loud voice. "WHO THE HELL ARE YOU?" Followed by. "STOP THE BLOODY CART." Robbie turned around to Jade who had two strangers at knifepoint; their hoods down and pressed against the back of the cart. Kate had a sword drawn and was holding it at the throat of one of them.

Robbie blinked. "Who the hell are they? Harry stop the cart." Harry pulled hard on the reigns and the cart screeched to a halt, shuddering violently, and throwing everyone around. Kate pulled her sword back just in time to stop it slitting the throat of the man in front of her. He swallowed very deeply.

"We are friends," the first one shouted.

"We want to join you," shouted the other.

"There are horses coming," shouted Rune. Harry lashed the horses and the cart lurched forward again.

"You Stay there," shouted Robbie, hanging on to stop himself being tossed out of the cart. The cart whipped off at speed as two arrows hit the backboard and vibrated. The two men ducked behind the board. Jade forced one down with her knee and lifted her bow. John sat on the other and took aim out of the back of the cart. The others wedged themselves as best they could as the cart lurched and bounced around, and took aim at the horsemen who were gaining on them. Trees seemed to whip past as the cart gathered more and more speed. Harry lashed the horses harder.

The cart swung violently round a bend, an arrow shot above them, everyone clung to the sides and tried to fire. The cart leaned into another tight bend; Eric rolled across the cart and was snatched back by John's large hand. The road straightened and they recovered their stance and took aim. Jade laughed and screamed with delight, as Harry yelled from the front. "Hey man, there is this totally deep river and no bridge, it's going to get wet sudden like." A volley of arrows fired from the back of the cart, and Marshals fell from their horses, more carried on at great pace.

"Robbie man, I really need to kinda talk if you could like mosey on up here."

Robbie released his arrow and turned to see what Harry was shouting about. He saw the river, the lack of road, and screamed on the top of his voice.

"JUMMMMP!" The horses reared up, and the cart sailed into the air. There was an almighty splash, and the cart hit the water throwing everyone over board, as arrows whistled from the bank and embedded themselves in the cart.

Robbie sank rapidly looking around for all the others as they went under water. The cart was sinking fast, and Harry was going down with it as he cut at the horse's harness. They struggled free and headed upwards with Harry clinging on. Arrows shot into the water above him as he swam away. Robbie spotted Rune and swam towards her; he grabbed and pulled her up with him. They broke the surface ten yards down being carried by the current, and he gasped for new air in his lungs. The broken bridge was out of range and he kicked in the water as Rune gasped new air. She moved towards him and smiled. "I was going to ask about bathing arrangements."

Heads were popping up all over. "Let's get to the bank." Robbie shouted and everyone followed him to the stony riverbank, he crawled out and pulled Rune up. He lifted her out and then heaved John up who collapsed gasping on the grass. Harry flopped down breathing hard as Rune pulled Alice and then Kate out.

Harry sat up. "Wow man that was as intensely cosmic as it gets, I feel very spiritual at the moment." He lay back and breathed in more air.

Jade dragged herself up the bank laughing and screaming. "Wow Harry that was totally awesome man, we have got to try that again sometime. What a trip, I have not had a buzz like that since I fell off your bike last year."

Rune shook her head as she helped her mum up the bank. Robbie counted the bodies on the grass gasping for air, twelve. Which meant that with him, it was thirteen? He looked back at the grass and spotted the patched tan cloak. He put his foot on the chest of the man gasping for breath and his sword to his throat. The man looked up. "Haven't we done this already?"

"Just exactly who are you, and why did you climb on the cart?"

"My name is James Ashford and that cart was my property, in fact it was the only possession I had until a minute ago."

"Where is your friend?"

"That friend was my younger brother Anthony, and he won't leave his horses, which I believe your good companion here saved, I thank you."

Harry sat up. "It's like a real pleasure man. I like beasts and things."

Robbie released his foot. "Let's get under cover; if they come down the bank over there, we are sitting ducks here." Dripping and starting to breathe at a normal rate, the group sat up and began to organise themselves. They moved under cover of the trees into a small clearing. Robbie looked across at James as he sat down, Jade was close to him her bow in her hand ready. "Ok James tell me, does that river get shallow enough to cross anywhere near here?" James wrung his cloak out.

"The nearest crossing is about eight miles north, it will take them at least two hours to get here, the ground is so boggy they would have to walk the horses. I think we are safe, they won't bother, not after you killed their boss."

Robbie collapsed next to Rune. "We better light a fire and post some lookouts."

Billy had a fire going in minutes and they hung their cloaks on nearby trees to drip. Martin and Rowan took first look out duty, Jade slipped off with Eric to hunt. Alice sat down next to Robbie, she still had her shopping bag round her neck, and Robbie peered in at the bread. "Looks like damp toast tonight." She smiled a sad smile.

"Robbie, we have lost some of our bows and a lot of arrows." Robbie thought for a moment. Billy leaned over.

"I can dive for them later and get most of our stuff out of the cart it won't be that difficult." Alice seemed relieved that she would get her bag back.

Slowly they began to dry out and organise, Billy and Harry took James back up to the bridge, Billy left his shirt to dry by the fire. Robbie slipped his off and when it was dry, he handed it Rune. She moved into the trees and took off her wet one, and slipped on Robbie's dry shirt, Alice did the same. They all kept close to the fire as they slowly dried out.

Billy, James, and Harry returned a little time later with the bows, arrows, and all their bags. All the blankets were soaking wet and most of the food was spoiled. The fresh veg Alice had bought was added to a large pan, which was not theirs, but James had found it in the river, and the food was set to simmer on the fire. Harry was very impressed with James and had nick named him Fish. "Man, he was under there for ages; it was like he could totally breathe water, whoa that was cosmic."

It appeared that James had officially joined them, without any word from Robbie, Harry's endorsement, and addition of a nickname had brought him into the group. Robbie sat with his back to a tree; Rune lay across his legs keeping close to the fire so she could dry her pants, her boots steamed at the fire edge. Billy sat down next to Robbie. "Thanks Rob thanks Rune. I was really worried back there. I knew he was going to go for me; my arm is so stiff I would have not been able to get my sword out quick enough."

Rune looked up from Robbie's lap. "I hope you thanked Blades? She was quite cool with that jump and those swords, she bought you enough time for Robbie and me to set up and cover you, and without her Billy you would be dead now."

Billy nodded. "I was out of line with you this morning. I am sorry, and yes I will make it up to Blades."

Rune smiled. "That was this morning it's forgotten, I will say this for you Billy, you were very brave today, the way you got the girls away from him and fronted him out was pretty smooth."

Billy laughed. "Smooth I was shaking in my boots."

Rune smiled at him. "It didn't show, maybe we should rename you Smooth Billy."

Robbie smiled. "Hey everyone seeing as Kate there lived up to her name, she will keep the title of Blades." Kate started to blush and put her head down. "From now on Billy the sword here will be Smooth Billy in light of his ability to fool you all into thinking he is brave."

Everyone started to laugh, and smooth stuck, Billy winked at Rune. "Smooth I can live with."

Shortly before dusk Jade walked into the clearing with Anthony, and a small hog on her shoulder. "Look who I found?" She threw the hog on the floor. "I also caught me a live hog, well he smelt like one in the cart, now he has had a bath he is bearable."

Everyone laughed including Anthony; James leapt from the floor and pulled his brother into a hug. After going back to the river and not finding him, he had been sure he had drowned. The hog was roasted over the fire and the group sat around to eat. Robbie cut off a chunk of meat and sat watch, so that Rowan could eat. Steph sliced off the meat and passed it round. Somehow, she had earned the role and title of Mother; everyone would politely nod when she passed them their food and say, "thank you mother." Steph smiled at them, and was in a way quite flattered at the respect she got from such a wide range of people.

That night they posted four guards to watch. The cloaks and blankets were almost dry, and so with four on watch, they could share the dry bedding evenly. Rune sat with Robbie and Steph, as the others settled down. Robbie laughed, and Rune looked him. "What?"

"Two nights ago, we were eleven, last night twelve and tonight fourteen; I wonder how big we will be in a month."

Steph leaned her head back and looked at the stars through the trees. "Excuse the pun, but it is like a river that starts as a few drops, and runs down a rock gathering other drops. Soon it's a stream running into other streams and by the time it gets to where it's going, it is a river with a huge amount of force." Robbie smiled as he watched the fire.

"You are gathering momentum Robbie, Knox is worried enough to set up town Marshals and put up wanted posters, you must have him very worried indeed." Rune sounded almost miles away, as if she was thinking as she spoke, she turned to him her eyes filled with concern.

"How did they know we would be there today?"

Steph suddenly sat up; she grabbed the small shoulder pouch and opened it. "Robbie it's gone." She opened the bag and showed him. The map wrapped in brown paper was not there somehow, someone had taken it.

Robbie smiled. "Well that will confuse him for starters, but as to how he knew, that Marshal said he had quicker ways of getting news than the post. I wonder what he meant by that?"

Steph turned her head. "You are forgetting Robbie that Knox wants to return to the old modern ways that he knew. He will be bringing in as much as he can to get this world back to as near as he could to his old life. Knox has not learned from the red death. My father always said it would be the one thing that brought him down; he has no idea how to live as we do. He wants all those comforts that made the people of the past forget who they were. We can never return to those times, we have to restore the balance with nature, because if we don't, she will do it again and man may not survive next time."

Long after Rune and Steph were asleep, he sat awake watching the camp. It was in a way painful to know that one of this group who each day he was growing to love, was going to betray them all. He stared at the fire as it died down lower, and he thought of each member of the group. In all honesty he could not believe that any of them would betray him. Trust only your kin and my daughters, seemed to sound through his head. Yet he did trust them all.

So far, there had been moments that required total faith and every one of them had come through for him. He began to fully appreciate and understand the burden of responsibility that his father had shouldered for years. Here he was on the edge of his own coming of age and yet now he was seen as a leader of men, and had become almost overnight a famous person throughout the land, it just seemed so surreal to him.

He got up quietly so as not to disturb Rune, and poured a drink from the pot on the fire and walked over to Jade and Rowan who were sat with their backs against a tree. They spoke quietly as they watched the darkness; Robbie came up and crouched at their side. "How goes it?"

Jade looked up. "It's pretty quiet don't worry nothing will pass us two." Robbie smiled at her, Jade had grown in stature over the past week, that little misfit who wandered around Loxley had found her place in the world and he was glad it was beside him. "I am going to turn in, wake me if you hear anything."

"Ok Robbie will do." He patted her softly on the shoulder.

"Good night Pebbles, night Rowan." He walked over to the sleeping Rune and sat beside her. He pulled his cloak round himself and let his head lean back on the tree trunk. Robbie looked up and watched the stars gently twinkle through the gap in the canopy of the trees. The night slipped on.

It was over an hour later, when Jade came back through the trees towards Rowan with two more cups. She lowered herself down at the side of him and passed him the drink. "Here this will warm you up." Rowan gratefully took the cup and cupped it in his hands. He stared into the darkness, his eyes alert and focused. Jade watched him, Rowan fascinated her and she found his company peaceful.

Jade's eyes slowly scanned over him, from his long black silky hair, which had two fine plaited braids down the front, that held his hair off his almost chiselled face, to the strands of blonde plaited hair that made a chain round his neck. She found him very mysterious and interesting, there was a story to tell about Rowan and she felt she wanted to hear it. Why was the left shoulder of his faded burgundy shirt torn and roughly darned? Why did he wear a woven leather belt, and not a thick strap one like the others? Who made the coloured plaited woollen bracelets around his wrists, and why did he keep his silver dagger in his boot and not in his belt? The knife in his belt was just a plain woodman's knife; she thought the silver dagger would be safer in the belt sheath than a boot.

The moon passed behind a cloud and he darkened. She leaned back on the tree trunk her mind filled with theories about her strange companion. Jade did not really realise that she was asking the question. "You loved her deeply, didn't you?"

Rowan moved in the darkness, and Jade could just see the light in his eyes as he peered through the dark. "That life is over, I have no past, and I am now Rowan of the woods and servant of the Green Lord." Jade thought that there was still an air of sadness to his words.

"Rowan, I mean no offence, but who was she that she could cast such pain and sadness across you? I have watched you since you have been with us and I admire your craft. You should have happiness in your heart at the wonder of the world around you, I am saddened that your life holds no joy."

"I have given up my past, and now only serve the present. Do not be saddened on my account. That life has passed, and is done forever."

"You say that Rowan, but you are not honest. I see how at night the pain returns; will you not share it with me? I would hope you would consider me your friend as I do you."

The cloud passed over, and the moon came back out. Jade saw the saddened eyes so deep and sorrowful, and yet he had the traces of a faint smile. "You do me great honour Jade of Avon, I appreciate your kind words, for they are indeed the words of a friend."

Jade gave him a big smile. "I can sew that properly if you want?" Rowan's smile widened and he leaned back to the tree. Jade relaxed again and stared out into the forest, she breathed softly as she watched the darkened gaps between the trees. The feeling of peace from Rowan washed over her.

"She was my younger sister, and they slaughtered her." Rowan's voice was almost a whisper, yet the pain in the words tore at Jade's heart.

A twig snapped in the forest a few yards in front of them, Rowan was up with Jade behind him, bows loaded and aiming. "Who goes there? Announce yourself or I will shoot." Jade scanned down the arrow as she panned the ground in front of her from right to left. There was more snapping of twigs and she saw movement, the arrow sung into the trees there was a cry of pain. Rowan stepped up to her side as she advanced towards where her arrow had found its mark.

The sounds behind her announced the presence of Martin and Billy, as both flanked wide whilst Jade and Rowan entered into the gap in the trees. Rowan spotted the dark lump on the floor, and he pointed his bow down towards it.

Carefully Jade pushed her foot to the body and gave it a shove. She pulled out a knife and slowly crouched down; her arrow was sticking out of the back between the shoulder blades. Jade lifted the arm and pulled, and the body rolled over snapping the arrow, she gasped. "You know this man?" Rowan was down at her side. Jade nodded. "This is Oscar Hargreaves, the bookseller from Loxley."

Robbie and Rune walked up to the trees holding burning torches, Rune gasped as she saw the face of the man on the floor. Robbie crouched down and looked over at Jade, who was looking very shocked. "Robbie I just killed Mr Hargreaves, I didn't know, it was dark and he did not respond to our call. I thought he was a Cutter."

"I have a funny feeling he was, check his pockets Jade." Jade slid her hands across him and then pushed her hand inside his jacket. She pulled out a package wrapped in brown paper and handed it to Robbie. Rune looked down at Robbie understanding the full implication of what had just happened. She was about to speak when Robbie nodded.

He slipped the package into his shirt and looked at Rowan. "We should bury him quickly." Rowan's eyes met Robbie's, and the understanding was there.

Martin and Rowan lifted the body, and walked off into the trees. Robbie headed back with Rune, Jade and Billy walked behind them.

"I cannot believe it Billy, we have known him all our lives, and how the hell did he get all the way out here?" Billy shook his head and looked up to Robbie.

"What is going on Rob? None of this makes sense, what does an old collector of books have to do with all of this? Why is he sneaking around in the dark?"

Robbie stopped and looked at Rune, he quietly asked. "Is your mum listening in?" Rune nodded. He turned to Billy and Jade. "We knew back at the stockade someone was passing information out to Knox, well I think that is a question we can now answer. I am not too happy to find we have been tracked, Billy from now on I want you at the back making sure that we are safe; Harry is not up to it. We cannot afford a mistake this important again; we are getting sloppy and need to clean up our act."

Billy nodded to Robbie. "There is a bright side to this though Rob, at least from now on Knox will be as much in the dark about us, as we are him." It was a good point and gave Robbie a little hope, he felt angry that he had allowed them to be followed. From the moment they had left Loxley, Knox must have known his movements, now he understood how Billy had been spotted by the Marshals, and why groups of Cutters had been in the woods near the priory. He felt a little relief, but knew that from tomorrow he needed to get his act together.

Robbie sat with Steph and Rune; he could see Alice and Billy talking across the fire. He knew Billy had been shaken, he had not said it but it showed as he watched him talking to Alice, Robbie knew that Billy would be more vigilant than ever. It was comforting to know he would be watching his back. Rune leaned on to him. "Come on Rob do not dwell on it."

He put his arm round her and pulled her closer. "We almost lost Billy and Alice today, and we only just escaped the Marshals. We have come too close; the whole point of this was to use stealth. Mason has been in our footprints from day one, I don't know if I am really up to this job, I still think my dad would have handled things better."

Steph sat up. "Give yourself a break Robbie, your dad and John tried everything to find out who was leaking information out of Loxley, and they came up short as well. We have a golden opportunity here to improve our situation; I have spent most of the day sat by the fire slowly drying out. It has given me enough time to think, and it appears that we travelled more distance in the cart in a few minutes, than we did in an hour on foot."

Rune nodded. "I was thinking that, we need to speed things up and get transport, it will put us further south than Mason realises, and it might just give us an advantage." She looked up at Robbie. "What do you think?"

Robbie seemed to be miles away he blinked at Rune. "How did he get the map out of Steph's pouch? It has been on her all the time, and if he had got it earlier, why would he still be around here? I would have left with it to get it to Knox."

"Maybe he got it tonight when I was asleep. I was further back than everyone else was; he could easily have crept in and lifted it. Maybe that is why he was trying to get away when Jade saw him and fired." Steph seemed convinced.

Robbie thought about it, considering the facts it was possible, except that Steph had missed it long before they settled down. "Everyone is getting too complacent; we need to sharpen up or Mason will have all of us before we know it." Robbie kicked hard at a log and it rolled into the fire, he leaned back against the tree and let out a long sigh. "How did an old man stay up with a cart, and where can we steal another?"

Rune sat up and looked at him. "Is it time to rob from the rich?"

"You know, I think it may well be, now if I knew where the hell I was, I would know where to find one."

"Ask Alice she never gets lost." Rune cuddled up to him. "It's getting cold, hold me close Robbie."

CHAPTER TWELVE

FAR SIGHT, GRAVESIDES AND GRAIN

The cold and the previous days soaking had taken its toll by morning. Billy piled the fire high to get a roaring blaze going as everyone shivered and ached. The group huddled around the fire moaning. The only thing to smile about was Hog had nipped off early, and had returned with three-dozen eggs. Eric went straight to work using the remains of Jade's cooked hog from the night before, and soon he was frying eggs and bacon as everyone sat drooling waiting in turn for theirs.

The smell wafted through the clearing and Rune stirred next to Robbie. She was somewhere under the blankets and cloaks, he had pulled round her in the night as she shivered, and he heard little muffled groans from underneath as she slowly and painfully by the sound of it, came to life.

The cloaks and blankets parted and a mass of red and gold tangled hair popped through it. "Oh Robbie, I hurt." A leg appeared further down as she stretched, and then an arm. "Oh this is awful." She slowly sat up and pulled her hair from her face, it stood up in every direction.

"Good morning." He smiled at her.

"What's good about it?" Eric handed Robbie two plates and nodded to Rune. She slowly came up from beneath the blankets.

Robbie handed her a plate and a fork. "Bacon and eggs My Lady?"

Rune coughed and took the plate off him. "God that smells good." Robbie smiled as he watched her tuck into the food. Steph sat up just at the side of them her eyes still closed, and sniffed.

"Oh please tell me that is bacon." She opened her eyes and blinked, Alice passed her a plate. "Ohhh fried eggs as well." A look of extreme pleasure passed over her face. "I feel like I have been without a proper breakfast for weeks."

Robbie stood up and stretched, and every bone in his body screamed. "Coffee ladies?" Both of them nodded.

"Mmmmmm yes please."

Robbie could hardly walk he was so stiff, and he staggered to the fire. He looked at the group who all appeared the worst for wear, except Hog who looked just about the same as he had yesterday. He picked up the pot and poured three coffees out. Bending back up was a painful affair. Blades walked into the camp in shorts and a vest with a towel rubbing her short hair. "Morning all," she chimed cheerfully.

Martin looked up at her. "Where have you been?"

Blades pointed behind her. "I have been for a swim."

"Are you mad its freezing?" Billy looked horrified.

Blades stood against the tree and lifted her leg up to her face, and pushing her arms up she stretched. Billy shrunk as if in pain. "I love to swim when I can." She dropped her leg and shook. "It really wakes you up and gets the muscles working." She did a high kick.

Robbie handed Steph and Rune their coffee, Steph watched as Blades practiced kicks and punches in slow motion. "You know she has a sort of oriental look about her don't you think...? I mean, I know she has blue eyes and blonde hair and all that but there is a quality about her."

Harry leaned over from the log he was sat on. "Her mum was half Japanese man, totally weird dude her dad, he would shrink trees so they were more his height and make him look taller."

"He did Bonsai?" Alice was very interested.

Harry's face went blank as he thought. "Dun know man, but he shrunk trees. Weird man and not cosmic at all."

"Harry Bonsai is when you shrink trees."

"Wow man, now that is totally cosmic."

Alice shook her head and rolled her eyes at Rune, who giggled as she sipped her hot coffee. Robbie was slowly coming back to life as the caffeine started to act, he stood back up and stretched again, it was a little less painful. Rune dragged her bag over and rooted around in it; she pulled out a mirror and squeaked. "God, I look a state." Robbie smiled as he headed off to find John, and Rune pulled a brush out of her bag and began to rake her hair to free up the tangles.

John was sat quite far out of camp in amongst some bracken; Robbie almost walked past him, and would have done if John hadn't greeted him. Robbie came up beside him. "I hear you had a good long chat with one of the local traders yesterday? Were you able to find out anything useful?"

John looked doubtful. "I am not sure what use the news I have will be, but I was told that this Mason bloke wants to defeat York and Loxley in the north, and Gloucester and Bristol down south, because there is opposition to him ruling over the whole country. There was also a place in Wales a Carly something, but I cannot remember." John stared into the trees as if trying to think.

"His army is huge now and he thinks he will just sweep the land. Those who oppose him are killed or kidnapped and end up dead. He is creating Marshals in every town so that he can impose order, and spy on the locals to stop them opposing him."

Robbie smiled. "If all your news appears to you as useless as that then please tell me John, because you have helped me a great deal thank you." Robbie patted him on the back. "I will get you some relief and you can have something to eat."

Robbie returned to camp and spoke with Martin, and he got up and went to replace John. Everyone seemed to be more alive now and they were happily joking around as they moved about and stretched the aches from their bones.

Rune sat on an old log her long red hair hung softly down her back, she had plaited two long plaits at the front of her hair and was pinning them back behind her head as he approached. Robbie smiled he loved to see her hair braided back.

She looked up sweetly at him and smiled; he bent down and kissed her. "I love you too." She softly spoke as her eyes danced at him. Robbie straddled the log and faced her, he told her what John had told him, and then he asked.

"Will your family have any more news than this? We need every scrap we can get." Rune sat still for a moment, he noticed how the colour in her eyes intensified. He felt spell bound as he watched the blue of her pupils intensify and the whites of her eyes became purple.

"Jett Hear me, Aunt Scarlet Hear me."

Rune's mind opened and the picture of Jett's eyes looked in, and another pair of black, lilac surrounded eyes opened.

"Rune my darling, how are you? Hey cousin I hear you."

Rune told them what she had heard and waited. Scarlet spoke.

"Tell your hooded man that we are grateful for this information, if Mason attacks us he will have to defeat Bristol first, I will send a messenger to them to warn them. Gloucester is a mighty opponent; the duke there will not bend to Mason's ways. Loxley is still safe although we heard that last night Mason's men arrived and set up camp in Hathersage, it will not be long before he makes a move. Tell your hooded man that most of the area is behind the walls now, and the gates have been sealed. His father has over a thousand men at his command. Loxley will not fall easily. Rune you must encourage your sister to accept her powers now, it feels like she is resisting them. Moreover, you are now almost at full power. You are becoming the centre of us all and we need Jade to join, to give us the power that will aid your hooded man. You will hear from grandmother soon and she will reveal all. I will talk to you soon my darling."

"Hey Rune, found me a hunk yet?"

"I have just the man for you Jett, he joined us yesterday I think you will really find him the man for you."

"Oh god really? What is he called and what is he like?"

"He is certainly all man and that is for sure, his name is Anthony".

Steph who was sat a few yards away burst into laughter; Alice gave her a funny look.

"Jett, I have to talk to Robbie now, but I will tell Anthony all about you I

promise."

"Great I can't wait, talk to you soon cous."

"Yeah, see you Jett."

Rune opened her eyes and smiled at Robbie. The purple faded back to lilac in the whites of her eyes. "Loxley is safe, your dad has over a thousand men and the gates are sealed."

Robbie breathed a deep sigh of relief, and put his arms around her. "Thank you, I really needed to hear that." She stroked his hair back and hugged him.

"I told you he would be safe... Listen Robbie my aunt says that the Duke of Gloucester is a tough opponent, and Bristol will not fall easily, my family are at Caerleon and will only be in danger if Bristol falls, so we have time yet to get south." She turned to Steph who was still chuckling. "Jett deserves a taste of her own trickery, but you almost gave it away."

"I am sorry sweetheart, but you did really surprise me, I thought you were talking about Rowan... When you mentioned Hog... I mean Anthony, I couldn't help laughing."

Rune smiled. "It will be fun when she meets him."

Steph giggled. "Oh, I think it certainly will."

Robbie watched the two of them without a clue of what they were talking about. Rune turned back to him and he pulled her close. "You know that thing where your eyes go purple?"

Rune looked worried. "Yeah!"

Robbie hesitated. "Well can you only do it when you talk to your family?"

Rune shrugged. "I am not sure why?"

Robbie winked. "It's really sort of sexy."

Rune smiled and pulled him back for another hug. "We will have to find out."

Half an hour later Robbie sat in front of the fire and addressed his men. "Well ladies and gents so far we have survived the trials that have been set us." Everybody smiled. "And yet last night someone walked into this camp unchallenged. No one knows how long they were here, but the fact remains that they should not have made it past our outer defences. That is bad enough, but to discover that the person was also from Loxley and has tracked us from day one is the worst news any of us should hear."

The whole group looked solemn. "Each of you is now worth fifty gold bits alive or dead. We are now hunted men and women, and we have become complacent and sloppy. From this moment on we must guard our every move and try to be as elusive as possible, to ensure that Mason Knox and his merry little bunch do not find us so easily again."

Robbie stood up. "We strike camp in ten minutes, Pebbles and Rowan you take point and head south. Billy clear the rear, and show Eric how to do it properly.

John, you run left and give pointers to Hog. Martin will you show Blades how to cover left?" He looked round the camp. "Everyone else fan through the middle. Fish I want you with me while we speak. Alright let's leave this camp like this place has never been touched; you know what to do, let's make it happen."

Fish wandered over to Robbie and Rune as they gathered their things. "Fish you know this area well?"

James nodded. "I have lived all over these parts."

"I need transport for fourteen, I want to rest everyone and move us all south as quickly as possible, you got any ideas?"

James rubbed his chin. "There is a farm about ten miles south west of here that supplies grain to Knox. He has large carts that will easily carry all of us. I would think that he deserves a visit more than most. He won't sell grain to any of the locals, he only sells to Knox."

Robbie smiled as Rune slid her arm in his. "I think Fish has found you a Prince John."

"Indeed he has... Billy!" Robbie waved him over.

Ten minutes later Robbie and Billy were sat with Fish, as he had drawn out a plan of the farm and the roads leading into it, one of the roads led into the woods, it was perfect.

Robert and John Lox stood on the covered platform high above the gates and looked out. The crunches of marching feet headed up the road from Hathersage. Len came up the steps his scarlet cloak and white hair blowing in the breeze. "Well gents, it appears the time has finally arrived." He watched as the army of two hundred foot soldiers tramped in lines of rank slowly towards the large dusty square before the gates of Loxley. Len closed his eyes and concentrated.

"Hear me daughter of the woods."

The group now seemed full of high spirits as they made their way through the trees. The sun was starting to rise and the day was warming, Robbie watched, as Martin instructed Blades. She was starting to settle into the group and he smiled as he saw Martin show her how to pass the lower trees without breaking them. He turned to Rune. "They have all settled well together don't you think?"

"Martin is wasting his time." Rune watched Blades as she wove through a dense thicket. "That one has been trained by someone far superior to him; she is just being good natured and going along with it." Rune smiled. "They are good people Robbie." Her face seemed to cloud and her eyes began to sparkle as deep shades of purple washed over the whites of her eyes. Rune seemed to swoon and Robbie caught her.

"Rune what is it...? Steph!"

Steph was already on her way up to them, and she quickly took hold of Rune and glanced at Robbie. "Somebody very powerful is trying to contact her." Rune seemed to recover a little as she put her hand to her head.

"I am fine, caught me off guard that's all." Rune closed her eyes as Robbie still clung on to her.

"I hear you Grandfather."

"Rune darling, I have no time to explain, you need your mother and Jade, get them quickly. I also want Robbie."

Rune opened her eyes; Steph was already turning to Alice. "Get Jade and fast." The group had halted and melted into the trees, concerned looks came back from between the leaves. Robbie pulled Rune close, as Steph put her hands to Rune's face.

"Sweetheart what you are feeling is a very great power, just relax and let it flow through you, do you understand?" Rune nodded, the whites of her eyes now had become such a deep purple it was hard to tell where the blue began or ended. Robbie slid his arm around as her feet steadied and she began relax and let the power to flow through her, she closed her eyes and focused.

"Grandfather do not sneak up on me like that, you almost blew me off my feet."

"Rune listen carefully, get everyone to join in a circle and hold hands, there are things here they must see. Your power is not strong enough yet and so I will need your mother and sister. Robbie must see with his own eyes what will befall here."

"Alright Grandfather, Jade is here."

Rune took the hand of the very alarmed looking Jade, and then she took hold of Robbie's, Steph completed the circle. Rune lowered to her knees and the others followed. She closed her eyes and relaxed, green wisps of light flicked in her mind.

"Is that you Jade?"

"Rune how are you doing this? Don't its freaky."

"My children relax and see what I see, open your minds and allow Lord Loxley to see and hear all before me."

"Granddad is that you, how are you doing this?"

"Jade please your mother will explain later. Just do as I say."

Rowan watched as the circle knelt down on the grass facing each other. Billy came up and Alice slid to his side. Rune opened her eyes and the wood flooded with violet light, it was blinding, and everyone fell to the ground shielding their eyes.

Robbie was nervous, and yet he felt the overwhelming presence of Rune all around him. It felt happy, loving, and gentle and his nose filled with scents of sweet flowers and wild cherries. He knew she was there and she loved him. He felt the surge of feeling he held deep down inside him flow to her. 'I love you Rune' coursed through his brain, and the pictures came. They were blurry at first.

Robbie looked around in amazement. He was stood at the side of his father and John high above the gates. He felt strange and disorientated. He looked at his hands they were older and thinner.

"Robbie relax you are seeing through my grandfather, I am here with you, there is nothing to fear."

He took a long deep breath, and he found himself back with his father. He looked out across at the road leading to the square in front of the gates. Row upon row of men with arms gathered in black shirts that bore the emblem of a bright red dragon. Each had a helmet of round steel and a shield of silver. A man in all black with a plume of yellow feather on his hat rode on a white horse slowly towards the gates. "Open the gates in the name of The Duke of Cornwall and newly elected Governor of England and its Isles."

John turned to Robert. "Newly elected, I didn't vote for him."

Robert stepped forward and looked down at the horseman. "This is the Loxley Estate and is private property. State your name and your business horseman, and remove your mob from our doorstep, at which point we will consider your request."

The horseman looked perplexed. "I do not think you quite understand, I am not asking you, I am telling you to open the gates."

John looked down at the horseman and back at his brother. "Not too bright this one, is he?" He looked back at the horseman. "State your name and your business or suffer the consequences."

"I am General Turner, the head of the newly formed army and protector of England."

"Well at this moment you are a trespasser, and you are the ones who will need protecting if you don't talk quickly. Why are you on our ground?"

General Turner suddenly looked a little unsure of himself. "My commander in chief, The Duke of Cornwall has a message for the Lord Loxley; I seek an audience with him."

Len Rimmer stepped forward. "Lord Loxley can both see and hear you, state your request and withdraw your men." Robert and John both looked suspiciously at him. Len winked at them and smiled. "Strangely enough my good friends he truly is here."

The General shouted up at the gates. "The Governor of England has banned all walled communities, and formally requests that Robert of Loxley lay down his arms and accept his venerable invitation to join him. In return the Governor, when he succeeds to the throne of England will award Robert of Loxley these lands and his rightful title."

John lent forward. "Are you telling me your boss wants to give us what we already have, is he mad?"

"Sir watch your words, our Governor is a kind and noble ruler, and if you soil his name such, I will be forced to act."

Robert Lox stood high and looked down at the General. "You sit at my door with an army, and threaten those who live here in peace under the arm of Lord Loxley. Go and tell that self-appointed lunatic that if he wants these lands, he will need a bigger army than this." Robert Lox drew an arrow from his quiver and fitted it to his bow. John drew his sword and held it up high. One hundred bowmen appeared along the high wall of Loxley, their arrows fitted, and hoods over their faces as they aimed.

Robert bellowed across the square. "Withdraw now or suffer the land of Loxley."

The General turned on his horse. "You have been warned," and his horse reared up and charged back to the army of black. The soldiers braced, and raised their shields. They began to move forward.

John dropped his sword and a hail of arrows flew into the air. Every arrow found its mark and the soldiers of Cornwall fell to the ground. The men of Loxley reloaded and took aim, the soldiers slowed as a bugle sounded. They began to withdraw backwards slowly. General Turner raised his sword. "I shall return Loxley."

Roberts bow sung, and the arrow shot through the air like a missile. It entered the knuckle, passed through the sword handle and came out of the palm of the General's hand. He screamed in pain unable to drop his sword as the blood splashed all over his legs. The horse reared and bolted, throwing him to the ground where he writhed in agony.

Robert turned to John. "I can't stand a man that waves a sword at me, next time he will think better." Robbie heard the voice of Len Rimmer.

"That will do for now My Lord."

Robbie felt a sudden lightness, and the pictures and sound disappeared. He opened his eyes.

H er face was very pale, and her dusky freckles seemed darker. Her eyes were the brightest and most beautiful of blue, and they floated in a stream of lilac. Her smile was all he needed at that moment, nothing else seemed to matter, he put his arms around her and pulled her close, and smelled the sweet violets. Her voice was soft and quiet and meant only for him. "I felt it, all of it, and now I know how deeply you love me." She squeezed him very hard.

Jade sat exhausted on the grass. "What the hell just happened to me?" Steph sat down beside her and put her arms around her.

"Jade my darling we are of an ancient line as I have said many times. All of us have certain gifts of which one is the ability to communicate using our thoughts. Rune has a greater power than all of us; she will become the centre of all of us, and through her, our power will be increased. You my darling have had to wait just as your cousin Ruby has had to wait. Now will be the time of you coming to power and soon you will learn what gifts have been bestowed on you."

Rune slid slowly out of Robbie's arms. "We should move, you have men to lead and our task is now more urgent. Loxley will only be safe for a short time before they decide to attack with more force."

Robbie stood up and looked at Alice and Billy. Billy smiled. "I am not even going to ask you what just happened... Rune next time your face decides to explode with purple light, warn me will you, it almost blinded us."

Rune looked at Billy and then Alice. "Was it that bad?"

"Lit the whole forest up and none of us could see a thing." Alice smiled. "It was kinda cool."

Steph stood up and lifted Jade to her feet. "Will you be alright now?" Jade nodded and walked over to Rowan. He placed his arm across her shoulders and walked her slowly up to the front and into the wood.

"Will you be alright Pebbles?"

Jade had a lost look on her face as she looked up at him; her voice was quiet and a little distant. "You called me Pebbles."

Rowan smiled. "Friends do."

Jade gave him a huge smile. "Let's get moving... Thanks Rowan." Together they picked up the path and headed south working their way quietly through the woods, leading Robbie and the group forward. Robbie walked slowly through the woodland his eyes keenly watching the others as they silently made their way through a particularly thick patch of undergrowth. Rune followed fifty feet behind him, her mother at her side.

"Your powers are almost complete now; you received your grandfather's gifts today."

Rune looked at her mother. "What gifts are they?"

Steph nodded. "Those gifts are not from our line, I cannot say what they will be, but I know that your grandfather saw in you the power to wield them. That Rune my darling is why you were chosen above Jett and Jade who are older than you."

"So, my grandfather has power of another line, not ours?"

"The line of your grandfather is even older than ours, and even now I truly do not know his full powers, but I do know he is very powerful and Knox fears him, as he also fears you."

Rune stopped and looked at her mother. "Me... Why does he fear me?"

"You are the stone on which all has been written Runestone Sapphire; your grandparents are the meeting of two lines of ancient power. Individually Knox might have had a chance to defeat them. But together you will be a match worthy of the fight."

"I have to fight him?" Rune was shocked and looked at her mother wide eyed.

Steph smiled at her. "Are you not already?"

"I am here because I love Robbie, and want to help him."

"Then Rune my darling you are already fighting him. You must understand

Rune there are not just sides at work here. There are also two ways of life, his and yours, and Robbie is fighting for a world that embodies the life he has chosen. You are a part of that life and so you share the same cause. At some point balance must be achieved, and Robbie believes that Knox will tip the scales away and destroy all that is good in this world."

"Robbie never chose this task; it was put upon him by the fellowship."

"Do you really believe that Runestone? Robbie chose this task the day he turned to his father and asked to go hunting. He was always destined to become a bowman, he had more talent than any, but when he asked if Joe would show him the way of a woodsman, we all knew he was the one. For there has only ever been one other who has excelled at both, he began that line when he took his mother's name above his fathers and called himself Loxley."

"What must I do to protect him Mother?"

Steph lifted her hand and touched her daughters face. "My sweet and beautiful daughter I felt the same emotions as you did today. You have already given him everything he will need to fulfil his task." Her eyes filled with tears as she spoke. "Did you not feel the joy and the love he has for you? Oh, Rune my darling, you have given yourself freely to him and that has brought power unknown in this world to his aid. Follow your heart and trust in him and believe me when I say, you will be the reason he lives."

"Hey chickens, I love this deep meaningful loving vibe, but like Robbie man is almost out of sight, and we really need to hustle man or we will lose the dude... Stephy baby, I love you and Rune too... gimmie a hug chickens." Harry threw his large arms around the two of them and squeezed. "Love man, it's like really happening you know?"

Rune smiled at her mum. "We love you too Harry." She turned to see Robbie just ahead in the trees and she ran across the grass, and between two trees to catch up to him.

Harry put his arm around Steph as they started to walk. "Man, I think like I am going to cry."

Steph squeezed him tight. "Come on you big softy."

Harry beamed as he pulled out his hankie and blew his nose. "Stephy baby, she is like really cosmic and special you know, man I really love that gig with the eyes, purple is a totally radical and cool colour."

Steph shook her head and laughed as she walked arm in arm with Harry. "You are really hopeless at times Harry... But I love you."

Rune took his hand and squeezed it; Robbie looked down at her and smiled. "It's been quite a day."

Rune nodded. "Sometimes I just start to feel like I am getting to grips with everything, and then the rug gets pulled out from under my feet again."

"Our lives seem so parallel at times; I really thought things were going well and then look at last night. Honestly Rune I am not sure what will happen next."

She squeezed his hand. "I think we will be fine."

Martin signaled and the whole group stopped, they went down in the grass and trees, as Jade slid back to Robbie. She moved soundlessly, and sat beside him and Rune. "We have reached a small lake, and Rowan thinks it's the one Fish warned us about. This is the edge of the woodland. There are just a few trees and then it's the farm lands and the grain stores."

"Are there any signs of soldiers or guards?"

"So far nothing, but Fish thinks this place is watched night and day, so we really need to be extra careful Robbie."

Billy crawled up. "Is this the lake?"

"Yeah, it looks like it. I think we should hold back and scout it out first before we make a move. Let's make sure Fish is right before we go in."

Billy winked. "Sounds like a plan to me Bro. Who are you sending?"

"What do you think?"

Billy looked around. "I am in, and Rowan, Fish knows the place and Martin is good, four of us should be enough."

"Ok Billy lets go look at the lake and see what's over it." Robbie and Billy made their way over towards where Rowan sat silently peering through the leaves.

Robbie signaled back to Martin who made his way forward to join them. Fish rolled in from the left.

The lake was not huge and could be skirted easy in fifteen minutes, it was approaching midday and the sun beat down on the grass-covered plain around it. The trees thinned and over the other side of the lake, the land fell away to field upon field of wheat.

To his left Robbie saw a derelict church and a road. The woodland stretched down to the roadside which skirted the edge of the lake, and Robbie followed the stonewall along the side of the fields until he spotted a large building in the distance. That had to be the grain store. Robbie looked at them all. "That is a bloody long way to travel without being spotted. It must be at least a mile, and the wheat is only about two foot high... is there no other way into this place Fish?"

"Down by the wall is a dyke. It's about three feet deep, and it runs right along the wall to the edge of the store, Tony and me have used it once or twice."

Robbie nodded. "I see, is that why you know it so well, you wouldn't happen to be well known to the bakers in these parts would you?"

Fish smiled. "A man has to live."

Billy looked down at the wall. "That gives us five feet of cover, might have known it would be wet, Harry was right about you. Fishy business and wet."

Robbie glanced back at the church. "Alright you four go and take a look, but be very careful, we will take up positions in the church, a little height will give us a place to watch out."

Blades crawled up to Billy's side. "Here take this." She handed him an arrow with a small rolled up leaf attached to the end of it just behind the tip.

"What's this?"

"My mum made them for me when I was a kid, they work better with paper, but leaves do the job just as well... If you get into trouble, fire this arrow back towards us. It will whistle and we will know and come get you."

Billy smiled at her. "That is pretty cool Blades, thanks."

Blades smiled a huge smile. "My pleasure."

Robbie slid back into the trees and joined the group, who were all sat back out of sight as the four scouts set off. He looked at who was left. "Harry, John, Blades, and Pebbles, there is an old church down there, which will give us cover, we need to check it is clear. John and Blades you check the right side and Harry and Pebbles you take the left. The rest of us will cover you from the trees."

They all moved into position and John and Blades slipped out of the trees and into the churchyard. Jade and Harry skirted around to the other side as Alice and Hog took up positions with Eric. Robbie and Rune moved slightly over to see how Harry and Jade were progressing. Steph guarded the centre ground.

Jade slipped silently over the wall by a tall yew tree and came up behind a large gravestone. She gave a quiet whistle through her teeth, and Harry popped over the wall. She slid forward through the long grass towards a large chestnut tree and took up cover ready for Harry.

When Harry did not come Jade looked back, there was no sign of him. "Harry," she whispered, and no response came back. Jade felt cold prickles run up and down her neck. She slowly lowered herself into the grass and slithered along the floor back to the gravestone. Pulling her knife, she crept around the tall grave.

Harry sat with his back to the wall, his hands on his ears, and murmuring quietly to himself. Jade slid in behind the grave and looked back to check all was clear. She looked back at Harry. "What the hell are you doing? Come on." Harry nodded and continued to murmur quietly; Jade kicked his leg hard.

"Hey baby girl don't hassle me like that it aint peaceful."

"Harry what the hell is going on? We need to get a move on; John and Blades will be almost at the church by now."

"Robbie made me do bad things man, I know they will know and screw with my vibes man." Harry looked from side to side his eyes wide.

Jade looked around cautiously. "Who will know Harry?"

Harry pointed into the churchyard and the dozens of gravestones set in row upon row. "Them man... This is not a cosmic place baby girl they know what I did."

Harry put his hands to his face and began to whimper. Jade looked around at the empty graveyard. "Harry there is nothing there, what the hell are you talking about?" Jade suddenly grasped the point. "Please tell me you don't mean the dead?"

Harry was up on his knees and shaking his hands about. "Shush man, don't talk to em."

Jade started to laugh. "Harry they have been dead for years, they cannot hurt you, don't be ridiculous." Jade felt the cold prickles run down her legs.

Harry screamed and pressed himself to the wall, he shook his hands in the air wildly. "Oh why did you have to talk to them man? Look what you done. They are coming man; this is not happening; they will mess with my funky vibes man."

Harry's eyes were wide open in terror, as he started to silently scream and he pointed at Jade. His mouth was wide, with just little bouts of squeaking emitting from his larynx.

Jade felt the laughter and desperately tried to push it back down inside her. "Harry get a grip nothing will...." She looked down at her legs and they had gone. Harry now screamed with all his might.

Jade threw herself forward at him; Harry spluttered and fell forward grabbing Jade's hands. There was nothing below her knees, Jade's eyes filled with tears. "Harry help me."

Harry pulled at her as tears welled in his eyes. "Let her go man, spooks and uncosmic monsters, this is so un-radical, hold on baby girl." He screwed up his eyes. "Oh man this is not happening they is eating your vibes." Jade began to cry as he pulled her up to him.

"Hear me Jade; oh thank god, I have got you at last. Jade relax this is the coming of your power, trust me you are safe."

"You mean this is supposed to happen? Oh Wow, Harry has no idea."

"Jade No!"

"I got you baby girl, I got you, leave her alone, hassle your voodoo elsewhere man, Oh baby girl don't space out on me." Harry could see Jade slowly disappearing, she looked back at the legs that had now completely vanished.

Harry whimpered and grabbed her head. "Don't look baby girl they have like totally vibed out your legs." Jade shook with what looked like fear, as she swallowed her laughter and Harry clung to her.

"Don't let me go Harry, please don't let me go, her eyes started to glow bright green. Harry screamed and shot backward crawling and whimpering under a bush. He stared as Jade slowly disappeared. He snapped his eyes shut, and shaking violently he hugged the tree and started to chant repeatedly.

A quiet voice whispered into his ear. "Harry... Harry.... You have done bad things, we want you." Two bright green eyes appeared right in front of his face. Harry let out a blood curdling scream, and fainted.

Jade sat laughing on the floor as Robbie and Rune dropped silently over the wall.

Robbie scanned the area and saw Harry under the bush out cold. Slowly he slid along the wall toward him.

Rune looked at the green eyes against the grave. "Robbie can't, but I can see you Jade," her eyes flashed lilac. "Are you alright now? I was trying to get through to you, but you were so scared you blocked me, I wish I had got you sooner."

"I am fine; look at me Rune how cool is this?" Two green eyes hovered in the air in front of her.

"You do realize you have terrified poor Harry?"

Jade giggled. "Sorry Rune." She laughed again. "It was just too good an opportunity to miss."

Rune giggled. "I saw it from his perspective, it was pretty freaky." She started to laugh and pointed over the wall. "Mums hysterical over there, I haven't seen her laugh so much in years, we had to stuff a scarf in her mouth to quieten her."

Robbie shook Harry and slapped his face. Harry opened his eyes, screamed and leapt up at Robbie hugging him tight. "Oh wow man; whoa I just had my vibes mangled from the grave man. It was freaky man, and the most uncosmic I have been man. I think they chomped on my karma or something."

Robbie held him tight and patted his back, and tried very hard not to laugh. Rune looked at Jade. "Right let's get you back to normal until we can work out how you did this."

"Awe Rune this is cool, do I have to?"

Rune looked under the shrubs at the quaking mass that was once Harry, clinging on to Robbie for dear life. "I think for Harry's sake Jade we need you back." Rune closed her eyes and began to concentrate. Jade felt the tingling in her back and legs and as she looked down, she saw her legs starting to reappear.

Robbie heaved Harry out from under the shrubs and sat back panting. Harry saw Jade and burst into tears, he lunged at her and pulled her tight. "Whoa baby girl I thought they had snatched you to some uncosmic place, to live with the freaks and un-radical mind benders who eat on your happy vibes."

Jade put her arms around Harry. "Come on Harry I am fine don't cry, you saved me, I knew you would." Jade looked down at Rune, her face showed the guilt that she felt. Harry loved Jade a great deal and the thought of losing her had pushed him to the point of insanity, which considering his starting point was not actually that far. She stood up and grabbed his hand. Very carefully and tenderly, she walked around the edge of every grave to the church as Harry chanted.

Rune looked over the wall at the red-eyed Steph, with a scarf still stuffed in her mouth. "I see now where Jade gets it from." Steph pulled the scarf out of her mouth.

"Don't tell me you did not think that was funny Runestone Sapphire? I felt it inside you as well." Rune grinned, Robbie stood against the grave with his head down as his shoulders shook.

The church was empty which considering Harry's total breakdown was a relief. Jade sat him in the corner next to a giant crucifix; she thought it might comfort him to feel protected. Alice tittered in the corner as Rune explained what had happened. Steph stuffed the scarf back in her mouth and watched from the door. Robbie went up to the bell tower to see if John and Blades could see how the others were doing. Blades had the long telescope out and she was watching them approach the grain store.

Eric sat on a pew at the back of the church. He was binding torn rags to the end of his arrows. Alice saw him and walked over. "What are you doing Eric?"

He looked up and smiled. "I figure that if all these fields are for feeding the army of Knox, I would put them on a diet for a while, you know if locals can't have it then neither can he." Eric dropped his arrows in to a can of paraffin on the floor.

Alice smiled. "That is smart thinking." She patted him on the shoulder and headed to the door where Steph stood on watch. The ceiling creaked as John and Blades moved about. Harry sat quietly looking up at the large gold cross, Rune sat enjoying the cool and restful atmosphere of inside the church. Jade came and sat with her.

"Is that my power to be able to go invisible?"

Rune looked at her. "You were not invisible Jade; you could be seen when you moved. I think you have the ability to be a chameleon."

"What does that mean?"

"I think you will be able to fade into any background, and as long as you do not move you will appear invisible, but the moment you move and your background changes, just for a few seconds you will be able to be seen."

"I can't wait to try it again; it will be great out in the woods."

Rune looked worried. "Jade please do not use it until you can control it, mum and me will help you practice."

Jade nodded. "Yeah, Ok Rune, can I tell everyone?"

Rune put her hand on Jade's knee. "I think Rowan should know, but keep it secret, these are special powers Jade and the less that know the better."

"Yeah, you're right it will be much more fun if they do not know, look how it freaked Harry out." Rune smiled.

"Harry loves you as much as he does Blades, don't ever forget that Jade, to him you are like his daughter, be nice to him."

"I didn't mean to hurt him Rune, I love him you know that. He is very special I will make it up to him."

Rune put her arm around her sister. "That was actually quite cruel." She started to giggle. "It was also very funny, poor thing he was scared out of his wits." Rune put her head down and held her hand to her mouth. Jade sniggered and the two of them sat silently shaking and hugging each other.

Blades sat up quickly, Robbie looked at her. "What?"

"Oh bugger." She turned and looked at Robbie. "Get everyone outside we will be leaving quite quickly."

Robbie looked out of the window to see flames billowing out of the grain store; the smoke rose and billowed in a thick cloud of black. It swirled as two carts came pelting through it. "MOVE!" He screamed and headed for the steps.

The group jumped up at the sound of rushing feet on the stairs. Robbie shot through the small archway and into the church. "Outside now." He tore down the aisle, and headed for the doors. Robbie burst out of the main door, down the steps and out into the road, everyone piled out behind him. He loaded his bow and took aim. Eric passed out arrows, and struck a match.

"Into the wheat," he yelled. Flaming arrows sung into the air in every direction. The wheat soon caught and flames began to leap up in the fields. Two carts were hurtling towards them. Rowan was knelt on top of the first one and took aim at a horseman behind the second cart. His shot was true and the man on the horse fell backwards on to the road and under the hooves of the others who followed. The whole group rushed out into the road and took up positions on either side.

As the carts drew closer, they took aim. Both carts passed at speed and a volley of arrows flew into the air, riders fell, and horses reared, and more arrows sung out. The following guards were caught out in the hail of arrows, Billy jumped off the last cart and ran back up the road with his sword in his hand, Blades and Harry were already in the midst of the horses, as silver and gold flashed in the sunlight.

Robbie, Rune, Alice and John knelt in the road and picked off those who attempted to approach Blades or Harry. The guards dropped to the floor as Harry in fierce mood spun his swords with skill and speed.

Two men who were left looked in fear at Harry, and turned and ran. Robbie lowered his bow as they sprinted back up the road to the grain house. Black smoke drifted across the road and they disappeared into it. Billy stood panting in the middle of the road, as Robbie walked across to him and patted him on the back. "Pretty smooth Billy." He walked down to Rowan and Martin who both stood smiling as they leaned up against the cart. "Two carts, well done guys." Fish wandered around the back of the cart.

"These are both full, we have about six hundred small sacks of grain, and Martin thought it might feed a few less fortunate than Knox for a while."

"I assume Fish you know just the place to take these?"

"Well, yes Tony has a place he wants to take it." Robbie turned to the others. Harry and Blades were cleaning their swords, on torn off pieces of jacket, Robbie looked at Eric.

"Eric, collect up all the spent arrows we may need them again, Hog, you drive the first wagon, Harry you follow, everyone else on the carts, and keep your eyes open and your bows ready." Eric wandered around pulling arrows out of the guards; he stopped in front of Blades who was wiping her other sword. "You were really amazing just then." She smiled.

"Thanks Eric, I noticed you took two off me."

Eric pointed to her nose and pulled out his scarf. "You have a little blood spatter." He gently wiped it off and smiled. "That's better." Blades looked down for a moment and blushed.

"Hey man, it's like split time." Harry pushed Eric, and he began to move back to the carts, Blades followed. As they approached the carts, Harry seized Eric by the back of his tunic and lifted him on to the front of the cart. "You ride with me man, I am watching your vibes, they aint too cool at the moment."

Blades climbed up on to the top of the cart and pulled an arrow out of her quiver. Robbie walked to the back of the carts and looked up the road at the smoke. He climbed up on to the back and up to Rune who was sat with her legs dangling over the top.

"Let's move it." Hog's whip cracked followed by Harry's, and the cart shuddered forward and began to roll.

Rune put her arm around him and pulled him close. "Well Robin in the hood, looks like we have just robbed the rich, and now we are off to feed the poor." She turned and gave him a kiss.

CHAPTER THIRTEEN

THE GREEN ARROW OF HEARNE

Hog sat at the front of the first cart as it trundled down the lane, Fish leaned back at his side and with his hands behind his head, and he hummed to himself. Robbie lay back on the grain and relaxed, he watched the clouds pass over him. He could hear Eric sat at the side of Harry watching the road. Rune sat at the side of Eric and looked at the smoke in the distance. Large clouds billowed into the sky.

"That was clever thinking Eric."

Eric looked down at the road and smiled. "Thank you Miss, I am glad it helped."

Rune smiled; he always called her miss despite her repeated attempts to get him to call her Rune. Eric was in many ways the baby of the group, and yet he had worked very hard over the past days to prove himself. Once again, spontaneously, he had come up with an idea that played a very important role for everyone. "How are you doing, are you settling in alright?" Rune's blue eyes watched him carefully.

Eric smiled. "I still cannot believe Lord Loxley asked for me Miss. My mum was so proud she told the whole village, I am trying not to let him down."

Rune patted him on the shoulder. "I can assure you he is very happy with you. Robbie is a fair man Eric, he saw in you something maybe others had not, and I think he was right, don't you?"

"I don't know Miss; I just know I will fight to the death to show him he was right."

Rune smiled. "I am not sure you have to go quite that far."

Eric chuckled. "No Miss." Robbie closed his eyes and smiled, Rune had such a good way with each member of the group and she was right, Eric had proven to be a good choice. All of them had done so well and to date no one had been hurt, which had been his biggest fear.

Blades sat and polished her swords; Jade was sharpening her knives and the sun was warm. The carts rocked from side to side as the afternoon slowly passed by. Robbie sat up and looked at everyone; they were all busy sorting out their weapons and cleaning up used arrows to reuse again. Alice had spread many of the blankets out on the cart in front to dry them off fully, and Billy sat at the front of the first cart above Fish and Hog watching the road ahead. Rowan was sat behind Robbie watching the road behind. From this high up both of them had a good view of anything that might come.

The carts slowed at a fork in the road and Hog turned off to the left, it was almost instantly noticeable that this road was seldom used, and the cart bumped from side to side over the lumps of grass that had sprung out of the tarmac.

Robbie dropped onto the road as the carts turned, and ran up the side to the front cart. He grabbed the side of the seat support, and pulled himself on to the seat besides Fish. "I take it this is a less favoured short cut?"

Fish nodded. "We are lucky to avoid any more carts, Knox uses that road as a supply run, we thought it better to avoid any of his other supply carts, all of them have soldiers on them."

"Good idea, we have done well to get this far. I think we have already doubled the distance we could have walked, how much further off is this place?"

"There by sun down, the sisters will welcome you." Hog nodded as he spoke.

Robbie looked at Fish. "What sisters?"

Fish gave a grin. "The Sisters of Good Hope, they have a large walled convent not far from here, that is who the grain is for."

"We are taking this lot into a convent? You have to be pulling my leg."

Fish chuckled. "Relax Robbie; I can assure you these ladies have met worse. They helped Tony and me when we were kids, our parents died and they took us in. These are good people Robbie; you have no idea how much good you will do with this grain. They will pass it out for miles and help a lot of people."

Robbie looked at him shrewdly. "Why do I think that these ladies somehow are quite used to you pulling up with gifts?"

Fish smiled. "They saved my brother's life Robbie; I have always done my bit for them."

Robbie patted him on the shoulder. "Then we will do ours." He swung off the seat and up on to the top of the cart. Alice was looking at Billy's arm, it was still very red, but the stitches of Rune's were still holding and the wound seemed to be knitting together. Alice was smearing some green looking paste on to it.

"What is that?"

"It's comfrey and calendula with a little arnica, it will help him heal faster." She looked at Robbie and smiled as she smeared it over the wound.

"You're in good hands Billy boy, we will soon have you swinging that blade of yours again."

Billy nodded. "I hope so Robbie, back there I was not that much use to anyone."

Robbie looked at Billy who seemed down. "Hey you will have a lot more opportunities; this is nowhere near over yet. Heal well before you swing that blade again."

Billy gave him a weak smile. "Yeah, I suppose so."

Robbie patted his good arm. "Good man," and moved off to the back of the cart where he sat at the top and hung his legs over to see Harry, Eric, and Rune. She smiled sweetly at him and her eyes danced, he blew her a kiss. "How are you feeling Harry?"

"I am feeling really mellow Robbie, I like beasts they have a sort of calming vibe you know?"

Robbie smiled, he had noticed the broad grin on Rune's face and she had chuckled. "I am happy you have found peace again my friend."

"It's cool man."

Robbie looked up at the sky and the birds that were flying across, there seemed to be an unusual number of pigeons these days, he turned and looked back at Rowan. "Hey Rowan fancy a pigeon shoot? We could use something for a meal later, a little roast pigeon would be a nice change."

Rowan got up, and walked back across the bags of grain. "It would make a nice change and give me some extra practice."

Pebbles jumped up. "I'm in."

John unsteadily got up. "Me too, I can eat quite a few."

Robbie looked across at the cart behind. "If we drop them on the road behind us, Eric can you and Blades gather them up and throw them to Steph and Martin?" Both of them nodded and dropped off the cart.

The four of them took up their bows and took aim. It was not long before Eric ran up the road behind the cart throwing the birds as he caught them up to Steph. Each time one was hit the others all cheered and clapped, Rowan and Robbie moved with lightning speed as they fired. Robbie out shot Rowan by two, and Jade was becoming more and more accomplished with her bow, moving targets were not easy, and although she missed a few times, which panicked Eric, as a sharp arrow fell to earth just in front of him. Jade seemed to hit a lot more than she expected and she whooped, and cheered with delight.

Everyone sat happily on the two carts; the shooting had provided a distraction and lifted their spirits. As the afternoon passed on, Pebbles sat talking with John as they discussed their shooting, and she gave him a blow by blow account of one bird in particular that had been particularly difficult. John sat smiling at her as she rambled on none stop.

Robbie had dropped off the cart and was now, sat at the front of the second cart with Harry and Rune. He put his feet on the kicking boards and leaned back happily, Rune cuddled up as they watched the trees now almost in full leaf; slip idly by on each side of the road.

In the twenty-six years since the red death, the Cheshire landscape had changed a great deal. The whole area had once been run and farmed by large corporations, and as they collapsed and the modern ways of what was now an old life disintegrated, nature stepped in. This had once been an area of broad open fields filled with crops, and neat hedgerows, kept bug and weed free with pesticides and chemical weed killers. Now nature had cast her fair hand over the landscape and the fields had become meadows of wild flowers and long grass.

The neat hedges were now thick trees alive with the chattering of happy birds, wild honeysuckle and sweet peas were starting to weave themselves into the hedges, ready to provide a summer of scents and pollen for the hard working bees. To the group on the carts, it was a scene of delight and tribute to the powers of the green man. To Mason Knox it was an abomination and land wasted not used by industry. Robbie felt relaxed and loved what he saw. He did not know of the stark transformation that had occurred, to him Cheshire was a delight with its overgrown hedges filled with life.

The carts slowed at a turn and Robbie looked up, the road continued but they had just moved onto a driveway. He leaned out from the cart and looked down the road in front; he saw a long eight-foot high wall that ran either side of the roadway. He stood up and pulled himself up to the top of the cart. In front of him was a large set of old black gates? Beyond the gates he could see many small red brick buildings and at the far back was a large church next to what looked like a very large three storey brick building.

The carts stopped and he jumped down at the side of Rune. Together they walked up to the front of the carts as everyone else started to drop on to the floor. Hog was already at the gates and had pulled a long rope that rang a bell somewhere over the wall.

Three bolts slid back, and a figure in black wearing a long white headscarf stepped out. She put her arms around Hog, and hugged as she would a good friend. Hog put his large arms around her and squeezed her; it was obvious he felt great affection for her.

Fish jumped down from the cart and ran over, he picked the nun up and swung her into his arms, she let out a happy shriek. Robbie and Rune stood by the carts as Fish turned and putting her arm in his, he walked toward them with the nun.

She was a little woman of about five feet. Her face showed great care and compassion, and also the hardness of life and her age, which must have been at least sixty. Her dark eyes sparkled with life and her smile was warm and welcoming. Fish walked her over with pride. "Robbie, Rune, this is Sister Mary, she leads this convent, and runs the House of Good Hope. Sister Mary, I would like you to meet Lord and Lady Loxley."

The Sisters eyes widened. "Welcome my children you are all most welcome. We have beds and some food."

Rune took Sister Mary by the hand. "It is nice to meet you Sister, we have brought a few supplies of our own, and I hope it is enough to repay your kindness."

Sister Mary looked at the two large carts filled with grain sacks; her delight was very apparent although she looked at Fish with a reprimanding look in her eye. "You came by these honestly didn't you James?" Fish looked down at the floor and shuffled his feet.

Robbie laughed. "These are gifts from the house of Loxley Sister, and shall we just say that these are the spoils of war."

Sister Mary looked up at Robbie. "This will feed many mouths My Lord; I cannot tell you what a difference this will make... Please come in all of you are very welcome." She turned and waved them all to follow, as Hog pushed open the large gates and returned to his cart. He lashed down on the reigns and the cart trundled forward, Harry followed in his cart, into the large yard and the others all followed on foot.

Rune placed her arm around Robbie, as he stood lost for words, a tear welled in her eye. They stood in a large courtyard, surrounded by hundreds of children. All of them wore rags and had no shoes to their feet; they were thin and white and looked very hungry. Their eyes were dull, lifeless, and filled with desperation. Nuns wandered round dressing wounds and administering medicines. Adults lay under tents on rough beds of straw with a blanket over them suffering the pangs of malnutrition and brutal beatings. It looked like a battle zone, and this was the side that had lost, the whole scene was one of utter devastation.

The whole group was completely unprepared for such a bitter scene. Alice wept on Billy's shoulder; Steph stood silently frozen her hands to her mouth. It was a devastating scene and Robbie swallowed as Sister Mary looked up at him. "We do our best My Lord, but we do not have great means."

Robbie looked down at her as two tears dropped to Rune's boots. "We have arrived just in time dear Sister." He turned to Fish. "You know these lands?" Fish nodded. Robbie turned to the others. "Rowan, Pebbles, John, Martin, Eric, we need food follow Fish and get what you can." They all nodded and spoke as one. "Yes My Lord."

They turned and headed for the gates. "Hog I want a roasting pit in the middle of this yard get to work." A sudden sense of urgency came over him; desperation drove from the pit of his stomach. "Alice, can you help with medicines?"

"I will see what they have Robbie and do my best." Alice and Billy started to head over to the tents. Steph came up at his side. "I will also help with the children and the sick."

Robbie looked down at the sister, who was smiling and had a tear in her eye. "Tell me sister what other troubles do you have?"

"We have a well, so water is not a problem, although the windmills have stopped and we have not got the power to pump water, we do it by hand which takes a lot of time."

Rune smiled. "I think we might just have the right man for that job... Where is Harry?" She scanned around and spotted him.

Harry was sat on the floor in the middle of about twenty children. "Hey little baby people." He looked up at Robbie and Rune. "Hey man these dudes are cosmic and cool." All the children gathered around Harry as he talked and smiled, and laughed with them. He made funny faces and all of them roared with laughter.

"Harry, we have problems with the wind turbines, do you think you can help?"

Harry looked up with two children on his knee. "Hey man they haven't invented a machine me and Blades can't fix."

One hour later Robbie and Rune sat with the sister under a long covered walkway, and looked out at the yard; Rune had a small mousy haired girl on her knee that clung to a teddy bear with only one leg. The little girl curled up and snuggled into her, as Rune stroked her hair. Robbie was shaken and shocked by the last hour. "How has it got to this Sister?"

Sister Mary watched him closely. "Well, My Lord, it was bad after the red death, but what you see is really the work of Mason Knox. His men are animals who kill indiscriminately and care not that the people they murder have children."

Robbie rubbed his face in his hands. "I have to stop this Sister." Harry ran past uncoiling a huge roll of wire, two dozen children ran laughing after him. Blades sat high up on the wind turbine with the back open as she worked on the motor. Rune and Sister Mary both smiled. Hog crossed the yard with a big pole across his shoulders with four young lads hung upside down from it laughing and cheering.

"I have not heard laugher here for a long time My Lord, your visit has brought something I cannot give these children."

Rune looked at the sister. "What is that?"

The sister smiled. "You have brought cheer to the children, and hope to my heart." She patted Robbie on the leg. "You are a good man Lord Loxley." She smiled and pointed upwards to the sky. "I should know, I work for the man upstairs." Robbie smiled and sat back in his chair, if only he could do more.

As the sun started to fall, the hunters arrived back. They carried four deer, and two boars into the yard, Hog already had a fire going and Billy sharpened his knife, and he and Rowan cleaned the animals and set them to roast. Harry was having trouble getting the wires he had taken from the old outbuildings and connecting them to the turbines. They had to travel along the roofline of the three storey building, which was the problem.

"Man, I really don't like height, it's not cosmic you know? That's like a birdie thing and I aint got wings man."

Eric looked up and took the end of the wire off him. "Where does it have to go?"

"It has to cross the roof man, and hook up with my baby girl there on the turbine." Eric grabbed the drainpipe running down the wall and started to climb. He shot up it at quite a speed, and Harry gasped.

"Man, he is like a totally cosmic monkey dude." Eric ran across the top of the roofline pulling the wire fed to him by Harry. He got to the end of the roof where Blades sat ten feet above him at the top of the pole on the turbine. Harry suddenly realised who was up on the roof and shouted up. "Hey man you keep your vibes cool, that is like my little baby girl there."

Blades tutted. "God dad," suddenly realising where she was, she put her hand to her mouth. "Sorry Sister." Eric started to giggle and threw the wire up to her. She caught it and began feeding it into the casing.

Eric sat on the top of the roof whilst Blades attached the wires and closed the casing, she pulled the brake off and slowly the propeller began to spin in the soft breeze. She slid down the pole and Eric helped her back on to the roof. They descended together to a very pleased sister.

All the power to the out buildings had stopped with the red death. Harry had used the overhead lines that had supplied the power and replaced the lines to the turbines. They were stronger and heavier, and he worked out that they would run for years. Light flickered on in the yard, Sister Mary jumped with delight.

Long wooden tables had been set up in the yard either side of the huge roasting pit. Sister Mary stood at the end of one of the tables as everyone sat with their heads bowed. Robbie and Rune sat opposite with the sister at their side.

Sister Mary started the prayer. "Dear Lord, we thank you for what you have brought us this day. We thank you for sending your envoys to our aid. Lord and Lady Loxley have brought with them many hearts of kindness to bless our lives, and bring us the hope we despaired would never come. Please bless them and protect them in all that they do. May Hearne protect you all?"

Rune looked up as everyone said. "Amen." The old Sister smiled.

"You believe in Hearne?"

"The Lord has his friends and servants all over this land Lady Loxley, you know more of that I would say than I do." Rune smiled.

The nuns provided cabbage, and potatoes, and everyone tucked in, and it was a feast to be remembered. Harry and Hog sat at the far end of the table surrounded by children, who all feasted, laughed, and chatted happily. Even John found he could eat no more, and stretched as he stood up from the table.

Rooms had been provided for all of them, and Alice and Steph had squealed with joy at finding a room that contained five baths.

Happy sounds soon came from the room as Alice, Steph, Rune, Blades, and Pebbles all sat immersed up to their neck in hot steaming water and thick soap.

Steph lay back in the tub her long wet hair hanging over the edge. "Oh, girls this is heaven."

The nuns lent them all robes and took their clothes to be washed, Jade squealed with delight when Rowan spotted her plodding up the corridor with wet feet. "What do you think?" She twirled around laughing.

Rowan smiled. "I think I see before me the fairest lady ever to walk out of a wood."

Jade spun to a halt. "Do you?" She looked almost embarrassed.

Rowan's eyes seemed to sparkle. "You are to me." Jade's face broke into a huge smile, she ran at him and launched herself up at him throwing her arms around him, and gripping him around the waist with her legs, Jade kissed him.

Rowan held her tight in his arms, a little shocked at first but also happy as she leaned back and looked into his grey eyes. "I want you to be happy Rowan, and I really want it to be with me."

"I have been for the last week my fair Lady Pebbles; you are the joy in my heart."

She pulled him close and kissed him again, Rune sat up in her bath and smiled, she looked at her mother who was also smiling. "We really need to show Jade how to block that stuff out."

Steph smiled. "Yes, but I am glad to have seen that, they deserve each other."

Rune lay back in the hot water. "I am so happy for her; he is a good man and somehow suited."

Steph chuckled. "For a man who loves peace I think his world will get somewhat louder." Both of them started to laugh.

The sweet smell of cherries and sweet honeysuckle drifted into his nose, and the warmth beside him radiated through him. Robbie opened his eyes and the sunlight streamed in to the small room. He lay with his eyes open and stared up at the paint peeled ceiling. He was clean and well fed, at ease, and relaxed as he lay on the soft bed. The sounds of sawing and children laughing came in through the slightly opened window, Rune disturbed in her sleep, he had fallen asleep long before she had come to him in the night. The feeling of calm and the smell of clean bedding, had somehow washed over him and he had slept very deeply, he now felt strong and refreshed.

Robbie sat up slowly and slid out of the side of the bed, Rune moved slightly, her red hair glinted in the light, as it slid over him and dropped on to the white sheet. He stretched and walked over to the pile of clean clothes folded neatly on a chair at the side of his bed. A thick black robe was cast on the floor.

He pulled on his pants and dropped his feet into his boots, throwing his shirt over his shoulder he walked to the door. He looked back at the pale white skin and shimmering red hair of Rune as she slept, she looked so peaceful. He opened the door quietly and stepped out; Jade was closing the door next to his quietly.

"Oops," she giggled as she saw Robbie watching her sneak out of Rowan's room.

She walked to him smiling. "Boy did he have some knots to work out." She started to giggle and ran off down the corridor, her bare feet slapping the stone floor. Robbie stood open-mouthed not quite wondering what to think.

Two slender pale arms came from behind him and round his stomach. "Don't get up yet come back to bed." She kissed the back of his shoulder.

Robbie turned looking quite shocked. "Did you see that?"

Rune blinked. "What?"

"She was in Rowan's room." He paused. "All night."

Rune started to giggle. "You're shocked... Admit it?"

Robbie moved his head from side to side. "I ... Was ... Just ... A little surprised that's all."

Rune laughed. "I think it's sweet, they really work well together, he is a loner and she is a misfit, and they are the two best woodsmen in the area, apart from you. I am really happy about it." Rune's expression changed. "You are not angry, are you?"

Robbie relaxed. "Not at all, I love Pebbles you know that, and I think Rowan is a man of great honour I have a lot of respect for him, it just surprised me a little."

She put her arms around him and kissed his chest. "Good, they both deserve happiness.... Robbie?"

"What?"

"Someone's coming."

"Meaning?"

"Close the door I am naked."

"What... Oh Hearne." He pushed the door and it slammed.

It was mid-morning and Robbie walked into the yard, there seemed to be activity everywhere. Billy had borrowed Harry's swords and he and Blades were fencing Samurai style. He watched Billy who was not used to using two swords, yet he handled them expertly. Blades was quite remarkable, she was nimble and agile, and spun as she fought countering all of Billy's strokes. She stopped and stepped back and showed him a wrist action to spin the sword better, Billy tried it, she smiled, and nodded, Robbie was glad to see them getting on well.

John and Martin were working on one of the carts; they had raised the sides of the cart to four feet and fitted two long wooden seats down either side. There was a framework of bent steel in hoops across the top, on to which they had secured a large canvass. Robbie understood that they could all sit in it and the canvass would keep out the rain. The higher sides he presumed would give them protection if attacked.

He stepped off the steps into the yard and walked along. Harry and Hog had found some spare wood and had already built a series of swings for the children to play on, Alice sat showing Eric how to make arrows, and Steph was sorting out supplies with Fish, which would be stored in boxes under the cart seats.

Rowan and Jade sat above the gates on the wall and kept watch. Rune came up at his side. "They have all been busy."

Robbie nodded. "Yes, I have good people around us Rune, we are very fortunate."

The children ran round laughing and screaming as Harry chased them, Hog now walked along a row of children who were now piled on to the completed swings and he pushed them in turn. It was a very different scene from the one that had met his eyes yesterday. He put his arm around Rune. "We have not done much but I think we have made a difference here."

"You will never realise the seeds of good you have sown here today Robert of Loxley." They turned to see Sister Mary. "I hope you will stay with us just one more night and let us celebrate the coming of Robin Hood."

Robbie smiled softly. "To be honest Sister, I think it will be hard for me to drag my men away tomorrow, never mind today. We would be honoured to give you another night. I am sure my men have quite a list considering their industrious mornings labour."

"We will eat in the Church Hall tonight at sunset." She turned and walked off. "I will have the sisters prepare My Lord."

Steph came smiling towards them. "Robbie, I have sent the pigeons you shot to the kitchens for tonight's meal, but I think you should look at these." She dropped three small rolls of paper into his hand. "Pigeons are faster than the post." He unrolled the first piece of paper and read it.

'Hood heading south on foot trap at market failed.'

'Progress at York slow will not be ready for at least ten days.'

'Loxley resisting, reports Lord Loxley still there. Can you explain?'

Rune leant over his shoulder as he read. "Well at least we know he will not know where we are now, all we have to do is drop any pigeon we see with a ring and we can interfere with his communication channels."

Robbie thought for a moment. "So, York is proving difficult and Loxley is obviously going to be hard, it looks like old Knox has got his hands a little full at the moment, and they do not understand why I am in two places at once."

Steph smiled at him. "This is the little bit of luck we needed, we intercepted these, Knox at the moment has no idea his trap failed, he does not know York is behind, or that your father is resisting. It will take them a few days to sort this out by which time; we have transport and will be where he won't be looking."

"I must admit Steph it is good news and we could certainly use it, we will leave here tomorrow at dawn and get as far south as possible. Get Harry to fit both teams of horses to the cart, it will give us greater speed and the pulling power to cross country, I am not convinced the clear roads are safe."

Rune squeezed him as Steph went off. "See you need to have faith Robbie; I want you to take a walk in the woods behind the convent with me later."

Robbie looked at her suspiciously. "Why?"

"Because it will be nice to be alone together under the trees." She smiled sweetly and headed over to the children. Robbie sat and watched her as she played with the children; she was caring and gentle as she spoke to them. Soon she had two little tots sat on her knee and a large group of children sat around her as she told them stories of brave Robin Hood, occasionally she would look up at him and smile, the lilac in her eyes would flash across the yard at him.

Billy sat down beside him stretching and flexing his sore arm. "She is very special Rob. You actually see the love in her."

"I really love her Billy; I worry she will get hurt."

"We won't let that happen Rob, you know everyman here adores her and you, it will be a hard fight for any man who would try to hurt her."

Robbie patted Billy on the knee. "I will tell you this much Billy, any man who tries will find a force in me he has not bargained for, and he will not live long."

"We have good people here Rob; don't think about something that won't happen." Billy stretched his arm and wiggled it. "It feels a lot better, that bout with Blades has done it good, I tell you what Robbie, she is small and young but she can fight."

Robbie watched her as she practiced alone. "I see Harry's fighting aggression in her, and I don't think I would like to face those Blades." Robbie looked up at Billy. "Tonight they are preparing a meal for us, I want to talk to everyone before we go in, will you tell everyone to meet up at the cart just before dusk." Billy got up and patted his shoulder and wandered off back to see Alice.

Robbie wandered back to the room a little later, and he lifted his belt and fastened it, checking his sword was comfortable on his hip. He picked up his cloak and threw it around his shoulders. He grabbed his bow and quiver, and headed back out to the yard where Rune was stood waiting. She linked his arm and they quietly slipped down between the Church and the accommodations block. There was a small gate at the back, and they slipped out into dense woodland.

"Just where are you two off to unprotected?" They turned to see Alice and Billy with Harry and Blades.

Rune sighed. "I wanted a few moments alone with Robbie, is that so much to ask for?"

"It is if it involves being alone in a strange wood." Alice folded her arms and looked resolute.

Billy put his hand on Alice's shoulder. "I tell you what Rune, do not go too far

in and we will scout ahead and try to bag some game." He handed her an arrow, if
you get into difficulty fire this and we will find you."

Rune looked down at the whistling arrow and smiled. "Alright Billy we won't go
far."

The group set off into the wood and Rune linked Robbie's arm as they walked
into the trees. "This is nice, just the two of us."

Robbie put his arm around her. "I love it under the trees; I feel I really belong
here."

"You do, you are the hooded man and a woodsman, and I am a daughter of the
woods, so this is our realm Robbie." She stopped at the edge of a small clearing
and pulled something from her pocket. "Happy Birthday Robbie." She stretched
up, kissed him, and then handed him the package.

It was his birthday and he had completely forgotten. "I cannot believe you
remembered... I had forgotten, with everything that's been happening."

Robbie unfolded the package carefully and looked down at the ring. "I got Jade
to make it before we left, do you like it?"

Robbie looked at the ring and saw a five pointed star set on a white background.
The centre had a sapphire blue pentangle from which each point of the star
radiated. Each point of the star was a different colour. Black, white, red, violet and
green, he looked at her. "This is very beautiful Rune; I do not know what to say."
She smiled and pulled him close and kissed him. She took the ring and slipped it
on, it was then he noticed it was the same as hers. "You have one?" Rune's ring
was set in platinum where as his was gold, but they were the same design. "We are
bound by these rings, aren't we?"

Rune smiled. "I love you Robbie and I will never leave your side as I know
you will never leave mine." He lifted his arms and pulled her close. He felt great
emotion rise up inside him as he stood and held her in his arms.

As he held her, a white mist rolled and swirled in from the trees, and the mist
seemed to whisper as it passed them. "Hooded Man, hear me." Robbie turned
and there through the mist on the other side of the clearing was an old man in
green. He leaned on an old and heavily carved staff, a crown of oak leaves and
acorns sat upon his pale green hair, and his long green robes appeared made from
soft leaves.

Robbie fell to one knee his head bowed. "My Lord Hearne."

The old man walked forward through the mist and as his robes fluttered, it
sounded like the wind in the leaves. His face was old and lined like bark, yet his
eyes shone like summer berries. The hairs of his long beard swayed like grass on
the prairie.

Hearne touched Robbie and Rune on the shoulder. "Rise my woodland children
so that we may speak." Robbie and Rune slowly rose up from the ground. Robbie

felt the power of Hearne in the air all around him and his stomach twisted with fear. This was the high lord, the king of the realm of woodsmen, who only ever appeared to them as a stag. Here Robbie stood before the man himself, revealed in his true form. The power and full force of life and death, and the circle of life radiated out of him, and it was a force of huge magnitude.

Rune trembled as she held his hand, her eyes flickered violet and Robbie squeezed her hand softly to reassure her. Hearne smiled. "You have done well my hooded friend; come let us sit and talk as men."

Hearne waved his hand and the mist parted revealing three large wooden stumps. Hearne sat down and the trees leaned over to be closer to him. Robbie and Rune lowered themselves slowly on to the stumps. "Be at peace my friends you cannot be harmed here." A wave of tranquillity came over him and he relaxed as his stomach unknotted, Robbie looked up at the Lord Hearne.

"My Lord I am honoured you have chosen to visit us, what must we do?"

Hearne smiled. "Your instincts have served you well thus far young bowman, do not concern yourself with other tasks, you have chosen wisely and I am proud of the choices you have made."

"I worry every day My Lord that I am missing something important that may cost all of our lives."

"To concern yourself for the welfare of others is a noble quality young bowman; do not fear the process of doubt, the path to truth is paved with it. It is a wise man who treads carefully through the marshes of doubt, and appears on the road of truth. Tell me what do you plan for the coming day?"

"We leave at dawn My Lord, and head south to aid others."

Hearne nodded. "This is wise my hooded friend, the eyes of the snake are blind for a while longer, use the time well to advance your cause. Travel by roads unknown, the covering of my children will not impede your wheels, they will only tie up and hold the wheels of the snake." As he spoke ivy slid from under his cloak and slithered around the floor like a snake. "You should head first to Gloucester, there is a task there for you, and then travel to the home of my daughters, there you will rest and receive support before planning to confront the snake."

"I will My Lord." Robbie kept looking down, somehow, he felt he should not be familiar with the high lord of the woodland.

Hearne lifted a hand and placed it onto Robbie's shoulder, his skin was brown and wrinkled and his fingers looked like twigs. "You are so likened to my first son young Robbie. He would be proud to know such a man of honour follows in his footsteps." Hearne withdrew a long green arrow out of Robbie's quiver, he was surprised to see it at first but then realised the touch of the green man had put life into it. "This must be the one for the snake; it has the power of my realm and will return the balance to you." He placed it on his lap and Robbie took hold of it.

"Will this kill him My Lord?"

"This arrow will be the last shot you take at him, you must decide what is done with it, life is my realm and so is death, the green arrow can give both, you must decide my hooded friend."

Hearne looked to Rune and her eyes flickered purple, he smiled. "My sweet precious daughter how happy I am to know you have such love for me and my realm, your power has gone beyond all I could have hoped for." Tears welled in her eyes and splashed purple on to the floor where small violets sprung out of the earth.

"Father of my realm I do love you and I rejoice that you have come here to see me."

Robbie watched Hearne smile like a proud parent who watches his child. Hearne stroked her cheek softly. "This hooded man has a love of all the things that you are my precious little Runestone, you have chosen well and I am happy to see you bloom into flower because of him."

Rune gasped as her tears flowed; Hearne pulled her softly to him, and stroked her hair as she hugged him. "I'm proud of you Runestone, you will do great things together, and my realm will be safe. With you on my side, the snake will not overcome you easily, and our hope lies in the total death of the old ways of modern man."

He released her and she sat down on the log, Hearne plucked a leaf from the tree and gently dried her eyes. He threw the leaf into the clearing, and a lilac tree sprung up. "I must return soon; I have many duties that occupy me." He turned to Robbie. "Hold out your hand my hooded friend." Robbie pushed forward his palm, and Hearne took two acorns from his crown and placed them into his hands.

"This is the love you hold for my child, and the love she holds for you, both are strong and yet grow stronger by the day. When you return to the children today place one on either side of the gates."

Robbie looked into his hand and then at Rune, she smiled, there was a crack and when he looked down, he saw two green leaves sprout from each acorn. "You should have no fear of leaving them, I will provide for all of them, your acts of kindness to these children will be rewarded, and this I promise."

Hearne slowly stood up and the sound of trees groaning filled the air. "I must depart." He raised his arms and pulled both of them close and hugged them. "Take care defender of my realm and guard well my daughters, especially this one." He smiled as he touched her shoulder, a caterpillar rolled off his cuff and landed on her shoulder; it spun into white silk forming a large ball. He lifted it and placed it into her hand.

"I love the sunset; this will keep the sun in your hair always my daughter." He took the last tear on her eye and lifted it gently off her face. Turning to Robbie, he placed it onto the ties of his cloak. The tear expanded and then contracted, and

Robbie looked down at the clasp of a small acorn of sapphire that held his cloak together.

The old man smiled. "Goodbye my children."

Robbie bowed. "Goodbye My Lord."

Rune smiled. "Goodbye father of my realm." He turned and walked into the mist and was gone. Rune slid her arm around Robbie's waist as he stood silently watching the trees. The clearing was no longer empty, in the centre was a large tree filled with lilac flowers, and the ground was covered in sweet violets. Rune held up the white woven silk ball and it split. A large golden butterfly unrolled its wings and fluttered, and then set. Rune looked down at the hairpin of gold, and gasped as it sparkled with tiny red rubies that reflected in the gold, giving it the colour of sunset and Rune's hair.

She lifted it up and slid it into her braided hair, a ring of violets sprung up around her braids, Robbie smiled at her with her sapphire blue eyes and violets in her hair she was the most beautiful thing he had ever seen, he pulled her close and kissed her softly. Taking her hand he turned, and walked back through the wood towards the small gate in the wall.

The trees parted in the thick white mist. "Oh man my vibes are shivering, this is not good, we are totally in a non-cosmic zone."

Billy looked around. "I am sure we have passed this tree twice already."

"We have, look that is the branch I snapped off, I am telling you Harry you are wrong, we need to go this way, you are just getting us lost."

"Hey chicken let's like mellow down; we don't do lost its not cosmic."

"But Harry you keep bringing us back here." Alice snapped another branch on the tree. "I am telling you Harry the right way is this way here."

Harry looked at the pathway and leaned forward to sniff it. "Man, that way smells funky, it could jangle my vibes."

"OH FOR GODS SAKE HARRY, IT'S NOT YOUR VIBES THAT ARE JANGLED, IT'S YOUR BRAINS!"

"Peace chicken, I had my karma chomped yesterday, it's like made me a little out of focus that's all."

"Harry you have been out of focus for years, if you ask me you are getting blurrier by the day. Are we going this way or not?"

Harry stepped on to the path and sniffed, Alice could take no more, she had been walking around in circles and had reached point break. "Harry I am telling you this is the right way, are you coming or not because I am leaving."

Alice spun round and walked down the path. "Hey chicken I was just focusing my vibes, I was going to like mosey on that way anyhow." Harry followed her down the path. "Say Billy dude, she gets pretty sexy when she's like mad, do you like get her mad often?"

Billy laughed. "Harry she is right, you are becoming weird."

Harry looked at Billy very seriously and then smiled he patted Billy on the back. "Billy my man, you're making fun of me aren't you dude? Wow man you had me goin there for a moment." Blades shook her head and laughed as she followed.

Five minutes later, they walked up to the small gate. "See?" Alice said smugly.

Harry stepped back in amazement. "Wow Alice baby, you are really cosmic, you are like a homing pigeon or something, that is so totally radical, you just knew. That is so cool baby girl, we should call you pigeon."

Alice shook her head. "I don't think so. I mean it Harry don't you dare say a word when we get back."

Harry's eyes got wider. "Oh wow. Yeah... I mean wow how blind am I? Alice baby this is cosmic at its highest. Pigeons never get lost and they carry information."

"And fleas." Billy sniggered, and Alice furrowed her brow at him. Harry snatched her up in his arms.

"Your head is like filled with information, and you stopped us getting lost, Alice baby cakes you are totally a Pigeon." Harry stood suddenly still nodding his head.

Alice pointed a long finger at him. "Don't you dare breathe a word?" Robbie and Rune came walking slowly out of the trees smiling.

Billy looked at them both. "You two look happy."

Rune nodded. "It is Robbie's Birthday."

Alice shrieked and looked mortified. "Oh, Robbie I just completely forgot, I am so sorry, what with everything that's been happening, it just slipped my mind." Alice looked distraught; she had never forgotten him before.

Robbie smiled at her. "Alice don't fret, I completely forgot myself, it was Rune who remembered."

Alice put her head down. "I should have as well." Robbie put his arm around her.

"Hey it's been a mad time, I bet you have a present for me stashed in your room at home, don't you?"

Alice gave him a soft smile. "I do actually; I just forgot to pack it."

"Well then when we get back you can give it to me and we will celebrate again."

Alice smiled. "Yes, we will. Happy Birthday Robbie." She kissed him on the cheek.

Robbie gave her a hug. "Thanks Alice." Billy put his arm round his shoulder.

"Happy Birthday Rob... you don't mind if I don't kiss you, do you?" Everyone laughed, and they pushed open the gate and walked back into the convent.

As Harry appeared, all the children came running down to him cheering. "Hey my little baby people, what you all bin doin?"

Robbie stood watching as Harry with about twenty children ran up the yard to the swings, Robbie turned to Rune. "Mad as a hatter that one, but you have no idea how much I love him." Alice turned back to them.

"We all love him Robbie." Her voice seemed to quieten. "He is very special." The children ran around as Harry dropped them all on the swings and began to push them in turn.

Rune sighed. "You know those kids are really going to miss him tomorrow when he leaves Rob."

CHAPTER FOURTEEN

THE RACE TO THE RESCUE

The day was drawing to a close; the sun began to slowly sink as Robbie and Rune walked up to the gates at the top of the yard. He looked at Martin sat on the top of the wall. "How is it looking Martin?"

Martin looked out across the roadway. "All quiet, and all clear My Lord."

Robbie slid back the bolts and looked at Rune. "Why are they all calling me lord again?"

"We are not in the forest Robbie, here you are Lord Loxley, in the forest you are Robbie in the hood. It is sort of sweet that they show you so much respect."

"I still prefer Robbie; I will never get use to this lordship stuff." Rune giggled as he swung open the gate and he stepped outside the convent. He walked to one side of the gate and Rune followed through to the other.

"Robbie if these are going to grow into big trees shouldn't we plant them away from the wall? Otherwise they could push the wall over."

"Good point Rune; let's say about four feet away alright?" Robbie stepped back so he was a little over four feet away and lined himself up with the gatepost. He looked over to Rune who was watching him carefully and following his lead.

Martin looked down from above with great interest, as Robbie took out his dagger and dug a small hole. Rune did likewise, and then watched as Robbie carefully lowered the acorn with two leaves into the hole. Robbie pulled in the earth and firmed it into position; Rune watching carefully did the same.

Robbie stood up and started to pat the soil off his hands, Martin leaned over the wall, as Rune walked across to Robbie and slipped her arm around him. "I don't wish to interfere with you two, but would it not have been better to have planted something just a little bit taller? Won't someone step on them before they have grown?"

Robbie looked up at Martin. "These are protected by Hearne; nothing will harm them." He walked to the gate with Rune, and turned round to look at them, he smiled satisfied with his work.

"Do you think we should water them Robbie? They are only small and I would hate them to die of thirst." Small drops of rain hit the floor at her feet; Rune looked up at the cloud that had rolled in from nowhere. A torrent of rain fell from the sky, and both of them jumped through the gates for cover. The other side of the gate was dry with no rainfall; Robbie pushed his head back through the gate and smiled at the soaking wet ground around their trees. Rune popped her head round and had a look. She smiled a satisfied smile.

Martin sat on the wall chuckling; he still could not see the point of two such small shoots. Robbie bolted the gates and walked arm in arm with Rune. She stopped and he turned to look at her. "We have done that right haven't we?"

He smiled and pulled her close. "Of course we have, a woodsman's way is the one of love, he plants all his trees with great care."

Rune smiled. "The way of love eh... is that why you love me?" Robbie smiled pulling her close.

"Those are our trees, it will be our love that makes them grow, and the more I love you the bigger my tree will get." She giggled as he pulled her close and then she kissed him.

Martin screamed out, and landed on the floor just in front of them with a heavy thud. Rune jumped back, and looked down at him. "What are you doing Martin? You scared the life out of me."

Martin pointed a look of shock on his face. "It knocked me off the bloody wall!"

Robbie and Rune turned round, and there outside the gate stood two enormous Oak trees. Robbie looked at her radiant smile. "See what a little love can do?" He turned to Martin, grabbed his hand, and lifted him up. "You see Martin the secret is to plant them small, that way the roots develop in the soil better, and you will always get a bigger better tree." He brushed him down. "Trust me I'm a woodsman."

Rune started laughing as she grabbed Robbie's hand and walked towards the cart leaving Martin looking positively astounded.

Ten minutes later the group started to arrive at the new fully kitted out cart. Robbie and Rune sat on the tailgate; Rune swung her legs as they waited, and the group gathered round. Robbie slipped off the tailgate and stood in front of Rune. "Is everybody here good? Yesterday when we arrived here, I think I can safely say our hearts broke." Everyone nodded. "I have never in my life seen such pain and devastation. Tonight, we will go into the main hall for our last meal with these good people, and they will be fed and happy for the first time in a very long time." He swallowed deeply. "I cannot express to you all how proud and honoured I am to count you as friends."

They all looked at him as he looked each of them in the eye as he spoke. "What you have done in a single day will stay with these poor people forever, I give you all my word that as Lord Loxley I will ensure that as soon as I return home, I will provide for these people always as a tribute to you."

Rune sniffled behind him, and Alice wiped her face on her sleeve. "We will leave here at dawn and we will travel to the aide of the Duke of Gloucester, but never forget what you saw here when you arrived, for that was the true face of the world that Mason Knox will build, remember these children when you fight. You have a feast that awaits you my good friends; you have earned it, go and enjoy it."

They all silently walked away from the cart; Rune put her head on his shoulder and her arms around his neck. "I am so proud of you Robert of Loxley." She hugged him hard. Robbie slid his arms around her legs and picked her up.

"Come on and let's enjoy the feast." He gave her a piggyback to the main hall doors as she hugged him and giggled.

The hall was a large amount of the bottom floor of the accommodations building. It was very high and huge chandeliers of candles hung in the air. The walls had been painted white, but Sister Mary by way of making it more at home for the children, had let them paint pictures of themselves on the walls. All the walls were filled with little faces of every child who had been here; it was easy to see how many had not survived. That disturbed Robbie a lot, as he sat down. The tables were laid out in a big square, with an empty centre, and as guests of honour, they all sat down at the end table and looked upon everyone else.

At the far end of the room Sister Mary stood in front of a wall covered with large white sheets, she banged on the table to get everyone's attention. "Our welcome guests of honour, I feel privileged that you have stayed for this meal, and I am happy that we have plenty to offer because of your extreme kindness. You are possibly now aware that all of the people who are brought to us have their picture placed on our walls, and as you can see not everyone can be here in person, but we believe that as long as we have their picture, they are here amongst us."

Robbie looked down at the table, the pictures of so many missing faces in the room saddened him deeply, Rune put her hand on his, and she felt the pain inside him. Steph and Jade looked across at him.

Sister Mary continued. "Your kindness has given us hope for a future, and we have no way we can truly show you how grateful we are except by adding you to our last remaining wall. Our children have spent all day in secret with the rest of the staff painting this for you, so I will reveal you one at a time; Harry has kindly given me all of your names."

She pulled the first sheet and revealed. "Little Eric," everyone cheered at the funny odd shaped little man with smooth dark hair and a huge bow. "Blades." She had spiky hair and two enormous swords. "Hog." A big man with a huge smile. "Mother," it was quite a good likeness. "Big John," they all laughed at John eating a whole deer. "Fish," he peered through the trees. "Runestone," Robbie smiled at the long red hair and the big blue eyes of a slender almost princess looking painting. "Robin Hood." A hooded man stood with a bow. The room exploded and she had to wait several minutes for them all to quieten down, she smiled at them all before she began again.

"Mad Harry," all the children screamed. "Pebbles, Rowan, Quiet Martin, Smooth Billy, and last but by no mean least Pigeon." Alice groaned into her hands as everyone looked at her.

"She totally is man, its major cosmic man." Rune laughed out loud and looked at Alice

"Pigeon, why pigeon?" Alice shook her head as if to say do not ask. Billy put his arm around her and chuckled.

"Come on it could be worse."

"Billy how could it be worse?"

"I don't know, he could have called you anything, what about chicken?"

"Hey man chicken is a sweet thing to say when you love someone." Harry beamed at Alice who suddenly registered what he had said and she smiled at him, he blew her a big kiss.

"They can call you pigeon baby cakes, but to me you will always be my chicken."

Alice's eyes filled with tears. "I love you too Uncle Harry."

Harry beamed. "Yeah, totally cosmic, you got my vibe baby girl." Harry pointed to the painting of him on the wall. "Look chicken, they really caught my radical side."

Alice looked at the wall and burst out laughing at the huge eight foot Mad Harry who looked like the abominable snowman dressed in a black coat. The swords looked like horns coming out of his head, and she screamed with hysterical laughter.

Robbie spent all night looking at the painting of a hooded man with a bow on the wall, above which the words had been painted 'Our saviour.' He was deeply touched by it and he knew that Sister Mary saw it, Rune certainly felt it.

Robbie left the meal early; he walked down the corridor and out in the empty yard. He stood at the bottom of the steps and breathed the fresh air. He took a long deep breath, and leaned on the post, he felt unworthy of the praise, his uncertainty about everything had grown each day and he wondered how long he could keep it up.

"You are troubled My Lord; can I help you?" Robbie turned and looked into the kind eyes of Sister Mary.

"I wish I had the faith that I see in you, I seem to spend so much of my days in doubt."

"Yet I see great faith inside you and your friends Robert of Loxley."

"I looked at all those faces on the wall in there Sister, you honour me when it is you who should be honoured for the lives you have helped and the lives you have saved, I am not worthy of such a tribute."

Sister Mary smiled. "Listen to me Robert of Loxley, because I have seen all that there is to see of people." She nodded as she spoke. "I have seen the good in people, and I have seen the worst. I am nearly seventy years old and I pray each day for another year." Sister Mary's eyes sparkled with life and hope.

"You are young and have so much time in front of you Robert, when you reach seventy, we will compare notes and see who has done the most." Robbie chuckled.

"I admire what you have done here, and when I return home, I will send you aid and help, I promise things will never be as bad as they were when I walked in here yesterday."

"You are a good man. When I saw you walk through my gate, I thought the Lord had sent me my angel of mercy, and in many ways he did. I will tell you Robert, that up until your arrival I was ready to quit." Robbie looked at her surprised. She nodded.

"I thought it was over, I was fighting a losing battle and I had made up my mind to close the gate forever. Before I opened the gate to you, I told myself this is the last one, and in walked my angel of mercy, who looked and said nothing, he just calmly gave orders and my mission was saved. Now tell me you do not deserve praise?"

Robbie was lost for words and just stared at the floor. "I have no words to express myself."

"You don't need them Robert; your heart is so big we all could see it. Why do you think there is so much love around you? Never in my life have I seen a woman care for a man as deeply as the Lady Runestone does for you. Look at the respect you command with your group, which is not because you led them, it is because they follow you. They follow you out of the love that they hold for you. You are very special Robert of Loxley and you should rejoice in what you hold in the palm of your hand."

Robbie looked at the smiling old nun. "What do I hold in the palm of my hand Sister?"

"You hold power, the power to do good, you are the most honourable man I have ever met, and I respect you for the even handedness in which you dispense it... There are many men who would abuse the power you have, and it would corrupt them. With you, it has not affected you, I see Robert the person he has always been, who loves a woman and is loved by all. Think very carefully about what I have said to you Robbie... I will see you before you leave, so sleep well tonight My Lord."

Sister Mary walked back up the steps and down the corridor, Robbie sat on the steps in thought, he was not aware of the silent figures of Rune and Alice who stood guard over him from the shadows.

Later that night, he lay in his bed with Rune curled around him, deep in thought. Rune looked up at him. "You should try to sleep."

"What will I be like when I am seventy?" Rune smiled and kissed his chest.

She sat up and looked at him, her eyes sparkled. "You will be old and wise, with long grey hair and wrinkles, and you will be as beautiful to me as you are now. I will love you more than I do now because for every day that we are together my love will grow." She smiled sweetly and he knew she was right. He put his hand on her cheek, she was so beautiful and he knew that he would love her forever.

She snuggled close to him and he held her in his arms until she was asleep. He lay in the dark and looked up at the ceiling; Sister Mary had given him a lot to think about.

It was just before dawn and Hog and Harry hitched up the team of four horses. Robbie and Fish spread the map out on the back of the cart and brought the lamp nearer to see. Rowan and Billy came up to see what was going on.

"Ok where exactly are we Fish?"

"We are here on Church Hill."

"Right, we need a road that will take us to Gloucester."

"This would be your best one but it's all overgrown, I doubt we will get the cart down there now it has been that long since anyone used it."

"Leave that to me Fish, that's our route, and we will be travelling with haste."

Everyone was appearing with their bags; Sister Mary had the kitchen provide supplies and they were loaded on the cart ready. Harry unbolted the gates and swung them open under the huge canopy of the Oak trees. "Hey man I know this sounds sort of freaky and weird, but how long have we been here? It's like I don't remember these trees at all."

Rune smiled at him. "Well Harry when we arrived two days ago you were suffering from having your karma chomped remember...? I do hope it's grown back." Everyone giggled.

"Wow yeah man that was an uncosmic day man."

Hog pulled on the team of horses and guided them out of the gates, most of the staff had come out to say goodbye, and many of the children looked sad and tearful. Robbie looked at the walls and noticed that overnight a whole grove of trees had sprung up surrounding the whole convent. Apples, plums, pears, and damsons hung in large bunches over the wall. Robbie smiled at Sister Mary and she winked at him. "I see you have spoken with your Lord Hearne." Robbie looked at the walls and the fruit.

"He gave me his word he would protect you."

"You see my noble friend; all of that doubt is for nothing. Put your faith in yourself and the love of this good woman beside you." Rune bent down and gave her a big hug.

"Take care of yourself Sister, this is not goodbye we will see you again."

Robbie took his bag of coins out of his pocket. "The children need clothes." He pressed it into her hand but she refused it.

"You have given more to us than you will ever know; I cannot take this, go with our love Robert."

Harry bent down in front of the children. "Hey my little baby people, what's with these tears? This is not goodbye I will be back when I have helped Robin Hood." He stood up. "Now what do we do when the world is hassle and we need to get our vibes back?"

All the children screamed at him. "Think cosmic!"

Harry beamed. "Peace chickens." He walked towards the gates with huge tears in his eyes and climbed on to the driver's seat of the wagon. He sat blowing his nose and wiping his eyes, as one by one everyone said goodbye to Sister Mary.

Alice hugged some of the children who were badly bandaged, her tears rolled as finally she stood up and Billy pulled her close. She kissed Sister Mary on the cheek. "Remember, change those dressings daily and keep using the cream I made."

Sister Mary hugged her. "Take care my child and look after each other."

Steph wept buckets as she hugged the children, and turned and left with her hankie up against her eyes, Rowan knelt beside a little girl with long blonde hair. He touched her face and she smiled. "You remind me of someone very special." Jade watched as he undid one of the woven coloured bands off his wrist. Taking her hand, he gently tied it to her wrist. "I am Rowan of the wood remember me and Hearne will protect you." He gave her a huge hug, and a tear welled in Jade's eye as she realised the small girl had to be the image of his lost sister. Rowan stood up and turned to Sister Mary.

"I will return here many times I promise, if you are ever in need call into the woods and I will hear you, and come to your aid, you are the protector of the innocent and Hearne will watch over you."

She smiled and took his hand. "Take care of each other and watch their backs they are very precious to all of us."

Jade gave her a huge hug. "We will, have no fear Sister."

The group finally came down to Hog and Fish, who both stood with their heads down. Sister Mary took them both into a big hug. "My dearest boys I am so proud of the company you keep; I must admit I have had my doubts in the past." She smiled a huge smile. "The good I have always seen in you has finally come to the surface; I am so proud of you boys. Look after yourselves and keep each other safe." Both boys wept as they hugged the sister who had been mother and teacher to them for most of their lives.

She patted them on the back and then pushed them back. "Go on now boys you have work to do. Be good for Robert and look after him for me." The boys walked through the gate and sobbing climbed on to the cart. Sister Mary dried her eyes.

As each one walked through the gate to the cart, they dropped their moneybags and then jumped aboard. Robbie stood at the gate as Rune climbed up on to the cart; he dropped his moneybag on to the pile of thirteen bags and smiled. "You cannot refuse what we all feel is right Sister."

She took his hands in hers. "Remember My Lord, have the faith to seek the truth and you will not go wrong." He pulled her into a tight hug.

"You have given me the gift of inspiration, and I will follow your example dear Sister and I thank you. Look after these children and we will return, my lord and your lord will protect you." Robbie climbed up and waved goodbye. Harry flicked the reigns and the cart lurched forward.

The gates closed as they reached the end of the driveway and everyone sat quietly wiping their eyes and blowing their noses. Just two days had passed since they had turned into the road that led to the House of Good Hope, and yet now it seemed like a life's time of love hovered above it.

Robbie sat at the back looking out at the road, and Rune slid up next to him, Billy sat quietly holding Alice in his arms a look of deep thought on his face, Steph dried her eyes on her hankie. Robbie looked back at everyone else. "Don't worry we will be back."

Robbie had not meant to waste an extra day at the convent, but as he thought of his conversation with Sister Mary the previous night, he understood that it was fate that had taken him there. His group had seen first-hand the work of Mason Knox, and they had acted as one sharing a close bond to ease a common pain. He was proud at how they had responded, and at how much they had achieved, the group were now closer than ever, and he knew that with just fourteen against countless numbers they would need to be.

The irony was interesting; he had walked into the hopeless and given them hope, now when he had felt at his most hopeless, they had given hope back to him. The picture of a hooded man on a wall came back to his thoughts and he smiled to himself. Maybe now he had a better idea of who the hooded man was, and what the hooded man should do. Robbing the rich and saving the poor had always seemed such fantasy notion, but now it was real. Knox would continue to murder, maim, and terrorise the people into submission and he had now seen the direct results, it had to stop and for the first time in a long time, Robbie knew what the hooded man really was.

He looked at Rune who was looking at him with a concerned look. "Are you alright Robbie, you look terribly pale?"

"I am fine Rune; I had very little sleep last night as I tried to work out what truly is the hooded man."

"What is it you have come up with?" Everyone was watching and listening.

"Us... All of us... Not just me, but everyone who pulls up a hood and loads a long bow and says here I am. Here is your hope, I will defend you because you cannot defend yourself. That is what all of us are and what all of us will do." Rune smiled a huge smile, and all of the others lifted their heads and smiled. She pulled him close and held him tight.

They travelled at speed down clear roads. Rowan sat at the front of the cart on top of the canvass and Jade at the other end, their route was clear and they approached the fork in the road that would see them leave the established routes. The cart slowed as it approached the lane, and Harry called Robbie up to the front. Fish sat next to Harry as Robbie leaned over.

The road was blocked, the hedgerows had grown right over the road and met in the middle, the floor was thick with Ivy, brambles, and grass. Harry pulled the horses to a halt. "Hey man the only thing that will make it down this road is a totally cosmic cat."

Robbie patted Harry's shoulder. "Have some faith my friend, Hearne is with us, now slowly drive into it."

"That's like really crazy man; we will be totally snared in a most radical way."

"It's all right Harry, do it." Harry flicked the reigns and the horses began to walk into the roadway. The trees lifted themselves up and the brambles and ivy scurried out of the way, tuffs of grass jumped on to the banksides and the road was clear.

"Whoa that is not cosmic man that is like jangled vibes."

Robbie grinned and patted him on the shoulder. "Alright Harry pick the pace up we need to move as quickly as possible." Harry urged the horses on, and the trees whipped up out of the way, clearing the road up to twenty feet in front at a time. Robbie moved back down the cart to the rear and looked out. The grass was jumping into the road and the brambles and ivy was slithering back into place as the trees leaned over and met again. Robbie smiled and glanced back at the white frightened faces.

"How the hell are you doing that Robbie?" Billy was as white as the rest.

"I am not, we have a little help from an old friend I met in the woods yesterday, let's just say we represent his interests, and so he has offered to help us." He winked at Rune who gave him a smile.

Eric dropped to his knees in the cart. "It's the great Lord Hearne, isn't it?" He bowed to the cart end. "Hearne help and protect us" Eric bowed very low and all of the others chanted under their breath. "Praise Hearne."

It was a strange moment for Rune to see this sudden outbreak of praise and loyalty towards someone who was actually the oldest surviving member of her family. Robbie noticed the puzzled look on her face, and he spoke quietly to her. "Odd, isn't it?" Rune blinked for a moment and looked at him.

"I have always known the men of the woods believed in him, I have never seen the devotion they show to him, it caught me quite by surprise."

Robbie sat back at the side of her. "Hearne to us is everything; he is our lord and master of the realm in which we live. He is in every leaf and stone and tiny creature that lives in the wood. To a woodsman he is the wood and we are his children. Whatever we take from his realm, it is only ever enough to cover our need. We do not take more than that because we know that he will continue to ensure we have our daily requirements." Rune looked around at all of the others who sat watching and listening to Robbie. "Hearne is not just some spirit, he is everything from life to death, he is the woods and he is us."

Rune watched, and as he finished they all said. "Praise Hearne."

Robbie smiled. "Now my good lady Runestone do you see why it is the job of true woodsmen to win this fight? Now you see why a hooded man was chosen. Mason Knox will cut back and burn down everything that holds our precious lord. Concrete and stone blocks and machines are not the world of Hearne; they are a threat to him. I want the world of my green lord to prevail." Rune stared out of the back of the cart at the trees as they moved back into place, and back to Robbie.

"I am of his line. I am the world you defend; I am the reason you will risk your life." Suddenly all the pieces fell into place and Rune realised that if Knox won, then over the coming generations the world would return to as it was, and eventually because of the greed and destruction the whole world would be thrown out of balance, and the world would fail. "Earth will die." Her voice was almost a whisper.

Robbie pulled her into his arms. "I will never allow that to happen." Rune clutched him tight, she now saw the full picture and it horrified her and she pushed her face into his chest to hide her fear. Robbie held her close and stroked her hair softly as the cart rattled along at an alarming speed.

They travelled quietly for well over an hour; most of them dozed as they swayed from side to side. Jade swung in from on top of the canvas and landed with a thump. Everyone jumped awake and she giggled. "Sorry guys... Look I don't know about any of you lot but I am bursting for a pee."

Eric looked up hopefully, as did John and Martin. Robbie looked at everyone. "What...? You are all grownups just say the word, I am Lord Loxley not some sort of toilet regulator, you do not need my permission, just go."

Martin leaned over and tapped Harry on the shoulder. "Pull up for a break Harry, will you?"

The cart slowed down and rolled to a halt, Steph stood up and stretched.

"Ladies left gents' right." Jade was already out of the cart and running into the trees. Everyone dropped off and wandered into their designated zones. Robbie walked around the cart on a clear grey surface. Twenty feet behind was impassable and the same in front. He stretched his arms and legs and wandered down to the horses that now leaned over to the verge and nibbled at the grass. The air seemed charged with electric, and he knew he was surrounded by the power of Hearne.

Jade slid down the bank and threw three rabbits on the floor. "Took em with a knife, thought about tea."

Robbie looked at her. "How do you sneak up on a rabbit without it seeing you...?" The penny dropped. "I know, so you have mastered it then?"

She gave him a huge grin. "Mum helped, I just wish I could block when I was having sex though, that's really hard and I just can't quite get the hang of it." She gave him a smile and walked off.

Robbie looked a little baffled and a little embarrassed. "What?" Rune was looking at him

"Does Jade have sex in your head; is that how you knew about her and Rowan?"

Rune smiled. "Yeah, she is having a bit of trouble blocking with that one; it's not easy trying to sleep with her going at it all night I can tell you."

Robbie looked panicked. "You can block though, can't you? Oh god please tell me your mother didn't hear us."

Rune started to giggle. "God Robbie stop panicking; you can be so insecure at times. I let a few things slip out at first, but your secrets are well and truly blocked with me."

"Oh good." Rune chuckled as she walked back to the cart to find the food box.

They all sat around the cart and had something to eat, whilst Fish, Rowan and Robbie tried to work out how far they had come. Rowan stood on top of the framework with Robbie's telescope and sighted each landmark. Robbie and Fish plotted it on to the map to cross-reference their position.

Fish looked at the map. "I knew we were moving Robbie but this has got to be a world record, the horses haven't even broken out in a sweat. We must be past Worcester."

Robbie winked. "As I have said, we have got a little extra help today." Fish looked very impressed as he glanced down at the map.

"If we keep up at this rate, we will do in one day what should have taken us five on foot."

"That is exactly what I am hoping. If we pop up somewhere we are not supposed to be, it will really confuse the enemy."

The sun was watery over Dean Hall. The young lord looked out of the windows onto the drive as the riders approached. Four soldiers wearing his father's colours dropped to the ground, and made great haste towards the front doors. There was a deep boom as the doors closed with muffled voices.

Young Sir Brandon walked across the almost empty room and sat in the only chair left by the fire. He clenched his hands nervously, as he heard the sound of feet on the stairs. A quiet tap on the door announced the arrival, and he looked up as Simmons stepped in.

"I am sorry to disturb you Master Brandon, but we must leave here now."

"What is it Simmons?"

The servant looked older than his fifty-five years as he bowed his head and looked at the floor. "I am so sorry sir, but the city has fallen and your father was lost in the battle."

Brandon fell back to his seat his face in his hands, and he shook with the silent tears that fell. Simmons gently placed a hand on his master's shoulder and gave it a gentle squeeze. "You are now the heir to Gloucester sir, you are the new duke, and if we do not get you away from here soon, he will find you and kill you, we must leave."

The duke looked up with tears in his eyes. "Let him come Simmons, I am not the fierce warrior my father was, what hope have I, a man of learning against a brute like Mason Knox?"

Simmons bent down on one knee. "I have served your family since I was sixteen years old sir. No matter how hard the times got, he was always a duke that was good and fair. Your father was a great warrior and lord of his people, but he wanted his son to be more than a man with a sword. He wanted his heir to be a man with the knowledge to keep his people alive, and you are now that man."

The duke watched the servant who had been by his side since birth shed tears of pain for the loss of a great man, and tears of love for the fear of his young son. He threw his arms around him and wept. The old servant held him tight as if holding his own son; softly he patted him on the back. "Come My Lord, we will take you to safety."

The big sergeant stood in the hallway as the duke came down with Simmons and threw his short burgundy cloak over his shoulders. The sergeant bowed and lifted a long package tied with burgundy cord; he knew it instantly; it was his father's sword and heirloom of the family. "My lord's last wish was for me to get this to you Lord Brandon."

Hesitantly the new duke took the sword of his father off the sergeant and looked to Simmons for guidance. "I think you should wear it in honour of your father My Lord." The old servant took the sword and gently un-wrapped it. He looped the belt around the duke and pulled the buckle of gold tight to his waist. The duke stood in the hall as the soldiers bowed to their new leader; he felt insecure and frightened and looked very uncomfortable. "Where will you take us Sergeant?"

"My orders sir from your father were to take you to Tintern to the Abbey sir, they have rebuilt it and will hide you until we can regroup. The army is scattered and we need help, your father thought that we could probably get you safely in Wales sir, the head of the abbey will help you."

"Thank you, Sergeant, I know you served my father well."

"He was a great man sir, and I will honour his memory in my service to you Sir, now if you don't mind Sir we really must go. Your horse awaits you outside." The sergeant stepped back and allowed the duke and his servant to pass. He nodded to the two soldiers by the door that stepped outside, and escorted him to his horse. The Sergeant turned to the other soldier. "Won't last the week that one."

The six riders swept out of the gates and down the road at great speed, the daylight was fading and they had to travel fast. A mile down the road the sergeant turned and headed up a small track, Simmons shouted up to him. "Why are we leaving the road Sergeant?"

"Too dangerous Sir there are enemy soldiers everywhere, we must cut across country if we are to get there on time." They galloped across the fields and headed for the woodland two miles in front of them.

Robbie and Rune leaned back after eating a very nice selection of cheeses and fresh bread. Jade threw an apple over and Rune caught it in her hand without opening her eyes. Robbie smiled; he knew she was watching from his perspective. "What do you think you will see?"

Rune smiled and opened her eyes. "How did you know?"

"I feel it; I know you are there as I feel your presence like you're sat at my shoulder."

"I just wanted to know what you see when you look at me."

He leaned over and looked into her bright blue eyes. "I see eyes as blue as sapphires that are filled with love and life, and I think they are the most beautiful eyes in the world. Your hair is as soft as silk and reminds me of the sunset in autumn that glistens on damp leaves. Shall I continue?"

She looked up and giggled. "Please do."

He stroked her face gently. "Your skin is as radiant as the moonlight on mid summers eve, and your lips are the pale pink of honeysuckle in the last days of September. You are beautiful Rune and I love you." She giggled as he slowly leaned down and kissed her nose. "Which is better, your view or my words."

"Your words," she whispered and reached up to kiss him.

"Hear me Runestone daughter of the woods."

"Grandmother is that you?"

"Rune my darling you must make haste and bring the hooded man."

"What is it Grandmother"

"Gloucester has fallen, the new duke is in danger, his father was killed and now he is about to leave to flee to safety, his party have no idea of the trap they heading for. I will do my best to divert them, but you must get the Hooded man here to protect him."

"I will Grandmother."

"Hurry child."

Rune opened her eyes as he pulled away from the kiss, they glowed deep lilac. "Wow my kisses must be getting better."

"Grandmother."

"Oh well never mind."

Robbie sat up and waited. Rune sat up suddenly and Robbie jumped. "Robbie

Gloucester has fallen and the new duke is in danger we must get to him and fast."

Robbie was up on his feet. "Mount up and quickly we are needed." Everyone gathered their things and hurried into the back of the cart. Robbie slammed the tailgate shut and jumped into the cart. "Hit it Harry."

The cart lurched forward and everyone slipped around. "Where to Rune?"

"Robbie I don't know, she did not say. She said the new duke is heading into a trap and she would try to divert them."

"Alright we will head that way and you try to find out exactly where this duke is." Rune nodded as Robbie turned and headed up to the front. "Ok Fish we need to get to Gloucester by the fastest route, can you do it?"

"We are on the road Robbie, this will take us down to Ross, and we just hang a left and it should be just down the road." Robbie patted his arm. "Hell, Harry how fast are we going?"

"Hey man I am sort of like just holding the reigns, these horses have gone seriously cosmic man, and they have vibes like I have never seen man."

Robbie sat back down in the back. "Ok has everyone got enough arrows? Check your bows and sharpen your knives. Billy how is the arm?"

"It is feeling great Robbie that stuff of Alice's is really good." Billy swung his arm around and flexed it; Robbie smiled and patted his knee.

"Good to have you back to full health bro." The trees were a blur as everyone got busy and sorted out their kit, Robbie wiped down his bow and checked the tension on the bowstring, and Rune followed his lead, and smiled as he gave hers a test and nodded. Pebbles looked down at Eric's empty knife pouch.

"Where is your dagger, Eric?"

"I don't have one; I only have a woodsman's knife."

Jade slid her arm up her back and pulled a long dagger out from under her cloak. "Here you can have one of my spares."

Eric looked at the long silver dagger with a bright silver handle. "Wow Pebbles thanks; I don't know what to say."

Pebbles grinned. "Don't cut yourself on it and if you get killed... I am taking it back." Eric went a funny shade of white; Martin started to laugh with John and patted him on the shoulder.

The cart flew at speeds unknown to horses, Hearne was true to his word and the trees flew apart to allow them through. It took them just over an hour and they were on the outskirts of Ross and slowing down as a cross roads approached. Rune's eyes began to glow violet, as Harry looked back at Robbie. "Hey man we are coming up to crossroads and I could really use a vibe on which way to find cosmicville."

"Hold on Harry it's coming." Robbie stared at Rune as she closed her eyes and connected with her grandmother.

High Meadow woods was just ahead, and as the duke and his party raced at great speed, the soldiers of Mason Knox entered the Abbey at Tintern. The horses pounded into the woodland and the light dimmed instantly, they slowed so they could see where they were going, white mist rolled in from the south. It was difficult riding as they picked their way through the trees, the sergeant now close to the side of the duke stared into the gloom as he tried to navigate the trees. "Watch your head here Sir the trees are quite low."

He moved to the right as the trees became so thick that they could only move away from the direction that they wanted to head in. "This is bloody hopeless Sir; we will have to head further north until I can find away round. It is strange; I never remember these woods being so thick before."

"We shall have to do the best we can Sergeant don't worry."

An arrow whistled through the trees, and the soldier in front left his saddle a long red-feathered arrow stuck out of his chest. The Sergeant grabbed the reigns of the duke's horse and pushed him forward forcing him down to the horse's head. He kicked his spurs and both horses shot forward. With his arm over the duke to protect him Sergeant Harrow rode with speed, Simmons lying low in his seat followed, as arrows whistled overhead. Three soldiers in the burgundy of their duke lay dead and the black-coated soldiers mounted their horses and began the pursuit.

Rune opened her eyes. "Follow the hawk."

Robbie slapped Harry's back. "Follow the hawk Harry."

"Hey man there is no.... Whoa that is one cosmic birdie man." The cart lurched forward as Harry flicked the reigns and they sped off. Harry followed the hawk as Fish stood up hanging on to the hoops and watched it fly over a field and into the woodland.

"Trees coming and they don't appear to be moving for us guys." The note of alarm in Fish's voice was enough and everyone leaned inwards, Birch branches shot through the open sides of the hoops and the cart jumped on the roots, everyone sat back hanging on, as they cleared the edge of the woodland and entered the trees. The hawk swooped down to rest on a tree stump, and Harry pulled hard on the break as the cart shuddered to a halt.

Robbie and Rowan were the first two out. "Everyone fan out you know the routine, until we know different this place is unfriendly."

Robbie headed across the trees and looked out on an open plain. The ground dropped in a steep slope, and then there was a large expanse of grassland. Five thousand yards away was woodland, he scanned the tree line for signs of life. Three horses at speed broke out of the trees, and galloped across the plain towards them, several seconds later a whole host of riders in black came out of the trees behind them. Robbie knew the moment he saw them who they were.

"Riders approaching," he yelled. "Three up front are the good guys, the really large group behind don't like us so make your arrows count, let's take cover and get ready."

The group moved like lightening along the forest edge, hoods went up and bowstrings felt the arrows as they fitted into them. Everyone took aim and waited, as the three riders flew across the plain below, Robbie watched as one of the riders broke free, he reared up on his horse and there was a flash of silver as he pulled out his sword. He turned and rode back to the chasers in black as the other two continued.

Robbie gripped the bow. "What the hell is he doing?" He took aim as the rider approached the mass in black. He judged the swordsman would go for the one on his right side first and aimed for the left. He pulled back as far as he could on the string and fired.

As the sergeant hit the man to his right with a mighty slice of his sword, the man on his left was unseated by Robbie's arrow, Rowan gasped with surprise. "That was well over a thousand yards."

The sergeant headed into the midst of the enemy taking four with him before he fell to the ground. The duke with his servant made the bottom of the hill, their horses exhausted. Robbie screamed on the top of his voice. "In coming riders hold your bows, on my signal." Robbie stood up as the dukes gasping horse came up the hill towards him. The young lord looked terrified to see a bowman right in front of him.

"Hog as they hit the trees, get them off those horses." The duke came past watching Robbie, and was suddenly unseated and pulled to the ground. Simmons pulled on the reigns as Hog leaped up and snatched him from the seat dumping him on to the floor at the side of the duke.

"Stay!" He barked, and snatched his bow and turned to the trees.

The enemy host approached the foot of the hill. "Get ready... Now!"

The hail of arrows unleashed from the trees, and the horses reared backwards as the force took the riders clean out of their seats. The riders behind had no time to react, as the bowmen reloaded with speed, and unleashed a second wave. Robbie loaded with immense speed, sighted, and fired with incredible accuracy. Some of the riders at the back realising it was a trap turned and began to retreat.

"Rowan, Pebbles, Pigeon, Rune, take the stragglers out." The arrows sung, and as the riders headed back, they were unseated and fell to the ground. The last volley of arrows flew out, and the few remaining riders hit the floor dead. The horses scattered in every direction.

Robbie stood on the edge of the tree line, he looked at the piled up dead at the foot of the hill. "Harry, Hog check them and finish it, Eric I want arrows, all of ours and any of theirs, I also want all their swords and knives, John and Martin give him a lift. The rest of you secure this area."

Robbie turned with Rune and walked back as the rest of the group jumped into action, he walked up to the duke and his servant who were sat on the floor and looked down at them. "I am assuming you are the Duke of Gloucester, if not I just saved the wrong man."

Simmons looked gratefully up at him. "This is the new duke, and I am his envoy Simmons, I have no idea what you were doing here, but I am very grateful indeed." He rubbed his arm, which seemed very painful.

Robbie stretched down and pulled him up, he looked at his arm. "I am sorry about Hog, he is a bit rough but he gets the job done, didn't want to risk you getting an arrow."

Simmons smiled. "Thank you, Sir."

"Rune could you see these gents to the cart and get them a drink they look like they need it."

The duke looked most put out as he staggered to his feet and Robbie returned to his men. "Just who are you?"

Pebbles walked past. "Like the clothes don't give it away." She dumped a large pile of blood stained arrows into the cart.

Rune smiled at him. "Let's just say we are friends of a friend; would you like to come this way My Lord?" Rune took them over to the cart and helped them into the back. Harry came up with the two horses and tied them to the back of the cart.

Rune walked back over to Robbie who stood in the tree line watching for any sign of others, he put his arm around her. "It is really starting now." He stared out as darkness started to fall over the fields. Rune slid her arm around him and pulled him close.

"You really handled that well Robbie, grandmother was very impressed, and she said there is a cave not far from here. The hawk will guide us, put two men on foot in front of the cart and walk the horses."

Robbie nodded. "Come on then, let's go and baby sit lord what's his face."

CHAPTER FIFTEEN

THE ROAD TO CAERLEON

The duke and his servant sat in the cart with the group of strangers as it moved slowly through the woods. Everyone was filled with high spirits, having fought their first true encounter with the army of Mason Knox. Simmons watched the jovial group, and although they were strangers, they had treated him kindly and he knew they were not to be prisoners.

Robbie held the reigns of the horse as he talked to Rune, and walked slowly forward watching the hawk that now led them to safety. "I think we should keep as quiet as possible; we do not know for certain how much this new duke knows, and trust only a few people outside of this group."

Rune nodded. "I think you are right; I am not sure we should inform the world of my line at all; they have been the secret guardians ever since the prophecy of Rhiannon was discovered."

Robbie looked over at her. "What prophecy was that?"

"Rhiannon, she is the Celtic goddess of the moon who many hundreds of years ago told of a time when the snake would grow legs and wings and destroy the world. It is the one my grandfather referred to when he told you that you were the heir to Loxley back in his house before the ceremony."

"A snake that grows legs and wings, I have already seen that twice now."

Rune looked concerned. "I saw their tunics tonight and I thought there is a snake with legs and wings. It frightened me to know something said so long ago could come true. It is so odd, all these years he has taught me things, and I never once realised he was teaching me about what was to come. I thought it was myths."

Robbie smiled. "Up until meeting your family I thought the same." He started to chuckle and Rune laughed.

"I suppose we do take a bit if getting used to don't we? You are brave to get involved with us lot."

Robbie glanced over at her smiling face. "Most of it I can cope with, it is a grannie who walks through walls that freaks me out."

She started to giggle. "So invisible sisters with big green eyes are alright?"

"Pebbles is cool, it's Harry who worries about that, and you know risking his karma and all his mangled vibes."

Rune looked back at Harry and covered her mouth as she started to laugh. "I really wanted to tell her off for that Robbie. It was really cruel, but all I could hear was my mum's hysterical laughter in my head, and I just started to giggle. Poor Harry it's no wonder he has his odd moments."

Robbie chuckled, as he looked up the track. "What's that? Is it a cave? Oh, I hope so I just want to sleep, I hardly got any last night, I suppose we had better sort his nibs out before we do anything else."

The cart stopped as the hawk landed outside the cave, Robbie and Rune entered with raised bows. The light was now fading fast and they peered into the dark to see if it was inhabited, as they came out of the cave, the cart was emptying. "Billy light a fire in there at the back will you, Hog, Fish, will you unload the cart, Harry sort the horses, Rowan, Jade keep a look out." He walked around to the end of the cart and looked at the duke and Simmons. "Won't keep you a moment, let us just get set up and you will be safe here for the night. If you would like to get out and stretch your legs, feel free but stay close to the cave where it is safe."

The group scrambled and very soon, a roaring fire blazed in the back of the cave out of sight. Alice found some candles in the store box and placed a few around to give more light, and then rolled out the bedding on the sandy floor. Eric got out the rabbits and fresh veg and went to work on a meal, and within thirty minutes everyone was set in position and the camp was up and running.

The Duke of Gloucester sat with Simmons utterly bewildered as John handed him a steaming mug of coffee. "That will warm you up a bit; tonight will be a cool one My Lord."

He took it gratefully and sat clutching it in the back of the cave. Robbie and Rune walked up and John handed them a cup each, Simmons stood up and held out his hand. "I would like very much to thank you Sir for saving my lord back there, I don't think we would have been able to out run them much longer."

Robbie took his hand and shook it. "It was our pleasure, sorry for the rough quarters for tonight, we had to change our plans at the last minute, it appears your Abbey is now in different hands." Simmons looked shocked.

"I cannot believe it that is a sacred place of sanctuary, he has no right."

Robbie crouched down to look at the duke. "It appears our young lord is in shock, had a bit of a fright tonight, he will need a meal and a good rest before we go on." He looked back up at Simmons. "As for right, it appears our friend feels he has every right, he is under the delusion that this country is his."

Simmons looked at his master and then at Robbie. "Who are you sir? I would like to know the name of the man who saved my lord here."

Robbie laughed. "Of course, so very sorry how rude of me." He held out his hand. "I am Robbie and this is Runestone, and these hooded good people are my companions at arms. I know who this is, but who exactly are you again?"

Simmons shook Rune's hand. "I am Simmons."

Rune gave him a wide smile. "Nice to meet you Simmons, please make yourself at home." Simmons looked around at all of the others sat with their long cloaks and large hoods down their back and slowly he put the pieces together. He looked at Rune as he dropped back on to the box. "He is Robyn in the Hood."

Rune smiled and crouched down. "He is and you are lucky that word reached him just in time, a few more minutes and I fear we may have lost your lord."

"But I thought it was all folklore and rumour, I would never have believed it." Simmons looked completely shocked.

Rune patted his arm as Eric came up with two steaming plates of rabbit stew. The duke slowly ate his as Simmons sat with Rune and talked. "Robbie is the true heir of the original Robin Hood. He is pure Loxley and to date the only one who has shared his extraordinary gifts with the bow, and woodsman's skills."

"So, he is the Lord Loxley we have all been hearing about? The one that Knox fears most, the bowman that the old prophecy says will vanquish him?"

"I would play the lordship thing down while we are out in the woods, out here he is a simple woodsman and just Robbie, but yes he is the bowman the prophecy spoke of. Eat your stew before it gets cold it's delicious." Simmons sat and ate his stew and attended to his master. He viewed the group with greater respect as they went about their duties.

Robbie sat with Billy at the cave entrance; Alice leaned against Billy's leg as the darkness fell. Rune came over and sat with them. She looked as tired as Robbie felt. "You should turn in Robbie, come on you are so tired, let Billy handle things for a while."

Billy patted his leg. "Go on Rob, I got you covered." Robbie wearily stood up, and Rune led him to a far corner of the cave where it was quiet. She had set up a small bed for him and he rolled under the blankets. She kissed him softly and he closed his eyes, and drifted in to a restless haunted sleep.

It was early morning and Robbie awoke in the back of the cave to the sound of Harry. He felt rough and ached and was still very tired. "Hey dude you ain't goin nowhere until Robbie says so. Come on man chill and be peaceful, we ain't going to mess with your vibes. Robbie is a cool and cosmic guy, and you should hang here man until he is ready."

"Get out of my way you big hairy man and just let me leave, I have to get to the abbey."

"Listen dude I don't want to get real radical with you, but if you aint peaceful like in a few minutes we will have serious karma conflict, you get me?"

"What's the problem Harry?" Robbie stood at the edge of the wall with his hair sticking up and his shirt open, the bright silver lion seemed to twinkle on his chest.

The young duke turned. "Are you in charge of this bunch of ruffians?"

"These ruffians as you call them saved your life last night; I think you had better change your tone before the others return." Robbie looked around the empty cave. "Where's the other one Harry?"

"He is like cleaning himself at the stream man. I like him; he is cosmic and sweet with us."

"I need attending to, could you bring him here to me immediately."

Harry turned to leave the cave, but Robbie raised his voice. "Harry, don't you dare... I want you to go outside and ask Rune to come in here please; don't let anyone else in this cave until I say so."

The young duke turned to Robbie. "How dare you prevent my man from attending me, who the hell do you think you are?" Rune stepped into the cave as Robbie spun on his heel and faced the young duke.

"I AM LORD ROBERT JOHN LOXLEY AND 51ST EARL OF HUNTINGDON AND HEIR BY DIRECT DECENT TO ROBYN IN THE HOOD, AND YOU WILL ADDRESS ME AS MY LORD WHEN YOU SPEAK TO ME."

Rune looked shocked. Not as shocked as the duke who trembled before the anger of Robbie. Robbie's eyes glared with fire. "Those men out there are some of the finest men I have ever had the privilege to meet, they answered the call to your aid without question, and I might add risked their lives to save yours. If you wish to leave, feel free, I am quite sure Knox will round you up within hours and slit your pompous throat."

Robbie spun around and walked up the cave, as he neared the entrance he stopped and turned around, his voice was much calmer.

"What is your name?" The young duke looked terrified.

"It's Lord Brandon Berkley My Lord."

"Right Brandon let me make one thing clear, under my command there are no titles, every man works as one, and for the duration of your stay you will also play your part. If your servant so much as fastens your cloak I will shoot him, do I make myself clear?"

The young duke nodded. "Very My Lord."

"It's Robbie, out here we are woodsmen." Robbie walked up to Rune who was speechless. "This twit needs a better cloak, have we any of those black robes left in the cart?"

Rune nodded. "Yes."

Robbie softened and smiled. "Please would you sort him something out? That red cloak is a beacon to the enemy."

Rune smiled. "Are you alright?"

"Yeah, I am fine, I just cannot abide ungratefulness." He leaned forward and gave her a soft kiss on the cheek. She smiled and her eyes sparkled, Robbie walked out of the cave into the assembled smiling group. "You all heard that?"

The whole group nodded. "Then you know that every man must play his part," he pointed to Simmons who looked very pale. "If he acts like a servant just once, you all have my permission to shoot him." Simmons paled even more and swallowed hard. "Eric the duke will cook breakfast this morning, show him how to."

The group beamed as they broke off to go about their duty. Robbie walked down to the side of the stream and washed his face. He stood up and looked out across the valley from Sisters Rock. It looked so peaceful in the early morning sunlight. The valley swept lush and green to the edge of the river as it snaked its way in to the surrounding woodland. How can such beauty contain such madness he thought to himself? Footsteps came down towards him and he turned.

Blades wandered down with a coffee, he took the steaming cup and sipped it, and she smiled. "You have no idea how much what you said meant to the rest of them Robbie, that was a very nice thing."

"It had nothing to do with nice. It was honest." He looked up at Blades. "Sorry I am tired and a bit snappy... how are you doing anyhow? I have not had much time to talk. Are you getting use to everybody?" Robbie walked slowly back up the hill to the cave as Blades filled him in.

"I love being with dad all the time, I can really get to know him better and Alice and Pebbles have been so kind to me, all the lads are great, even Billy seems to talk to me more. I really love Mother; we talk for hours she is so clever and Eric is sort of sweet."

Robbie raised an eyebrow. "Don't let your dad hear that, he already thinks Eric is uncool and not cosmic."

Blades giggled. "I really like Eric, but not that way. He is the same; both of us are the youngsters of the group so we talk about how to fit in."

"I think both of you have fitted in really well considering the others, both of you have made a very real contribution. Neither of you have anything to prove now, I consider you both as equals in this group, you tell Eric that."

Blades smiled and happiness seemed to radiate from her as they approached the cave entrance. "Thanks Robbie." Blades wandered into the cave for breakfast. Robbie sat on the back of the cart and Rune came out with a plate of fried eggs and beans. He looked at the dark crispy edged eggs surrounded by watery looking beans; he slipped his fork in and tasted it. "Not bad considering it is probably the first thing he has ever cooked. Where did the eggs come from?"

Rune leaned against the cart. "Funny you should ask; we were just trying work out how Hog can find fresh eggs no matter where we are. He just walked into camp miles away from nowhere with his arms full."

Robbie cleared his plate and sat back. "I am not sure I am too bothered I really enjoyed that. I will have to let his lordship know." He slipped off the cart and took his plate inside the cave, he could not help but smile as he crossed to the fire to see the red faced and somewhat sweaty Brandon busily frying eggs as the group went back for seconds.

Simmons seemed quite anxious about his master's welfare, and was using all his self-restraint to hold himself back, and of course avoid being shot by one of the others. Robbie smiled at Eric. "That was really good Eric, I enjoyed it, you must let Brandon help you again... Simmons, can I have a word outside? Billy, Rowan, you as well."

Robbie sat at the cart with the map laid out and held down with a few rocks. They were just above Monmouth and needed to head south to get to Wales; their big problem was that the only road they could use went through Tintern, and right past the abbey. Billy looked at the map. "We could lose the cart and go on foot but that will treble our travelling time. What we really need is a diversion to make them look one way, whilst we pass another." Robbie pondered the point.

"I would prefer to keep us all together if possible, we are in strange surroundings and I don't want the risk of us being separated permanently."

Pebbles and Alice came out of the cave holding their noses, Jade looked repulsed. "Can't you do something about your brother Fish? Robbie, do we have to keep feeding him beans? It will be a good hour before we can go back in there." Other members of the group were emerging and looking sickly, Rune looked positively green.

"We have to do something about Hog Rob, no offence Fish but it's disgusting, I am sure he does them and then walks off... are you sure it's not dysentery?"

Robbie smiled. "That has just given me a great idea... Hog come here I need you." Everyone looked startled and moved well away from Robbie just in case. Hog came out of the cave and over to Robbie.

"You want me, Robbie?" There seemed to be a dubious odour around him.

"Hog I need you to find me a sack full of something foul smelling, you know dung and stuff."

"Ok Robbie." Hog wandered off into the bushes and Rune gave him a strange look.

"What are you up to?" He smiled.

"You will see. Alice don't roll up the blankets, and can you make sure everyone has a scarf?" She looked puzzled and Billy leaned forward.

"Just what exactly have you got in mind Robbie?"

Robbie smiled a devilish smile. "Remember the watering cans?" Billy nodded. "Well, it will be worse." Robbie chuckled, as he walked off to find Harry.

Everything was packed on the cart and ready to go, when Hog returned with his sack. He had barely made it in to the camp when they all started sniffing the air. Everyone was made to bind their faces with scarves, and then get in the cart and wrap up in a blanket. Rune had nipped off with Alice into the bushes; they stepped out as Hog put the bag down. It fell over and the contents spilled out, Alice and

Rune, who were a few feet away, retched violently. Rune covered her mouth but it was too late.

Robbie shouted as Alice began to throw up with Rune. "No don't waste it do it in the sack."

Rune had a look of abject misery on her face as she looked at Robbie and suddenly understanding what he had just shouted, she looked at the sack and vomited again. It took another twenty minutes before a green and pale looking Rune and Alice would even come near the cart.

Finally, when everyone was on the cart with their scarves firmly in place over their mouths and noses and covered with blankets, Robbie rolled down the canvas and sealed them inside. Hog sat on the tailgate with his sack, and Robbie without his cloak jumped up into the front with Harry. "Let's move."

As Harry moved off, Robbie lifted the canvass behind the driver's seat and pushed his head into the cart with the confused looking group. Rune was looking an awful colour and as he looked down at her, she rolled over and turned her back to him.

Robbie looked up. "Rowan, Billy, Pebbles, if their guards stop the cart be ready, I am hoping that Hog and his bag is enough, if they lift the cover just moan."

The cart rattled down the road through Monmouth and headed for Tintern and the abbey, Robbie pulled an old blanket over his head and shoulders as the cart approached the guards. A long barrier was set across the road, and six soldiers in black tunics watched them as the cart slowly moved up to them. They came to a halt as the soldier eyed them suspiciously.

"What's in the cart?" His eyes looked up and down the large frame of Harry who smiled weakly. All the other soldiers watched as they walked slowly up and down checking the cart out.

Robbie climbed down slowly and hobbled around to the soldier. "Speak up sonny I am a bit deaf," he shouted.

The soldier looked at him. "Why the mask?"

"Dysentery."

The soldier stepped back a bit; he looked very suspiciously at Robbie and then began to walk around to the back of the cart; muffled moans came from inside. Jade and Rowan crouched by the tailgate wrapped in a blanket. Both of them had knives ready and their bows were an arm's reach away covered and ready. Billy waited at the back of the cart just behind Harry, his long silver sword drawn. Alice watched nervously as the shadow of the soldier walked down the side of the cart to the back.

He reached the back and the air was foul, Hog sat holding his sack. He looked up at the soldier, and a deep whining sound emitted from between the tailgate and Hog, he gave an embarrassed smile and loosened the top of the sack. The soldier stepped back. "God that's disgusting." He covered his nose and fanned the air in front of him. "Are they all like that?"

"Worse." Robbie croaked.

The soldier wretched, as he stepped backward. "God, get that stinking heap out of here."

Robbie nodded. "Yes Sir," and he headed back to the front of the cart and slowly climbed on. Harry flicked the reigns and the cart moved forward. Jade's arms moved as she pushed her knives back into her belt. She smiled at Rowan and he relaxed and pulled off his blanket. He pushed the long silver dagger back into his boot, and gave her a wink and smiled. Billy popped his head through the canvass and looked up the road.

"Robbie you are a genius." He gave him a huge happy smile, everyone inside the cart moved as knives and swords were put back into sheaths.

Once round the corner and out of sight, Harry flicked hard and the horses picked up speed. They flew down the road putting as much distance as they could between them and the abbey. Robbie put his head back inside and looked around at the smiling faces. "Everyone alright back there?" He looked at Brandon. "Soon have you nice and safe again." Rune looked the other way and refused to look at him.

Harry pulled the cart off the road into the trees and ran down a small track into a clearing surrounded by thick birch and small oak trees, the cart bumped over the large tufted clumps of grass. Hog jumped off the back removing his putrid sack. Robbie jumped off the front and ran round the back of the cart; he undid the ties and let them all out.

All of them collapsed on the grass and gasped for clean air. Hog put his sack down about fifty feet away, as Rune climbed down off the cart looking very pale, Robbie smiled at her and she walked away. "Oh come on Rune, don't be mad, it was a safe way of getting us all through."

She walked to the trees and took deep breaths and continued to ignore him. Billy came up to Robbie pulling down his scarf and smiling. "Don't worry bro she will be fine in a bit... Just as a matter of interest what was in that bag?" Robbie shrugged. Billy looked up the path. "Hey Hog what did you have in the bag?"

Hog smiled. "Cow dung, dead badger, dead sheep, and Rune sick." He tipped the bag out and it spilled on to the grass. Rune and Alice put their hands to their mouths and flew into the trees. One or two of the others also disappeared.

It was sometime later when everyone was fit to travel, Hog now smelt so bad that everyone insisted on him travelling on the tailgate. They hurtled down the side of the River Seven and finally, as midday passed, they pulled in at the side of the river. They all stretched their legs as they jumped out, and walked around to get the blood flowing. Some of them sat at the riverbank and washed their faces; very few of them ate anything. Fish came out from behind the cart and walked up to

Hog who stood at the edge of the river. "That was clever brother, and it probably saved our lives but now." He gave Hog a huge push, and he fell headfirst into the river. Hog spluttered as he came back up, and stood dripping in front of Fish on the bank.

"What did you do that for?" Fish tossed him a bar of soap.

"You stink, wash yourself or you are walking." Everyone started to laugh, and even Hog broke into a smile and started to rub the soap on his clothes and his hands and face. Even Rune seemed able to give a little smile, she turned to Robbie and he turned away and walked over to Simmons and got the map out. Her face dropped and her eyes clouded over.

Robbie spread out the map, he felt angry inside at Rune for being so stupid and ignoring him, he glanced up and saw her down hearted and dispirited as she walked along the bank of the river. His heart pulled a little and he started to feel bad, but he thought to himself, 'No a little while longer won't hurt her she acted stupid. I was trying to get everyone safely through.'

He looked down at the map, Fish had pinpointed them to be just outside Caldicot they were just over an hour away from Caerleon, and he breathed a sigh of relief. Billy wandered over towards him. "So how are we doing, are we there yet?" He looked at the map.

"We are not far from the castle and some peace and safety, I must admit Billy boy I am looking forward to a day's rest, I have hardly slept in the last few days, and what sleep I have had has been disturbed with dreams. It will be nice to know someone is watching over us for a change."

Rune wandered along the bank watching the water peacefully slide past the bank. Ducks and geese paddled along the edges level with her, and then disappeared into the thick clumps of reeds and tall flag.

She felt lost, confused, and suddenly very hurt, why had she been so silly and ignored him? She had hurt him and her regret fuelled the pain inside of her. A single tear fell to the ground and a small violet sprung up. She knelt down and looked at it, how curious she thought. She had seen it happen when she was with Hearne, but she had naturally assumed that it had been his doing. She reached out her hand and touched it. The plant divided and became two; she smiled and touched it again. The plants divided into four, she giggled and turned, two small white feet stood on the grass before her. Rune jumped and looked up.

"Hello my daughter of the wood."

"Grandmother." Rune stood up and embraced her. "You surprised me."

"Listen my child you have now received most of your powers and in time they will strengthen, I see you have noticed your effect on the world, that is good for there lies your true power."

Rune looked at the lady stood before her in a long white robe with a white hood over her head. "I do not understand Grandmother, what is my power? I thought I was the centre of the circle."

"So you are my daughter, as I was to my generation which is now fading."

"Fading how do you mean? This is not making sense."

"All of us have limited time Rune when measured in the span of the world. My time will come to an end and your time will begin as you inherit the mantle I will pass to you, fear not we still have many years before your full time is here."

Rune's eyes opened wide and she felt frightened. "Tell me Grandmother, what will happen to me? Why have I been chosen when my sister is older?" Her eyes began to fill with violet.

"Calm yourself daughter of the woods you will have your time with your woodsman and his children and their children's children, and you will also know the joy of life in every form."

Rune began to cry. "Grandmother please tell me I will not have to endure three lives without Robbie, because I cannot bear the thought of that. I love him and want only to be with him, do not tell me that I will have to see him die and live on." Rune fell to her knees and wept bitterly.

The lady in white knelt down beside her. "Rune please you must not upset yourself; please listen to my words for you have no choice in what has been preordained for you. It was not my choice and it was not your woodsman's choice, but everyone has a purpose, and yours could be such joy if you would open yourself to it." Her grandmother placed a hand on her shoulder. "Calm yourself my child; do you not know who you are?"

Rune hung her head as the tears slowly stopped dripping to the floor, where a wide carpet of violets now grew. "I am you; I am Nature."

The white lady softly stroked her hair. "You are the flowers in the morning and the wind in the trees, you are summer berries and the late sunset breeze, all of the world that grows will be your domain, because your life will be theirs, you will be the mother of all the Lord Hearne creates."

Rune looked up at the white hood from which in just a single moment, blue flashed across, Rune rose slowly to her feet and looked at the white hood. Slowly she raised her hands and took hold of the hood, Rune slid the hood back to reveal the face of her grandmother.

Her grandmother smiled. "See my child you will bring life to the world." Rune stared at her own face beneath the white hood. The golden red hair and the sapphire blue eyes were hers in every likeness she pulled the hood back up over her grandmother, and her arms dropped by her side.

Her grandmother took her hand. "Runestone there is hope in this world and in others do not despair for you have so much more to gain, not everything will be as it seems, please trust me for you will one day understand everything fully."

Her grandmother pulled her speechless body into an embrace. "I must leave you now for soon you will go to the castle and bring another sister into our fold. Your powers are stronger now than you have ever known, use them wisely and protect the woodsman."

Rune stood like a statue frozen in time, her mind spun as the thought of having to live life after life alone without him. The shock of knowing was too much to cope with, and the pain in her heart welled up inside her, knowing that only one part of her life would be the happiness she wanted. The rest was going to be a long and enduring pain of grief and loss. Her grandmother the white lady of the wood walked into the trees and was gone.

The time had seemed to slow down, and unmoving Rune stood in a small glade in the wood at the edge of the river. Her eyes glowed lilac and then violet, slowly the colour deepened. The leaves in the trees began to move and vibrate, small stones rolled into the river down the bank. Grass began to sway as the breeze picked up; the ground below her feet moved and started to vibrate. Rune blinked and then opening her mouth she screamed as loud as her lungs would let her. "Robbbbbbbbbbbbbie!" It came out as a terrifying wail.

A huge force unleashed, and the trees splintered, cracked, and broke away from the ground as they were tossed in the air, leaves stripped off twigs with the force of the wind that suddenly erupted into the wood. Grass lay flat as though forced to the floor, the river rose up, and a mighty wave crashed to the other bank flooding the land. She fell to the floor and was still.

The young duke walked up to the cart and stood in front of Robbie, all his men noticed, turned, and watched him. "I owe you an apology Robert of Loxley and also your men."

Robbie looked at Brandon, who although older in years appeared younger in attitude. "I will have loyalty from my woodsmen and they have mine, your comments were out of line My Lord and so I said my piece. I respect the fact that you have considered my views and changed your opinion, it is a sign of a true man."

The duke looked at him. "I have lost my father and inherited his mantle, and it is a task that I was neither wanting nor prepared for, I should have shown those who defended me more respect as my father would have done."

"We have common ground then my friend on which both of us can build from. I too was handed a mantle I was unprepared for, so let us draw a line under this and begin again." Robbie offered his hand. Brandon took it, and shook.

Steph suddenly staggered slightly, and Robbie did not need her to tell him, she put her hands to her head and fell. Alice grabbed her but Robbie was already running along the riverbank. The wind began quite strongly, and within seconds it blasted the whole area. Robbie was thrown backwards forty feet, and grabbed the remains of a tree stump. The group were blown to the ground, as trees and branches flew above them, and bounced into the other trees, the cart slid, and rolled over dragging the horses. All of them held tight to each other with fear in their eyes. The wind dropped as quickly as it had begun, the swollen river dropped back and sloshed up the bank dowsing everyone. The stillness that followed was eerie and calm.

Robbie struggled to his feet and he saw her lying still in the middle of a circle of devastation. He staggered through the stumps and the branches that littered the site and fell gasping beside her. She was as pale as snow as he dragged her into his arms. "Rune my darling, my life, what has happened?" His tears fell as he lifted her cold limp body to his, he looked down on the face that to him was joy, was life and every happy moment his future would bring. "Rune don't leave me." He rocked her in his arms as he wept his head down and his soul on the edge of splintering.

Alice came running up and fell to the floor her eyes blurred with tears. "No," the only word she could squeeze from her throat. Her eyes widened. "Robbie look." He lifted his head and through blurred eyes, he saw violets appearing all around him, she opened her eyes and his heart broke with the joy. He sobbed giant tears as she lifted her arm and touched his face.

Robbie pulled her close and held on to her as tightly as he could as he buried his face in hers. "Robbie I am here; I won't leave you." Her arm folded round him and squeezed him. "I am so sorry my darling." He wept into her shoulder and she slowly raised herself up and pulled him around her. Alice stood up still crying, and slowly walked back through the torn and uprooted trees and left them alone to heal.

Harry sat on the grass holding Blades in his arms; he had caught her and shielded her through the blast. "Whoa baby girl that was totally the meaning of cosmic." He lifted her up and inspected her to ensure she was safe an unharmed. She pulled him into a hug and held on to him.

"You totally saved me big cosmic Daddy."

Harry burst in to tears and looked down at his daughter. "Wow baby girl your vibes is all grown." He wept as he hugged her.

Logs rolled, trees parted, and carts moved, as everyone appeared from wherever they had been blown to. Jade crawled out from under a huge bowed stump and looked up at Rowan. She gave him a huge smile. "Wow Rowan can my sis kick ass or what?" She leapt into his arms and hugged him.

They had sat together quietly on the grass holding each other and not speaking. He softly stroked her hair as she held him. Robbie leaned back and looked into her beautiful blue sparkling eyes. "You alright?" She smiled sweetly and nodded. Robbie leaned forward and kissed her. "I am sorry Rune." He squeezed her and then looked around at the fifty-foot wide circle in the devastated forest. "Rune?"

"Yes, Robbie my love."

"You know the next time we might fall out for a bit?"

"Yes."

"Couldn't you just break a plate or something?"

She started to giggle, and his heart filled with the joy of a sound that made his world whole again. He slowly stood up and helped her to her feet. "You know Rune, you really need to control your temper, I loved these trees." He slid his arm around her and together laughing, they walked back to what was left of the camp.

They were stood around the cart, which had been tipped back up the right way when Robbie and Rune stepped out through the trees, and walked towards them. There was relief and smiles all around. John patted Robbie's shoulder as he passed and Martin nodded a smile, Jade ran up and hugged him and then turned to Rune, Rune swept her into a tight embrace. "God sis remind me never to get you mad."

Rune held her sister as she looked up at her smiling mother with a cut lip. Steph pulled her close and held her tight. "Oh my daughter, my Runestone you frightened me."

"I am sorry Mum."

"You have your full power Rune; you must be careful and control it with extreme caution."

"Yeah sis at least I only moan in your head at night, you almost blew mine off." Jade smiled at her and winked.

Rune smiled. "Let's hope I have the power to block you, I really need a good night's sleep, Jade can't you just leave him alone for one night?"

"Are you joking? Look at him he's a hunk." Steph and Rune smiled at the wide eyed and giggling Jade, as Rowan walked up and she slid her arm round his waist. "I like em strong and silent." She looked up at Rowan and blew him a kiss.

It took a while to sort out the cart; the steel hoops were badly bent and twisted and it took Hog and John a while to force them back, they were a little crinkled but they held the canvass and everyone could get in now. They finally drew back on to the road as Robbie and Rune sat at the front with Harry, who kept sniffling and blowing his nose.

Everyone in the back seemed jovial considering Rune's emotional outburst had flattened an entire area of woodland, and almost killed them all. Lord Brandon was trying to get to know everyone, he was still very much the odd one out, but they understood he was trying to make amends. "So, you are Big John, and you're Quiet Martin, what are you wiggly Eric...? Oh no, little Eric, and then there is Pebbles and Rowan, Smooth Billy, Pigeon and Hog, which leaves just Fish, Mother and Blades, is that right?"

"Hey man and don't forget me, I totally am the link in the cosmic chain to these guys." Brandon leaned round.

"You can have no fear Sir, it will be a very long time before I can forget you Mad Harry, a very long time indeed." Everyone smiled as Harry swelled with pride.

"If you have to make an impression Robbie man, make it a cosmic one."

The cart trundled along, and in the distance set on a hill above the town surrounded by forest stood a very large castle. Robbie smiled at the sight of it, Steph smiled more and a tear came to her eye. "Look girls we have come home."

Rune watched as the castle rose high into the air as they got closer, Harry turned the cart on to the driveway that led in a straight line down the trees. The castle gates grew before them and Rune stood up as they passed over the drawbridge and under the high stone archway. The hooves clattered as they hit stone, and the cart rattled into the enormous courtyard and slowly came to a halt.

"Aunt Steph, Rune, Jade." A slender young woman in black robes edged with violet ran down a steep flight of steps, her long raven black hair flowed behind her as she ran, her pale white face was a beacon of excitement, she leapt into Steph's arms and Steph with tears in her eyes hugged her tight.

"Oh, how is my little jovial Jett? Oh, my darling I have missed you so much."

"I have waited all day and I thought you would never get here, welcome home Auntie."

Steph let her go, and she turned and jumped at Rune. "Hey Cous welcome home." Rune pulled her close.

"Oh, Jett it's so nice to be here."

Jett let go and pulled Jade into a hug. "Hey Jade remember me, I bet you don't, I am the one who used to push you round Avon in your trolley, welcome home, me and you are going to cause so much trouble together, it's going to be great."

Steph walked on to the steps and looked up. A warrior of a woman with long red hair and dark black eyes looked down and smiled, her eyes flickered with lilac. "Stephanie." She opened her arms and ran down the steps pulling her sister close. Steph wept with her sister.

"Oh, Scarlet I can't tell you how good it is to be back, I have missed you so much."

Robbie put his arm around Rune as she dried her tears. Scarlet, came toward them. "Lord Loxley I am honoured you come to my home." She bowed and

Robbie noticed her ring; her face broke into a big smile. "Rune, Jade, you have grown so much and look at you both, so beautiful."

"Hi Aunt Scarlet." Jade gave her a hug and looked at the large golden sword on her side, Rune stepped up.

"Aunt Scarlet it's so nice to be here." Scarlet pulled her close.

"Oh Rune, you have so much power now, and you have grown so like my mother. Come everyone there is food and drink, we have plenty of room; you are guests of the house of Caerleon now." Everyone slowly dropped off the cart and made their way round to the steps.

Rune and Robbie were almost at the top of the steps when Jett shouted up. "Hey Rune?"

Rune suddenly stopped and looked panicked. "I can't believe I forgot."

Jett stood looking at each of the group as they got off the cart. "So, which one of these hunks is Anthony?" Rune closed her eyes, and Steph some way ahead burst into laughter. A large unshaven brute of man smelling of fresh soap looked down at her.

"That's me." He smiled.

Jett smiled back. "Wow aint you a big boy?" As Rune entered the door, she heard her voice shout from outside. "You are a naughty girl Runestone, I will get even."

Robbie pulled her close as they entered through the thick wooden doors of what was her family home. She looked up at the crest on the wall in the entrance hall, her family crest a multi coloured five pointed star set in a white circle surrounded by black. "Home." She said more to herself, it did not feel like it, her home was Loxley; a strange feeling came over her.

"Father is that you? It's not possible. Father I am here."

Harry pulled the cart round to the side, and tethered the horses; he lifted his black hat off the pole at the side of the brake and walked to the steps. Looking up he saw a pair of bright red eyes watching from the third floor window. He swallowed deeply. "You are a bad man Robert of Loxley, you like made me do bad things and now I got evil eyes wherever I go. It is not cosmic man, I had happy vibes, now I just got bad evils. First green and now red, oh man this is so not cosmic." He put his hat on and pulled it over his eyes and ran up the stairs. "Hey man, don't leave me alone with those evils."

He sat in the chair his hair was long, lank, and dirty, the drawn features of his face, resisted death. He was covered in filth and his torn dirty clothes stunk. His head hung limp and to one side, how much more he could take, he did not know.

Was it a week or two? He had suffered so many beatings that the time had seemed to stop and the process now felt like one long unrelenting moment of pain. "Peter you are dying, your body is done and you will leave this world forever, why not tell me what I want to know?"

The man leaned over him and his long white hair that was once dirty blonde fell to the arms of the chair and softly stroked the red and bleeding wrists clamped in the manacles.

Peter's mind flicked back into life for a moment, a young woman with straight blonde hair and bright green eyes sat in a bed in the corner. "Peter look, you have another daughter." She held up the child and he saw the red hair and bright blue eyes. "She will be Runestone Sapphire, isn't she beautiful Peter?"

The pain in his face smashed the thought out of his head. "TELL ME WHAT I WANT TO KNOW LANE, OR I WILL KILL YOU NOW."

He raised his head and his bright blue eyes stared up from the filth on his face. "Kill me then, I care not." Peter's head dropped back to his chest. "I am dying anyway; this will not last much longer for me Mason."

His thoughts seemed to slide into oblivion, and his mind drifted into nowhere, *'where are you?'* came his own quiet voice from inside his head. *'Runestone where are you?'* His mind tried to call to the pictures so they could return and he could see her once more.

'Rune please do not leave me, come back. Rune where are you?'

"Father is that you? It's not possible, father I am here."

"Rune I need you where are you? I miss you, please do not leave me come back."

"Father I am here, I won't leave you, I have everyone, we are coming to get you please, please father I beg you fight him, do not give up we are almost there. Give me a few days and I promise I will find you, do not give up on me, and fight him. Father... Father don't go please stay Father..."

Peter Lane slumped in the chair a smile on his face, the door slammed hard as Knox stormed out of the room.

CHAPTER SIXTEEN

MAPPING THE LIES

Robbie held her, concern in his eyes. "Rune what is it...? Rune, talk to me... Rune!"

"Robbie leave her... She is fine, oh Robbie you have no idea how fine she is." He turned to see the half shocked half happy face of Steph. Rune's eyes started to flicker bright purple, he held her tight.

Steph stood breathless, as Scarlet came back up to her side. "I am so happy for you sister; I knew her home would intensify her power. I cannot believe she has found him, after all we have tried."

Scarlet gripped her sister's shoulders, as Steph stood motionless her hands to her mouth and waited holding her breath. The colour in Rune's eyes drained and she blinked, she slightly swayed, but Robbie had her. "Oh Robbie...Oh that was hard." He held her tight and she looked into her mother's hopeful face and smiled. "Mum I've found him." Tears welled in her eyes. "He is close, I have found my father."

Steph rushed to her and threw her arms around her. "I know, I saw him, Oh Rune, I saw him and he is still alive. After all of this time I had lost all hope, oh my darling thank you."

Robbie smiled as Scarlet smiled back at him. "Looks like we have work to do young Master Loxley." Robbie nodded.

"It's the reason I am here."

Harry came bounding up the steps and stood close to Robbie. "Hey man did you see anything like uncosmic and red coming in here?" Harry stared around the room and bent down to look under the table.

Robbie looked down at him. "Harry what the hell are you doing? It's Peter, Peter Lane."

Harry shook his head. "No man his are blue and totally cosmic, what I saw was red and man they were karma chomping, I tell you." Harry looked back at the door. "It's your fault man, you did this to me. You made me do bad things man; my vibes have been jangled ever since."

Steph and Rune walked holding each other into the main hall, Scarlet followed.

Robbie turned to Harry. "Harry what the hell are you talking about? I am talking about Rune's dad."

"Wow man, nice dude, his karmas cool, he aint seeing evils."

"Harry, Rune has been able to contact him, we know he is alive and so we might have a chance to get him back."

Harry looked down at Robbie and then suddenly pulled him into a big hug. "If you save my main dude, I will owe you forever man."

Robbie looked at the sad eyes and very serious look of his uncle; he smiled at him and squeezed him back. "Hey Harry we are family, of course I will help. I am doing it for Rune as well remember, but Harry this is still secret so keep it that way."

"Hey man you don't need to tell me; I am the cosmic secret keeper."

"Ok Harry, come on and let's get something to eat." Both of them walked down the huge hall to the long table that was laid out with food. Everyone sat around the table eating, and talking, Simmons who now indoors was back to his duties, had made the formal introductions to Scarlet. She now sat talking in depth with Brandon, who in more civilised surroundings seemed to have found more courage.

Robbie sat at the huge wooden table and looked at the large amount of food laid out in front of him; Harry was piling his plate high. Robbie took some roasted chicken and a few vegetables. Jett slid in at his side. "Not hungry then?"

He smiled. "It's not that, it sounds strange, but where I come from things are quite simple. I suppose I am not use to so much choice, it is sort of overwhelming."

Jett smiled. "It's not like this all the time, its mum showing off because her sister is here; I think it's like some sort of sibling rivalry. Probably get cheese on toast tomorrow." She stabbed at a potato with her fork and bit pieces off. Her black eyes watched him as he ate. "I was told I must call you My Lord, Rune said you would prefer Robbie. So, which is it?"

"What would you prefer?"

Jett's face lit up and she smiled, her eyes twinkled with violet. She reminded him very much of Rune but also a lot of Jade. "Oh wow, Robbie you really are as cool as Rune says you are. I think we are going to get on great, don't you?"

He chuckled. "You know what Jett; I think we are."

She took a large bite of her potato. "So how cool is it being the real Robin Hood?"

"Actually, just between me and you and without sounding to much like Harry here, it's so cool, it's cosmic."

Jett beamed and bounced on the seat, laughing, she slapped him on the back. "Alright Robbie."

Jett was good fun and he laughed along with her as she joked about life at the castle, when Blades joined her dad and Jett noticed she too had the same sort of samurai sword set her dad had, Robbie noticed the serious side of her. Jett loved swords and had remarkable knowledge of their design and manufacture.

Blades slipped one of her golden swords out and handed it to Jett. She walked from the table and into a wide area of space. Robbie watched her with interest as Blades showed her the stabbing and lunging positions of a Japanese fighter. Jett balanced the sword in her hand and then spun it, she smiled and nodded to herself, she did a few practice swings with it and looked up.

"Hey Harry, can I borrow your swords for a minute?"

She looked at Blades. "Fancy some practice?" She passed the sword back to Blades as Harry pulled his out, and passed them over to her.

Jett took the measure of the swords. Blades squared and bowed to Jett. She smiled and bowed back and took her stance both silver swords in her hands.

Blades made a few small lunges and Jett countered with ease as she got use to the weapons. Blades came at her a little faster, and Jett once again countered.

Robbie somehow felt that Jett was also getting the measure of Blades. Jett raised the swords, and it began.

She came at Blades at terrific speed swishing and twirling the swords, the room flashed with gold, silver, and the ring of metal on metal. Blades defended with skill and smiled as the blade's movements became so fast that it was hard to see who was hitting at whom.

It was exciting to watch as they flew at each other, both of them enjoying the thrill of the fight. They seemed evenly matched and neither could outwit or out fight the other. Finally, after about forty stunning minutes and breathing hard they both lowered their blades. Both of them smiled and Jett put her arm around Blades. "Best work out I have had in years," she gasped.

Blades nodded and smiled as she breathed. "Me too." They returned to the table and discussed their moves; somehow it appeared to Robbie, that a very good friendship had just been forged.

Slowly the main hall emptied as each member of the group was shown to their room. Robbie wandered around getting to know the place, he ascended a small flight of stairs that took him up to a balcony at the far end, and looked out over the hall.

The walls were large blocked grey stone, and contained weapons of all types from all ages; the huge stone fireplace was so big you could easily have driven the cart into it, a large fire roared in the hearth. Once again, the same symbol as his ring cropped up everywhere. It was on several of the tables, and set into the floor in coloured stone, surrounded by a thick black circle. Most of the walls had large paintings from over a vast span of time, and all of them were women from fierce looking fighters to graceful and elegant women who smiled serenely.

Three chairs of red velvet stood against the wall, it was dim up here and Robbie sat in the far right chair and stretched his legs out. It was quiet now with just the sound of the fire burning and crackling in the hearth. He felt peace flow inside him and he closed his eyes and relaxed, the fire sparked and silence surrounded him, it felt like heaven.

Robbie drifted around as if floating; occasionally he would hear the fire crackle in what felt like some distant area of the house. He slowly drifted back to reality with the sound of footsteps coming through the entrance and into the main hall. A deep voice spoke.

"Matthews there you are, I am looking for Lady Scarlet have you seen her?"

"Yes sir, I have just left her, she is in her study with the Lady Runestone and her Sister Lady Stephanie."

"They have arrived, but we did not expect them for at least another week, this is good news. Is he with them also?"

"Oh yes My Lord, he is here now in the castle, and quite incredibly he has brought Lord Harold."

"Who?"

"Harold of Loxley sir."

"Oh Harry, how fantastic, how is the mad old dog?"

"It has been some time since I have seen him sir, but I believe I was right then, and I am still. He grows stranger by the day sir."

"Ha! Harry is back well that is fantastic, I will return in a few days and get drunk with him, just like old times. Right this Loxley, is he really as commanding as they say he is?"

"To be honest sir I found him very calm and respectful, not at all a brash warlord I am happy to say."

"Can he be trusted though that is the question?"

Robbie opened his eyes and jumped. A small figure with brilliant white hair sat in the chair opposite. She was wearing red tinted round-mirrored glasses. She smiled and raised a thin pale finger to her lips.

"Sir I feel there is no question of trust, he saved Gloucester from attack and brought him here undetected, he has been appearing all over the place, only three days ago he was in Winsford at the top of Cheshire and before that Kirklees. He has some power, although I am not sure what, and he wears the ring."

"She has given it to him so soon? That is a surprise."

"I believe Lady Runestone would only offer it, if she truly knew that he was the one. I have seen his eyes sir, and he is truth there is no doubt."

"Excellent Matthews, I am overjoyed to have this news, I will return to my men and update them and return here within two days. Stock up the mead, Harry and I will be re-living old times."

"Yes sir."

The footsteps clattered back out of the main hall and across the entrance hall, and died away. The small figure sat wearing a grey oriental jacket, and silk trousers smiled at him. "Hi... You are him, aren't you?" Her voice was soft and quiet, just a little louder than a whisper.

Robbie leaned forward in his chair and sat up straight crossing his legs. "I am Robbie yes... I am presuming that you are Ruby?"

Ruby gave him a big smile and nodded. "Yes, I am, and I am very excited to meet you Robin Hood, Cousin Rune has talked of you a lot, well she has to Jett, but I listened in."

"Has she now, I hope that she has not been too unkind about me?"

"Oh no... Oh Robbie, she loves you very much, that means you must be very special indeed. Rune is the centre of us all, for her to love you as she does, is a good thing."

Robbie smiled and felt a warmth glow inside him. "Well Ruby, I will tell you this, I love her as much if not more."

"I know, I feel it coming from you when her name is spoken. I feel a lot of things because it is hard for me to see things." Robbie noticed the long white pole with black tips leaning against the wall.

"Have you lost your sight Ruby? I am sorry I did not know."

Ruby slipped off her glasses and looked at him, her pupils were blood red and glowed slightly, she slid her glasses back on. "Light hurts my eyes so I use other ways of seeing. I can see in the dark better than you or anyone. The sun hurts me, and so I wear my glasses."

"Ruby I am sorry I meant no offence."

She smiled. "I am not offended Robin Hood, I am special, I know because Rune has told me, and she is the one who really sees everything."

"You seem to like Rune a great deal."

"I am only just getting my powers, and I do get lonely here at times, Rune has talked to me every day for the last three days, although I have not met her yet, I can feel her in the castle and I know I will see her tonight. I am very excited Robbie; it will be nice to have a cousin."

"Well, I hope you will include me as a friend Ruby, and you should know if I am here, I will always come and visit you."

Her small pale face seemed to radiate joy. "I would like that very much Robin Hood, I hope we will be good friends."

"I am very sure we will be. With your permission, I would ask a favour."

"What can I do for you?"

"I don't suppose you know where my room is? And possibly help me to find it, this is a very big castle and I think I may get quite lost."

"I know which one is yours; I would very much like to show you."

"Good it's a deal?"

It was ten minutes later when Robbie walked round the corner with Ruby on his arm chatting away like old friends. She chuckled at his jokes and loved hearing the story of Jade and Harry in the graveyard, she laughed all the way round, and down the long corridor. As she turned the corner with Robbie, Ruby took a sharp intake of breath. "Are you alright Ruby?" She had stopped suddenly and her head moved slowly from side to side as if she was sensing the air.

"Oh, Robbie she is coming."

Robbie turned back and saw just the end of the long corridor, where Rune had appeared. "There you are," she shouted. "I have been looking everywhere for you." She started to run up the corridor.

Robbie turned towards her and revealed Ruby at his side. "I have been given the tour by my new friend here."

Rune slowed her pace, and a huge smile broke out across it. "Ruby?" She was small, thin, and very pale, almost fragile looking with her white stick to guide her and her long white hair, and yet she dropped her stick and with arms out stretched she ran straight down the centre of the corridor.

"Rune!"

Rune went down on her knees and pulled the small figure, which for the last three days she had secretly helped with her unbearable loneliness, into a huge hug. Robbie smiled as he watched her hold on tight to his new little friend. Ruby cried tears of joy to feel the person, who had connected to her on such a deep level, finally hold her. It seemed like an age before Rune would release her and her tears flowed as she held her. "Oh, Ruby my darling I have wanted so much for this moment to come, I am here now, and I will never let you be so afraid and lonely again, I promise."

Robbie stood smiling at the scene before him; Rune looked up violet tears on her cheeks, and smiled at him.

"I believe that the good Lady Ruby was escorting me to my room."

Rune slid back to look at Ruby. "I see you have met my hooded man?" She whispered very quietly to her. "Was I right or was I right?"

Ruby smiled. "You were Rune, he is gorgeous... It's a shame you met him first."

Rune started laughing, and Ruby began chuckling. Robbie looked down at the pair of them. "What?" Both of them laughed more, and taking one hand each, they guided him to his room.

Rune smiled. "I will see you in a bit; I just want a word with Ruby." She kissed him softly on the cheek and the two of them wandered down the corridor.

"Goodnight Robin Hood, I will see you tomorrow."

"Goodnight Ruby."

Robbie entered his room and was quite surprised. The room was quite large with a big fireplace and a large wooden four-poster bed. He had a carved wooden table, and a carved chair with a deep red velvet cushion. The whole room seemed to be of carved wood in a woodland theme. He liked it and felt at ease the moment he entered. Deep green velvet curtains hung at the window and he looked out over the trees to the sea. In the very far distance, he could see small lights, and he wondered what would be lit up so far out to sea. He stared out as if drawn to them.

He was so exhausted and it was not long before he slipped under the covers and lay spread out in the soft cool fresh bed, his whole body seemed to ache, and he sunk into the softness and felt snug. He closed his eyes and was gone.

It was late morning when he stirred. Rune moved as he went to sit up, he scratched his head. "What time is it?"

"Who cares, this bed is so much more comfortable than mine."

He looked down at the mass of red hair in front of him. "What do you mean, than yours?"

She pulled herself close to him and hugged him. From in amongst the mass of red hair two blue eyes peeped at him. "I am next door; Aunt Scarlet seems to be a little old fashioned about this sort of thing."

"We are old enough, how can she object?"

Rune kissed his stomach. "Who cares, my mum is cool with it, the weird thing is that according to mum she was at it at 14. At least I am almost 17 and you are my first, how can she tell anyone how to live?"

Robbie lay back on the pillow. "We are guests here though, aren't we?" Rune smiled as she pulled her hair apart to look at him.

"I went to bed for a bit and then I snuck in here through the adjoining door, mum gave me the key," she laughed. "You are too polite you know that?" She sat up and looked at him. "I will go back if you want me too?"

He looked at her pale naked shoulder, she lifted the blankets. "No, I don't think so." She squealed and jumped on him.

Rune sat at her dressing table and brushed her hair, the door that adjoined the rooms was open and she could hear him pounding around. "Robbie what are you doing?"

He popped his head around the doorframe. "Where the hell are my clothes?"

"Have you looked in the wardrobe by the door?"

"Why would they be there when I dropped them on the chair?"

"Maybe one of the maids has taken them to be washed."

"What maids?"

"Robbie you are in a big castle, there are staff to help with the upkeep."

He did not look happy. "I don't want some maid doing all my work. I can look after myself. I am a woodsman for Hearne's sake. I don't want a Simmons running after me, pulling on my boots."

"Robbie you are a lord now, you have to understand that."

"I am Lord of Loxley and in Loxley everyone mucks in."

Rune started to laugh. "You are so like your dad at times. I tell you what find some clean clothes in the wardrobe, and after breakfast I will explain to the staff what it's like up north and tell them to leave your room alright."

"Will you...? Great."

Rune looked at him with a surprised look on her face. "You're really serious about this?"

"Of course I am, why wouldn't I be? I am not some pampered twit."

She smiled at him. "I love this... you know... how you are...so...so?"

"A true woodsman first?"

"Yes." She got up and put her arms around him. "I love the fact that you are not afraid to be who you are, so many people pretend to be something they are not, but you really are Robert of Loxley the woodsman and the best bowman in Britain." She kissed him.

"Well I don't know about Britain, I am pretty good for Loxley."

When he appeared downstairs with Rune on his arm, he really did look like a lord. He had hated most of the clothes in the wardrobe, and found after a long look, a deep green velvet shirt that laced at the top, and a pair of green canvass pants. There was a nice brown suede waistcoat, that fitted him well, and so after much debate he dressed.

Rune wore her long flowing deep purple top with a matching skirt, she pulled a fine golden belt around her waist and she looked a picture, everyone looked up as they appeared. Matthews greeted them. "Good morning My Lord, My Lady." He led them to the table, where most of the group were in clean new clothes as it appeared everybody was having theirs washed. Robbie relaxed a little, if it was all right for Hog's to be washed, then he would accept equal treatment.

Scarlet looked up and smiled. "Good morning Lord Loxley, how did you sleep? I hear the bed in your room is particularly comfy?"

"It was indeed Lady Scarlet, we slept well, didn't we my dear?"

Rune gasped a laugh and nodded. "It was wonderful."

Steph who was wearing a huge smile looked down at her food; Jade and Jett giggled, and Ruby chuckled. Scarlet scowled and quietly said to Steph. "Do you let them sleep together at home? She is not old enough yet."

Steph put her hand on her sisters. "She is almost 17 and much older than we were as I remember, she is a young woman with a great power, do you want to tell her what she can and cannot do?"

Scarlet thought about it and whispered. "I had not thought of it that way." Steph nodded, and smiled at Robbie.

The morning was slow and Robbie wandered around getting use to the castle, he bumped into Alice who was laughing because she had just heard that Harry had locked himself in his room. "That's a bit mean, isn't it? I know he goes on a bit, but being happy he is locked up is not funny."

Alice laughed more. "No Robbie, you see he keeps seeing red eyes watching him from dark places." She chuckled so much she could not talk for a minute. "He says it is your fault for the grave of Robin Hood. He thinks the real Robin is haunting him." Alice burst into fits and had to sit down holding her tummy. "It's Ruby Robbie, he hasn't met her yet, so he just sees her eyes peeping from dark places." Alice almost rolled onto the floor. "Rob, he thinks the evil eyes are after him." All restraint left her and she collapsed in tears, even Robbie was laughing.

Half an hour later they stood on the battlements as Alice dabbed her eyes with a hankie, where she would intermittently chuckle. They looked out across the sea and Robbie looked to the area where he had seen lights the night before. He pointed for Alice as he told her about it. "Maybe it is just a small town that you can see."

Robbie peered across the bay where in the distance he could just see a faint outline of a dark coast. "If you had a candle, or oil lamp lit that far away in the dark, you would barely see it. These lights looked big and they must have been bright to show up all the way over here."

"So, what do you think it was?" She looked a little nervous.

He looked at her. "What else could it be? It has to be something to do with Knox."

"Excuse me Lord Loxley, Lady Loxley, but both of you are required in the conference room, would you care to follow me please." Matthews turned and went through the door. They quickly followed him down the steps, several corridors and the main hall, before being shown a small door.

They stepped through into a small stone room with a large round table. A large map of Britain was laid out on the table and small figures in either green or red were placed on the map. Robbie studied it with a keen eye as he walked around the table. York was almost under attack, as was Loxley, Gloucester was all red and a large group was building up around Bristol. All the area around Caerleon was covered with green troops, and they seemed to be working down towards Bristol.

A large red square was at Weston Supermare, and Canterbury, as well as London. Robbie looked up at Scarlet. "What are the red squares?" He noted the one at Tintagel.

"They are camps of troops with a minimum of ten thousand men." Rune sat quietly with Steph and Jett as he walked round the table taking in every detail of what Knox had. He noticed isolated pockets of green, at Oxford, Chelmsford, Worcester, Stratford, Nottingham, Lincoln and Barnsley. His eye drew to Glastonbury where there was a single green figure. "What do we have behind his line, can we use them?"

Scarlet smiled. "Not yet, but that is a sacred site they are safe, he won't attack there it is also sacred to him." He looked up at Scarlet.

"How accurate is this?"

"We cannot be exact, there are more pockets appearing every day to defend against him, these are the ones we know of."

Robbie stood back and thought as he looked at the map. Rune got up and came to him; she slid her arms around his back. "What are you thinking Robbie?"

"I think he has had more time to prepare than we have, he must have started planning this the moment the red death hit, look at Cornwall and Devon they are completely red. But look at south Wales it's all green." He looked at her as she looked down at the map. "Loxley and York are safe; he knows they will not fall like Gloucester did. Worcester and Stratford look like they can handle themselves, so he will not rush there. London is so big; he knows we will not attack it. Bristol is not too far from his reinforcements and so I would think he would strike there first. That way he controls the river up to Gloucester, and that will prevent us getting men over to the main land." Robbie looked at Scarlet. "What do you think?"

Scarlet looked impressed. "That is exactly what my husband thinks, he is currently increasing the men to go to Bristol, and has put extra men on the roads through to Monmouth, and he insists it is vital to hold the river."

Robbie smiled. "Your husband sounds like my sort of guy; I should try getting drunk with him to find out."

Scarlet looked even more surprised. "You and him will get on famously, I am sure."

"What else has he in mind?"

"At the moment nothing he is too busy with all the planning for these."

"So he wouldn't mind if a few hooded men were to have a small raiding trip of their own, I do feel we should give Mason a taste of his own medicine." Robbie looked up at Steph and winked.

Scarlet looked down at the map. "Just where exactly would you want to raid?"

Robbie looked up at her. "Not that long ago he decided to raid a very special area of mine, it did not please me, I thought me and the guys would raid somewhere close to his heart, see how he likes it." Robbie pushed his finger into Tintagel.

Scarlet looked at him alarm in her eyes. "Robbie, are you mad?"

He calmly looked up from the map. "No that's Harry's department."

"You are joking, aren't you? That place is a fortress, he has spent years rebuilding it back to its former glory; we have looked at it a thousand times. It is impossible."

"You do not have the sort of specialised people I do. I will not use the tactics of an army, which is what he built it for. I am a woodsman and stealth is my way. He has a fortress in the middle of a sea of his own troops. He thinks exactly the same as you, which can only mean one thing Scarlet."

"What?"

"Complacency, his troops have stood guard for years knowing there is no way anyone will be mad enough to attack it. That means a small squad of specialists could slip in and out without him knowing."

"Well Robert of Loxley you are either very brave or very stupid, and I am not quite sure which?"

"Well Lady Scarlet what I will say is, in my group we have equal amounts of both." He squeezed Rune's waist and she smiled. "I will have Peter Lane here within the week, just let me see everything you have on Tintagel, I need to talk Harry out of his room. Does anyone know where Ruby is? Oh, and by the way, nobody outside of this room is to talk about this, not even to close friends I want this to be the biggest surprise Knox will ever have."

It was sometime later when Robbie knocked on Harry's door. "Harry it is Robbie let me in." The key turned in the lock and the door opened slightly; his dark brown eyes appeared at the gap. The door swung open and Harry walked back to his chair and sat down. Robbie walked in with Ruby. "Harry you look a mess."

"Hey man don't please, I am havin a real bad trip at the moment and it aint cosmic."

Ruby sat on the bed in front of Harry. "Harry this is Ruby, she is Rune's cousin."

"Hey baby girl, I have heard about you from Jade and Rune, it's nice to meet you, wow those are really happenin glasses." Harry gave a soft smile; his eyes were dark and his face seemed pale. Ruby lifted his large hand in her small white one and shook it.

"It's really nice to finally meet you Harry, I have heard so many nice things about you I really wanted to come and see you and make friends."

Harry smiled. "Whoa that's really sweet and cosmic. My head has been like somewhere else baby girl I am sorry, I shoulda dropped in at your pad and done the hey man thing."

"Ruby is a very nice person Harry, but she does not have many friends and she gets very lonely."

"Wow that's a bummer man... Hey... Wow, you could be one of my dudes, and then you would have cool vibes and be happening forever."

"Sorry Harry, what was that you just said?" Ruby looked confused.

"What Harry was saying Ruby, was that he would also like to be a friend?"

Ruby smiled at Harry. "OH... Harry I would really like that."

"Peace chicken, it's happening." Harry smiled at her.

Robbie moved to the window. "Ruby has a few problems with her sight Harry, would it be alright to pull the curtains? The light hurts her."

"Man yeah, don't want my little chicken here in the hurts vibe place."

Robbie pulled the curtains and the room descended into darkness. "Alright Ruby, you can take your glasses off now."

"Arrrrrrrrrgh! Eyes man... Evils to chomp karma."

"Alright Robbie, I have put them back on." Robbie pulled the curtains back open. "Robbie he's gone." Ruby looked at the empty chair where Harry had been moments ago. Robbie opened the wardrobe door, Harry sat with his fingers in his ears and his eyes shut chanting to himself. Robbie looked at poor Harry. He had been having such a hard week, he felt so sorry for him that it was hard not to laugh.

Harry opened one eye and saw Robbie and Ruby watching him. He took his fingers out of his ears as his wide eyes panned round the room. Robbie sighed. "Harry, will you get a grip. Ruby has red eyes, which is why she has to sit in a dimly lit area. In bright light she is blinded. You have been seeing Ruby, who as you can see is not a karma chomper watching from the shadows."

Harry climbed out of the wardrobe and put his arms around Robbie. "Oh man I needed to hear that, I thought I was going to go to a very uncosmic place, and have my vibes mangled by mind bending karma chompers." Robbie patted him on the back.

"Welcome back Harry. Do not forget you got a new friend now so be sweet."

"Hey man, I love baby people they are cosmic and cool, I am always sweet." Robbie left Harry and Ruby to get to know each other.

Later on, Robbie sat in his room surrounded by pictures, drawings and maps of Tintagel. He carefully scrutinised every detail as he formed a plan in his mind, it was a few hours later, Robbie walked into the conference room where Scarlet stood looking down at the table next to a tall stocky man with a long black ponytail. He looked up and smiled. "Here is the very man now." He stretched out his hand. "Phillip, I am Scarlet's husband."

Robbie took his hand and shook it. "I have heard a lot about you sir, it's nice to meet you."

"Call me Phil everyone else does, well apart from Matthews. So, what can I do for you Robbie?"

"I need eight ropes at least sixty feet long, four climbing hooks and a decent size boat with two lifeboats." He smiled.

"You really mean to go then?" He looked surprised. "We just thought it was a wild idea."

"I have found three ways in and two ways out, and I think I know where Peter is, so I will brief my crew tonight and attack tomorrow at dusk. I would like to take Ruby she has night vision skills we could use, but I would understand if you said no." Phillip was impressed.

"I wish we had more men of Loxley down here; we have spent years looking at that place and you come up with all this in a matter of hours."

"We look at things differently in Loxley."

Phillip nodded. "I would appreciate being in on your briefing if that is alright? More out of interest than anything else." Philip looked bemused. "When I see how you are going to do this, I will let you know about Ruby."

"Do you have a smaller room than the main hall? Too many places to listen, I want to keep this quiet."

Philip looked at his wife and shrugged. "Yeah loads."

"Great, I will see you after the evening meal, and we will gather everyone together. I will go and brief Billy now." Robbie walked across the hall and saw Alice sat at the table reading a large book. "Hey Alice, have you seen Billy?"

"He is probably some place drawing his map, he is more worried about getting lost in the castle than me," she seemed really glum.

"Hey, what's up?" Alice looked up from the book and the tears welled in her eyes. Robbie moved over and sat down beside her. She pulled her arms round him and put her head on his shoulder.

"It's Billy." The tears flowed as she sobbed, and Robbie pulled her close.

"Hey come on, it can't be that bad?"

"I don't think he loves me anymore; he just gets angry with me all the time."

Alice started to shake as she wept deep and sorrowful bitter sobs. Robbie felt a pain deep within him, he loved Alice, she was special to him, and even Billy had no right to hurt her. He held her close and rocked her gently as her pain surfaced.

Robbie blinked his own tears away. "Come on, tell me all about it."

Alice began to talk and it all flowed out. She told him about how he started losing interest after the hunting trip, and how he would come to the barn and leave straight after sex, whereas before they had stayed together all night and talked. She had asked him if he was seeing anyone else and he had become really mad. Alice explained how on the day in the woods they had fallen out because he kept watching Blades, and then when Robbie had asked her about him, she had been ashamed to tell him.

"He spent so much time talking about Blades; I started to think he was seeing her behind my back. I got angry with him at the convent and asked him again, I saw him go into the woods and I thought he was meeting her. Well, she is such a good swordswoman I could understand it, he is obsessed with swords and never stops talking about them." Alice gave a big sniffle.

"Since we have been here, all he has done is talk to Jett, and she is just as good with a sword. I tell you Robbie he is probably with Jett now."

"Who is?" Jett came in to the main hall with Rune. As soon as Rune saw Alice in tears, she ran over and put her arms around her.

"Alice sweetheart what on earth is the matter?"

Robbie looked up at her. "Billy."

"He is out in the garden we just passed him." Jett pointed behind her.

Robbie got up. "I am going to sort this out, Rune stay with her." Robbie passed Jett and headed for the garden.

Jade stood against the tree and faded away. She looked down at her hands that were now the same as the bark. She turned and walked into the trees, and her arms were the same as the leaves. She chuckled to herself. She came to the fat oak and pushed her arms flat against it and watched them take on the colour of the bark. She heard voices and smiled to herself, slowly she slid around the tree to see who she could jump out on.

"This is the whole map of the castle, get to him as quickly as possible and he will get it to Mason."

"Alright Lord Knox."

She could not believe her eyes. "HOW COULD YOU?" Screamed out of her, the horseman jumped and kicked his horse, as she lunged for the stirrup, a sword blade sliced through the air and she felt a slice of her hair come away.

The horseman shot off dragging her as she clung to the strap, and she felt for her knife, pulling it out she plunged it into his leg, and he wailed in pain pulling back on the reigns. The horse reared and she let go falling to the ground, Jade was back up in a flash and this time she was ready, two knives came out of her belt, and she launched them with skill, speed, and accuracy. The horse reared as the knives hit home and the rider fell backwards to the ground, the two long silver daggers stuck out of his back, and he hit the floor dead. Jade walked slowly over as her full visible self came back into view. Rowan sprung through the trees and came running up a lock of her hair clutched tightly in his hands. Jade bent down and pulled the map of the castle out of the dead man's hand, then pulled out her knives and cleaned them on his shirt.

Rowan snatched her into his arms and pulled her close. "Oh thank Hearne you're alright." He hugged her tightly, and her feet dangled loosely off the floor as her eyes filled with tears. Her voice held a bitter pain to its tone.

"Rowan how can I tell him?"

Rowan looked at her closely. "Tell who what Pebbles?"

She started to sob. "Robbie." She held up the map and then looked at the dead man. "Billy." Tears streamed down Jade's face.

"Billy what Pebbles?"

"He is the traitor." She held up the map of Caerleon Castle, and showed it Rowan. "I just saw Billy give this to him, his real name is Knox."

Rowan stared in disbelief. "Are you sure?"

Jade nodded and burst into full tears. "I missed it, all this time I have protected Robbie and I missed it Rowan, I promised him, and now I have let him down."

Rowan pulled her close. "Pebbles you have not let him down at all, you have probably just saved his life... Come on we have to get back and bloody fast, Billy is still about."

Robbie walked out into the garden; most of the group was out on the lawn practicing their archery and swordplay. Blades was showing Eric how to handle a sword. "Anyone seen Billy?"

Martin looked up. "He just ran down to the stables."

"Cheers Martin."

Robbie started to walk down the lawn as Billy came out of the stable on one of the horses. He galloped hard up the path and Robbie waved and shouted him. "Hey Billy slow down I want a word."

Billy saw him and smiled, Robbie smiled back, Billy changed course but picked up speed. As he rode closer, he drew out his sword and lifted it high, Robbie's expression changed. An arrow whistled over his head and hit Billy right in the wrist, the blood spurted as he dropped the sword, and the horse veered off towards the trees. Robbie turned fast and looked back.

Rune looked down from the top of the steps with tears in her eyes, her bow still held tightly in her shaking hand. She dropped it and ran towards him, on the other side of the garden Rowan and Jade broke out through the trees and came running over towards him.

Robbie looked down at the sword just one inch from his foot stood upwards out of the ground. Rune was getting nearer, tears streaking down her face. "Rune, what the hell is going on?" She hit him at full speed and he fell backwards on to the floor with Rune on top of him. She kissed him as she wept and lifted him into her arms. Rune sat and sobbed holding him tight, he put his arms around her and held her close. She could not speak; she just held him shaking hard and wept.

Rowan and Jade gasped as they arrived, and Rowan smiled and bent double as he tried to breathe so he could talk. Jade collapsed down and threw herself around Rune and Robbie, and gasping for air, she too started to weep. Rune pulled her close and hugged her. "Thank you. Thank you, Thank you." Rune sobbed into Jade's hair.

Robbie looked up completely confused at the madness around him, and started to get angry. "Will someone please tell me what the bloody hell is going on?"

"Robbie?" Rowan gasped. "Billy is Knox's son."

Robbie looked up at Rowan, and started to laugh. "Guys?"

He looked at the sword in the floor as Rune squeezed him tighter, Robbie stopped laughing, his face suddenly became very serious. "I knew it."

He hit the floor with his fist, Rune and Jade let go and sat back; Robbie sat up and looked at the three of them. "Billy was the only person who could have mapped out Loxley Woods, because only three people knew how to get to Joe's hut from that side of the woods, and the other two were Joe and me."

Robbie put his head in his hands. "How could I have been so foolish? Oscar Hargreaves was ahead of us, not following us, he was waiting to meet Billy that is why he took two watches that night, I knew. There was no way we could have been followed out of that village; the documents must have been taken when we were drying our things by the fire; Billy was keeping it stocked up while we all set up camp. I knew, and just didn't want to believe it."

Robbie looked at Rune and she looked back quietly through damp eyes.

"Beware the snake that grows legs and wings... It's been round his neck for ten years." Rune pulled him closer, as he looked at Jade. "Pebbles you are bleeding."

She lifted her head and she had a small cut to the side of her cheek.

"I am so sorry Robbie, I suspected him, but never thought he could. I should have killed him when I had the chance." She pushed the map of the castle into his hand. "I went after this instead."

Rune looked at her sister. "You saved his life, if you had not let me know Billy would have taken his head clean off." Rune looked at the sword still stood up in the floor. Jade got up and pulled it out of the ground.

"I am having this... This is what I will kill him with."

CHAPTER SEVENTEEN

FRIENDS IN LOW PLACES

Robbie moved around the room picking up his papers, and sorting them into order. He laid them in neat piles on the bed as he organised in his mind, which maps and diagrams he would need first.

He looked at the door that connected his room to Rune's. He stopped and looked at her, she was beautiful. The long red hair he loved so much was braided around the sides, and wove its way into a long ponytail. It was currently across her shoulder and hanging down in front of her, her blue eyes glinted at him as she stood watching him. She smiled but he could see the concern in her eyes.

"Hi... How long have you been there?" She stepped into the room and came and slid her arms around him from behind, and put her head on his shoulder.

"Long enough."

He put his hands on hers that were resting on his heavy belt. "That's nice." He leaned his head back and on to hers; she softly kissed his cheek. She had such a great way of being able to know just when he needed a little extra something, and her embrace was just the thing he needed right now.

"Robbie?" Her voice was soft and quiet in his ear. "You know, we all understand how you are feeling at the moment; you can leave this until tomorrow."

He squeezed her hand. "No... Nothing has changed; we go ahead with the raid. There is one man across that water worth bringing back, and I will not let him down."

Rune increased her hug on him. "Talk to me Robbie, I can feel how much you are hurting, please let me help."

Robbie turned slowly to face her; a tear welled in his eye. "I can't Rune, not yet, give me time." He put his head on her shoulder and gritted his teeth, as the wave of emotion that stirred inside him subsided.

"Oh Robbie, I am so sorry, I hate seeing you hurt, I feel it as well don't forget, but you know I am here for you, and so are all the others you are not alone in this?"

Robbie released his hug and looked into her bright blue eyes; he gave her a soft kiss. "I know... Now come on we have a very special member of the family waiting for us somewhere across the water. It's the one thing that Billy did not know about, so it's still business as usual." He moved back a little and stopped. "Thanks Rune, I love you."

Robbie walked down the steps into the main hall with Rune; he looked across at the group all gathered around the long polished wooden table. Jade went to stand up, and Rowan put his hand on hers. "Let him do this on his own, he needs to."

"Good afternoon everyone, I am sorry to keep you all waiting, but there is quite a lot to sort out. I was going to hold this in a less public place, but it appears that need is no longer an issue." He placed the long rolls of paper on the table and looked at everyone.

"I think Mason Knox has had things far too much his own way up to now. Who is up for a little pay back?"

Everyone smiled and looked at each other excitedly, Martin looked at Robbie. "What you got in mind Robbie?"

Robbie unrolled the huge plan of a large fortress on to the table in front of them; they all leaned over to look at it. "The Cutters have been raiding this country for years, I think it is about time someone raided them back, and I know just the men to do it." He looked up at their smiling faces.

Robbie looked back as footsteps entered the hall. "Sorry we are late; it appears that we did not get the message until now."

Robbie turned his back to the table, and looked at the Duke and Simmons as they walked up to him. "My Lord Brandon, Simmons, I was not aware that you wished to be included now that we have returned you to safety."

Lord Brandon looked at little put out. "Well, My Lord Loxley, it appears to me that I have cooked these men meals, and attended to the washing of their pots, as well as give them a few fencing lessons over the last few days." Several of the group nodded. "Was it not you who said every man must pull his weight? Well, here I am."

Robbie looked around the table at the others, John and Martin nodded at him, and so did Blades and Rowan. "Alright Brandon you are in." Robbie turned back to the group, as Brandon and Simmons took their places with the others.

"As I was saying, I think we should pay Mason a little surprise visit and steal one of his prized possessions, and it appears to me that this particular building is the perfect place to start."

Jade and Ruby leaned over the table to look at the plans. Jade looked up. "Cool where is this place?"

"Tintagel." There were gasps all around the table as the others looked in disbelief at the plans, and then each other. Martin gave Robbie a shrewd look. "This is not a quiet country house Robbie; this is his stronghold. It is on high cliffs and almost surrounded by water, we are woodsmen, not boatmen."

"Well, that is not exactly a problem; I have been sailing up and down this coast for years, although the coastline around there can be tricky. I presume you will anchor off shore, and drop smaller boats into the water to reach the cove?"

Brandon came around the table and unrolled a map. "If you drop anchor here it is reasonably safe, and you will be out of sight of the castle. That headland there is very high, it will hide you nicely."

Robbie smiled. "Ok Brandon you can skipper the boat and plan the landing, I will lead the assault."

Brandon smiled a huge smile. "I assume we will be doing this at dusk?"

"We will. Is that a problem?"

"It will be tricky in bad light, but I will manage it if it means I get one back at Mason."

Robbie patted his shoulder. "That's the spirit." Brandon seemed very pleased, and looked down smiling to study the coastal map in more detail.

Robbie moved back to the plans of the fortress. "We have two ways in that are quick and easy, and one that's a bit hairy... Two are over the wall, and one is through Merlin's Cave here under the castle."

"Let's start with the walls." Robbie pointed to the map. "These cliffs to the sea are rugged but not impossible to scale, there are two blind spots on each corner of the walls, here at the north end and here at the south. Because of the cliffs, I am assuming they will have converged their guards over by the land locked sides here."

Rowan peered down at the plan. "From here and here we can take all their guards on the parapet out with bows very quickly and quietly."

"Exactly, so while two teams do that, I will be coming in from underneath through Merlin's Cave to gain access from below. Our prize is down in the basement, kept nice and secure."

John leaned over. "What exactly is our prize?"

"Glad you asked me John, there are two." He looked up at Rune's smiling face. "The first is that local fishermen have seen small boat loads of gunpowder being delivered there, and the second prize is a very important member of our team who is a prisoner there, and I intend to bring him back with us. They plan to move him shortly; I want to get him while we can."

Jade looked at Robbie with a very startled look on her face and a tear rose in her eye. "You are going to get my dad?"

Robbie smiled softly. "Yes Pebbles, we are going to bring him back to where he belongs, here with you."

Jade jumped on to the table and scuttled across all the maps and papers, and kneeling on the table she put her arms around Robbie. "Oh Robbie, thank you." Rune touched her shoulder, all the others smiled as they watched; Steph held her hand to her mouth as her eyes glistened.

Robbie pulled Jade close as she wept, and looked at the others. "Any questions?"

Eric looked up at Robbie. "Just how exactly do we get all the gun powder out?"

Harry looked at Robbie. "Hey man, I got your vibe. Whoa this is going to be totally radical and cosmic."

Simmons leaned over to Eric. "Ever heard of a man called Guy Fawkes?"

Eric shook his head. "No."

"Well, when we get back, I will tell you all about him, and where he went wrong, which has taught us how to be right."

Eric nodded. "Ok then."

Simmons looked at Robbie. "I have some experience with fuses, I did work for a long time for a duke warlord who loved blowing things up."

"You will be with me and Harry then."

Rowan looked again at the map. "This can be done Robbie I have no doubt, but we will need to be very coordinated. That will not be easy."

Jett walked round to Robbie's side. "Rune with you, Jade on one team me on the other, total communication, you need me, which is great because there is no way I am missing this party."

Robbie tapped her on the shoulder. "What about your Aunt Steph?"

Jett smiled. "You still need me. Aunt Steph will be down below with Pete, there is no way you could ask her not to be."

Robbie looked at Steph who had been very quiet all the way through; she gave him a slight smile. "I would like to be there when you get him, yes." Tears ran down her face.

Robbie looked at the silent figure of Lord Philip stood next to his wife. "It's up to you, they are your daughters." Philip looked at all the hopeful faces around the table and at both of his daughters. "Pete is family, we will play our part."

"Hey Flash, you get to be with me."

Robbie looked at Harry. "Who is Flash?"

"I am." Ruby squeaked.

"Hey man, watch this it's like really cosmic."

Ruby took off her glasses and turned away from everyone. Suddenly white light flickered out of her eyes illuminating the wall in pulses. "Whoa, how cool is that? See Flash, man that's cosmic."

Rune leaned over to Robbie. "It's her new power, I have been helping her control it, believe me if you look her in the eyes when she does that, it will be the last thing you ever see, she has the power and I might add the personality of sunshine."

Robbie smiled as he still held Jade in his arms. "Right, we know where, we know how, and what we will do. We leave tomorrow afternoon and sail down the coast;

Lord Brandon here will let me know the departure time by the morning." He slowly looked round the room.

"I will work out the teams and brief all of you after breakfast. I want to see knives and swords on every team member; we still have a stock in the cart. Make sure you all have enough arrows, and I want clipped flights. We are woodsmen and even though we will not see too many trees, we are all still expert at stealth." The group gave a nod. "If that is everything, go and prepare and I will see all of you after breakfast, and remember all of you. We need each other so get sharp I don't want to lose any of you."

They all nodded and started to disperse; Robbie pulled Jade away from him, and looked into her watery green eyes. "I have a really cool job for an invisible friend; don't cry any more I need my tough little Pebbles."

She smiled. "I have not let you down yet, and I never will... Thanks Robbie." She kissed him on the cheek and Rowan lifted her off the table and into his arms. He looked at Robbie and put his arm on his shoulder.

"I have seen much in this week alongside you. You have become more and more like the lord you are, and I am proud to be beside you my good friend." With Jade wrapped around his waist, and her arms round his neck, Rowan walked out of the hall.

Philip patted him on the back. "You have surprised me Robbie, now I will surprise you. I have three groups of men hidden in his realm. At dusk tomorrow you will have a diversion that will draw all eyes away from the sea and in land, use it well."

"Thanks Philip we will."

"Good luck, and take care of my children." Robbie nodded. Steph came up to him and quietly put her arms around him, she gave him a huge hug.

"I am so proud of you, and every day I am cheered that my daughter has such a worthy man to care for her."

Robbie pulled her back. "By tomorrow night, you will again I promise."

The light was fading, and Robbie walked into the garden. Alice sat alone in the last of the sun on a small bench in the rose garden. He walked into the heavily scented square and sat down beside her. Alice had very red eyes and held her hankie close to her face; he took her hand and held it tight. "How are you doing?" Alice sniffled.

"I will be alright; I just wish I didn't feel like such a fool."

"You are not a fool Alice, none of us believed it was possible, I grew up with him just like you did. He was family, and you never expect that."

Alice started to whimper, and tears began to form in her eyes. "I really loved him; I wanted so badly to be with him forever."

Robbie put his arms around her. "I know, I am so sorry Alice, I too honestly thought that with you and Billy, and Rune and me, we would all be happy and run Loxley together as the perfect team."

"Oh Robbie, I don't know what to do, I feel so horrible inside, I let him touch me and all along he was planning to kill us all, I am dirty because of him." Alice wept bitterly into his shoulder.

"Listen to me Alice... And listen good. No matter what his plans, or what cruel deeds he had in mind, just you remember that it was his doing and not yours. Your love was pure, good, and clean, you are a person of great quality and you cannot be soiled by him. Do not ever think that you can be, the likes of him are not worthy of you." Robbie sat with Alice until long after dark; he held her close and talked softly to her as he stroked her hair. Jade and Rune sat in the shadows out of sight and watched on guard.

Robbie sat in bed with Rune curled up by his side, ate toast, and drank coffee. "You know if this is the life of a lord, I could cope with this." Rune smiled.

"You don't have to be a lord to have breakfast in bed, Jade and I do it all the time at home, we take it in turns to get up and cook, sometimes mum does it to surprise us."

"It should be compulsory."

"Well, you are lord of Loxley, when you get home, you can make it law."

Robbie smiled as he put his empty plate on the table and swallowed the last of his coffee. "Maybe I will."

He slid down and she curled around him and smiled. "I am so happy Robbie."

He pulled her close and felt the heat from her radiate into him. "Yeah, me too." He paused. "What's that on your thigh it feels rough?"

"It's your crumbs, you should pass a law for use of bigger plates." She squealed as he pinched her, and pulled the cover up over them. Rune giggled.

The group finished breakfast at the table, and Robbie came down back in his now clean woodsman clothes. He carried a large bundle with him, which he placed on the table and then sorted through them. "Right let's see, Flash, Jett, Skip and Fuse. Oh, and Hog and Fish." Robbie passed out the woodsman cloaks in Lincoln green with a wolf's head crest and two black crossed arrows. "You are now all officially bowmen of Loxley congratulations."

Everyone clapped as each one swung the cloaks round and fitted them over their shoulders. Robbie winked at Ruby. "Rune has lined your hood double to keep out more light." Ruby beamed with delight as she drew her hood over her head.

"I am Ruby in the Hood now."

Everyone laughed. "Well my merry group, we have two more new names as you see, hooded men have to have nick names by order of Harry, so I took the liberty with my good ladies advice, and Lord Brandon is now Skip. Simmons will be Fuse. Good work related names we will all remember."

Robbie unrolled the plan of Tintagel fortress again on the table. "Right here are the teams for tonight. There will be three teams, one group of six, and two groups of five"

"That's only 16, and there are 17 of us." Alice looked worried.

Robbie smiled at her understanding that she thought he might leave her. "Sorry, and one boatman. We will need someone to prepare for our getaway and that will be Skip in his vessel." Alice smiled, and Robbie winked at her.

"Ok group one, the north wall. This wall is high and needs to be scaled quickly, Eric and Blades will lead the climb, your lack of fear at heights at the convent impressed me. Eric will drop two ropes down, and Blades will cover. Alice, I know has no fear of height because she has climbed every tree in Loxley with me as kids. Jett and Martin you will follow."

"Once on the top Alice and Martin will use bows, Blades and Jett as we have seen are formidable with swords, and I hope skilled with knives. You must be fast, quiet, and not seen. I need every guard on that tower taking care of." All of them nodded. "Eric you will secure the stair, and at the given signal work your way down to the far end of the dungeon... It's a tall tower Eric, if any of you meet anyone there are plenty of windows, take care of them and push them out, the sea will do the rest."

"Right group two, this is the south tower. It is not that high because of the steep cliffs. Rowan and Jade will lead, and drop ropes, both of you are skilled with the bow, and so you should be able to cope until the others arrive. Fish, John and Hog get up as quick as you can. The stair at the top of that tower leads right down to the door that leads to the cave and the small jetty where my group will be coming in."

"Jade will lead using her particular camouflage skills. Jade you must get down to me as quickly as possible and get that door open." She nodded a steel look on her face. "Hog you follow Jade; I will need you as soon as I am in."

"Group three will be Rune, Ruby, Harry, Steph, Fuse and myself. We will come in by boat through the cave and up to the jetty; Ruby and Rune, will be our eyes in the dark. Once inside Harry, Hog and Fuse will head for the store with Jade, and rig the explosives here." He pointed to the plan.

Steph, Ruby, and Rune, you will come with me down the corridor, and hopefully we will meet Martin and Eric. The corridor will need to be covered whilst Steph and I locate the cell and release Peter." Robbie took a long breath.

"Right, this is the important bit. When the first groups are dropped off the extra boat will be brought into the cave with us, the tide will be low so we will be fine. Once Peter is out, all of you will have to move down as quickly as possible, and out into the cave. Get in the boats, and we will set the fuse. We have to fit all of this in before the incoming tide, because as the tide rises the cave will fill up and our escape will be cut off."

Rowan looked at Robbie. "How much time will we have?"

Robbie looked at them all and smiled. "From landing to leaving, we will have about seventy minutes, let's say an hour. It's slim but to a group of experts such as you lot it's doable."

John whistled. "That's not slim Robbie, that's bloody anorexic."

"Yes it is John, and if we pull it off, it will be the biggest shock to the system that Mason Knox will ever have, so I think it will be worth the gamble." Robbie looked at each one in turn. "I have faith in every one of you; do you have enough faith in me, to follow me in tonight?" Rune put her arm around Robbie.

"I am in."

"Me too." Ruby squeaked.

Every one nodded in turn. "In."

Robbie smiled. "Thanks guys I won't forget this. Right all of you, I want those patches off your cloaks, tonight we go in as men of Loxley, so be proud and show them what Loxley stands for." The whole group smiled and nodded.

"We will kick his ass don't you worry Robbie," everyone patted John on the back.

"Ok Skip, your boat awaits you down at the dock, take a couple of the lads and get it prepared. It's your boat what time do we cast off."

Skip, looked at the group. "I want you all on board by three thirty at the latest."

"You heard the skipper, let's hustle and get prepared." He winked at Skip.

Laughing and joking they all broke apart and headed off to prepare, Robbie stood by the table with Rune at his side, and watched his men with pride.

"You have a good team there Lord Loxley; I do believe they would follow you to the end of the earth." Matthews stood on the steps and smiled as he walked down towards them, he held out his hand. "I wish you and your men the very best of luck sir; you truly are the most natural leader of men." He shook Robbie's hand.

"Thank you, Matthews, I will need all the luck I can get."

The walk from the castle to the harbour led from the bottom of the garden through a small gate on to a cobbled road that wove its way through the woods, down to the remains of the town. The town had suffered during the red death, and nature had in turn reclaimed some of what was once the busy town of Newport. All that remained now was a busy inner circle of the once thriving town, which centred on the harbour.

The seagulls screamed and swooped as tiny boats landed their fish on the old sea battered harbour walls. The air was fresh and Robbie breathed it in and tasted the salt. Every man who was attached to the castle had been briefed that white arrows on cloaks meant high rank, and as Robbie walked down with Steph, Rune and Alice, any man in green that passed would clench his right fist and proudly bang it up against his top left shoulder.

It took some getting used to, as there were rather a lot of them, and they all felt obliged to do it back, so the conversation seemed to stop and start as they all passed yet another group of woodsmen. "My shoulder is starting to hurt," said Alice rubbing it, and once again rapping it for another group who passed.

"I must admit, I will be glad to get on board and rest my own arm." Rune saluted again. "This is ridiculous."

"Do you think so? I was thinking how good it could be in Loxley." Robbie smiled mischievously, and she grinned back at him.

The boat was Lord Philips private yacht, and it was quite a vessel, it was seventy foot long and dark blue. Rune gasped as they walked up the gangplank. "Philip seems to be doing alright."

Philip had his own crew attending, and they ran about all dressed in black as Skip gave his instructions. Skip seemed like he was in heaven, he had a broad smile and laughed and joked, and then belted his orders to the crew. Robbie sat on the deck and watched as he slowly got the yacht ready to sail. "I think we have found Skips place in life; he actually has some authority at last."

Steph smiled. "He is so young for the responsibility of his position."

"What and Robbie is old? Skip has at least seven years on Robbie."

Steph looked across at Rune. "Yes, but Robbie has lived a life with contact with his father. I see Robert Lox more and more in Robbie here; Skip was privately educated and kept away from a father who wanted his son to know a better side of life. The saddest thing is that Skip wanted to be with his father, but grew up elsewhere. He has no idea how to be the position he now is, Robbie although he hasn't realised it, has been guided all his life."

Robbie thought about what she said. He had to admit, he had once or twice smiled to himself as he heard himself giving orders out like his dad did the farm hands, and maybe she was right.

Skip shouted to the crew and the anchor began to rise. Ropes were thrown from the harbour walls and gathered in, and sails began to rise on the masts. Slowly the yacht began to move off from the harbour wall. "I think we should all get below just in case of prying eyes." Robbie got up and the group followed.

Below decks was quite plush. It was very beautifully fitted out with neat fitted cushioned benches, and a nice wooden table and cabinets and cupboards. Jade was fascinated by the television; she had no idea what it was, and pushed all the buttons even though nothing happened.

Eric was very quiet in the corner and Blades nudged Martin who smiled. "I really enjoy the way the boat goes up and down, it tickles my tummy and makes me feel all wriggly inside. What about you John?" Martin nodded at John, who noticed the faint green shade slowly arising in Eric's face.

John smiled. "It makes me hungry; I always fancy fried eggs and mashed tomatoes and dripping butties at sea." Eric's hand went to his mouth, and he fled up the steps and on to the deck.

Rune smiled at John and Martin. "You two are awful with the poor lad."

John gave her a broad grin. "I love that lad to bits; we wouldn't do it if he couldn't take it." He gave Martin a big smile. "It's better up; he will be lighter for climbing." Martin chuckled with Blades.

It was going to be a long slow journey. Skip took the yacht out to sea so there was no chance of being spotted; he planned a wide arc that would bring them back in just below the point of Tintagel. Robbie got the plans out on the table and went over it repeatedly asking questions all the time, until he was happy everyone knew their own specific tasks. As the light started to fail, Robbie went up on deck.

The headland was in view and the fortress was obscured, sails dropped and the yacht slowed down. Skip turned the wheel and swung the boat to face out ready for the escape. The anchor splashed into the water as the crew pulled the two long black boats that were tied on a long line behind them, down the side ready to be boarded.

Everyone gathered in the boats, and as Robbie got ready to climb down, Skip pulled him over and gave him a hug. "Good luck, and may Hearne protect you all my friends." Robbie patted his arm.

"One hour, be ready." Skip nodded and pulled up Robbie's hood.

He stepped in to the boat and grabbed an oar. Harry pushed off hard, and silently the boat slipped away from the yacht. They pulled on the oars as the light faded and headed around the headland, Alice sat up front and watched as they came round the bluff and Tintagel Fortress came into view. "Bloody hell." She gasped. "It looks like Knox has added a small city to it."

What was once a beautiful area of natural wild coastline was now a walled city? The fortress stood tall on the top of the cliff, and in front of it for miles was building after building. A concrete jungle of buildings sprawled all over the sides of the cliff and across on to the moors.

Robbie turned his head and looked at the fortress as Rune steered the boat along the cliff line. They very carefully moved along the cliff at the southern end of the fortress. A ledge led to a steep bank, and the remains of an old walkway for tourists was about ten feet up. Using the oars, they steadied the boat safely up against the wall.

Rowan and Jade were out in a flash, as John and Fish scrambled out and dragged Hog up on to the wall. Rowan gave the signal and Robbie and Harry pushed off. Rune steered down towards the second boat where Blades and Eric were already scaling the tall north tower wall like two insects.

Jett and Martin pulled the boat, and Alice jumped out. "See you later guys." She threw the rope to Rune, who pulled it round behind her as Fuse, Steph, and Ruby climbed out of the first boat and into theirs. Ruby took the rudder and Rune sat beside Robbie as they rowed towards the mouth of the cave.

The sea was a little rough and he noticed a slight trace of lilac as Rune closed her eyes and the sea calmed down a little. They slowly moved into the mouth of the cave; it was very dark. Ruby took off her glasses and put them in a pocket inside her top. Rune concentrated. "Pull your oars in a little, it narrows here. Ok, a little to your left Ruby. Everybody it gets real low soon so bend forward until I say when."

They all leaned forward as flat as they could, and the boat flowed forward on the current. It was cold and damp and as Rune spoke her voice echoed. "Alright we are through, you can sit back up again, Ruby sweetheart will you pan round so I can see the whole cave. Right guys the jetty is just to the right, Harry if you lean out you might just feel it.... Now."

Harry felt wet wood on his hands. "Alright everyone the jetty is high; there is a ladder we will have to climb. It is about five feet up, so climb up, and when at the top stay still until we can reach you. I will guide each one of you on to the ladder."

Two sets of fingers came over the top of the wall on the north tower, and then a hood slowly rose. Two eyes peered slowly round, Eric pulled himself up, and taking a large steel hook out of his belt he leaned forward and gently hooked it on to the front of the wall. He gave the rope a tug, and the rope tightened.

He looked to his left and pointed, and raised one finger. A pair of eyes came above the wall six feet to his left. They scanned the scene, spotted the guard with his back to them, and then with the speed of a cat pouncing, Blades appeared with a long silver dagger. It took less than a second and the guard lay on the floor, Eric was over the wall and had attached another hook.

He crouched low as he looked around. A bow and a quiver was silently passed over the wall and he took them, Martin slipped down beside him in the gloom. A few feet over, Jett slid down quietly besides Blades, followed by Alice. Martin and Alice loaded their bows as Jett and Blades pulled out their swords.

Alice scanned the ramparts; two guards stood talking fifty feet to their left. She signaled to Martin as Eric headed for the steps down to the tower bottom. Martin took aim, and Alice signaled him to take the one on the right, he nodded as she raised her bow. There was a faint swish and the two guards fell silently. The group moved back to the stairwell. They watched the wall along the south side, and the five guards who walked slowly up and down.

There was a ripple of dark colour against the wall at the top of the south tower and two green eyes suddenly appeared. The guard walked slowly past and then made a quiet grunt, he slid stood up back to the wall, and hand with woollen wrist ties appeared over the wall, and gripped the back of the guard's collar and held him upright, the other guard walked up.

He looked at the guard stood against the wall and an arrow hit him in the back, a hooded figure with a large fat arm came over the wall and seized him by the front of his uniform, with a huge heave; the guard lifted into the air and disappeared over the wall.

Two green eyes beamed as they surveyed the area. There was a tap on the wall and the wrist holding up the dead guard pulled. The place where he stood was empty, apart from two dark huddled lumps, where Rowan and John now crouched. Two more guards walked towards each other, the huddled lumps moved silently and low along the base of the wall to the corner of the tower.

As the men approached each other, two green eyes appeared flat against the wall at their meeting point. They looked at each other and smiled, their eyes widened in surprised as they fell towards each other and bumped heads. Two dark figures rushed forward and seized them; Jade reappeared between the two guards, a knife in each hand and firmly stuck in each guard.

Rowan and John lifted them up and over the wall, they both stood against the wall out of sight as two more dark figures appeared and dropped silently down beside them. The final guard walked over to the door and gripped the handle. Two arrows swished from the north wall, and hit him in the back, the door opened, he fell in, and a pair of green eyes followed and closed the door.

A body fell silently from the top window of the south tower and landed in the sea. Hog and Fish followed through the door, Jade was already three flights ahead, her eyes glowing as she talked to Rune.

In the total blackness of the cave, they were all safely off the jetty and walking slowly up the stone steps. Ruby led the way and Rune with her own eyes closed watching through Ruby's was at the back whispering directions. They approached the steel door. "Jade's on her way, the south tower is ours, and so is the north." Robbie smiled in the dark.

Rowan and John backed to the tower door, as Blades and Martin headed down the north tower steps after Eric. Jade moved silently into the room, the large steel door was in front of her, and she peered around the corner. There were two guards, one asleep with his head on the table; the other sat reading a book opposite him. Jade leaned over the man as he read the book. It was as if he knew she was there, because he slowly turned his head. A voice from nowhere spoke. "Wasting your time mate the butler did it." Two green eyes appeared in mid-air in front of him, he went to scream, but the long silver dagger entered his heart and he flopped on the table.

"Now Harry Potter, that's my kind of book, I love the classics." The pages of the book next to the sleeping man flicked over. "God Hermione was cool." The sleeping man jumped slightly, and Jade reappeared and wiped her knife on his shirt. Her eyes glowed green as she pulled the bolts on the door and swung it open. Ruby stepped in, and the others followed, Rune came in last. She looked at Jade. "You're not serious, are you? Ginny was way cooler."

Hog and Fish appeared at the door. Harry and Fuse grabbed Hog, and Jade followed as they headed off to the powder room. Robbie grabbed Steph's arm. "Come on the cells are this way." As Robbie entered the long dimly lit, grey corridor filled with doors, he saw Eric standing guard at the other end, he smiled as Blades and Martin appeared. He ran with Steph, followed by Rune towards them.

Robbie and Steph turned the corner and Blades and Martin fell in behind them as they headed to the cells. Robbie stopped at the cell door, and looked in through the small window. He slid back the bolt and looked at the three men lay on the floor. "Come on, you're free get the hell out of here."

Steph was two doors down pulling the door open, tears in her eyes as she fell into the room and grabbed the half dead longhaired dirty man on the floor. "Pete I am here, oh my darling what have they done to you?" She squeezed him, and for a moment, he thought it was a beautiful dream.

It was the voice of the other, which told him this was really happening. "No offence Steph but we don't have time for this... Rune we got him let the others know." Rune nodded with a huge smile on her face and headed back.

"Steph darling is it really you? Is Rune here?" Steph held him tight and wept.

Alice and Jett sat quietly in the dark next to the door. Jett's eyes glowed lilac. "They have got him; let's get the hell out of here." Alice let fly her arrow; it hit the door just above Rowan. He patted John's leg and began to move. From out of the hills at the side of the walls, burning arrows started to rain down on Mason Knox's small city. Rowan hesitated and watched as they landed and started to burn, alarm bells rang out all over the city and he backed quickly into the passage. All of them fled down the steps to the bottom.

Rune stood at one end of the corridor, and Eric at the other. Martin appeared at his side as the alarm bells started to ring. Fish loaded his bow and stood next to Rune, doors all along the corridor opened and men ran out only to fall dead as the arrows sung. Robbie darted into the cell and lifted Steph up, and looked down at Peter. "Hi Pete, I am almost your new son in law, I am here with my Uncle Harry can you walk, or maybe run?"

Pete blinked. "Err...I... I will try." Robbie helped him to his feet, and pulled his arm around his shoulders. "Blades we are coming, let's go." He yelled as he came out of the door. Steph supported her husband on the other side and almost lifting him from the ground they ran back down the long stone corridor with him.

Jett and Alice stood next to Martin Band Eric, and slowly walked forward unleashing their arrows on anything that came passed a doorframe. Jett slid out her sword as Blades came running up, her two golden swords already stained with blood.

Alice turned to face down the corridor and cover Robbie and Steph with Pete.

Jett and Blades led the way checking each door as they approached, and stepping over the bodies. From the other end of the corridor, Rowan and Fish checked out the rooms and moved slowly towards them. Rowan fired and a voice screamed.

By the time, Robbie and Steph reached the long corridor, there was a guard on every door along the corridor, and Robbie seeing his chance threw Pete on to his shoulder and ran with him to the other end. Everyone fell in behind him, Robbie yelled as he ran. "Ruby get on the cave steps and light the way; Rune tell Jade we are leaving."

He reached the end of the corridor and sank back against the wall lowering Pete to his feet. "So dad, are we having Fun?" Robbie winked; Pete smiled, and looked up.

"Princess?" Rune pulled her dad close.

"Oh dad, what have they done to you?" Her tears spilled down his back as the others came flying up.

Rowan panted. "There are more coming down the stairs Robbie, I think we should bar the doors while everyone gets in the boats. Time is going to run out if we don't move soon."

Robbie nodded. "John carry Pete get him in the boat, you too Steph, Fish, Eric go now." They disappeared through the door. Rune dried her eyes, as Robbie looked round.

"Alice, Martin, Jett go." Rowan and Robbie stood either side of the corridor doorway. "Rune as soon as everyone is out of here scream out, and we will be right behind you. Get Ruby at the bottom of the steps to light the way, when that first boat is full get it out of here, no waiting alright?"

"Got you Robbie." Robbie loaded his bow and took aim down the corridor. The door at the bottom opened and soldiers appeared with crossbows. Robbie and Rowan fired. Rowan smiled.

"You are a fun guy to hang out with Robbie." He shot another arrow.

Robbie chuckled. "Wait for the main event it gets better... Speak of the devil."

Harry, Fuse, Hog and Jade came round the corner at high speed. Jade skidded to a halt as the others passed through the door and headed down the stairs.

Something fizzed in her hand. "Harry made this quite quickly, so if I was you, I would run." Robbie took one look at the fizzing sparks that were getting very close to the round object in her hand, and looked back up at Jade.

"Pebbles sweetie, aren't you supposed to throw that at them?"

"What? Oh yeah!" Jade launched the bomb down the corridor towards the soldiers who seeing it, turned and ran back. The three of them dived through the door and hurtled down the steps.

Rune was on the jetty with Ruby. "In the boat!" Robbie yelled as he thundered down the steps towards her. The three of them came skidding up as a mighty blast shook the cave. Robbie dived head first into the ice-cold water and came up next to the boat. Jade popped up followed by Rowan. Rune reached over. "Leave us Rune," he gasped. "We will push the boat."

Jade, Rowan, and Robbie swam to the rear of the boat and flicking their legs, they pushed the boat, as Ruby flicked her eyes to light the way. The boat moved towards the narrow passage; Rune shouted to everyone. "Lie down." The top of the boat buffeted against the roof and dragged down the passage.

Robbie, Rowan, and Jade flapped their legs as hard as they could to get force and speed behind the little boat, as it groaned on the passage roof. Harry and Hog lay in the boat on their backs and pushed their legs against the ceiling of the cave. The boat dropped in the water a bit. Walking along the ceiling with a lot of effort the boat finally bobbed back up in the mouth of the cave.

A huge hand grabbed Robbie, who was now almost exhausted, out of the water and lifted him into the boat. He sat gasping as Rowan and Jade appeared. "Paddle." Hogs gruff voice echoed in the cave.

The tide was flowing in fast, and they heaved on the oars to get the boat out of the cave, but the current was washing against them. "Rune we need help." Robbie gasped, his energy failing as he pulled on his oar. "Quickly the castle is going to blow."

The cave was filling up fast, and the ceiling of the roof was beginning to come a little too close for comfort. Harry and Hog stood up getting ready to push the boat down in the water as the others fought on the paddles to get the boat nearer the mouth of the cave. Robbie looked back at the swirls of water pouring into the cave. "Rune, for Hearne's sake do something, we are not going to make it."

Rune sat still and her eyes began to colour violet. The boat vibrated and they started to move forward, Robbie looked over the side, and the sea was rolling back on itself and sucking the boat out of the cave.

A huge wave smashed in through the opening and drenched them all; the boat drifted backwards, Robbie now gasping for breath pulled with all his might on the oars. "Pull!" His voice echoed as the others wrenched with all their failing strength.

They came near the cave entrance, and Robbie could see Rune her eyes burning deep purple as she focused all that she had on the water. Hog and Harry pushed their arms against the roof of the cave and pushed down lowering the boat in the water, and trying to walk it out of the cave.

Robbie looked at Rowan as they pulled back on the oars with the last of their energy depleting. The cave suddenly glowed violet, and as Robbie looked up, he could not see Rune for the intense purple light that streamed out of her. The sea seemed to boil as it spun round and round under the boat, the boat shook. Harry fell forward onto Rowan, and Hog crashed backwards over Robbie. The boat gave a huge lurch forward as the light radiated out from Rune.

There was sudden force, and the boat shot forwards like a missile, every one gripped the sides as the boat skipped like a stone across the waves into calmer waters. The boat slowed down and Rune opened her eyes and smiled. "Sorry guys need more practice."

They pulled hard on the oars, and began to gain pace as they moved away from the mouth of the cave. Robbie looked up at the city where flaming arrows still showered down as the alarm bells rang out, fires were burning all over, and the sky was bright with orange and red. Robbie gave a long sigh of relief.

There was a huge rumble in the cliff, fire exploded up into the sky, as thousands of pieces of stone launched themselves into orbit. Everyone stopped rowing and watched, as the fortress of Tintagel fell in upon itself, and slowly slid into the sea. Jade ducked as hundreds of tiny pieces of stone fell out of the sky and bombarded the little boat. "Ouch, oh God Robbie this hurts."

Rowan relaxed as he dripped into the bottom of the boat, he grabbed Robbie's shoulder. "You were right that was quite a main event, you don't disappoint Robbie." He started to laugh and Robbie chuckled. Tired and exhausted he collapsed in the boat as everyone laughed in relief.

They drifted along watching the flames as half of the Mason Knox Empire lay wasted and ruined, the yacht came along side, and they exhaustedly climbed on board. Jade was first off and ran down the deck to the cabins at the end, Rune watched, and hesitated, Robbie smiled at her. "Go on, I will be there in a while." She smiled as her eyes filled and she turned and ran up the yacht.

Skip patted Robbie on the back. "Bloody hell Robbie, you scared the hell out of me there for a minute." Rowan smiled at Skip

"Not just you." He patted Skip on the shoulder. "Well done Skip you did brilliantly."

Peter Lane sat holding a very stiff brandy, as Steph curled around him; he sipped it and smiled his blue eyes twinkling with exhausted happiness. He trembled slightly as he sat in rags and covered in filth.

The side of the cabin clumped as footsteps banged along the side deck, the cabin door flew open and Jade came down the steps into the room in a flash. "Dad... Oh my Daddy." She fell screaming and crying into her bewildered father's arms, and hung on to him for life itself. Loud bitter painful wails came out of her, as he shakily put his arm around his daughter and wept with delight.

"Oh Jade, my little bundle of joy, I have missed you so much." Steph squeezed his arm and cried with joy at seeing the father of her child reunited. Peter looked up his eyes blurred with his tears as Jade sobbed into his shoulder and there, Rune stood shaking and crying. He smiled. "Hello my beautiful princess."

"Oh Daddy, I thought I would never see you again." Rune knelt down and with his free hand; he pulled her close and wept more, as she put her arms around both her mother and father for the first time in ten years and sobbed long deep sobs.

John and Martin sniffed. Blades and Alice openly wept on each other shoulders,

Hog wiped his eyes and Eric bawled like a baby. It was some time before they all stopped and started to talk.

Robbie sat with Rowan on deck and watched through the window, both of them happy to see the joy on the faces of Rune and Jade. "We did a good thing today Rowan my friend."

Rowan patted his leg. "We certainly did, but none of us would have done it, if you hadn't led it Robbie." Harry walked up and sat down; he put three glasses on the deck and pulled the cork out of a bottle of rum. "Man, you guys are so cosmic at the moment, you could fly." He poured out three tall measures and passed the glasses to Robbie and Rowan. "Here is to the two greatest men I have ever known, you guys are way more radical than me, and they call me Mad Harry, whoa man you guys are totally insane."

"That doesn't help Harry... Cheers." They clunked glasses and took a drink. Robbie and Rowan gasped and coughed; Rowan looked up at Harry. His voice was coarse and husky. "God Harry, where the hell did you get this from?"

"Radical aint it? Me and Joe only make the good stuff." Robbie noticed the varnish peel where he had just coughed.

CHAPTER EIGHTEEN

FLAMES AND FAREWELLS

Robbie lay back on the deck of the yacht above the cabin; where below the celebration of a family reunited could be heard. He was exhausted and very wet, his body seemed to ache and weaken by the second, and he was thoroughly spent. He looked up at the stars as they slid from under the passing clouds. He had felt a pain in his chest all day, he was filled with anger and sadness and his insides felt twisted. He suddenly felt a strong sense of separation and loneliness sweep over him.

The simple truth was that Mason Knox has planted his own son as a spy shortly after the kidnap of Peter Lane. Even then, all those years ago he was planning the downfall of Loxley. Robbie breathed out a deep sigh. "Why did it have to be Billy?" All the fun of the days when they played together, or sat up all night talking of their plans for the future flooded back. Robbie's pain was hard, Billy would have loved tonight, it would have been right up his street. Robbie sat up and leaned forward, he wanted to scream and let out all the pain that was flowing around inside him. The strange thing was that he missed Billy, and knew he would give anything to have him back at his side; he would even forgive the brother he loved so dearly.

He put his head in his hands and squeezed his tears back down inside. "He is not worth them." He said to himself angrily. He gritted his teeth and bit hard to contain it all.

Two hands touched his shoulders, and her warmth seemed to radiate through him. "Please Robbie let it out, don't let him twist you like this." Her arms came around him, and he shook to hold in the explosion that was about to go off in him. Rune pulled him back up and turned him around to her.

The moon washed over her pale skin, and her eyes were as warm as the heart that beat within her. He loved her more than life itself, and as he looked, he felt the cracks appear inside him. "Don't ask me I can't."

"Robbie you are too good a person to let that snake he has put inside you twist you to bitterness. Please if you love me, listen to me and release him."

She pulled him close as he shook to hold himself together; she put her hand on the back of his head. Rune winced as she connected to his pain and she began to shake. "What are you doing Rune?" Startled he looked up at her face that was twisted with grief.

"I love you too much to see Billy destroy you, if you won't release him, I will take him from you."

"Please Rune, don't."

Her eyes were fierce. "Then let it out Robbie, and be the man of truth you are." She pulled him close, and he felt her warmth. Her eyes began to change from lilac to violet and as he closed his eyes and pressed against her, he felt her presence move inside him. It was warm, comfortable, and very loving, he felt at ease with the world.

"Hear me my love I am here with you. You will be safe, now release him."

The hurt, the shock, and the feelings of devastation began to flow in a stream through him. The betrayal that chewed at his insides came up like a flowing volcano, and before he could find the strength to contain them, they rose to the surface. The pressure started to build inside him.

"Hear me Mother... keep everyone down in the cabin, no one should see the pain Billy has caused, let me help Robbie."

Robbie pushed his head deeply into her shoulder, and it began to flow out. His silent screams of anguish and pain passed through her, and she clung to him, surrounding him with the love she had for him, as he wept bitterly and silently into her. His body shook with force as it exploded out of him, and he lifted his arms and pulled her tighter. Every happy memory he had that was now tainted with the betrayal of the one he called brother, flowed out of him.

Her violet tears spilled on to him as she shared the pain within him. Each tear was a moment of love in her life with him, and she used them to cleanse him and rid him of the suffering that was now passing from him. As he started to quieten, she rocked him gently, and the violet light of her eyes started to soften, and slowly they faded back to lilac. Rune lowered her head to his.

"It is done Mother."

Robbie lay in her arms and did not move for an hour. Rune held him tight and would not let go; the yacht entered the channel heading towards the town below the castle. Rune kissed him softly on the side of his face and he moved. He slowly lifted himself up and she smiled sweetly at him. She did not need to talk; she still had a connection and he felt the surge of love inside her still surrounding him. *'You will be fine now my love,'* seemed to echo in his mind.

His eyes were red and his face was pale, she pulled up his hood to keep out prying eyes. The yacht glided slowly into the harbour wall and stopped with a gentle bump. The noise from below rose as the happy group celebrating their success made their way off the yacht and up the hill.

Rune stirred when everything was silent again. "Come Rob, you're exhausted let's get back to the safety of the castle." She helped him up and holding him tight, she guided him off the yacht and on to the harbour.

The journey back up the hill to the castle felt long and hard, everyone was exhausted, it was now the early hours of the morning and the street was almost empty. The guards on duty bowed their heads and saluted the passing troop, the word was already back at Caerleon, and the soldiers felt huge respect for just seventeen men had struck a blow to Mason Knox that hundreds had not achieved in years.

As they entered the main hall champagne corks popped, Philip pulled Peter cloaked in a Loxley cloak, into his arms and held him close for some time. The alcohol flowed, and the tired spirits of everyone was lifted, and soon a party for heroes returned was underway.

Rune lay Robbie gently onto the bed and undressed him, he was utterly drained and spent. She pulled the covers over him, and then returned to her father and mother. Steph was concerned, Rune had been so overwhelmed by the force of his pain a little had leaked out. The small amount that she had lost control of was enough for her mother to understand how deeply his pain ran, and Steph had blocked all the others from feeling it.

"Thank you Mother." Steph lifted a concerned hand to her face.

"Will you be alright my darling that was a lot for you to handle alone?"

"I will be fine when I am back with him." She turned to her father. "I know this is your night Father, but I cannot leave him, please forgive me."

Peter Lane took his daughter in his arms. "I love you my princess, and I understand, for the small part I have seen of him tonight, I can see why you love him. There is nothing to forgive, he is the reason I can see my daughters before me, go to him."

She squeezed him tight. "Thanks Daddy." Rune turned and ran up the stairs towards their room. Robbie was fast asleep when she slipped under the covers beside him, he murmured and she pulled him close and held him all night.

The group gathered around the table and Lord Philip raised a glass. "My good friends let us drink a toast to the man who defied all the odds and did it anyhow." Philip looked around the room. "Where is he?"

Rowan stepped forward. "I am sorry My Lord, but as you know Lord Loxley has many affairs to attend to, and I am afraid something has arisen that needed his urgent attention, he asked me to please offer his excuses and apologies."

Steph smiled at Rowan and raised her glass; she mouthed 'Thank you,' to him. Rowan nodded back.

"Well then, I am sorry he is not here, but what the hell, the man is a bloody hero." Lord Philip raised his glass. "Ladies and gentlemen... Lord Robert of

Loxley." The response was deafening as everyone sang his name out with pride.

The castle stood gleaming in the sunlight of the new day. The stones seemed to shine in the bright light, and the whole town appeared to be uplifted. The news that the Hooded Man had walked into the home of Mason Knox, and stolen his most valuable prisoner and released all the others, was the talk of the town.

The first boat out of the cave contained 19 extra passengers. Ruby had led them down and packed them all in. Lord Philip had brought them all up to the castle, fed them, and issued them with clean clothes, having let them all bathe first.

Robbie woke up next to Rune, he felt rested and his insides felt lightened, he looked down at the eyes that had been watching him sleep. They twinkled and he knew she was smiling. "Hi."

He moved up the pillow a little. "Hi." She crawled up to him and kissed him.

"How do you feel?"

"Better... Thanks."

"You are a huge hero this morning."

"Oh dear."

She started to giggle. "You really hate it all don't you?"

He smiled. "Don't you?" He sat up. "All that bowing and scraping, and yes my lord this, and yes my lord that, oh Rune I get so tired of it. There were seventeen extremely brave people there last night, not just me, and they are all lucky to be alive."

"Jade wants to see you."

"Oh god she doesn't does she?"

"Yep, and she is louder than ever."

"Not yet please, I need coffee and clothes, I just need you and to be quiet."

"Ah! She is outside with breakfast as we speak... Are you ready...? Come in Jade."

The door burst open and the tray rattled, as she rushed across to the table and placed it at the side of the bed.

"Hey Robbie you are a huge hero, and you should be because what we did last night was just about the most cosmic thing I have ever known. My dad is so happy to be home, and I cannot even start to begin about how happy I am because of you, and what you did. All the soldiers are treating the guys like lords, which is right because they all deserve it. I think we should drop all this nonsense and kill Knox, and then you should be king of England. Rune should be queen because you are the only one who has stood up for everybody and helped everybody, and there isn't anyone I would like to see more on a throne than you, because you would be so cool with everyone like you have always been with me. Wow Robbie your body is almost as sexy as Rowan's."

She dropped on to the bed and handed him a coffee. "And by the way, did I tell you I love you."

Robbie smiled. "Good morning Pebbles... I love you too." He took his coffee and sipped it.

She bent forward and kissed him on the cheek. "I just wanted you to know." She slid off the bed and walked to the door. "Oh, and by the way Rune... You are having a laugh; Hermione was way cooler than Ginny... See ya." The door banged shut.

Rune giggled. "She really does mean well you know, and she adores you Robbie."

"I know... I just wish she would whisper like Ruby does." Rune started to laugh at him, and he smiled and stared for a moment into space.

"What?"

"How is your Mum?"

"Oh Robbie, I have not seen her so happy in years, dad needs feeding up a bit but she will love the attention she can give him." Rune went quiet for a moment. "I cannot tell you how many nights she has cried herself to sleep over the years. It will be nice not to hear that anymore." She patted his leg softly; he took her hand in his.

"So what do we do today plan another war?" Robbie breathed a long sigh and relaxed on the pillow.

"I think actually, there are some people waiting who would like to thank you. We came out of that tunnel with a few more than eighteen last night."

There were nineteen drawn and white faces in a row waiting to meet Lord Loxley. They all sat down one side of the table eating breakfast, while the rescue party sat with very heavy heads down the other, sipping just coffee. Robbie arrived at the top of the stairs in his slightly damp woodsman's clothes. Rune had a thick green velvet dress on and they made the perfect couple. Everyone stopped, as they came down the stairs, and Rowan got up and walked over to meet him. "My Lord there are some people who have waited all night to pay their respects to you."

"It's alright Rowan, I will see them."

Rowan turned to face everyone. "Gentlemen may I present to you Lord and Lady Loxley."

Robbie walked down the line and spoke with each of them. "How long were you there for? We shall do what we can to help, if there are others we will find them." Every one of them squeezed his hand in gratitude, and when they reached the end of the line Robbie looked back at them all. "Please my friends finish your meal; if I may I will join you?"

Robbie, and Rune sat at the head of the table, and talked to everyone as they drank coffee and had toast and marmalade. Rowan sat at the side of them next to the rest of the group and told him how Lord Philip had given each of them fifty gold bits to get food and clothes, and find accommodation. Robbie was very impressed.

They all finished their meal, returned, and shook his hand again. "Bless you My Lord, My Lady," they would say or, "we will never forget this." Slowly the room emptied, apart from his companions.

Robbie stood up. "I am proud of what you did last night; you are all truly heroes in my book. All of you were exceptional, thank you my friends your loyalty alone has humbled me." The whole group smiled and nodded, John looked up.

"I will die for you My Lord if you ask me to; such is the love I hold."

"Hear, hear," they all murmured.

Rune watched his face change as the statement impacted on him. "I would risk my life for any of you and that is the truth, for you are all my kin in my heart. Thank you John, you have honoured me more than any ever has."

Rune rose up and walked down the table; she bent down and kissed John on the cheek. "That was the nicest thing I have ever seen happen to him." She followed Robbie as he walked out into the garden, John blushed as everyone smiled; Martin patted him on the back.

"Best looking woman that will ever kiss your ugly face that is mate." The whole group burst into laughter, but although John laughed, he knew the sincerity in her voice was real, and he was deeply touched.

He stood at the top of the steps and the sun shone brightly down on him. He wore no weapons, and his shirt hung loosely flapping in the breeze. His shirtfront was slightly open and the silver lion glinted in the bright light of a new day. He stood tall with his hands on his hips, just a young boy of seventeen and as his hair blew around his shoulders, he seemed to grow in stature.

The gardener stood leaning on his spade on the edge of the tree line, and he knew just by looking that this was a man of power; he truly was a great lord of his own realm. He stood and watched as Rune came out and stood beside him linking his arm. The gardener stepped back into the trees and bowed. "My Lord Hearne has provided our saviour," he spoke quietly to himself as he raised his head to Lord Loxley.

"What you thinking?"

He looked out over the garden and its exquisite beauty. "I think when we return home, we should build a house close to the woods, and get mum to help me create a garden of paradise like this one."

Rune squeezed his arm. "A home for us you said."

"I did, and I will build it from all that is nature." She smiled, and kissed his cheek, he turned. "It is a new day Rune; many lives are in danger and we must act soon or thousands will suffer. I need to talk to Skip, he knows of things about politics and government that I do not. I am beginning to understand where my direction lies and he was not sent to us by chance. He is important to all of us and so is Rowan, he is a man of mystery who has some value to all of us."

"We have a long way to go yet Robbie, last night was just the start."

"Last night was just me starting to get angry." He turned to her. "Rune you have gained incredible power and I have something although I am still not sure what. Together we are a force of our own; we must now help everyone who wants to push Knox back into that hole we made last night."

"This will not be easy Robbie."

"I am from the north where nothing has ever been easy, that I can handle. I am the Hooded Man Rune; it is time to be completely that and that alone. Lord Loxley can wait, we have communities in danger and I need woodsmen to save them."

"And only the true hooded man can lead them?" She smiled at him; she had felt the conflict in him ever since the night when he was made the lord of his land. She had understood the turmoil, as he had strove to be a lord to his people and Robbie to his friends, and the hooded man of the woodlands. Rune watched, as the three dissolved into one and he chose his path, on which he would lead the country back and end his inner conflict.

"It is what I am Rune, it is what I have always been, I am a woodsman who wears a hood." He smiled. "I just happen to be called Robbie, which is convenient. Come on, we have to learn to fight fire with fire not sticks, they burn too easily."

Robbie and Rune walked back into the main hall where the group had started to finally come to life. Alice sat at the table with her head in her hands; a large glass of something that fizzed was in front of her. She looked up at Robbie as he approached, her eyes were sunken and her face was very pale. For Alice the previous night had been more a case of drowning her sorrows, rather than celebrating.

Robbie drew an arrow out of a quiver as he passed, and walked up to the table. He looked at her. "God, are you alright? Alice you look awful."

She weakly smiled. "Robbie that does not help, and stop shouting."

"Sorry...I'm not... Alice I need your help; you know the arrows we used to make as kids for great Uncle Walter?"

"Yes, he used them to hunt those escaped elephants from those zoo things."

"Well, I need about a thousand, and I will need someone to show the arrow maker round here how to make them, can you do that?"

"Thinking of hunting a few elephants Robbie?"

"Not elephants, but something equally as big, a Knox... These arrows will have to be at least two and a half times as long as this one and we will need the sharpest point possible on them. I need something that will puncture just about anything. Remember John, and his boar buster arrowheads? Well, they have to be better."

"Alright Robbie, I hear you, let me have this and then I will go and sort it out."

Robbie smiled. "You know you look like Harry does in the mornings."

"Cheers Robbie that has just given me a reason never to drink alcohol again."

"Ok where is Fuse?" Robbie disappeared, and Rune shook her head and sat next to Alice. "Oh you do look peaky, are you going to be alright?"

Alice nodded slowly. "I will live, I am not sure I deserve to, but yes I will live."

It was much later in the day when Rune, Rowan, and Alice found Robbie. He was stood at the top of the battlements looking down a long telescope.

"Where did you get this? It's a real beauty." Rune eyed the scope with delight, her grandfather had taught her all about the planets and stars, and she had shared many hours as a small girl with him looking up at the night sky.

"Matthews helped me get it up here, he can be a funny sort of bloke but I do like him." Robbie glanced back at Rowan and Alice. "Look at this."

Rowan peered down the scope and stepped back as Alice took a turn. "What is that Robbie?" Rowan looked a little concerned.

"That my dear friend is a weapons plant, Knox is making weapons. The old technology as Fuse has pointed out does not exist to recreate some of the weapons of the old modern era, so he is turning his hand to improving some of the first weapons man ever made. He is making cannons."

Alice took her eye off the scope and looked very worried. "I have read about them in books, Blackbeard the pirate had several on his ship."

Rowan still looked a little confused. He had grown up in a woodland without books. "Just what exactly are these cannon things?"

Robbie turned and pointed to the back of the courtyard on the battlement. "Those."

The old disused cannon sat on its wooden wheels with its long black metal barrel pointing across the yard. Rowan walked over and inspected it. He stared down at it trying to understand what it actually did. Robbie walked over and picked up the steel metal ball that sat on the floor beside it. He handed it to Rowan, who instantly felt the weight, and it was heavy.

"Imagine Rowan..." He picked up a large stone off the floor. "What would happen to that glass window if I threw this with great force at it?"

Rowan glanced at the window and then the stone. "You would smash the glass."

Robbie nodded. "Well now imagine that the steel ball in your hand is the stone, and the walls of this castle are the glass." Robbie patted the cannon. "And this is me, get the picture?"

Rowan slowly lowered the ball to the floor and walked back to the telescope, he peered back through it. "We need to get to Bristol."

Robbie patted him on the shoulder. "Or plan another boat trip."

Alice came up to the scope. "How did you find out all this Robbie?"

"I have been watching all day with Fuse, you know he is a whiz on weapons. There is not much he does not know about the modern and past history of warfare; I find him more and more a useful member of this team." Robbie walked back to the wall and looked out across the bay. "You see something that has been on my mind for days, is why would Knox want gun powder? I know that Joe has some because I have helped him refill his cartridges for that old shotgun. I did think at first that Knox might be making guns, but when I saw cannons through the scope this morning I knew."

Alice suddenly realised. "You knew Loxley is made of wood; Knox will have to use something very powerful to smash through it." Alice looked suddenly sick again.

"Don't worry he has been building that over there for months, according to the locals the lights only started a week ago, which must mean he has only just started production. I think he is working day and night to produce as many as possible, and soon he will start to move them across the country, that will be when he is at our mercy." Robbie smiled at Alice.

Rune came over to his side. "How will he be at our mercy?"

"That's easy, Harry." Rune looked completely confused and a little worried, anything that relied on Robbie's half mad uncle was a subject of great concern.

"Just how does Harry fit into all of this?"

"Harry rides a motorbike; he knows every decent road surface in this land. Knox will not be able to transport heavy objects like cannons across country."

Rune smiled. "He will need the old road system, and with Harry's knowledge we can predict his route and attack them."

Robbie smiled. "I love a woman with brains, especially when they are this beautiful." He kissed her.

Robbie sat a little later, at the table with Harry and Pete. "No man, I tell you, last time I went that way it was like wheels of glue man."

"Harry dude, you got it all wrong, look we cruised it back in 17 when we went looking for those spare carbs."

"Yeah, wow man, you are like amazin, how cosmic was that trip? We totally buzzed for week's man."

Pete smiled. "Yeah, Stephy loved that week, it was the first holiday we ever had."

Robbie leaned over. "Guys no disrespect meant, but could we focus for a moment, I really need to know how Knox will bring cannons up to Bristol. At the speed you two are working he will have flattened it and be knocking at the door here before you decide."

Pete smiled. "Yeah, sorry man, he can only use this road, the old M5 is out of action, because two nutters tried to move a petrol tanker down it with flat tyres and it blew up from the sparks, it brought three bridges down."

Harry burst out laughing. "Oh wow man, that was cosmic, I thought we were totally dead dudes, I was ready for my cosmic rebirth, it was amazin and really radical, it looked sort of spacey and cool at sunset."

"So this is the road?" Robbie's eyes fixed on Pete for clarification.

Pete was smiling; he shrugged his shoulders. "What can I say we were young? Yes Robbie, this is the only clear road to Bristol, the old A37. Knox will have to travel east on the old Bath road, and turn on to the 37, and come into Bristol from the south."

"Cheers Pete that really helps, you will work out the other routes as quickly as possible, won't you?"

"Hey man you can totally depend on us we are the cosmic couple; we radiate cool vibes and mellow happenin." Pete smiled at his best friend.

"Right Harry, just focus alright?"

Robbie picked up the map and headed off to find Philip. He was in the conference room just getting ready to leave for Bristol.

"Am I glad I caught you; I need to show you this?" Robbie spread the map out on the table, and showed him the route that they all thought that Knox would use to get to Bristol.

"If he gets those cannons to Bristol, you will not have a chance. Philip, you have to find and stop his convoy, there is nothing more important than this. I would say that they would have covered wagons with gunpowder in them. All you will need to do is have one group use flaming arrows to ignite the trucks, once they start burning the gun powder will do the rest."

Philip studied the map. "I have a few men in that area that could pull this off, leave it with me and I will send word when we find them. What will you be doing in the mean time?"

"Oh well me and the gang are considering another little boat trip, I thought we might let him know we are back in town for a bit."

Philip smiled. "Well good luck, somehow I think I will hear all about it before I get back." Robbie walked out to the courtyard with Philip, where his horse was waiting for him. He climbed up and saluted Robbie. "I will see you soon my friend."

Robbie nodded. "Keep your head down and watch your back eh...?" Philip smiled and pulled on the reigns, the horse turned and galloped through the large arched gate, he raised a hand to wave as he rode off.

Everyone was gathered around the cart and Robbie walked over, six large wooden boxes sat in the back. Hog heaved another one into the cart as Fuse smiled. "I have managed to find those items you wanted sir, actually we are very lucky I have far more than we needed. The box with the red cross on it is a little sweaty, so I would suggest we use that first."

"This is excellent news Fuse, all I need now is for Rune and Alice to arrive and we will be ready, can you get this down to the yacht and we will meet you there shortly? Take Hog."

Martin looked at Robbie and back at the boxes. "What is in the boxes Robbie? And why is it going to the yacht?"

"Don't worry about the boxes, they are a little surprise gift from us to Mason. As for the yacht, I thought a little moonlight sailing would be nice for all of us." He winked at Rowan.

He headed back in, to go and get all of his things together; Rune arrived as he sorted things out in his room. "We got them; he has only been able to produce you 200. He has ten men working flat out to get you the rest as quickly as possible, Alice was really clever, she showed all his men a much better way of doing it, I hadn't realised how much she knows about all of Loxley's production."

"Yeah, winters drag in our house, first sign of bad weather and dad had all of us in the barn working. You would be surprised at how skilled we all were before the age of ten."

Rune slid her arms around him. "Busy day then? Keeping yourself nice and busy."

He turned and smiled. "I am fine now; you were right I had to let it out and it has done me some good." He pulled her close. "Thanks, I am not sure how I would have got through it without you, it hurt a lot more than anyone but you realised."

She stroked his fringe back from his eyes. "I will always be here to help Robbie, I will never leave, you do know that don't you?"

He softly kissed her, "I know."

The darkness was approaching when Robbie gathered his team together, and headed down to the harbour for the second night running. People stood and watched as the group all hooded with Loxley crests on their cloaks, walked up to the deep blue yacht. Skip was stood at the wheel ready, as the crew ran about getting the yacht in final preparation for the journey. The group was chatting happily, as they boarded and made their way to the crew cabin.

Robbie approached Skip who was barking his orders out at crewmembers, as the gangplank was drawn up and the ropes were cast off the harbour and on to the yacht. "It's going to be a nice night for a sail Robbie, the conditions look fantastic."

Robbie came up to his side and looked down the yacht as it moved away from the harbour, and headed into the channel that would take them out to sea. "You know what to do Skip? Take us in a wide arc. I am quite sure they will be watching us now, so let us look like we are off elsewhere before we swing round. You are sure we can slow down enough to do what we need and then speed off now aren't you?"

"Just leave the boat to me Robbie, you focus on your task at hand and we will do fine, I promise."

Robbie patted him on the back and made his way down the deck to the boxes that were sat on top of the cabin. He opened the box with a big red cross on the top, and took out one of the objects; from another box he took a shiny clear roll and what looked like some rope. As he neared the cabin, he pulled one of the new longer arrows that Alice had helped to create.

Everyone sat in the cabin talking as Robbie came down the stairs. "Ok listen up, I need you to pay extra attention than normal, I have something a little different to show you." Robbie placed the new arrow on the table, and they all peered down at it.

Martin examined it very closely. "Hell Robbie do we shoot this, or just throw it?"

The arrow was two and a half times longer than a normal arrow. The tip was a large almost harpoon like blade, and the feather flights were a lot longer than normal, the arrow was a monster.

"I use to make these when I was a kid with Alice. We had an uncle who would shoot these at elephants that had escaped into the wilds. This is a very specialist tool for a very specialist job."

Robbie placed the other objects onto the table. "Cool bangle." Pebbles picked it up and looked at it closely

"That is not a bangle; it is called as I believe cellophane tape... Fuse here used it a lot in the old days. It is not easy to get hold of, so please go easy with it. This as you all know is fuse cord, which means that this can only be dynamite." He placed a brown looking candle on the table.

"Tonight people, we are going to give our dear old friend Mason, a blast from the past." Robbie smiled. "Fuse will show you all how to prepare your fuses." Robbie cut a piece of fuse and inserted it into the dynamite. "Then you tape the dynamite just behind the tip of the arrow using this really fantastic cellophane tape, wow that is cool." Robbie bound it to the arrow with speed and ease.

"At the given moment you light the fuse and then shoot. The arrow lands, and then bang, Mason finds he has more problems.... You all understand?" Everybody nodded. "Right, we have about an hour and forty minutes to assemble our arrows so get to work, everything you need is in the boxes above the cabin, let's get busy."

Over the following hour, they all had a lot of fun. Cellophane tape was an instant success, as most of them laughed at each other for losing the end of the tape or sticking their hair to the arrows. Rune was in fits when Jade stood up and most of the arrows she had prepared all jumped out of the box and followed her. They hung from her hair, and Rune had to snap them off one at a time.

The time was almost upon them, and Robbie divided them in to pairs. "Ok we will travel slowly past the target, you both load your bows, and then one of you will light the fuse and tap the bowman on the shoulder. That person will fire, by which time the lighter will have taken aim. The one to shoot first will then light the second shooters fuse and they will fire, and so on and so on, alright?"

The whole group nodded. "Alright everyone please be careful, just one of these arrows will sink the yacht if it goes off on board, and it is a long swim home. Be careful, and no messing about, I want you all focused. We will be approaching the target close by so be ready for anyone firing at us. If they do, send them one of these, I somehow do not think they will hang around for long. Right let's get on deck."

The group came on to the deck and lined up in pairs, as the yacht began to slow, and they approached a heavily lit area. "All those buildings and everything in that brightly lit area is the target so spread you arrows wide for maximum effect. Don't forget these are bigger heavier arrows so pull back as far as you can on the string, get ready to light your fuses."

Fuse had been passing them all little red glowing sticks. Rune held hers ready as Robbie raised his bow; they drew alongside the massive complex built on the docks and the anchor slipped down almost stopping the yacht.

"Light em," shouted Robbie, and he saw his arrow fizz as he pulled right back on the string, one of the buildings had its door open and he took aim and fired.

The arrow shot with incredible pace, and another seven followed his in different directions, all over the plant. Robbie watched his go straight through the open door. He grabbed the lighting stick, and Rune pulled back on the bow. Her fuse began to fizz, and he pulled away, and lifted another arrow, her own arrow followed his.

There was a massive explosion, and then another, and then another. Bright orange and yellow flames burst out of the building he had shot into, the walls ruptured and fragments exploded into the sky. They were blasted at least a hundred feet up, and the air rained down splinters.

The boat was moving very slowly, Robbie took aim further into the site. "Get them as far in as possible." He screamed as Rune lit his fuse. He pulled as hard as he could on the bow and aimed high, the arrow whipped into the air right over everything that had been hit. He pushed the lighter on to Rune's fuse, as a man appeared on the dockside with a crossbow. Rune twisted and shot, she hit him right in the chest, and the arrow lifted him three feet into the air and he disappeared out of view.

Explosion after explosion went off, more flames, screams, and fire burst out of all the buildings as the yacht moved slowly along the bank. Any figures that appeared soon ran screaming, as they were chased by a lit, highly explosive arrow.

Nine of the huge warehouses were engulfed in flames; Robbie counted at least twelve more. "Concentrate on the ones not burning." He screamed over the noise of the explosions. Rune sent another arrow high into the air and he watched it drop behind one of the buildings. Whatever she hit, it was big.

A ball of fire two hundred feet high erupted into the dark. The sound was ear splitting, and fire engulfed every building within two hundred feet. They all stopped to cover their ears, as a ball of fire after ball of fire erupted into the sky. It was so bright that the whole coastal area was in daylight. The ground shook so violently that ripples crossed the water and the boat rose and sank throwing everyone off balance. They all grabbed the handrails to stay upright.

Burning debris started to rain out of the sky, as Jade and Jett danced along the top of the cabin whooping and cheering, Robbie threw his arms around Rune, hugged, and kissed her. Whatever she had hit, it was highly explosive and one arrow had taken out just about all of the factories. Flames and black smoke billowed in to the sky.

"Let's get the hell out of here Skip." Robbie yelled over the dancing members of the group. Harry and Pete danced with Alice and Steph down the opposite side of the yacht whilst all of them shouted at the top of their voices. "TOTALLY COSMIC MAN," and laughed and danced some more.

Rune had a huge smile on her face as the sails went up, and the yacht began to pick up speed and move into the centre of the channel. Eric appeared from nowhere screaming. "ROBBIE!" He threw his arms around Robbie's smiling face, and that's when it hit.

Eric gasped. "Robbie…" Robbie grabbed him; he looked across the bank to see the shadowy outline of Billy holding a bow, he turned and ran, as Eric slid to the floor. The whole world had stopped, as Robbie looked down in shock. "No!" It was just air passing his lips; Robbie fell to his knees pulling Eric towards him, the long red feathered arrow stuck out of his back.

Rune was beside him in a flash, Rowan stood above Robbie his bow trained on the bank. Robbie stared into the face of the young boy in whom he had placed so much confidence. Eric swallowed hard, and gasped for air. "Robbie you're safe."

Robbie held him as he would a child. "You saved me Eric." Eric smiled.

"You are my hero Robbie."

"Oh Eric, it was not your time."

"Tell my mum I was brave for me." Eric coughed as the blood came to his lips. "Look after him Miss." Robbie shuddered, as Eric went limp and the last air inside him passed his lips. The tears blurred his eyes, as he looked at the group all now gathered round. "We've lost him."

John fell to his knees and cried, as Robbie pulled Eric's body close and wept. Rune leant over him weeping, Blades sat with her face in her hands, as she wailed in grief. Martin held Alice into his chest as he stood frozen, and tears streamed down his face, and the yacht sped away into the darkness.

His body was finally taken from Robbie and laid on top of the cabin by John. He straightened his clothes, and then folded his cloak around him. The Loxley crest flickered in the moonlight, as gently John with tears in his eyes, pulled the hood over his face. He picked up Eric's bow, and rested it on top of him.

Everyone stood down either side of the yacht weeping. John looked at Robbie who was weeping as Rune cried into his shoulder. John raised his head and spoke with a loud but very shaky voice.

"Hearne take this man who is my friend into your keep; guard him well because he is a true Bowman of Loxley." Robbie lifted his head and pulled Rune gently away from him. Everyone looked at him through tear filled eyes. Robbie looked at them all one by one.

"He was valiant and true to all of you. He was my friend and yours, honour him." Robbie clenched his right fist and slapped it hard in salute into his left shoulder. Every one followed and bowed their heads, John and Martin wept and their shoulders shook as they stood before him.

The yacht drifted into port with the flag at half mast. A large group had gathered on the harbour and they all cheered, as the yacht pulled alongside the harbour wall. Ropes were thrown out to tie the yacht, and the cheers of the crowd died down as they saw the men of Loxley stood either side of their fallen comrade with their heads bowed.

The gangplank was pushed out and the crowd separated, as two men with a small fattish man dressed in black, pushed through towards the yacht carrying a rough wooden box. Robbie looked up and saw the men approaching the plank. "Stop!" He yelled, as he passed his men and he made his way down the yacht to the small fat man. "You, what are you doing?"

The small man looked sheepishly at Robbie as he came down the gangplank towards him. "I am the undertaker My Lord... I ... Err saw your flag at half mast and brought you a coffin for your fallen comrade My Lord." He smiled, and nervously pointed to the box of rough splinter ridden pine.

The anger rose quickly in Robbie. "What the hell is that crate?"

The crowd stepped back nervously; the undertaker shook. "It is a box for the burial of a soldier My Lord."

"He will not leave this vessel in that egg crate, get me something more fitting."

The undertaker pulled at his long black scarf that hid where his coat did not quite meet at his stomach. "But My Lord this is what all the common soldiers are buried in."

Robbie's temper blew, and he drew out his sword. It shone, and rainbows danced reflected on the undertakers frightened face. "Common! Who the hell do you think you are? Do you know who I am?"

The sight of a sword of such quality was frightening enough, but the look on Robbie's face was enough to terrify anyone. The crowd took another step back, and the undertaker shook more violently. "You are Lord Loxley, My Lord."

Robbie pointed to the yacht with his sword. "That man there is my man; he is a true man of Loxley who died to save his lord tonight." He swung the sword under the chin of the undertaker. "You go and find me a box that is in keeping with the life of a lord for I owe him that much." He pushed the sword into the chest of the undertaker. "That man was braver in his short life than you would be if you lived ten." He looked at the crowd. "He is a true hero, and all of you should honour him."

He looked back at the undertaker. "Get me a fitting tribute to that hero or I will take this sword and cut you in half and feed you to the fish... Now go!" Robbie swung the huge sword up, and dropped it in to its sheath. The undertaker ran at great speed back up the harbour followed by his two apprentices.

At the top of the gangplank, Robbie stood his face fierce, as he saw at the top of the street the undertaker and his men reappear with a white satin wood casket. It had brass handles, and it was made with precision and skill. They came to the harbour and stood before Robbie.

He looked back over his shoulder. "John, Martin, attend to our man of Loxley." They fell out of the vigil that the others all held, and came up to the harbour, and collected the casket and took it back on board.

Eric was placed very gently into the casket, Blades still weeping ensured he was tidy and neat, as she burst in to more heavy tears and wept bitterly. Rune pulled her close and held her as she sobbed John, Martin, Fuse, Harry, Rowan and Pete gently lifted the box on to their shoulders.

Robbie pulled out his sword and held it before him. He stepped forward as the pole bearers came up the gangplank, and he walked slowly in front of the casket up the street towards the castle. The people of the small town bowed their heads as he passed, some of them wept for such was the passion of his honour and respect for his fallen man, that they were touched and wept openly. The white casket glowed in the darkness, as it was carried with high honour up to the castle. Rune holding a weeping Blades, and Steph holding Alice followed. At the top of the street Jade and Jett lit, two arrows and fired, them out to sea in salute, and Eric of Loxley entered the castle for the last time.

Just after dawn in a small clearing in the woodland next to the castle, a grave was dug. The casket was set on poles and adorned with flowers, Robbie and the entire group gathered around with their heads bowed.

Robbie searched inside himself for the words and the strength to deliver them.

"I stand before the remains of a young boy. A young boy who gave his life to ensure that I stand here before you all today, it was an act of love that I cannot even begin to repay, for he is gone, and I will never be able to tell him of how proud I was to stand beside him."

Robbie began to tremble as the emotion took him. "I chose this boy to follow me into uncertainty, and I bare the guilt of his passing, he was a true man of Loxley, a true bowman and woodsman, and I lay him here under the watch of our Lord Hearne."

He lifted his head as the tears ran down his cheeks. "This boy has honoured me with his life; I will avenge him and honour him with a life. I call upon Hearne to protect his remains and welcome him in to the spirit of the trees. Hearne protect him."

Everyone repeated. "Hearne protect him," and the poles were removed as young Eric was lowered into the hole. The soil was moved back in, and the grouped bowed their heads one more time to their friend and comrade. John and Martin placed his bow and quiver on the grave.

Robbie stood still as everyone walked quietly away. Rune dried her eyes and slid her arm around Robbie. "I need you to contact Len and ask him to have Eric's mother informed, I want it known in Loxley that this man was a hero and should be praised."

"It is already done Robbie; his mother will be cared for don't worry."

"He gave his life for me Rune; I don't even know where to begin in understanding that. He had so much to live for, and he gave that to me, what must I do now? This young boy, who just wanted to shoot a bow for me, has shown me an honour that goes beyond my understanding."

"Would you have taken his arrow?"

Robbie looked into her eyes. "Gladly."

"Then do not question what he did, but honour him as you said by living and making a difference. You have to finish what we have started, if you do not, he would have died in vain Robbie." Rune bent down and touched the earth, and violets sprung up all over the grave. She stood up and looked at him. "Do not dishonour his sacrifice, remember him with affection and fulfil his dreams." Hand in hand, they walked back toward the garden and the castle. Robbie's heart was heavy; he felt the loss of Eric more than any, for he had chosen him knowing he was not trained or ready. Eric had in his time proven his worth, and his value beyond measure. He had earned the respect of all the men, especially Big John, who had become very fond of him and had guided him through everything they had faced.

It was a solemn mood in the castle that night as they all raised their glasses and saluted the empty plate at the table. They had come so far without loss, but now as the battle to prevent Mason Knox from ruling England came closer; they all knew in their hearts that countless more lives would be taken.

Blades took the loss of her friend badly and did not come down to the meal that night, Rune spent several hours sat talking with her, she even managed a smile when she told Rune how her father had taken her to one side, and told her he had been wrong. He told her that Eric's vibes had actually been quite cosmic.

CHAPTER NINETEEN

A VERY WELCOME DAY OFF

The weapons making plant of Mason Knox still burned as dawn broke. Thick black smoke drifted in the sky, and spread right across the bay and far out over the sea. The sun struggled to penetrate it as it fought its way through the blackness.

Robbie sat on the castle battlement wall, his legs dangling over the steep drop, a cup of coffee clutched tightly in his hand. He had not been to bed and had spent half the night sat watching the burning inferno across the bay down the coast. He prayed it was enough to save Loxley, his precious home could be completely destroyed by cannon fire, and he just hoped he had been able to stop Mason before it was too late.

He breathed a deep sigh, he was tired and he leaned back and stretched out his arms, as he pulled the muscles to stretch out the aches. His dark tired eyes looked down as he watched the small fishing boats chug out to sea, heading toward the black cloud that hung in the air.

Life seemed to be going on regardless, to the town's people they were all heroes, who for two nights running had struck bitter blows to the empire of Mason Knox, yet Robbie still felt uneasy. The thought of knowing that he had planted his own son as a spy ten years ago meant that he was still very prepared. He was ready for a war that would bring chaos to the lives of those who still fought for a daily life of survival.

"There you are I was worried when Rune said you had not gone to bed."

Robbie turned and looked at Alice. "I couldn't sleep so I thought I would sit here and think for a bit, it is over a day now and it is still burning."

Alice climbed up on the wall, walked along the high edge of the tower, and sat down beside him. She patted his leg. "It's been quite a rough time Robbie."

He took her hand and held it. "It's not been so hot for you recently, has it?"

"I am Ok now the initial shock is over, if I am honest Rob, I was becoming very unhappy, and I am probably better off now."

Robbie lifted his arm around her shoulder, Alice was very special and now seeing her start to recover lightened his heart a little. "We are all better off Alice; none of us were safe while he was in the camp. I can relax a bit knowing Mason is now in the dark about us."

"I still cannot believe he tried to kill you, I never thought he would, honestly Robbie. I thought that you two no matter what happened would at least respect each other, you know just because of your past together, you were like brothers."

"It has surprised me a little, I can tell you. I never thought he would, I know it sounds odd, but we were brothers we loved each other, I cannot remember a time when he was not at my side. It feels so odd now Alice."

"What will you do now if you meet him?"

Robbie looked at her. "Alice I will have no choice, if I don't, he will kill me. You know that don't you?" Robbie knew how much she had loved Billy, and he knew her well enough to know that it would be hard for her to see him die. He watched as she looked down at the gardens far below in the grounds.

Her voice was quiet. "Yeah, Rob I know." He gave her a squeeze.

"Come on it's going to be a bright day, do not think about it, let's go and find some breakfast."

Just under an hour later, Robbie and Alice sat chatting at the table as they tucked into a hearty breakfast. He had not eaten a great deal over the last few days, and now he felt starving and helped himself to more eggs. He had been keeping a low profile since they had returned from the yacht and had spent most of his time alone or with Rune.

"How are the group holding up?"

Alice watched him as she buttered her toast; he knew she could read him well. "They do not blame you if that is what you mean. Eric was part of the team he knew the risks, just like all of us do. They actually respect you more for giving him the chance, most of them were not sure he should come. But to be honest Rob, we all think you were right to bring him, Eric proved himself in a tight spot a few times."

"I am responsible Alice. I lead them."

Alice put her toast down and looked at him. "Rob, Eric was a little timid at first, but that night at Tintagel you didn't see him I did. He went up that wall like a spider, and dropped like a shadow over the wall. Eric was confident and very skilled. Down in the corridors there was not a sign of fear in him, he was relaxed and sharp, he faced the enemy and did what he had to do. That was no boy down there that was a man of great courage and skill." She smiled. "You gave him that Rob, your trust allowed that young boy to grow into a man. You gave him his honour and his self-respect, that was very important Rob, and I am not sure that you realise just how important it was to Eric."

Robbie sat quietly listening; Alice always had that knack of making him see things clearer. She took a bite out of her toast and chewed. "I will tell you something else as well, if it hadn't been Eric, you can bet your last bit it would have been one of us." He looked up at her. "I would take an arrow for you any day if it kept you beating Knox." He stared at his eggs.

John and Martin came down for their breakfast and wandered over to the table. Martin patted him on the back as he passed and John gave his shoulder a squeeze. "Nice words for him yesterday boss, we all appreciated them thanks." He patted Robbie hard on the back.

"So what are we up to do today?" Martin smiled at Robbie.

"I have a lot to sort out today, so I thought it would be nice for all of you to have a day off, I believe there is a nice little tavern in the town, and you all being heroes and loved by the people." He smiled. "I think a little basking in some glory will do all of you good."

John beamed and licked his lips. "Been a while since I had a good ale, what you say Alice love, fancy a drink with all us heroes?"

Alice's eyes twinkled. "I think I might just."

John slapped the table and laughed. "You watch her Martin my boy, she can handle a pot when she wants too." Alice beamed at them as she bit into her toast and her eyes danced.

Rune was sat in bed when he arrived with coffee and toast; she smiled as he entered with the tray. "Oh Robbie, that is so sweet, thank you." He sat on the bed and put the tray on the small table at the side. He leaned over and kissed her. "I have given everyone the day off; they are going into the town to let off some steam."

Rune sipped her coffee. "I think it will do them all good, things will get tougher by the day from now on. So... A day off eh...? What sir do you have in mind?" She put the cup down at the side of the bed; Robbie smiled as she slid down under the covers.

"I thought it would be nice to go for a walk in the forest, I want to feel the leaves above my head I have missed it." He smiled at her twinkling eyes. "But a little later on I think." Rune giggled as he slid over towards her.

It was a glorious and warm day, the group all gathered in the garden and in high spirits; they headed off to the small gate that led down the old cobbled road to the town. They laughed and joked as they made their way down the steep hill into the small town, in search of the village tavern. Alice and Blades giggled as Pebbles and Jett messed about, and joked about how they could easily leave John standing when it came to drinking.

John rubbed his ample size belly and laughed as he winked at Alice. "Plenty of room in here girls, I have the capacity and the thirst." Jett laughed at him.

"I might not have the girth old man, but I certainly have the stamina." She rubbed his large belly and giggled.

Robbie was right, they all were big heroes and the sight of Loxley coats of arms on their cloaks gained them instant respect. People stopped them and shook their hands, the landlord of the 'the Boatman's Rest' gave them their first pint free, and the whole group sat out in the sun and laughed and joked. They talked to the people who passed them and offered their sincere respects for the loss of their comrade, and over the day, they got somewhat drunker, and sang happy songs of the woods and began to feel a return to normal.

It was late spring and late April was allowing the sun to shine brighter. The mighty Oak trees of the woodland were now finally breaking their buds and unfurling their leaves as the sun tempted them out.

The tall skeletal figures of the woodland trees were covered in pale green and Robbie knew as he looked around, soon the bright sun would become a dappled shade. The ground seemed bumpy and covered with a cloth of green lush moss, and it was only as they wove their way through, that he realised that this part of the wood was once the town.

Broken walls and smashed decayed buildings were now covered in a dense green woolly moss, and bluebells sprung from every crevice as they began to open the first of their flowers. He stopped with Rune holding his hand and marvelled at the glory of the woodland. "Oh Rune, isn't this place beautiful?" He looked up to the sky and watched the birds flapping from tree to tree as they hurriedly built their nests for the summer eggs. He took a long deep breath, and breathed in the fresh clean air filled with dank stone, and mingled with the scent of the damp earth.

Rune pulled him close and smiled. "I really love the way you love the woods. You make them even more alive by just being here in them." He smiled a huge big smile at her.

"All my life I have yearned for the trees, I cannot explain to you what it is like. I suppose it's about being out here, and lost in amongst the trees that just draws me in. I just seem to know that whenever there are leaves above my head, I feel alive and at peace with myself. Does that make any sense to you at all?"

She looked at him with her bright blue crystal clear eyes. "More than you will ever realise Robbie." She smiled and pulled him close and kissed him.

"Oh Rune, this is so perfect, you and the woods are all that I will ever really need, why can't everyone see them as I do and understand their beauty?" He leaned back in her arms and stared to the sky. "Just look at that canopy of finely interwoven twigs. Man could never in a million years create something so wonderful. Nature is the creative genius of the world, why would Knox want to destroy it? He is as mad as they come and so short sighted."

She pulled him back. "Do you really love nature so deeply Robbie?"

Robbie looked at her in wonder. "If she was human, she would be just like you?"

Her eyes sparkled with tears as she pulled him close and held him tight.

"Robbie I love you, have you any idea how much you mean and how special you are to me?"

He pulled back and looked into her damp eyes; he lifted a finger and wiped the tear from her eye. It fell to the earth and the bluebells burst into bloom. "Rune I know after Eric we are all worried, but I will not leave you. Rune you understand, don't you? There will never be another for me." He softly kissed her. "You are everything in my life and will be forever, you are my life and my love. Even my love of the woods is secondary to you, you are everything."

She pulled him close and held him tight and she wept. Robbie gently stroked her hair down her back as he held her. "Hey come on, things will be fine I promise. Really, Rune I mean what I said; when all of this is over, we will go back to Loxley and build a cabin. I will grow old in your arms surrounded by all our children and we will be happy forever. Trust me I am Lord Loxley; I will make it the law."

Rune giggled and he pulled her back to see her smiling face. "I am the hooded man, with the sword of truth believe me, we will be fine."

She wiped her eyes and more bluebells flowered. "I know, I am just being silly, it has been a hard few days I think it has got to all of us."

"It's a new day Rune, so come on let's enjoy our time off." He gave her a huge smile, and took her by the hand and walked deeper into the woods pointing out the marvels that nature had created.

The trees began to get older and older as they walked; their old trunks creaked and groaned as the breeze above gently shook their limbs. The fat old trunks showed their age with open hollows, which contained nesting birds or stores for the squirrels. Robbie marvelled at every one of them. They came to the top of a steep bank and looked into the small hollow of green moss. It was a perfect circle set within the trees and was surrounded by the oldest trees of the wood.

Robbie held Rune's hand as they walked down towards it, and Rune's eyes flickered lilac. She stopped and became very nervous, he glanced back at her. "Robbie I am not sure we should go any further." She pulled on his hand. He stopped and looked at her and saw her eyes that were now a shade of violet.

"What do you sense?"

"There is a great power here, a very ancient power, I am not sure we should disturb it Robbie." She shook her head and he nodded, he knew that if she warned him off, he would be better to follow her lead. He took her hand and turned.

"Welcome my children do not be afraid my granddaughter is right, but there is nothing here that will hurt you two."

Turning back, he saw the figure of the white lady stood in the centre of the open circle. He looked back at Rune who did seem very nervous; the white lady lifted her hand.

"Come Runestone, you have nothing to fear, our last meeting was hard for you as it was for me, but you will be safe. Today is a new day for it heralds the start of the age of dreams."

Robbie held her tight and they made their way into the circular clearing. The white lady waved her hand, and mossy hummocks rose in the ground. A crystal decanter appeared with two glasses, as Rune watched it with suspicion.

"Welcome to my home woodsman, welcome home granddaughter, rest a while and we shall speak, for there are things to tell." Robbie and Rune walked into the circle and sat together on one of the raised hummocks. Rune seemed wary and stayed close by his side. The lady in white poured two large glasses of a clear pink coloured liquid, and handed it to them. Robbie still could not see her face, and again he felt something familiar about her as he had in the priory.

He lifted the glass and smelt the scent of roses, and as it touched his lips, he tasted elderflower. The liquid was ice cold, and yet somehow, he felt a surge of energy inside him, and his whole body seemed to tingle with life and he felt strong and powerful. Rune's eyes flared deep purple as she swallowed and then they faded back to the pale lilac of normal.

"I have watched and listened to you today woodsman, for you are in my domain now. I am pleased that you love my home and marvel at its wonder; you do me, and my granddaughter great service in the love of her and my realm. It has made me very happy."

"Grandmother you spoke of a new day and a new era, what do you mean?" Rune seemed to relax slightly and Robbie watched carefully as she spoke.

"It is the reason you are here my precious child." The white lady of the wood lowered herself on to the hummock in front of them, her hood was low and her face was still unseen. "My time here will fade over the coming years and a new mistress will replace me, for I am Opal and the Whitelines of sleep are fading. As the new age of dreams comes into power a new mistress more suited to the task will take power, and the age of dreams will command until the dawn of awakening comes."

Robbie felt a little lost. "So, there are ages of events that shape the future?"

"Woodsman, there have been three ages so far; all differ in spans of time. There was the age of power when we came forth and helped to build a world of joy and harmony and man. Then came the age of knowledge, and man grew but was leaderless, and the first true king was brought forth. He was followed by the age of sleep where some of us were imprisoned and we had to sit by and watch man grow unaided, and lead the destruction of our world. All that we built was turned slowly to stone, and machines became the love of man, not beauty. He forgot the gifts of life we had given to him and he destroyed the love of the wild."

Rune looked up at the Opal surprised. "You did it, you brought the Red Death?"

"There are some more powerful than I my dearest granddaughter, but yes it was one of us who brought a death to slow down the destruction of this world. They were imprisoned as we were, but some of their power was older than time, and they used it to slowly release themselves from the bonds that held them. The power used was great, and they brought the red death forth. It was the signal to us all that the new age was coming."

"My Lady it destroyed most of those who lived in this land, how could anyone do something so evil?"

"Woodsman, you know of my father of the woods, you have both sat before him. He has the power to twitch just one finger and Loxley will burn, and all you hold dear would be gone, would you call that evil?"

"I would yes My Lady."

"The snake you fight would take Loxley and turn it into stone, and kill your precious woods, would you call that evil?"

"I would yes My Lady."

"So to see all you have built and loved destroyed, and soiled, is that then an act of evil?" Robbie and Rune now began to understand the Lady of the Woods. Robbie lowered his head and nodded. "You see my dearest of children what Humankind has done to our creation? My realm and that of Lord Hearne's will disappear if we do not do just as you are doing now. We have to defend it, for if we don't, we will die too."

Her pale white hand came out from under the cuff and touched Robbie's hand; her voice was now soft and filled with compassion. "Dear Woodsman, there is so much ahead of you that cannot be revealed, but now is the time for the dreams of Humankind to become enlightened, and lead the way to a world that we all desire. I felt tears when you spoke to my granddaughter, because the dream you hold for your world is hers and mine. You above all hold the answer for everyone in your heart."

She sat back and Robbie looked up at her, she raised her hands, and lowered her hood; Rune looked at her with tears in her eyes. Her hair was as white as snow, and her blue eyes glistened with violet tears. Her face was white and pale and showed the signs of great age. Robbie noticed how like her in many ways Rune was; and he could see she was of her line. The white lady smiled.

"Come to me my dearest Granddaughter." Rune slipped to her knees and her grandmother pulled her close. She held Rune tight as her tears dropped onto Rune's red shimmering hair. She looked at Robbie with sadness. "I have felt your love of my realm and of my granddaughter woodsman, they are true and noble. The age of dreams is almost here and we are powerless to guide it. We can only help to guide you, all our hope rests with the love of one man."

"Why can you only guide me My Lady, do you not have the power to save all you have built?"

"My power is fading as others grow stronger my dear woodsman. We are faced with two men who both hold power and can determine the fate of the world. It was written at the start of time that this age would be given to humankind, and now you and the snake have a powerful dream each."

"You are telling me if I fail, then Knox will build his dream and the earth will fail, and you and Lord Hearne will be gone forever?" The old lady stroked her granddaughter's hair as she held her in her arms. She held her as if this was the last time she would ever see her, and would have to give her up forever, the pain and loss in her eyes showed, and she seemed to age before him.

"The fate of my lord father, and my entire family lie in your palm woodsman, will your dream be stronger than the snakes?"

"I want it to be, I want Rune and myself to see a life together, and create something for our children."

More tears welled in the old lady's eyes, and she released Rune slightly and looked down into her pale face. She smiled at her granddaughter. "My dear sweet Runestone I have seen them, and they are truly blessed."

Rune looked into her grandmother's old and saddened face and smiled. "My children from Robbie, you know?"

Her grandmother nodded. "You must help him bring his dream above that of the snake my child, because there is a joy in your future that will surpass even mine." She looked up and smiled at him. "You really should call me grandmother woodsman."

"I am sorry My Lady... Grandmother."

Rune laughed and hugged her. "Oh, thank you Grandmother."

"Never doubt yourself Runestone my child, follow your heart as you did in the wood today and both of you will come through with the hopes of everyone on your side. Follow the lead of this woodsman, for he has over the last few days taken his steps in the right direction, follow him child." She lifted her hand to Rune's face as she spoke and touched her soft white skin. Her grandmother released her and slowly stood up. She kissed Rune on the cheek and turned to Robbie, she touched his chest. "Here beats the heart of a lion, let it ease from recent pain, for he is now safe in the forest of woodland spirit with my lord father and he is happy."

Robbie blinked. "Eric is safe?"

"Your Lord Hearne will protect all of those who fight for him woodsman, you know that."

Robbie swallowed deeply, and placed his hand on hers; he felt the pressure in his chest ease. "Thank you, knowing he resides with my lord is comforting to me."

"You are a good man woodsman, and your devotion to those around you does you great honour."

She turned once more to Rune. "It is time for you to begin the age my child, and I must leave you now, heed my words well." She kissed Rune on the cheek and turned. "Farewell woodsman, be true in all you do and we will meet again."

"Goodbye Grandmother." She raised her hood, and walked into the trees and faded away into the leaves.

Rune slid her arms around and him pulled him close. "I want six girls."

He laughed aloud. "Aren't you forgetting something?"

"No What?"

"A little hooded man?"

"Ok six girls and a boy." She smiled the most radiant smile he had ever seen and she kissed him. She meant so much to him and seeing her happy lifted his spirits higher.

"We will see." He kissed her back and slid his arm around her as they walked up the bank and back into the forest.

"You know Robbie technically there could be a hooded woman, you know something like Roberta in the Hood." He started to laugh and she giggled as he pulled her close and walked back through the wonder of Caerleon Wood.

Rune and Robbie walked arm in arm out of the trees and into the garden, Alice and Blades both sat on the top of the steps grinning happily, Blades tried to wave but fell over, Alice laughed hysterically, and pulled her back up. She smiled and waved. "Oh dear, maybe a day off wasn't such a good idea." Robbie waved back as Rune chuckled.

"Hey Rume, hey Ruddy." Alice waved vigorously.

"Nope it was definitely not one of my best ideas." Rune waved at the two girls who started to giggle.

Blades smiled a happy smile as they approached. "I got kissed by a French man."

"Really how was it?" Rune smiled at Blades.

"French!" Alice burst into hysterical laughter; Robbie looked at Rune with a help me sort of look.

"Come on you two coffee and food." He lifted Alice who could hardly stand to her feet, and she swayed. "Wow Ruddy, everything is really moving fast." He held her tightly, and slowly walked her into the castle, Alice leaned back. "Hey Babes tell Rume about magic."

Rune looked down at Blades, who had some command of her feet but not a great deal more than Alice. "What's magic?"

"She means Maggie."

"Oh, who is Maggie?"

"It's dad's old chick." Rune seemed a little surprised.

"You mean an old girlfriend?"

"Yeah...?" Blades seemed to stop and then turned a very odd colour. "Rune...? I don't feel very well."

It was sometime later when Rune reappeared; Robbie sat with a pale looking Alice, who was considerably steadier, sipping black coffee. "That poor girl, you would not believe how a girl as small as Blades could hold so much liquid inside her, I was shocked, and thought she would never stop."

The coffee cup chinked on the table, and Alice ran at high speed out of the main hall. Rune smiled at the laughing Robbie. "Go on Cousin Ruddy, I have done my bit."

"Ok Rume darling, I will check to see if she is alright."

It was a while later, when Alice sat on the bed in her room looking exhausted. "I will never drink with Harry and Pete again."

Robbie pulled her into a hug. "You will and you know it, still it's better out."

"Oh, please Robbie, don't talk about it." She blanched and he laughed.

"You will never learn will you Alice?"

"Actually, I really had a great time today, Maggs was a lot of fun, she is as weird as hell but she is very kind, I really liked her."

"Who is Maggs?" Alice sat up and looked at him.

"Oh of course, you and Rune won't know, will you?"

"Know what Alice?"

"Maggs or Maggie is one of Harry's first ever girlfriends, she is the one Harry use to get all the stones for in Loxley. Apparently, she was at Steph's wedding and is Jade's godmother. Her and Harry go way back, and he had lost touch with her when he met Blades mum. He thought she had been killed by the Cutters, because their town had been burned down."

"She is here in this town?"

"Yeah, she was one of the traders on the market, she does jewellery. Harry was freaked when Jade's head disappeared because she was drunk, and he legged it into the crowd screaming something about how it was all your fault, and how you made him do bad things. He just ran right into her, and she went bonkers."

"Jade's head disappeared?"

"Well, no she had her hood up, don't be silly, it must have been Harry, he had drunk a hell of a lot. He kept ranting about green evils coming to get him and chomp his karma, and off he went. The next thing we know there is loads of commotion, and this woman is in the middle of the square kissing Harry like he is the most gorgeous man on the planet, well he would be if he was on this planet if you get my drift?"

"Wow... What is she like?"

"God Rob, what do you think? This is someone who thinks he is really gorgeous and cool... She's as mad as a hatter."

Robbie started to chuckle and Alice smiled. "Actually, she is quite sweet, thinks she is a bit of a psychic, kept telling me I would have six nieces."

"What?"

"I know, she is as loony as a fruit cake, but she would have to be if she is Harry's girlfriend."

"So where is she now?"

"Harry stayed back to help her pack up, she will be leaving on the boat soon to go to the next market somewhere near Southampton I think. She does some sort of travelling spring market thing."

As the evening arrived, Robbie sat in the balcony above the main hall; it was becoming one of his favourite places, as it was isolated and dim. He had been spending quite a bit of time out of sight with Ruby who had become very attached to him. She had just left for one of her lessons with Rune, when Pete and Steph appeared.

Pete sat down beside him. "Just seen Flash she said you were up here, don't mind if we have a chat, do you?"

"Not at all what's on your mind?"

"I take it you have heard about Maggs?"

"Alice did say something about her, why is there a problem?"

Steph leaned forward. "Oh no problems Rob, Maggs had almost all her entire family wiped out by the Cutters, she is sound. Well, we can trust her let's say." She smiled.

"Alice did mention she is madder than Harry, which I find hard to believe."

Pete started laughing, and Steph nudged him. "Ignore him Rob, she is very sweet, a little eccentric but very sweet. Maggs is living with her mum on her farm somewhere over near Canterbury. She has said it will be fine for us to crash there."

Robbie considered the point. "It would solve one of my biggest problems, we need to lay low just before Mason goes to steal the crown, and we are becoming a little too popular at the moment round here."

"This could well be the solution Robbie." Pete looked at Steph. "If we have somewhere close as a base, we will be able to get up close and check out what security is like in the place. This could be the opportunity we are looking for."

Robbie thought for a moment. "It does sound ideal; I will have a chat with Harry later when he comes back, cheers guys."

Pete patted his leg. "Come on the foods here."

Steph and Pete headed down to the table, and Robbie sat in the chair in the gloom thinking. Getting close was his biggest problem, what he now needed was a way into the Cathedral to get to the crown before it was placed on Masons head.

After the meal Robbie looked across the map in the Operations Room. The red figures were now streaming out of Cornwall and spreading across the country. Skip studied it carefully and looked at Scarlet. "He seems to be building a very large force at London, do you know why?"

"I am afraid we have no idea; Philip is finding it very hard to get anyone inside there. We think he is cleaning it up and rebuilding it as the seat of power. We do know that there is a lot of work going on around Windsor."

Rowan leaned off the wall. "Windsor will be where he rules, and then starts to slowly rebuild the country from."

Robbie looked back at London and then at Bristol. A wall of green men spread out from the city in a wide arc, as Philip was trying to push Knox back and protect the city. "How is Philip doing? He does seem to be advancing."

Scarlet smiled. "He is very taken by your methods, and has tried using a few of the old woodsman skills. He has had surprising results, we are pushing forward daily, and for now Bristol is safe. Your new arrows have been very successful with the convoys."

Skip nodded. "If we can keep the weaponry equal, we will at least have a chance."

Robbie looked up the map at Loxley and York, there was a huge force gathered around both of them. "Why has he not attacked here yet? He has the force assembled and yet he is not using them, I do not understand him."

Rowan came closer to the table. "He is a man of self-worship, you once said Robbie he thought he was invincible and his arrogance would defeat him. Can you not see he is given us the date of his attack?"

Robbie looked at Scarlet and then Rowan. "When?"

Skip slapped the table and every one jumped. "Of course, I should have known better, every king and politician through the ages has done it. It all makes perfect sense now. This is not war, this is politics."

Rowan smiled at him. Robbie looked at both of them. "When you two have finished your mutual debate would one of you like to tell us what the hell is going on?"

Skip smiled. "I am sorry Robbie; it's just this has been done in politics a thousand times before. When you have to do something that is big, you create a mass diversion to take attention away from what you know will cause a ripple, in this case the crowning of an illegitimate king.

A cold shiver ran down Robbie's back. "So as the crown is lowered on to his head, there will be a full scale attack on the rest of the country, to suppress all those who would oppose it?"

They all looked at each other and Scarlet shrugged. "It does make sense." Her dark eyes did twinkle and she smiled. "Although... He has made one very big mistake, and Rowan my dear you are very correct... We now know when."

"Well, we would if we knew the date of his crowning." Robbie felt frustrated

"Have no fear Robbie my husband has his spies all over, we will know long in advance of the date. However, we now have the chance to even the scales, his eggs are all in one basket sitting idle, and waiting to be broken. I think we should plan a little scrambling."

"I wish you would not talk about food Scarlet, I missed tea and you're making me hungry."

"Robbie my dear, are you hungry? I will ring for refreshments; in the mean time we need to get our forces working together."

Robbie looked at Loxley and the red men all gathered at Hathersage. "You know Hathersage is set in a wide valley, it would not take much to surround it. I would not think that they would expect an attack, and the Loxley bowmen do not easily miss their mark."

Scarlet smiled. "Now My Lord Loxley we are thinking the same. If we all attack him on the eve of his crowning whilst they are busy sorting themselves out. We could create chaos and defeat his men before he has a chance to muster them into position."

Rowan smiled. "He will be so busy preparing his coronation, he will not be quite on the mark as normal, it's brilliant."

Skip looked doubtful. "We need to communicate faster than we are, this message will not get there quick enough."

Robbie stood up as Matthews arrived with a large tray of sandwiches. "It will if we use the post." He took two large cheese sandwiches off the tray, and took a bite out of one and smiled.

The post service had interested Robbie from the moment he had first heard about it. Somehow, everyone on the west coast had embraced this old-fashioned idea of being able to transport letters. Small offices had been set up in towns with fresh horses, and the riders would hurtle in, hand over the letters and jump on a new horse to continue at speed.

From what he had heard, there were now over two hundred fast riders pacing up and down the country that were not stopped at all. They just shot through the towns, and people would step out of their way to allow them through. To Robbie this seemed to be the chance he was looking for. These riders knew all the hot spots and avoided them. Horses allowed them to cross country, so roads did not govern them, as long as he had a reference point, he could deliver orders to any group of woodsmen anywhere in the land, and Philip had all of the reference points.

"Scarlet I need you to work out where every force is, and what their precise locations are. I am going to write some letters, I will need Jade, have you got a local smithy I can borrow...? Oh Rowan, Skip, could you pop into the town and find out where these postal riders are based, we will need at least six?" Skip looked a little confused but he smiled and nodded. Rowan was already two steps ahead and knew exactly what Robbie had in mind.

Everyone was sat around the table when Robbie entered the main hall, Rune smiled as he walked up and he kissed her on the top of the head. He slipped on to the bench at the side of her. "Ok everybody we are sending a post run from here tonight, so if you have anything to say to your friends and family get it wrote down and I will see it is delivered."

Everyone seemed really overjoyed as Robbie passed out paper. "These apparently are Pens, they are much more accurate than ink and nibs, Fuse does seem to be coming up with the most wonderful little things from the past."

Everyone eyed them carefully, then put them to the paper and gasped; John scowled at his. "Where do you dip it in the ink?"

Rune giggled. "You don't, my granddad uses these, they are full of ink you just write until they run out, see the black line in there? That's ink."

John shrugged. "What do you do when the ink runs out?"

Jade beamed. "We used them as dart shooters when we were kids." She smiled at Rune as fond memories of their tricks on their mother flooded back.

Robbie handed out the paper and then looked at Jade. "How quickly could you knock up a ring with the Loxley crest on it?"

Jade shrugged. "It will take a few hours; it depends on what exactly you want."

He walked over to a glass case that contained an old envelope from some past history of the family. It had a bright red lump on it with the shape of a coat of arms pushed in as a seal. Robbie pointed to it. "I want to do that."

"No problem, have we a smithy handy? I will need a little help."

The whole group sat silently as they wrote. Blades gave John a lift, as he had never really been taught much reading or writing. He took his orders from Robert Lox and did whatever needed doing around the farms. He quietly told Blades what he wanted, and she wrote the words down in a very neat handwriting. Her dad was her only relative apart from Robbie and Alice, as she did not know the others. Harry sat quietly muttering his words as he wrote:

'Dear Jess. Now do not be angry with me because Robbie and Alice have been very uncosmic with their attitude, and mangled my vibes once already.'

'I should have told the family I know, but I did not want you getting heavy with me on the short times I am home, so please be chilled and cool when you read this.'

'I have been looking after my cool and radical baby girl for three years. She is a totally hip chick called Katie and is sixteen.'

Harry looked up and sucked his pen as Rune and Alice both smiled, and Blades beamed at him from across the table. Robbie was scratching away on a large pile of letters, and consulting a long list as he wrote to each of the leaders of the woodsmen, who were doing their best to hold back the troops of Mason Knox. He finished the large pile of letters and started thinking. He looked at Rune and smiled, and then he took a clean sheet of paper and he began to write slowly as he thought.

Dear Mrs Tanner,

I am aware that you have already been informed of the death of your son Eric; However, I feel the responsibility of his loss and feel I should write to you.

The young boy who left Loxley with me was a very different person on the night that we lost him. In his brief time with us, he grew in stature, and was an essential and very well loved part of this outfit.

Myself, and the others, were devastated when he lost his life protecting his lord. Your son committed the bravest act I have ever known, and his actions humbled me greatly, when he threw himself in the way of an arrow meant for me.

I have no way of knowing how I can repay such a debt to your family, but you have my assurance that on my return I will humbly try to, and I will ensure that your son will be honoured above all others.

Eric was very brave in several raids that we undertook and he showed courage and skill beyond measure. We were all very proud of his achievements and valued his friendship. He is dearly missed.

Your humble servant,

ROBERT.

Lord of Loxley

Rune slid her arms around him as she put her head on his shoulder. "That is a very kind thing to do." She kissed him softly.

"Do you think it is alright? I have never written letters before."

She squeezed him tight. "I think that will become a treasured possession of the Tanner household, and I think it is very beautifully written for a first real letter, you have touched me and I would think that it will mean a great deal to his mum."

"I hope so Rune, I have thought that it should have been me who told her face to face."

"You have great heart My Lord." She kissed him again.

When all the letters were written, Alice and Robbie sorted them out into piles depending on what was going where. The Loxley pile was quite large, as most of them had written to several people as they seized their chance to let everyone know how they were. Alice had written eight.

Jade arrived back looking hot and sweaty; she still had a small file in her hand as she cleaned up the edges of the silver. "It's not my best work but for a quickie, I think it will serve its purpose."

Robbie looked at the ring of silver, which had the crest of a wolf's head and two crossed arrows on it. He was very impressed, and smiled as he showed it to Rune. "This is excellent Jade, if this is a rush job, I must get you to make me a good one when we get back so I will have my first heirloom of my own household."

Jade beamed a broad happy smile. "I am glad you like it Robbie, it should fit you alright, I have made that many over the years I can usually tell a ring size without measuring. If it doesn't, I can adjust it."

Robbie slid the silver ring on to his finger; it sparkled in the light and fitted perfectly. Rune lit the red candle as he folded each letter, and she dripped the wax on to it as everyone watched. Robbie pushed his ring into the cooling wax and there was the imprint of the seal of Lord Loxley. Jade beamed with delight.

"I have got to make me one of them... Wow how cool will it be, the seal of Jade? I could even use green wax." Robbie smiled and put his arm around her.

"I think this is the coolest ring ever."

Rowan walked in with six scruffy looking riders who all had small leather bags round their shoulders. "Gentlemen and ladies, this is Lord Loxley."

The six scruffy riders all bowed to him. Robbie looked at them, most were barely sixteen, and were dressed almost in rags. They had dirty faces but a look of determination about them. Robbie walked along the line showing them the sealed letters with a red wax impressed seal on the back. "This is my seal, and any letter that contains it is of the greatest importance, do you all understand?"

They all looked at the seal and nodded. "You must get these letters to their destinations; I take it all of you can read?" They all again nodded. "Alright then if you see Lady Loxley by the table, she will let you know the destinations and you will be able to choose the routes that you know the best."

All of them walked over to Rune, and after a few minutes, they selected their pile of letters and placed them in their shoulder bags. As each turned to leave, Robbie stopped them and lined them up, he handed each of them three golden bits, they looked into their hands with wonder.

"You will all wait and rest up at your destinations for replies, when you return here to this castle you will each receive three more bits. I cannot stress how important these letters are; you must at all costs get them through and fast, is that clear?"

They all bowed. "Yes My Lord."

Robbie nodded. "Alright, off you go and good luck, have a safe journey, Hearne will protect you." All of them turned and ran out to their horses, and in seconds they were gone, Rowan patted him on the back.

"Now we must wait and see."

Robbie sat down at the table. "Hearne will protect them; we must now plan our next move. We have to prevent him from making it to Canterbury, and find a way to slow his work in London, I also think now would be a good time to think about retaking Gloucester."

Skip sat up next to Fuse. "Is that possible?"

Robbie smiled at him. "He has halved his troops there, as he moves everything towards Bristol, I have instructed those at Worcester to head south, and we have quite an army of our own based here. I think My Lord, we should get you your seat back."

"It would be a great honour to my father's memory Robbie if I could in any way return his sword to its home."

"Then with the grace of Hearne, we will try."

Skip looked at Fuse and smiled. "It would make him very proud, wouldn't it?"

"I do believe it would Master Brandon."

Robbie stood up from his seat. "I have spoken to Lady Scarlet, and she is aware of the plan to recapture your city back. You will need to liaise with her and use all of the help she can provide."

Skip looked at all of the group, and back to Robbie. "You will not be doing this with me, will you?"

Robbie walked over to Skip and put his hand on his shoulder. "My Lord, I have watched you since the moment I picked up your pampered backside off the woodland floor. I am pleased to say that the man I rescued is no longer present." Robbie crouched down. "I see before me a true lord of great worth, and a valued friend. This is not the end my dear friend, I have a few other things I must do and then we will be of need to each other again."

Robbie lowered his tone. "You have a remarkable man at your side that is as loyal to you as my men are to me. Respect him and use his wisdom and you will see in yourself what I now see in you."

"What do you see in me Robert of Loxley?"

"I see a well educated man, armed with all his father could give him to lead his own people, if he would just trust in himself. Be the skipper of your own vessel, for when you take up the wheel and bark out those orders, your authority is there. Use it wisely and I think you will surprise yourself."

"I truly am your friend My Lord, but I fear I will never be you."

Robbie smiled. "That is an honour to me, to know you hold me in such high regard thank you. Now listen to me my friend. If I ride in victory into Gloucester, it will be mine and not yours, and I will not do that to a friend. Follow my lead and use your advisors well, and you will see then as you ride into Gloucester that you are in part your father. Trust me."

"You are a great man Robert of Loxley; how will I ever earn the loyalty of men such as you have?"

"You already have." Skip looked up at Blades, who suddenly looked nervous. Blades looked round at the others and then back to Skip. "You are one of us Skip, and as one of us we would all risk our lives to protect you."

Everyone shook their heads in agreement, and Martin patted Blades on the back. "Hear, Hear!"

"See My Lord, you have loyalty, you need to look in the right places, that's all." Robbie patted his leg. "Have a little faith, it usually brings with it great courage."

Robbie stood up. "For a day off it has been a very long and busy day, get some sleep all of you for tomorrow I wish to go sightseeing in London."

Jett smiled. "Ooooh Blades, I think we will have some sword play at last."

CHAPTER TWENTY

THE SMOKEY ROAD TO LONDON

Robbie sat at the table looking at the map as Rune appeared at the top of the stairs, she wore a long powder blue night dress, and a long white house coat, she started to walk down them and he looked up at her and smiled. She looked like a princess as her hair swung from side to side across the lacy garments. "Robbie you have to get more sleep than you are, it is only just gone five. I woke up and you were not there, I hate that. You know a woman likes to wake up being cuddled."

He smiled and yawned, a wide gaping yawn. "Then in future, when I want to get up, I will put my arms around you and then wake you."

"If you do, you won't be getting out of bed, anyhow what are you doing sat here all on your own?" Rune looked down at the map that showed what was left of London. "So, you really do intend to go to London and see if he is there?"

Robbie stretched. "He isn't."

"What makes you say that? Do you not think that he would be there overseeing the building work?"

"Billy was only across the coast, so I would imagine he is with his father, after all they have been apart for ten years. I would think if Billy pops up anywhere else then his father will not be far away." Rune moved across to him and sat on his knee; she slid her arms around him and hugged him.

"I was serious you know? You should be getting more sleep than you are, why don't you come back to bed for a bit, and at least have a few more hours. None of the others will be up before seven."

"I like it down here in the morning, I like the peace and quiet it helps me think, I don't want another mistake, I let my guard down last time."

She kissed him softly. "That was not your fault; you have to stop blaming yourself Robbie."

"I just don't want another loss, Rune they are like family to me even though we have not been together all that long, I feel a closeness to them like I have known them for longer. I just cannot make a big mistake like that again."

"Come on back to bed for a bit and promise me you will have some more sleep."

He kissed her softly. "All right I will." Standing up he lifted her in his arms and carried her giggling up the stairs.

Rune was right, it was eight before any of them surfaced; she sat on the bed with a full breakfast tray as he opened his eyes. She leaned over and softly swept his hair from his eyes.

"See you were tired, you have slept like a log for three hours, now come on and have a good breakfast it will get you set for the day."

He sat up as she put the tray on his lap. "You sound like my mother."

"That's because mothers are always right, and so am I." She smiled and took a piece of toast and dipped it in his egg.

"Hey, I love to do that."

She smiled. "If you slept more, you would have been faster." She chuckled and ate the toast.

Rowan was looking at the map when Robbie came down. "I see the information on London is quite accurate. Most of the city centre is ruined. It would appear that the only part of London now intact is the east side."

Robbie yawned. "Yeah... Harry was down there last year, he reckons that there are a few wild gangs in the centre that kill anyone who goes near, he used to sell them moonshine so he got on with them well. It would appear that Bracknell across to Staines, remain pretty much intact and Knox moved in there about five years ago and started cleaning it up."

Rowan looked back at the map. "There is a lot of green land around here Robbie it looks like our kind of country, its parks, woods and lakes."

"It is exactly our kind of country that is why I am going to go visit his home."

Rowan looked across the table at him as he lifted his cup. "You do realise there will be hundreds of his soldiers all over the place? We will encounter quite a few."

"All his troops are using the old M4 as the main road in as it is quite clear, Knox had all the debris removed years ago just for this purpose, I figured we would run parallel and have a look at what he has got. Maybe let one of our special arrows off and give them something to worry about." He smiled at Rowan and poured himself a cup of coffee, as he yawned again.

"You should get more sleep Robbie."

"Oh, don't you start, I have already had Rune on my back about it."

"It's a long walk Robbie; it will take us at least a couple of days, maybe three."

"We won't be walking, we will be using horses, Phil has told me to use some of his, it will help us travel faster and we will not need roads, we can go across country."

By midday, they were all packed and ready to go; Jett and Flash had also joined the party as they now saw themselves as officially members of the crew. Scarlet kissed them good bye, as a warrior herself she was sorry not to be coming, but her role was there now, and the duke needed her assistance and advice on his own little adventure. He took Robbie's hand in his.

"Good luck, and be careful your road has many enemies."

Robbie smiled and pulled him into an embrace. "Yours my friend is as equally full, but I will take care as long as I know you will."

Robbie pulled himself up on his horse, and they all moved off slowly down the long drive out of the castle. It felt good to be on the move again and he could feel the spirits lift of everyone as they made their way at a gallop to the bridge over the Severn River, and into Bristol.

The whole of one side of the road that had once been a motorway was filled with troops heading towards Bristol, row upon row of carts filled with men slowly made their way east. They waved as they realised who was passing them, and stood up and cheered as Robbie and his men passed by.

Bristol was a surprise as most of the city was intact, and for the first time ever, Robbie got to see what a city looked like before the red death. The streets were clear with paving and tar roads, the buildings were intact and not crumbled wastelands. It felt eerie as they slowly trotted down the quiet streets; soldiers suddenly jumped and stared in disbelief as they saluted Robbie as he passed. He could see them turn and hurriedly talk to their fellow soldiers, as they explained exactly who he was.

Robbie and Rune stared at the long rows of large glass fronted shops, many of which were still open and had windows filled with goods, some of the shops seemed to have closed many years ago, and their windows were filled with naked dummies. Jade chuckled as they passed them, and even Robbie had to smile at what seemed like such a strange land and life.

His world felt like a million miles away as he looked at the concrete that was hot and dusty in the sun, how could anyone live in a world such as this? Did they not miss the softness of grass under their feet, or the dappled shade of leaves above their heads? His insides stirred and suddenly he felt home sick and wanted to walk in his woods in Loxley.

They came down a large road through what was once a crowded city centre, and Robbie looked at the rows of tents set up on the verges. Soldiers were running about gathering their kit and preparing to move out to their specified locations.

They passed along the long line of large carts filled with men, and one of the soldiers stood up and shouted. "My Lord Loxley?" Robbie slowed and turned to see a man in a woodsman uniform with a red lion crest wave to him. He turned his horse and came alongside a cart filled with men in similar attire. The soldier bowed. "If you may, My Lord would you permit me to be rude and ask to shake your hand." He looked up at Robbie.

"Since when has it been rude to shake the hand of a man? I would gladly shake the hand of any man who faced the forces of Knox." Robbie held out his hand to the soldier. "What is your name woodsman?"

The man's eyes lit up with glee, as all the others in the cart looked astounded. "My name My Lord is Joseph Tucker."

Robbie gripped his hand firmly and shook it. "I am pleased to meet you, Joe Tucker, it is an honour to shake the hand of any brave man." He nudged the horse a little. "This is Lady Runestone, and her sister Jade." He moved along as Joe shook their hands.

"I am honoured beyond measure My Ladies." Jade giggled, and Robbie moved down to the next man and shook his hand. The soldiers all cheered having all took it in turns to shake the hand of every member of Robbie's party before they moved off, and Joe got three cheers from his troops in honour of the hooded man.

Robbie smiled as he rode on and Rune beamed at him. "You show off, you loved that."

"No I am not, I meant what I said, I am proud to shake the hand of any woodsman in this land."

Jade grinned. "Big head."

Robbie started to laugh as they made their way following the road signs out of the city and heading for London. They rode with speed down what was now the old M4, as they approached the outskirts of Chippenham and they came up to a heavily defended check point. A large man in woodsman attire waved them down and they slowed as they approached, Robbie opened his cloak and flung it back over his shoulders, and approached the guard slowly.

"Sorry sir it is policy, would all of you mind dismounting while I ascertain who you are and what your business here is, most people seem to be heading in not out of the city sir."

"I have business outside the city, sorry but you have not given me a name woodsman."

"Quite right sir, I am Able Bowman Bents sir, and you are?"

"Lord Robert of Loxley, nice to meet you bowmen Bents." Robbie pushed out his hand, as the bowman looked a little lost for words.

"My Lord I am sorry I had no idea; I had not seen your emblem and mistook you for one of the captains, please forgive me My Lord."

Robbie took his hand and shook it. "Nothing to forgive Bent's, you are doing your job like all of us and doing it very efficiently, I have no complaint, have you met the Lady Runestone?"

"No My Lord, I would be deeply honoured to shake the hand of any of your party, the words of your deeds have given us a great deal to talk about." Bents smiled and his fat red cheeks glowed with admiration and pleasure.

"Well let us see, here we have Lady Runestone; this is Pebbles, and Mother,

Hog, Fish, Jett and Flash." Robbie walked down the line as he introduced everyone. "Quiet Martin, Big John, Rowan, and Pete, he has not earned his nick name yet. Lady Alice we call her Pigeon, Mad Harry and Blades, we have a few more but they are off on other business."

"I am so honoured; all of you have inspired us in our work. Could I offer you some refreshment and some food and water for your mounts?"

"That is very decent of you; yes, I think we would appreciate it." Robbie smiled at the other soldiers on duty.

Bents sat with them on the crash barrier, as a very young boy carried a shaking tray around and offered them all tea. The horses drank from a large trough and chewed on a bale of hay. Bents talked endlessly about how they had heard of Tintagel and then the weapons plant at Weston Super-Mare, and how proud everybody was of what they had achieved, and how the whole army wanted to live up to them.

It felt strange for Robbie that, everyone knew every detail of his life over the past week. The whole group seemed lifted by the experience, and as they said goodbye and departed, Robbie felt a wave of hope flow over him. They travelled on up the road and Steph came up by his side.

"Rowan thinks we should leave the road soon, it's not far now before we will start to encounter their forces." Robbie nodded and looked up the road for a way to get off. The road was wide, grey and empty; it ran straight for miles, without a kink or a curve. Either side the banks rose and fell as the grass and the trees came up to meet the road.

It felt very strange to him; here was the natural world he loved so much almost violated by something that was in no way natural or in character with any aspect of the world as he saw it. It became for Robbie, a symbol of what he thought Mason Knox stood for, the rape and misuse of a land that was tortured into submission, and suffocated to death. It made his stomach twist just thinking about it.

There was a river not far ahead and when he arrived at it, he crossed over the bridge, and then headed down the embankment into the fields; it came as a relief to get off the road and back on to living soil. His stomach seemed to settle as he looked around and they all followed in a long line behind him. His mind turned from Knox to Bents the guard.

Rune looked at him and smiled. "What's on your mind?"

Robbie looked at her. "I find it strange that everyone seems to know every detail about us. That man knew everything we had done."

"You are the Hooded Man Robbie, you are now a hero to every woodsman in the country, look at what you have achieved in just a week, you have saved Skip, destroyed the home of Knox, and completely blown apart any chance Knox had of using cannons against us. Philip and his army were just holding back until you arrived, and now they are pushing forward and pushing Knox back. That is in less than a week, of course they know about you."

"I honestly had no idea, I am just trying to get this over with, so I can go home build a house, get married have kids and live a normal life."

Rune smiled. "So, you're going to get married, are you?"

He smiled at her as she beamed. "I am assuming you will marry me eventually?"

"I might, we will have to wait and see, won't we?" She kicked her heels and her horse shot forward; Jade came up beside him.

"I am not wearing a skirt."

Robbie looked at her. "What do you mean Pebbles?"

"The wedding, if I am a bridesmaid it will have to be pants."

"Ok, pants it is." Jade smiled and kicked her horse, to catch Rune. Both of them laughed and giggled as they made their way up the hill to the top of a rise and in to some trees.

Robbie dropped down and walked with his horse, as he wove it through the woodland along the path. He enjoyed the dappled shade of the woods, and he breathed the fresh cool air. They followed the ridge for a few miles and came close to the edge of the woodland. Through the trees, they could see the large road to London as it snaked its way in front of them.

Robbie stopped and tied his horse to a tree; he walked through the new young sapling trees to the top of the hill and looked out on the road. A long convoy of slowly moving carts came up from a side road and slipped onto the large motorway to London. The convoy was miles long, and filled with heavy wooden carts and marching troops.

Rowan came up at his side. "Bloody hell Robbie that is one hell of a convoy."

"Isn't it just...? We can't hit it from here, we will have to get closer, but we will definitely need to slow that down and as soon as possible."

Rune came quietly alongside them. "Robbie Jade has just told me we have company; twenty woodsmen are creeping towards us from the east."

"Ok they are more than likely friendly so let's be gentle with them, let's spread out and melt into the place and wait for them, you never know they may come in handy." Robbie looked round at everyone. "Ok let's see how much you have forgotten in the last few days, let's get to work. Hog you stay high profile with the horses."

Within a second, the woodland was empty. There was no sight or trace of anyone, except Hog, who was holding and feeding all the horses. He smiled at the horses as he stroked them down, and talked quietly to them.

The lead woodsman made his way through the undergrowth towards Hog; he checked his line of men as they made their way into a half circle surrounding him. Slowly he lifted himself up in the undergrowth; he raised his bow and stopped.

A silver knife touched his throat. "You better have a very good reason for wanting to shoot my man, otherwise blood will be spilt here, and it will be yours. Can you not spot a woodsman of Loxley?"

The man swallowed hard as the blade pushed tighter against his throat. "A cloak does not make a woodsman."

"Indeed, I see you wear one, and yet here I am with a knife to your throat. Name yourself and quickly I am wasting precious time here."

"I am Brian of Catlow Hill, and these are the men who defend it."

"Then you are in luck Brian of Catlow that I am the one who has caught you, because with the noise that your group make, I am surprised Mason Knox has not caught you already." Robbie pulled his knife away and moved back. "Tell your men to lower their weapons, and stand up... I would also advise no sudden movements from any of you."

Brain Catlow whistled a bird like call, and his men stood up and lowered their weapons; he turned slowly around and was confronted with a wall of hooded men all holding bows. They were pointing at all of his men and were ready to shoot. Robbie stepped forward. "You know who I am?"

Brian Catlow fell to one knee and shook with terror. "I do My Lord."

"Why do you stalk woodsmen when there is a convoy of Mason Knox down there that should be attacked?"

"Your horses were reported, and we thought you were his scouts My Lord."

"An easier target than the convoy no doubt... Alright get off your knees, you are no good to us down there, we need you and your men up here."

Brian jumped up quickly, a look of relief on his face. "Anything at all, just name it and we will do it."

"How good are your men with these bows, I hope they are better than they are at stalking?"

"We are fair to middling My Lord."

Robbie looked around at them; it was obvious many had seen too many winters. "How many are fair?"

"Bout half of us." Robbie gave a sigh as he looked at Rowan, who clearly had his doubts.

"Fish get ten of our special arrows out and a few lighters. Right Brian how close can you get to that convoy without being seen?"

"I can show you from here My Lord." He walked over to the edge of the trees and pointed to a small copse not far from the road. "We can get in there easy enough."

"How fast can you get out safely?"

"Quite fast, why My Lord?"

"Alright Brian, plan to be faster, we are going to give you some special arrows, they have dynamite attached, you know what that is don't you?"

"Yes My Lord." He said nervously and looking quite worried.

"Listen carefully now all of you, all you have to do is light the fuse and fire, these are longer arrows than you are used to, so pull your strings back on your bows as far as possible, you will have time to aim and shoot. Do not drop them just shoot them. Aim for every other wooden cart, these points will go right through the wood and so if someone tries, they will not be able to pull them out. As soon as you shoot, run and get as far away as possible."

Brian nodded slowly as Robbie waved the arrow in front of him. "We will ride for one hour and then we will attack up ahead, so wait here for an hour and then attack, by then the sun will be going down and you will have a good chance of escape. Do you all understand me?"

They all nodded at Robbie. "Alright we will move ahead and good luck."

Robbie pulled his horse off Hog, and mounted as Fish handed one arrow each to the shooters. He gave them a hand full of lighters. "These burn for two hours so light them before you get into the woods down there." He patted Brian on the back and walked over to his horse.

Rune dropped her hood and looked at them; they all seemed surprised as they looked up at her. "This task has been set you by the Hooded Man, all woodsmen serve him, do not dishonour them or him. Serve the master of the woods as he has asked you."

They all fell to their knees. "We will My Lady Runestone," Rune gasped at the fact that they knew her, she pulled up her hood and rode off with the others.

Brian looked round at his men and felt his throat. "God he is good to catch me out like that." All the others laughed and a voice from the back spoke.

"Who you kidding?"

Robbie and the others pulled out of the woods at full gallop, they had one hour to make it appear as if they were in two places at once, he rode as if a devil possessed him across the fields keeping the road always in sight in the distance. Fence after fence, they jumped and finally after forty minutes he slowed down to find a suitable site.

He spotted the point he needed as the small hill rose up a few hundred yards from the roadside. It was densely covered with trees and would provide good cover. They made their way slowly up to the back of the hill and dismounted. Hog pulled the horses into the trees, and waited with them as Robbie led the group up the hill through the trees and towards the road.

He knelt at the top of the hill and looked out through the trees and across the road. "This will be fine, now remember you will all have to light your own arrows, so lay it on the bow string and then light it. Drop the light stick, and raise your bows aim and shoot, Fuse has made sure we have time so watch you own fuse and see how close it is to the dynamite. As soon as you shoot head back to the horses and mount up as quickly as you can."

All of them nodded. "Alright get your arrows and when you hear the explosions down the road there light yours." They all spread into the undergrowth in a long line along the bank. Robbie looked at the sun as it started to fade; he knew it would not be much longer. He peered up the line at Rune in the undergrowth, and he winked, she smiled.

Ten minutes later to the west was a blinding flash, followed by a loud boom, all the soldiers on the road looked back as another flash and boom followed.

Robbie lit his arrow and watched the fuse; he took aim at the wooden side of the cart loaded with explosives.

He fired with pace, and the arrow streaked off, within seconds it had split the wood and entered into the cart. Rune's was gone and she was heading back. He ran into the trees behind her and saw all the others heading backward. The flash was blinding, and the explosion shook the earth, and deafened him throwing him to the floor. He shook his head and scrambled to his feet, as another almighty explosion shook the floor. He broke the edge of the trees, and grabbed Rune throwing her on to her horse. He pulled on the saddle and was up, taking the reins he steadied the horse as another massive explosion lit up all the trees. Splinters rained down on him.

Checking every horse had a rider he nodded to Rowan, who charged off across the fields. Everyone was away, and he turned and followed as another almighty explosion went off. He lay as low as he could on the horse and galloped for his life, more explosions went off behind him as he joined the group. Rowan was heading for a patch of trees and everyone burst in through the new leaves and pulled to a slow pace as they worked inwards around the trunks.

Rowan, watched from the edge of the trees to make sure no one was following. The whole road was lit up with fire, and he could see the scattered bodies of dead men. The wooden carts were smashed and broken, others lay overturned and burning, Soldiers crawled stunned up from the trees. Jade was laughing with Jett.

"Whoa cous that was scary, it blew me right off my feet and I could not get back up I was laughing that much." Jett beamed at Jade.

"I will tell you this cous, you know some pretty wild guys that was totally awesome."

Robbie checked, as he looked round, brushing splinters off his sleeve. "Everyone alright, no one hurt? Ok, let's look sharp, Jett, Jade, focus you are both precious, we will party later... Rowan, how's it look?"

"It's clear, they seem a little preoccupied for the moment." He smiled as he walked his horse through the trees toward him.

"Right let's move with purpose."

They came out of the woods on the bottom of Lambourn Downs and rode up the hill slowing near the top, Robbie sat on his panting horse and looked out across the south. Over the small woods and fields in the distance two areas glowed in the falling dark on the road where fires still burned, it was only about sixty carts but it was a start, and he was happy no one was hurt.

They rode across the top of the downs looking for shelter of trees, it was about an hour later when Rowan spotted a dense wood through the failing light, and they walked their horses into it. A good way in was a small clearing and they tied up the horses and set up camp. They posted four lookouts and Mother started a meal, Robbie relaxed a bit, somehow it felt a little like old times back in the woods and under the trees, Jade slowly walked bandy legged up toward the fire and dropped a pile of firewood.

"God my ass is sore; I wish I had worn knickers now."

"Jade!" Steph was shocked.

She smiled at Rune. "I am sore in places only Rowan knows." Rune and Alice both burst into laughter, as Jade raised her eyebrows, smiled, and walked bandy legged into the trees.

Steph looked over at the laughing Rune and Alice with a scowl. "You should not encourage her." Rune laughed more and Steph smiled as she stirred the stew in the pot.

Robbie sat in the trees with his back to a stump, Rowan sat a few feet away as they watched the darkness. Rowan's eyes gleamed in the dark as he turned to look at him. "That was too close today; we should have been further away." Robbie nodded in the dark.

"Yeah, I know, I was just thinking the same."

Rowan moved and Robbie turned to him. "Do you remember when we saved Skip Robbie?"

"Yes why?"

"I will never forget it, as the guard turned back and charged at the men of Knox, he raised a sword and went for the man on the right; you hit the man on the left."

"Yes, I remember that Rowan, why is that important?"

"Robbie that shot was over a thousand yards, and you were still deadly accurate, I would have missed or been very lucky to hit him. I have never seen a shot like that in my life before."

"I have a good bow."

"You have more than that my friend; you have a gift beyond all of us."

"Why does it matter?"

"Think what you could do from a roof top with explosives, and a castle to aim at."

"Are you thinking of London and his castle at Windsor?"

"Robbie, Fuse told me that not that long before the red death, Windsor got badly burnt, it caught fire and burned so quickly they had to rebuild a lot of it, I just think for safety reasons it would be better to attack from a distance."

"I must admit after what we have been up to his guards will be nervous and more alert. You think we should strike fast do damage and pull out quickly?"

"I do. We are lucky only to have lost one of us; I do not see the point in losing another. We can hit it three or four times if we have to, we already know it will burn."

"You are right Rowan; I will look at it with you tomorrow, when we get near."

They both sat silently in the dark for a while; Robbie heard Rowan move and turned to him. "Robbie, you really love Rune, yes?"

"Yes I do, does it show?"

Rowan laughed. "Just a little... Robbie I really have fallen for Jade, I think I will ask her to marry me when this is all over."

Robbie smiled to himself in the dark. "Jade is very special Rowan. I really am happy for you my friend; I know Jade loves you dearly."

"I don't want to lose her."

"Rowan don't worry about Jade, she is one of the best we have, you won't lose her easily believe me."

He heard the sigh of Rowan, and knew he was thinking the same thing he had a million times. Each day they entered into danger, and each day they had come out unscathed. But just what if Rune got killed, he remembered the day in the woods near Joe's place when she had stubbornly told him she would not wait in safety. She had been adamant she would follow him, and he knew now things had not changed.

Without risk, they would achieve nothing and the world he loved would fall. All his hope lay now in forcing a dream on to Mason Knox and defeating him, there really was no other option. Robbie stared into the dark and watched a fox as it slowly passed by. It sensed them sat in the dark and stared for a moment its eyes bright. Knowing somehow it was safe, it slowly moved on to another part of the forest to hunt, and silently disappeared.

In the middle of the night, John and Martin patted them on the shoulder and took over. Robbie watched as Rowan slid down next to Jade and pulled her close under the blanket, she smiled and wriggled up to him. He smiled to himself as he slid down next to Rune and she too wriggled back to him. He pulled her close, and held her tight and felt the warmth of her body next to his as he drifted into sleep. Rune moved to the sound of laughter and opened her eyes. Robbie's arm was still round her and she felt him move as more laughter came across the clearing. Robbie sat up and rubbed his eyes.

Flash stood in the clearing with her long white pole, and wearing a blindfold. Her head moved slowly from side to side and slightly jerked. The long pole twitched, as Jett and Jade tried to sneak up on her from either side.

Robbie tapped Rune on the shoulder, and she raised her head and watched. Flash moved very slowly as they got nearer, you could almost feel her concentration in the air. She suddenly moved with incredible speed, the white pole was a blur as she spun and took both Jade's and Jett's legs out from under them.

The pole broke apart and she spun bringing the two parts of the pole down at great speed, but stopping just above their throats.

Rune sat right up. "That was unbelievable."

Jade and Jett lay laughing on the floor, as Ruby removed her blindfold and put her glasses back on, laughing at the two girls who rolled about on the ground.

Robbie put his hand on Rune's shoulder. "I just thought the pole was for walking with, that is some fighting pole and some talent, did you teach her that?"

Rune looked back at him. "No, I have just showed her how to control her eye power, although considering who her mother is?"

"I tell you Rune this lot are full of surprises." He got up and walked to the fire, the coffee pot was hot and he poured two cups, and came back and sat down. He passed a cup to Rune and sat sipping his drink, watching Ruby as she practiced, and Blades gave her a few pointers.

"We will see the castle today." She looked up as she braided her hair.

"Will we be attacking or just looking?"

"Rowan thinks we should shoot explosives from long range, and then get out."

"He is a smart man Robbie."

"You agree with him then, you think it will be suicide to go in?"

"If you are asking me, should we kill half the group to bring his house down the answer is no, we should not. This is not Tintagel; this will be heavily guarded." Her voice was sharp and she looked back at him with a glare in her eye.

"Good, I agree with you. You know Rune you can be quite grumpy in the morning."

"I just think we should be smart from now on, he knows we are coming remember? We did sort of advertise the fact last night when we blew up his carts. Do not rush Robbie, think it all out like you did Tintagel, look how smooth that went, that was your doing and preparation. Just don't be in a rush is all I am saying."

He nodded. "Yeah, you are right."

"I know."

"Oh, don't start all that again."

She started to giggle. "It is right though."

A little later, Robbie stood on the top of the hill above the wood; the hill fell softly into wild meadows that gently moved in the early morning breeze. He held up his telescope and looked out over London in the distance, he could see the castle, and it was still a long way off. It would be half a day at least on horseback before they would be close enough to really get an idea of the place.

Mounting their horses, Jade moaned as she lowered herself gently into the saddle. Rune looked at her. "Will you be alright?"

Jade winked and whispered. "Alice has leant me some really thick knickers."

Rune started to laugh and shook her head. "You are one in a million sis." Jade smiled and set off up the hill pulling Rowan's horse behind her. Rune grabbed the reins of Robbie's horse and followed, smiling at her sister.

It had been over an hour as they slowed down, the road was in sight and still full of moving traffic, and now the castle could clearly be seen. Everything across the old motorway had been levelled to the ground. There was half a mile of flat rubble; it was the same all around the castle apart from the large green park.

Robbie looked in disbelief. "How the hell will we get close to that without being seen?" Rowan looked dispirited.

"We have had a wasted journey; there is no way we can get close without being picked off. He was expecting us to come and he has been busy preparing Robbie."

Rune leaned forward on her horse. "Maybe there is a way; there is something I would like to try. I think we should get a little bit closer, don't quit too quickly guys, I have an idea but it will only need you two, and my sister."

Robbie looked at her. "Tell me what it is?"

She smiled and blew him a kiss. "Trust me?"

Robbie looked at her as she turned her horse and moved off, he looked at Rowan who shrugged and just smiled. "Don't know what you are smiling at, honestly she is getting as mysterious as you are."

Rowan laughed and moved off behind Rune, Robbie followed. They picked their way through town after town, which were now deserted and empty. All the buildings lay ruined, collapsed, and covered with grasses and shrubs. It was slow going and took over two hours to get close enough for Rune.

Finally, she pulled up and dismounted. They all followed as she walked through an old factory to a large rectangular green mound. The structure was huge and covered with ivy, and bushes, trees grew all along it. Rune walked up to the ivy and touching it with her finger, it swung open like a giant green curtain. She gave the signal, and they all approached.

Behind the curtain, was a huge empty space of concrete, which had yellow lines marking out spaces all-round the edges. She led her horse under the curtain and into the dark damp space. All of them followed wondering what this place must have been, and as they entered the curtain swung back. "We will be safe here, nature guards us." Robbie looked around and saw the steep slope heading up towards what looked like another level, and he walked up to it.

"What is a car park fee?" Jade looked around. "It says we have to pay and display whatever the hell that means."

Pete smiled at the innocence of his daughter. "This is where people would park their carts while they went off and did stuff; they had to pay for so much time here."

"Sounds silly if you ask me, it is not even a nice place to stop." Pete smiled as Steph put her arm round him.

"She is so lucky not to have known it you know?" Pete shrugged.

"I wish I hadn't, I am glad she grew up away from it all, just the bit I remember was awful."

Robbie got to the top of the slope, and walked around the corner towards the wall of green curtain. He parted the growth and looked out at the castle. It was just less than half a mile away, across a barren landscape of crushed rubble. A wall below defined the outer edge of the flat land. Rowan came up to his side and looked out. "It's a shame we are not nearer this would be a perfect place to shoot from."

Rune looked out through the growth, she touched it and it drew back so they had a better look.

Rowan smiled. "You and Jade got more in common than I realised." Rune smiled at him.

"That is why only you and she will see what we do; you already have some knowledge of the families' gifts, most of the others do not know. My mother is organising them as we speak, Jade will be here shortly."

Jade came happily round the corner with a bag of special arrows, and a small box of lighter sticks. Rune looked out at the castle set like a gem on a plate of dust. "Right here is what we will do. You tell Jade where you want to shoot, pick a window she can see. She will light your arrows and I will tell you to shoot, aim high. Once the arrows have gone Jade keep watching where the arrows must go I will need your vision. I will guide the arrows with a little influence all right. Please be aware I have not tried this yet, so if it goes wrong, we may have to leave quickly."

Robbie loaded his bow ready and Rowan fitted the arrow to his string. Robbie looked out. "I will take the top window on the right; you take the top on the left Rowan, alright?"

Rune's eyes began to colour from lilac to purple. "Light the arrows and watch the windows." Jade lit two of the sticks on Harry's old lighter. She pushed them on to the fuses, which began to fizz. She looked out at the castle as Rune's eyes turned a vivid purple. "Fire!" The arrows sung high into the air, Robbie watched as they vibrated and suddenly a strong breeze got up and they shot like missiles towards the castle. The two arrows separated and both entered the chosen windows. Rune gasped, and the breeze dropped.

Inside the castle lit up as the dynamite exploded, and flames burst from the windows as they all smashed and balls of fire stroked up the walls. "Alright again name your targets." Rowan took aim.

"Top window of the left tower."

Robbie looked. "Bottom window of the long block." Jade lit the fuses.

Rune's eyes glowed purple. "Fire!" The arrows again sung out, they flew up in the air side by side and then suddenly they shot off at immense speed, and separated finding their mark. They watched, as there was a thunderous explosion. Men were blown off the battlements and black smoke started to billow out of the castle roof. Rune gasped and breathed deeply. "Double your arrows I cannot keep this up, I have not practiced it. Jade I need a bird can you see any?"

Jade looked around. "There is a pigeon down on the floor over there."

Robbie cut the flights off the arrows and fitted them to Rowan's bow. "This will be a new experience for you." He cut his own ready.

"This time Jade, look at the pigeon not the arrows. Do not light the fuses until the bird is high in the air. Robbie, Rowan shoot at the bird, do not worry you will not hit it."

Jade looked at the pigeon as Rune's eyes began to glow deep purple. It jumped, looked about and then took off. "Oh wow." Jade could see what the bird could see. Quickly she lit the fuses and watched the bird in the sky.

"Fire!" Four arrows shot into the air, they rose higher and higher, and followed the bird. Suddenly they plummeted to earth like lightening and separated. Each arrow hit a different part of the far side of the castle. Jade could see soldiers with buckets of water running around, there was an almighty flash, and the soldiers were blown to the floor and covered in fire. Brickwork flew up in the air and crashed down on them as walls collapsed and flames and smoke engulfed everywhere. Rune gasped and the pictures in Jade's head stopped.

"Oh, wow Rune that was so cool, I could see everything the bird saw it was awesome, Robbie I saw the arrows hit and the buildings collapse, it was incredible."

Rune swayed and Robbie caught her. "Are you alright?"

Rune smiled. "Dizzy... Tired, it took a lot of strength, I need to rest I will be fine in a bit."

Robbie sat down and pulled her on to his knee, she leaned against him and he held her tight, her eyes still fluttered purple and she closed them. He pulled her head on to his shoulder. "Rest my sweet you will be fine."

Rowan and Jade watched as the castle burned, columns of smoke rose spiraling into the sky and met to form one huge dense cloud. Robbie sat stroking Rune's hair and rocking her gently. Rowan pulled an arrow from his quiver. "Jade get your bow, and warn the others we have company."

Jade looked out of the gap and saw the long line of troops heading their way across the rubble, and then turned and shot off down the ramp. Rowan took aim and let fly with his bow, there was a muffled yell. "You stay there Robbie and take care of Rune; we will deal with this."

Jade came flying back with Steph and Pete, they took up position all along the car park wall and cleared a place to shoot. Four bows sung out as they fired, and down below everyone was in their places covering every side of the building; Jett drew her sword and smiled at Blades. "They are all around us." John shouted.

"And there is a bloody lot of em."

Jett smiled. "Goodie... Any that get through are Blades and mine, you lot focus on arrows." Blades drew her swords and wiped the blades together. Ruby walked over to them and broke her long pole apart. The three of them stood ready their backs to each other in the middle of the car park waiting.

The first two to break through met Jett, they hacked at the ivy with their swords and stepped in, she came fast and without mercy. Her sword flashed and was a blur, as she made contact and stepped back, and the two men fell dead. To the side of John, a hole appeared, and Blades was there in a flash, John winked and raised his bow.

Her golden swords spun in her hands with great grace, and the four men all tried to parry her blows. Their swords sheared off under the speed of her blades and before they knew what had hit them, they found her swords had run them through. By the time they hit the floor, she was already moving to the next, she looked back and saw Jett fighting off three. Ruby was spinning like a top; her steel white poles making contact that buffeted and beat each man so quickly, that by the time she had hit their windpipes, most of their limbs were broken. More men with swords piled in, and Blades somersaulted over them and landed behind them before slicing at them. "Dad a little help needed."

Harry dropped his bow and slid out his swords, he ran towards his daughter, Harry was aggressive and waded into the group, and limbs fell to the floor as he screamed. "Off my baby girl."

Jett whooped and laughed as she tackled each swordsman, her yells and screams echoed as she lunged and swiped at speed with her sword. Her speed, aggression and howls terrified most of the men, but by the time they stepped back away from her it was too late, she had got them and had already moved on.

Hog had put down his bow and now just hit the men coming through so hard their necks broke on contact, John and Martin stood side by side and anyone who seemed to be getting an advantage on a swordsman ended up with an arrow in their back.

Fish and Alice covered from the other side, working in tandem as they shot and reloaded, slowly working along the edge and taking out any who entered. Robbie and Rowan appeared at the top of the ramp followed by Jade and Pete. Their arrows flew like rain and the soldiers piled up at the bottom of the ramp as they approached. Jade pulled her knives, and picked off any too close to Jett or Blades, a large group entered in front of Ruby. She snapped off her glasses and all of them screamed and fell to their knees as their eyes burned. She put her glasses back on and turned to take on another. He looked at her glasses and ran back through the ivy and away. She spun on the spot and took out a large man who was sneaking up on her. He stretched and grunted as she spun and hit him on the throat, as he fell to the ground, she saw Robbie's arrow in his back and she blew him a kiss. Jett was now at fever pitch. "Come to me boys, I want you." She blew them a kiss as she bounded toward them; they dropped their swords and ran screaming through the ivy. John and Martin seized their chance and arrows followed them, they landed on the cleared rubble zone dead.

Blades and Harry were back to back, swinging, and spinning in unison, men fell left and right around them, and suddenly they stopped. No one was left standing, and they lowered their blades and looked around. Harry put his arm around Blades. "Hey baby girl you was totally cosmic."

She patted her dad on the back. "Yeah, dad I am fine and totally cosmic." He smiled at her but there was a slight look of concern in his eye.

Jett was smiling in amongst a large pile of dead soldiers; Flash was picking her way towards Blades. A body groaned and moved, Flash shot round and her stick hit the throat, he groaned no more. Robbie, Jade and Pete stood looking at the pile in front of them, Rowan walked through the pile of the dead stabbing the odd one to finish them. Alice wiped her brow and put her arm round Fish.

"Nice one partner." John and Martin smiled and patted each other on the back. Robbie looked carefully around.

"Stay sharp this might not be over yet, I do not want any accidents." Everyone moved into covering positions as Robbie shouted out. "Martin?"

"Clear this side, Robbie."

"Alice?"

"Clear Robbie." She looked as she wiped the sweat off her bow.

"Jett?"

"All clear Robbie." She crouched down and cleaned her sword as she watched the street in front.

"Ok keep your wits, we leave in five minutes, we have done what we needed to. Harry, Hog sort the horses."

Jett kicked one of the bodies and looked up and Jade. "Shame about that one he was quite cute."

"Still would be if he had picked the right side."

Robbie ran back up the ramp, Rune was now stood with her mum. She smiled as he pulled her into his arms. "I will be fine now; it just took a lot of strength and I needed to rest a second." He squeezed her harder. "Honestly Robbie I am fine." He kissed her and smiled.

"You missed quite a party, I tell you what, don't mess with Jett when she is armed, bloody hell she is scary, I am glad she is on our team."

They walked down the ramp and Steph gasped. "Hell Robbie, how many was there?"

Jett stepped over a rather dead ugly man. "Just over a hundred."

Steph looked at her. "You have to be joking?"

Jett pointed her sword at a large pile. "Count if you want." She beamed a satisfied smile.

Robbie leaned over. "See what I mean, do not piss her off."

Jett smiled. "I was just warming up, god you guys are wild, I love hanging out with you lot it's just buzzing." She spun her sword and dropped it in its sheath.

Rowan, John, and Martin, slipped out of the car park and looked around. They quickly crossed the square of ground in front and took up covering positions behind an old crumbled down wall. Robbie led the team out with Jade, Harry, and Fish, covering the rear. They moved quickly into the cover of the old factory and all mounted up, Rowan gave the all clear, and they headed north away from the centre of the town and looked for the cover of woodland.

Once out in the country they picked up the pace and got as far from London as possible, after an hour of riding hard they slowed their pace to a cantor and idled along keeping their eyes peeled. They soon found themselves heading over the Downs again and the road came back into sight. The convoy had slowed as guards now sat on the top of every wagon holding their crossbows. Robbie looked through his telescope at them, all were watching nervously. He turned to Rowan and handed him the scope. "How many specials have we got left?"

Rowan smiled. "Enough."

"A thousand yards, eh?" Robbie winked at Rune.

"Maybe a bit nearer." Rowan handed him the scope back.

The men on top of the cart saw two arrows smoking towards them, there were huge screams, as they all jumped in every direction. The arrows hit hard and sunk deep into the wood, as the soldiers ran screaming into the grass. The cart lifted twenty feet in the air and burst into bright orange flame. Cart after cart all along a long line jumped into the air and ignited, soldiers were blown into the air and the road was littered with smoking splintered wood.

Rune sat on top of the hill, watched and laughed as Robbie and Rowan followed by the others rode up the hill, Jett and Jade were laughing loudly and waving their bows. He pulled hard on the reins and came around to her side. "Rowan owes me a beer, one thousand and two hundred yards direct hit."

Rune looked at the smouldering road and smoke; she looked back to London where the black smoke still rose into the sky. "You know Mason must really hate you about now." Robbie looked at her.

"Nowhere near enough to match me for him using Billy." He pulled on the reins and signaled. "Let's go home you lot."

CHAPTER TWENTY ONE

THE POWER OF NATURE

As Robbie and his party headed back to Bristol with the smoking wreckage of the carts strewn across the road behind them, Sir Brandon Berkley, the Duke of Gloucester, made his way up the western side of the Seven River towards his home.

Three hundred woodsmen had left Bristol heading north towards the city of Gloucester, and the woodsmen of Warwick were already heading south. One hour earlier fifty woodsmen had silently dropped in to the grounds of Tintern Abbey, and much to the surprise of the guards and the Abbot, the men of Mason Knox lay dead within minutes.

By dawn the following morning, Woodsmen had crossed the Seven by boat, and silently surrounded the reduced force encamped on the doorstep of Gloucester. As the sun started to shine, Lord Brandon gave the signal and the arrows flew. There was panic and the army of Mason Knox was caught out.

As they tried to flee north their only route of escape was cut off by the woodsmen of Warwick, and throughout the day as fighting raged, Brandon aided by his new lieutenant Simmons, coordinated the clean-up operation to bring the city back under the control of the duke again.

Sir Brandon Berkley was a hero of his own people and truly his father's son, for he had masterminded a one day attack and won a city it had taken Mason Knox three weeks to defeat. He sat on his horse and for the first time in his life, he seemed to hold himself with authority and looked like the duke he was.

Brandon rode through the streets a hero, and his people threw flowers and cheered as he made his way to his ancestral home. The battle had done a great deal of damage, and he was saddened to see houses and buildings of value burned out and ruined.

He looked across to Simmons, as he rode up the drive to the manor house. "This was not my victory Fuse, it was Roberts. I may have given the order but he planned it."

"I believe you are right sir, but knowing Lord Loxley a little, I would say that this was his way of giving a favour you may one day need to return, and one of your victories could be his."

"I am not sure what you mean Fuse."

"Your father gave you a mind for politics, and before this is all over, I feel that Lord Robert will require your expertise in that area to aid his victory, that will even the score and you will both be lords of equal standing. He is a man of great honour sir."

"He is also a friend."

"I would say sir, he is, probably the truest you will ever have."

Jade moved delicately in her saddle. "Will we make it back to the castle tonight Robbie? It's just that my bum is killing me."

"My dear Pebbles, we are trying but the light is fading, although we are not far from the road and the check point, it still could be some time before we make it to the castle. Would you like to stop here and rest your sores for a while, I am quite sure Alice has some cream that may help."

Jade smiled. "I suppose I could get Rowan to rub it on for me."

Rune started to giggle. "Jade, I hope you never change."

Rowan and Martin came, riding up. "There is a barrow with a stone circle up ahead and just to one side is quite a deep wood, it would make a good place to rest up for the night." Rowan smiled at Jade. "There is quite a nice large pool which would cool the feet, and other hot areas."

Rune and Robbie laughed aloud. "What say you Pebbles; would you like to sit and cool off?"

She smiled at them. "Yes please."

"Alright Rowan lead us on to the place of Pebbles relief if you please." Rowan turned his horse, and at a pace, they all followed.

Robbie leaned on the tree as Jade and Blades, and some of the others splashed about in the cool water. He stared up at the hill and the circle of stones silhouetted at the top of it. This was an ancient site of ritual and he had never thought much of the thousands of years of worship that had existed in the country before. He knew the stones were placed during the times of Celts and Saxons, they were so big and yet somehow without all the device's men had used, they had built this place of worship to the Earth Faith.

It made him realise how close he was to those times, from what he knew of modern times, man had created metal monsters that somehow did everything for them, yet here in the middle of nowhere, man with just his hands and his sweat had built something that had out lasted everything modern man had built. Rune came up behind him and put her arms around him. "It's beautiful, isn't it?"

He tilted his head as she rested her head on his shoulder, and pulled her arms on top of his belt and held them. "That was built long before modern man, and yet here it still stands."

She nuzzled into his neck. "You know they had pretty much the same life as we have now? Like us they had to live off the land."

"Yet here it still stands, how many buildings have we seen that are broken and decayed and covered in weeds? The red death was a small passing moment in the span of the time these have been here."

"What are you trying to say to me, Robbie?"

"It gives me hope Rune, that all of us can build something that will last for thousands of years as these have."

"That is a dream worth having Robbie, grandmother would be pleased."

He turned and slid round in her arms. "Is my dream stronger than his?"

"I have thought a lot about what grandmother said Robbie; I just don't think it will be about just the dream. I think that the love and the meaning of the dream have to count, you know like whom benefits and will all lives be fairly treated, and communities aided? Your dream is for the good of everyone, his comes from the desire to benefit only him. Your dream has got to count and be victorious."

"Nature is not always fair Rune, a hedgehog may dine on slugs and worms, but the fox may dine on the hedgehog. Even a fox, can be snatched by an eagle, there is always something whose greed will win over."

"But Robbie that is the law of survival, an eagle will not snatch ten foxes and swap them for cows, you only take from the wood what the community need to eat, you could have taken more and sold them for greater profits but you did not, that is fair and just. It is a reflection of the person you are, and so is your dream for all of us, can you not see that?"

"I just want a home with you, which is my true dream."

"Is that not the dream of everyone? To hold that sense of belonging that family brings, Knox has no sense of family, he gave his own son up for power and wealth. Listen to me Robbie, your dream is pure because it comes from the greatest power in the universe."

"And what power might that be?"

"The power you hold in the palm of your hands, which is what my grandmother told you."

"What do I hold in the palm of my hands Rune?"

"Me... And I love you... And you love me, it is the only power you need Robbie. You are surrounded and protected by it, please believe me when I tell you, that no matter how hard it gets, you will be victorious."

She lifted her arm and pulled his head forward, and kissed him. He slid his arms round her and pulled her as close as he could, and they kissed for a long time, Rune pulled off. "Wow!" She gasped. "Down tiger." He started to laugh and she smiled. "We need to get back to the castle and have this talk again."

Rune stood in his arms and he leaned against the tree and stared at the stones in the dark, an owl hooted up in the trees, and the foxes called to each other, maybe she was right. Mason Knox had cast his own child into a house full of strangers just so he could gain the upper hand. How would that have made Billy feel, knowing he would not see his own father again until he had achieved what his father wanted?

Robbie thought of the many times he had seen Billy stare up into space for hours, had Billy been thinking of his father? Did he secretly hate him for what he had done or was he planning his triumphant return? It all spun around in Robbie's mind, he could not lose sight of the fact that Billy had a kind and almost noble streak in him. He had seen it so many times, so where would Billy be in the plans of Knox if they were to fall down, or would even Billy fight his father for power? The small violet flower of hope began to blossom inside Robbie, and he thought this might just work after all.

He looked down into her bright shining eyes, and he could see life and love.

"Rune I am so glad that I found you."

Arm in arm they wandered back to the fire. Jade and Blades sat shivering wrapped in towels. "Feeling better?" Jade nodded as she shook.

"I still think a soothing cream would have been easier."

Rune winked at her. "And more fun." Jade smiled as she shivered. It was calm in the wood, or maybe it was the influence of the stones on the hill. Robbie watched as Jade snuggled up to Rowan for warmth, and looked at the happy face of Steph as she slept with Pete's arm pulled close around her. Blades sat on her dad's knee, and he pulled his cloak around her to warm her and Ruby slept side by side with Jett. Maybe Rune had a point; all everyone needed was just a little love.

He slid down and pulled her close, her small warm frame pressed against him. He knew that there was a great deal of love around him and he would be protected. He was tired, and his eyes felt heavy, they closed and he drifted as pictures flashed before his eyes.

His sleep became uneasy, his mind was filled with images of mist covered standing stones and decaying broken buildings. Ravens screamed in the trees and the leaves withered and turned brown. The grass was dying and turning yellow as it decayed on the floor, the soil rolled back and concrete towers pushed through the earth.

He stood alone on the edge of the dying woodland. Before him was a fortress of grey slimy, algae covered stone, he shivered as he slowly approached it, and carefully looked all around for signs of life. He felt the hairs on the back of his neck begin to rise, and he knew he was not alone. Robbie looked up at the stone tower topped with a winged figure, he could not climb, it was too smooth and the algae was slimy, he would not have a grip. His breath came in gasps of white smoke as he got colder, and he began to shiver. Robbie rubbed his hands up his shoulders as he tried to get warmth inside him; he turned slowly round to try to understand where he was.

Robbie stood frozen to the spot as he suddenly realised where he was. Loxley Wood lay green as it grew for miles in front of him, he could see the trees leading up to the edge of the high white escarpment. The trees were slowly turning yellow and dying, moving backwards towards the high place he loved so much. His heart started to beat faster, and he began to move forward under the dying trees.

Robbie could feel his stomach twist as his heart beat fiercely inside him. Panic shook him, and his mind reeled, he had to stop it and to find a way to keep it alive. He began to run faster into the wood, his only thought was catching the edge of the green leaves and trying to hold on to what life that was left.

Branches snapped and crashed to the ground as he ran, they landed in front of him and impacted, breaking apart as the wood split open with a foul smelling decay. He jumped over them as he tried to run faster, his lungs now gasping for air as his throat burned. His stomach writhed as the foul reek that surrounded him made him retch and gag, he struggled, the panic in him tearing at him and forcing him forward.

Tears began to well in his eyes. "Please don't do this, let my wood, my love live." The thoughts screamed out of him.

Rune woke and sat bolt upright; Robbie thrashed wildly on the floor beside her. She turned and tried to hold him. "Robbie... Robbie wake up." Her eyes flickered violet as she touched him her heart went cold. "No, Robbie!" She started to panic. "MOTHER...! ROWAN!" She screamed at the top of her voice.

Figures came out of the dark at speed, as Robbie thrashed locked in a sleep he could not be woken from, Steph fell beside her daughter.

"Rune what is happening, why is he not waking?" Tears were forming in her eyes as she pulled him to her and held him close; Robbie shook violently in her arms.

Rune looked in her mother's eyes. Steph saw the horror that sat behind Rune's bright blue pupils. "Oh Mother... It's... Her... She is attacking him." The colour drained from Steph's face and her eyes opened wide. Her voice was almost a whisper.

"Rune that's not possible." Steph slightly trembled.

"She is free again, I feel her... Mother the black one is returned."

Everyone watched shaken and panicked unable to understand the conversation between Rune and her mother. Jade was down on her knees, tears rolled from her eyes, staring at Rune. "You must do something Rune; you must help him."

Rowan leaned forward. "Rune listen to me, we must help him, there must be something you can do to free him from whatever terror is in him."

Rune looked at her mother. "I must join him." Steph gasped and clutched her daughter's arm desperately.

"No... It is too dangerous, you are nowhere near ready, please Rune I beg you."

Rune's tears were rolling faster on to Robbie. "I love him; I cannot leave him to her."

Rowan gripped Rune's arm and shook her, his voice contained heightened desperation. "Rune if you can help him do it, and do it now, we cannot lose him."

Rune blinked, and her tears slowed, she looked at Rowan whose fierce eyes showed fear for the first time since she had met him. "I need more power... The stone circle."

Rowan pulled Robbie out of her arms and lifted him over his shoulder.

"Come on.... Now...! Hurry!" Rowan shot off at high speed, running into the trees, Rune was up on her feet in a flash. "My sisters of the wood, I need you." She turned and ran after Rowan into the trees.

The tree cover broke as Rowan burst through them like a bullet; his breath was laboured as he ran hard up the slope towards the tall circle of stones at the top of the barrow. Rune was not far behind as all the others followed. She ran driven by the fear of losing her reason for life; Rowan crashed to his knees and carefully lay Robbie down on the grass.

Rune ran into the circle and collapsed gasping for breath. "Rowan leave the circle... this is just for my sisters now." She gasped each word out as she panted, and looked back at her mother, cousins, and Jade as they arrived gasping for air.

"Mother, take his head, Jett right arm." Rune swallowed more air as she tried to breathe. "Jade left arm, Ruby his feet... hold him still and spread eagled, I need a star."

She stood up and looked at the faces of all the others, they were white and frightened. "You must not come in to this circle, if you do you will risk his and all our lives... do you understand?" They all stared at her wide-eyed as if entranced. "DO YOU UNDERSTAND?" She screamed at them, and they all blinked. All of them swallowed deeply and nodded. "Only my sisters of the wood can help him, leave us inside this circle and no matter what happens stay away from the stones." They backed off more out of fear of Rune.

"Ok... Sorry... Robbie is being possessed by a dark evil force; I am going in to get her. If she comes out and you're in the circle she will kill you, my sisters I can protect, you I cannot... Step away from the circle and you will be safe."

Rune walked into the centre of the circle, as Robbie lay outstretched on the grass. Steph placed her hands on the sides of his head. Jett and Jade held his hands firmly, and Ruby held his feet apart. Rune walked into the centre and stood straddled over Robbie's waist, she looked down at his pale contorted face.

She turned to each of the girls and then at her mother. Steph nodded, "we are with you Runestone." Rune lowered herself down on top of his waist. She stretched her legs down and Ruby took hold. She took a deep breath and leaned over him lying on top of him face down. Her forehead lowered to his and she stretched out her arms and covered him. The girls took her wrists and held her tight. "All right sisters, do not let go, hold on to us both no matter what happens." Rune's eyes began to glow as she looked at Robbie's closed eyes. "Hold on my darling I am coming," she whispered softly. The whole circle glowed violet as she summoned her power.

Everyone took two steps back as purple light swirled into the air around the inside of the circle, Rune closed her eyes and the circle went black. Alice felt Rowan's hand, and grabbed it in fear, as Rune focused her mind.

"Hear me sisters. I am the centre of the circle and command you. Come to me we are in need, Scarlet hear me. Stephanie hear me, Gwinne hear me."

"We hear you, command us Runestone."

"Jade hear me, Jett hear me, Ruby hear me, Amethyst hear me, and Crystal hear me."

"We hear you, command us Runestone."

"Grandmother guide me."

"I am with you my granddaughter; I will protect all that surround you."

"Hear me my sisters and lend me your powers for I face the dark alone."

Everyone looked on in the dark; Martin put his arm around Alice who was weeping as she squeezed Rowan's hand. "Come on love he will be fine." She trembled in the dark silence and then gasped.

A single shaft of red light came out of the sky and hit Rune like a spotlight. Then a bright white beam appeared at its side, the two beams began to revolve around each other. A shimmering silvery white beam appeared and shot down to them, which was followed by a violet beam.

Alice watched as they spun round and around, Jade opened her eyes and green light spilled out into the centre. Jett followed shooting blue light. Ruby opened her eyes and brilliant white illuminated the whole circle. The different coloured lights spun faster around the circle mixing and blending.

Steph opened both of her eyes, and golden light wove its way into the middle of the other beams and began to weave together all the other beams of light into a single pulsing rainbow surrounded by a net of gold, it dropped and hit Rune square in the back. She shuddered, and the light streamed through her, and she began to glow and pulsate on top of Robbie.

Robbie staggered on gasping and retching as he fought through the decayed and rotting wood that was falling before him; he knew the stream that was now dry as the water evaporated off hot steaming rocks. Desperately he clambered over, his eyes cast up to see where life still was.

The whole forest was dying around him and he looked from left to right and saw the trees either side were dying as a circle slowly drew in. "The Escarpment."

He gasped as he vomited, his nostrils filled with the rotten vile stench of decay that surrounded him. He shook violently as he staggered to his feet, and began to half run, half crawl up the stony slope towards it. He could see the foliage of the trees now forming one last protective circle of green at the top that somehow was resisting. He tried to move quicker but he was exhausted from the fight of his journey, his body ached and screamed in pain. He scrambled up to the top, and his heart froze, as he dropped to his knees.

There at the top of the escarpment in the centre of the ground tied and bound, was the huge stag. He fell forward onto his hands; his eyes did not quite understand what he was seeing. In front of the stag was a giant bird of raven black, it stood with its wings outstretched and in its right wing tip was a long snake like silver dagger.

The raven spun round to face him, and he was shocked to see it was a woman. Her eyes were small and dark, and pierced into him from her pale pallid face, her dark withered lips smiled with evil intent. She stood silently watching him, her long black robes flowing on the floor around her. She lowered her arms and the cloak of raven's feathers fell by her side.

"You're too late boy of the woods, he is mine." Her voice was soft and yet somehow it contained an evil so deep it made him shudder. His mind struggled, as everything inside him seemed to collapse, and despair overcame him as he looked into the eyes of the stag.

"You have lost, I have returned and your dream is but a nightmare now boy. You are powerless against me." Her laugh, as she leaned back her head, was evil and terrible, and Robbie retched with fear as terrors arose in him that was as black and ugly as she was.

She looked back at him, the smile of hideous evil on her lips. "I will kill him, and you are powerless to stop me, and then all this world will be mine for my sons to inherit. Did you really think the heir of a worthless bowman could defeat me? I who have cornered and forced into sleep all the powers of this world. You are all fools."

He watched the grass die as the circle shrunk past him, and now the only patch left was slowly receding towards the stag of Hearne, tied and bound on the floor before him. She raised the dagger high in the air, and the despair in him grew, his dream of life and love of nature was going to die. "Nature," he whispered to himself.

In front of the stag on the floor, in amongst the dying yellow grass, a small violet pushed up and burst into bloom. The cold seeped out of his bones and he felt her warmth, a breeze blew past his ear. "I am here my love, I will not leave you, I am life and the Runestone."

Energy returned quickly to his arms and legs, and he stood up swaying and faced the vile dark figure, she looked down at the violets that grew from his feet and spread across the floor.

"What is this?" She yelled pointing a long pale finger with a claw like black nail.

Robbie's eyes flared purple as he stared at her.

"Your dream is a lie; you will never defeat me." She screamed and a blast of cold air hit him with huge force, yet he did not move, his feet held as he leaned back and absorbed the impact. "My lord has our love and our dreams of truth; you will not easily conquer us all."

"Your lord is weak and will die boy." She plunged the dagger downward toward the stag. The golden rainbow of light from his blade flooded the whole area as he drew the sword, and with one flowing, sweeping movement, he hit the dagger and the blade shattered as it flew with two fingers from her hand.

Robbie swept back the blade as treacherous screams filled the air, and as he struck back with skill, the ropes sliced apart and the stag jumped to its feet. Black clouds swirled around him and upwards into the sky, his ears were deafened by the screams and suddenly it was gone, and calmness surrounded him.

Raven black feathers floated softly down to the floor; Robbie turned in his daze to see the stag stood at the edge of the clearing. He bowed, and the stag lowered its head, the grass beneath its feet began to grow and the trees sprouted leaves on their torn and splintered trunks.

He was exhausted, then as the stag turned and left the clearing, Robbie fell to his knees and hit the grass utterly spent. He rolled over; his arms outstretched and looked at the sky, he felt he was spinning round and everything went black.

Alice held her breath as Martin's arm tightened around her and Rowan's hand squeezed, the coloured lights spun faster and faster, and out of nowhere a bloodcurdling howl shrieked, and then screamed. Lines of black appeared coiling upwards in to the sky as the wailing and moaning continued, there was a huge blast of bright violet and everything went dark. Alice gasped as the sudden silence surrounded her.

The faint light of lilac flickered, and she moved forward to see better, Robbie's face was a glow with the colour of violet as Rune looked down at him, Alice watched as she sat up on his waist slowly and weakly. Rune leaned back over him and softly kissed him. He opened his eyes, and her radiant violet tinted eyes looked down at him, she smiled and her eyes filled with tears. "I love you." She leaned forward and kissed him softly.

She pushed her arms under him, and put her head at the side of his and wept. He hurt all over as he slid his arms around her and pulled her tight as she shook with her tears. "I love you too my Rune."

Seeing him move, Alice burst into tears and ran into the stone circle. She fell to her knees and peered over at him, as he stared up, he smiled. "Hey?"

Alice smiled through her tears. "Hi."

Rune sat up still on his lap and he raised himself up and hugged her, Alice wrapped her arms around both of them and wept. Jade and Jett lifted themselves from the base of the stones where they had been flung. Jade saw Alice around the two of them and crawled over. Kneeling up she joined the hug.

Steph sat with her back to the stone, as Peter knelt down in front of her. "You alright sweetheart?" She looked at him and gave him a faint smile.

"No." She burst into tears; he grabbed her, and pulled her close. "Oh Pete I was so frightened I thought I would lose her." He held her tight as she wept and sobbed.

Jade looked at her sister and smiled. "Wow sis you are brave, I was so frightened I peed myself." Rune smiled, and touched Jade's face with her palm.

"Thanks sis, you helped me save him." Jade smiled.

"I love him too you know?" Robbie raised a weak arm and pulled Jade closer as he pulled Alice close. "I love you all too." He lifted his head and Rune smiled at his eyes.

Alice stared. "Robbie why are your eyes all purple."

Rune touched Alice on the shoulder. "He is still very weak; I am still inside and protecting him." Her eyes also flashed lilac. Alice nodded and hugged them both.

Jett lifted Ruby who was still trembling. "Who was that woman Jett?" She slid her glasses into her pocket.

"Don't really know sis, but if I meet that bitch again, she will lose more than a few fingers."

Robbie was still very pale and trembling, his whole body had been weakened and he clung to Rune. She herself was still using power to protect him and held him tightly in fear that she would return. She was also exhausted, twice in one day she had harnessed great power, and her body was not use to it, her strength now came from making sure Robbie was all right. No one had realised how the black one had used Robbie's own life force to increase her own power over him. It had drained him to the point of death, and now he was barely strong enough to stand.

Rune had got to him just in time, and had drawn life from her whole circle to support him and strengthen him, without it he would be dead, although his resistance to her had been surprisingly powerful, which now confused her. Robbie was mortal with no mystical powers, and yet he had lasted ten times longer than a normal man, had he drawn power from the sword? She could not work it out.

Pete lifted Steph into his arms. She clung round his neck with her head on his shoulder as he walked towards Rune and Robbie. Steph looked down at her daughter and sniffled, Rune's eyes still flickered violet and lilac. "I did not know you were a weaver mother."

Steph smiled. "That is the first time I have ever used it, and I hope I do not have to again, I have no idea how you just did that Rune, you have a greater power than I think you realise. You are very brave; I am proud of you." Rune smiled as she looked at her mother.

"Thanks Mum... I could not have done it without you."

Rowan scooped Jade into his arms and she smiled as she put her arms around him. He gave her a kiss and carried her down the slope to the trees. Robbie was just too exhausted to stand, and Harry picked him up gently, as John lifted Rune. "Come on you two, I think you need rest you look exhausted." John smiled at Rune. "I don't know what you did girl, but you did good there is no doubt about it." He carried her to the camp and lay her down gently on her bed. Harry lowered Robbie who was drifting in and out of sleep.

"Tell him I am here man if he like needs me, won't you?"

She smiled. "He will be alright Harry; he just needs a lot of sleep and a good breakfast. Don't worry I will make sure he knows you are here."

"Cool man, hey you know I really dig those funky eyes vibes, it's like is totally funky." Rune smiled.

"Thanks Harry."

Rune pulled Robbie close and held on to him as he drifted into a deep sleep. He felt her presence deep within him all night, as Rune lay in the dark holding him tight, she felt very weak and very tired, her eyes soon began to flutter, and it was not long before she was fast asleep beside him. A lady in white stepped out of the trees and waved her hand, everyone lay down and rested. She placed her hand on top of Rune and it glowed with a silver aura.

She moved her other across to Robbie, and it glowed a faint lilac colour. She stood up and looked at all the group who were now fast asleep, and she smiled. She sat on a log beside Rune and Robbie and watched them, a tall stag stood silently in the trees opposite. As dawn broke, she stood up and walked over to her daughter who lay fast asleep with her husband Pete, she kissed her finger and then pushed it gently on to her forehead. The white lady stood up and walked from the camp, she waved her hand and everyone moved in their sleep. Jade opened her eyes and smiled. "Night Grandmother."

Rowan sat up and stretched, as John came through the trees. "Ready for a coffee are you, John?"

John nodded and sat by the fire, Rowan got up and built up the fire, and filled the coffee pot and put it into the centre of the fire to boil, he looked over at Robbie and Rune fast asleep rolled up together close to the trees. "I have no idea what happened last night John, I don't think we ever will truly know, I just think that we should keep a better eye on him from now on, he is more of a target than I even realised." John nodded.

Robbie woke just as everyone was almost ready, he was still very weak and they sat him on his horse, and Rune jumped up behind him. It was just gone five, when they all left without eating. They rode at high speed down on to the road into

Bristol. They clattered through the streets and over the long bridge up the road to Caerleon. Robbie hardly noticed the journey and when he woke up he was lay in his bed in the castle. It was four in the afternoon.

Rune was asleep in the chair at the side of the bed, her head was to one side and her long red and golden hair glinted in the sunlight as it lay across her shoulder, and over her white gown. He ached all over and did not move, he just lay there and watched her taking in every detail of her face and body. She was to him the most beautiful creature he had ever seen, and he loved her.

She woke with a start after about fifteen minutes, and her pale eyelids flicked up and flashes of blue lit her cheeks for a moment. She smiled at him a warm and loving smile as she straightened in the chair. "Hi gorgeous." She leaned over on to the bed. Robbie pulled back the sheet and she slid in.

"Hey there beautiful." He kissed her and she snuggled beside him. "How long have I been out?"

"Almost all day, she almost killed you. You barely had any strength when we revived you."

He squeezed her tight. "Who was she Rune?"

"They call her the Dark One, only my granddad knows her proper name. She is the most powerful dark sorceress there is, and both of us are lucky to be alive."

"How did I survive? I felt myself dying and knew she would kill Hearne, and then suddenly I was fighting."

"You remembered something very important that she could not defeat Robbie, and it helped me to get to you and fight her."

"What did I remember? My mind is so clouded it is hard to think."

"You spoke my real name, and you knew that you loved me. Your heart opened up to me and I found a way to connect that made us one. Together we had the strength to defeat her."

"She will come back wont she?"

"Yes Robbie, she will be back, she has been revealed to us, and we will be prepared for her, you can trust she will never try to possess you again. She had quite a shock when we blended." She turned and looked at his ashen face and his brown eyes. She smiled and kissed him. "Hold me close Robbie, and don't let go."

"I will never let go."

It was getting late when Steph brought a food tray into the room and placed it on the table. Rune was curled tight in a ball in his arms fast asleep. Steph smiled at her. Robbie looked up at Steph as she sat in the chair. He spoke quietly. "She took a big risk, didn't she?"

Steph nodded. "No more than any of us would have done, but yes for her so new to her powers it was a giant leap of faith. The Dark One would not be my choice for an opponent."

"I felt others helping her who I did not know, who were they?"

"Rune is the centre of the circle and the mistress of all of us, there are a few of us, and you have not met all of the circle yet. You will in time, she was clever to think of it, I had forgotten the rest of the family. I have wondered if she has contact as we do not, they are hidden from everyone."

"So because she is the centre she can find them?"

"Robbie in all honesty I am not sure. Rune is not like the rest of us, she has powers and qualities that even I her mother is unaware of. Last night I felt her true power for the first time, I am scared of the Dark One because of the dark force she has inside her. Nevertheless, I will tell you something Robbie, as strange as this may sound, Rune frightened the life out of me last night. Her power was such I found it hard to bear when it passed through me."

"But how could you be afraid of Rune?"

"I do not fear my daughter Robbie, I fear what she holds. It's like a bottle of acid, the bottle is harmless and nothing to worry about, but the acid inside is deadly and burns all it touches. What was bottled in Rune last night was too concentrated and pure, I was afraid of it. I was not the only one, it terrified Jade, and she actually wet herself with fear, this from a girl who has never in her life shown fear of anything. Rune is the most powerful thing I have ever encountered."

"I do not see that at all. She is the most kind and loving person I have ever known, look at her Steph, look how frail and gentle she is."

"My dad has always told me that the most terrifying force in the universe is pure love, maybe that is what I felt last night, concentrated purity of love. Robbie, I do not know, this is even beyond me, I just know what I felt, and it scared the hell out of me."

"She is very precious to me, and I think I would have died last night without her."

"There is no doubt Robbie, by the time we got to you I thought it was over, and that is when I felt it, Rune channeled something mammoth into you, and you began to come back. I was absolutely certain you were a goner, so were Jade and Jett, I think she simply opened her heart and out it all came. It surrounded you with a protective force more powerful than the sun; I will never really understand what she did or how she did it. I just know it frightened the life out of the Dark One."

"This Dark One felt the pain of the blade and Hearne was saved, which is what is important, I cannot believe someone would want to kill him."

"Hearne has a lot of power; she would not have caught him easily; I can only think it was by chance. She showed her hand very early in the game if you ask me, it was a mistake I would think she now regrets."

Rune stirred at the side of Robbie, she lifted her hand and stroked his face and smiled, her eyes flashed blue. "Oh, you're awake, how are you? I was dreaming about us talking by the stones." She smiled. "Do you remember?"

"Oh yes... But I think maybe we should discuss that later."

"Why... Don't you want to make love to me?"

"I think you should talk to your mother first... She is there in the chair."

"God she isn't, is she?" Rune buried her head in his chest.

Steph started to laugh. "Maybe something to eat would be better; you know build up his strength a bit... You know, I have no idea where you and Jade get this from, it must be your father's side."

Rune slid round and sat up in bed. "It's funny that, because he says exactly the same thing about your side of the family... Is there anything you would like to share mother?"

"Eat this while it's still hot." Steph passed them both a plate. "I will be having a long chat with your father... Come on, eat you need your strength, both of you still look peaky to me." Steph closed the door quietly behind her and Rune giggled.

"She is pretty cool for a parent don't you think?"

"Your mum is one of a kind that is for sure Rune. She loves you and Jade so much you know, both of you are really lucky."

"Yeah, I know we love her too."

The figure of a very muscular man paced up and down in the hall waiting. He stopped and walked to the full-length mirror, and looked at himself to see if he was presentable. His long blonde thick curly hair fell down behind his shoulders, and the side braids where his hair was scraped back into the black back tie were straight and neat. He smiled a charming smile from his tanned olive skinned face, and his dark European brown eyes sparkled. He was happy and walked back to the bottom of the large wooden stairs and waited.

Simmons looked down at the bulky frame of the man, with his white frilly silk shirt, and long black coat with deep cuffs and golden edged trimming, which showed he was a man of great means. The black leather boots that led up past his knees, tapped on the polished wooden floor impatiently. He slipped his hands in his wide black belt as he stood and waited. Simmons looked at the doorman. "The man looks like a pirate, who did he say he was?"

"He is Ambassador Jacques Phillips of York sir."

Simmons looked again. "Alright show him up, and I will let his Lordship know."

The Duke of Gloucester was sat in his chair by the fire when the knock came. Simmons opened the door and the Ambassador stepped in. The doorman bowed. "The Ambassador from York, My Lord."

The ambassador walked right past him and up to Brandon, and grasped his hand very firmly; he had a grip like a vice. "Thank you kindly for seeing me at such short notice your Lordship, I am on an errand of great urgency and have been informed that you could assist me." His dark brown eyes searched deeply into Brandon's.

"I am very pleased to meet you too Ambassador, if I can aid York in any way I will of course oblige, would you like a seat?" He gestured to the red velvet chair on the Wilton patterned rug.

"Thank you, your Lordship and please call me Jacques."

He sat in the chair opposite and Brandon resumed sitting in his own chair. "Tell me Jacques how can I be of service?" He crossed his legs and studied the man as he rested his arm on his knee.

"My Lord, I have been sent from York by my father who is currently under siege by the self imposed army of Mason Knox. It is our understanding that the man is set to attempt to crown himself King of Britain. We at York oppose this and we are attempting to gather together the true lords and heirs of the land to meet and oppose publicly this illegitimate heir to the throne. I have been informed you share our opinion."

"Who else have you spoken with to arrive at your conclusion Ambassador? You are very aware I take it, that what you have just divulged to myself could get you easily killed?"

"I am aware, but I will not die easily rest assured My Lord." Jacques sat back and gave Brandon a broad and confident smile.

"I am not sure you are aware of this, but your father and my father worked quite closely on several matters in the House of Lords before the end came, you can relax Jacques you are amongst friends here."

He smiled. "Good, I will not be needing this then." He pulled a large silver revolver out of his pocket and placed it on the small table to his side. "I only have ten bullets left and I don't want them wasted."

Simmons smiled. "Why sir is that a peacemaker?"

"Aye, and it fires straight and true, my father brought it back from Canada, my mother and he were stationed over there before I was born, Calgary, he was the British Consulate there."

"A most remarkable weapon sir, the colts were always problematic and kept jamming, but these they were expertly crafted." Brandon coughed. "I am sorry sir you know I have a weakness for antique weapons." Simmons sat down in the other chair, and the duke eyed the gun cautiously.

"As I was saying Jacques, you are amongst friends here. If you would care to join us, we will be having dinner presently and of course, you must accept my hospitality, this will be a safer place for you to stay, we are still clearing roads to Bristol to create safe passage."

"That is very gracious My Lord; I would be pleased to accept your kind hospitality."

"You are aware I take it that there have been several large scale attacks on Mason Knox in recent days, and he has been dealt several bitter blows?"

Jacques leaned forward in his chair. "You mean the Hooded Man?" He gave the duke a broad smile. "Now there is a man after my own heart. Is it really true about Tintagel?"

Lord Brandon seemed to rise in his chair with pride. "Oh yes, I can assure you it is very true indeed. He has since demolished a very large weapons factory in Weston Supermare, and today we had news he has completely demolished Windsor Castle. We believe Mason intended to use it as his seat of power, and he has caused so much destruction and havoc for Mason on the old M4 road, that Mason has had to stop his supply runs temporarily whilst he finds another route. The Hooded Man is indeed very active in these parts."

"They say he is the lord from Loxley come down to fight Mason. There is some prophecy about a bowman who will lead the country back to a real king. We cannot get through to Loxley it is sealed tight; I have lost ten men trying to contact them."

"Well, I can assure you my dear Jacques any message you have for Loxley, you can be sure we will be able to deliver it for you, we have a direct line of communication." Jacques leaned forward excitedly in his seat.

"Will they back my father in a revolt against Mason? That's what we need to know." Just a hint of a satisfied smile crossed Brandon's lips.

"I don't think you have quite grasped the tree as it were to speak, my good man it is not a case of asking for his support it is more a case of you asking to join, you do not seem to understand, Loxley is here and is already leading the revolt and he has been for some time. Plans are already on the table to stop Mason Knox."

"Then I must find him and talk to him."

"All in good time Jacques, we intend to see him shortly to speak with him ourselves. We have a few items of unfinished business with Lord Loxley, and will be travelling shortly to meet him."

Jacques slapped the arm of the chair. "This is great news, I knew when I arrived here things would turn out for the better, I wish I had brought some wine to celebrate."

Brandon smiled. "You are in the house of a duke my dear Ambassador; we have only the best claret in England." He looked up at Simmons. "I think a little toast to our union is quite in order."

Jade bounded into the room and jumped on the bed. "Hey guys are you ever going to get up I am bored?"

Rune uncurled from Robbie. "Oh, Jade we had a rough night we just wanted to sleep."

"Yeah right, that's not what mum thinks." She grinned with mischief.

Robbie brushed his hair from his eyes. "Where is everyone Pebbles?"

"They have set up some targets out in the garden and are practicing their shooting. Jett and Blades are at it again with their swords, and Harry is trying to knock Ruby over and getting battered.”

Rune looked at Jade as she pulled the bedding up a little and tucked it around her. “Why aren’t you out there with them, what is Rowan up to?”

“He is trying to beat Alice... Like he has a hope... Oh guys I miss you, I was really scared last night I would lose you, I just want to spend some time with you, I need to know you are fine.” Rune leaned forward and put her arms around Jade.

“Oh, come here... Look we are fine, it really did wipe us out and we have slept nearly all day, tell everyone we will have some supper with them in a while and we will come down, Ok?”

“Cool.” She crawled up the bed, and kissed Robbie on the cheek and then hugged Rune. “You guys are the best... I am really glad you are safe.” Jade bounced off the bed and headed out of the door.

Rune turned to him. “I am sorry, you don’t mind, do you?”

He pulled her close. “No not at all. Actually, I could do with stretching my legs a little, and it will be nice to thank everyone for last night.” He slid off the bed, pulled on his pants, and stretched. He felt a lot stronger, and dropped his feet into his boots.

“Well back to normal again, I wonder what we can blow up next.”

CHAPTER TWENTY TWO

TABLES AND SWORDS

The mist swirled through the trees and across the square, as the sun set its first slender beams of the day over the horizon. David Williams walked slowly along the path at the top of the great wall; he patted his men on the shoulder as he passed. "Stay awake Jenkins it's at times like this you can expect the buggers." The soldier nodded and smiled, and looked back out across the trees.

David walked along toward the large observation platform above the gate. He could see the Sergeant at arms, Henry Benson peering in to the mist through his binoculars; he came up the steps and across the deck to his side. "Not much to see Henry?"

"These things are bloody useless in this; I will be a lot happier when it lifts, and I can see the sods coming." David peered back, his men had been on high alert for ten days and nothing had happened, since Robert Lox had sent General Turner off with an arrow through his hand.

"I hate this Henry; I don't know which is worse, standing up here all day or bashing them off the walls when they do get here."

"I go for bashing em off sir, keeps me busy like, stops the boredom."

David smiled and patted him on the shoulder, "I think I will go and find out where the hell the coffee is, I don't mind freezing my butt off, but I will be buggered if I have to do it without a coffee." David walked down the steps and across the top of the walkway.

"In coming rider!" The voice screamed down from the high observation tower above, David spun on his heels and ran back up the steps. "How many, can you identify them?"

The soldier peered out across the top of the trees. "Difficult to say sir, there is I think just only the one, and they are coming at speed." The sound of galloping hooves echoed through the mist getting louder and louder.

A small figure on horseback shot through the trees and on to the large open square in front of the wall, a very high pitched voice screamed. "Open the gate there is six of em after me." The horse reared and screeched to a halt panting for breath. The figure of a small girl sat on the horse dressed almost in rags, and covered in dirt with a small bag over her shoulder.

David nodded and the Sergeant at arms shouted down. "Open the gate."

David slid down the handrails of the steps; his feet not touching even one. He spun round the ladder, and slid to the floor as one of the large wooden gates started to open. Six riders came out of the trees in black tunics, their horses strained as they pulled up hard, but it was too late, arrows flew and they fell dead as the sniper archers took them out.

The small girl rode into the compound behind the gate and slid down off her horse, she glanced back behind her as the heavy gate started to close. "You cut that a bit bloody fine mate."

David looked at the small girl covered in mud with a very dirty face. Her hair was, pushed under a woollen hat, which had several holes in it and thick lumps of matted hair poked out. She was just sixteen and yet she somehow appeared older.

"I am the Master of the Gates, state your business here and I will decide if we allow you out of this compound."

"Alright keep your hair on, I am a postal rider. I have important documents for..." She looked at the letter with the red wax seal on it. "Robert Lox, John Lox, Leenard Rimmer, and David Williams. I also have a few less important items for other members of this community; they are from Lord Robert of Loxley."

David Williams's eyes widened. "You have letters from Robbie? I am David and Master of the Gates, let me see."

She pulled the letter back. "Can you prove it?"

"Sergeant, will you please tell this bag of rags, who the hell I am."

The Sergeant looked down. "You are David Williams sir, and Master of the Gates."

The small girl smiled, and held a letter out for him. "Letter for you sir."

David took the letter off her and looked at the seal of Loxley on the back; he broke it open and started to read. "Your lord and his lady are fine." He noticed every soldier smile. "He has gathered together a group of others and he has..." David stopped talking, and stared at the letter.

The Sergeant looked, back over the edge of the rail and down at David. "He has done what sir?"

David looked stunned, as his eyes left the paper and he looked back up to the top of the gate. "He has only gone and blown up Tintagel Fortress."

"Beg your pardon sir, did you say Tintagel? You know.... What's his faces' home?"

David nodded up to the sergeant. "He bloody well has Henry." He turned and looked at the girl. "I would kiss you if you weren't so dirty, I have no idea how you got through to us, but bless you girl, you have brought us great hope. What's your name?"

"It's Michelle, but everyone calls me Rags." David smiled at her and began to walk for his horse.

"Well Rags if you follow me, I will take you to the others you have mail for, and see you get a hot meal and your horse is cared for, follow me we still have a short ride ahead of us." David jumped up on to his saddle.

Robert Lox sat behind the desk in the small room at the rear of the Village Hall; he rubbed his tired eyes with frustration. "Len, I need to know he is alright, is there nothing you can do to get through?"

Len sat opposite a worried look on his face. "Robert, I have told you, she is blocking everything at the moment and will not allow anything to pass. Rune is now very powerful and even I cannot force my way in. I am sorry Robert; you have to understand that Rune is now the centre of the circle, she controls the flow to every one of us, and if she has put up such a strong defence around everyone she must have good reason."

Robert sat back and sighed. "Just tell me again what you think has happened, I find all of this confusing."

Len sat forward and leaned on the table. "Last night something very powerful tried to penetrate Robbie, I have my ideas but until I can contact Rune or Steph I do not fully know. Rune called upon all the sisters of her circle, which surprised me, she drew a lot of power from them and blended herself to Robbie. I am amazed that she knew how to do it, but Opal has all sorts of ways of giving power and knowledge, and I think she gave both of them a little extra something a few days ago to help them. Whatever it was, it did work. Rune spliced herself into Robbie and helped him, it saved both of their lives and now either Rune or Opal has placed some sort of protection on them until they are fully recovered. I expect contact with Rune soon; she has talked with me several times recently."

He sat back in his chair, and closed his eyes; he was worried as he felt a presence he had not felt in a long time. It had only been fleeting, but it had been enough to get him up in the middle of the night and walk to the farm to consult with Robert.

"Alright Len, I am starting to get the picture. My lad is safe and alive you are completely sure of that?"

"He is alive Robert, so are Rune and the others, the last thing she sent me was simply I am very tired and I need to rest, we are all safe."

Robert nodded and closed his eyes as he leaned back. It had been a tense and worrying night and now he felt drained.

They heard the footsteps across the main hall, and then came a soft knock at the door. Robert opened his eyes. "Come."

David walked in with Rags. "Excuse me Robert, ah! Len, we have just been looking for you. Gents we have mail." Len turned in his chair as if he did not quite hear right, and looked up at Rags, who smiled.

"You Mr Rimmer then?" She handed him the folded sheets of white paper, one from Rune, and one from Steph. There was a small one from Jade; she had been making the ring for Robbie and so only had time to quickly write, 'I am great and I love you and miss you.' Len looked at the letters of carefully folded paper sealed with the seal of Lord Loxley.

Rags moved over to the desk. "You I take it are Robert Lox his dad?" Robert nodded; he was so surprised he could not quite muster the words. The letter from his son was thick, and he turned it over to see the red wax seal. Robert smiled and he broke open the seal and opened the letter up.

"Scuse me Sir, but I have letters for Jess and Beth Lox, as well as John Lox, where do I find them? I also have a letter for Mrs Nellie Tanner." She noticed his watery eyes. "He is fine sir, put these all in my hand right personal like, nice lad not bad looking I can see how he pulled that Runestone bird, I wouldn't have said no either." She gave Robert a big smile and he nodded.

"Thank you young lady, please go with my brother in law to my farm, where you can deliver the rest of your letters. My wife Jess will sort you out some food and we will care for your horse. I will come up to the house shortly with a reply for my son. You will find Mrs Tanner is there as well, she works for me."

"Right you are squire, see ya." She turned and walked out passing Len who was already engrossed in his letter from Rune. Nothing in detail had been told of Eric's death or how he died, Robbie had insisted that only the basic facts be given to Loxley. He had no idea after the attack on Tintagel what condition Loxley was in, and so he and Rune had agreed to keep the facts minimal. Len now read about the two attacks from Rune and she apologised for not telling him sooner, but Robbie was in command and he alone had the final say over what was given.

Robert brought his hand down on the table hard, and everything including Len jumped up in the air. "WHAT?" He read on in complete disbelief. "THAT FOWL RANCID SNAKE, I WILL KILL HIM!" Roberts's eyes flared as he dropped the sheet of paper, and stormed round the office cursing and swearing. Len picked up the letter and read, his eyes widened as the words Billy appeared in the letter.

Robert had hit fever pitched as his rage intensified, Len stood up and tried to calm him. "Robert please, you must calm down, there is nothing you can do here hundreds of miles away."

Robert was purple, and he spoke through gritted teeth. "I gave that slimy worm a home, raised him as a son, and he was plotting the death of us all." Robert breathed deeply. "So help me Len, I will kill him, I will tear his arms and legs off and that is a promise."

Len had no doubt, the enraged Robert Lox was terrifying to behold. Robert flopped back into his seat. "Oh Len, how the hell am I going to tell Jess? She loved the boy; this will break her heart and what about John? Oh hell, Billy was messing with Alice, John will bloody kill him, and you know what his temper is like?"

Jess sat quietly at the table holding the letter from Robbie to her heart as the tears rolled down her cheeks. Robbie had already told her, Beth walked quietly in through the door, her eyes were red and her face was ashen. Alice's letter was held loosely in her hand. She crossed the kitchen and sat beside her sister-in-law. "Jessie love, I am so sorry." She pulled her close and held her tight as Jessie wept and sobbed. Beth cried too as her sister pulled her tight and they shared their sorrow. The enormous crash from the barn was enough to work out that John had now also discovered the truth; Rags flew out of the barn and down the path to the house.

"It's got nowt to do with me mate I just bloody deliver em," she shouted. Rags flew into the kitchen. "Hey misses help me, that man is a maniac."

Beth looked at Jess as both of them looked at Rags, Beth turned to Jess. "Oh, bloody hell Jess, she has gone and told John."

John came storming out of the barn his face red with rage. He pulled his horse down the driveway toward the house, his bow and quiver were across his back, and his large silver sword was hanging from his belt. He stopped at the shed, opened the door and pulled a large silver axe out, and slid it into his belt on the opposite side to his sword.

Beth and Jess came out of the house screaming at him. "John where are you going? John don't be stupid we do not know where he is." John pulled his horse too, as Beth caught up to him. "John this is daft, you cannot go running off into nowhere, no one has any idea where he is."

John's rage was at fever pitch, and he was a terrifying site to behold, and yet Beth seemed to have no fear of him at all. "I will find him and tear his skin off, messing with my little girls' affections, and trying to kill Robbie, I will bloody well kill him and roast him." Beth looked at him and then screamed.

"JOHN HENRY LOX!" The slap across his face echoed around the farm, Rags clenched her teeth and closed her eyes as she watched from behind Jess. John went instantly quiet as Beth wagged an angry finger in his face. "Now you listen to me John Henry Lox, I will not tell you to calm down again." Beth's eyes had narrowed sharply and her brow was furrowed and her face was red.

John rubbed the smarting side of his face. "Don't hit me Beth baby that hurt."

"Then just you behave and stop scaring me." Tears welled in her eyes. "I don't want you riding off all mad and getting yourself killed. I could not bear to lose you."

John opened his arms and pulled her close, and she blubbered into his huge frame. "Come on now baby don't cry love. It will be all right I have plenty of time, I will just hunt him down and rip his skin off later."

The huge frame of John Lox stood in the centre of the yard, and he held the weeping figure of his wife. Jess smiled, Beth was the only person alive who could strike John and not be attacked, she breathed a sigh of relief and looked down at the small girl cowering behind her skirt. "Come on you, it's safe to come out now. Let us leave them a minute and I will get you something to eat. So what's your name?"

"It's Michelle miss, but everyone calls me Rags."

"Why doesn't that surprise me? Well Rags, I think a bit of food and maybe a bath and a comb may improve your situation. I think Beth has a few old bits of Alice's that would help. I know we have some boots somewhere that will fit you. How can you ride with your toes sticking out like that?"

"No choice miss, it's the job, we don't get paid money, it's usually just food, except Lord Loxley of course, now there's a gent, paid me three gold he did."

"Well of course he would, he is my son, and been raised with respect and manners."

"Yes miss."

Rags sat at the table having had a bath and washed her hair, which had now gone from a matted dirty brown to a matted strawberry blonde. Jess combed it out as gently as she could, and then pulled it into a long plait. She had sorted out some of Alice's old clothes, and Rags now began to look more like the female she was supposed to be. She had on a pair of heavy brown cord trousers, which were patched at the knees, and a collarless mustard coloured shirt with a green woollen top pulled over. Jess gave her Billy's old brown cloak. "Not the height of fashion but it has to be better than this lot; at least you will be warmer and dryer. All you need now is these." She dropped a pair of long black riding boots on to the floor and two pairs of socks.

Rags was overjoyed. "Oh, thanks Miss Lox you are a real diamond, these are great."

Rags sat with Jess for most of the afternoon and talked of her life on the road. She was the only one who would come to Loxley, as the rest were afraid of the soldiers. Rags was rated as the best horse rider of all the postal kids, she knew all the short cuts, and could get across country faster than anyone could. Rags used roads that no one else did. She told Jess she would have been quicker but she had come via Lincoln, which had slowed her down, and it had taken her three nights to get here. "I will be back in two," she had commented

Rags curled up on the sofa and went to sleep as Jess sat and wrote her reply, it was almost five in the evening, when Robert Lox arrived with replies from him and Len. Rags slipped them into her bag and mounted her horse; she smiled at Jess as she pulled her new cloak around her. "Thanks Miss Lox you are a real lady."

Jess smiled. "Remember Rags, stay safe on the road and when you return come straight here, by the next time you come we will have a proper postal rest room for you."

"I am a Loxley and back only postie now miss." She smiled and kicked the horse, and off she shot to the gates. David took Rags out by a new safe door that had been designed just for slipping out; he gave her his letters and wished her good luck. She sped off across the fields and into the woodland, and up past the old stone circle and was gone. He closed the gate and silently asked Hearne to protect her.

Alice sat with Jett and Flash up in the dim balcony, they looked down as Robbie and Rune sat eating lunch with some of the others. Alice rested her chin on the balcony rail as she talked. "He only spent three hours with us last night and he was exhausted, can it really do that to you?"

Jett tilted her head to one side and looked at Alice. "Mum reckons he is lucky to have lived, she said most mortal men would have died a lot sooner, Rune pumped a lot of power through him to keep him going, she is lucky she did not damage herself."

Alice watched carefully as he ate, and smiled as he talked to the others. "He still looks very drawn and pale to me; I hope we hang around here for a bit so he can rest up."

Flash leaned forward. "I think he is terrific and I just know that he will recover. He is the Hooded Man and Hearne will protect him."

Jett was not too sure. "Hearne wasn't much help the other night; if it wasn't for Robbie she would have killed Hearne and we would be looking for a new green man today."

Alice was confused; she sat back and looked at the two of them. "This was just a dream though wasn't it...? I mean Robbie wasn't really there because we could see him in the circle."

Jett gave her a sort of wincing look. "In our world things are not quite that simple, that Dark One took the essence of Robbie to the other side and recreated a wood like Loxley. She somehow had captured the essence of Hearne and then her power played it into Robbie's mind; can you sort of grasp that?"

Alice nodded. "I suppose so."

Jett continued. "If she had killed Hearne in the dream or Robbie, the shock to their body would have been so horrific, that they would have died here."

"I see... Yes, that makes sense to me, so when Rune spliced with Robbie her spirit sort of entered him, and she then used his mind to find the dream, which let her into the world?"

Jett nodded. "It's not quite that simple, but to be honest even I find it hard to explain."

"I think I get the idea of it; I didn't know you know? They kept it so quiet. I had no idea that Rune had all these powers, I mean there was a weird thing with lights in the woods on the way here; I just wish she had trusted me and told me." Ruby placed her hand on Alice's back.

"Do not be disheartened Alice, Rune had no idea of the power she really had until last night, I felt the surprise inside her, so Rune could not have told you if she wanted to."

"I suppose not." Alice sighed.

The clatter of hooves sounded in the courtyard outside. Robbie was talking to Fish. "All I know is that it is a very big Cathedral, so it must have a balcony, and we have to find a way of getting up there so we have a high enough position to strike from, without plans Fish it will be impossible."

"My dear Lord Robert." Robbie looked up and smiled. He put his arm on Fish's as if to say we will continue later, and he stood up. Skip was soaking from the heavy rain and dripped all over the floor as he walked the full length of the main hall.

Robbie embraced him warmly. "Skip my friend it is good to see you." He smiled a broad grin and leaned back to look at his face. "Did I not tell you that you would be the hero of your own city?" He pulled him close and patted his back. "I am so pleased Skip, we heard all about it."

Robbie broke apart from him. "Thanks Robbie, it was nice to get it back I owe you big."

"You owe me nothing, we are friends and friends help each other." Rune came over and gave him a close hug.

"Oh, Skip it's good to see you so soon."

"Likewise, Runestone, I know it's only been a few days but its felt like much longer... Hi Guys." The whole group sat at the table and smiled. Robbie gave Fuse a hug.

"Nice to have you both back in the fold my friend."

"It is very nice to see you too Robbie."

Jett leaned forward on to the balcony rail. "Aye, aye girls what have we here?" She peered down at the new figure stood behind Skip and Fuse as Robbie welcomed Skip. "He is quite the dandy in his frills and his long black coat."

Alice leaned on the rail. "Oh, I don't know, I think he is sort of hunky, he looks like a pirate. I love pirates; I've read every book ever written about them."

"Looks a little sort of girlie to me, maybe Robbie should watch himself." Jett laughed as Alice scowled at her, and then looked back down. "I wonder who he is."

Skip turned. "Robbie, we have brought someone who has been trying to reach you for some time. This is Jacques Phillips; he is the Ambassador to York."

Martin leaned over to John. "He's a big'un; we might have a playmate for Hog." John gave an evil grin.

"Jacques this is Lord Robert of Loxley." Robbie stepped forward and put out his hand.

"It is a pleasure to meet you Ambassador; York has been in my thoughts a lot recently." Robbie grabbed his large hand and shook it.

"My Lord, I cannot tell you what a honour it is to finally meet you, I have heard many things about you sir." Jacques beamed as he shook Robbie's hand.

"Most of what they say is lies, isn't it lads?" He winked at John. "If you please Ambassador this is the Lady Runestone of Loxley."

Rune smiled as he took her hand and kissed it. "My Lady the pleasure is all mine."

"Oh... Ambassador, it is very nice to meet you, won't you please remove your wet coat and join us," she waved to the table.

Jett giggled from the balcony. "I bet that raised her goosebumps, god he is smooth I will give him that."

Flash chuckled as Alice watched him slide his coat down and throw it on to a chair. "Corr... he's a dish." She beamed with her chin on the rail. Jett's face appeared very close to hers.

"Alice you are not serious are you? I would rather do it with Hog; at least he is a manly man... Well, that's as long as you don't have to breathe near him."

Alice's eyes moved to look at Jett. "Don't you think he is sort of sophisticated?"

Jett snorted. "Who wants that? I want a hunk with muscles and the fencing skills of my mum, fearless and rugged."

"Well, if you are not interested Jett, that means I can have the field clear for me." She watched from the balcony.

"So, Ambassador tell me of York, I have heard interesting stories of local governors and a very well-run city for trade."

"Yes, My Lord. My father was very quick to spot the potential for trade and provided more than adequate facilities for them, as a result it has brought a great deal of goods into the city and allowed us the benefits of links to the rest of the country. My father has spent most of his life in politics, and really it was just an extension of his own life to introduce government at a local level from day one, we are all very proud of his achievements and the city is thriving."

Robbie sat back and thought for a moment. "Your success is why Mason has targeted you, just as he has us at Loxley. We appear to both have the same problem Ambassador; we are too successful it appears."

"I think you are right Lord Loxley, which is why I have been trying to contact you for several months now. We knew this was coming and have been trying to organise some sort of resistance to Knox, it has not been easy, he has us almost surrounded, but we have been sending out raiding parties and have had some limited success."

They talked until quite late, when Rune reminded Robbie that he needed to rest,

Robbie was starting to look tired and when he had left, the others continued to talk. Alice fell asleep on the balcony her head perched on the rail.

Robbie established very quickly that York was a fortress and hard to attack, but what worried him was that the people of the city were exactly that. There were no woodsmen in York; all of Mason's men were now camped in the vast forested area that had grown around the south of the city.

Jacques impressed Robbie; he was a good tactician in warfare and listened carefully to what Fuse had to say. He could see strong understanding between them, by the end of the evening, Robbie had taken the measure of him, and as Rune slipped into bed beside him, he asked. "What do you think of him?"

"I found him very down to earth and likeable once he dropped all the lord and ladies' bit, he is very well educated, and certainly knows a lot about what is going on in this country. I think he will be useful; he certainly doesn't like Mason."

She snuggled down. "Can we trust him Rune?"

"Only time will tell, I hope so for Alice's sake."

Robbie looked down at her. "What has Alice got to do with him?"

Rune smiled. "Didn't you see her up on the balcony?"

"No."

"She never took her eyes off him once all night... Bless her, I think she is more than a little interested in our new Ambassador, you better find him a name and quick, the lads will only accept him if he is named."

Robbie sat confused; this man had to join because Alice fancied him, and not because he was useful. He shook his head and slid down to cuddle up to Rune, there were times when he found the whole female thing far too confusing.

It was late the following morning when Robbie and Rune woke. Jade brought them some breakfast, and they sat in bed talking as the rain bounced off the windows, Robbie was forced into wearing more lordly attire when Rune pointed out his pants and top were starting to stink, and she sent Jade off to the kitchens with his clothes to be washed. Robbie scowled at the thought.

Everyone looked up when he appeared at the top of the stairs wearing an open burgundy shirt and black pants. He looked very much like a wealthy lord, even though he had only his sword belt and boots on with them. Rune had sat and brushed his hair, something he loved and now all groomed and neat he came down to his men.

The heavy rain prevented any of them from going outside and they had all been talking when the subject of wrestling had been raised. It had appeared that Jacques two older brothers had seen wrestling when they lived in Canada, and had when Jacques was born shown him all the moves. He was now a very competent opponent, and he was as yet undefeated.

Robbie came down to the main hall to find the group excitedly gathered as

Jacques and Hog stripped down to their trousers, where twisting and grappled each other in a make shift ring, as Fish umpired the competition. Jacques grunted as he twisted and threw Hog in the air off him.

Harry sat sweating on a chair and beaming with delight having beaten Hog once, and losing to Jacques four times. Martin did point out that Hog had not really been ready and had won on all five other occasions with Harry.

Jacques was very muscular, and it appeared very strong as he slammed Hog down to the floor. His dark olive skin glowed with the sweat, as Hog writhed and twisted and wriggled free. Jacques showed no fear at all as Hog who was large and ferocious came back at him quickly. He grabbed Hog, and spun him and pulled him up in the air, and squeezed him in his arms as a giant grizzly bear would. Hog soon found himself flat on the floor and Fish counted him out as the whoops and cheers arose from the group.

Robbie did notice how Alice seemed to be the one making most of the noise as she cheered for Jacques. John peeled off his shirt and entered the ring as Rune came down and sat at the table.

She smiled as she saw all the happy faces of the group as they laughed and joked as John made his way menacingly towards Jacques. "It's good to see them letting off steam again; being cooped up here is not much fun for them."

"Are you not enjoying yourself here?" Robbie looked at her as he raised a cup and took a drink. She smiled at him for noting how quickly he seized up on her comments.

"I miss home, and although I never thought I would say it, I miss my loom and weaving. I have seen some lovely things here, and I have had some great ideas for clothing, especially for you." She watched him as she spoke. "Don't you miss it Robbie? Tell me you cannot wait to walk in the greenhouses, or wander down to Joe's cabin and hunt in the woods round Loxley."

Robbie put down his cup and sighed. "It has been seventeen days since we left, and yes there has not been a day pass that I have not thought of Loxley." She slid her hand over to his and gave it a squeeze.

The group roared as John lifted Jacques into the air and slammed him to the floor. He wriggled quickly back to his feet, with surprising agility for a man of his size. The crowd cheered as the two faced each other and prowled around in a circle looking for their opportunity.

Robbie looked at the large arched windows and watched the streaks of rain running down them. "It would be nice to be under the leaves today, I do not mind the rain too much."

Rowan walked laughing up the hall as he watched John wriggle and squirm, as Jacques tried to push him to the floor. Rowan moved the heavy sword down the table as he slid down next to Robbie and Rune. "How are you two feeling now?" Rune smiled.

"I think we are recovering well; I feel a great deal stronger and as you can see, Robbie actually has some colour in his face today."

Robbie nodded and patted him on the shoulder. "I feel fine now Rowan, why do you ask? I can see you have something in mind."

Rowan leaned in to them. "We are having a lot of trouble getting information on Knox, but it appears that a lot of the church members are starting to travel to Canterbury. Robbie the time must be near and I think we should consider moving soon."

Robbie thought deeply as he watched the others. "I must admit I had hoped to be on route by now."

Rowan looked at the group and then back to the two of them. "Skip appears to be here for a while, he has left his cousin Rupert in charge in Gloucester, and so I thought if we have him, why not use him."

"You mean sail round to Canterbury?" Rune looked at Robbie as she spoke; it appeared she had the same in mind as Rowan. "It will give you more time to rest and we will be undetected and safe."

Robbie looked at the two of them. "I am fine; I wish you would all stop trying to mother me, but yes if it makes you all happy, we will ask Skip if it can be done, I do enjoy sailing actually, it is sort of a new thing for me going on water."

"It does make more sense Robbie. We have too much attention here, and if we can sneak out and sneak back in on the other side of the country it will give us quite an advantage." Rowan watched Robbie as he spoke.

"I must admit Rowan it seems everywhere we go people pop up, look at the last trip out we almost got ambushed by woodsmen. This friend of Harry's has offered us her farm to lay low, so if we can get as close to there as possible and then sneak in it will be useful. I want some time watching to size things up before going in."

Rune smiled as John pinned Jacques down and everybody cheered. "Knox will be prepared for this one; we must have upset him a lot recently. I would imagine he will have half his army lying in wait."

Robbie frowned. "I know, I have been thinking that, but his army will be all round the outside, whereas we want to be on the inside. We have to find a way past his forces and into the cathedral, and we will need to be inside early and lie low in wait. Have you ever heard of sewers?" Robbie looked at them as if he had just mentioned some everyday item.

Rune shook her head, so did Rowan. "No, what's a sewer?"

Robbie leaned in very close and talked quietly. "Sewers are apparently big tunnels under all the major cities, Harry and Pete used to use them when they were selling moonshine. They would swap the moonshine for gold, and then go round a corner out of sight and drop down these sewers to escape. It appears most of the gangs they dealt with always wanted to come after them and rob their gold back. Harry and Pete always got out of the cities using them, so what if we use them to get in and out of the cathedral?"

"It sounds alright, but I would want to see one and how it works. I am not keen on being trapped in the dark underground." Rowan leaned back as the others started to head back to the table with a victorious John.

Jacques patted John on the back. "That is my first defeat in ten years, congratulations my friend you fight with great heart. Lord Loxley good morning, you have a group of strong able fighters, I have never met such men of skill and ability; I have felt my equal here, which is not something I have in York."

"You fight well ambassador you are quite the sportsman."

Scarlet walked up the hall. "Rune darling can I have a quiet word?" Scarlet looked startled as she glanced down at the table. "Whose swords, are they?"

Robbie looked at the large handle encrusted with fine jewels sticking out of the sheath of the sword in front of his.

Jacques turned and looked up at her. "That is the sword of my father; it has been in my household for hundreds of years. Would you like to see it?"

Scarlet looked a little shaken. "Not yet, and who owns that other sword?"

"Oh, that's mine sorry, I usually keep it in my room, but Jacques here was going to chance his arm with me and a little sword play." Skip looked apologetic as he lifted it off the highly polished table.

Scarlet turned to Robbie. "I need to talk to all three of you and Rune now. Bring your swords." She turned and hurried from the main hall. "Jett!"

Robbie looked puzzled at Rune. "Have we upset her?" Rune shrugged.

"I have no idea; something bothered her though, I felt it. I suppose we should go and see."

The four of them got up and Jacques slipped on his shirt, and they walked down the main hall and over to the conference room. Scarlet stood outside the door as Jett ran up with a large bundle of cloth in her hands.

Scarlet looked at them all. "Follow me." She turned, and abruptly walked down a slim corridor that seemed to go down in a gradient underground, parallel to the great hall. It was dimly lit and at the right far end was a thick wooden door. Scarlet pulled a heavy golden key out of her pocket and unlocked the door.

"In there!" She stood holding the door as they all turned left; under what was the steps above in the main hall. They walked into a large room and Scarlet turned on a light, Robbie screwed up his eyes, he was not used to electric light and it seemed very bright at first and his eyes had to get used to it.

Rune smiled as she looked on the symbol of her family. Robbie looked at his hand and the ring given him on his birthday by Rune, she smiled at him and her eyes sparkled as she came over to him.

In the centre of the room was a huge round table of highly polished stone. It was white with a huge five-pointed star of different colours, set on a white background, the edge of the outer circle was black and edged with solid gold, and the whole table seemed to shine in the bright light.

Scarlet took Skip by the arm and led him round the table; she stood him in front of one of the star points, which was coloured white and outlined in a fine black line. "Take out your sword and lay it with the tip of the sword at the point of the star, with the hilt pointing to the centre of the table." She then led Jacques to a violet coloured point of the star. "Take out your sword and do likewise." Rune walked Robbie round to the top of the star that was a black colour. He slid out his sword and laid it on the table, as Scarlet unrolled the cloth in Jett's hands, and withdrew a bright golden sword and laid it down on the red point of the star then stood back.

"Gentlemen I am Lady Scarlet, keeper and guardian of the table of swords, you have been sent here to me not by chance but by destiny, all of you were chosen a long time ago for this time and this task, and as proof you were destined to receive the five remaining swords of power."

Robbie looked at the other two who looked at each other confounded. Scarlet walked over to Robbie. "The Sword of Truth once owned by Gawain knight of the round table." Scarlet touched his shoulder and then walked on to Skip. "The sword of justice, once owned by Gaheris who was wronged by Gawain, and was sent to Arthur who knighted him and set him the task of bringing fair play to the court." She touched Skip's arm and walked on to the sword lay on the red point. "The Sword of Knowledge, a sword never once used in combat for it belonged to Merlin who had no need of weapons of man. This sword has yet to be passed to its true owner; it is held in my keep until all the swords are placed here. Scarlet walked round to the next point of violet and Jacques. "The Sword of Courage as handled by the very brave Sir Tor who was valiant in all that he did." She rested her hand on Jacque's shoulder; she walked on to the last star point, which was green and stopped.

"The last sword is missing, the sword of honour. It was carried by a man who lost his and fought his way back through redemption and pain, to finally in the last moments of his life recover the high honour he once held, and seek his lord's forgiveness, the lost sword of Sir Lancelot."

Robbie looked at the four swords and their owners. "What does this all mean?"

Rune walked up to the table. "I am sapphire blue the centre of the circle, and when all swords are placed all of you will be linked together through me."

Robbie looked at the centre where all the points of the stars met and formed a bright blue pentangle; Rune came up to his side. "All of you will soon have a guardian of your sword. Black is Jett who is present. White is Crystal who is hidden, red is Ruby who is almost ready, violet is Amethyst who is also hidden, and green is Jade who will come when the sword is found."

Scarlet walked back to the table. "These swords are swords of power only given to those who can wield them fairly; they have the power to defend what is right for this land. I have lived in fear that they would not come in my time, so my heart was shocked today, but now it rejoices to know that soon you will all gather together and help lead this country to balance and harmony." Robbie felt a little lost, looking at the others he felt they too felt the same; Scarlet lowered her voice and smiled at them.

"Gentlemen welcome to this table, for now you are amongst us we will meet regularly to discuss with each other the affairs of this land. You're all now the true heirs of this kingdom charged with one task and one task alone."

Jacques looked across at Robbie and then over to Skip; he swallowed hard and looked at Scarlet. "What is this single task we must do My Lady?"

Scarlet smiled. "It is now your task to share power, and find the last sword. When that is done and the true identity is revealed to me of the owner of the sword of knowledge, your task then will be to find and set up the true King of Britain."

Rune walked up to Scarlet's side. "We have an impostor who is about to set himself down on the throne. We must leave for Canterbury and at all costs, we must stop him, a war is coming my heirs, and now we must act fast and swift to ensure that we lead it and we win it. The true king is coming and when the time is right, we will set him where he belongs, on the throne of this land."

Robbie looked over at Rune and she nodded to him, he looked at the other two. "Skip I want you to go down to the harbour and ready the yacht, we are planning a little sailing trip, and if this bloody weather will just lift we will hopefully set sail just before dawn."

"Excellent Robbie, where are we sailing to?"

"I want you to plot a course that takes us round the south of this country and brings us round to Canterbury. Can you do that?"

"No problem, we are sailing not riding, how wonderful."

"I think considering our rising popularity round here it is the best way of just disappearing for a while, and keep Mason in the dark a little while longer."

Jacques looked to Robbie. "My Lord what should I do?"

"Firstly, Jacques you can stop calling me My Lord every minute, its Robbie. I only ever use the title lord at home, or if I want to shout at someone or gain advantage for my men. You will be coming with us; it appears my good man you have been chosen to play your part. Although if you are coming with us we must first find you a suitable title lets go and see what the rest of the outfit think."

They gathered their swords and headed out of the room; Jett came up to Robbie's side. "Hey Robbie how cool is this I am the guardian of your sword, if anything happens to you, I get to inherit it." She beamed up at him and he looked cautiously down at her.

"I think you said that a little too joyfully for my liking Jett." Rune started to giggle and he put his arm around Jett. "Great why is it I never get the quiet one?"

Rune put her arm around him and smiled. "Look on the bright side you haven't got Jade." Robbie smiled.

"I do not see the difference." Jett beamed up at him as she looked at him.

"I know you love me really Robbie."

Robbie walked into the main hall as Rags passed out letters to everyone in the group. She looked tired and exhausted, but she turned and bowed as he entered and held up a large bunch of letters, Alice stood smiling by her side.

Robbie looked at her as he took the letters from her and then to Alice. "I see she's met Beth and mum. Aren't those my old boots? That is definitely Billy's old cloak." He smiled. "I would think you are dryer and warmer, what is your name postie?"

"I am Michelle, but everyone calls me Rags My Lord."

Robbie put his hand in his pocket and pulled out four golden bits. "There you go, as promised payment for a job well done; there is an extra one there for being first back."

"Begging your pardon My Lord, but I don't want it."

Robbie looked surprised. "Rags you have earned this fair and square; I am very impressed that you have been to Loxley and back in very difficult conditions so fast. You really have excelled, and you deserve your fair wage."

Rags put her head down. "You have a very kind family My Lord. They fed me and washed me, and made my hair nice and gave me new clothes. I felt proud to deliver their letters after what they did. Your mum is the sweetest person I ever knew, and they have a room for me so I can just ride to Loxley and back, I don't want your money My Lord because they has paid me ten times over with kindness." She looked up and she had tears in her eyes. Rune smiled and put her arm across her shoulder.

"The people of Loxley have done that for many families Rags, which is what makes Loxley so special to all of us. You have earned your wages for doing the most dangerous of all the runs, do not offend your Lord Loxley by refusing what he gladly gives."

"I would never offend such a great lord My Lady." Rune placed the money into her hand.

"Here go to the kitchen and have a meal, and then we will find you a bed, you look exhausted. I am sure there will be other letters for Lord Loxley's personal messenger later."

Rags wiped her eyes. "Thank you, My Lady." She left the hall and was guided to the kitchen by Matthews.

Rune slid her arm around Robbie. "Another fan, you are building quite a club Robbie." Robbie smiled at her.

"Yeah, but there is only one fan I truly want." Rune smiled and shook her head. "God you can be smooth when you want to."

Robbie looked laughing at the others. "Listen up everyone, we set sail just before dawn tonight, so read your mail and then prepare, I want everyone on board by two. Full kit and clean your weapons, we have another surprise visit for our dear old friend, you will all be briefed on board." Everyone nodded. "Our ambassador will be joining us as a new recruit so I expect you all to welcome him into the fold, he will be known as Bear from now on. I feel he tends to hug like one."

Everyone started to laugh as Alice leaned over to Jett. "Oh god I hope he does," and they both started to giggle.

Robbie looked down at Blades who was sat reading a letter. "Has someone written to you Blades?"

She smiled a large happy smile. "I have Aunties." She lifted the two letters. "Auntie Beth and Auntie Jess. They have sent me really nice letters Robbie, they sound wonderful."

He crouched down. "Beth is one of the nicest and kindest people I have ever known. Alice is very like her you know, and my mum, well she is going to love you and spoil you so much Blades, you will love Loxley it's a very special place."

Blades beamed with happiness. "I really can't wait to see it; dad had told me so much about it. It is a very special place for him, he always talks about it."

"It's home for him and home for me, and soon it will be home for you, there is no place at all like it. Finish your letters and I will see you later." He kissed her on the head as he winked at Harry who sat with a large smile on his face.

Robbie sat in his room and read the letters from his parents. Talking to Blades and reading their words, he missed them more than ever, and he felt the pangs of home in his stomach. He had been away too long, and he wanted to return as soon as he could, he put the letter down as Rune slid smiling beside him. "Missing it aren't you?"

He smiled and pulled her close. "I want to get back soon Rune; I belong in the north its home.

CHAPTER TWENTY THREE

THE VILLAGE ON HONEY HILL

By eleven that evening, Robbie was sat at the table with Rowan and Skip, looking at the maps. "Where the hell is Honey Hill?" His eyes scoured the map all around Canterbury.

Rowan and Skip leaned over and stared down. "Isn't that it with a love heart drawn round it?" Skip smiled. "I am assuming this is a cosmic place?"

Rowan and Robbie smiled at each other, and Robbie peered down, there very faintly on the map in small black print was printed Honey Hill. "He is so like a child at times, fancy putting a bloody love heart round it. Alright now we know where the place is, Skip how close can you get us?" He slid the map round so that Skip could get a better view.

"I know the estuary relatively well, although it has been some time since I was over there. The water is deep around Whitstable although I will have to avoid the bay. I don't want to ground her; it will all depend on the harbour and what condition it is in. it might be better Robbie to drop anchor and come in using the row boats."

"You don't fancy the harbour then? We would be really exposed in small boats."

"It's not that, it is more a case of keeping the yacht secure, that area was hit badly. There really is not much left down that whole coastline, everything is destroyed. There were many fires and a great deal of that coastline was burnt to the ground. It is grown very wild, apart from Canterbury, obviously the church used a great deal of resources to protect it, but there really is not that much left. It is one very big green and wooded space."

Robbie sat back and thought for a moment. "Green and wooded I like, that is my kind of area, it will help us to disappear. As for the yacht, it is your vessel Skip, you command the waves and we will go with your judgement on it. We will have the two small boats so we can drop a landing party and then follow with the rest of us if we have too. I do expect to run into a few unfriendly faces, I will expect Knox to be on the lookout."

Rowan studied the map carefully; Robbie could see he was already looking for escape routes and ways into the city, it was something that had always impressed him about Rowan, he liked the way he would learn as much as he could beforehand, and he worked things out in the same way as Robbie. Out of the entire group, Rowan was the one he found a deep bond with.

Members of the group were starting to appear as they prepared, and one by one they came down and dropped off their bags. They sat at the table and helped themselves to drinks. Rune and Alice came down the steps with Rags, she was looking a lot better now she had been fed and rested. Rune smiled as she approached the table, Rags saw the letter on the table and opened her bag as she came up to Robbie. "Feeling better now Rags?"

"Yes thank you, My Lord." Rags smiled as he passed her the letter.

Robbie slid the map across the table. "I need this letter here before I get there, I will be leaving at dawn. Do you know this place?" Rags looked down at the map and studied the area. She pulled a pencil out of her bag and a small piece of paper and made a very small copy of the map.

"I know the church place, had loads of letters from them about that king thing on May 1st, so it will not be hard to find this, I am pretty well known over there because of it, so I will get through no problems."

Robbie looked at Rags with an unusual look in his eye, and Rowan was staring at her. "What king thing is that Rags?"

She looked at Rowan. "You know the big parade with him on May 1st. we have been rushed off our feet taking invites out all over the bloody place, its why them Cutters have been leaving us be."

Robbie grabbed her and gave her a huge kiss. "Rags you are an absolute angel."

Rags looked stunned. "You ain't to bad yourself Robin Hood." She touched her lips. "Corr you just snogged me."

Robbie looked with glee at Rowan and grabbed his hand. "Yes, we have got him right where we want him." Rowan carried a broad grin.

"We have six days to prepare."

Robbie turned back to Rags. "Ok Rags, get that letter to Maggs at Honey Hill as fast as you can and wait there for us to arrive."

She gave him a huge smile and winked. "That Rune chick is a lucky gal, see you in a bit." She spun round as the entire outfit started to laugh, and she ran to her horse in the yard and jumped on, and with a clatter of hooves she was gone.

Robbie was suddenly in very high spirits as Rune slid her arms round him. "I need to keep a closer eye on you, My Lord."

He pulled her tightly up to him and gave her a long slow kiss. John and Martin whistled slowly, she was impressed as he slowly released her and caught her breath. "Wow!" Violet flickered in her eyes.

Robbie smiled. "Still worried?"

"Phew... No." She fanned herself with her hand.

"Rune we have him, finally we have him, we know where and when, all that needs to be done is to alert everyone, and we can start to push him back into the sea.”

She was happy to see him smiling again and she pulled him close, his eyes danced as she gazed deeply into them. “I am so happy for you Robbie.”

“Oh, Rune do you know what this means? Just another week and with luck we can go home.” He squeezed her tight and swung her round, it had an overwhelming effect on the others, who somehow were all bitten with his happiness and spirits rose higher.

The journey down to the yacht was not the quiet affair they had planned. Loaded up with all their weapons and their shoulder bags they joyfully walked down to the harbour and the waiting smiles of Skip, who as always had a hive of activity preparing the yacht for sea.

The rain seemed to have eased a little and everyone headed below decks and into the cabins to settle down for the night. Rowan sat on a chair and stared out at the clouds as Jade curled up on his knee, and Robbie made his way to the cabin where Rune was already slipping into the cabin bed.

Robbie lay in the dark looking out of the tiny porthole at the clouds that were lit by the moon as they passed below it. The boat gently rocked and Rune breathed softly beside him, he felt a strong sense of relief as if everything that had been building to this point was now finally about to happen. He looked down at the sleeping Rune in the dark, the moon lit her pale face and light bounced through her hair and he smiled to himself. Happy and relaxed he slowly drifted into sleep.

The sound of seagulls called in his head, and he heard the flapping of the sails above him as he opened his eyes. Rune sat smiling and brushing her hair humming quietly to herself, in front of the small mirror on the little dresser. He closed his eyes and listened to her, as he lay happily in the bed. She came over and sat beside him, he felt her soft warm lips on his and he opened his eyes.

“I promised Mum I would help with breakfast, come on sleepyhead get up and help us.” It was a little while later when Robbie sat on deck with the others all eating fried eggs, bacon and tomatoes as the yacht bobbed along far out to sea. Skip had taken a wide course to avoid being detected, and as the yacht with its sails bellowing in the wind skimmed through the waves, Robbie enjoyed the company of his group of companions, and the wind through his hair.

He finished his food and headed up to the wheel. Jacques was at the wheel whilst Skip ate just behind him, John and Martin sat back with their fishing rods over the sides as they tried for a catch. Robbie soon realised money was at stake as Martin tried to convince John his line would catch first.

His eyes scanned around, and for as far as he could see there was nothing but crashing waves and grey skies, it was surprising to him considering his woodland roots, that he enjoyed sailing so much. Maybe it was the excitement of something so different, or maybe he just knew that sailing was the cutting edge of the force of nature, Skip looked up and smiled.

"I thought we would put down anchor just short of the estuary and wait for dusk when we get there. It will give us a little cover and make us less obvious going in."

Robbie nodded. "You're the skipper, and this is your domain my friend."

The afternoon was spent above deck. Rune brought some cushions and blankets up on deck, and they sat together having close time, which to be honest they had not had a great deal of. The last few days they had been together but Robbie and Rune had been so exhausted that they kept drifting in and out of sleep. She curled around him, they talked softly, about Loxley, and the farm and her weaving, and clothes making, he began to see a different side of her.

It was more of the homely side of her that enjoyed cooking and clothes designing. Rune had a great knowledge of garden plants and she talked about the sort of garden she had always wanted to create, Rune also wrote poetry and short stories she would read to Jade, Robbie listened fascinated as she revealed the other side of her life to that of her role with her woodsman.

As dusk began to descend the yacht silently slipped down the channel and headed past Herne Bay towards Whitstable, Robbie watched with his telescope as they passed the crumbled ruins of all the towns. There were no signs of fire or smoke, just an endless line of looming green sculptures where nature had dressed all that had remained after the long fires. "It looks dead Skip, but it is your vessel sing out when you are ready."

Robbie walked down the deck checking that everyone had all their things. "Ok all of you; I want Rowan, Jade, John, Martin and Alice off first. Get into the trees and clear the area, I want to make sure we have total security before completely leaving the yacht. All of you should now be aware that from now on the area we travel in is to be regarded as highly hostile, stay sharp and keep your wits about you."

Skip decided to take the yacht up to the quayside. The first mate steered the vessel alongside it and the first group jumped off and ran into the trees. The rest followed and crouched low, Rowan gave the signal, and the first mate gave his orders, as Robbie and the others headed into the trees that had now taken over the whole town.

The yacht was to drop anchor at a safe distance and wait, Robbie moved closer to Rowan. They gathered their bearings and agreed the fastest route, and Rowan led off with Jade and Jett close by. Harry and Martin watched the rear as everyone else fanned out either side, they moved silently in the growing dimness as the light began to fall.

They quickly got the lay of the land and by using Flash; Rune could project the paths up in front to Jett, Jade, and Steph. Keeping everyone in a close group, they were able to work through the dark until the trees broke and they found themselves on the edge of wide-open meadows. The sky was clear and the moon was full, Rowan looked at Robbie. "That's a lot of open space between here and the next line of trees to get caught out in."

He watched the long grass as it swirled and swayed from left to right, carried by the breeze in the silvery moonlight, it looked so peaceful and beautiful, yet he was not so stupid as to realise it was the ideal spot for a trap. Robbie agreed.

"How about you and Jade scout ahead, and we will hold back here until we know?"

The grass was long and they both disappeared into it, Jade literally disappeared as she faded away crawling forward. Two guards sat watching the open ground in amongst the leafy shrubs at the edge of the clearing. "What the hell are we doing sat here in the dark? Three bloody days doing nothing but sit and watch birds eat flies, I tell you Stan if he is going to come it will not be this way."

"Suits me Bob, I have no wish to meet him, just being on that road and being almost blown up was enough for me. I don't care who the king is as long as I get paid."

Stan nodded in the dark. "Yeah mate, we are better off here, nice and safe."

The silver dagger touched his chin. "So, you would not want to die for your king?" Stan swallowed hard.

"I don't want to die at all," he squeaked.

Bob was very quiet and Stan began to panic. "You haven't killed Bob, have you? He was a decent bloke; he only joined because they said they would kill his kids."

"Bob is fine and will continue to be so unless he makes the mistake of not doing as he is told." Bob fell out of the trees bound, gagged, and hit the ground with a muffled thump. Jade fell like a cat silently beside him. She smiled at Stan.

"Bad night or what?" She peered around through the dark.

Rowan's voice came from behind Stan. "It's Stanley, isn't it?" Stan nodded slowly; he did not want to make a fast movement with a silver dagger at his throat. "Alright Stanley tell me this... Is this it, or are there more of you?"

Stanley was so frightened that his voice was almost impossible to hear. "It's just us ... Honestly." Jade slid her bow round and pulled it over her head, she pulled an arrow out of the quiver, and Stan closed his eyes and waited to die, as he shook from head to foot. Jade pulled back the string and fired, the arrow whistled over the meadow and landed in the grass just short of Robbie. He leaned forward and pulled it from the dirt, and slid it back into his quiver.

He gave the hand signals and the group moved silently in pairs into the grass. Stan opened one eye and realised he was still alive, Jade looked down at the large wet stain in his groin. "I did that once, makes your legs sore if you don't change fast." She smiled and slipped into the bushes, Stan saw other figures creeping past and then a hooded figure rose out of the grass in front of him.

Robbie crouched down. "Well, what have we here?"

"This is Stan, Robbie."

"Not a good place to be on guard tonight Stan, I see we surprised you a little." He looked at Stan's wet pants.

"What do you want doing with them Robbie?" Robbie glanced at the two eyes staring from above the gag round Bob's mouth.

"Oh, please sir show mercy... We are just a couple of farmers, we mean you no harm, you have no choice round here sir, if you don't join em they kill your kids, please sir I beg you, Bob here has a family."

Bear crawled up and his huge frame rose out of the ground like a mountain. "I don't mind carrying one of them, if Hog will the other." Robbie nodded as a gag appeared around Stan's mouth; his arms were drawn around his back and tied. Bear looked down at the two of them. "Hog gets the wet one." He grabbed Bob, and threw him over his shoulder and walked into the trees.

The ground began to slowly rise, and Robbie knew that soon a road would be reached; it was then just a case of cross the road and up the hill to the farm. A moss and weed filled barrier appeared in front of them, it had to be the wall that once marked a clear edge to the roadside. Robbie scratched with his knife and stone appeared, this was the road, it was just the rows of trees twenty feet wide that made it confusing.

He slipped over the wall with Rowan, and wove through the dense trees. There was the wall on the other side of the road, they carefully slipped over and into a line of young saplings, and then there were the fields, and the one in front was planted with rows of cabbages. The farm was some way up the hill; he could see a pale light in one of the windows, he was just about to move when he spotted a pair of eyes staring out from the cabbages. They glistened in the moonlight, one winked, there was movement and Rags sat up. Rowan had not spotted her and stepped back bringing up his bow. Robbie stretched out his hand to Rowan's arm. "It's Rags."

She crawled out from the cabbages. "You took your bloody time; I have been sat here half the night."

Robbie knew something was wrong. "What is it Rags?"

She pointed a dark thumb backwards. "There are ten of them with Maggs and her mum. I was in the stable when they turned up and slipped out here, I heard em say something bout you might come this way, and they wanted somewhere to hide in case you did."

Robbie patted her cheek. "Thanks Rags we owe you one."

Rags smiled a cheeky smile. "Wot no kiss?" She winked and Robbie gave a chuckle.

The problem was they were in the house, and he was not sure where. They could not just storm into the house because they would be going in blind. He looked at the others, Rowan stared at the house. "We can't use bows inside it is just too close, we need to draw them out, but again not knowing where they are, we will need every window covering."

"Or we can use the vests on those guys to pretend like we are their own men and just walk in and throttle them. I do not need anything if I move fast and stand still quickly." Jade smiled, she had a great point, she was invisible and Robbie and Rowan had two black vests with red dragons on to prove they were the good guys.

Ten minutes later Martin, Alice, and John slipped along the wall of the road up to the house. Jett, Rune, Rags, and Blades came quietly through the cabbage fields to the rear of the house and took up position in the yard hiding in dark corners.

Robbie and Rowan walked noisily up the road wearing two newly acquired black vests with red dragons on the front, as they approached the door a face popped round it. "Who the bloody hell are you two? Keep the sodding noise down, all right?"

Rowan smiled. "What kind of memory have you got; I thought you would never have forgotten us two, don't you remember us?" He started to laugh and looked at Robbie. "He has no idea." He turned back to the puzzled looking guard. "We are the ones who blew up your boss's house."

His neck clicked as Jade twisted, and he fell silently to the floor, Rowan and Robbie, walked in wearing big smiles. They pushed open the door to the Kitchen, where an older woman with pink hair and a woman of about forty with long blonde curly hair and buck teeth, sat quietly at the table looking very nervous.

Two guards stood by the window holding cups in their hands, Rowan smiled at them. "Great the pot has boiled; you know it is getting quite cold out there, froze my butt off tonight." The other two nodded as he walked past and lifted two cups. Robbie came up behind Rowan; it was fast and painless, as they slipped down to the floor dead. Robbie put his finger to his lips as the blonde curly haired woman brought her hands to her mouth.

He winked. "I am assuming you are Maggs?" She nodded. "Robert of Loxley, nice to meet you... Now tell me are the others upstairs?" There was a heavy bump on the floor, Robbie's eyes moved up to look at the ceiling. "No matter I think Pebbles has found one."

There were footsteps across from a room in the front, to the room above them. It was silent for a second and then there was another bump, Robbie looked back at Rowan. "You know hanging out with you she is becoming very good don't you think?"

Maggs touched Robbie's arm and swallowed. "There are like three in the barn."

Robbie winked, and then smiled as he looked at Rowan. "That still leaves two, where the hell are they?"

Robbie stepped carefully out of the back door; he looked around before stepping forward. Rune leaned forward her bow in her hand into the moonlight and winked; she moved back and disappeared into the shadows.

Rowan and Robbie walked into the yard with three hot cups of coffee; they walked over to the barn and slid the doors open. "Brews up lads, come on get em while they are hot." As the three men walked down the centre of the barn smiling and rubbing their hands, Robbie and Rowan stepped aside opening a wide gap.

Three arrows, two from Rune and one from Alice, shot through the gap between Robbie and Rowan, and the soldiers buckled, and fell to their knees and keeled over, Robbie sipped his coffee as Rune quietly rushed in, he handed her the other cup. "I was just saying to Rowan here, this is a good size barn."

She took a swig of the coffee and handed it back as she ran up the ladder. "You forgot the sugar that must be Alice's" Rowan smiled and shook his head.

"How could you forget she has sugar?"

Robbie shrugged. "I have been rushed... By the way there are two on the roof... Nope make that one." A body landed just in front of the doors. Another fell into the yard with a heavy thud. "My mistake, the roofs clear."

Hooded figures loomed out of the shadows and assembled in the yard. Harry slid down his hood, as Maggs came running out of the door and flung herself at him jangling wildly with bangles and jewellery.

"Oh, there he is my big brave baby boy." She kissed him hard on the lips as he held her tight. Everyone seemed to cringe at the sight, of her flapping frilly shawls and wild erratic hair filled with feathers and beads, and a kiss that sounded like a plunger being drawn off a sink.

"Hey baby cakes, it's like really wild and cosmic being able to rescue you with my dudes here." Maggs beamed as she slipped down Harry, she looked like a midget next to his tall frame. "Hey guys this totally radical and cosmic chicken is Maggs."

Everyone was trying their hardest to keep a straight face under their hoods, which had suddenly seemed to go back up, and they all nodded and mumbled. Rune was very quiet next to Alice, and shook slightly, Alice kicked her and a high pitched shriek came from under the hood. Maggs rattled over to Robbie with a wild smile on her face.

"Wow you really are the main man...? Robin Hood... That is oh so groovy." She nodded her head up and down as she spoke, and her earrings and necklaces of which there was a copious amount, all rattled in tune.

There were soft titters behind him, he held out his hand. "It is very good of you to offer us space. Yes I am Robbie, and this..." He turned to an empty space, where Alice and Rune had previously been, Rowan stepped forward.

"Sorry My Lord I asked Rune and Alice to secure the perimeter." He smirked.

"Thank you, Rowan. Well, it really is nice of you to offer us a place to stay, I will leave you and Baby Cakes here to get reacquainted, and take care of my men and sort out a guard for you."

"Oh, isn't he so sweet Harry?"

"Yeah man, he is like totally cosmic."

Robbie turned and walked into the barn where Rune and Alice hid in a corner and sniggered, pushing their fists in their mouths. Her bright blue eyes flashed in the dark, Robbie felt cross with her. "Rune that was not funny." She nodded her head, her fist still in her mouth as Alice shook in silent fits.

His smile broke out across his face and she leapt up and threw her arms around him laughing and giggling. Everyone came in chuckling, John patted his back, and Rowan just stood in front of him and smiled as Jade slid her arms around him. Robbie looked at them all and shrugged. "What?"

Skip came up and patted his back as Rune carried on shaking. "True diplomat Robbie, how you kept a straight face I will never know, I couldn't have done it."

Alice looked up tears in her eyes. "Told you, mad as a hatter." Everyone burst out laughing.

Robbie and Rune finally settled down in the top of the barn, she snuggled up to him and sniggered. "What now?"

Her eyes danced and her smile was big. "Oh, Robbie you can be so funny at times." She squeezed him as she started to chuckle. "I have no idea how you kept your face so straight." Titters broke out across the barn, and Rune started to shake. "I do love you, Robbie." He smiled as he pulled her close as she quietly howled into his chest.

The following morning Robbie woke to the sounds of, "chuck, chuck, chick, chick, chuck, chuck, chick, chick."

He opened his eyes to see Rune's bright blue smiling eyes watching him. "I am not going out there forget it." He turned over and closed his eyes. Rune giggled and moved toward the ladder, Robbie stretched up and looked out of the small window. Rune, Jade, and Jett walked into the yard.

"Oh my darlings, good morrow, and joyous blessings."

The three girls smiled. Maggs was in a long flowing tie-dyed yellow and lilac dress, which she had tied around the waist with long silk green shawls. Her hair stood out like a huge curly bush, with beads and feathers sparkling and flapping in the breeze. She held a huge basket of grain in her arms and she blew kisses and chucked at the chickens as she fed them. "I like to communicate with my animals, it like really builds respect you know?"

The three smiling girls nodded; Jade looked closely at the chickens. "Is it like a psychic thing?"

"Oh yeah darling." She nodded vigorously as she spoke, which made her rattle; Robbie smiled as he watched from the window. He looked back. "Hey lads Jade, Jett, and Maggs." They all beamed and got up, and crowded around the window grinning.

Jade looked at Maggs. "So, you could tell them in your mind to stand in a line and they would?"

Maggs looked uncertain. "I am not sure; I have not really tried that." Jade winked at Rune and Jett smiled.

Maggs stared at the chickens, and Rune's eyes flickered lilac and then violet. The chickens all looked at each other, and then suddenly moved to form a perfectly straight line. Maggs gasped, and lifted her hands to her mouth. "Oh wow, how cosmic is that? I have the gift."

Robbie and all the others shook with silent laughter. Jett put her head down and her shoulders shook. Jade smiled at Maggs. "You have power Maggs that is totally cosmic... Make them stand on one leg."

Maggs focused and stared at the chickens, and Rune's eyes went violet. The chickens all looked at each other and then lifted one leg in the air. Maggs went down to her knees and spoke very quietly. "I am blessed with truly cosmic energy, how groovy is that...? It's so wild."

She looked stunned; Jade knelt down by her side. "Maggs one day you will be worshipped." Maggs silently nodded. The three girls came laughing into the house and headed up to the bathroom.

Maggs walked in silently, Harry looked up. "Hey chicken." She came around the table and sat on his knee.

"Harry baby, I have discovered a higher cosmic power." She slowly nodded as she spoke and her bangles rattled.

"Whoa Chicken, that is completely now and very cosmic." Harry nodded with great understanding.

"Groovy."

It was later that morning that Maggs took them to a place where she told them they would be completely safe, and well away from prying eyes. They headed through the woods at the top of the slope, and came out in a clearing. "How groovy and radical is this?" They all looked at a wide circle of fifteen tall pointed tents. "It's my tepee village. You won't get hassled here, and you can have a big fire because the trees are so big and thick no one can see through them, how cosmic and funky is that?"

Jett looked at her. "Totally!"

Robbie smiled. She was completely bonkers but was very kind. "Maggs this is perfect, we are all very grateful thank you."

"Oh, Rune sweetheart, he is such a love isn't he, you can tell he's a Lox, as cute as my big baby boy Harry Pops."

Rune smiled. "I think so Maggs." She put her head down and bit her lip.

Everyone wandered around picking their tepee, Rowan walked passed one, and two small arms and a mass of curly blonde hair shot out, grabbed him and dragged him in, wild giggles came from inside. Rune looked at all the blankets, and shawls scattered all over the carpet inside what was a very large tent, and she pulled Robbie in, she slid her arms around him and kissed him. She dropped her bag and pulled him down to the floor. "Come here Robbie Pops." They both started giggling.

Most of the morning was spent settling in and getting the camp organised. Rowan was nowhere to be seen, and judging by the giggles from his particular tepee, everyone thought it best he was left. Martin and John skirted the forest to find that two hundred yards in was a large twelve-foot mesh fence that circled the whole camp. There was only one way in, which was via the path they had arrived on. A fire was soon burning in the large circle surrounded by huge tree trunks to sit on.

Hog sat on guard in front of one tepee, as Stan and Bob sat inside relieved at still being alive, especially after seeing the speed and efficiency with which the group had dispatched the others. Coffee pots were placed, and food was cooked, and soon the sounds of a camp were all around as everyone made themselves at home. Robbie came out of his tepee in his pants and bare feet; he fastened his shirt as he walked to the circle.

He poured a coffee and looked at Alice. "I want you to teach Bear some wood skills." He looked around for a very missing Rowan. "Where is Rowan?" They all looked up at him.

"Jade."

"Oh... alright then Alice you take Bear and give him some training, try and teach him some bow skills." She gave Robbie a huge thank you smile and skipped off. Rags was sat watching him. "What?"

"If you have no letters for me, I am just sat here, can I learn anything to help?"

"What weapons have you used?"

"Done a bit with a sword."

"Ok then, Jett can you give Rags a few pointers with a blade? We need to improve her skills."

"Cool I kept a few swords from last night, here kid, let me show you a trick or two."

He sat on the log at the side of Pete and warmed his feet. "Tell me more about sewers Pete."

Pete smiled. "Oh, the stories I could tell Robbie."

Later that afternoon Robbie and Rune walked with Steph and Pete up the steep slope of the neighbouring hill with Rowan and Jade. Steph and Rune had taken advantage of a tepee filled with shawls, and Rune had one tied round her waist and one over her shoulders. Steph seemed to be reliving some part of her past and had tied a silk scarf round Pete's head, which she loved. Looking more like Maggs was probably good cover as they all walked at a gentle pace up the hill; Rowan laughed and joked with Jade up in front. Steph smiled. "It is so nice to see Jade so happy; I have not heard her laugh so much in years."

Rune smiled. "I am not sure about Jade, when Rowan came to us he was so quiet and never smiled, now look at him." He grabbed Jade and threw her screaming into the air and then caught her. She threw her arms around him giggling wildly and he kissed her.

"They are perfect for each other. She is wild on the outside and kind and loving inside, and my friend Rowan is kind and loving on the outside yet has the insides of a man of the wild." Rune looked at Robbie almost surprised.

"Robbie that was beautifully put, and just so perfect a way to describe them both." He watched them and smiled to himself, and looked around. They had come quite some distance from the farm, which sat at the bottom of the long gradient of tall grass. Bright blue cornflowers and scarlet poppies nodded in the slight breeze, and he thought about how this would once have been short lush green grass for grazing. Robbie much preferred it the way it was, a honey coloured hill of tall grass that swished on his legs, covered in speckles of bright colours from the millions of tiny flowers that all waved as he passed in the glorious sunshine. Rune smiled as he glanced at her, he gave her a soft squeeze on the hip. "This is our last big hurdle, it will challenge us all, I just hope we can make it without loss." Rune pulled him closer.

All of them stood at the top of the hill and looked out across the sea of trees to the tall bell tower of the cathedral. It was a gloriously hot and sunny day, and the sun bounced off the stonework giving it a bright sand yellow appearance. "Wow that is tall." Rune gasped.

Robbie sat in the grass and stared at it. "It's also a way in."

Rune sat down beside him. "You have got to be joking Robbie, it must be hundreds of feet high."

Pete sat beside him with Steph, and Robbie looked at them and then to Rowan. "Alice and I could climb that, and maybe even Blades."

Rowan shifted on his feet. "During the day maybe, but what about in the dark?"

Robbie pulled out his telescope and pulled it open, he put it to his eye and looked at the tower brickwork, he followed it up to the top of the tower. "It can be done if we use the inside corners where the walls come out, and then get on the roof and make our way to the tower."

He passed the scope to Rowan. "That is no easy climb Robbie but I can see what you mean. There are several ledges you could use; how long would it take you."

"About an hour and a half maybe."

Rune looked at him. "Robbie if you are seen all the way up there you have had it. You will be sitting ducks."

He put his hand on hers. "Rune it is only the first of many ideas, we will look at as many ways as possible, but in four days' time when they lower that crown, I have to be in that building there. Find me a safer way in and I will take it." Rune watched as he sat and stared out across the trees at the huge building, with its large arched windows and its finely carved stonework. He knew he was missing something, but he could not put his finger on it.

"Why don't we just blow it up like we have everything else?" Jade stabbed the ground with a dagger. "A couple of well-placed arrows while he is in there, and all of us could go home."

Steph patted Jade's shoulder. "That is a house of worship, I know you have not been raised in that faith, but to the people who travel there, it is as important to them as Hearne's wood is to us. If we blow it up, we will just create a whole new line of Mason supporters and we do not want that."

Pete stood up and stood next to Rowan. "What we really need Robbie is a closer look, at the moment there does not seem to be enough detail from here to really get a feel for it."

"I think we should get a little closer tomorrow and check it out properly."

Robbie lay back on the grass and closed his eyes; he could see the tower in his mind and tried to find any weak spot that could be exploited. He felt Rune lean against him and he lifted his hand to her, he knew how worried she was, and he understood it because he felt the same. The task was reaching its final moments, and he needed answers.

It stayed in his thoughts all day, and as he sat by the campfire and watched the flames as they flickered in the dark, everyone around him was laughing and joking. Maggs sat with a guitar and played really badly, which was made worse by the fact that her singing was terrible. He breathed a sigh of relief as Bear took the guitar off her and offered to play. Bear was worse, and his singing was as bad as Maggs, it was too much for him and he got up and made his way back to the tepee.

His disappointment increased when he found it empty. He pulled off his pants and shirt, and slid under the blankets, and pulled several of the many pillows down and propped himself up.

Robbie sat in the dark with the dull sounds of outside in the background, and closed his eyes; the truth was he had run out of ideas. He needed information and without it, he could not make a plan, Tintagel had been so different because there were plans, maps, and even a few drawings to give him an idea. He had none of that now and the clock seemed to be ticking, he slipped into a depressed and weary sleep, his mind swirling with problems and doubt.

He felt her beside him as he came out of sleep, and opened his eyes and she was smiling at him. He sat up and rubbed his face, and she leaned forward and very gently kissed him. "Come on silly wake up its important."

"What is it Rune?"

She slid a bundle of folded garments under his face and then placed three large sheets of paper on top. "What is this?" He tried to focus but just walking up; his vision was not quite what it should be?

Rune beamed with delight. "That is twelve black Knox vests, and the paper contains a plan of the cathedral and the compound that Knox has built round it."

Robbie unfolded the paper and looked with delight. "How the hell did you get this?" He looked at her bright happy face.

"Are you not happy with it?"

"Happy. Rune I am ecstatic." He lurched forward and grabbed her pulling her close. "You know what this is don't you?"

"A safer way in." She kissed him. "Come on have a close look, I have spent hours getting this to scale."

Robbie sat up and lit another candle to increase the light in the tepee. He unfolded the paper out fully, and stared down at the thick dark lines, Rune pointed to the plan.

"Look he has done what he did at the castle in London. Five hundred yards of land around the Cathedral has been cleared and flattened. A large ten foot wall has been built all the way round, and then there is a ring of houses that are all still occupied, another wall and then the woodland."

The black vests would get them into the compound, Rune had repaired them all so the arrow holes no longer showed, and had them washed and laundered.

Robbie unfolded the floor plan of the cathedral.

There were several high places to shoot from, and a lot more exits than he first realised. He looked at the seating plan of those of importance and those of lesser importance, and there in the centre was the ceremonial seat where he knew Knox would be seated to receive his crown. Robbie looked at her. "I am astounded."

"Thought you might be, you should talk to those around you more Robbie. Hilda is a cleaner at the cathedral, she spends all day Friday and Saturday there mopping all the floors for the big service every Sunday, apparently people travel from miles around to attend."

"Who is Hilda?"

"Hilda is Maggs mum Robbie. On Fridays and Saturdays Maggs has a stall on the church market ground, they travel down together and Hilda goes off while Maggs sets up her stall. The day after tomorrow is market day, so you will be able to walk right up to the front doors and have a really good look, so tomorrow you need to look at what streets lead to the forest for escape routes."

Robbie pulled her close. "This changes everything Rune; I cannot tell you how important this is to the plan. This could be the difference between us loosing half the team or not, thanks."

She held him close. "I have my moments Robbie."

The following morning, they followed a map given them by Maggs, and made their way through the woods toward the cathedral. Robbie took a small team, as he wanted to keep it as tight as possible. Rowan, Martin, and John went ahead and scouted in front whilst Jett and Jade joined him and Pete.

Robbie was starting to get a feel for the ever changing woodlands around the country. He had now travelled through many different types of wood, and each one seemed to offer its own special character. Loxley, he knew so well with its bracken and bramble and dense elder in amongst the birch, beech, and oak.

Here the wood changed regularly, and he could tell in an instant whether the woods dated before or after the red death just by the size and scale, and also what was low growing. There were large areas of tall thick trees, where very little grew at ground level, these were the elders of this wood, and the dense patches of thick saplings that provided good cover over the uneven floor. Here he knew buried below them was the last remnants of Humankind, in this area nature had taken it back as her own.

They moved quickly and quietly taking note of every patrol, of which there was quite a few. They were badly trained and noisy, and they heard them coming long before they crossed their paths, by which time Robbie and the group was well out of sight. They reached the outer wall within twenty minutes; it was a very badly built wall and Jade almost carved her way through in minutes. It was poor quality lightweight cement, and Jade looked at Robbie. "Hit this hard enough and the lot will fall down." She pushed her dagger hard and a small hole appeared that she could see through, Robbie bent down and looked. There was the housing, and the small streets that would lead up to the cathedral.

It took seconds to drop over the wall and have a look; they all walked in pairs along the streets getting the lay of the land. Pete watched the floor for any signs of drains, and he found one just down from the east wall of the cathedral behind the giant wall of the compound. It was situated up a small alleyway, and he quickly pulled the lid up and dropped down inside pulling the lid back on. Robbie leaned against the wall with Jade, whilst Jett stood with John and Martin further down.

Half an hour later there was two taps on the drain cover. Jade checked all was clear and tapped back, the lid lifted and Peter appeared. Within seconds, he was back above ground and smiling; he dropped the lid back and leaned against the wall. "I followed it down; it goes right under the wall and into the woodland, it took a good shove to lift it but it is free over the other side and we will be able to find it fast enough, I marked it in a way I will recognise."

Rowan slipped out from one of the side streets. "We should move out and head back, it is getting very full of soldiers over there, its best we don't advertise."

Robbie nodded and signaled the others; they made their way back to the wall. They were over the wall in seconds, although Robbie crouched on top for a few moments looking over to the compound. There were many soldiers in black vests pouring into it, he turned and jumped down and headed back through the woodland to Maggs place.

Back at the camp Hog and Fish had taken Bear off on his first official woodsman hunting trip. Robbie arrived back to find everyone in high spirits as a large boar roasted over the fire on a spit. Maggs sat with Harry close to the fire, and she beamed with her horsy buckteeth smile at everyone. Fresh veg was boiling on the fire and everyone seemed to be really relaxed. Robbie sat down next to Alice. "Everything alright?"

She smiled and patted his leg. "Yeah, everything is going to be great." She stared at him for a moment. "Remember sitting next to the compost eating fruit and getting all worried about Loxley?"

Robbie smiled. "Yeah, that feels like years ago."

Alice nodded. "You have done so well Robbie; I was just sitting here watching this lot and thinking about it. You have pulled together good people who love and care about you; it is something to be proud of Robbie."

Robbie put his arm around her. "I have had you behind me all the way just as you promised. You know Alice; I should say it more I know, you are very important to me; I have always seen you more as a sister than a cousin. You are very special."

She smiled. "I love you too Robbie don't ever forget that. You know... If things go a bit crazy on Sunday." Alice put her arms around him and hugged him. "You have always been there for me Robbie and that has always meant such a lot to me." She kissed him on the cheek.

"We will both get through this together as always." Alice gave a vague nod.

"If I tell you something, and ask you to not tell anyone, not even Rune would you promise me Rob, it really is important to me?"

Robbie looked at her concerned; there was something about the way she asked, which was not quite Alice. "What is wrong?"

"Rob if you see Billy on Sunday, will you kill him for me? I am not sure I will be able to even though he has hurt me so much. Promise me, you will not hesitate, aim and shoot, for me."

It was not what he had expected and it threw him a little. "Don't think about Billy any more Alice, that is done with let him rot."

Alice's eyes filled up with tears. "You must promise Rob. If you love me as your sister, promise me you will not hesitate, take the shot for me and mean it."

Robbie put his hand on hers; the sight of her in tears and the hurt in her voice upset him. He loved her dearly and she was so important to him. How could he? But how could he not? Billy's treatment of Alice and the suffering he had seen her go through, had hurt Robbie more than anything else.

"I promise Alice, you know I will not break my word to you?"

Alice nodded. "Thanks Robbie I needed to know you would... Robbie?"

"What is it Alice something is chewing at you? I know you well enough. Won't you tell me what is wrong? There is something else please Alice tell me." The tears flowed as Alice shook.

"Robbie, I think I might be pregnant." She turned and pushed her head into his shoulder and sobbed. Robbie was lost for a second and found it hard to find the right words; he pulled his arms around her and held her tight. Rune noticed and turned to walk over but he nodded to her, and she stopped.

"Are you sure?" What else could he ask? She had just hit him with the one thing he had never expected.

"I am late for my period," She squeaked quietly from his shoulder. Robbie held her tight and rocked her gently; she put her arms round him and wept long bitter tears of anguish.

"How late Alice?"

She gave a big sniffle, and looked up at him with large red watery eyes. "Just over a week...Robbie I am never late." She burst into more tears and sobbed. "I have been such a fool." She buried her head back in his arms.

Robbie held her tightly in his arms and he kissed the top of her head. "Loving someone is never foolish Alice; it is the best part of all of us." He felt her tremble as she wept and he stroked her hair. "Do not go blaming yourself for this; we all thought you and Billy would last forever." He rocked her in his arms, and she sniffled as he held her tight and tried to swallow his own tears.

The thought of Alice having the baby grandchild of Mason Knox was not something he wanted to think about. But he loved Alice, she had been there for him all his life and he knew he would stand by her no matter what. As she quietened down and dried her eyes, he took her hand and looked her right in the eye. "First clear shot I get, he is gone, I promise you Alice."

She snuggled into him, and he sat and held her safe in his arms for a while. Rune watched from across the fire, he nodded to her to let her know Alice was fine.

Alice quietened down and sat up. "I think I will have an early night, Rob." He stood up with her and she smiled weakly. He pulled her back into a hug.

"Don't go getting upset anymore whatever happens I will be with you. You have my word... It is up to you, but personally I would talk to Rune, I give you my word she won't hear from me."

He too lay in bed a lot earlier that night and thought of Alice. She was so kind, gentle, and loving and she deserved so much more than this. Anger began to rise inside him. Billy had hurt her, which had burned her deeply, but this was different, the coldness of Billy's actions toward her lit fires inside him and his anger began to smoulder.

Rune came in very late. She slipped into bed beside him and cuddled up against him. "I have spent most of the night with Alice talking; she told me she made you promise not to tell me."

"I had no choice I am sorry."

She kissed his cheek. "I understand Robbie; I know how close you two are. She says she will have it and raise it as a Loxley, will you be able to handle that?"

Robbie was surprised and turned to her in the dark. "How do you mean?"

"That child will be a daily reminder of him Rob."

"I would never blame a child for the sins of it parents, I will only see the child of Alice, nothing more."

Rune snuggled up and was quiet. He could see her bright eyes twinkling in the dark and he knew something else was on her mind, he put his arm around her and she snuggled closer and put her head on his chest. He looked at her. "What?"

"Will you really kill him Robbie after everything?"

Robbie let out a long deep sigh. "First clear arrow I have is Billy's. I promised her Rune, I don't have a choice."

CHAPTER TWENTY FOUR

HOODED FRIENDS FOREVER

The country was now slowly dividing into two. Apart from Cornwall it seemed the complete western side of the country was in support of Robert of Loxley. Most of the east was in support of the church or Mason Knox. The church had made a stand behind Mason Knox, and was telling everyone in the few churches across the country that this man would save them from the life of hardship they faced.

The postal riders were now all in support of Loxley and were making regular stops to let everyone know of the gains he was making to stop Knox stealing the crown. Woodsmen were meeting in secret as Caerleon Castle coordinated them into groups ready for a large-scale attack on the soldiers of Knox.

Knox had a far superior army; he had spent years in preparation and Robbie had only really begun his fight in earnest over the last week. In Loxley stockade, the Lox brothers were piling carts with weapons as they kited out every available man and women who wanted to take up arms. There were now over three thousand within the Stockade who were armed and ready.

A corridor of green had now appeared up the western side of the country as the woodsmen loyal to Loxley watched every town. The Marshals of Knox suddenly found that their men were disappearing fast, and their offices would mysteriously catch fire, and they began to leave as woodsmen replaced them and looked out for the town's folk's best interests.

With two days left to go, the movement behind Robbie had grown considerably, although he was not aware of most of it. Scarlet was now communicating directly to Len and passing back information to Rune whom would give Robbie a daily update. Robbie now spent his time sat at a picnic bench Harry had brought up to the site. Rowan was becoming more and more Robbie's number two as he discussed plans with Skip, Bear, and the others.

Rune Alice and Steph would sit with him, and he would discuss things over with them for another perspective. Slowly the time had passed, it was now April 29th, and the date for attack was closing.

Maggs and her mum had gone off early that morning with Harry to set up her stall in what was now called, 'The Church Market.' It was set in the grounds of the cathedral, Steph had joined them with a large pad, and some sketch pens that Maggs had found, she was going to draw the cathedral for Robbie so they could get a closer look at the detail of it.

Jett accompanied Rowan, Jade, and Flash with Blades, all dressed in shawls to wander about and size up the guards. Pete, John, Martin, and Bear were scouting the streets around the compound for more information on routes in and out, as well as what sewer access there was.

Robbie had decided it would be better for him to stay at the camp, and he advised Alice and Rune it was better for them. Billy was on his mind and he knew they would be spotted quicker than the others would by him. Alice seemed to have settled down now and was back to her old self.

Robbie sat at the bench with Rune as Hog walked Stan and Bob up to the table, Rune took out her knife and Stan flinched, she cut the ropes from their hands and Robbie invited them to sit.

Rune walked to the fire and returned with four cups of coffee, Stan and Bob gratefully accepted them, and rubbed their wrists where the ropes had been. "Well gents, you have been very well behaved; although I am not foolish enough to think you would run. I know as well as you do that you would not get a mile before you were dead."

Both of them lowered their heads and agreed. "What should we do with you two I wonder?" Stan lifted his head, he was in his early fifties and had lived a hard life that showed on his face, he had small tuffs of hair at the sides but the rest had fallen out, his face was dark from the sun and very lined. He looked old and frail.

"If you beg my pardon My Lord, we were hoping we could stay here."

Rune smiled. "Why would you want to remain here, is your loyalty not to the army of Knox?"

"We have no loyalty to him My Lady. We were dragged out of bed in the middle of the night, and told fight or die. They said if we ran away they would kill our kids, only we knew they would come and we had told our families to head to my brothers in Norfolk if they took us."

Robbie watched them as Stan spoke; Bob nodded in agreement with Stan. "So your families are safe, and yet you did not run?"

"No disrespect My Lord, we are being fed regular, and we thought over here we would be out of harm's way and not have to fight. I know that sounds wrong but it was the best of a bad situation." They both hung their heads in shame; it was a pitiful sight to watch.

"So now we have you here and you are faced with being a prisoner with us, or being killed for deserting your posts by Knox. It does appear that you are in quite a jam Gents."

Both of them looked at Robbie with sad eyes, Bob summoned up the courage to talk. "I don't want to die, who would look after my wife and kids My Lord?"

Rune looked at them sadly, she felt very sorry for their terrible situation. "What is it you want us to do with you both?"

Bob seemed almost surprised at her question. "Oh, please My Lady, give us a chance, we can help out round here, and if you send us back, we are dead men don't you see that?"

She smiled. "But how can we trust you, technically you are the enemy?"

Stan seemed to be very offended by her remark. "I am no one's enemy, and I have never been in my life, tie us up and keep us in the tent if you must. I might not be as high and mighty as you, but I am still a man of my word."

Robbie held up his hands. "That is not called for Stan, what my good lady meant was that you were captured by us wearing enemy clothing, you were seen by my men as legitimate targets. Frankly you are very lucky to be alive, you saw how my men deal with men in black vests at the farm, I lead this outfit and I am the one who will need proof that you will keep your word, it is I who will decide your fate."

Stan put his head down. "I am sorry My Lady I meant no offence, but everyone in these parts who has known me will tell you, I never break my word."

Robbie looked at Rune, she nodded to him and he knew. "You will be given a trial, if you hold to your word when we leave here you will be free, if you try in any way to leave this camp or enter the tree line my men will have orders to shoot, do you both understand?"

Stan and Bob nodded. "You will not regret this My Lord and we are grateful."

Robbie looked at Stan. "I want your word you will help us and do nothing to harm or endanger us; I am taking a big leap of faith in you two." Stan looked at both of them sincerely.

"You have our word My Lord; we will aid you as much as we can until you leave."

"Alright then Gents, there is food by the fire and pots to clean, so have a good meal and then clean the area and stoke the fire. Hog will be watching you."

They stood up and bowed, and rushed off to the fire, Robbie looked at Rune and she smiled back at him. "They will be fine; I can see their hearts are good."

"I hope so Rune, I have enough to think about without having to worry about those two." She bent down and kissed him. "You will be fine stop worrying."

Steph sat a few feet from Maggs on a small stool and began to sketch the building. It had been some time since she had done any drawing, but her hand moved with skill and precision as she slid the pencil across the paper. Maggs came over behind her. "Here you go darling wear this." She slid the crucifix over Steph's head and winked at her. "If they see one of these, they don't hassle your vibes girl."

Steph looked at the wooden cross on a long black cord around her neck and smiled to herself as she began to draw again. She had been there for just under an hour when one of the guards who walked past looked down at the sketch and stopped. "Hey that aint allowed." He looked at Steph as she looked up from her work; the crucifix flopped on to her pad!

"Oh, I am sorry sir I didn't know, Sister Mary at the convent asked me to, knowing I would be here, she will be so disappointed."

He walked around to her side and looked down at what was a very detailed and impressive picture. "Wow, you are good... Sister Mary, eh?" He considered the point for a moment. "You going to be working it much longer?"

"Not much it's almost finished."

He looked from side to side and down at the picture. "Hurry up and finish it, and then draw something else. Make sure you tell the good Sister how Christian I was."

Steph smiled. "Bless you, she will be very happy." The guard nodded and walked off, Steph looked over at Maggs and smiled, Maggs gave her a knowing wink.

As Steph finished her drawing, Peter Lane was passing directly beneath her in a long brick tunnel with a small stretch of water running down the middle. He had covered his face with a rag dipped in lavender oil, and had it tight across his mouth. He held the little lantern high as he saw in the distance a metal ladder bolted to the wall, he looked back at Martin and John. "That's it just down there... Where is Bear?"

John smiled behind his scarf. "Took his mask off to put more oil on it, he is throwing up back there, he'll be right when it's up." Pete nodded and moved forward, the rats squealed and ran off as he kicked them out of the way.

Jade sat on Rowan's knee with her arms around him. She put her head on his shoulder and he rocked her slowly. Her eyes looked past his long hair as she whispered softly in his ear. "Two across the rear every forty-five seconds, three grouped down the east side, takes those one hundred and ninety eight, that is the blind spot on the far wall, one, two, three, four, five, six, seven, eight, nine, ten, eleven. We will have twelve seconds to cross the gap."

Rowan wrote on a small piece of cloth on her leg under her shawl. A guard came slowly past. "I love you too darling." He turned and kissed her, as the guard walked away.

Jett sat on a barrel next to the ale stall talking to the two off duty soldiers as she swallowed yet another large mug full of strong ale. "Corr! You have the job of watching all the balconies, you must be really important?" The guard's chest swelled with pride, and she smiled at him. "That really turns me on that does." He beamed as the silver badge on his black vest glistened.

Jett leaned over close to him. "Give me a kiss for being so sexy." She moved forward and kissed him roughly, she pulled back and looked at his pal. "You give me one too." He could not wait, and was across like a flash, Jett gave him a long slow passionate kiss; after all he was quite good looking.

She parted from him. "Wow.... You must be way more important than him," and she kissed him again. "More drinks," she yelled. Maggs friend poured two large tankards of strong ale and handed them to the soldiers. She gave the tankard of liquorice water to Jett and winked. Jett downed it in one and slammed it on the small table, the guards struggled and then lay their heads down on the table.

Jett smiled and stood up. She walked across the market, and as she passed Steph, she dropped two, shiny special duty badges on to her pad, Steph snatched them quickly and put them in her pocket. "Six," she quietly said to herself.

Jett walked across the compound toward Blades and Flash. She saw the fast hand sign and looked up at the building behind Blades. Jett ducked her head quick and pulled the shawl round her and over her head; she reached the wall and pressed flat against it. Blades was about three feet away, her back turned slightly away from her. "Did you see him up there?"

Jett leaned forward and pulled up her boot. "I saw him, what you wanna do?"

"We cannot attack Jett, I know you want to, I wouldn't mind a pop myself, but if we do, they will know we are here. Can you let Jade know?"

"I better had I suppose." Jett gripped her other boot and looked at the floor, she closed her eyes. "Hear me Jade."

Jade kissed Rowan passionately, pulled away, and looked at him. "That's another twelve just in the doorway... God I really love spying." She pulled him close and twisted him round as she squeezed his bum while she kissed him. "Oh God that is about twenty in the office across the path... Don't get any ideas about slinking off with Robbie tonight, after all this you're mine until sun up."

She moved closer and stopped. Jade suddenly pulled him up against the wall fast, and peered over his shoulder. "Stay still." She raised herself up on her toes and watched. She slid the hood on his bright purple cloak over his head. Rowan looked at her face. "It's Billy, isn't it?" She nodded as she touched the cut on the side of her cheek, she slowly lowered her hand and slid it into her tunic, and

Rowan gently grabbed her wrist.

"Jade! Swallow it now. I know how you feel, but save it for Sunday." Her arm slackened and he let go. "Come on, let's warn the others, where is he?"

Jade slid the brightly coloured shawl over her head. "Big hotel behind you, balcony third top window from the left." Rowan walked with his back to him across the compound towards Steph, he looked down at her picture. "Very nice." He lowered himself to look closer and whispered. "Hotel balcony, top on the left, cover up." He stood up. "Too expensive, never mind Honey." He put his arm around Jade and walked off.

Steph slid Harry's black hat up from behind her shoulders and pulled it down over her head. She folded her pad, stood up, turned, and walked out of the compound. Harry read the note on the picture left on the stool as he folded it up.

He pulled his cloak hood up and then crouched down behind the stall and peered through the goods at the hotel. Billy stood and looked down at the crowds and watched, dressed in fine black clothes and drank wine from a crystal glass. His long blonde curly hair seemed to glow in the sunlight. A young woman in red came out and slid her arm around him, and topped up his glass. She smiled and kissed him

Harry's blood started to boil, and he scowled, if he was closer, he would have the perfect shot, but only Robbie would hit him from here and he was back at the camp.

The group all stood on the edge of the wood and waited. Jett came running through the trees fastening her pants. "Sorry guys that bloody stuff makes you pee for England." They all smiled and began to walk on through the long grass toward the farm lane. Rowan was lost in thought and Jade looked up at him. "Rune knows, she caught Jett telling me."

Rowan looked at her. "He won't do anything stupid will he?" She shook her head.

"Robbie will get him, but he will not jeopardise the attack on Sunday."

Rowan walked on slowly. "You want him, don't you? I felt the way you tensed."

Jade looked at the floor. "I thought about fading and going for him yes. I love Robbie and Alice; they are two of my best friends and he has really hurt them. You saw Alice last night; I hate him Rowan for what he has done." She looked up at him. "You know the night on the boat when my dad came back?"

Rowan slowed his pace and nodded at her. "Rune took on a lot of Robbie's pain. My mum blocked it, but she was so upset and happy at having my dad back she leaked. Both Jett and me got a blast of what Robbie felt." A small tear ran down her face. "I would kill him just for that small bit that I felt; it hurt me deeper than anything else in my life ever will." Rowan pulled her close to him as they walked into the farm.

Rune sat on the grass sewing a tear in her shirt, she stopped and looked up at Robbie, her eyes flared violet and flashed across her cheeks. They faded to blue with lilac whites, and she watched Robbie as he looked up from the plans, their eyes met for just a moment and she looked down at her sewing. Robbie watched as she looked up again and smiled. "Rune... He is here isn't he, Billy?" She nodded slowly at him and he looked down at the plans and spoke no more.

It was late evening when everyone returned from the market, Stan and Bob had cleaned the site and prepared a meal. Robbie now had the bench inside his tepee and had several candles lit, as he slowly went over things in his mind. Rune looked over his shoulder. "Why Blades and not me?"

Robbie looked up, his eyes were tired. "I don't want you inside if it gets bad Rune, I want you where you can get free and escape."

Rune slid on to his knee and looked him right in the eye. "I will not say this twice so listen to me Robbie. I will be inside right at the side of the man I love, I will not live alone without you, if we die it will be as we started, we will die together... Change the plan put Blades outside." She smiled and kissed him. "You need me inside I can communicate with everyone at the same time and send them pictures of what is happening."

Robbie nodded. "Alright we stay together." He pulled her close. "Please don't do anything to risk yourself; I have no intention of living alone either." Robbie scratched out Rune's name in the church square and wrote Blades, he scratched Blades out in the cathedral and wrote Rune.

Rowan came into the tepee with a sheet of paper in his hand. "All the troop positions for Sunday; they have spent all day rehearsing. Robbie there will be a hell of a lot of them." He looked down at the paper and read all the notes collected by Rowan and Jade, he started to mark them on to the plan.

"I expected more to be honest." Rowan stared at him and shook his head. "I need to eat; we will talk later." He walked out of the tepee as Steph came in with her pad. She sat at the side of him and flipped through the pages.

"These walls here where there are no windows, is where your large balcony will be toward the back. Look at this." She flipped the next page on her pad. Robbie was very impressed with the quality of the drawings. "Right Rob, the internal balcony has a small corridor at the back see it on your plan. Well, that runs along these windows, if you get into trouble, you will be able to smash the glass and drop four feet on to this roof above the main entrance. As long as you have outside cover, all of you can slip down this drain pipe here."

Robbie nodded with Rune. "That is great Steph, well done, that gives us another way out which was one of my concerns." She smiled at him.

"You know Rob you are either very brave or very mad, and with Harry as a family member I am inclined to think you are both." She patted him on the shoulder. "Look at the drawings and see what you think." She put the six silver badges on the table. "All guards entering the cathedral must wear these, that is Jett's little gift for you, she is a talented girl."

Pete was last with his plans of the sewers. "The good news is that we can get inside the cathedral with no worries at all. The bad news is that the entrance in the woods has collapsed, so we have to go in from the alley. The odds are very high that with the increased security the whole place will be crawling with guards."

Robbie sat back as Pete left and stretched. "I think I will eat and then decide how to play this." Rune rubbed his shoulders and he moaned happily. "Oh, that's so nice."

The group was sat by the fire, as Robbie and Rune came out. The light was fading and their faces danced with colour from the flames, he sat down on a large log as Bob passed him a plate of stew. Everyone was silent as they ate, and Rune slipped down beside him and looked around. Robbie took a mouthful and chewed. "From now until four tomorrow is your own time. We will gather here then, and I will brief you all and then we will prepare." He looked at all of them sat around the fire as they shared their meal together.

"This is the hardest thing any of us will ever do. The odds are against us from the start, I have been honoured to know you all and fight beside you, I pray that Hearne will protect all of you my dearest of friends." He got up with his plate and walked back to the tepee.

Everyone sat by the fire and stared at their plates, the time had come and they all knew the odds of survival was low. One by one, they finished their meal and broke apart to head to their tepees and prepare themselves for the worst.

Robbie ate alone at the table with a heavy heart, he was asking his friends to make the ultimate sacrifice and he found it hard to accept. He sat staring at his plate no longer feeling hungry, and it was sometime later when Rune came in that he moved. She stood behind him, slid her arms around him, and put her head on his shoulder. "Leave this you have all day tomorrow, you are too tired to think, come to bed Robbie and get some sleep."

He lay in the dark as she slid under the blankets and curled up next to him. He felt her warm body wrap around him, and he stirred and pulled her close kissing her. "Don't leave my side for a moment tomorrow Rune; I do not want to lose a second with you." He looked down at her in the dim light, and he thought of every moment in his life where he had watched her.

The pictures flooded his mind of those beautiful blue eyes that peeped at him through the clothes on the rail at her house. The way the sun had bounced off her hair and glinted in the woods as they hunted. The paleness of her skin as she had run down the bank at Joe's into his arms. Her slender figure as he watched from Alice's bakery as he shovelled snow from her yard. He loved her so much and yet could not get the feelings into the words to tell her, and he desperately wanted to tell her.

Rune's eyes glowed in the dark and turned violet; her soft fingers touched his eyes and pulled the lids down. With his eyes closed and her warmth all around him, he relaxed and lay in her arms. Suddenly inside him she was there, he felt her presence surround him and pass into him; it was a glorious wonderful feeling as he basked in her love.

Robbie opened his heart, and unleashed everything he had ever felt for her, and a wonderful warmth grew inside him. She squeezed him as it flowed out and she saw for the first time the real depth of his love for her. He opened his eyes and she was smiling as violet tears ran from her eyes. "My words are not big enough Rune."

She held him close as their feelings mixed together and she whispered.

"You will never need words, just show me my love." She softly kissed him.

It was three in the afternoon on the last day of April, and as Robbie prepared to face the group and brief them on the attack in Canterbury. Further north on the moors and in the woods, green-cloaked woodsmen surrounded the town of Hathersage.

The army of Mason Knox was preparing for a strike, and the troops were relaxed as they sat in their hundreds of tents and awaited their orders to move out. Robert Lox stood on the edge of the trees above the pass where most of the troops were billeted, whilst John Lox led his men at arms down through the trees and the scrub into the back of the village behind the church. One of his men slipped inside and took hold of the bell rope ready to give the signal as Loxley's men at arms, spread silently around the town and every house.

General Turner sat at his desk in front of the bay window, his hand heavily bandaged as he looked at his battle plan for the fall of Loxley. He lifted the glass of claret to his lips as the glass window shattered, and the long white tipped arrow came across the table and pinned him to the chair. He coughed and put down his glass, as he stared out of the broken window at John Lox in his hood and then fell forward, his chin on his chest.

The church bell struck up and hooded men arose from the grass and the trees. Hathersage rained arrows and the soldiers in their tents screamed as the high speed arrows came through the top of the tents and pinned them to their beds and the floors.

The village ran to the screams of wounded and dying men as the heavy hail stopped, and the hooded men melted back into the grass. A door opened and a man ran from it across the street, he hit the door opposite dead, a long white feathered arrow between his shoulder blades. In quiet dark corners men screamed out as they confronted the fearsome figure of John Lox with his sword, as he and his men swept slowly through the town.

The long drawn out process began as Knox's army met the will of hunters with patience, over the rest of the day; any movement was hit with an arrow. As darkness fell arrows lit with flames began to rain down on the houses and buildings of Hathersage. Screams echoed around the valley as men chanced flames or arrows, and by midnight, the whole village burned and every soldier was dead. Hathersage was no more.

Knox's army surrounded the city of York, as row upon row of men in black vests marched into position. The men of York stood on the walls knowing they were outnumbered; their men with crossbows loaded waited for the onslaught to begin, and as the drums beat and the large army moved forward, their three

General's fell from their horses pierced with long arrows. Out of the trees and up from the long grass, hooded figures rose and fired, the men of York cheered and opened fire from the high walls as the large army of Knox was caught in front and behind.

Woodsmen from all over Yorkshire and the north, had received the call to arms of Robert of Loxley, and shots of precision took out man after man in black vests. Leaderless the men panicked and turned on each other as the fight to the death continued. Four hours later York was surrounded with piles of the dead and the hooded men faded away without a word.

The men of York looked on speechless, and the captain above the gate breathed a sigh of relief. An arrow hit the doorframe above his head and he jumped back. The captain looked at the white paper wrapped around the arrow with a red wax seal on it, carefully he unwrapped it as his men looked on, he unrolled the letter, broke the wax seal, and looked down and read the neat handwriting. He looked up at his men, as one of them plucked up the courage and asked. "What does it say sir?"

He looked at the letter and then looked back up, and held the letter out.

"Compliments of Lord Robert of Loxley, the Hooded Man." The soldiers all looked at the captain and back over the walls at the dead and the dying.

"I'll be buggered." Came from somewhere within the assembled soldiers.

Skirmishes broke out across the rest of the country as the army of Knox moved north. It did not go all well for the woodsmen as many of them lost their lives in fierce battles across the midlands, and Knox had now pushed hard up past Yorkshire, where his army still ruled supreme over the men of the woods.

During that time, Robbie sat at the table his head in his hands. No matter which way he arranged everyone it was a suicide mission, Rune slid her arms round him.

"Oh, this is hopeless Rune. We can get in and probably do the job, but no one will come out alive." He leaned back in the chair and she held him tight.

"Robbie please take a break you are pushing yourself too hard, please just go outside in the air for a few minutes and relax. Then come back with fresh eyes and see what can be done." She looked down at him with a very worried look on her face.

He nodded and got up and walked outside, the sun was weak and the air cool, with a gentle breeze. He walked toward the trees, his feet were bare and his shirt flapped open, as he stood under the leaves and breathed deeply, enjoying the freshness of the air, and the feel of the woods on his bare feet. Two green eyes watched from the trees, he smiled. "Hi Pebbles." Jade faded into view.

"You do not have a sword, dagger or bow, Robbie you should know better." He sat down on a stump and sighed; Pebbles came close and sat cross legged on the grass in front of him. "What's up?"

He gave a long sigh. "I have to ask all the people that I love and care for to do something which at the moment will probably end up killing them all, that my dear Pebbles, is what's up."

"Oh, I see. That is pretty heavy Robbie."

He looked at the grass, saw an old acorn and flicked it with his toe. "I need all of you inside to cover the guards while we deal with Mason, the problem is that with no one outside and about a thousand men forming a guard of honour, no one will come out alive."

Pebbles nodded. "I see your point, but do you think we care? We will do it if you ask because the alternative is we all go home and die anyhow Robbie. That is what Knox means on the throne to every woodsman in the land." She smiled. "I love Rowan."

Her beaming face somehow lightened his heart. "I know you do and I am happy for you Pebbles, I think he is a great man of honour and his friendship like yours, is very important to me."

She looked up and then hesitated, and then she looked up again. "I want to live Robbie and I want Rowan to live. I have always felt different from everyone at Loxley. You was the only one who saw me for who I was, but you loved my sister and not me. Did you ever realise how in love with you I thought I was?" She smiled and Robbie sat back surprised, he had never ever thought.

"Jade I had no idea. You know I loved you as one of my best friends." He was lost for words.

She leaned forward and touched his hand. "Robbie it is alright. Although I loved you with all of who I thought I was, I did not know really, who Jade was until I met Rowan. I do love you and I always will as my closest friend and my future brother, but I have found something that I never thought I would, and you were the one who helped me. I could die tomorrow Robbie, but I would, knowing that the person I love more than life itself would be with me... Rowan."

She squeezed his hand gently. "Rune feels the same as me about you, and that is why tomorrow when you stop Knox you will have those who love you by your side. Because of love, I love the woods you sent me to learn about with Joe. I love the man who for me is the woods, and I love the man he respects above all others, because he is also my greatest friend." She sat back and smiled. "Put the lot of us in together and we will find a way out I bet you. Just have a little faith in yourself and us. Do not ever forget Robbie you can work wonders with a bow, but you will work miracles for Rune."

She got up off the grass and patted him on the shoulder. "Keep close to the camp you are not armed, Martin is five trees back under that fern, but he thinks we don't know." She walked back into the camp humming to herself.

Robbie smiled as he stood up. "Watch out for those ants Martin, they bite."

He sat up in the grass. "How did you know?"

Robbie chuckled as he walked back into the camp and headed to the fire, where he poured a drink as Fish announced. "Incoming."

Robbie turned to see who had arrived. Steph stood up and ran to her sister. "Scarlet what are you doing here?"

"Hey sis thought you could use the help, and I am so bored coordinating this bloody war when I want to be in it. Where is Robbie?" She kissed her sister on the cheek as Robbie came up to her. "For a man about to go into the fight of his life you look very relaxed Robbie, I must get Rune to tell me her secrets." She laughed and gave him a hug.

"Scarlet it is wonderful to see you, but why are you here?"

"Oh, be nice Robbie, I am having such fun. I thought you would need an extra sword or bow and so I brought both. Here is my sword and I have one hundred bowmen in the trees by the sea."

Robbie's eyes widened and he pulled her close and gave a huge hug. "Scarlet you are wonderful, thank you they are much needed."

"How are my girls?" She looked round the camp.

Robbie pointed to a large tepee. "They are in there preparing, go on I can see you have missed them." Scarlet smiled, and walked over to the tepee and popped her head in the flap, the girls screamed with delight.

Rune walked over smiling and slipped her arms around him. "Better?"

He pulled her close and smiled. "You knew, didn't you?"

Her bright blue eyes danced with delight as she kissed him. "I might." She hugged him. "You see, all you need to do is have faith and trust in the protection of Hearne, he is with us Robbie we fight his corner."

Robbie sat back by the table that had been placed back outside in the light, and as he worked on his new plans and he looked up. Rowan and Jade walked arm in arm on the edge of the forest. Blades was practicing her fencing with Jett, they seemed to have become such good friends, Flash although only small was practicing with her pole with Hog who had become very proficient under her guidance, Alice was over in the corner of the camp showing Bear bow skills, whilst giving Maggs and Rags a few lessons. Fuse sharpened swords and knifes, while Skip gave Fish a few lessons more. Scarlet sat with Steph, Pete and Harry by the fire talking, and Bob and Stan were working on a cart and loading it with empty beer barrels, which bows and extra arrows could be stored in. John and Martin were nowhere to be seen; But Robbie knew they were watching keeping everyone safe. The whole camp was alive with the sound of friendship, there was laughter and talk and he thought there was a lot of love in the air.

It was just after four when Robbie stood before them all. He looked around at their smiling faces as they all settled around the fire to listen to him. "As I speak, all over this land there are woodsmen fighting to quell the surge of power of

Mason Knox." They all gave a grin.

"Mason Knox will cut down every tree and kill every woodland in his bid to rebuild this country to his benefit, and if he takes the crown tomorrow, we will be powerless to stop him. My dear friends if he gains power the balance of man will be tipped back to as it was before the deadly red death where man killed all that was kin to Hearne. We cannot return to those days, we must protect this country until the time of a rightful king who protects the balance comes forth." Rune smiled as she watched him.

"I ask of you now to help me defeat him, in a task that will be very dangerous against huge odds. We are all that stands before him, and the destruction of all that we love. It was once told me that we will never be able to enjoy the power of love until we can end the love of power, here today in this small circle I have seen the true meaning of the power of love, for it flows through you all."

He slowly watched all of them as he looked around the circle before him, and he took his time, as they all nodded and thought of his words. "Will you join me tomorrow to defeat the love of power?"

They all nodded their heads and John spoke out. "We bloody well will Robbie."

Robbie smiled. "Thank you, John." All the others giggled as Martin patted him on the back.

Robbie cleared his throat. "Alright I want to use everyone so that they play to their skills, we will divide into teams. Two teams of nine, one team of three and a pair." He looked at his list.

"First team of nine will be bowmen. Pebbles, Fish, John, Martin, Mother, Rowan, Pigeon, Rune and myself, our job will be to take and secure all the high ground inside the cathedral. The Second team of nine will be swordsmen. Scarlet, Hog, Bear, Fuse, Skip, Pete, Harry, Blades and Jett, your job will be to cover all the floor space, and help remove any guards that could threaten the bows. Flash, Maggs and Rags. Your job will be to secure the main doors once everyone is in. Harry and Blades will assist you." Each of them nodded in turn.

"Bob and Stan have offered to drive the beer cart, which will help all of us get as much weaponry in as possible, we will be supported by our fellow bowmen of Caerleon; who are currently camped down by the sea. They will move on to the roofline all around the cathedral at dawn tomorrow. Pete will lead us in via the sewers, which I am informed is not pleasant, but it will get all of us in undetected. We will come up under the crypts and move to the bell tower. Rowan and Jade, your first job will be to get that tower clear. The rest of the bow team will clear the balconies." They nodded.

"Floor team you will all see me after and I will go over the seating plan and the best places to conceal yourselves and cover all the exits. Door team you will wait in the crypt, until everyone is in the cathedral, as the service begins, you will use Harry and Blades, and take out the guards and close and bolt the doors. It is my hope we keep Mason in and his army out.”

Robbie sat back on the front of the table. “It will be close and tight in there, stay alert and keep your eyes on each other. It will all go on my signal; I will stand in full view of Mason Knox and challenge him, so all of you must follow my lead and stay hidden until the very last moment.”

He paused for a second. “You are all of great value as people, and I care for every one of you so please only strike and reveal yourself at the very last moment. I will worry about Knox you keep his guards busy. Bowmen protect your sword men, and sword men protect your bowmen. Stay sharp and alert. I will see all the bowmen in one hour and the sword men after. Door crew I will see you first. We attack at dawn, go and prepare, and then get some rest.”

He watched as they all began to talk and got up and wandered into their tepees to sort out their things, Rune came up smiling. “We will be fine don’t look so worried, trust me.”

Robbie’s face broke into a huge smile and he nodded. “I know you know stuff.”

She slipped her arms round him and he gazed into her eyes. “You’re a handsome man when you smile Robin Hood.”

He leaned back and looked at her closely. She smiled. “What?”

“I have been so busy that I forgot, but I have wanted to ask you something.”
“What is it?”

“Well, you know we have been sort of... You know... As busy as Alice and Billy were, I just wondered?”

Rune smiled. “I am nature Robbie I bring life when and where it is needed, our time will come you will see.”

“Six girls, and a boy?”

She winked at him and then smiled. “You will have to wait and see won’t you?” She walked off chuckling to get her sword and bow cleaned up and ready.

“I am not calling him Robert.” He called after her, and she just chuckled more.

The following hours were very busy as Robbie briefed the teams. Rowan and Scarlet stayed by his side the entire time. Robbie covered all the high shots, and then moved on to the floor space, he showed them where it was likely that guards would wander into them.

Able Bowman Bents was brought up much to the delight of Robbie, who shook his hand with vigour. He had volunteered to lead the bowmen on to the roofs around the large oblong compound and coordinate from there.

The detail was set and now it was a case of just waiting for the sun to lower itself enough to give them enough cover to begin and move towards the city.

Robbie noticed Harry looking very nervous by the fire, and he thought he knew why. He wandered across the site to where Maggs was trying out a hooded cloak. “Robbie baby, darling isn’t this just positively groovy?” She smiled with her huge front teeth which reminded him very much of the horse he had used at Caerleon.

"Could I ask you a favour Maggs?"

"Oh, sweetheart I would do anything for you, what is it baby cakes?" She laughed which reminded him very much of the gasping horse Brandon had ridden in the woods.

"You don't happen to have a spare pair of those purple round glasses do you; I think they will focus Harry's karma, he had it chomped you know?"

Maggs looked over at Harry looking pale by the fire. She nodded rapidly and her whole body struck up a tune of tinkling jewellery. "Poor baby boy, his vibes have been most un-positive because of it. Here give him these they have my new cosmic abilities in them, tell him if animals start to do as he thinks, it's because these have the power." She nodded and rattled in tune again.

Robbie tried not to smile. "You are blessed you know Maggs." He heard Jade titter as she passed.

Maggs eyes went very wide. "You know Robbie, others have said that." She nodded a lot slower, and played a ballad.

Robbie turned smiling and walked across to Harry. "Hey Harry, how's it going?" Harry looked up at Robbie and smiled.

"I am like drifting with the flow of cosmic vibes you know?"

Robbie crouched down in front of him. "Harry you have been truly a tower of support, and I know I have asked you to do bad things for me."

Harry waved his hands around as if fighting off a bee attack. "Hey man, what's with you jangling my karma, I told you already don't talk to em."

Robbie put his hand on Harry's shoulder. "Harry, I have seen the green evils too."

"Whoa dude." Harry looked quickly from side to side. "They follow me man, they are slowly chomping on me, so I will be all karma chomped and I will like go to the land of uncosmic monsters and the unfunky voodoo man."

Robbie handed him the glasses. "Here use these in the crypt. These have hooded cosmic power and the green evils won't be able to see you or chomp on your karma, Ok?"

Harry took the round purple tinted glasses and slid them on. "Whoa man these are like radical man I can feel the vibes just flowing."

Robbie smiled and stood up, he turned to walk away and stopped and looked back at Harry. "Harry... You have never eaten any of those small brown mushrooms that grow near Joe's, have you?"

Harry jumped about on the log shaking his arms about. "Whoa man yeah, it was like totally cosmic. This old man with acorns for eyebrows, came up to me and he rolled me up in a bed of moss, and he like looked down at me with really long twiggy fingers, and said you will have freaky babies Harold." Harry looked suddenly very serious. "It was intense, and then the trees sang me to sleep, it was very cosmic dude."

Robbie regretted asking and he left Harry deep in thought about his weird dreams and walked to his tepee, as he passed Pebbles, he looked at her and she smiled. "Lay off Harry, I need him saner than he currently is tomorrow." She smiled and nodded.

"Ok Robbie."

There was at least four hours to go before setting off and Robbie collapsed on the bed, his head felt like it was spinning. Rune sat on his waist and leaned forward massaging his temples, she smelled of honeysuckle and sweet violets, and he closed his eyes and drifted as all his worry and aches and pains flowed away. "Oh Rune, that is so good." His body went limp and he drifted into sleep, and dreamt of old men in the woods with leafy beards and acorn eyes, and mushrooms for ears, it was most cosmic.

CHAPTER TWENTY FIVE

THE FACE OF MASON KNOX

There was three hours to go before dawn, as Robbie and Rowan crept along to the sidewall that looked over and down a side street towards the cathedral. Two sets of guards in pairs walked towards each other, Robbie and Rowan slipped back off the top of the wall. They listened as the guards met and then quietly talked. "Nothing to report, all is quiet and boring."

Robbie signaled to Flash sat further down in the trees watching him. Movement behind him brought up Jade and Jett, Robbie silently pointed, gave his orders and Jade and Jett went left and right. He gave another signal and Bear and Hog came silently through the trees.

Robbie turned to Rowan and winked and pulled up his hood, together they silently jumped on to the top of the wall, where Jade and Jett appeared left and right, the four guards met and nodded.

Four hooded figures dropped out of the sky with silver daggers, and as the guards looked up; they were snatched from behind and felt the cold steel of

Loxley. Two sets of large arms came down as the soldiers were thrown flat to the wall, and the four dead soldiers shot upwards and out of sight, there was a soft thud on the other side of the wall.

Four dark hooded shapes crossed the road and flattened themselves against the buildings, on either side of the street that led to the inner wall of the cathedral boundary. Jett and Jade slipped down the street toward the large inner wall, at the end by the corners they slowly peered round. Jade signaled back and more hooded figures came over the wall out of the darkness and down the street.

Every doorway down the street now had a dark hooded shape pressed against it, as Pete and Robbie hurried to the small side street and the manhole cover. Pete went to work quietly lifting the cover as Robbie and then Rune, stood either side of the alleyway. He dropped through the hole with a gentle thud, Robbie signaled and two cloaked figures dashed past and dropped through the hole, Rune signaled and two more appeared only to disappear down the hole. The process continued as each of them passed and dropped down.

Robbie signaled Rune and she slipped on to the floor dropping her legs to

Rowan who guided her down. Robbie pulled away from the wall and ran to the hole, he dropped silently down and Rowan stretched up off the metal rungs he stood on and very quietly replaced the cover.

Robbie gasped for his breath as he tied the rag of lavender around his mouth. The stench of rot and decay was overpowering, and his eyes started to water.

Rowan lit a lamp and patted him on the back, Rune looked back at him and he could tell her stomach was churning just by the look on her face.

A small line of lights bobbed along in front as Pete led the way to the Norman Crypt below the cathedral; Robbie looked at the shadows on the tiny red bricks that curved in an arc above his head. He felt something near his foot and looked down; rats ran down the side of the water that trickled down the centre of the tunnel. He stepped back and kicked a rather large fat one out of his way, it squealed and ran off past Rune making her jump; Robbie took hold of her hand from behind and gave it a gentle squeeze. He felt her relax as she pulled him down the passage, towards a bright light where Pete had placed several candles to mark the grate that led into the crypt.

Robbie looked up as Hog and Harry lifted Rune into the crypt, and then dropped their hands to him. They grabbed him and he shot out of the sewer and into a large stone room filled with rows of large stone oblongs, that had statues lain on top, they were very old and had strange markings carved across the top of them.

"Marvellous aren't they?" Fuse whispered excitedly as he as he scraped the dust and dirt off to look more closely at the inscriptions.

"Hey man don't go messing with them, it aint cosmic, they jangle your vibes dude."

Skip scoffed. "Harry they are dead, they can't hurt us."

Harry slid on his glasses and smiled. "Hey man, I am like cool, and my vibes is safe, you see." He wagged a finger at Fuse. "When they chomp your karma man these are staying with me." Harry pointed to his bright purple tinted glasses and nodded in a very serious way.

Robbie smiled and patted him on the back as he passed, he looked at Jade who was smiling and Robbie pointed at her. "I mean it Pebbles not tonight." She shrugged and sat on one of the tombs.

The chamber was tall and carved stone, tall pillars rose to the arched ceiling, and Robbie looked down to the far end which was some distance away, where a set of stone steps led upwards. Martin and John were on either side with Alice and Rune.

Rowan came up to his side as he reached them and walked quietly on to them, they halted at the thick wooden door. Rowan pressed his ear to it and listened, he slowly turned the large metal handle, which squeaked a little and Robbie held his breath, Rowan pulled the door open a small jar and peered through into the darkness. Jade came up to him and smiled at him, he winked at her and silently pulled the door wider as she faded away and slipped through.

A few minutes later, there was a quiet bump, and the door opened. A dead guard fell into the gap, Rowan grabbed him and heaved him down the steps to Hog, who threw him over his shoulder and walked down the crypt, there was a faint splash as the guard landed in the sewer.

The door swung quietly open and Jade smiled at Robbie. Rowan and Rune slipped across the main hallway to the steps to the bell tower, they took up their positions as Alice and Martin led by Jade headed on to the steps. Slowly they all crossed on to the stairway that spiraled up the tower and Rowan with Jade shot off to the top, it was now their job to clear the stairway and then keep watch from above.

They all headed up the stone stairs led by Martin and Alice, as they approached the balcony that ran across the back of the cathedral they slowed, Robbie and Blades slipped in through the low archway as Alice and Martin took up their stance and covered them.

Four guards stood facing out across the high roof of the cathedral. Behind the two furthest away from the doorway, between the old dusty seats two hooded figures rose up, one was quite tall, the other short. They moved like lightening and two of the guards twisted as the daggers went in, the other two turned as the arrows hit them.

Robbie pushed his guard aside, and lunged at the guard who wobbled and looked like he would fall from the balcony. He grabbed him by the shirt at the front, and heaved back as the guard swooned over the rail, two small hands snatched at his waist and Robbie felt the pressure on his wrist slacken as Rune heaved the guard back with him.

Her bright eyes glinted in the dark at him as they lay the guard down out of sight. Fish, John, Martin and Steph dropped their hoods and swung back their cloaks to reveal black vests with a red dragon on them, all of them had small silver badges on their vests, and they stepped up and took the place of the dead guards.

The rest of the group slipped into the back of the balcony and kept out of sight. They sat back, lifted their legs and waited, Rune took the silver badges off the dead guards and handed them to Scarlet, as Bear and Harry pulled the bodies on to the stairs and silently headed for the crypt where Maggs, Flash and Rags sat with Hog. Robbie sat on the floor with Rune and Alice and peered through the rail at the rest of the huge cathedral; he laid his bow on the floor and made himself comfortable.

Able Bowman Bents signaled, and a group of his men slipped over the wall and ran into an alleyway at the side of the hotel. They grabbed the drainpipes and rose like monkeys off the floor up to the roof, another flick of his wrist and again another group slipped up the side of the building containing all the priesthood. Up they shot towards the roof, he watched the pacing Knox guards turn and head off down the street, his third wave flooded across the road and into the shadows at the side of the barrack house.

He slipped back down the wall and headed with the rest of his troops around the outer wall to the other side of the Square and the house of the archbishop next to the Central headquarters of Mason's Army. They came over the wall in pairs and split as each headed for their allotted building. Further down the roadway small groups sneaked into the alleyways on the opposite side of the Church Square, they scrambled up the drainpipes and on to the roofs and lay flat or crouched down waiting for their moment.

The sun was starting to rise as the last of the men slipped into position, 80 of Caerleon's best bowmen were now in place and sitting in wait for their moment to arrive. Bent's sat down with his back to the outer wall and looked at the men who sat in the cover of the trees. "Won't be too long lads, settle down but stay sharp, that lad in there is depending on us." Just over the wall a squad of guards marched down the road from the barracks to meet and escort the bishop in his preparations of the ceremony.

Rowan and Jade now in black vests with silver badges, stood at the top of the bell tower and watched as the sun rose in the sky. A bugle sounded out and minutes later sound rose out of the barrack buildings as the soldiers woke up and prepared for the day.

Jade's eyes were fixed on the top left windows of the hotel, from here she could hit anything that passed the windows, Rune's voice drifted into her head

"Jade please, I know you love Robbie but that will not help him, we need Knox here, please restrain yourself."

"Sorry Rune, I couldn't help myself for a minute, I hate Billy for what he has done and seeing his window just got me angry, you know he has some other woman in there with him, don't you? I hate what he has done to Alice; he will die today and I hope it will be me who gets him."

"Alright Jade, just wait until he is in the cathedral."

"I will Rune."

Rowan smiled at her. "What did Rune say?" Jade seemed surprised.

"How did you know I was thinking to Rune?"

"Your eyes flicker little green flashes, didn't you know?"

Jade smiled. "Cool, no I didn't." She blew him a kiss across the bell tower and he smiled and turned around to watch the troops now assembling on the square below.

The very large area that had been cleared by Knox suddenly seemed to be becoming a sea of black vests and silver spears. Rowan watched as lines of troops marched in rank and file on the ground, their officers screamed at them as they paraded and the lines closed in and their steps began to beat in rhythm as they marched endlessly round.

Rowan watched thinking of Robbie's words when he had mentioned how he thought Knox was far more prepared than most people expected. Rowan now saw and understood the insight that Robbie had, as over a thousand troops seemed to march around the square and up the streets.

Robbie sat with each member of the team as Jett and Scarlet who had slipped off, now returned with black cassocks, which Jett passed around all the sword team. Robbie showed each of them their places down below, where there would be adequate cover and give them an advantage of surprise on any guards.

The time passed slowly as the sun rose, and Robbie watched the few guards below as they paced up and down. He could hear the crunch of marching feet outside and he knew that the mass army of Mason's guard was assembling, Rune grabbed his hand and he turned and smiled at her.

"Robbie relax, will you? We are all here together no matter what, and I am here and I feel stronger than ever before, you know grandmother spiked us don't you?"

He turned to her and looked at her softly smiling face. "What do you mean spiked us?"

Rune's grin broadened. "The drink in the forest at Caerleon was enchanted; it gave us both extra strength and vitality, I must admit I did wonder how you could resist the Dark One for so long."

"That drink was magical?"

"She is a daughter of Hearne; I should have realised." She squeezed his hand. "I am glad she did, I could have lost you without it."

Robbie smiled at her. "Better get used to the idea of me hanging about for quite some time." She leaned over and kissed his cheek.

"I can live with that."

Robbie relaxed, and as the sun rose and the light streamed in he could now see more of the cathedral. It was huge and bigger than anything he had ever seen, he looked down at the pews and the huge columns of stone that ran along the outer edge to the roof that towered above them.

At the far end was a vast space in front of the altar steps, which was where he presumed Knox would be crowned king, the windows above the altar were as tall as trees, although they were partially obstructed by a wall of carved wood that crossed above the front of the altar in a decorative arch. As the time passed, he studied the wonders of the cathedral, Rune noticed him looking and leaned over. "I never realised it would be so big."

"I could hide another hundred men in here Rune, it's so vast." The large doors below them opened and light flooded up the centre of the cathedral, Robbie tensed as soldiers marched in and came down the central aisle. They had their usual black vests on, but they all now wore a ceremonial helmet of highly polished silver with a bright yellow feather. Each held a shield of round steel with a red coiled dragon on it, and they all had a shiny silver sabre. Thirty soldiers made their way down each outer side of the pews, each spaced evenly along its length next to the large pillars. There were another nineteen soldiers down either side of the central aisle, and Robbie could hear more underneath, he knew there would be a long line back to the doors that would come rushing in as soon as trouble started.

Feet clattered up the steps towards them, and Robbie signaled to the others at the back who sat still in their black robes, with their heads down as if silently praying, as the four guards came in to replace the four already on duty. The first one looked at Robbie as he walked across towards him; Robbie saw his expression change as he realized Robbie was in woodsman attire. Robbie raised his finger to his lips and pointed to the praying clergy. "Shush!" He smiled, and the guard noticing the vicar's smiled back and nodded. The four fake guards of Robbie's men turned and slid their daggers deep.

The new guards slid silently to the floor and Fish, John, Martin and Steph picked up the helmets and shields and turned back to face forward at the top of the balcony. Robbie nodded to Scarlet, as people started to wander in, and clergy in black cassocks led them to their allotted seats.

As each member of the group passed Rune, she handed them a bible off a pile in the corner. Holding it solemnly in their hands they wandered down the steps and into the crowds as they moved in to their allotted places. Robbie watched from the top of the balcony through the wooden rail, as all of them found their spots and stood with their books in their hands against the walls as if in silent prayer.

Harry and Blades had readjusted their swords so they now pointed down under their robes; the others had slid their swords back a little so that they were not obvious under their cassocks. Robbie now slid extra quivers with bows to the front of the rail, making sure each one of them would be able to snatch their bow and arrows in a second. He breathed a deep sigh as his plan started to come together and the final preparations fell into place. He looked up the left hand side of the church, Harry and Skip were in position, and Scarlet walked across to the corner of the Lady Chapel, she was ready.

Up the right Jett, Fuse and Blades, all stood with their heads down as though reading waiting for their cue. Pete stood at a small door holding it open for two soldiers who carried a large golden chair through it, as he swung an incense lantern. They seemed to think he was blessing it, and smiled at him, Robbie silently chuckled; Pete had nerve that was for sure.

The golden seat was carried to the steps just above the front of the main aisle and situated slightly to one side of Robbie's right, in front of the altar rail. The choir now started to file in behind the carved wooden screens on either side of the altar.

A second golden chair slightly smaller in statute, was carried in and set beside the large golden chair, Alice leaned over the pew. "I think Knox has got a wife; look we may even have a queen."

Rune looked up at her. "I never really thought about him like that, but I suppose Billy had to come from somewhere."

Alice smiled. "Told you he was a son of a you know what."

Rune smiled. "What's this Alice no swearing in church?"

Alice giggled quietly. "Silly isn't it, but I thought I would hedge my bets... You know just in case, don't want Sister Mary finding out, do we?" Rune smiled.

"I suppose so but considering why we are here I would have thought swearing would not matter quite so much."

The time ticked by as all the seats filled with what looked like lords, ladies, and vicars from the church. Everyone seemed to be wearing their very best clothes and fanned themselves as they all spoke quietly to each other.

Robbie nodded to Scarlet and then Jett, as everyone stood up. A bugle sounded outside somewhere and drums began to beat at a slow rhythm, the time was almost upon them; Robbie patted the legs of Martin. "Alright folks let's get ready for the show, and remember follow my lead."

Rowan and Jade quietly slipped into the balcony; Rowan tapped his shoulder as he passed. "He is here Robbie. You are going to love this; he turned up in a golden carriage, this is definitely a man who loves himself there is no doubt."

The line of bowmen all prepared. Rowan was on Robbie's left hidden behind a pillar; Jade who had faded away stood up with her bow against the rail. Rune slid along the floor at his side, as Steph pulled at the stitches of her top on his right. She removed the documents to prove Mason was a fake, as Alice sat on the floor a few feet down from her.

Martin, John, and then Fish lifted their bows to lean on the rails ready, and all nodded back at Robbie, he watched through the rails as the organ struck up and the choir began to sing. Robbie felt the moment coming and his heart beat faster as he waited for what felt like an eternity.

The congregation began to sing and shortly after, the procession appeared below him as two figures with long thick red cloaks, walked from under the balcony and into view up the centre of the cathedral. Eight young women in white walked either side of each of them holding the long heavy cloaks, and behind them came the archbishop in a heavy purple robe and two other bishops in deep maroon. Other members in various shades of cassock followed. Robbie's mind wandered a bit, as he thought of the ceremony at the Village Hall when he had become the hooded man, it seemed quite similar to him.

Knox and his wife were seated in the thrones of gold, and the women in white fluttered around them, ensuring all was correct. Robbie moved from side to side but he could not see Mason at all, as the bishop's and attendants obscured his view.

The archbishop raised his hands as the hymn stopped and everyone sat down in their seats. He opened his prayer book and began to speak; Robbie could hear his voice but did not really absorb the words; he was now focused entirely on trying to get a view of Mason Knox. The ceremony continued for sometime; Robbie was only partially aware as he strained to see Mason.

More vicars appeared around him and prepared him as the bishop spoke a prayer, he ended and the congregation all voiced a loud. "Amen." Robbie's hearing seemed to slip back into his mind.

The bishop turned as two men carried two red cushions bearing the crowns of England down from the back of the altar, they glittered and sparkled in the candlelight and a faint ripple of sound passed through the congregation. They came both sides of Knox and his wife, and the bishop spoke, it was suddenly loud and clear in Robbie's ears.

"Do you Mason Knox swear before God to uphold the laws and the church for the sake of the people of England and its border countries?"

"I will." His voice was deep and cold, and it cut deeply into Robbie as he heard it, he felt the anger rising within him.

"Do you swear to be just and rule this land with truth, and dispense to your people as a considerate monarch should?"

"I do." Robbie was becoming more and more frustrated, as the bishop and his attendants blocked the view; he grabbed the rails and peered through.

"Do you Mason William Knox accept this office and swear to rule as first monarch of the new age of man."

Robbie pulled up his hood, grabbed his bow and leapt on to the rail with his back foot against the pew, as he sighted the arrow in anger and bellowed with all his might and authority down the cathedral. "By what right does this church place a butcher on the seat of this fair land?"

There were loud gasps as everyone turned and looked up at Robbie high up on the balcony edge hood up with his bow loaded and his arrow pointed right at the bishop. Eight hooded figures stood by his side, all with bows pointing down, the bishop spun round as the two attendants stepped across in front of Knox and his wife.

Robbie looked the bishop in the eyes. "You would put a murderer on the throne of England to rape pillage and destroy all that is good in this land? Answer fast Bishop my arrow grows impatient."

"By what right do you challenge me outlaw?" The bishop's eyes met the dark eyes of Robbie below his hood.

"I challenge you as Lord Robert of Loxley and 51st Earl of Huntingdon a true line of Celtic blood and not a Saxon impostor. I challenge you Archbishop, as a man who stands for those in England this snake would kill and destroy. By what right does this church deem itself worthy to crown a king that will destroy all that England is?"

Knox bellowed from behind the bishop. "I am of true blood to the line of Arthur and rightful heir to this throne Loxley."

"No true blood of a king as great as Arthur would hide behind the skirts of a man, he would step out and face me as all true English men would, show yourself snake."

"I share the line of Igraine mother of Arthur, Loxley you cannot deny me that? I am heir to this throne that you now choose to steal; this is not grain Loxley that can easily be taken."

Steph pushed her hand high in the air and waved it. "I am Stephanie Rimmer of Caerleon Knox. You know of my father, and I have his proof here that you are of Igraine's daughters' line, but not of Arthur's, the true heir is alive and protected Knox, you are not the heir to the throne of England." She waved the papers wildly in the air, and the congregation all began to murmur. "My Father proved you once a fake and he is very much alive and well to do it again, you have no claim to this throne and this crown. Your line is derived from a union of a Germanic Saxon lord and Celtic queens blood Knox, Arthur the one king was pure Celtic, you are not descended by direct decent."

The long green arrow trembled in Robbie's hand. Knox struggled behind the attendant's and he heard a sword drawn, movement at his side caught his eye, as Knox bellowed.

"Give me that crown and kill them." Robbie watched the arrow from Alice's bow as it headed to the far right of Mason Knox. The silver sword swiped quickly but not quick enough, and the arrow skimmed the face and took off part of the ear. Robbie stared as his eyes met Billy's, as he fell to the ground blood rushing from the side of his face.

"Robbie take the shot, ignore Billy, Mason is after the crown." Rune's voice felt loud as she shouted into his ear, and she raised her bow.

His eyes snapped back to the struggling Knox who was snatching for the crown behind the struggling attendant's. "I don't have the shot I can't see him; Rune I cannot shoot he is cowering."

Rowan screamed to Martin. "Look out." The soldiers were pulling crossbows from the pews, the bowmen of Loxley opened fire, as black cassocks and bibles; fell to the floor and swords flashed at the sides of the cathedral.

Flash, Maggs and little Rags heaved as the large doors swung shut. Bear and Hog ran down and thrust them together ramming the large bolts shut. The congregation screamed in panic as arrows rained down with accuracy from above and soldiers fell.

At the sides of the cathedral swords clashed as Harry and Blades waded into the soldiers and Scarlet screamed as she charged at four waving her large golden sword. Skip with the sword of Justice gleaming in the light, and with years of sword training, took on their officer who fought with skill; he smiled as the blades rung out on collision.

Robbie moved from side to side as Knox fought to get through to the crown. Rune was now at his shoulder her bow almost touching his as she shadowed his movement. Robbie's teeth were gritted, as his anger rose up and he could not get the shot.

Billy bleeding heavily made a run for the door at the side of the choir, and as he grabbed the handle a white-feathered arrow hit the door, he turned the handle and as the door gave, he looked back and into the eyes of hatred that belonged to Alice. Fear rose quickly in him and he pushed the door and fell through.

"Going somewhere Billy boy?" Jett smiled as she drew her golden sword from its sheath. "I will enjoy this." She licked her lips, as she slowly advanced; Billy pulled his sword up and smirked.

"Well little girl let's see if you match up to a Knox."

"My pleasure." Jett came at him with speed and ferocity, Billy countered but it shook him. He wiped the blood from his face and smiled as he shook himself and regained his composure. He picked up a large brass candlestick, and he lunged at Jett striking hard with his sword and swiping fast with the candlestick.

Jett was a swordsman of great skill, she laughed as she twisted and spun her blade moving like a streak of fire in front of Billy. He was Loxley trained and no slouch, and he countered her advances using his sword and the candlestick. The two fought with great speed and agility, Billy spun and swung the candlestick with ferocious speed and strength.

Jett stepped back, and countered with her blade and very quickly, she snapped back her wrist, and countered the candlestick. It was heavy, and Billy had strength, he brought it up fast and her sword slid down it, as his arm swung round and it hit her on the side of the head.

Jett saw stars and fell backwards, Billy came at her and she spun on the floor, bringing her sword up and blocking his strike. He laughed at her and then spat blood at her, as he made another lunge. The door exploded open, and an incense burner swung wildly, and hit Billy in the face, he screamed in pain, as the burning incense smashed out all over him.

He staggered back and grabbed the side door, and screaming in pain, he slipped through, as Pete grabbed Jett by the scruff of the neck and lifted her up off the floor. Both of them headed to the side door, Jett flung the door open wide, the arrow lifted her right off her feet, and she flew eight feet backwards, as Pete slammed the door closed, and forced the bolts across shut. Jett hit the floor and slithered, a long red line drew itself on the white marble. Arrows rattled on the door outside, as Pete gasped and turned towards Jett.

"Robbie, we cannot let him get the crown, for god's sake shoot the bloody bishop and then shoot him." Rune screamed as she followed his line with her bow. Knox was hitting out, and forcing his way toward the crown dragging the bishop as cover, Robbie shouted to Rowan.

"Rowan the crown, take the man out with the crown, Rune blow it, blow the crown away, I need a moving target."

Rowan loaded his bow and took aim, in amongst the fighting crowd of church officials that contained Knox, half of them fought to protect the crown, as half fought to pull it to Knox. The congregation was spilling out all over in panic trying to get out, as the soldiers battered on the main door trying to get in. Bear and Hog hit anything coming down the aisle their way, and Ruby spun with her sticks at anything that got past.

John fell back an arrow in his leg, and crashed writhing in pain on the pews, Alice's bow sung and the soldier who was reloading his crossbow fell dead. Rowan got his mark and fired, as Rune's eyes flickered, the arrow hit and the vicar fell backwards throwing the crown. A gust of wind erupted in the cathedral, as the crown lifted up in the air above Mason Knox, who suddenly jumped free of the crowd to try and catch it. Alice's bow sung with Martin's, Robbie closed his eyes.

"Hearne, I call upon you to guide my arrow, make safe this crown for the true king of England." He fired, and opened his eyes.

The crown spun in the blast of the wind in the air as it passed the carved wooden arch. The green arrow swerved above the crowd, and as Mason Knox placed his hand on the crown in midair, the arrow entered the back of it, and with an almighty golden flash, it pierced the gold of the crown and pinned it to the wooden wall.

Knox screamed a horrific wail in agony as the arrow turned gold and glowed hot, his body twisted as he screamed, and his eyes met for the first time with Robbie's.

Robbie and all of them gasped, the long curly white hair and the pale blue eyes were Billy's. They were older and now contorted, as he hung from one hand, his legs kicking in the air. Billy was without doubt the double of his father, Robbie shook his head to free the shock, and pulled another arrow from the quiver, he fitted his bow and aimed. His bow fired as Mrs Knox jumped up from the seat to her husband, the arrow hit her right in the back splintered her spine, and pierced her heart.

Her arms gripped the neck of Mason Knox, and he screamed in agony, as her weight was too much, he looked up at Robbie and Rune, and his eyes exploded with deep red light. Rune gasped and waved her hand in front of Robbie as her eyes went suddenly violet. "He has powers?"

It was like a shock to Robbie as he felt something pass him like a soft breeze but almost electrical, his own eyes flickered lilac as Rune's shield kept him safe.

Knox defiantly stared, his eyes glowing red, he screamed a loud howling scream, as he felt his hand rip, as it tore off the golden arrow. He dropped to the floor, and was snatched quickly by a soldier as Rune took aim, Knox was dragged over behind the Lady Chapel and Rune's arrow hit the soldier who was pushing his wife's lifeless body toward him. Rune was almost in shock. "We missed him!" Robbie grabbed her arm and shook her.

"Get sharp Rune, we saved the crown, there will be no king crowned here until Hearne is ready to give that crown up, look."

Rune looked down the cathedral and smiled, the whole carved wall of the cathedral had sprouted leaves and was bursting into bloom with lilac flowers, Ivy ran up the walls towards the roof, and the floor was starting to crack as small oak trees began to rise all along the inside walls.

Jett leaned up against the wall as Pete slid a table against the door, he pushed it hard, and then came over and looked at the arrow. "God that is nasty it's almost come right through."

"Cheers Pete, I really needed to hear that." Her face was pale and beads of sweat formed on her forehead; the top of her cloak was soaked in blood, as she peered at the red feathers at the end of the shaft sticking out of her shoulder. "Get it out of me Pete. My bravery is running out."

He smiled and stroked her face. "I will snap off the shaft, the point is almost through on the other side, so a good push and it will be almost out alright?"

Her lip trembled as she shook her head. "You won't tell if I cry will you Pete?"

He smiled at her. "Cry all you want; your secret is safe with me."

Pete looked around and saw a small brass collection plate, and he picked it up and laid it on the floor, he took out his knife and cut into the arrow shaft. Jett closed her eyes and breathed in sharply with the pain, two small tears leaked from her eyes. The shaft snapped off clean. "Ok so far so good."

He put the plate against his shoulder and pulled Jett slowly forward, the broken tip touched the plate. He took a firm hold of her. "This will hurt, I am really sorry in advance, you are a brave girl Jett I will give you that."

She looked up at him her eyes glistening. "Pete wait." She swallowed hard and more tears welled in her eyes, as she looked at him and trembled. "Pete I am frightened."

He put his hand on her pale white face. "Me too, but I won't lose you... Honestly." He gave her a warm smile. "Big chunk of bravery needed... Are you ready?" He winked.

"Do it."

Pete put his arms around her, and slammed her against him with all his might.

He saw the arrow point shoot out of her back, Jett screamed into his shoulder, and he held her as tight as he could as she sobbed, and shook, his own eyes filling with tears as he pulled the end of the shaft out of the hole in her back.

She pulled her right arm up around him as her left hung limp, and the pain coursed through her. He held her tight and she shook violently. Pete gently rocked her. "I am so sorry Jett, there was no other way." He hugged her and kissed her head. "Forgive me?"

Jade stopped on the balcony as Rune shuddered. "That is two things I owe you now Billy."

Pete pulled her back as she sniffled. "I can tell you this Jett, I would have screamed a lot louder, hell you are tough." He stroked her hair out of her eyes, and wiped her tears on his cuff. "You are going to be alright now, I thought for a moment back there I had lost you." Working fast, he rolled a spare choir top up and made a pad to dress the wound.

Jett sniffled. "Thanks Pete... You know for getting it out, seeing it stuck in me like that was doing my head in."

"Come on let's get you out of here." He lifted her up, and carried her to the door. "You ready for this, on a count of three. Three!" He kicked the table from under the handle and pulled the door open.

"**R**owan let's get the hell out of here, send the signals." Rowan and Jade sped up the steps to the bell tower. "Rune let Flash, Jett and Scarlet know it's time to leave." She fired two arrows together and took two crossbowmen out. Robbie saw his crew working backwards fighting with swords, and he started to cover them as they came back. Robbie fired with speed and precision, as he hit anyone within three feet of one of his swordsmen.

Pete came out of the top door with Jett on his shoulder; a guard fell with Rune's arrow in his back. He ran down into the crowd, as Robbie and Rune took anyone near him out. Bear and Hog, beat back any who tried to come near, as the group slipped through, and headed for the stairs to the balcony.

Rowan and Jade stood at the top of the bell tower and loaded two explosive arrows each on their bows, the fuses fizzed, and they both fired into the masses of troops on the ground. The arrows went deep and the soldiers panicked and fled from the smoking fuses, the explosions were huge and men blew into the air screaming.

The roofs were suddenly lined with hooded men, and arrows rained down on those who were still in the cleared compound around the cathedral. Jade loaded her bow and lit the fuse. "Go Rowan." She turned and sighted her bow at the top left hand balcony of the hotel; she smiled as she released the arrow. "I hope you are in there Billy, if not I can wait." She flew down the steps as the windows exploded out of the hotel, and flames burst through the roof.

The bowmen realising what was happening, ran across the top of the roof and launched themselves into the air across the gap and on to the roof either side. The whole top of the hotel was destroyed, it fell in, and flames burst into the sky.

The compound was almost deserted as Robbie climbed out of the window on to the roof above the main door archway. The others followed up the stairs and came out of the windows and on to the roof; Robbie guided them to the drainpipe. Alice and Rune went first dropping and taking up a defensive stance on the ground with bows raised, the others slid down, and looked at the scorched earth and burning hotel, as the dead littered all over. Bowmen lined the roofs all around the compound, and anything that moved was hit with an arrow from above, as the bowmen of Caerleon protected their heroes with pride.

Bear and Hog moved backwards as Rags and Flash stood at the bottom of the stairs. "Go Rags." Flash pushed her backwards. "This is my specialty, come Bear, Hog, get your big bums out of here." They walked backwards as the soldiers cautiously came around the corner. "It's alright boys you go I will be fine."

The soldiers came to a stop. Two of them smiled at the sight of little flash with her white pole, she looked at the massed group of large burly men with swords.

"Hi guys, you want to play with me?" They looked confused and then started to laugh, Ruby took off her glasses and looked at the floor. "I don't like being laughed at."

Her voice was quiet and yet cold, the soldiers stopped laughing and began to advance. Flash looked up and the whole cathedral was bathed in bright white light, it pulsed out of her and the soldiers screamed in pain, as their eyes and faces burned with the heat of the sun. "Shame on you for picking on a little girl." Flash wagged her finger and then put her glasses on.

The burned and smoking soldiers fell dead to the floor, as she turned and ran off up the stairs.

Harry waited nervously at the foot of the drainpipe, Blades knelt at his side a gash across her arm, John lay on the floor as Alice tore a bandage off her cloak, she had cut the arrow out, and had plastered the wound with thick paste, and Rune sewed four quick stitches to seal the wound. Alice bound his leg, as Hog slid down the pipe and pulled his bow off his shoulder.

The group sat in a wide arc in the empty ground at the side of the cathedral's two out buildings. In front of them the floor was littered with the dead, across the compound the wall was blown down, and Robbie could see Bowman Bents, with his men guarding the way to the trees and the woodland.

Ruby jumped out of the window and ran across the roof to the drainpipe. "Hey baby Flash you feeling cosmic?" Harry opened his arms wide, and Flash screamed out as she jumped from the roof.

"Whoopee!" She landed safely in Harry's arms. "Wow Harry that was amazingly cosmic."

Jett coughed, as Jade leaned over with Scarlet; Rowan bound the wound in her shoulder tight. "I almost had him Jade, I almost had him."

Jade stroked Jett's hair. "Next time we stay together, and we will finish him."

Jett smiled. "Yeah."

Robbie looked round. "Alright let's get ready to hustle."

Hog lifted Jett into his arms. "Is that alright, I am not hurting you, am I?"

Jett smiled. "Hog you stink and you fart too much, but apart from that you are a real sweet guy." Hog smiled, and then farted.

Bear lifted John on to his back, and on Robbie's command, they started to move, they moved with purpose across the compound past Bents who saluted, and into the cover of the trees. Rowan and Jade watched the rear, but there was nothing. They were almost at the farm before Robbie slowed down and began to walk.

Rowan patted him on the back. "Some cuts and bruises and a couple of bad wounds but you did it Robbie, you brought us all out again."

Robbie patted Rowan. "You were fantastic in there, all of you were." A small warm hand slid into his and he turned to her as she slid her arm around him, she smiled sweetly at him her eyes danced.

"What did you ask the arrow?"

"I told Hearne to watch the crown until the true king came, only the true heir to this kingdom will be able to pull out that arrow and put the crown on. It just came to me as I tried to get a shot at Knox, how can the bowman herald the coming of the true king? Only by making it impossible for anyone to use the crown until he does, I just figured Hearne would know how, so I asked him."

Rune squeezed him tightly. "It was your last shot at Knox, and yet you used it for the benefit of everyone."

"There is more than one Knox now, killing Mason would not have ended it, Billy wants the glory as much as his father does. I only had one arrow, and I cheated them both out of the crown in one shot. That is what Hearne meant when he said he would leave the choice up to me, he knew what was in my heart, and I was the one with the doubts but not him. He knew Rune; he knew what I would do."

Robbie slowed and looked back. Alice seemed in a daze as she came up beside him, he slid his arm around her and pulled her close. "You Ok?"

Alice sighed and looked at him with a weak smile. "I suppose so... I almost had him Robbie, but I know it would not have made me feel any better."

John lifted a hand from the stretcher at her side and took her hand. "You are a true lady Alice of Loxley. Don't you worry my love, there is a lord out there waiting for you, and you have to look on the bright side, let's face it if he ever wants to get an earring you have a quiver full waiting for him." He gave her a broad smile, and squeezed her hand.

Alice started to giggle. "I could do the other while I am at it." John chuckled. "That's the spirit."

Jett tried to sit up and groaned and lay back. "Hey Robbie did you see Pete with that incense thing, man he could swing it, I bet Billy looks like a pepper pot... Pete was so cool the way he appeared, I think we should call him Smokes."

The whole group started to laugh, as Steph pulled him close, and chuckled. Rune smiled, as she looked back at all the smiling faces coming through the trees. "I think that's total agreement, Smokes it is."

Robbie looked at her smiling face and dancing blue eyes, she had made it through by his side again. She gave him a knowing smile, slid her arm around him and kissed him on the cheek. "Can we go home now?"

"I think a party at the castle is in order and a quick visit to Sister Mary, but then yes, I want to go home and sleep late and have breakfast in bed for a while. Then we build an army, after today there is going to be one hell of a war Rune, we will have two to fight now, Knox and the Church."

The door exploded open as Billy flinched. "Watch what you're doing fool." The Soldier trembled as he tried to neatly sow what was left of Billy's ear back on; his bare back was peppered with large red burns and covered with an oily cream.

Mason Knox had his hand wrapped in a cloak, and he kicked at the table as the door slammed behind him. "I WANT HIM DEAD!" He screamed at the top of his voice, and then slumped on to one of the beds.

Two medics rushed over, and slowly peeled back the fabric to reveal a split in his hand from behind his knuckles, down to the joint of his index finger. Billy screwed up his face as he looked at it, and looked at his father who was watching him.

"Your mother is dead." He seemed quite unconcerned as he spoke to his son. Billy appeared equally as unaffected and looked back up from his father's hand.

"What do we do now?"

Knox smiled. "I may not have the crown but I am still ahead in the game from that tree picker. I want you to go north and supervise there, I will take care of that pile of logs they call Loxley myself."

"We still need the sword?"

"Let me worry about that, just keep your eyes and ears open, and see what can be found about this so called heir to the throne. I will see your grandmother shortly, it is about time she stopped bloody talking and started being a bit more active."

Billy's broad grin crossed his lips. He flinched. "What the hell have I told you?"

The black clouds rolled in with the wind and rain across the sea, and pelted down on to the circle of twenty stones set deep in the ground, on the wild moor below the high cliffs and rocky outcrops.

The grass was almost flat as the wind blew across the top of the sea, and on to the land. Bits of twig and tufts of loose grass, bounced along the floor looking for somewhere to wedge themselves, and the large heavy raindrops tried to batter them into submission. The silent stones, which had weathered the storms of a thousand lifetimes stood silently waiting for her, they knew she would not be late for she had never kept them waiting before.

The tall slender figure came over the rise, as the wind whipped her long waist length brown hair around her face. She slid her arms up wiping the wet hair back, and smiled as her slate grey eyes saw the stones again for the second time this year. She pulled the pale blue cloak around her as protection from the wind, and she strolled as if on a leisurely walk on a summer's day.

Entering the stones, she felt the calmness grow within her, the power of her lord was strong here. Callanish had always been a place she loved, but with hope today, she would know if it was time to go home. She walked to the centre of the circle and raised her arms, the wind dropped and the rain eased; silence fell across the whole island.

Holding her arms out, her eyes began to glow blue, and her breathing slowed as she closed her eyes, and the sun opened a cloud, and pushed through its first rays of sunshine in weeks.

"Hear me Mother."

"I hear you my daughter, and I have great news."

"Oh, mother can I return to my homeland at last?"

"Melanie my child, come home and bring with you my granddaughter and grandson, I have missed them so."

"He has done it? Has he Mother?"

"There is no king in this land and his quest for truth starts now, as does yours my daughter. The lost sword must be found before we can reveal the one who will lead."

"I have heard things Mother; they say it has left France and is on its way here."

"Find it my daughter before the snake does, for he has lost a crown and will want all the swords in order to make his claim again. He craves the power, and has never understood what we all know to be true. He will never be able to join as we have where one mind becomes one for the good of all."

"I will return to my children and prepare mother, and I will wait for the time when I too am written onto the Runestone and be free to feel my family again."

"Come my dear daughter, I will prepare the way."

"Rune, are you alright?" Robbie looked at her as she sat on the log next to the fire, she had lifted her hand to the side of her face.

"I just had the strangest sensation, I felt someone who is a stranger to me, but that is not possible, I am the centre of the circle, and know all of them." She looked worriedly at Robbie. "What do you think that can mean?"

The Adventure will continue:

Heirs to the Kingdom Part Two
The Lost Sword of Carnac.

Be warned lords of the realm that in days to come the land will burn red and your people will die.

Then will the snake grow legs and wings and come forth to you with offers and treaties, and he will cover his true plan to unseat you. Your people will start to die again.

He will poison the land and rid the world of the green one, and in doing so destroy everything.

Gather the swords of the heirs of this land, and bring them to the daughters of the table in the woods, for there is the only hope of saving what is important, and the true swords man of your land will fight again to restore the balance of power.

Look for the bowman, for he will lead them together and forge anew a world that will be truly for earth and man.

Heed my words for if you stray from them the world is doomed.

(The prophecy of Rhiannon as translated by Geoffrey of Almesbury AD 426)

More Author's
From
Violet Circle Publishing

Mike Beale. (Children's Book)

Crumble's Adventures.
ISBN: 978-1-910299-06-7
Digital ISBN: 978-1-910299-08-1

Colin Smith (Play)

Heaven knows I'm Miserable Now
ISBN: 978-1-910299-16-6
Digital ISBN: 978-1-910299-23-4

Ted Morgan. (Poetry and verse)

Wordsmith's Wanderings.
ISBN: 978-1-910299-04-3
Digital ISBN: 978-1-910299-09-8
Peregrinations of the Wordsmith
ISBN: 978-1-910299-18-0
Digital ISBN: 978-1-910299-21-0
Silhouette Soldiers
ISBN: 978-1-910299-19-7
Digital ISBN: 978-1-910299-22-7
A Menu of Memories
Digital ISBN: 978-1-910299-32-6
Digital ISBN: 978-1-910299-33-3

Robin John Morgan. (Fiction/Fantasy/Slice of Life)

Heirs to the Kingdom.

Book One, The Bowman of Loxley.
ISBN: 978-1-910299-00-5
Digital ISBN: 978-1-910299-10-4
Book Two, The Lost Sword of Carnac.
ISBN: 978-1-910299-01-2
Digital ISBN: 978-1-910299-11-1
Book Three, The Darkness of Dunnottar.
ISBN: 978-1-910299-02-9
Digital ISBN: 978-1-910299-12-8
Book Four, Queen of the Violet Isle.
ISBN: 978-1-910299-03-6
Digital ISBN: 978-1-910299-13-5
Book Five, Crystals of the Mirrored Waters.
ISBN: 978-1-910299-05-0
Digital ISBN: 978-1-910299-14-2
Book Six, Last Arrow of the Woodland Realm.
ISBN: 978-1-910299-07-4
Digital ISBN: 978-1-910299-15-9
Book Seven, Bridge Of Sequana.
ISBN: 978-1-910299-17-3
Digital ISBN: 978-1-910299-20-3
Book Eight, The Circle of Darkness.
ISBN: 978-1-910299-26-5
Digital ISBN: 978-1-910299-29-6

The Curio Chronicles.

Part One, Abigail's Summer.
ISBN: 978-1-910299-27-2
Part Two, Curio's Summer.
ISBN: 978-1-910299-34-0
Digital ISBN: 978-1-910299-35-7
Part Three, Curio's Christmas.
ISBN: 978-1-910299-38-8
Digital ISBN: 978-1-910299-39-5

Other Works.

Rise Of The Raven
ISBN: 978-1-910299-30-2
Digital ISBN: 978-1-910299-31-9
The Countess Of Darkness
ISBN: 978-1-910299-40-1
Digital ISBN: 978-1-910299-41-8

Han's Cottage.
ISBN: 978-1-910299-36-4
Digital ISBN: 978-1-910299-37-1

Find out more about our authors and their books at
www.violetcirclepublishing.co.uk